Audrey Howard

PROMISES LOST

THE SHADOWED HILLS

BCA

LONDON NEW YORK SYDNEY TORONTO

This Omnibus edition published 1997
by BCA
by arrangement with Hodder & Stoughton,
a division of Hodder Headline PLC

CN 9424

Printed and bound in Great Britain by
Clays Ltd, St Ives plc

CONTENTS

PROMISES LOST

I would like to dedicate this book to all
the ladies who have written to me saying they
enjoy what I write, and even those who haven't.

Part One

The two girls were picking blackberries when the gang of men came upon them. They were extremely pretty girls, one about fifteen or so, the other a few years older, with hair so rich and tawny the sun's rays seemed to set it alight; but where one had hers fastened at the back of her head in a neat chignon, the other's hung, curling and heavy, about her shoulders and down her back, falling across her small breasts in a gleaming curtain of copper.

They were absorbed in their task, their heads constantly turning this way and that, their eyes darting along the thickly branched hedgerow in their search for the most luscious fruit and they did not notice the men as they came round the bend which led from Lane End towards Wray Green.

The smaller of the girls had a crooked walking stick for reaching the higher fruits and there was a smear of blackberry juice at the corner of her plump, pink mouth. The berries she and her sister picked were dark, heavy and glistening in the sunshine.

"I wish I'd tied my hair up, Alice," the men heard her say.

"I did tell you but as usual you wouldn't listen," Alice replied tartly.

"It's just that it wouldn't have dried so quickly if I had. You know what it's like when it's been washed. The only trouble is I can't see what I'm doing. I'll be in the hedge in a minute."

"I did warn you, Sara. Why don't you tuck it behind your ears? You look like a gypsy with it hanging about you like that. What if someone should see you?"

"Who, for goodness sake?"

"One never knows who one will meet, Sara. I have told

you time and time again a lady should always be groomed as though guests were expected."

"Oh Ally! We're blackberrying for heaven's sake."

"It doesn't matter."

There was silence again as the girl with the stick lifted it above her glowing head, dragging at a heavily laden branch.

"Why are the best ones always at the top," she gasped, wincing as her flesh snagged on a sharp prickle. "Dammit!"

"Sara! How many times must I tell you, ladies do not swear, *ever*, and where you pick up such language is beyond me."

"Father says it, Ally. You've heard him yourself."

"That doesn't mean you may, Sara Hamilton, and if you don't stop eating those blackberries there won't be enough for Dolly to make a pie let alone jam."

The men had stopped, those trailing at the back of the group colliding into those at the front but they began to smile and elbow one another as they saw the girls. The very air about them became electric with their male excitement. The dust in the rutted lane was soft and thick, rising in little puffs as they moved, muffling the sound of their approach and the two girls continued to gather the fruit, unaware as yet of their presence. There were a dozen of them, big men with broad shoulders, sturdy legs and strong, thick-muscled bare arms and they walked arrogantly, evidently considering themselves to be a cut above other men, their heads high, their gaze insolent.

Their dress was distinctive, almost a uniform in its similarity, each man wearing a pair of moleskin trousers, a double canvas shirt, a white felt hat with the brim jauntily turned up and a gaudy neckerchief apiece. Only in their waistcoats did they differ from one another, for though the cut was the same, each one was of a different rainbow hue. They were well scrubbed, some shaven, shorn and barbered for what was obviously a special occasion, others smooth-faced, one or two with thick, ferociously curling full beards.

The girls suddenly stopped what they were doing as they sensed they were no longer alone. They turned at the same time and, seeing the men, shrank back together in visible alarm. The golden-honey flush of their sun-warmed faces paled and they clutched the baskets in which they had been collecting the blackberries to their breasts as though they might afford them some protection. They both took a step backwards, moving deeper into the dry ditch which ran beside the lane and the hems of their light summer dresses were hidden in an eruption of white meadowsweet, golden buttercups and the bright crimson of poppies.

It was autumn and on either side of the bramble hedges stretched golden fields ready for the harvesters. The dusty stream of the lane flowed to the right and the left between hedgerows heavy with fruit, not just blackberry, but sloe, thick and purple-clustered. The sun was hot and the day was still but for the chattering of the finches which flashed about the ditch and hedge further up the lane. It remained still but the stillness was abruptly laced with tension, with a menace which could be felt by both the girls and they huddled even closer together.

"Now then, there's a foine soight to be sure." The voice of the man who spoke was soft and lilting with the unmistakable brogue of the Irish in it but its softness did nothing to dispel the alarm of the two girls.

"Ye're roight there, Racer. I've not seen a foiner since that maid we persuaded ter be friendly . . . sure an' when was it then? Aye, I have it now, so I have. T'was at the fair when we was in Preston. That'd be a month or two back, I'm thinkin', an' a roight owd shindig it caused, an' all. Jesus, Mary an' Joseph, I nearly had me jaw broke, so I did, by that boyo who thought she were his. I can still feel that . . ."

"Never mind yer bloody jaw, Billyo, an' let's not be dwellin' on the charms of another lass when sure haven't we the two prettiest little darlin's I've clapped eyes on in many a long day right here ter hand, so ter speak. An' all alone too. Now then, Alice, was it? Would yer not loike it foine if we was ter help the pair o' ye wi' yer blackberryin', if yer catch me drift."

He winked lewdly. The smaller girl put her hand to her mouth, doing her best to press herself even further back into the long, supple stems and dense leaves of the hedge. There were hooked prickles on the stems which caught at the smooth, bare flesh of her arms and tender neck, raising tiny specks of blood but she was unaware of the pain as the greater threat began to move, almost as one man, slowly towards her. They were smiling, that mindless smile of anticipation the male hunter assumes as it approaches its female prey, not even aware that they were doing it really, not sure as yet how exactly they meant to proceed with these two defenceless girls but knowing they intended having a bit of fun while they did it. They wouldn't harm them, not really harm them, for they were only young lasses, but perhaps a kiss or two, a joke, a bit of a lark before the really serious business of enjoying themselves at the ale-house in Kirkham began. The Bowling Green was where they were headed but a small diversion on the way would not be unwelcome. It was the end of the month, pay day and they were off on a randy and what better way to start it than with the novelty these two lasses promised. They were not drunk yet. That would be rectified when they reached Kirkham which was no more than a mile from the railway track they themselves had helped to lay.

They were taken aback and not a little amused when the older girl squared her shoulders and stepped forward boldly, rather in the manner of an indignant governess facing up to a pack of rebellious schoolboys. Her chin rose and her eyes snapped with the light of pure outrage. Her first nervous alarm appeared, at least for the moment, to have dissipated. She still had her basket in one hand and taking the stick from the limp grasp of her sister, clasped it firmly in the other, brandishing it with the apparent intention of braining any man who moved an inch towards her.

"Get out of my way," she told them fiercely, turning to look from one to another, from one rough and covetous face to another while beside her Sara did the same, searching for something, perhaps a man not quite so . . . so . . . she didn't even know what word to use to describe what she meant for she was young and had been reared in ignorance of men's ways. And these were no ordinary men. Hadn't everyone in the county of Lancashire heard what happened when navvies went on the riot? Though Sara had been only a child when the Preston to Wyre railway line was built, the opening of which had taken place five years ago in 1840, she dimly remembered the outrage and – in deference to her youth and innocence – the whispered comments of those who had lived beside the violence it had created. Tales of drinking and brawling, of theft, of men humiliated and women insulted. Tales of gangs of navvies overwhelming the ale-houses in the villages along the track, fighting and swearing and disrupting the quiet lives of those who had known nothing more dangerous before their arrival than a bit of poaching and an occasional show of harmless fisticuffs when the inn discharged its customers.

Nothing was safe from them, nothing. Not property, not livestock, and certainly not women!

It was the age of the railway. Only twenty-three years ago a crowd of three hundred shouting, singing navvies had helped to lay the first rail of the Stockton and Darlington Railway and eight years later in 1830 when the Liverpool and Manchester line was opened it was hailed, and rightly so, as one of the greatest feats of engineering of its time. Now, just over twenty years from the start of that first line there were no fewer that three thousand miles of railway track up and down the country. Two hundred thousand men employed, it was said, men who, when one track was finished, went on the tramp to find another. Labouring men who grew into an élite group called "navvies", from the word "navigator" given to the canal builders of the previous century and inherited by the men of the railways. Labourers, true, but not to be confused with the rabble of common workmen whom, the navvies boasted and with truth, they could out-work, out-drink and out-fight any day of the week. They came from Ireland and Scotland, Lancashire and Lincolnshire and Yorkshire, hard men and often brutal, criminals, a few of them, for the railway was a refuge in which it was easy to hide. They had false names, nicknames such as "Tramp", "Redhead", "Bible John" and "Happy Peter" and no questions were asked of them as long as they looked powerful enough to do the hardest, the most hazardous work in the country. They followed the rail wherever it went, working with one contractor until he ran out of work or higher wages were promised elsewhere. Two and sixpence or three shillings a day was considered fair and now, with what was left after the "Tommy shop" had been paid jingling in their pockets, these men were off to spend it and, more than likely, none of them would return to his job until every last penny was gone. A navvie was paid once a month and not being of a thrifty nature nor inclined to save for the future, he lived on credit until pay day. A subsistence allowance, in the form of a ticket which could be exchanged for goods at the Tommy, or Truck shop, was given to him by the "ganger" in charge. At the end of the month the value of the ticket the navvieman had received was deducted from his wages, often leaving him as badly off as he had been before he was paid.

Nevertheless these men had a few bob left in their pockets

and were bent on spending them as fast as they could swill ale down their throats! It was September. They had come, some of them, with their ganger direct from the building of the track between Manchester and Sheffield which was to be opened for traffic in December. They had, at least in this group, survived the construction of the infamous Woodhead Tunnel through high and wild moorland where the wind was bitter even on the mildest day. One thousand men living in forty stone shelters in the bleakest bit of the rough Pennine country, but they had come through and were now to begin work on the small branch line which, its owners seeking to develop the "excursion" trade, was to run from the Preston and Wyre Railway, leaving the main line at Kirkham and moving across flat country to the small fishing hamlet of Lytham. Excursions were the thing now, cheap and very popular with the masses who, until the advent of the railway, had never been further than their own back street in their lives. "Cheap trips", such as the one in which two thousand Sunday school children and their teachers had descended on Fleetwood in one day!

The building of the Lytham branch line would be like a holiday after the Woodhead Tunnel, the navvies told one another cheerfully, for the hardships they had suffered there had been appalling and what better way to begin than with what was left of their wages burning a hole in their pockets and two pretty girls to have some fun with?

The men began to move in that aimless, shifting way animals employ, one following another, standing, moving from foot to foot, each man waiting for the next to make a move, grinning foolishly as the one at the front who had been addressed as Racer held out a placatory hand to help the girls from the ditch.

"Will yer not let me help ye up, me pretty?" he leered, his eyes on the girl called Sara, the young one. "Step up 'ere an' let's be havin' a look at ye, an' yer bonny sister. She is yer sister, in't she? To be sure ye're the spit of each other even if she is a bit prim fer my taste. Now *you* . . . will yer look at that hair, boyos. Have yer ever seen the loike of it 'ceptin' on an angel in heaven? Like a new guinea piece, so it is, shinin' in the sun an' I've a moind ter . . ."

Before he had even finished speaking Alice lashed out with her stick and the blackberries in her basket went flying with the violence of her movement. Racer only grinned, revealing the stumps of his rotting teeth. Sara recoiled, moving rapidly from alarm to blind terror. Her eyes were enormous in her white face, the clear pale green of them becoming unfocused as the pupils narrowed to pinpoints.

"Well now, she've some spirit, an't she, lads?" Racer said, referring to Alice. He winked over his shoulder at the circle of flushed faces behind him. "T'other's a mite quiet but we'll alter that, won't we? Sure an' won't yer say good-day to us, girleen? We mean yer no harm, do we, boys?"

"You touch me or my sister and I'll split your head open with this stick. How dare you threaten us. My father will have the law on you if you don't let us by at once." Alice was beside herself. She was a lady and did not take kindly to being spoken to by ruffians and though she was often irritated beyond measure by her young sister, and by· what she considered to be her unladylike behaviour at times, she was not about to let anyone insult her as this fellow appeared to be doing. Sara was what Alice called "soft", a trait Alice deplored but she was Alice's sister and not to be addressed by any common labourer who came along. She held the stick in her two hands now, swinging it from side to side, shifting from foot to foot, ready to strike out at any hand which attempted to lay itself on Sara or herself. They were no more than a hundred yards from the small house in which she, Sara, their father and their servant Dolly Watson lived and if she were to shout loud enough Father would hear her, but the trouble was Father was not there and Dolly was subject to the intermittent and convenient deafness of the elderly. Father had dawdled off an hour ago on his placid old mare to visit Fanny Suthurst who lived on the far side of Wray Green. A bad attack of the rheumatics, Fanny had, or so she said, though Alice was of the opinion that the old crone called the doctor out merely for a bit of company. This last attack had seized her up "something chronic" she said, so that she could barely move and though there was little Father could do, after all Fanny was over eighty, he had explained in his kindly, patient way, "soft" like Sara, just the sight of him would give her comfort since it was a signal that help was at hand, which was half the battle. A great one for faith, was Father, though Alice had no time for it, and it was his belief that if a patient was treated as though he or she were important, he or she instantly felt better. Twaddle, Alice privately thought it. Fanny wouldn't be able to afford his fee, naturally, but, like many a dozen of his patients, would offer in payment a neatly plucked chicken or a rabbit one of her grandsons had trapped and skinned, a practice Alice deplored since a skinned rabbit or a plucked chicken was useless when it came to paying coal bills or providing a much-needed pair of shoes for either her or Sara.

The face Sara Hamilton looked for, the expression she looked for, leaped out from the rest and though she was doing her best to withdraw from this terror which had come upon her, she made herself painstakingly fasten on it. It was younger than the others and though not handsome in the classic sense it had a boyish appeal, an engaging good-humoured look about it which was very reassuring. A face which had not yet completely matured into manhood but strong and with something about it which said its owner was not one to be meddled with lightly. The jaw was blunt-angled, the mouth was firm and, at this moment, unsmiling, the lips somewhat flattened as they pressed against his teeth in a grimace of disapproval. The skin was smoothly shaven and a deep amber brown. The thickly lashed, narrowed eyes were a warm copper colour, like those of the marmalade cat which was for ever under Dolly's feet in the kitchen, she grumbled. He was, unlike the others, hatless, and his hair, though he had evidently made some effort with water and comb, fell about his head in a riotous mop of sun-glinted chestnut curls. He was taller than the rest, the length of him in perfect proportion to his weight. Tall, straight-boned, his body shaped by his trade to that of a strong and healthy young animal, he stood at the back of the group, hesitating, not sure what to do, only knowing it must be something.

Please . . . her eyes beseeched him, recognising what was in him and it was as though she had spoken out loud, as though the thoughts in her head were in his, her feelings of terror and outrage felt by him, a link forged between them at precisely that moment which neither was yet aware of. There was an endearing smear of blackberry juice at the corner of her soft mouth and Jack distinctly felt his carefree, young man's heart flip over! She looked so frightened, her eyes enormous in her small, pointed face, trembling away from the threat of what he and the other men might do to her. He wanted to stride forward, take her in his arms, protect and soothe her and tell her she had nothing to fear, ever, while Jack Andrews was about, but of course that would not do.

Instead he grinned, his square white teeth startling in his brown face. Shoving his big hands deep into his trouser pockets, he sauntered through the group of men in front of him, pushing carelessly aside those who got in his way as though any offence he might give was of no consequence since his fate was sealed anyway. With unhurried composure he turned his back on the two girls so that he stood face to face with Racer. He braced his well-muscled shoulders which had not yet quite gained their full strength, the power which would one day be his, and his amiable grin deepened.

Racer, shorter, squatter, was forced to glare up at Jack which set the Irishman at a slight disadvantage and his expression became irritable. His thick neck was the same width as his head which sat in the centre of his shoulders like a cannon-ball. He had the massive build and the scarred, knocked-about face of a man who has been in many brawls, winning most, and the picture he and the younger man presented was of a bull mastiff being challenged by a sleek and impudent whippet. He looked perplexed. He studied the other man's smiling face, evidently expecting some witticism for Jack Andrews was known for his humour. They all liked Jack despite the fact that he was not Irish as they were for nothing was too much trouble for him. He worked alongside them and did more than his share. He was always the first to help a mate in need, to put his hand in his pocket towards the "tramping bob" collected for a destitute navvieman. Only a farthing or two from each man in the gang but enough to make up the shilling which was customary to help another on the tramp to find work. And he'd bought Racer many a jug of ale when Racer was skint. There was great loyalty and comradeship amongst the men who worked on the railways. They might be looked on as troublemakers – and frequently were – a malevolent scourge by the villagers and farmers who lived in the vicinity of the track-laying but amongst their own they were steadfast, always standing shoulder to shoulder against outsiders.

Jack Andrews was such a man. He was as fond of a drink as the next man, could sweet-talk a pretty woman with the rest, though not with such force, and would get into a fight, particularly if his mates were involved, as willingly as any other. He was not what Racer and Billyo called a "serious" brawler, for his sense of humour and fair play and what he smilingly called his "conscience", whatever that was, often got in his way, but he never interfered with or tried to restrain the others when they were excited by the liquor they poured down their throats.

So what was up with him now? Why was he standing there, smiling cheerfully, his eyes glowing with goodwill, blocking Racer's view of the two tasty wenches with whom he meant to spend an enjoyable half-hour or so. Heaven-sent, these two were, as was any wandering female who crossed Racer's path. You didn't often find village or farm women out alone since their menfolk kept them close when chaps like himself and his gang were on the randy and Racer meant to make the most of the opportunity. There were women in the camp, "wives" of the navvies who followed their men from shanty town to shanty town, bearing them child after child but they were not available to any man except the one with whom they had "jumped the brush". These two were!

"Now then, Jack, step outa me way, there's a good lad fer I mean ter show these pretty lasses how an Irishman treats a lady." He turned to wink again at his comrades and they nudged one another, grinning lewdly.

"Yer surprise me, Racer, 'onest yer do. Why yer should weant ter be troublin' these . . . these young ladies" – turning to bow in the direction of the two wide-eyed girls – "when there's a real woman waitin' for yer at Bowling Green is summat I can't understand. Kitty'll have bin on pins fer hours, dyin' fer a sight of yer ugly mug an' if yer don't look sharp I reckon she'll be up them dancers wi' French Joe an' then where'll yer be."

He continued to grin lazily but there was a certain tension about his mouth and his eyes were deep and watchful.

"Sure an' what the 'ell do I care fer that owd slag when there's two dainty little pieces ter me hand, Jack Andrews. So stand aside, lad, an' let the dog see the rabbits." He couldn't have chosen a more apt illustration for both Sara and Alice were staring at him with the wide, unblinking eyes of hypnotised animals caught in a trap.

Jack would not give up. "These two'll be no fun, Racer, believe me. Look at 'em . . ." and a dozen pair of eyes did so, studying with avid interest the softly budding breasts, the tiny waist and neatly curving hips of the younger girl, the more mature fullness of the elder. They were both dressed in white, plain and modest, their dresses of fine cotton material. The younger had a sash of apple green velvet about her waist. The only incongruous note to their comely appearance were the sturdy black boots on their feet.

In direct contrast to the menace in the dusty lane, the flesh-crawling emotions of fear, of excitement and anticipation, the sunlight fell in a slumbrous golden haze in which midges danced madly and bees droned as they blundered from flower to flower. It was hot and tranquil, a day to lie and dream amongst the yellow wheat ears which moved gently on the far side of the hedge. A day to breathe in the silky fragrance of the fading summer, the sweetness which broods breathlessly on an unexpectedly warm autumn afternoon. A solitary robin sang and two fields away a team of red oxen pulled a plough, the rattling of their chains clearly heard on the peaceful air. A far cry indeed from the violence which threatened to spill over in the lane at this inflammable moment.

Racer was becoming impatient and beside him Billyo's face took on the truculent expression the others knew only too well. He and Racer were a well-matched pair, strangely alike in appearance, though if what Racer had between his ears could be so described, he was the "brains" of the two. Racer began arguments, fights, brawls, or indeed any activity which was to hand, be it at work or play and Billyo followed.

"Bugger off out of it, Jack. Sure an' if yer don't fancy a bit o' fun then leave it ter those as do. Go on, be on yer way. Me an' Billyo an' the rest only want ter be friendly wi' these bonny colleens but if yer not interested then don't stop those who is."

Jack sighed and took his hands out of his pockets. Big hands they were and already balling into fists though he still smiled, a merry smile that brought forth an answer from several of the less vicious of the men. There were one or two who were not as brutalised as Racer and Billyo and they were a mite uneasy at the thought of interfering with these two terrified lasses. You could tell they were decent girls, not like many of the buxom country women who, bored with the rustic charms of farm labourers, thatchers and hedgers, welcomed the attentions of the bold Irish, enjoying their wit, their roguish impertinence and were only too happy to be seduced by it.

"Don't bother with 'em Racer," Jack said softly. "See, little 'un's no more 'n a bairn." As he spoke and as though to emphasise his words he turned to Sara and Alice who, despite her growing terror, still brandished her stick, ready to use it if she got the chance. The men at his back did not see his lips move nor hear the words he mouthed at her.

"When I move, lass, take yer sister an' run like t'wind fer home." Alice blinked then nodded briefly to show she understood, and Jack thanked God for her quick intelligence.

"Ter the devil wi' yer, Jack Andrews," Racer roared, "yer nothin' but a great windbag wi' nowt in yer pants ter show yer a man an' I'll thank yer not ter interfere, so I will. If yer've not the stomach fer a wee bit o' fun then step aside unless yer askin' fer a fight."

"Now yer come ter mention it, Racer, I reckon I might be." To the amazement of the rest of the men and indeed Racer himself, Jack smiled warmly and so did they for there was nothing – apart from a lassie with her legs open to them – they liked better than a brawl. In fact, if they had to choose between the two they would be hard pressed to say which appealed to their masculine nature the most. The girls, for the moment, could be put to one side, so to speak, for wouldn't they still be there in the short space of time it would take Racer to flatten Jack Andrews. He could look after himself, could Jack and was a grand fellow to have at your back in any kind of set-to. He was handy with his fists but the bull-like strength of Racer would overwhelm him before he could so much as brandish them. And then there was Billyo, for it would not be a fair fight, man to man, but a free-for-all in which any man might take part.

Turning away from the girls, the men moved into the customary shuffling circle which forms when one male is about to take on another and as they did so Jack drew back a fist as hard as the iron rails he himself helped to lay and drove it with all his young strength into Racer's enormous stomach, doubling him up and driving the breath out of his body with a gasp.

At once Alice abandoned the stick, and took hold of her sister's arm, dragging her for several yards along the bottom of the ditch. Clambering up its side, her left hand grappling with her long skirt, she heaved the almost senseless Sara along with her, racing her up the lane towards safety. Their pounding feet raised a soft milky dust as they ran.

Racer was still hanging with his head between his knees and so did not see them go but Billyo did and at once he began to bellow like a wounded animal. Unfortunately, so slow moving was his brain he could not quite make up his mind what to do next, chase the girls or reach for Jack Andrews and by then it was too late. The others, themselves bewildered by the turn of events, watched open-mouthed for several lost moments as the girls disappeared, then, in frustrated rage, they turned almost as one man on Jack Andrews, the source of their blighted hopes. A couple of them dithered in the direction in which the girls had gone, but the sharp slap of flesh on flesh brought them eagerly back to what was, after all, at least for now, their favourite occupation.

They began, slowly, to murder Jack Andrews. They were mindless, maddened not so much by the loss of the girls, for there would always be women to be found somewhere but by the simple and brutal pleasure they took in pitting their strength against Jack's.

He did not go down lightly. He was strong and young and the very number of them helped him at first to defend himself. Fists aimed at him hit another by mistake, who in turn struck out in response and for several minutes there were two or three disgruntled scraps going on round Jack, Racer and Billyo who were the main protagonists. The two older men were panting, slit-eyed, beyond reason as they rained hammer blows on the younger, striking Jack's flesh in obscene unison, trampling on him with their hobnailed boots when he went down, dragging him upright in order to knock him down again, mangling and mauling him as they slowly reduced him to a bundle of wheezing, bleeding rags.

It would have gone on until all life had left him. Racer and Billyo had gone out of control and those who might have attempted to restrain them were themselves involved in their own grievances.

When the horse and rider erupted explosively among them they were confused and alarmed, though still aiming blows at one another as was their habit.

"What the devil is going on here?" a voice thundered. "Stop that at once, d'you hear me." Though they were not the sort of men to heed authority, especially when their bloodlust was up, something they recognised in the voice of the man who spoke seemed to send a message to their inflamed minds and all of them, with the exception of Racer and Billyo, slowly fell away from one another and stepped reluctantly back from the scene of the carnage.

The horseman, though he himself was not a man of violence, to which anyone in the village of Wray Green would testify, knew his mare would instinctively avoid the man on the ground as he drove the animal at the two who were still steadfastly engaged in kicking him to death. With another roar he and the horse sent them both toppling backwards into the dust of the lane, but like beasts they turned in his direction. A man, a horse, a raging tiger for that matter, it was all the same to Racer and Billyo. Something to take the iron blows, the lethal feet, the butting heads, even the snapping teeth they were both determined to inflict on someone and for several moments it looked as though not only Jack Andrews but the horseman and his mare would be finished by the red-misted murder in the hearts of the two deranged Irishmen.

But as quickly as it had begun it was over. They took some handling, did Racer and Billyo, the combined strength of the remainder of the gang finally overwhelming them. By the time they were able to see him clearly the horseman had dismounted and was bending over the recumbent figure on the ground. They shook their heads to clear their brains and almost at once the navvies were miraculously transformed from brutish brawlers to the sheepish status of schoolboys who had been caught in an unruly schoolyard game of fisticuffs. And the wafer-thin, elderly man who had ridden the mare at them was the incredible cause of the transformation. They waited humbly for him to speak.

"Here, you two," he called, unafraid of their dreadful appearance, their purpling eyes, bloody noses and cut lips. "Lift this lad . . . gently, dammit and take him . . . for god's sake I said lift him gently. I don't like the look of that leg . . . My house is just up the lane. Tell my servant to have a bed ready in the kitchen, she'll know what you mean . . . that's it . . . carefully, carefully, and the rest of you can get on your way and be quick about it. I've never seen such disgraceful behaviour in my life."

"Sorry, Doctor . . . begorra, we'd no idea, had we, Paddy . . . will yer not let . . .?"

"I'm not concerned with your regrets and I don't want to know why you were beating this man to a bloody pulp but let me say this. It's pretty obvious you're off on a randy. Now I don't care what you do to each other but if I find you have interfered with anyone in this village the next time I am called to that camp of yours to set a broken bone I shall be forced to refuse. Do I make myself clear?"

"Yer do that, Doctor . . ."

"Aye, ter be sure . . . sorry, Doctor . . . sorry . . ."

"Sure an' we meant no harm, not really . . ."

They all – except Racer and Billyo – cast agonised glances in the direction the girls had gone, hoping to God and the Holy Mother that they were nothing to do with this man, for without his ministrations many of the men who had worked on the Preston to Wyre line would be unemployable. The work was dangerous. Gangs of men, half disciplined, if at all, hacked away at great banks of earth which promptly fell in on them. There were explosions, for the men were careless, casually smoking their pipes near open barrels of gunpowder. Trucks were derailed, pinning boys beneath them and stone fell in cuttings, crushing the fragile bones of arms and legs. Navvies had a kind of unspoken bravado, a daring which caused accidents where none should be and it was this man, this doctor, unlike many others of his kind, who turned out time and time again to put them to rights. Usually so mild-mannered, here he was shouting the odds about Jack Andrews who looked as though he'd never get to his feet again! Glory be to God, what if he should find out about the two wee girls who were obviously inhabitants of Wray Green? Thanks to the Holy Mother they hadn't touched them. Aye, and thanks be to Jack Andrews, poor sod, who didn't look as though he'd last the day, God love 'im.

2

He was stark naked when he came to, bound firmly as though with ropes beneath crisp white sheets which smelled of soap and the fragrance of fresh ironing. The combination brought back memories of his mother as she bent over the enormous pine table in the centre of the kitchen which was the glowing heart of the cottage where he had been brought up. She would be "giving what for" to the newly washed shirts he and his brothers had worn and which moments before had been whipped in from the clothes line which stretched from post to post across the back of the cottage. Snapping in the brisk wind they would have been, the wind which always blew across the peaks and moorland in which the village of Woodhead was set. Four vigorously laundered shirts standing out like flags amongst the pegged sheets which would be placed so as modestly to hide her own pair of bloomers and stays. His mother was a Lancashire woman, constrained and hardworking and a fiend with the wash-tub. She could not abide muck. Muck was her enemy and no matter where it landed she attacked it with relish.

"Let's have that shirt off thi', our Jack," she'd say in her broad-vowelled northern accent. "Tha' looks as though tha's bin down't coal pit, so tha' does, an' only clean on this mornin'." She would cluck her tongue reprovingly. "An' whilst I'm at it the rest on yer can strip off an' all. Clean 'uns are fresh ironed an' airin' by't fire."

"Aah, Mam . . ." they would all protest half-heartedly, knowing it would do no good. Down the track one of them would be sent to the racing deluge of Withens brook to fetch the water and before you could say "soap" it would be heating on the fire which was never allowed to go out. If none of them was about she could be seen – unlike many of her slatternly neighbours – at all hours of the day tramping sturdily down the track with her empty buckets and up it again, more slowly, when they were filled. She was always at it, washing and scrubbing and polishing, proud of her spotless doorsteps, her shining windows which winked in the sunlight, the neat net curtains, carefully darned again and again, which she had brought with her from Manchester on her marriage. Proud of the high gloss on her mahogany chiffonier which had once belonged to her mother in the tiny cold parlour, the gleaming brass face on the tall clock and the beautifully embroidered red velvet cushions – done by herself as a small girl – on her sturdy kitchen chairs.

Madge Andrews, Madge Broadbent as she had been then, had, in many folk's opinion and particularly her father's, come down in the world when she married handsome, red-haired Chris Andrews, for she had been the only daughter of a small but respectable cotton agent and could have done better for herself. She could read and write and, her mother being dead, had run her father's home conscientiously and to perfection, seeing to him and her brothers' needs until dashing Chris Andrews had come into her life and swept her off her normally steady and circumspect feet. Chris had been no more than what her father sneeringly called "an odd job" man doing a bit of casual joinery at the offices in Lower Mosley Street, with no particular trade and with no intention of learning one, preferring, he said winningly, to be his own gaffer. That was what he was, winning, charming, warm-hearted and Jack's mother loved him until the day he died of a fever, regretting nothing she had relinquished for him though he had, in turn, given her nothing but four strapping sons, hardship and his total devotion.

Jack was the youngest of Madge Andrews's boys. He was ten years old when his father died, his brothers Harry, Will and George twelve, fourteen and sixteen respectively. They were all working by then, even Jack doing a bit of stone-picking or rook-scaring, for Chris Andrews's careless application to his position of "man of all trades master of none" had brought in barely enough to feed himself and Madge, let alone four sturdy boys with appetites to match. Chris did a bit of fence-mending, ditch-digging, clock-repairing, patching up farm implements, but mostly the men in the villages and farms saw to their own repairs and when he died his "wage" was hardly missed.

The three older boys had become farm labourers, Harry and Will over at Great Hill Farm and George further down the valley at High Shine Farm. The cottage in which the family lived was rented to them by the farmer at High Shine and because George, who was then sixteen, was courting the farmer's dairymaid, they were given permission to remain there. When he was eighteen, the farmer said, knowing he had a good steady worker in both George and his Emily, and were married, the cottage would be theirs for as long as George worked for him.

By the time Jack was fifteen and working in the slate quarry up beyond Snailsdon Moss the cottage was filled to overflowing with George and Emily, George and Emily's children, four of them in three years, and with himself and his mother. Harry and Will, thankful to escape, had moved over to rented accommodation near the sheep farm at Great Hill and were both "walking out" with local maidservants, ready to settle in the tied cottages the farmer would provide when they were wed.

But George's wife, despite her training as a dairymaid, had not the scrupulous passion for cleanliness Madge Andrews was used to and the cottage was a constant battlefield between the muddle Emily would have allowed it to sink into and the fanatical determination of her mother-in-law to prevent it. The two brothers, George and Jack, were for ever caught in the crossfire. George had no choice but to put up with it. Jack, forced to sleep on a truckle bed in the kitchen, since the cottage had only two bedrooms, desperately sought a way out. The slate quarry was steady, relatively well paid and the hard manual work suited his rapidly developing body but he longed to know more, to see more of the world beyond the village, to have adventures, to do more than trudge the five miles up to Snailsdon Moss six days a week, quarrying slate for twelve hours a day with no prospect beyond that, drifting on the same domestic trail as George and Harry and Will.

They had all heard – as who had not – that the railway was to go through. It had been speculated about ever since the year Jack's father had died, the year the railway company was formed, though those in the area were unaware of its exact timing. The Sheffield, Ashton Under Lyne and Manchester

Railway Company, it was called, or so they had heard. The plans had been commissioned by then, and an engineer by the name of Charles Vignoles appointed to carry them out, though again the folk of Woodhead were not privy to this information. All they knew was that there was to be some sort of ceremony at Saltersbrook, a place a mile or so east of Woodhead, so why not go and see what it was all about for any sort of event was welcomed in this part of the world where the escape of Fred Armitage's pig was considered exciting. They weren't even exactly sure what it was all about but it was a nice day and they'd nowt' else to do!

They were dumbfounded as they watched some elderly gentleman by the name of Lord Wharncliffe cut the first sod on what was to be a tunnel running from their village of Woodhead in Derbyshire to Dunsford Bridge in Yorkshire which must be at least three miles and all under the roughest terrain, the bleakest, most inhospitable bit of moorland to be found in the high country of the Pennines. Sheep, bogs and heath, that's all there was there and how it was to be done was a mystery to the simple farm labourers, shepherds, wallers and the quarrymen who had come to see the ceremony, Jack amongst them.

Jack was immeasurably excited, he didn't even really know why at first. He had never taken a great deal of interest in railway building though now, as he watched Lord Wharncliffe put his spade in the ground and listened to the words of the elderly gentleman on the progress this was to bring, it struck him quite forcibly that he was right. This was the beginning of another age, another era in which the railway train with its ability to carry people and goods at amazing speeds from one part of the country to another would play an enormously powerful role. And here was his chance to get in on it. To make something worthwhile happen in his life. He didn't quite know what but whatever it was it wouldn't take place if he stayed in Woodhead and it could hardly be worse than quarrying slate for the rest of his life. He was fifteen years old, tall, strong, well nourished by his mother's boiled mutton, rabbit pie, pig's trotters, hotpots and stews, the vegetables he and his brothers had grown in the bit of garden at the rear of the cottage, the milk and cheese George brought back from the farm, just the sort of handy lad the ganger in charge was looking for, he said, and while his mother's attention was elsewhere he had signed on, properly signed on, for Jack Andrews, thanks to his mam, could read and write, to engage in digging out the Woodhead Tunnel.

When the first shaft was sunk at the western end of the tunnel Jack was among the men who helped to sink it. Despite the warm bed which was his within easy walking distance at the cottage each night he chose to stay amongst the men with whom he worked, sleeping in the tents provided, or bivouacked in huts run up with loose stones and mud and thatched with ling from the moor. There was constant rain that winter, making mining difficult and the construction of access roads almost impossible. More and more men were taken on as navvies until there were a thousand of them. At its highest point the moor across Woodhead is fifteen hundred feet above sea level. The tunnel went through the millstone grit, the shale, the red sandstone, the slate and clay at a height of one thousand feet so that the shafts were often five hundred feet deep and when it was completed Jack was to wonder how he had survived it. There were many men killed and injured but Jack not only survived but grew from gangling youth into manhood. Six years it took to build, that killing tunnel, the tunnel which was generally ankle deep in mud but on more than one occasion knee deep in mud. Water ran down the sides of the walls and men, parched by the work and close atmosphere underground, drank this foul and muddy effluence and became ill with gut-wrenching dysentery. But Jack, having had the benefit of a mother with good sense who had brought him up to be the same, had resisted the practice, carrying a jug of watered ale with him and had remained in good health and sound of limb.

Now, here he lay, smashed to pieces by the fists of the men he had called mates and all over a slip of a girl with the eyes of a frightened doe and the soft and trembling mouth of a child and . . .

"I think he's coming to, Dolly," he heard a light voice whisper and at once he was dragged back from the confused thoughts which circled in his head. His aching head, he realised, groaning a little as he moved it an inch or two on the pillow, doing his best to turn it so that he could see who it was who had spoken. He was conscious of the crackling of a fire, the full, contented rumble of a cat, the resonant ticking of a clock and the rustle of material as someone bent over him. His eyes were still closed and he was surprised to find that he could not get them open. The lids seemed to be glued together and he began to panic, struggling to part them, to get a look at where he was and who was beside him but more to reassure himself that the kicks he had received to his head had not blinded him. He could vaguely remember the fight . . . aye, with Racer and Billyo who had wanted to interfere with the young girl . . . girls, though the older one could hardly be called that. Liked them young, did Racer . . . Oh God, what if he . . . he couldn't remember, his last memory had been the sight of a boot being aimed at his head – bloody hell, it ached – and then nothing, nothing but those wide and incredibly green eyes . . .

A hand as light and gentle as a dove's wing settled on his forehead. There was a fragrance – what was it? – roses, and another of beeswax . . . the smell of beeswax he remembered from his mother's parlour, and overlaying the two was the aroma of baking – steak and kidney pie – yes, just like his mam used to bake. In fact it all seemed so familiar he might have been back in the kitchen of the cottage up by Woodhead.

He tried again to open his eyes, moving his head more frantically on the pillow and at once whoever stood beside the bed leaned closer and two small hands were placed one on either side of his face, holding him steady. Immediately he became calm, recognising them, though he couldn't have said why. It was her, the young one, the little one, the soft and gentle one, the one whose fear had brought to the surface all Jack's unsuspected but natural male need to protect, to shield the vulnerability of a female from others and, by God, he'd done it but at what cost?

"No," she was saying, "oh no, please, you mustn't move, must he, Dolly? You have been hurt and you must lie still or you might tear the stitches." He could feel her compassion flowing in strong waves, like the sea upon the shore, cooling his fevered body as the salt water will cool the sand, soothing his anxious mind which toyed with pictures of Jack Andrews being led about like a child for the rest of his days.

"Don't try to move, or speak either," she went on, a little breathlessly, as though, like a child, she was excited to be helping in this important business of nursing. "Yes, I know you can't open your eyes but really, if you could see yourself . . ."

There was a small chuckle, quickly suppressed and he wanted to smile at her but of course he couldn't. "Oh glory, that sounds daft, doesn't it, but if you were able to look in the mirror you'd know what I mean. It's very bruised, two enormous black eyes and stitches where . . ." She stopped and cleared her throat and he had the distinct impression there were tears there though her hands continued to cup his cheeks as gently as before. "My father's a doctor, you know, and he sewed you up and . . . oh, a few other things but nothing that won't mend, he says. No, please lie still," as he began to struggle feebly, wanting to know what the "few other things" were, "you can trust Papa, really you can. He's the best doctor in the world, everyone says so." There was a wealth of love and pride in her young voice.

Still Jack did his best to open his eyes. He could faintly make out red and brown moving shadows against his eyelids but though he did his best to lift them they were just too heavy and he lay still, longing for the cool hands to remain where they were. He licked his dry lips, a movement weak and painful, for his mouth felt as though it had been run over by a herd of cattle. As though it was not his own at all and he couldn't control properly what he did with it.

"See, leave lad alone, Miss Sara, I'll tend to 'im," a disapproving voice tutted. "Tha's done enough already. Besides, it's not fittin' for a young lady to be . . . be fussin' over a chap what's not fambly. You don't find Miss Alice hangin' over him like you're doin'. She knows better. Now leave 'im be. I can do what's needed."

"Oh please, Dolly. I helped Father with him yesterday."

"Aye, I saw thi'." Whoever it was sniffed in what was evidently outrage. "And I don't like it an' neither would tha' mama. I told tha' pa so an' all an' he agreed wi' me so kindly step aside an' let me tekk over."

"Oh Dolly, *please*. He saved us from . . . from . . ." She gulped painfully and her hands trembled on Jacks' face and he longed to lift his own to them, to comfort her evident distress. "He wants a drink, Dolly, so won't you let me give him one. After what he did . . . please, we're only wasting time. He's thirsty, aren't you?" and Jack managed a small nod though he didn't want her to go, even to fetch the drink his parched mouth and throat needed.

"Fetch some water, Dolly," he heard her say firmly and

from somewhere in the room there was the sound of a deep resigned sigh. Elderly footsteps crossed the flags, there was the sound of the rustle of skirts and of liquid being poured into a container.

"I'll give it to you on a spoon," the young voice murmured gently, while behind her he sensed the hovering presence of the woman, a much older woman, it seemed, and heard her muttering in that particular way the elderly have when they wonder out loud, knowing they cannot be reprimanded for they are, after all, talking to themselves, on what the world was coming to when a young lady takes it upon herself to . . .

The girl's sweet breath fanned his face as she bent closer to him and when the hands left him he felt bereft. "Can you open your mouth just a little?" she asked anxiously and when he did, feeling it was going to tear even more at the corners, she carefully tipped a sip of water, sweet, ice-cold water, refreshing delicious water between his lips and across his tongue where it slipped down his throat. There was another and another, each one as gently administered and after each she asked, "another?" until at last he felt revived enough to shake his head.

"When you're feeling better, if my father says you might, we'll try some soup. Dolly makes it from shin of beef and it's very nourishing. Now, Papa says you must sleep as much as you can. It's the best healer, he says and . . . what is it? Do you want something else? What is it you want?" she asked again, sinking back on her heels beside the bed.

His voice was cracked and hoarse when he managed to answer, just as though Racer and Billyo's boots had stamped on his windpipe, but Sara Hamilton clearly heard what he said.

"Nothing . . . only your . . . hands on me face."

"Of course," she said, as though it were the most natural thing in the world. He sighed thankfully as she returned them and his mind and body were soothed by her touch as he fell into a deep and healing sleep.

The next time he awoke it was night-time. He could tell because the red and brown shadows behind his eyelids had turned to a blackness which frightened him at first. He lay still, telling himself it was all right because he could still smell roses and beeswax and hear the rumble of the cat's purring. It was quiet except for that and the steady ticking of the clock but his senses became more alert as he thought he could detect the sound of someone breathing. It was only light, but steady, long-drawn out, the sound a sleeper makes in the depth of tiredness.

He felt better, not in his poor battered body which he could tell had been subjected to a severe beating, one of those at which Racer and Billyo were so adept, but in himself, in his mind which was clearer. He lay still but with a great effort, just as though he were lifting a barrowload of the stone and muck he dug out and cleared hour after hour on the track, he managed to turn his head, open his swollen eyes and there she was!

Sara! That was her name. He had heard her sister call her that yesterday – was it yesterday or the day before? – on the lane where they had been picking blackberries and here in this room, which seemed to be the kitchen, the old woman had addressed her thus.

Jack Andrews couldn't explain what had happened to him when he had seen Sara Hamilton shrink away from the men – and him – her small, booted feet deep in the wild flowers growing in the ditch, her rosy mouth stained with blackberry juice, her terror clouding her lovely childlike face. He couldn't explain it but he knew it was something which would be important to him. He was twenty-one years of age and the pleasures of a woman's body were not unknown to him. There had been a dairymaid, young but experienced with whom, for a month or two, he had thought himself to be in love. Mad for her he had been, or at least for her ripe, pink-tipped breasts, the white sheen of her belly and the thick tangle of dampness which she revealed to him with her spread legs. Mad for her in that short period of time in which the track the navvies laid had run beside the farm where she worked, then, when the gang moved on she had slipped from his mind as easily as the other women with whom he had loved and, for the most part, laughed.

But this one was not of that order at all. When she had focused her beautiful, sea green eyes on his, the terror in them had flooded his own heart with pain. The direct appeal in them had been irresistible. Something had caught in his throat. His insides had lurched quite mysteriously and his heart had tripped before it softened to a gentle awareness as though something had been revealed to it which it instantly recognised.

Now she lay sprawled in the chair beside his bed, a plump marmalade cat on her lap and both were deeply asleep. She wore a white nightgown. Her head had fallen to one side and her lips were slightly parted. Dark fans formed a crescent on her cheeks where her eyelashes lay and her hair, like molten, fiery gold in the light of the flickering candle, streamed across one shoulder almost to the floor. She had one bare foot tucked underneath her, the hem of her nightgown slightly bunched and the glowing flesh of her bare ankle gleamed like satin, fine and shapely. She had a shawl thrown across her shoulders, a fine woollen shawl in soft colours of palest honey and apricot and cream. It had a silken fringe which mingled with her hair, drifting with it to the spotless flags of the kitchen floor.

She was beautiful. He had never seen anything more delicately beautiful than Sara Hamilton. He had thought so then and he thought so now as his half-opened eyes studied her through the swollen, battered slits of his lids. Her sister had been attractive, like her but older, more . . . more sharp, hard, but there was something . . . something extraordinary, something unique about this young girl whose hands had calmed him to rest and he knew, as he watched her, that if he spent the rest of his life with her, he would never be able to explain it. She was only small, light, light as a bit of swansdown, or the snowdrops he had seen pushing through the grass in the spring. But warm, glowing, not pale like swansdown or snowdrops but the lovely blushing colours of a summer's evening sky. She was not tall, a little wisp of a thing who, were he to take her in his arms would fit just beneath his chin. She was only a child, fresh and innocent, an inexperienced young lass who would know nothing of men, but whose warmth and compassion when she had put her gentle hands on his face had been the personification of all that was womanly. Thank Christ her sister had been quick-witted enough to get her away, and herself of course, since their treatment at the hands of Billyo and Racer would not have been pleasant. He trembled to think what might have been done to her . . . over his dead body, of course, for they would have had to kill him first, which they had tried to do, he mused, chuckling wryly deep in his chest; even that hurt him. Hell's teeth, he was in a bloody mess and what must he look like to this child who was evidently watching over him? He had always had success with women. They seemed to like him and he certainly liked them but his good looks, if you could call them that, had gone, at least for the moment and would she remember him as he had been before the fight in the lane beyond the house?

She stirred in her sleep and he held his breath as best he could for he did not want her to waken. What was she doing here, anyway, he asked himself, watching over him in the night when she should be in her own bed? She must be exhausted. Couldn't the old woman have taken a turn, or her sister, though he was glad they hadn't. And where was her father, the good Doctor Hamilton whom they all knew at the camp? Why wasn't he here to keep vigil at his bedside, if vigil needed to be kept, which he doubted. Jack Andrews was strong and healthy and would soon mend and Sara Hamilton had no need to watch over him. The other way round, more likely, for a beautiful girl like her must be the target of every man's desire in Lancashire. Jesus God, what was the matter with him? What had happened to him . . . she was young . . . too young . . .

There was a small sound on the far side of the room as a door opened and into Jack's restricted vision came the tall, thin frame of the doctor. He sighed disapprovingly when he saw his daughter but even through eyes clogged and swollen, Jack could see and feel the power of his love for her. He put a gentle hand on her shoulder and at once she stirred, stretching and purring like a little kitten, looking about her with sleepy eyes, smiling up at her father in welcome. She lifted her hands to her hair, threading her fingers through it, pushing it to the back of her head then allowing it to tumble freely again about her back and shoulders. She stood up, much to the annoyance of the cat.

"Papa, I must have fallen asleep." She reached up to kiss his cheek.

"You shouldn't be here at all, child," her father scolded her lovingly. "This chap's in no danger and would have been safe on his own until I got back."

Jack kept his eyes hooded, watching Sara, knowing that neither she nor her father were aware that he was awake.

"I just slipped down to see if he wanted a drink. I must have fallen asleep . . ."

"And in your nightgown, too. Sara, you really must learn that you are–"

"I know, Papa, a lady. Alice tells me so a dozen times a day but this has nothing to do with proper behaviour, not really. He saved us, rescued us from . . . an unpleasant experience and I feel we owe him more than . . ."

"I know, my darling child. I understand. I am in his debt too, and those men and the contractor at the camp will be left in no doubt that if order cannot be kept then they must find themselves another medical man. We have a lot to thank this chap for and we will when he wakes. Dear God, when I think . . ."

He shuddered and Sara shuddered with him, recoiling from the pictures which had so recently been real, the red, sweaty faces, the dreadful grinning ugliness, the rotting teeth, the feeling of filth, of something obscene which she had not fully understood.

"If they had hurt you, my darling, they would have had me to answer to."

And me, Jack said to himself. It did not occur to him to wonder why the doctor did not include his elder daughter in his statement!

"Well, they didn't, Papa, only this poor man." Sara's youthful voice was very earnest and Jack could imagine how bright and lovely her eyes would be in the candlelight. "But because it was me and Ally, because we were the cause of it I want to help him. Help to get him better. You do see that, don't you?"

Richard Hamilton smiled and cupped his daughter's cheek.

"Oh yes, I do, Sara Hamilton. I do see that. Now will you go to bed and leave me to attend to this poor fellow's needs. Has he had a drink yet?"

"Yes, some water." Jack felt her warmth as she bent over him. Her rippling hair touched his face and to his shame and horror the dark centre where his manhood lay stirred lazily. Jesus, that hadn't been damaged at any rate, but what if this girl and her father should notice it beneath the tightly tucked sheet that lay over him. Oh Jesus, what could he do to distract them, this good man and his innocent daughter who would be shocked to see the growth of his erection? Unable to think of anything else, indeed he was incapable of anything else, he let out a hoarse groan and thrashed his head from side to side on the pillow.

Agony struck him and the groan became genuine as what seemed to be every part of his body flared with it. At once the doctor was beside him, his hand to his forehead. His daughter moved hastily backwards to allow him room and Jack physically felt the sweetness of her presence leave him and he was quite bewildered at his sense of loss.

"What is it, old man?" the doctor asked him. "Where does it hurt?" Then, seeing that Jack's eyes were half opened, he smiled grimly. "That was a damned stupid question, wasn't it, since there's scarcely an inch of your body those two bullies missed. Just lie still and I'll give you another draught to make you sleep."

He turned his head to Sara who still hovered anxiously at his back, and so did Jack and the doctor clucked his tongue impatiently.

"I said lie still, lad. You've taken a heavy blow to the head, several heavy blows and I doubt thrashing it about like that will help."

"What . . . damage? How . . . where?" Jack managed to mumble through his torn lips.

"You've a broken leg, I'm afraid. A fracture of the tibia which is at the front and the inside of the leg. No doubt caused by the same boots which damaged your head but I've set it and it will mend in time. You've lost fifty per cent of your body skin and what is left is so badly bruised you're going to look like a ripe plum for many weeks. I'm a bit doubtful about your ribs so I've bound them up just to be on the safe side and your face looks like a prize fighter's, but apart from that you're as fit as a flea. It's a good job you're as strong as you are. A lesser man would have come off considerably worse." He smiled broadly, then winked. "Now then, drink this," and, like his daughter had done with the water, gently spooned some cool liquid into Jack's mutilated mouth.

"Thank . . . you," Jack managed, doing his best to see Sara who was no more than a dark shadow at her father's back, then, thankfully, for his body was on fire with pain and his head felt as though it were clamped in a vice, he let the calm blanket of the drug-induced sleep wrap about him.

Sara Hamilton gazed down pityingly at the unrecognisable face of the young man who had so amazingly come to her and

Alice's rescue. She could still see him as he had been before he had strolled so casually through the group of ogling men and just as casually offered her and Ally his protection. Why had he done it? Why had he whispered to Ally to run, "run like the wind"? Oh yes, she could remember those words though at the time she had been deeply locked in terror, and she could remember his eyes which had sent her some message, though she could not have said what it was. One man against a dozen and yet he had smiled, at her, and at them, his brown eyes crinkling at the corners, his mouth stretched in a lopsided, endearing grin over his strong white teeth. Oh yes, she remembered that, too, and his multicoloured waistcoat which had been of green and blue, all shades from lime to mint, from peacock to aquamarine, from the blue of a cornflower to the pale colour of a duck's egg. Beautiful, it was, suiting his darkness, of skin and eyes and the rich russet of his hair and now it was in ruins, bloodstained and torn, as he was, and how was she ever to thank him, for that was how those men would have left her and Alice had it not been for him. Young she was, and inexperienced, ignorant of the details of physical, sexual abuse, but old enough and intelligent enough to know it would have changed her for ever.

"Go to bed, darling child," she heard her father say. "He'll do until morning."

"Is he really all right, Papa?" Her voice trembled with deep distress.

"Of course he is, Sara. Don't upset yourself, sweetheart. I know how deeply you feel the hurt of others. I worry about it . . . well . . ." He shook himself and put a hand to her shining hair, pushing it back with great tenderness from her anxious face.

"He's a strong and healthy man. He'll be in that bed for a week or two and be as stiff as a board and sore as the devil when he gets out of it but by this time next week he'll feel a great deal better. How he'll fare later I don't know but he'll manage."

"I'll help him, Father," she said resolutely.

He smiled and pulled her to him, tucking her head beneath his chin as Jack had just imagined doing. "I know you will, my pet, but I mean when he gets back to the navvie camp. I'll say this for them, though. They may be brawlers and drinkers and troublemakers but they're loyal and supportive with their own."

"Even one they've almost killed," his daughter murmured against his chest.

"Don't exaggerate, Sara. He's far from dead, and as for the damned navvies, by now, after they have drunk themselves into a stupor, they will have forgotten all about it. In fact they'll probably be wondering where whatever his name is has got to!"

3

Sara Hamilton missed her mother as fiercely as if she had died yesterday instead of two years ago. Two years last Easter and despite the time that had elapsed she still looked for her when she came into the house, even thought she caught a brief glimpse of her at the bottom of the flower garden now and again. Her shawl would be slipping gracefully from her narrow shoulders and her faded copper curls, from where Sara and Alice had got their own colouring, would be falling in an enchanting tumble about her head. Enchanting, that was what her mama had been, with a nature which was warm and sunny and inclined to laughter and Sara would have been startled to learn that she was exactly like her. It was for this reason that Richard Hamilton guiltily loved Sara so much more than his older girl, who tended to be somewhat grand, stiff, ladylike in her dealings with others. There was no spontaneity in Alice who was four years older than Sara, for she could never quite allow herself to relax her guard against what she considered to be a lowering of the standards of her mama's well-bred family who, though she had never met them, she knew she would have admired enormously.

Sara could remember the shawl about her mama's shoulders. Even now it still retained in its folds the faint scent of the pot-pourri her mama made from the petals of roses and scattered amongst her clothing. The shawl was part of Sara's childhood. It had been bought for Eleanor Kingsley by her ardent bridegroom and worn on her wedding day twenty-two years ago, a fine wool in pastel shades of honey, apricot and cream with a long silken fringe. The scented shawl, Sara had called it as a child and just before she died her mama had told her that she was to have it though Alice had not been pleased.

It was twenty-two years since Dolly Watson came to live in Wray Green with the lovely, intelligent young woman who had been Sara's mother. At twenty-one still a girl herself really, Eleanor Kingsley had come from Cheshire where her own mother's family had been landowners. She had met Richard Hamilton, then in his late thirties, at the home of a mutual friend, Richard having gone to Cambridge with the older son of the house, and within two months they were married.

"Eleanor, I absolutely forbid you to leave your home for that wild country beyond the Ribble Estuary," her mother had told her coldly, expecting to be obeyed, for though Richard Hamilton was a gentleman he was not a wealthy one and in Mrs Kingsley's opinion came from what was only a step away from barren wasteland. Besides which, Eleanor's Uncle Frederick, Mrs Kingsley's older brother, was a baronet and surely her only daughter could do better than a country doctor?

"Mama, it is farmland, not wild country. Richard has a dear little house there and a good practice and I shall take Dolly with me. She will see I come to no harm."

"If you go, Eleanor, do not expect anything from your papa and me. You understand what I mean?" her mother asked her. "I do not approve and will take it badly if you disobey me."

"I'm afraid I must, Mama."

They had been happy, Eleanor and Richard Hamilton, Dolly could vouch for that and her two daughters had been a joy to Eleanor, especially the younger, though she had done her best not to let her preference show. She loved them, petted them, educated them to a standard which was somewhat above the level girls of their class normally achieved. The piano, French, the dances she knew, reading from the many books she had brought with her from Cheshire and even some of those her husband favoured. Sir Walter Scott's *Waverley* novels and Sir Edward Bulwer Lytton's *O'Neil, the rebel* being great favourites. They could write a fair hand and were aware of what their mama called "current affairs". Eleanor and Richard Hamilton were firm champions of Chartism and the betterment of the working classes. Their girls were acquainted with the reports of riots in Birmingham and other parts of the country, and the reasons for them. They were familiar with the movement to repeal the Corn Law and of its cold reception in parliament and though Alice merely pretended an interest in the philanthropic ideas of her parents to please her mama, Sara's tender heart was touched by the plight of the "poor", not aware that in the eyes of the middle-class society of the parish, the Hamiltons were as poor as church mice themselves.

Alice and Sara, having inherited their mother's gift with a needle, and with her to teach them everything she knew about sewing, became as talented as she was. Mention a stitch and Eleanor Hamilton could create it and so could they in time. Appliqué lace work, step stitch, scalloping, shell stitch, feather stitch, French knots and button holing. She could make a charming bonnet out of nothing more than a scrap of velvet, some lace and a silk rosebud; renovate lace and ribbons and though, from the day Doctor Hamilton brought her as a bride to Wray Green until the sad day she left her home in her coffin, she employed no dressmaker, she was considered to be the best-dressed, the most fashionable woman in the district.

She was loved and respected by her husband's patients on whom she lavished her whole-hearted but increasingly fragile strength and support whenever it was asked for and when she died, giving birth to a tiny, dead and unexpectedly late daughter, the village mourned her deeply, and every last one of them, from the oldest, Fanny Suthurst, to the newborn infant of Dora and Tom Wilson, turned out to line the route which led to her last resting place. Not the gentry, of course, if you could call them that, for they were treated by a more conventional medical man than Doctor Hamilton, but the cottagers and farm labourers, the cowmen and dairymaids, the ploughmen and their families whom he doctored very often without charge. He did not get on with the "gentry" as they liked to think themselves, nor they with him for they saw him as "odd", radical in his views, a traitor to his class. When he had brought his new wife home to Wray Green, since none of them knew of her well-bred connection and she felt no need to tell them, the Hamiltons were not included in the social world of the Benthams, the Armitages and their like. It mattered to neither Richard nor Eleanor. Their lives were complete with one another and they needed no one else and if it were to damage the success of their daughters' future in the middle-class society which was rightfully theirs, neither of them appeared to be concerned about it.

Sara wore the shawl on the day Jack Andrews gingerly heaved himself into a sitting position in the narrow truckle bed in the corner of the kitchen. It had turned colder, the morning hushed and waiting as October came in and gently ushered autumn towards winter. A fine mist drifted through Richard Hamilton's garden, blown from the morning fields by an errant breeze, swirling lightly beneath the branches of the horse chestnut tree. Sara had gone to pick Michaelmas daisies which were at their best at this time of the year, she told Jack with that bright enthusiasm she applied to everything she undertook, from helping Dolly to make coconut macaroons to playing with the marmalade cat. Teasing it, more like, Dolly grumbled, her own eyes fond as she watched her. Alice agreed, as she always agreed, Jack noticed, with anything that prevented her sister from enjoying herself. It was not ladylike behaviour to loll on the kitchen mat dangling a cotton reel on a bit of thread for the cat to play with, she snapped and Sara was to get up at once and do something useful.

"I'll go and pick some Michaelmas daisies then. Is that ladylike enough?" Sara asked.

"Rudeness does not become you, Sara. Mama instilled in us the need to be polite at all times, you know that, and I'm surprised at you."

"Oh Ally . . ." Sara was upset at the mention of her mother, Jack could see that and he longed to leap to her defence, to shush her and pet her back to her usual glowing delight in everything about her, but he was merely a spectator in this family and had no right to speak out.

"That's enough, Sara."

"See, Miss Sara," Dolly said placatingly, "put tha' shawl on, lass, it's parky out," deflecting the sharpness of Alice's tongue from her sister in a way Jack noticed she frequently did.

When Sara returned, the shawl slipping carelessly from one shoulder, Jack thought he had never seen anything quite so exquisite as the pink-cheeked young girl with her arms full of flowers. She wore a fine woollen dress of a colour somewhere between honey and cream, the shawl complementing it to perfection. The freshly picked flowers of pale and dark lilac,

strong purple and white were a splash of brilliance against
the subtle shading of her outfit but outshining them all was
the glory of Sara Hamilton herself. Her hair was tied at the
crown of her head with knotted ribbons of narrow cream
satin, the long ends caught in the tumbled mass of vivid
copper curls which, despite their confinement, fell halfway
down her back. In it sparkled droplets of moisture, catching
the firelight, diamonds which were mirrored in the pale sea
green of her eyes and on the ends of her long brown lashes
which in some light were tipped with gold. Her cheeks were
flushed to a brilliant carnation and her mouth was ripe, rosy,
smiling across the room at Jack, her earlier distress forgotten.
His heart gladdened, softened and his eyes welcomed her.

Dolly had modestly draped a light crocheted shawl about
his shoulders, one of her own which she had made in the long
winter evenings before the kitchen fire. It was a lovely shade
of blue and he felt an absolute fool in it but, bearing in mind
the tenderness of his badly lacerated flesh, he was grateful
for its lightness. Besides which, he knew she was aware that
he was a man and her girls were not accustomed to seeing
half-naked men lounging about the kitchen, and neither was
she. She liked things decent, did Dolly.

The weals, the torn and bloodied skin of his chest and
back and shoulders, the bruises which were turning from
livid purple and black to brown and green and yellow,
were not a pretty sight. He was feeding himself for the
first time, carefully spooning into his mouth the good broth
in which chunks of mutton and fresh vegetables floated. He
ate slowly, fastidiously almost, making none of the smacking,
sucking sounds with his lips as some common men did. On
the tray which Dolly had laid across his lap there was a
plate with slabs of fresh-baked bread neatly cut into cubes
to accommodate his awkwardness and Dolly watched him
approvingly, wondering where he had learned his dainty
manners.

Alice had gone to sit in the small front parlour which
she insisted her family use, though it was a waste of good
coal in Dolly's opinion. Mind you, she supposed her mama
would have approved, for though Miss Sara preferred the cosy
comfort and homely warmth of the kitchen it was only proper
that two young ladies such as Miss Alice and Miss Sara and
their papa, who was a gentleman, despite his lack of wealth,

should relax of an evening in their proper place, which was certainly not the kitchen!

Jack slowly lowered his spoon as Sara entered the room. His free hand clutched the shawl more firmly about him for he knew his body was a hell of a sight and how could such a lovely creature bear to look at it? Up to now the old woman had kept him firmly trussed up beneath the sheets, tucking them firmly under his chin so that only his battered face could be seen. A triangle of flesh which had hung above his right eye and which the doctor had sewn back as neatly as his own wife might have done, was healing nicely beneath its bandage and his eyes were fully open and had lost much of their puffiness. But he knew he still looked a bloody awful spectacle and certainly not one for a young girl such as Sara Hamilton to be forced to look at.

She didn't seem to care. Her face lit up with pleasure.

"Jack, how wonderful. You're sitting up and feeding yourself and don't you look fetching in Dolly's shawl?" she teased. "The colour suits you."

"Now then, Miss Sara," Dolly reproved, "don't you mekk fun o't lad. That there shawl's just right fer 'im. Warm an' light against 'is poor . . . well . . ." She scowled for it was against her nature to reveal the warm-hearted woman who breathed beneath the crusty exterior Dolly showed the world.

"I'm not making fun of him, Dolly, but you must admit he looks very— "

"Give over, Miss Sara. Now mekk thissen useful an' pass Jack that custard."

"I'll feed him if you like," throwing off her shawl and letting it slide to the bed where Jack lay. At once he was draped in its lovely perfume and it was his turn to scowl. For the past week she had taken it upon herself to spoon the broth and gruel, the light egg custards Dolly made, into his torn mouth and now he'd have to forgo that enchanted, tormenting pleasure, though he'd not let her know it. God, but it had been a joy, an exquisite torture, a pain and a rapture he could never describe to have her so close to him.

"Let me hold your head, Jack," she would say, "while I slip another pillow beneath it." It was both heaven and hell to have her glowing that special blinding smile which was so peculiarly hers into his own dazed face. She had a way of opening her eyes wide, like a child who is enchanted by what it sees, then narrowing them into laughter which she was determined to share.

"Lie back and don't fidget," she'd say, arming herself with the bowl and the spoon and sitting on the edge of his bed as though he were not a man but a log of bloody wood. Lie back and don't fidget! It was a bloody tall order when a girl as sweet-smelling, as dainty, as glorious as Sara Hamilton was leaning over him the way she innocently did. The soft swelling of her breast in its well-fitting bodice almost touched his shoulder, for Christ's sake. In the shadowed corner of the kitchen where his bed lay her eyes were the pale greeny-grey of the wild mignonette which grew on the barren wastelands near his Pennine home, her eyelashes, brown in some lights, copper in others, almost meshing as she concentrated on her task. He found himself watching her mouth with enormous fascination, for in her effort not to spill the soup from the spoon she pursed her lips then parted them as he did, as though he were a child to be encouraged, smiling a little at every successful mouthful.

"That's right, Jack," she would say softly, her back to Dolly, creating a small, cocooned world in which only he and Sara existed. "Sip it slowly. It will make you strong then we'll have you out of that bed and on your feet again. Dolly makes the best soup in the world. Ask anyone in the village for there are more than a few who have recovered from illnesses and accidents on Dolly's soup."

"Now then, Miss Sara," Dolly would say, but Jack knew the old woman was pleased and that was how Sara was, pleasing people without trying.

He never took his eyes from her face, as absorbed with her expressions, with the mobility of her curving mouth, the shining smile in her eyes, as she was in feeding him. Their glance would meet but she would not notice as the tiny frisson of something electric passed between them for she was too young for such things, he told himself miserably. Her smile would widen innocently and whatever was in her eyes was nothing more than the affection a child feels for someone it trusts. He would look away guiltily for she was a lady and was doing what any well-brought-up young lady was taught to do in helping those in need. It was bred in them, the belief that they should give aid and succour to those less fortunate them themselves. All ladies did "good works" among the poor and sick, especially one such as Sara Hamilton since she was the daughter of the local doctor and that was just what Sara was doing for him. Being charitable and by God, though it was a rejoicing in his heart, it played havoc with his masculinity. His body just could not help being stirred by her nearness, her warmth, the smell of her, the soft closeness of her golden rosy flesh, the tangle of loose curls which escaped from their ribbon and brushed against his face, and it was a damn good job, he told himself fiercely, that he could now feed himself.

But if her proximity in the task of feeding him had been a rapturous torment to him, the hour or two each day they spent alone with each other in the kitchen were the happiest he had ever known. Someone must stay within call, Doctor Hamilton had said in that first week after his beating, since Jack was completely unable to move, indeed must *not* move until the doctor was satisfied with the condition of his cracked ribs and the healing of his broken leg. A tricky break and one which would need watching and on no account was Jack to leave his bed while the doctor was out on his rounds. Therefore, either Alice, Dolly or Sara must be on hand to see to his needs and during the night when they were all in bed Jack had only to ring the handbell provided for him and the doctor would come down to him. Even the unconventional man who was father to Sara and Alice was aware that it would not be fitting for either of his daughters to attend to his patient in their night attire!

When he began to sit up for more than half an hour at a time, Jack was decently arrayed in a clean, much-mended nightshirt which belonged to Doctor Hamilton, made years ago by his nimble-fingered wife, but almost beyond repair. It had ruffles at the neck and wrists and with the rather rakish bandage about his head and the deep, still bruised amber of his face and throat he only needed gold earrings and a cutlass between his teeth to look like a pirate, Sara joked. Though Alice was supposed to take a turn in seeing to the needs of the patient, she didn't care for it, Jack could tell. It was beneath her cool dignity to feed a common navvie, to hold his head while he drank, to shift his pillow and smooth the sheet which was over him, and though she knew she should be grateful to him for saving her and Sara from the navvie gang, at the same time she resented the position he had put her in by doing it. She was polite, dignified, correct, but her manner said that though she was prepared to put up with it for the time being she did not like having him in the corner of her kitchen or indeed in her home.

Alice was away from home quite often, doing her best to infiltrate the "good" society which, with her breeding, she felt entitled to enter, calling on any pretext at the home of Mrs Bentham or Mrs Armitage who both had daughters the same age as Alice. If they were disconcerted to find her "calling" on them, they were too polite to show it and now and again Alice was gratified when she was invited to take tea, though very often Mrs Bentham and Mrs Armitage were not "at home" when she called. It did not deter her. She was determined not to be overlooked; after all she had a great-uncle who was a baronet which, when they knew of it, would make her welcome in any home. She watched and waited for her chance to take walks with Lilian Bentham and her governess, pretending to be just "passing" and as she was going their way perhaps . . .? She was assiduous in her application to the goal of being finally included in the round of sociability which was her due and to the correct social formulas which would achieve it for her.

Dolly was getting old. Not that she would admit it, even to herself, and her legs ached "summat fierce" when she had been on them for a few hours. She had been over fifty when she came to Wray Green with young Mrs Hamilton but she still did the heavy cleaning, the cooking and baking though, much to her chagrin, she had found herself forced to give in to Miss Sara's pleading to be allowed to help. There was no money in this house to pay a girl to give a hand with the chores and though nothing had ever been said, by her or the doctor, it was a good long time since Dolly had received a penny piece. In fact, not since Miss Eleanor, God rest her lovely soul, had died. Not that Dolly complained nor even cared about wages. She'd a bob or two under her mattress should she need a petticoat or a new pair of shoes but as she never went over the doorstep except for a breath of fresh air in the garden of a summer's evening, what did she want new shoes for? Her old ones would do her for as long as she needed them. She was up early and in her bed early and in between, perhaps after their midday meal, she liked to sit in Miss Eleanor's parlour – that's if Miss Alice wasn't there, of course – put her feet up and have forty winks. It was grand to see Miss Eleanor's things about her, her piano come from Cheshire with her, bits and pieces of dainty furniture and chinaware, and Miss Sara had only to call out if that there lad needed anything.

Jack was an intelligent young man, quick-witted with a keen sense of humour. He had an endearing, lively nature, slightly reckless as all the men in the navvie camp were, with a bold confidence six years of working among such men had bred in him. But with Sara he found himself increasingly tongue-tied. In those first few days he was in great pain but through it all he sensed her at his side, sitting patiently waiting for him to speak, to ask something of her, anything, she only wanted to help him. He smelled the roses and felt her warmth, her sweetness and it gave him great comfort at first. When he could see properly he was conscious of the soft sympathy in her eyes, her eager readiness to ease the agony of his devastated body, her gentleness and her womanliness, if that was the right word, doing what men in pain dream of a woman doing and it bowled him over, made him awkward, almost to the point of boorishness at times, though she didn't seem to notice.

"Tell me about your life, Jack," she said one warm afternoon when Alice had gone off to "call" on Charlotte Armitage whom she was determined to have as her friend since they were about the same age. Dolly was snoring in the parlour and Sara had sunk into the chair by the fire with a bit of sewing in her hands. The back kitchen door stood open and the autumn sunshine lay across the kitchen table in shimmered beams in which dust motes danced. Jack lay on his side, his deep brown eyes gazing through the bars of sunshine to the girl on the other side of the room.

"Tell me all about your family and where you come from and what you did before you went on the tramp." She had already picked up some of Jack's navvie vocabulary.

"There's nowt to tell really." His answer was terse since how could his rough upbringing mean anything to a girl brought up as Sara had been? How he slept rough in hedges and ditches when he was on the tramp, which sounded "romantic" to those who did not have to do it. The ginshops he had frequented and dog fights on which he put bets. The sprawling camps beside the railway tracks he helped to lay; the buxom, swearing, drunken women who lived in them with men who were just as brutalised. Human, they were, but different beings to Sara Hamilton.

"Oh, don't be silly, Jack, everyone has a mama and papa, sisters and brothers and I want to hear about yours." She took a couple of neat stitches before glancing up to smile at him, a vibrant smile of interest and goodwill and he looked away hastily but not before Sara had seen the strange expression in his eyes.

"What is it?" she asked in immediate sympathy, not recognising what an older, more experienced woman would have seen at once.

"Nothing . . . nothing."

"Are you in pain?"

"No." And to divert her he began to talk about his past. "Well, me mam came from Manchester," he said reluctantly.

"Did she? What did her family do?"

"Her family?"

"Mmm, her father."

"He was in cotton, so she said."

"Was he, and what about your father? Was he in cotton too and where did he and your mama meet?" applying to his life the rules and conventions of her own world where ladies and gentlemen were introduced at the home of a mutual acquaintance as her own mother and father had been.

"Nay, I don't know. Pa was a joiner, a repair man, a clock mender, a thatcher." He chuckled reminiscently at the memory of the well-meaning but feckless man who had been his father. "Put him to any job and he'd have a damn good try at it. Turn his hand to 'owt, could Pa but he . . . well . . ."

"What? What is it?" She stopped sewing, turning to look at him again as though she sensed some distress in him which, if it was in her power, she would do her utmost to ease, then rising in that impulsive way Jack had come to know she crossed the room and sank to her knees beside his bed, her face clouded with his pain.

"What, Jack? Tell me."

"He was . . . Mam said her pa called him a . . . ne'er-do-well."

"And was he?" She was very direct.

"He loved me mam." His tone was defiant.

"Well, there you are then," she said in triumph as though that should be enough for anyone. It was enough for her romantic young girl's heart and her soft eyes told him so and somehow he felt better about his pa and the careless way he had treated his ma. Love made up for a lot of things, or so Sara appeared to be telling him with her ardent gaze and he supposed she was right in a way, but by Christ, he'd not let this lovely young girl live the life his ma had been forced to live. If it could be done and given the chance to do it, he'd work his fingers to the bone, fight and claw his way up from navvieman to ganger, to subcontractor, to contractor to give her what she was used to, what she deserved and what she should have. He'd stand on other men's backs, kicking away those who got in his path, cheat and lie and steal to get where he wanted to be if there was a hope that Sara Hamilton would be beside him when he got there. He'd started at the bottom, if you could call the high quarry in the Pennines where he had begun at eleven years old the bottom. He could read, thanks to his mother, which surely must give him a head start on the illiterate fellows with whom he had been carelessly happy to carouse and womanise before he had met Sara Hamilton. He'd lived rough and hard but was there not a need for a man who . . . who . . .? His thoughts were jumbled, darting about in his head like a flock of birds and it was perhaps at that moment that it began. She was fifteen, she had told him so, and was still a girl but he could wait. He *would* wait. It would take time to . . . to carve out a life, a decent life to which he could take her, before he could offer her . . . Oh, God, Jesus God, but his heart ached with loving Sara Hamilton!

He glanced up and she was watching him, smilingly, encouragingly, her compassionate mouth as soft and pink as the first flush in the dawn sky and his virile male energy warmed his body beneath the sheet. She brought a stirring to his blood which was nothing like the desire he had felt for other women. He could not describe it, nor explain it except to say that ever since he had seen her in the ditch in the lane she had filled his thoughts and his eyes so that he saw no one else. She put a shine in his life and set ablaze a fierce masculine yearning which he had never known before since it was not just a physical yearning but one of the mind and heart and soul. She was a young girl but one day soon she would be a woman and Jack Andrews wanted nothing more than to be there when she was.

He forced himself to smile for surely his thoughts were

mad, wild, lunatic. Yet despite her youth, her warmly ebullient spirit, her laughter and lovely light-hearted singularity, there was something . . . something steady about her, something practical, an inclination to look at the reality of life as it was. Not like Alice who twittered on about ladies and gentlemen and making calls, whatever that meant, and doing what was "correct" in the social class to which she believed she belonged. He'd seen Sara smile when Alice babbled on and it occurred to him that Sara Hamilton would become the sort of woman a man would be glad to have at his side in any kind of life to which he might introduce her. Fighting in *his* corner, so to speak.

He rubbed his chin and felt the stubble, not removed for ten days, rasp beneath his fingers.

"I could do wi' a shave," he said without thinking and at once she stood up.

"Of course you could, Jack. Why didn't I think of it before?"

"Nay, Miss Sara, please . . ." horrified at the idea that she was about to offer her services as a barber.

"Oh, don't worry, Jack, I'm not going to do it. Not with Papa's razor which is of the cut-throat variety. I wouldn't even know how to sharpen it. He has seven, one for each day of the week and I'm sure he wouldn't mind."

"Nay, Miss Sara, I can't expect your pa to . . ."

"If I put the lather on you and held the mirror do you think you could shave yourself?"

He was in such a state of helpless and appalled panic mixed with excitement, a fierce male excitement at the thought of being involved in such a personal and intimate exercise with her he could scarcely get his breath, let alone argue and while he stared in horror she was off out of the kitchen and up the stairs, clattering on the treads and across the landing, then, within seconds, back again. She carried a bowl, towels, a shaving brush, soap, a shaving mug, a round, wooden-framed mirror on a stand and a lethal-looking cut-throat razor with a tortoise shell handle.

"Now look, Miss Sara . . ."

"Sara, please, Jack. You wouldn't like it if I called you Master Jack, would you?"

"Well, no," he admitted feebly, his heart beginning to flutter about his chest and into his throat.

"Right then, sit up and we'll have a shot at it." She began to giggle infectiously and her sweet breath touched his face as she leaned over him.

"I'll shave messen, Sara Hamilton," he told her firmly. "No lass is goin' to barber me if you please." He sat up awkwardly, twitching away from her as she put out a hand to help him.

"I wouldn't dream of tackling it, Jack." She laughed, her face rosy at the very idea. "I'd probably remove your ear or one of my own fingers at the very least."

"Right then," allowing her to tie the towel about his neck.

"Would it not be easier if you removed your nightshirt?" Her voice was innocent and though he glared suspiciously up at her he could see no motive in her other than the wish to be helpful. And what motive would she have, Jack Andrews, you great daft lummox? he asked himself ferociously.

"No, it would not," he answered loudly to cover his confusion. "Now hold that mirror steady and pass me the soap and brush."

Propped against several pillows and draped in a large towel, Jack began to lather and then shave his face, screwing it this way and that in the strange way men do when they are removing a growth of beard. Though it was painful lifting his arms he found he could make a fair job of it. He was inordinately pleased with what he saw in the mirror and when her laugh rang out he was startled and not a little offended.

"What?" he demanded truculently, feeling devastatingly ill at ease to have been performing such a personal, male task beneath the interested gaze of a young female. At least one like Sara.

"Do all men pull such faces when they shave?" she begged him to tell her through her laughter, doing her best to keep the mirror still. She was standing beside the bed but it was difficult to gauge the height at which he needed it and it seemed to her that the only way to do it properly would be to sit down on the bed beside him but he was glaring up at her so ferociously she didn't dare.

But the laughter continued to bubble up in her and he felt his own not far beneath the surface.

"I don't know what other men do," he replied huffily. "I don't watch them when they're doin' themselves up for a randy."

"Is that the only time they shave?"

"Aye, I reckon so."

"And you?"

"No, every day or me mam'd clout me."

He grinned then, looking up at her so engagingly the hand that held the mirror did a little dip.

"Can I sit down, please, Jack?" she asked him, her voice breathless for some reason. "This mirror is heavy and it will keep bobbing about."

"Well . . . all right. I've nearly done."

"You look very handsome," she said quite unthinkingly as she lowered herself to the bed. Their eyes met and to Sara's surprise Jack flushed a bright crimson. His hand trembled and the nick which appeared in his chin because of it began to flow with blood, dripping in bright splashes to the towel.

"Goddammit," he growled, tearing his eyes away from hers. At once he apologised and she said it was quite all right, anyone would swear if they cut themselves and she'd go and fetch something from her father's dispensary, or perhaps some fresh water and he said no, this would do if she could just find something to put on the cut to stop it from bleeding. What? Oh, a bit of paper would do. In between her evident amazement at his irritability and her hesitant reaching for this and that, Jack knew he had alarmed her.

"I'm sorry, lass," he mumbled again when the towel and all the other paraphernalia had been cleared away.

"Well, that's all very well but I don't even know what it was that upset you," she said indignantly. "I was only trying to help."

"I know, an' I shouldn't have cursed like that."

"Why were you so cross?" She was clearly bewildered.

"I wasn't, at least not with you. It's me, I'm just wanting to be out o' this bed . . ."

She was instant contrition. "Oh, of course you do, Jack, and I'm sorry too. You must be longing to get back."

"Aye, well . . ." wanting to stop her for that was the last thing he wanted. To get back! "I'll lie down again, I reckon."

"Can I help you?" reaching for pillows and smoothing the blanket which lay over him.

"No . . . no, thanks." He did not think he could stand much more of her closeness.

"Perhaps a . . .?"

"No! No. I'll just sleep a bit."

"Of course, and I'll sit here and . . ."

"No!" His voice was harsh but with a great effort he softened it for he couldn't bear to think of upsetting her again. "I . . . well . . . I'd fall asleep easier if you were to . . ."

"Leave you alone?" There was a strange wistfulness in her voice.

"It's not that I don't want you to, but . . ."

"What is it, Jack? You can tell me. Is there something bothering you?" Before he could stop her, or even think of anything to say which might, she dropped to her knees beside his bed, put her elbows on it, propped her chin in her cupped hands and looked down seriously into his freshly shaved face. He did look handsome, she thought, despite the bruising which still discoloured his flesh. His eyes were the deepest, warmest brown she had ever seen, like the horse chestnuts which scattered the garden at the back of the house and when he blinked he seemed to do so ever so slowly, his long, long lashes lifting and falling in the most fascinating way. Really, he had a most pleasing face, a kind face, a face which was gentle and smiling and at other times creased in a broad infectious grin she found quite delightful. Dolly had washed his hair at his own request and it tumbled in heavy russet curls across his forehead and over his ears and though she couldn't see it at the moment she knew it clustered in tighter curls at the nape of his brown neck.

"Do you miss your mother, Jack?" she asked him solemnly. "Is that why you're sad?"

If he was startled he tried not to show it. Jesus, he was a man and men didn't miss their mothers and yet . . . now he came to think of it, he would like to see his mam and feel that awkward embrace she drew him into. This girl, with her complete lack of constraint, had a way of bringing to the surface emotions, good feelings, real feelings, feelings of which no man should feel ashamed. He was a man but that did not mean he should not love his mother.

"I do miss her now and again, Sara," he said, looking directly into her sympathetic eyes, eyes which at times he did his best to avoid lest she see what was in his. "She's a grand woman an' looked after me an' me brothers when me pa died, even before," he added ruefully.

"I miss my mama, Jack," she said simply.

"I know you do, lass, but your pa's a fine man an' . . . he

loves you, anyone can see that." He did his best to keep his voice steady.

She sighed deeply and again her breath touched his face. Of its own volition his hand rose and cupped her cheek gently and she rested it in the palm of his hand.

"Alice does her best, I know she does, but it's not the same."

"I can see that, lass." His hand continued to cup her cheek and the strange thing was that there was nothing in it that was sexual. It was just one friend commiserating with another and when the voice at the door rapped out neither of them jumped or even felt guilt.

"May I ask what is going on here? What are you doing hanging over Mr Andrews's bed in that unladylike manner, Sara, and Mr Andrews, I think you are overstepping the bounds of propriety in the way you are handling my sister. Sara, come away at once and Mr Andrews, if you are going to abuse the hospitality my father has allowed you then I think it's high time you were on your way."

Sara sprang to her feet and her face, which had been soft, dreaming, innocent, at once flamed to a bright and shamed crimson. Jack felt his heart turn over for her, for her confused humiliation, and it was at that moment he began to realise that Alice Hamilton could be a dangerous opponent in his hopes and dreams for her young sister. She was not looking at Sara but at him and it was there in her eyes. Jack Andrews was nothing more than a coarse navvie and the Hamiltons were of a social class to which he could never aspire and if he thought he might do so through her sister he was sadly mistaken.

4

It had become summer again overnight and the day was warm.

"Jack, Papa told you that you weren't to move even an inch from that chair and what he will do to me when he finds out that I allowed you not only to stand up but tramp about the garden I can't imagine. Beat me probably or send me to my room on a diet of bread and water." Sara twinkled mischievously. "And it will all be your fault," she continued. "Oh please, Jack, do sit down again. See, put your arm across my shoulders and let me help you back to your chair and if you behave yourself I'll bring you another glass of lemonade and some of Dolly's coconut macaroons. They are freshly made and you know how you like them. You said so yesterday."

Sara Hamilton smiled up at Jack Andrews, slipping his arm across her shoulders, putting her own about his waist. Her head came barely to the point of his shoulder and if he had put his full weight on her he would have had the pair of them on the ground and they both knew it, but she really did seem to enjoy nursing him back to health.

She was willing to be involved with even the most unsavoury side to his injuries, if Dolly had let her, bathing his scraped flesh which, in one place on his left shin, had festered; the application to his bruises of the mixture her papa made up, the removal of the stitches from his face, the changing of his bandages and the washing of them and his soiled bedlinen. Sara was only too pleased to look after this tall, amusing and, emerging from his knocked-about state, attractive young man who inhabited their kitchen. His right leg was still in the splint Papa had applied but already, five weeks after the fight in the lane, he was doing his best to hobble about with the aid of a crutch. Sara thought he was the most agreeable young man she had ever come across. Not that there were many, if the truth were told, but Jack, despite his awful beating, was cheerful and brave and though she wanted him to recover, of course she did, she would be sorry when he left. He had brightened her calm, unruffled day-to-day existence and she had been glad of the chance to help to make him better for the service he had done her and Alice. He had become very dear to her and she would miss him.

Of course she knew he was not what Alice would call a gentleman as Papa was a gentleman, though, unlike many of the labouring men of the village and indeed the whole country, he could read and write. His broad Lancashire accent gave him away for what he was and though he was always polite and respectful he was never humble. He had not the polish which was inherent in her papa but did that matter one iota, she asked herself sternly, when she considered how courageous he was, how courteous and good mannered? He made her laugh. He was not afraid to tease her, allowing her to believe that without her ministrations he would never have recovered, which of course she knew was not true.

Jack let himself be led stiffly back to one of the deep cushioned chairs which had been placed beneath the benevolent shade of the horse chestnut tree which spread its roots and its canopy across two-thirds of the garden at the back of the house. It was enormous, having been planted at the beginning of the seventeenth century when the species had first been introduced to the shores of Britain. Already, as autumn took hold, its leaves were changing from green to yellow and gold and the ripening "conkers" or horse chestnuts would be their distinctive rich glossy brown in a week or two.

"There, are you satisfied now, lass?" Jack grinned as he lowered himself gingerly into the chair, keeping his eyes from straying to Alice Hamilton who sat on his left and whom he had distinctly heard wince at the use of the word "lass". It was because of her sharp and disapproving presence that, with the doctor's help, he had heaved himself up and staggered off towards the wall at the back of the garden beyond which, in a square hardly bigger than a handkerchief, the good doctor was vigorously turning over a patch of soil. The Hamiltons, though they were known as "quality", at least by the villagers, were barely more prosperous than many of the doctor's patients, living, or rather lurching from what Jack had gathered, from day to day on an occasional fee paid, on the eggs and chickens and rabbits tendered in lieu of a fee and the vegetables the doctor himself grew

"I like to work with the soil, Jack," Doctor Hamilton had told him as he puffed on his pipe only a couple of evenings ago. He had given Jack his arm, staggering with him and the crutch from the back door of the house across the lawned garden, beneath the tree and beyond to his vegetable plot where he had propped the invalid against the wall. The sun in the west had vanished behind the house roof but there was enough soft, dusky light to make out the neat rows of Doctor Hamilton's thriving cabbages and carrots and turnips, those sown earlier in the year and which stood proudly to attention beneath their creator's scrutiny.

"I see a lot of death in my job," he continued, "so it gives me enormous satisfaction to make things live and grow. And why should not a professional man enjoy the simple pleasures a labouring man knows, I say, though there are those who would disagree with me. They all grow what they can in the bit of ground about their homes so I'd a fancy to see if I could do the same. I found I was quite good at it. My wife used to laugh at me and say I should have been . . . well," he humphed, "she was a great one for . . . for laughing and Sara's the same, you may have noticed."

"Aye, yes . . . aye . . ." Jack humphed a bit himself then, "I liked a bit o' digging messen when I were at home and me mam were always glad o't veg."

"And so is Dolly. She can make a tasty meal out of a bit of scrag end and a handful of vegetables."

"I know. I've tasted it."

"So you have, and thrived on it. You'll soon be able to leave us, Jack," imagining the lad was itching to be on his way. "That leg's healing nicely."

"Listen, Doctor, if I'm any trouble ter thee, tha's only to say, you know that." His accent broadened with his anxiety and Jack almost leaped from the dry stone wall where he had been leaning in his eagerness to let the doctor know he had no wish to impose on his kindness and hospitality for a moment longer than was necessary but Doctor Hamilton pushed him gently back, laughing and shaking his head.

"Stop it, Jack. Really, I've never met a man less willing to take what he considers to be charity. After what you did for my girls I'd give you the shirt off my back and the food from my mouth."

"Nay, give over." Jack was embarrassed.

"No, it's true but it will be several weeks before you are anything like ready to take up your previous employment so you must resign yourself to staying with us for a little while yet."

"I reckon I could swing a pick wi' the rest of 'em. Good as new I am, thanks to you . . . and Sara."

His voice caught on her name but her father did not appear to notice. He leaned his elbows on the top of the wall, smoke from his pipe wreathed like mist about his head. From the trees sleepy birds called just as though they were bidding one another goodnight and Jack felt the sadness enter him as he had never known it before. He had to go soon. His chest still hurt when he took a deep breath and his body was a half-healed map of bruises and contusions. How he would manage the tramp to Moss Side where the track had reached was still to be determined. When he got there could he swing his pick and wield his shovel, manhandle a wheelbarrow, lift heavy sleepers and rails? There would be embankments to climb and holes to scramble into, ground to be levelled and if his leg did not heal properly, and soon, he would be unemployable as a navvieman. But he must not think like that. He must make himself well by exercising as much as he could, which was why he was doing his best to shuffle about the house and garden. He had plans that needed to be put into action, a vision to seek out, men to see about his future and he couldn't do it sitting on his arse round here, could he? He was stiff and awkward but surely that would wear off the minute he set his long legs in the direction of the track-laying which led in the direction of the sea-bathing resort and fishing village of Lytham? Four and three-quarter miles of track and it would be finished by the start of the new year, he had heard the ganger say, and when it was he must be off to find more work. There was plenty to be had, for in this ending year of 1845 and the beginning of 1846 it was said that almost five thousand miles of new lines were to be authorised, here in the north-west and even further afield. Birmingham, Wolverhampton, the Stour Valley,

Buckinghamshire, Oxfordshire and further south. Plymouth and Falmouth, if he wanted or could manage to tramp that far, which of course he didn't, not now. There were lines stretching their tentacles north across Cumberland and up into the high reaches of Scotland but it was nearer to Wray Green he was aiming for. The Kendal and Windermere Railway from where, if she was willing, he might tramp to visit Sara. It was all there, waiting for men who were ready, men with guts and the incentive to grasp it and though he had always had the former, now he also had the latter.

Sara! Sara, the girl whose spirit had fascinated him from that first day he had come across her. Sara of the gentle healing hands, the serene and lovely face. The quick laughter, the warmth, eyes lit with resolve and determination as she did her best to withstand her sister who as yet had her firmly under her thumb. Dear sweet Jesus, if there is a way to win her show it to me . . . help me . . . help me . . .

Sara sat down in the third chair beneath the tree and began to sew some scrap of material, a sleeve, she said, which was to go into a dress, a winter dress she was making for herself. Alice was the same, the pair of them for ever plying a needle, or unpicking something, so he was told, that had once belonged to their mother.

"We get most of our fabric from things that Mama wore, Jack, and it was she who taught us to sew," Sara had confided one day. "She was the most beautiful and talented seamstress and made all her own clothes and ours. Gowns, capes, gloves, bonnets and . . . well, other things . . ." since she knew Alice would disapprove if she mentioned undergarments in the presence of a gentleman.

Now he closed his eyes, leaning his head against the cushion Sara had put there for him. He could see the shadows of the gently moving, still heavily laden branches of the horse chestnut tree at the back of his eyelids and he allowed his breathing to deepen as though he were asleep. For several minutes he could sense Alice fidgeting in the chair beside him then, as he had hoped, she stood up.

"I'm going to pick some flowers for the table, Sara," she murmured in a low voice, for arranging flowers was a task a lady did and Alice Hamilton was well suited to it.

"Good idea. Those chrysanthemums are just ready for cutting. I thought I might take some to Mama's grave."

"Of course. But don't go alone, Sara. One never knows if those brutes are still hanging about."

Brutes! Jack almost snorted with laughter at hearing Racer and Billyo described thus but he remembered in time that he was supposed to be asleep. But that was how Alice saw them and *him* and she missed no opportunity to let him see it. To point out the difference between his station in life and hers. He was here on sufferance, her attitude told him, and the sooner he was recovered and on his way the better Alice Hamilton would like it. Ever since that day when she had come home and found Sara kneeling by his bed in what she plainly thought was an indecent manner she had done her best to see that they were never left alone. She wouldn't have left them now had she known he was awake, he was well aware, as from between almost closed lids he watched her glide away in that stiff-backed way she had. This was his chance to be alone with Sara and he wanted desperately to seize it. He didn't know what for really, since it was only to say that he must go soon. To say goodbye. Goodbye and thank you . . . and . . . Jesus, if only he could . . . if only he was the same as her, the same class . . . if he had the right to tell her . . . ask her . . . could she? He loved her and all he wanted was the right to tell her so as a man such as her father would have the right, to speak to her, ask her . . .

Ask her what, you fool? You're a navvie. A rough, half-educated lout who has known nothing but hard work, grinding poverty, hardship and endurance on the high Pennine land where your father took your mother and you saw what it did to her. He had not, of course, known his mother before her marriage to his father but he had heard her speak of it and though she had never complained he had known it was better then. A piano, she told him. A flower garden, lace tablecloths and fine bone china. Water from a pump, a girl to scrub, books to read. She had not been gently bred like Sara, coming from a working family; not the rank of which the well-educated Doctor Hamilton was a member, but moderately successful and certainly not dirt poor like Chris Andrews had been.

He sighed deeply and beside him Sara put down her sewing.

"Are you asleep, Jack?" she asked softly.

"No."

"Are you in pain? I could get Papa to . . ."

"No." He sounded angry even to himself.

He opened his eyes to stare into the blue glazed silk of the sky. Three lapwings tumbled across it and he was struck with the utter serenity of the day, the garden, in contrast to the turmoil which cannoned inside himself.

"Shall I leave you to have a rest then?" she enquired anxiously.

The turmoil deepened, boiling into a confused and painful mixture of emotion. Anger was one, resentment was another. There was stubborn arrogance in Jack Andrews, for he had been brought up by a proud and independent woman who had taught him he was as good a man as any. Just because they were poor did not mean they were inferior to the men of class and wealth, she had told him. Hold up your head, tell the truth, work hard and though one man is the employer and the other employee, this did not make the former superior to the latter.

Aye, Mam, that's what you told us and I for one believed you but what you failed to explain was that when a working man loves the daughter of a gentleman the whole bloody argument gets chucked out of the window. This lovely girl who, her sewing discarded, turned so compassionately towards him had no more conception of what living as a navvie's "wife" would mean than she did of growing wings and taking to the trees like a bird. Either situation was just as foreign to her and best he get away from her as soon as he could. His leg would hold him upright long enough to get him to Moss Side and then, perhaps with the help of the gang with whom he had laboured for nearly six years, he might be able to do something, ride one of the horses which hauled the waggons of spoil, maybe, until his leg was strong enough for him to resume his previous job.

Dear Christ, it was hard, this pendulum state of existence in which at one moment he was ferociously intent on clambering upwards in life so that he might eventually claim Sara Hamilton for himself, then at another swung to the point where he could clearly see the futility of it all. Six years he had been a navvie and still was, never having much concern for bettering himself, enjoying the carefree, gypsy life, the comradeship of his mates, the lack of responsibility only an unmarried, untroubled man knows. Now, in the space of a few weeks, it had all changed and the cause of it sat innocently beside him.

He frowned ferociously, his youth and good humour vanishing as a cloud will hide the sunshine and Sara longed to put out a hand to his where it clenched on the arm of the chair. He was so obviously displeased about something but for the life of her she didn't know what. He was like that at times, scowling and stern as though all the merry humour and good spirits had been squeezed out of him by something she could not even guess at. One minute he would be lively, ready to tease Dolly by untying her apron strings as she passed by his chair, the next gazing sadly out of the window as though he had just received the news that someone he loved had died. And when she asked him what the matter was he turned away from her as though she were an irritating child. He would soon be on his way and the thought was alarmingly hurtful. What thought is that? she asked herself. That he was to go soon, or that she would be hurt by it? Either really, or both, and the foolish thing was she didn't really know why except that he had brought something clear and shining into her life which she was reluctant to part with. Every morning when she awoke the first thing that came into her mind was Jack and the day was good right from the start, which was very odd since her life had always been a happy one, apart from the death of Mama. It would be again, when Jack went, but somehow she could not quite picture it. In the first days when he had been restless with pain she had sat with him on many nights and Papa, Alice and Dolly had known nothing about it. She had been drawn by some compulsion to watch over him, telling herself that he might need something, a drink or . . . well, whatever it was, she would be there to get it for him. Alice would have been horrified had she known but he had been so vulnerable in those first few days, which she knew sounded silly since he was such a large young man, but his bruised and swollen face had made her hurt inside and his sweat-drenching agony when Papa moved him seemed to go through her body as it did his. His eyes would fix on hers in the most extraordinary way and she would try to give him strength and comfort, to smile soothingly as though he were a hurt child. But he would tear his glance away, glaring into the corner of the kitchen until her father had finished his examination.

"Can I bring you a drink, Jack?" she asked him now, watching the shadow of the branches above their heads flicker across his almost healed face. Several leaves spiralled downwards, a glowing golden yellow, each one made of delicate leaflets shaped like a tiny pear, floating gracefully to land on Jack's chest and he brushed them off impatiently, glowering at them as though they had personally offended him.

"No, for God's sake. I'm not a bloody invalid."

Sara was shocked and deeply hurt. For some reason she felt like bursting into noisy tears but instead she clamped her lips tightly against her teeth, so tightly she could hardly answer him.

"Well, you have certainly given a good impression of one these last few weeks," she said tartly, the strong core of her resolve which lay buried deep in her youthful spirit rising vigorously to the surface.

"Oh aye, an' what's that supposed to mean?" Jack sat up violently, turning to glare at her, his expression so maddened by something she thought he might be going to strike her.

"Only that you seem to have no difficulty in allowing me and Alice to dance attendance on you every hour of the day and night."

"Dance attendance on me! Day an' night? Bloody hell, woman – I beg your pardon – but dost tha' think I enjoy havin' a young lass runnin' around after me? Dost tha'?" His face contorted in frustrated rage and Sara was not to know the true cause of it. "No one's waited on Jack Andrews, not even me mam, since I were a nipper." His accent broadened the angrier he got. "I see ter messen an' always have done an' 'avin' ter be tied to a bed like a bairn an' spoon-fed like a babby don't sit right well wi' me. Fetch me, carry me, bring me, I can't abide it . . ."

"I have never heard a more ungrateful statement in my life and if that's all the thanks my father is to get then I wish he'd left you lying in your own blood in the lane."

"Not tha' pa, girl." Jack's face twisted in pain and horror at being misunderstood. Jesus, if Doctor Hamilton had not come by when he did Jack Andrews would be a cripple now. Maimed and disfigured for life and though his face would always have a scar above his eyebrow and there was a possibility he might be left with a slight limp he was in a hell of a lot better shape than he would have been, thanks to this girl's pa.

"Not tha' pa," he repeated. "God in heaven, dost tha' think I'll not be thankful to 'im fer the rest o' me life, Sara Hamilton, an' you an' all fer the way tha've looked after me but . . ."

"And what about Dolly and Alice?" Sara asked violently, surprising both herself and Jack with the force of her words and their delivery. She put a neat pintuck in the shoulder of the sleeve, knowing as she did so she would have to do it again since it wasn't even straight but Jack was making her so . . . so bloody mad she didn't really know quite what she was doing, or saying.

"Alice?" He was clearly astonished. "Dolly, aye, but your Alice? What's she got to do wi' owt?"

"Has she not done her best to bring you back to health?" She bent her head to her work and with sharp white teeth bit off the thread of the cotton, composed as a madonna though inside she was seething. She didn't know why. For a moment Jack was diverted as his gaze rested on her soft pink mouth but as she looked up at him, her green eyes as icy as grass with frost on it, he snapped his jaw together in scorn.

"Give over! She does nowt but . . ."

"Yes?" Her expression became even more intense and she showed every sign of jumping up and clouting him about the face in defence of her sister.

"Hell's teeth, dost tha' think I'd have survived if your Alice had had the nursin' of me? She's nobbut a la-di-da, high muck-a-muck old maid, full of her own importance with no time fer the likes o' me. I'm nowt but a cow-pat beneath her dainty shoes an' the sooner I'm outa here the better she'll like it. She's done nowt, nowt, compared to you and Dolly and what I want ter know is what tha' meant by dancin' attendance on me day *and* night. Are you tellin' me that . . . that you came down at night . . . when I were asleep?"

"Yes, yes I did and what of it? You were very . . . poorly." Her tone was defiant and she lifted her chin and stuck it out at him.

"But . . .?"

"Why shouldn't I?"

There was a deep and breathless silence as Jack Andrews and Sara Hamilton faced one another across the slowly narrowing divide which stood between them. Neither moved nor seemed inclined to speak as glowing brown eyes fastened on bewildered, iridescent green and asked the question which Jack himself was incapable of uttering. Blindly she began to recognise what it was and her heart moved with the loveliness of it, the unexpected, unbelievable joy of it but Sara was still a young, untried girl and had no experience, nor had even developed the instinct which a woman has to tell her what to do next. If they, she and Jack, had been on their feet facing one another it might have been done for them. A step, a lifting of her face and arms to his, a bending of his head to hers and, without thought, with without the need to think, it would have been done.

But Jack was awkward, fastened by his injuries to his chair and without a strong hand to help him found it hard to get up, and Sara was restrained by her inexperience, her innocence, her upbringing, from offering it. Nevertheless, given a moment or two, perhaps a reaching out with his rough, brown hand to hers, it might have been accomplished but even as their eyes and hearts grappled with it a vituperative voice heavy with displeasure brought them back from that first hesitant step and they both turned guiltily to Alice.

It was as if Alice, though she had seen nothing untoward between her sister and the navvie, and having nothing really to be disapproving of, picked something, anything, about which to make a fuss.

"Sara, I have told you a dozen times not to sit about in the garden without a bonnet. What will people think if they should see you, and isn't it about time Mr Andrews moved indoors? We don't want him to catch a chill on top of his other . . . infirmities."

"Oh Ally, a bonnet! Who on earth is going to see whether I am wearing a bonnet or not?"

"One never knows when a caller may— "

"Here?" The incredulity in Sara's voice emphasised Alice's sad lack of visitors.

"And may I ask you not to keep interrupting me when I am speaking to you. Now give me a hand to get Mr Andrews— "

"His name is Jack, Ally."

"And mine is Alice, Sara. Now come along, it's becoming chilly and if Mr Andrews is ever to get back to his employment, which I am sure he is eager to do, we must see that he keeps up his recovery."

"Alice, he can barely walk, let alone work!"

"That will do, Sara."

"Aye, Sara, don't argue wi' Miss Alice. She's right an' sooner I'm off the better."

Jack was well aware of Alice Hamilton's growing animosity towards him, her tendency to mock him, to say and do things which, in her opinion, would show up his lack of breeding. She resented his continued presence in her home and he had a strange feeling that she knew of his feelings for her sister. He did his best not to let them show, that sudden breathlessness with which he was afflicted when Sara came near him, the light of near worship which he was sure glowed in his eyes but it was very difficult to keep his burgeoning emotions to himself. Alice sensed something, he was sure, and naturally, since he was nothing but a common labourer the sooner he was out of her sister's life the better. Not that she would imagine in her wildest dreams that there could ever be anything between Jack Andrews and her own gently bred sister, but best be shut of him and as soon as possible.

The warmth of the autumn sunshine was indeed cooling. The pale light, amber-coloured, fell through the golden leaves of the horse chestnut tree. Doctor Hamilton had evidently lit a bonfire, gathering the fallen leaves which had drifted across the wall to the vegetable garden and the smoke from it trailed straight up into the soft, still evening sky. Rooks were beginning to clamour in the nests they had built in the spring and the aromatic fragrance of the burning leaves told Sara as nothing else could that soon the year would be dashing sadly towards its end. Jack would be gone.

Sadness settled over her like a wet and heavy cloak, frightening her, for why should the thought of Jack leaving Wray Green make her sad? A moment ago, before Alice came, it had all been as clear and sharp, as vivid and dazzling as sunshine on snow and now, suddenly, she was not even sure what she meant by "it". What? What had passed between her and Jack, if anything? A glance, the start of a smile, secret, just theirs, a feeling of great delight but for the life of her she didn't know why. Jack was scowling at Alice, evidently with great displeasure and Alice's face was set, cold, tight-lipped with some anger she was doing her best to contain. Sara wondered at the strange and unfamiliar feelings Jack's jutting jaw and lowering eyebrows evoked in her.

"No," he was saying, evidently in answer to something Alice had asked him, "thanks, but I'm off fer a chat wi' tha' pa." He clutched the arms of his chair in an effort to stand up without anyone's help and certainly not Alice Hamilton's. Automatically Sara rose and extended her small hand to him but he waved it away impatiently.

"Don't be silly, Jack," she snapped, surprising herself with her own irritation. "Take my hand and Alice will— "

"Give o'wer, lass, I can manage messen. I've ter get used to it if I'm ter get back to't gang an' sooner I do that the better or I'll be stuck 'ere on me . . . well, another few days, I reckon, an' then I'll be on't tramp."

"No, Jack, oh no, you can't mean that," Sara cried, horrified at the very thought of Jack being taken from her. "You're not fit yet, not by a long way. See, you can hardly get out of that chair."

"We'll see about that," Jack muttered grimly and with a great heave he had himself on his feet. Sweat stood out on his brow as he put his full weight on his injured leg. His face lost every vestige of colour and as he went down it was Sara's hand he reached for and Sara's cry which tore at his heart.

5

Even at the last Doctor Hamilton did his best to delay Jack's return to the navvie camp.

Winter had fallen with a vengeance over the past week, just as though those last and unexpectedly warm days of autumn must be made up for and the air was cold, damp, with a drizzle which clung to the greatcoat, new when Richard Hamilton was a bridegroom and which now fitted very snugly on Jack's broad shoulders. It was almost ankle length with a high collar and flapped pockets in which Sara had packed enough bread, cheese, fruit, plum cake and cold cooked bacon to last him until he reached Land's End, never mind just beyond Moss Side, he joked. The coat was a serviceable brown wool and would be the focus of much ribaldry and covetousness when he reached the camp but it was warm protection against the stark weather.

It was eight weeks since Jack's beating in the lane, the savage beating from which, despite his youth and strength, he had not yet fully recovered.

"If I don't get back to work there'll be no work to get back to," he told the anxious doctor. "They reckon line ter Lytham'll be finished an' ready to open by new year, or not much beyond, an' then we'll all be on the tramp."

"Why don't you stay here until then, Jack? You know you're more than welcome."

Well, there's someone'd give you an argument on that, Jack thought wryly, the cold aversion on Alice Hamilton's face clear in his mind. He often wondered how two sisters could be so alike to look at, for there was no denying Alice was very attractive, and yet be so totally different. It was in the expression, he supposed, one so warm and glowing, the other cool, distant. There was beauty in the gentle blossom time of summer, midsummer, the month of June when Sara was born, but the delicate tracery of frost on branch and stem, the icy brilliance of January, the month of Alice's birth, was equally lovely. They were alike in colour, in the fineness of their skin and the blazing copper of their hair but their natures were as differing as summer is to winter.

Doctor Hamilton leaned forward impulsively and laid a hand on Jack's shoulder. He had taken a great liking to this good-humoured young man and would be sorry to see him leave. Jack had kept apologising for what he called "putting" on them, saying that he would eat them out of house and home but the truth was that since his leg had allowed it he had, taking after his pa apparently, performed many tasks about the house, mending everything that would not function properly from a run-down clock to a chair with a broken leg and the bellows which made the kitchen fire draw. He had sharpened knives which had been blunt for years and put together again a pair of wrought-iron candle-holders and snuffers which had fallen apart with age. From a piece of elm wood he had carved for the doctor a smooth, simple but graceful candle-holder for when he had to get up in the night with a place for a tinderbox in its base since the new, phosphorous-tipped "match" was expensive and could not be afforded by the impoverished Hamiltons. Even Doctor Hamilton's own instruments, the handscales and weights he used to measure powders accurately, had not been ignored and several cracked ceramic mortars were now as good as new.

As his leg grew stronger and he could get outside with the help of his crutch, Jack took to mending fences and repairing the dry stone walls which divided the garden at the back of the house. Hinges which had set the teeth on edge for want of oil no longer screeched. Latches fastened and unfastened neatly, window frames through which the wind had whistled were now trim and draught-free, all jobs which, being an "unhandy" man, the doctor had been grateful to have done.

It was the beginning of November when Jack set out along the railway track which led from Lytham Junction Halt, a mile west of Kirkham, to just beyond Moss Side where it had now reached on its journey to Lytham. Doctor Hamilton had been called out there on a number of occasions to attend to sick and injured men and could give a full report on the track's progress. He had, as Jack had instructed him, asked for the man called Whistling Tom, or simply Whistler, a name given to him on account of his talent for imitating the calls of wild birds and for whistling through his teeth as he worked. Whistler was a decent man, a man with a wife and family, a man Jack had helped more than once when Whistler's wife had been refused tickets for the Truck shop and if anyone could now be trusted to repay that help it was Whistler.

"I just want somewhere to stay while I get me bearings, tell 'im. Him an' his missus have a grand hut ter themselves, not just one of them shanties the single men throw up an' I reckon I'd best keep out o't road of Billyo an' Racer until this damn leg o' mine's a bit stronger." He smiled crookedly, for none knew better than he how a weaker man, no matter how small that weakness, would fare at the hands of bully boys like the two brutal Irishmen who had so nearly killed him in September. They could possibly have completely forgotten the incident of Sara and Alice after all this time and be vastly astonished to see their old mate Jack Andrews back in their midst, probably wondering where the hell he had been but best take no chances, he told the doctor. If Whistler and his wife would put him up – he had a few bob in his pocket and could live on Truck while he earned some money, he said with the optimism of youth – he would hopefully find work he had done before the fight, and he would manage.

"And if you can't, Jack? What then? That leg of yours is still weak and will stand no strain on it. I know you have exercised it as I have shown you but it has had no real test."

"There's that diggin' I did. I shaped then."

"Yes, I agree but you stopped when I told you. You won't be able to stop and rest when you are laying railway track."

"Well, 'appen I could work the horses."

"That's boys' work, Jack and not well paid. Not what you're used to."

"Aye, I know that but it'll keep me going while I'm messen again. An' that'll not be long."

"You will take care, won't you, lad?"

"Nay, you make me sound like some broken-down old nag or a bairn that can't look after hissen." Jack laughed but the doctor only shook his head.

"You know what I mean, Jack, but I suppose you must be

on your way. You have your own life to make and there is nothing for you here." The doctor wondered for a brief moment at the sharp spasm which crossed Jack's face but it was gone so quickly he had no chance to get a grip on it as Jack turned smartly, stamping on his injured leg as though to prove its efficiency.

"You're right, sir, an' as you can see I'm as fit as a flea so I reckon I'll be off then, if that's all right with you."

Jack's health was fully returned to him, his body and face healed and his cracked ribs mended. Only his leg was still suspect, having a sudden inclination to give way beneath him at odd times but that would improve, the good doctor told him. He might be prone to a slight limp when he was tired, but slight enough as to be almost unnoticeable. Aye, it was time to be off, Jack told himself as he felt the doctor's eyes on him and but for the girl who had just gone up to her bed he might have tried to do it weeks ago. He had not spoken to her even though he had sensed a change in her manner towards him. Still warm-hearted and eager to help him but there was a certain shyness, a constraint which, though he was not absolutely sure, seemed to him to be the awareness of herself as a female and Jack Andrews as a male. She was too young even to think of courtship, not yet sixteen, but that would resolve itself with time and until that time came he must curb his longing to let her know, in words, what his true feelings for her were. She was his heart and his soul and he would give both to save her from a moment's suffering but these were words which were too strong, too powerful, too passionate for a girl on the threshold of womanhood. He must discipline himself, hold back his longing to drag her into his arms and declare his love for her, subdue his natural masculine yearning to take her for his own, be patient until she was ready, and loving her as he did he would know when that moment came.

Feeling the elderly man's eyes upon him he looked up and grinned in that endearing way the Hamilton family had come to know. The cat purred on his knee and his big hand fondled a spot behind its ear which made it purr the louder. Somehow Sara had washed the bloodstains from his moleskin trousers and with that special skill her mother had passed on to her and with scraps of vivid material from a dozen different garments, while he lay in bed during those first weeks she had fashioned him a new waistcoat. He had been dazed with pain and the drugs the doctor had administered to him and he had scarcely noticed what she sewed but it seemed that in the attic at the top of the house were boxes of Eleanor Hamilton's gowns of silk and velvet and brocade, twenty-odd years out of fashion since she had brought them with her from Cheshire on her marriage. There were shawls and undergarments, bonnets and mantles, those she had "made over" from what she had laughingly called her "trousseau". Being the clever seamstress that she was she had enough clothes to last her until the end of her days, she had told her ardent bridegroom. She had not envisaged, and neither had he that "her days" would not lie beyond twenty years of happy marriage.

Now, thanks to the thrift and clever fingers of her daughters, but more particularly Sara, Jack sported a rainbow waistcoat which was the twin of the one ruined two months ago. He looked as dashing and decently dressed as he had then and had even allowed Dolly, refusing Sara's offer quite brusquely, to cut his curly crop of chestnut curls "before he began to trip over it" as he whimsically put it. Alice had not been best pleased to see the cloud of reddish brown silk which lay about her kitchen floor in thick, gleaming strands, the sun which lay across it turning it to fire and had been sharp with Dolly, but Jack could see that she saw the incident as one step nearer to his departure and was gratified by it.

So he was shaved and clean, fastidiously so, Doctor Hamilton thought, wondering again how the lad would fare on his return to the navvie camp.

"Nay, don't tekk on, Doctor," the "lad" said. "You've not ter worry about me. I'm a grown man an' I'll steer clear o' them buggers – I beg yer pardon – what did fer me last time."

For some reason his glance moved to the ceiling and Richard Hamilton wondered at the sadness in them.

It took no more than five minutes to make his farewells and the whole time he was conscious of the quiet figure of Sara Hamilton standing behind Dolly like a small and white-faced statue, her eyes the transparent green of moss beneath water. She bit her lip as though to stop it trembling and her hand was as cold and light as a snowflake as he took it in his.

"Sara." It was all he could manage.

"Jack." She was the same. She was calm as he shook hands with her father, her face expressionless, polite with him as though he were a guest who had been made welcome but was now to be on his way. Nobody special really, just a young man her father had doctored and only Dolly, who knew her better than anyone since she was her mother all over again, was aware of what was in her.

"If you're ever this way again, Jack, let us know how you are." The doctor nodded kindly, watching with a professional eye as his patient straightened his tall frame, noticing anxiously how he still favoured that leg of his.

"That I will, sir."

"Goodbye, lad," Dolly tutted, as though he was leaving just to be perverse but there was a softness in her eye which spoke of her regret. At his going and at the obvious pain it was bringing to Miss Sara. She would get over it, of course, which was for the best, since nothing could come of it.

"A pleasant journey to you, Mr Andrews." Alice bowed her head regally, a lady seeing a common man on his travels. It was all she had to say as she turned away from him, intent on letting him see that she was a busy woman who had done him great honour in interrupting her tasks to bid him farewell. She sighed in great relief, even he could detect it, glad to be shut of him he was well aware.

He did not look back and Sara did not stay to watch him walk away along the lane where he had saved her from Racer. His coat tails swung jauntily. His head was bare. His chestnut hair stood up on his skull, aspangle with raindrops, curling crisply, a bright blaze of colour in the dismal greyness of the day.

They felt quite lost without him, Dolly and the doctor told one another as they sat down on opposite sides of the hearth, oblivious for once of Alice's disapproving lift of the head. The parlour fire was lit and there was no need for her Papa to sit down with Dolly in the kitchen but in the regret at Jack's going Richard Hamilton did not appear to notice. The fire burning brightly on the hearth was the focal point of the kitchen and around the warmth of it hovered many of the activities of the house. The fire was never allowed to go out, night or day and while he had been at Lane End Jack had found it a source of deep satisfaction to sleep, with the marmalade cat sprawled across him, on the truckle bed he pulled up to it. The hearth was enormous, wide and deep, an ingle fireplace with stout oak surrounds backed with smoke-blackened stone which led up the chimney. Horizontal bars were supported by "dogs" and a brazier, or fire-basket, was filled with burning logs. Next to the fire was the black-leaded oven where Dolly did her baking and roasting and above that was the hotplate. The oven was heated by lighted brushwood and apple logs. There were more than a dozen utensils hanging about it, pots and pans and skillets, kettle tilters and even a chestnut roasting box. Bright copper pans of all sizes stood on shelves, graduating from the smallest milk pan to the one in which a large joint of mutton could be boiled.

There was a dresser groaning with blue and white "everyday" crockery, bright blue check gingham curtains at the window and in the window bottom a row of vivid winter geraniums, bright and showy, potted and grown by Doctor Hamilton. An enormous bowl of pot-pourri, the leaves and petals gathered and dried by Sara, stood in the centre of the kitchen table and still resting in the corner of the room was the truckled bed in which, somehow, Jack's large frame had slept at night. On it, neatly folded, were the blankets he had used.

Sara glanced hastily away from it, going immediately to the door which led into the small hallway, making for the stairs with a muttered excuse which none could understand, except perhaps Dolly whose eyes softened as they watched her go.

It was Sunday and what was for Doctor Hamilton a quiet day, for it seemed the good folk of his practice, most of whom attended church, were less likely to call on the physician unless it was a dire emergency. Alice, in that rather cloying and false manner she assumed when she spoke of her "acquaintances" among the upper class of the district, begged her father to take a walk with her and Dolly was well aware that she did so in the hope of bumping into one or other of them and in so doing introduce her father into the company to which the Hamiltons belonged. The walk would doubtless take them in the direction of the Bentham home, Laurel House, which lay halfway between Wray Green and Bryning. It was a pleasant stroll from Lane End and would "do Papa the world of good" she told him. She was acutely conscious that her father was not interested in the soirées and dinner parties to which Alice longed to be invited, saying bluntly that the people who gave them had the brains of sparrows and the airs and graces of duchesses but Alice didn't care. Mrs Bentham, as the parish's leading hostess, gave frequent parties and balls and Alice wanted nothing more than to be included. To fall, oh, joy of joys, beneath the handsome and well-bred gaze of Anthony Bentham and to this end she was for ever begging her father to make more effort in becoming better acquainted with the family and others of similar standing in the community. It was the cross she had to bear that her own modest home was completely unsuitable to accommodate the grand and lofty Benthams in any form of hospitality, should they accept it, even for the taking of simple afternoon tea. Where were they to sit, she agonised to herself, since her mother's parlour, or drawing-room as she liked it to be called, was far too small and cramped a room in which to fit the splendour of Mrs Bentham and her eldest daughter Lilian. Alice was nineteen and longed for nothing but to be married and Anthony Bentham was the most eligible bachelor in the area.

What she hoped to achieve by sauntering past the imposing gates of Laurel House was not clear. Perhaps that Mrs Bentham might be glancing from her window and run eagerly down the drive to invite Alice and her papa inside, Dolly thought to herself in amusement, but as the day had fined up her father agreed to indulge her.

It was half an hour later when Sara crept quietly down into the kitchen and settled herself opposite the old woman who was half dozing in her chair. Sara had her sewing in her hands, a froth of soft blue wool material which was to be her new winter gown. It was a misty blue, a pale hyacinth blue, simple in style, and when it was finished would have a round neck, long tight sleeves, a neat, well-fitted bodice carried to a point at the front and a full gathered skirt. Down the skirt about six inches apart were narrow flounces of the same material, each flounce scalloped, each scallop bound with a deeper blue satin which was repeated in a tiny collar and in the cuffs. It was this touch of ingenuity which would give the gown its style, its simple elegance, its air of having come directly from the house of a French couturier though Sara, having no knowledge of such things, was unaware of it. She was fifteen, not sixteen until next June and had been guided by her mother up to the day she died. Since then her mother's teaching and her own instinctive good taste had influenced what she made and wore. She knew what suited her, young as she was. Altering, unpicking, shortening, lengthening, tacking, snipping and assembling the shapes into a whole, she and Alice had acquired a wardrobe of garments, all derived from what her mother had worn, a wardrobe that any girl would have been proud of. The smartest, most stylish, most dashing young ladies in the parish, it was said of them and there was many a remark passed by those ladies who envied them that it was a mystery where the money came from for such fripperies.

The silence stretched on as Dolly who had awoken watched Sara's fingers thread a needle then, swiftly but skilfully, put in two dozen running stitches which would catch the hem of the skirt in position until she fashioned the invisible ones which would finally hold the finished hem. It was the first stitch her mother had taught her as a child and as Dolly studied the girl, into her mind's eye, the eye of an old woman who has seen many things and remembered all of them, came the image of Eleanor Hamilton, her smoothly shining tawny hair close to the curls of her little daughters.

"Careful, my darlings. Tiny, tiny stitches, fairy stitches that no one can see," she would exhort them as, with tongues out and brows furrowed they did their best to emulate her cleverness with their childish fingers. Naturally Miss Alice was more advanced than Miss Sara, being four years older but they wanted to be just as their mama was. Especially Miss Sara. Miss Sara had loved her mama and had wanted more than anything on earth to be like her and she was. In looks and in all the facets of her mama's sweet nature, but where Miss Eleanor was submissive, gentle as a dove and fragile as a snowdrop, Miss Sara had more of her grandmother Kingsley in her than Dolly would have liked, and Dolly should know. A strong woman, Eleanor's mama, a woman who ruled her husband and family with a rod of iron but where old Mrs Kingsley had little of the milk of human kindness in her, thank God Miss Sara, her granddaughter, overflowed with it.

She'd taken a shine to that Jack Andrews, Dolly could see that and was surprised Miss Alice hadn't noticed but then to Miss Alice the idea of her sister having any feelings for a low-down chap like Jack would be too ludicrous for words and her mind would not even contemplate it. But how would Miss Sara fare? It was in her nature to be whole-hearted and loyal, her affection once given never withdrawn, but she was a sensible lass who knew the rules of the social strata and where her and his place were in it.

Feeling Dolly's eyes on her Sara looked up into the seamed, compassionate face of the old woman who had been part of her life since Sara was born. Always there had been Dolly, brusque and busy about the house, declaring she didn't know where the muck came from and if Miss Sara didn't wipe her feet she'd take a switch to her. Untrue, of course, and let anyone else try and they'd have Dolly to deal with, for there was no more loving, caring, stout-hearted woman than Eleanor Hamilton's servant, though she went to great lengths to disguise it. Many's the time she'd sit Sara on her lap, grumbling and awkward, telling her not to be such a "cry-babby" as her tears over a skinned knee or a splinter dripped on to the immaculately tucked bodice of one of the dresses her mother was always making for her. Aye, ungracious and curt was old Dolly, but open-handed with her comfort, her loving arms and clumsy kisses. Dolly had been devastated, ready to curse a God who would take such a good and lovely woman as Eleanor Hamilton and leave a slut like Jessie Wilmot who lived in the village and had more children than Dolly could count on two hands, each with a different father. Since then she'd been sharper, cautious with her affections, as though afraid if she showed them the recipient might suffer the same fate as Miss Eleanor, but they were still there, deep and eternal.

Sara put down her sewing and sighed forlornly.

"I shall miss him, Dolly," she ventured sadly.

"Aye, I know that, lamb an' sorry I am 'cause I know and tha' knows . . . well, it's best he were off. He didn't fit in wi' . . . tha' knows what I mean."

"Why, Dolly? Why didn't he fit in? What's wrong with Jack?" Sara's face was rosy with indignation.

"Nay, don't be foolish, lass." The old lady shook her head and the cat on her knee looked up at her as though in complete understanding.

"He's a good man, Dolly." Sara's voice rose with a passion Dolly did not care for.

"'Appen he is. A good man but not a gentleman."

"Because of what he does?"

"That's part of it. Them navviemen've a bad name, lass, an'

just because this 'un can read an' write an' has nice manners it don't mean he'll ever amount to much."

"That's not true, Dolly." Sara's face became even pinker and her eyes narrowed into green slits of outrage. "He told me all sorts of things, about what he's going to do, on the railway, I mean. He says there are opportunities for men of . . . of vision who are prepared to work hard and . . . and grasp what is offered. That sort of thing. And as for the rest, his mother came from a good family. Not that I give a damn about that, but her father was— "

"Mind tha' language, if tha' please, Miss Sara. It doesn't matter what her pa was, it's him what counts and he's nowt but a navvie, and as for . . . for grasping opportunities, why hasn't he grasped them afore now? Tell me that. Six years a navvie and still a navvie so to my way o' thinking he's bin a bit slow in getting somewhere. He's a good lad, a nice lad but he'll never be anything other than what he is an' your pa'll tell him so when he comes back."

Sara stared goggle-eyed with amazement at the old woman's wise face.

"When he comes back?" she repeated.

"Give over, Miss Sara. I've known thee since the nurse put thee into my arms fifteen and a half years ago. I've changed thi', bathed thi', wiped tha' . . . well," she concluded hastily, "I helped tha' mama to fetch thee up an' there's not much goes on in this house I don't know about where you two lasses are concerned. Miss Alice . . . well, she's Miss Alice and'll always do't right thing. She's different from thee an' her mama an' sooner she finds herself a husband the better. Any husband'll do as long as he's a gentleman an' will treat her right. She'd be happy wi' that. But you, well, I don't know of any chap I've seen in these parts what'd suit you but I do know this though. Tha'll not be satisfied wi' second best."

With this mysterious statement Dolly closed her mouth grimly, snapping it to like a trap with a mouse in it, crossing her arms over her sagging bosom and the struggling cat. She sniffed disapprovingly, almost ready to fetch it a clout if it didn't behave and it subsided defeated across her lap.

Sara took up her sewing and for the first time since she had watched Jack stride off so enthusiastically up the lane she felt a little warmth creep into her heart. It was as though Dolly's rejection of Jack and his future, and yet her certainty

73

that they would see him again, had restored life to it, making it beat a little faster with some emotion she did not recognise. There was a stubborn resolution in her to prove Dolly wrong. To show her that despite his lowly beginnings, which were not his fault anyway, he would demonstrate to Dolly, to the world, that he had the makings of a gentleman in him. Not a gentleman, as her father was a gentleman, born to it, bred to it, but a truly gentle man who would be admired for what he was, what he had become, for there was no doubt in her mind that all the things Jack had told her he meant to do, he would do. When he had gone, no more than two hours ago, she had been frighteningly overwhelmed by a great emptiness within her. A hollow, aching emptiness his going had cut out of her but now, as the remembrance of his sweet smile closed like a fist about her heart, she felt that emptiness fill up again, fill out again, overflow with something lovely he had left behind. A leap of gladness moved inside her and her mouth began to tug in a smile. There was no doubt she would miss him terribly but if he were to come back . . . if he were to come back as Dolly seemed to think he might . . .

Dolly saw the smile and her heart sank. It was so familiar. It was Miss Eleanor's smile. The one she had worn when her Mama had absolutely forbidden her even to meet again the impecunious doctor, fifteen years older than she was, let alone marry him, but she'd done it just the same. She'd left behind her comfortably luxurious home, her friends and family and set out to a life which was vastly different to the one in which she had been brought up.

Now her daughter had that same look about her. A secret, shining look which worried Dolly to death. Not that she thought Jack Andrews had done or said anything to Miss Sara which her papa could not have been privy to. Despite his background Jack had not been the sort of man to take advantage of an innocent young girl and if he had Dolly would have known about it, of that she was sure. She knew every facet of Miss Sara's nature, which was open and honest, and if she had been guarding some private thing between her and Jack Andrews Dolly would have been instantly aware of it. Just as she had when Miss Eleanor eloped with Doctor Hamilton.

The first letter arrived a week later and at the sight of it, though she had never seen Jack's writing before and could not have known it was from him, Sara's face lit up like the glowing flame of a candle to which a light has been put.

It was beautifully written, every word spelled correctly and might have come from a man educated as a scholar. She read it out to them with the bright and lovely innocence of a child, unaware of Alice's frozen, forbidding expression, only too pleased to share with her father, who seemed as delighted as she was, the overflowing contents which described all that had happened to Jack since he had left them. She was not to worry about him, he said. His health was as good as it had ever been and his leg was strong again. He was laying track which had already reached the spot where it passed the hamlets of Lower and Higher Hestham and was having no trouble keeping up with the other men who, even Racer and Billyo, had been surprised and pleased to see him. He had *not* reminded them of the last time they had met, he said whimsically, and Sara could imagine the humour in his face as he wrote it and the deep curve of his smiling mouth, smiling herself as she read the words to them all. He had a cosy little billet with Whistler and his wife and was going to lay aside every penny he could of the twenty-four shillings a week he had received. He did not say why. He had heard there was work to be had up towards Oxenholme. A line to be built between Kendal and Windermere which he would try for. Again he did not say why though Dolly knew, of course.

On and on the letter flowed, charting the wonders of what he meant to do in the great new world of railway building. He did not say why.

Sara sat down at once to reply.

6

She next saw him on Christmas Day. They were just sitting down to a Christmas goose given to Doctor Hamilton by one of the obliging grandsons of Fanny Suthurst when the knock on the door sounded.

The doctor had asked no questions on how Albert Suthurst had come by the goose and Albert had offered no explanation but Dolly's eyes had lit up when she saw it. She exchanged a conspiratorial glance with her employer then, without a word, took the bird from his hand, hung it for a day or two in her cool larder, plucked it, singed it, drew it, cut off the neck and feet, trussed it and made her own delicious sage and onion stuffing to accompany it before putting it in the oven.

It was on the table, its aroma drifting to the rafters when they heard the rap on the door and three of the four faces round the table fell, for it could only be a call for Doctor Hamilton. The fourth took on a look of ill-humoured pique, just as though whoever was knocking did so with the express purpose of annoying Alice Hamilton.

"Well, I think it's just too bad that your patients find it necessary to call you out on Christmas Day, Papa, and I for one will give whoever it is a piece of my mind."

"Alice, don't take on so. I can't think who it could be since as far as I know all my patients are on the road to recovery. There are no infants imminently due and they would let themselves get to the very crack of death's door before calling me out today of all days. It must be serious."

"Well, whoever it is, kindly tell them that you are just about to sit down to dine and will be along presently. I don't know, these people imagine you to be at their beck and call night and day and what thanks do you get, tell me that? If some of them were to pay your fee I wouldn't mind but no, a rabbit or a few eggs . . ."

"Alice, please," the doctor pleaded with her, "do allow Dolly to answer the door and find out who is there before you make statements which you may regret."

He stood on the back doorstep, his large frame filling the doorway, still wearing the old overcoat Doctor Hamilton had given him. Traditionally, and to Sara's delight, it had snowed lightly the night before and the dazzle of it was at his back. There was a light dusting on his chestnut curls which had grown since Dolly had cut his hair and across the shoulders of the overcoat, and his moleskin trousers were damp to the knee as though he might have floundered through a small drift or two.

"Hmmph," said Dolly, who had opened the door, her eyes doing their best to hide the smile in them with a look of disapproval. She rattled the door latch as though she would dearly love to shut the door in his face but Jack just stood there, his eyes going at once to Sara. Her own were a vivid blaze of pleasure, like emeralds in the rosy glow of her face and if her father or sister had been looking at her they would have been left in no doubt as to the state of her feelings for Jack Andrews.

Doctor Hamilton sprang to his feet, his face showing his own pleasure but Alice's mouth thinned dangerously and her eyes hardened. I thought we'd seen the last of you, they appeared to say, their green depths, so like Sara's and yet not, narrowed and hostile. She was already in a state of icy displeasure because she had been overruled on the question of where they should dine. To her mortification the house had no dining-room and the parlour was too small and already too crowded with her mama's lovely furniture to allow a dining table to be put in. But to eat, like common working people, in the kitchen was the sign of poor and slipping standards and her resentment simmered just below the surface over this and over Jack Andrews's intrusion as he stepped shyly over the threshold.

"Jack, come in, my boy, come in," the elderly gentleman beamed. "Dolly, stop hovering in the doorway and let Jack get by you. Shut the door, woman and keep the cold out. I do believe it might snow again. See, Jack, take off your coat. Help him, Sara, please." He grinned boyishly, as pleased to see his former patient as though he and Jack were closely related. "It's done some stout service, that coat, and still is by the look of it. It *is* good to see you, old chap, and obviously in the rudest of health— "

Alice lifted her chin imperiously as she interrupted. "As Papa says, you look well and one can tell your work suits you, Mr Andrews," and why not since you are from the labouring classes. "You look very well, but I wonder that you took the trouble to make the long walk here," since what is there here for a man such as yourself? She might have spoken the words out loud so obvious was her meaning, but it appeared to escape the notice of both the doctor and Sara.

"A Happy Christmas, Jack," Sara said, as though that was just what it was now. She had stood up as he entered the kitchen, hopping about like an excited child. She was wearing blue, the hyacinth blue of the dress she had been making during his weeks of convalescence. Light from somewhere struck sparks from her hair and it formed a fiery nimbus about her small head. She wore it in a braid, one single rope as thick as his wrist and it fell in a live ripple of escaping tendrils across her left breast to her waist. On the end of it was a froth of blue ribbons. She darted to help him with his coat, laughing as his arm caught in his sleeve, reaching to brush the snow from his hair and eyeing admiringly the smooth, freshly shaved glow of his cheek and chin, the wide smiling curve of his lips.

Jack spoke at last, directing his words towards the doctor though his gaze still clung tightly to Sara's. They were both bewitched by this meeting, speaking to one another without knowing they did so in that secret, special way which seemed to spring up from nowhere between them, green eyes glowing into brown, the expression in them identical, the message clear, at least to Jack who was more experienced than Sara.

"I hope you don't mind, sir," were the first words Jack spoke, "intruding like this on tha' family but I thought . . . well, it were no more 'n a mile or two to tramp. Even in't snow it was nothin' an' it bein' Christmas Day there was no work bein' done an . . . well," he floundered, "tha've only to say an' I'll be on me way."

"My boy, we're delighted, aren't we, girls?" turning to glance at the rosy smiling face of his younger daughter, passing over the stiff one of his elder. "And delighted to see you in such obvious health. No trouble with the leg, then?"

"No, sir. It's not kept me from layin' track. Not for a minute. Truth to tell I've bin doin' some extra work."

"You musn't overdo it, Jack."

"Oh no, Jack," Sara echoed, looking round for somewhere to lay his coat then flinging it unceremoniously on to the rocking chair as though she had far better things to do than bother with it. Jack was here. Jack was here and her day was complete because of it.

"Nay, I'll be careful, sir," his glance still firmly fixed on Sara. "but I needed extra cash, tha' knows. I've a scheme or two up me sleeve an'— "

"Well really, Papa, are we to let a good meal spoil just because . . ." just because this interloper has turned up. Alice had no need to finish the sentence for Jack knew exactly what she meant. Nothing had changed then, his wry expression seemed to say.

"I suppose you had better fetch another chair from the drawing-room, Mr Andrews," Alice went on ungraciously but Richard Hamilton, concerned with patting Jack's arm and his shoulders with professional interest and telling him how pleased he had taken the trouble to come, again failed to notice.

"Aye," Dolly added. "Tha's right, Miss Alice. That's a good goose goin' cold on't table and them roast potatoes'll want eating before they lose their crispness. There's nothing worse than soggy roast potatoes. I'll have to heat gravy up as it is."

Grumbling and testy but her eyes still inclined to be soft when they rested on the "lad", Dolly circled the table, watching Miss Sara with irritated concern for if she didn't wipe that expression off her face, sit down and stop smiling in that foolish way it would not be long before her pa and Miss Alice noticed summat was up. She crashed plates and tureens about unnecessarily, doing her best to camouflage the strange intensity which stretched between the lad and Miss Sara behind a screen of domestic activities, passing the knife and fork to the doctor with curt instructions to "get carving".

"Fetch them hot plates, Miss Sara, if tha' please, and you, Jack Andrews, sit tha' down and pour us all a glass of my cowslip wine. It's been standing since I made it last May an'll be strong, so think on, no more than a glass fer Miss Sara." He had brought in four parcels with him and she eyed them suspiciously but he continued to clutch them to his chest as though he was afraid to let them out of his sight. "An' will tha' put them parcels down or are tha' to hold 'em in thy lap right through dinner? Tha's ter stay ter dinner, I tekk it? Aye, I thought so."

It was a merry meal, made so by the delight of Doctor Hamilton, Sara and Jack to be in one another's company again. Alice Hamilton's tart remarks interspersed with stony silence were taken for granted since it was a condition of her nature to be critical and was so usual it was scarcely noticed. They agreed, the three of them, that it was the best Christmas dinner they had had since ... well ... Doctor Hamilton looked wistful and Sara patted his hand and Jack knew they were thinking of Mrs Hamilton but just the same it was a grand meal. Dolly, who had begun to nod over her own plum pudding in which she had put a glass or two of her cowslip wine, smiled in gratification. Jack had noted Dolly's warning about the strength of the wine and had replenished everyone's glass – except Sara's – the moment it was drained, not feeling the slightest qualm in doing so, his reasons kept to himself. The laughter rose and loosened tongues so that even Dolly found herself telling a joke or two, innocent jokes revealed innocently to her by someone she couldn't remember, she kept saying. Alice became flushed and bright-eyed and, apart from several references to inebriation which made Jack smile inwardly for she looked pointedly at him when she made them as though she fully expected him to fall face down into his mince pies, she appeared to be resigned to his presence.

Jack regaled them with tales of life in the navvie camp, those that were fit to be repeated in the presence of ladies, even going so far as to mimic one or two of the more comical characters. He described Whistler and his "missus", refraining from telling them that the pair were not actually married, having only "jumped over the brush" as was customary in navvies' camps. They had three living children, were clean and respectable and they, and Jack, all managed to squeeze into a small, roughly built stone hut which lay halfway between Wray Green and Lytham. The camp sprawled along the line but Whistler and Mary's place stood a small distance from it, he explained and though he did not voice it to these good people it meant that apart from when they worked together he had little commerce with the men, with Racer and Billyo, with Fighting Jack and Brown Punch and those with whom he had once caroused. He meant to tell Sara later – hoping for half an hour alone with her while the others had an after-dinner, wine-induced snooze – describing to her how he was putting away every farthing he earned, except what he paid Whistler's Mary for his grub and the corner of her small home he occupied.

They sang songs. "Hark the Herald Angels Sing", "The Holly and the Ivy", "Good King Wenceslas" and "Greensleeves" which, though it was not a Christmas song, was a particular favourite of Dolly's. There was a fire in the parlour, of course, and after shooing Dolly, who had prepared the meal, the doctor who deserved a rest on this one day, and Alice who, not accustomed to wine, was in a slight and unusual daze, out of the kitchen, Sara and Jack cleared the table, washed the plates and pots and put away the detritus of the meal in total and vibrant silence. Sara's face was a vivid pink and in it her eyes had the brilliance of emeralds.

When they had finished, the table cleared and the bowl of pot-pourri returned to its centre, when the last dish was put away and there was nothing else to do Jack turned to Sara, his hand outstretched, and as if she were waiting for it her hand rose to take his. It was as though she were mesmerised as he led her to the chair by the fire. With the delicacy and instinct of a man who truly loves he placed her in it. Holding both her hands he knelt at her feet, his face sweet and somehow shy as he looked up at her with all that he felt for her written there.

"Sara." His voice was rapt, reverent as though he were in church, kneeling at the feet of an angel.

Sara's face softened into an ethereal loveliness which the trust she had in him awoke in her. Her eyes melted from the brilliance of emeralds into limpid pools of sea green silk and her long lashes drooped slowly in a way which delighted him.

"Jack," she whispered. "I thought they would never go." She leaned towards him innocently, offering whatever it was he might want of her and his heart slowed with his love for her. Her smile ran through his veins, setting him on fire and he was reluctant to go on. She knew he must leave the district soon, for the railway track which was being laid between

Kirkham and Lytham would be finished before long. There was to be an official opening of the railway station at Lytham in a few weeks' time and he wanted her to be there to see it. He wanted Doctor Hamilton to realise that Jack had a bright future before him and the finishing of the line meant the start of that future. The opening of the station would be the symbol of his hopeful prospects and with this in view surely, when she was old enough – and he was prepared to wait – Doctor Hamilton might be persuaded to treat seriously Jack's proposal for his younger daughter's hand. Jack wanted to do it properly. Follow the rules and keep to the conventions her society demanded of a prospective suitor. There must be nothing hidden, nothing underhand in his wooing of Sara Hamilton but she must be spoken to first. She must be made to understand his love which was patient and limitless. She was no more than a girl and he must be careful with her, not startle her with any urgent declaration of how he felt about her but it was hard not to stand up and sweep her against his eager body, kiss her until she responded, hold her and guard her and imbue in her his need to know that she belonged utterly to him. His. His possession. His woman and one day, his wife.

"It's been a hard, long time, Sara, since last I saw you." He looked up into her face, his own serious with the strength of his love which he allowed her to see without reserve for the first time. His mouth tightened, for he was nervous and he reached with one hand to push his hair back from his forehead. "I thought I'd not get through these last few weeks an' if I hadn't had your letters I'd never've managed it. They were grand, those letters."

"And so were yours, Jack," she said simply.

"Times I've wanted ter walk over 'ere but I had ter work. Earn as much money as I could."

"I know. I know how important it is to you, Jack."

"The money means nowt' ter me, Sara. It's what it'll bring me that's important." He looked at her meaningfully, hoping she would know what he was referring to but her smile was uncontrived and as natural as fresh-picked flowers.

"Did tha' miss me, lass?" He could not stop himself from asking.

"Yes, I did, Jack, enormously. Each day . . . somehow I couldn't stop looking for you though I knew you couldn't come. Sometimes I even thought I saw you in the lane, just like I sometimes think I catch a glimpse of Mama."

He was not sure he wanted her feelings for him to be likened to those she felt for her mama but he knew she was sincere, saying whatever was in her heart without guile.

"You were in my thoughts always, every minute of the day." He smiled ruefully. "'Tis a wonder I ever got any work done I was in such a daydream."

"Really, Jack?"

"Aye, Sara, really." His big hands rose to cup her face and the smile slipped from his. Into his eyes came the serious expression Sara had come to know so well, the one Jack Andrews assumed when his emotions were deeply involved. She had seen it several times, particularly when he spoke of his mother. She studied him carefully and at that very moment she saw it, and as he watched her he recognised it in her, the knowledge of what they were saying to one another. Up to this moment she had still been the child, the young girl befriending the man who had rescued her from the unimaginable horrors of his own workmates. There had been overwhelming gratitude, a genuine pleasure in his company, an attentive interest in what concerned Jack Andrews. Now, in a sudden illuminating awareness she saw what was truly in him and it overjoyed her. It was as though, deep beneath the layers of bone and muscle and flesh which made up the outer surface of Sara Hamilton, there had been hidden from her the glowing heart of her essential being, the one which had known right from that first moment in the lane that here was the man. The man. Jack!

"Jack . . .?" Her voice was wondering and the light of love which glimmered in the depths of her green eyes grew and intensified until it was strong and steady, a flame which would never be put out.

"Aye, my lass. 'Tis me. Jack Andrews and you know what's happened, don't you? I can see it in you, what's been in me these weeks. I've held back . . ." He gulped, his throat constricted by some emotion which threatened to get the better of him.

"Jack," she said again as though everything there was to say was in that one word. "How long have you known?" She smiled a little, her eyes enormous, overcome almost to the point of tears with the serious but beautiful truth of it and by the enormity of how easily they might have missed one another.

"Ever since I saw thi' in't lane. I knew then, but lass, you were so young."

Neither noticed the past tense since Sara Hamilton's childhood, girlhood, was gone now as her woman's eyes acknowledged Jack Andrews's love and revealed hers for him.

"I didn't know, Jack. I've always . . . liked you but now . . ."

"What? Say it, Sara. Never hold back from me for I couldn't stand that. The truth, always. Never hold back from me, girl. Whatever you feel, good or bad, tell me. There can be no secrets betwixt thee an' me, my Sara, ever."

"I know . . ." She hesitated shyly.

"Dost tha' love me, lass?" he urged. "Like I love thee?"

"Yes, Jack, I do." It was spoken with the reverence of a bride at the altar taking her marriage vows.

He drew in his breath and threw back his head, the strong line of his throat tense and straining, the tendons in it standing out like rope.

"Oh Jesus God, I've prayed for that, my lovely girl, waited and prayed and now it's come I'm . . . unmanned."

"Unmanned?" She put out a hesitant hand, not at all sure it was correct to place it on him in this lovely thing which had come to them. Was the female, herself, permitted to touch the male, Jack, without first . . . well, whatever it was, must it first be invited by Jack or could she just touch him? Her finger, of its own volition, rose to his fierce eyebrow and gently ran across it, feeling the thick and unfamiliar arch of it. She shivered, then as he lowered his head to look at her drew it back hastily. His eyes shone with a glistening light which she did not at first recognise.

"Nay, don't draw back, my little love, for there's nought I want but to feel your hand on me and to put mine on you but it's the joy of it which is making me . . . when I say unmanned, I want to weep with it. I could never bring meself to believe, you see."

"It's true, Jack," she said solemnly, "and please, don't weep. There's nothing to weep for. Would you instead . . . if it's permitted . . ."

"Yes, my love, my little love . . ." savouring the words on his lips.

"Kiss me, if . . . that's all right."

"All right . . . Jesus!"

He rose and lifted her from the chair with big, gentle hands, standing her before him with a decent six inches between them. He wanted her close, closer, but was afraid to be too precipitate for fear of alarming her. Her womanhood was so newly found and must be treated with the deepest respect. He took her face between his hands, cupping her cheeks, looking down for several seconds into her clear eyes, his thumbs lightly caressing her cheekbone.

"I love you, Sara," he said, his voice rough but soft, then laid his closed mouth on hers in her first kiss. Her lips were full, soft, closed as his were but ever so gently he moved his on hers and at once they parted and her sweet breath was in his mouth.

"I love you," he said again without taking his lips from hers, then slowly, looking down with aching tenderness into her dazed face, he put her gently from him. He continued to smooth her face, her chin, her brow, her hair, his eyes dreaming over her and when she sighed in blissful content he smiled.

"Did you like that, lass?" he asked her.

She lifted her hands and placed them about his where they cupped her face, looking up at him with the trust, the truth, the simple honest truth which was what she had to offer him.

"Oh yes."

He put his arms about her and tucked her beneath his chin, enclosing her in the shelter of his strong arms, resting his brown cheek on the softness of her tawny curls, sighing with the glory of it though his loins ached with his need of her. She was so young. He kept repeating it to himself, so new to this he must treat her with the honour her youthful innocence deserved but, dear God, he longed to be more to her at this first moment of awakening than she would ever realise.

"We'll be married, Sara, true an' honest, you know that, don't you? When the time's right. When I've made me way an' you're a year or two older." His hand was at the back of her head, his fingers deep in the richness of her unruly hair. The braid had come unplaited and part of it rippled like warm silk over his right arm which held her to him. There was considerably less than six inches between them now and he was uncomfortably aware of it but, Jesus, she felt so lovely in his arms he couldn't bear to let her go.

"You know you're mine now," he added possessively.

She nodded, her face raptly pressed against his beating heart, her arms tight about him, her hands clasped at his back.

"We'll have a house, a home fer thi' an' me and the bairns we'll have." His voice was quite matter of fact as though she knew all about marriage and bairns, then, horrified, for was she not a gently bred, gently reared girl and might not his outspokenness offend her, he put a gentle finger beneath her chin and lifted her flushed face to look into his. "Jesus, I'm sorry, lass, I reckon I shouldn't have said that but . . . well, you're to be me wife one day and I just . . . and you a maid who doesn't . . . ." He struggled with his own thoughtlessness while Sara stared uncomprehendingly up into his face.

"What is it, Jack?"

"Lass, when— " He stopped abruptly, his face flaming.

"Tell me, Jack, for there's no one else will in this house."

"Nay, Sara, it's not fer me to . . ." He took a deep breath to steady himself, his eyes intent on hers, then, seeing the trust in her he sighed.

"Well, when a man an' woman love one another . . . has no one ever told thi', sweetheart?" he asked beseechingly, which was a foolish question he knew when he considered the women in her life. One the brusque old servant, herself probably a virgin, the other a dried-up old maid who was Sara's sister. Nineteen years old Alice might be, which was not a great age, he was well aware, but that was what she reminded him of. A dried-up, disappointed old maid whose bitterness and envy of those who had husbands while she had none was souring her until she was dangerous. She had great influence on Sara, which frightened him, but it was a gold guinea to a farthing that not only did she herself not know the true facts of what went on between a man and a woman, she would not have disclosed them to her sister if she had.

"Well, I've seen . . . there was a dog with . . . it was Fanny Suthurst's grandson's lurcher. Albert takes it about with him and one day, when I was in the village the dog was . . . there was another, a female and they were . . . the dogs, I mean . . . Albert was laughing and . . ." She bent her head to avoid his gaze.

Jack looked down gravely to her bent head then, putting a gentle finger beneath her chin, lifted her face to his.

"I love thi' true, my lass an' when I tell thi' about what will happen between thi' an' me it will be nowt like what goes on with animals and that's God's truth. It will be the most wonderful thing ever to pass between a man and a woman. A man and woman who love truly, that is. When the time comes thee an' me will . . ." and with the utmost grace and delicacy Jack Andrews described to Sara Hamilton the mystery of their two, very different bodies and how they would fit together when they loved one another, not only with their senses, their hearts, their two entwined souls but physically. Her eyes grew bigger and her mouth opened in a circle of awe but he could see she was not frightened. On the contrary she was fascinated by the idea.

"Jack," she said earnestly.

"Yes, Sara?" smiling down at her, wondering what she was going to say. After all it was rather unusual for a young girl to be given such intimate details of making love by the man who eventually was to have the joy and pleasure of it.

"I'm tempted to ask you if we . . ." She blushed a little but her eyes were steady on his.

"Aye, my love, I know what . . . well, I feel the same for we love each other true an' it's the most natural thing in the world to want to show that love . . . to find pleasure, and it will be a pleasure, Sara."

"I'm sure it will, Jack," and he wanted to smile at her seriousness.

"But we must wait. I wanted thee to know the consequences of lying with a man. There'll be childer but before that you'll have my ring on tha' finger." It was spoken with deep pride. "Now I must go, lass . . . no, don't argue, my love, 'tis a fair tramp an' I must get back before dark. I reckon it'll snow before long an' if I'm not at the hut Whistler's Mary'd only fret. Aye, a grand woman is Mary. She puts me in mind of me mam, cluckin' about me shirts an' me wet feet an' will I not wear me muffler? I'm right well looked after, my little darlin'."

He seemed to rejoice in the last words, his expression telling Sara that that was what she was to him. At last, his deep brown eyes told her, he could say what he felt, speak the words of endearment which he had spoken to no other woman. Her own eyes shone luminously, joyously into his and he groaned inwardly as he tried to restrain himself from folding her into the very depths of his arms where, he knew quite well, she would feel the swelling of his male desire for her. Despite the sensitivity with which he had enlightened her on the mechanics of lovemaking he was not awfully sure she understood exactly what her body was doing to his but he was willing to suffer it. His loins might ache but his heart was as soaring and deliriously enchanted as a meadowlark. He could not give her up, not yet, not until he was forced to by the arrival of the others.

They continued to stand in the gentle embrace Jack thought suitable until, from the parlour, came the sound of voices as if those who had collapsed there were coming to and Jack and Sara reluctantly stepped apart. When Dolly stumped into the kitchen, her old eyes everywhere at once, she glared suspiciously at them, her disapproving manner telling them that if she had known Alice wasn't with them she'd not have let them out of sight for a minute. She'd had her forty winks and when she awoke from them she had been alarmed to see the doctor and Miss Alice doing exactly the same as herself, and where were that lad and Miss Sara? had been her first anxious thought. Jack was a nice enough chap and one Dolly would have looked kindly on if he'd come courting her granddaughter, if she'd had one, but he was not for Miss Sara. He'd treat a woman right would Jack Andrews but Miss Sara was not only a woman, but a lady.

"Now then, what are you two doin' hangin' about on that there hearth-rug? Why aren't thi' in't parlour with Miss Alice and tha' pa, Miss Sara? And as for you, lad, tha'd best look sharp if tha' wants ter get to that camp o' thine before dark."

"Aye, you're right, Dolly, but . . ."

"Nay, no buts, me lad. Wrap up warm an' be off with thee."

"But I've not given out me Christmas presents yet, Dolly," Jack protested. "There's one for thee an' all," he added winningly.

"Christmas presents! No one said owt' ter me about no Christmas presents," Dolly objected, deeply offended, not by the fact that Jack should give her a gift but because she felt she had somehow been tricked by this engaging young man and after she had just given him the rounds of the kitchen, an' all.

"It's not much, Dolly . . . well, I'm trying to save, tha' know . . ."

"Save! What for?" Dolly's mouth pursed distrustfully. Since when did the likes of navviemen save?

"Oh, this an' that," Jack answered airily.

"This an' that! And what's that supposed ter mean?"

"Well, I've things I need for . . . well . . ." Jack floundered and behind him he felt Sara's hand squeeze his. Returning the squeeze he let go of her and moved across the shining flags of the kitchen, giving Dolly a wide berth as though he expected a clip round the ear. He reached for the parcels which he had placed carefully in the corner as he sat down to eat. Handing her one of them he said politely, "This 'un's for thee, Dolly."

"What is it?" she asked, taking it in her hand as though it were just about to explode.

"Open it and see, Dolly," Sara begged her, her eyes shining like stars in the firelit glow of the kitchen.

It was nothing but a simple handkerchief, a fine square of lawn edged with a bit of lace and embroidered in one corner with the initial D, white on white.

It might have been the crown jewels, the joy with which Dolly received it, especially when Jack explained he had purchased the material himself and that Whistler's Mary from the camp had made it.

"Whistler's Mary?" Dolly looked slightly apprehensive for surely anything that came from that camp must be suspect but it was spotlessly clean, beautifully made and embroidered and Dolly marvelled that such a thing could be fashioned amongst so much muck and confusion.

Brought from the parlour, Alice and Doctor Hamilton were presented with similar gifts of handkerchiefs, Doctor Hamilton's large, plain and businesslike, Alice's dainty, fragile, like the ones ladies used, Jack had thought. They thanked him, the doctor profusely, Alice carelessly tossing it to one side, for she could have made the thing herself, and much better, and her distasteful expression said so.

When Sara's gift was put into her hands, a gift so much bigger and so much more interesting-looking than anyone else's, Alice eyed it suspiciously, and it was then that the first inkling of what lay between her sister and Jack Andrews was revealed to her. She watched her sister carefully lay the parcel on the table and begin to untie the string, then peel back the wrapping paper, so slowly, so gingerly it might have contained a live animal. Her eyes were filled with wonder and with something else Alice Hamilton did not as yet fully recognise but she was certain she would not care for it when she did.

"What can it be, sweetheart?" her father asked smilingly, turning to look at Jack as though he would never cease to be amazed at the versatility of his patient.

It was a sewing box, made from a piece of walnut, a simple rectangular shape with no embellishment anywhere on it but it had been put together with such care and expertise it was impossible to see where the pieces which made it up were joined. Only a fine line was visible where the lid fitted to the box and at the back where two tiny hinges lay. It had been polished and polished until every grain and pattern in the wood stood out, the whole shining and complete, exquisite in its simplicity.

Sara looked at it in silence, her face suddenly gone pale and still, her long lashes hiding the expression in her eyes.

"Open it, Sara," Jack encouraged, almost in a whisper and when she did so, her hands trembling, it was found to be lined in a fine blue velvet. There were small pockets to hold thimbles; there was a pincushion of plain polished walnut, the cushion made of the same blue velvet as the lining. There was a thread winder and a measuring tape, all hand-made except for the one thimble, a cheap silver thing with a heart etched in it.

She couldn't speak and neither could anyone else. It was so clearly a thing of the heart, from the heart, a giving, a declaration of what Jack Andrews felt for Sara Hamilton that no one in the room could be left in any doubt as to what those feelings were.

"I made it messen, Sara. I found this bit of wood in Holme Chase a while back, a lovely bit of wood an' right away I wanted to . . . There's this shop in Lytham, sells all sorts. She 'ad a bit of velvet and . . . well, me Pa taught me about wood . . ." His voice died away as no one spoke but there were really no words needed from the girl he loved.

She stretched out a finger, gentle, unbelieving, enchanted,

and smoothed it over the lid of the lovely box then, turning enormous, glittering eyes to Jack, she began to weep.

Alice Hamilton's face became as hard as though carved from stone and her lips thinned frighteningly. Dolly sighed. Smoothing her hands, work-worn in the service of this family, down the crisp immaculately ironed skirt of her capacious apron, she turned away. Crossing her arms over her bosom she sat down heavily in her chair and when the marmalade cat sprang up to its usual cosy place on her lap, it was surprised and outraged when, with little ceremony, it was pushed off again.

7

They did not meet again at the house and Richard Hamilton gave orders to his younger daughter that she was no longer to communicate with Jack Andrews. It had taken him two days, and hour upon hour of Alice's insistent exhortation that he had no other choice, before he could come to terms with the scene which had taken place in the kitchen, not only come to terms with it but actually believe that it had happened at all. He had taken a great fancy to the lad over the weeks he had lived in his house and would be eternally grateful to him for defending his two daughters from the navvies but his gratitude did not stretch as far as Jack evidently hoped it would. He had admired Jack's stoicism, his wit and humour which had never deserted him even when in great pain. He had liked the lad, found him an agreeable companion, astute and surprisingly articulate, with a keenness to learn. It had not occurred to him to guard either of his daughters for he had trusted Jack and Sara to act in a proper manner. He had imagined, if he had thought of it at all that with Dolly always on guard and Alice constantly at Sara's side, which she had been in the past, his daughters were adequately chaperoned. The letters that had passed between Jack and Sara in the last few weeks he had thought to be those of friends, not just from Jack to Sara but to them all and when Sara read them out while they sat about the supper table it had not crossed his mind to ask to see them. He himself had entreated the young man to "keep in touch", "let us know how you are," "call in if you are passing" and had been delighted to see him on Christmas Day.

Their farewells had been cool and it was made very evident to Jack that he had made a grave mistake in revealing, with the simple splendour of his gift to Sara, his feelings for her. There was no entreaty to "call again", to "pop in if you're passing", merely a stiff nod, a polite thank you for their Christmas gifts and a hope that Jack would continue in good health, and at their father's back Jack carried away with him the image of two faces, one that of Alice Hamilton, rigid with enmity, the other of Sara, white, tear-stained and slack with sorrow.

"Well, you've done it now, Sara Hamilton," Alice hissed, "or at least that navvie has." Her voice was hoarse with loathing. "How you could so demean yourself in allowing that . . . that lout to make advances to you as he so obviously has, is beyond me. You, a lady, our dear mama's daughter, to let a man who consorts with thugs and loose women lay his hands on you makes me cringe with shame."

"Don't, Alice . . . please don't. Jack and I did nothing wrong, ever."

"Do you expect me to believe that? I saw the way he looked at you and why, if there is nothing between you, should he give you that sewing box? Why did you not get a trumpery handkerchief like the rest of us? I can hardly believe that . . . that my sister should resort to such . . ."

"Oh, please, Alice . . ." Sara's face was streaked with tears and she sniffed inconsolably. She was a small child again under the brutal attack her sister launched on her and, with the triumph of those who imagine they are being cruel to be kind, Alice continued viciously.

"You are too young for this sort of thing, Sara, far too young and that oaf knew it, taking advantage of your innocence."

"No, it was I who— " Sara bit her lip until she drew blood but Alice pounced with the sureness of a beast of prey.

"Aha, so there was something. He did . . ."

"No! No! It was he who told me that we should wait until we are married before we . . ."

"Before you what?" The air was quite electric, nasty with Alice's breathless insistence on worming from her sister everything there was to know about her and Jack and Sara trembled like some wilting flower which has been caught in a fierce wind.

"Nothing . . . nothing. We love one another."

"Love one another! You make me feel sick, Sara Hamilton. How could you possibly love that person? Dear God, have you no shame?"

Sara, whose head had bowed lower and lower under the

onslaught of her sister's frenzied attack, raised it suddenly and her face cleared and became filled with a light which was lovely to see.

"There is nothing shameful in loving a man, Alice, nor in having a man love you but then you wouldn't know anything about that, would you?"

Alice's face blanched with insensed rage. She could not have been more amazed if the marmalade cat had stood on its hind legs and asked her to dance. Sara *never* defied Alice. In the years since their mother died Alice had quite naturally, and without argument from any of the other three members of the household, taken her mother's place, as mistress and as guardian and mentor of her young sister. Sara had been almost like her daughter for though there were only four years between them Sara seemed to need Alice's guidance and Alice had been only too pleased to provide it. Now, within the space of a few hours Sara was defying her, being insolent, nay, being spiteful about Alice's failure to gain for herself a husband of her own, for that was what Sara meant. Alice would not forget this day, nor would she forget Jack Andrews who had brought it down on their unsuspecting heads.

"How dare you? How dare you speak to me like that? You forget yourself and all that Mama taught you. I am thinking only of you when I say you shall not see him again and Papa agrees with me. He understands our position in this community."

"What position is that, Alice?" Sara asked desolately.

Alice was appalled. "I cannot believe this, Sara Hamilton, I really cannot believe it and I can only assume you are under the influence of that man whom we took in. Heavens, thank goodness we found out in time, for it would be a catastrophe if you had continued your association with him. I said so to Papa and he is to— "

"What? What is Papa to do? What has he said?"

"It is not for me to tell you, Sara. That is Papa's job and you will find out soon enough."

Sara watched numbly as Alice swept regally from the room. She was ready to weep again at the beauty of Jack's gift, at the wonder of how he had fashioned it, and when. He worked twelve, fourteen, sometimes sixteen hours a day, he had told them so, back-breaking, bone-breaking labour which would kill a lesser man and yet when it was done he had still found time to carve and put together the delicate symmetry of the sewing box she held against her as though it were a star plucked from the firmament and therefore of inestimable value. His hands were big, rough, scarred with the harshness of his work and yet somehow he had created this delicate object and he had done it because he loved her.

But his efforts had ended, she knew quite positively, in disaster, for her papa's face, her papa's voice, though he had said nothing untoward as yet, had told her that he was . . . well, displeased was too weak a word to describe what her papa obviously felt. Shocked, offended, hurt by what he saw as a betrayal of his trust. She had not given a great deal of thought to the complexities of arranging a marriage between herself and Jack since she was still in that first bewitched state new lovers know when just to be in the same room with the beloved is enough. Today is enough providing the object of one's love is in it and tomorrow can wait for a while. She was not even sixteen until June of next year and too young to marry. At least to marry a man who . . . well, if Jack were a man of her own – dear God, she hated to say it – her own rank, or status . . . a gentleman, in fact, she would have been considered quite old enough since girls married as young as fifteen if the groom was suitable and wealthy enough to support a wife. And, of course, Jack wasn't, not yet. She had hoped that, given a year or two and the furtherance of the plans he had hinted at in his letters, she and Jack might persuade her father to allow them to be married one day in the future, but now, through Jack's generous but ill-timed gift it would all be cut off and disposed of before it had time slowly to become acceptable to him. To Papa. She could tell, had known at once that she and Jack would no longer be able to continue their relationship, not with Papa's blessing, that is. That it must now be conducted in secret, for though as yet Papa had had nothing to say except "Go to bed, Sara, I will see you in the morning," the implication was there. The implication that Jack had overstepped the mark of what a well-bred gentleman would instinctively know as the bounds of decency.

He said so, gently, sadly but with an inexorability that told her he meant every word and that he expected to be obeyed. She was not to write to Jack again and if Jack wrote to her the letter must be handed, unopened, to him. The new postal service which had been adopted only five years ago and was paid for by means of a pre-paid adhesive stamp, though it was a boon to those who corresponded with one another, was no benefit to Doctor Hamilton since it made his duty to protect his daughter from this unwanted suitor that much more difficult. He was sorry that he must treat her like this and he said so, for she was a good girl but she had been led astray by a man with charm and manners, certainly, but a man who could never be considered as a husband, if that was what Jack Andrews had in mind. Best finish it now, he added firmly. Sara had only to see the navvie camp beside the track to Lytham to realise how ill-advised a friendship with Jack Andrews was. He could do no more than appeal to her judgment which, despite her immaturity, he had always trusted. He trusted her now to defer to him in this matter. He had, he was the first to admit, been remiss in not considering that she was almost a young lady and therefore was ready to mix with others, as Alice had pestered him to do, in the station in life to which their mama had been born. He meant to contact Mrs Bentham or one of the other ladies of the community so that matters might be taken in hand at once to introduce both his daughters into the class of society which was their due, imagining in his naivety that any hostess of good taste would be only too glad to take on his own pretty, presentable girls.

He and Sara were in the parlour where Dolly had lit the fire, well aware of the impending encounter between Doctor Hamilton and his daughter. Over the fireplace a small portrait of Eleanor Hamilton hung, painted the year before her marriage to Richard. Over twenty years ago when she herself was twenty years old and but for her expression, which was serene and gently smiling, it might have been a painting of Sara. She was in a gown of soft, creamy silk. Her hair fell in lustrous ringlets over her shoulder and for a moment Richard Hamilton faltered.

Dear God, he anguished, why did you have to take her, the words silently battering against his sorely troubled heart, for only a mother, another woman, would know how best to deal with this.

He turned back to his daughter, studying her expressionless face.

"Do you understand what I am saying, my dear?" he asked her gently.

"Oh yes, Papa."

"Good," visibly relieved that she had agreed so readily. "And you will . . . well, I hesitate to use the word 'obey' but you know what I mean."

"Yes, I do, but I'm afraid I can promise nothing."

He blinked. Sara had always been so sunny-natured, so warm-hearted she was inclined to bestow her hugs and kisses quite without thought if Alice had not been there to restrain her. Alice had done her best to curb Sara's childish enthusiasms, which he had sometimes regretted, but a lady must show restraint, at least Alice said so. Her nature was vital, joyous, her charm headlong, her loyalties fierce but she had always been amenable, eager to please, both himself and Alice. An obedient, dutiful daughter.

"I'm not sure . . ." he began.

"Papa, I love you dearly, you know that, but I cannot promise to obey you, not if it means my giving up my . . . my friendship with Jack." Her youthful dignity overwhelmed him and he wanted to draw her into his arms and tell her to go ahead and do whatever made her happy, for her happiness was all that mattered to him but he knew he must be strong.

"Neither of us has done, or said, anything dishonourable," she went on, "anything of which we should be ashamed. I know Jack is no . . . he is not . . . Oh, dammit, Papa, what stupid words we are forced to use to describe one another and one of them is 'class', but he is honest, truthful, a hard worker and means to get on. He can do it, too, for he is intelligent and educated above his – oh Lord, how I hate this – his station."

"Sara, stop there at once for you know it cannot be allowed."

"Why not? Why not, Papa? He will make a fine husband."

"Stop there at once! Husband! Do you imagine for a moment that I would allow one of my daughters to live as those . . . those sluts at the camp live? You have not seen it as I have. The appalling conditions the women exist in. They look after their men but they are not looked after. They are beaten for no other reason than it entertains their masters. They take part in all the . . . the obscenities and are as blasphemous as their men. They fight as the men fight and are frequently injured."

"Jack wouldn't let me be."

"They consort with any man for the price of a few pence."
In his horror Richard Hamilton forgot he was speaking to his
innocent, gently reared child. "They start as young as twelve
or thirteen."

"Please, Papa . . ."

"They sell drink along with their bodies. They eat half-
cooked rotten food and live in filth, most of them. Their
children are neglected. They are depraved, Sara."

He bit off his words violently, just as though his teeth had
locked about his tongue, the sudden realisation of what he
was saying overcoming him at last.

He went on in a quieter tone, its very quietness telling her
he meant what he said. "If I have to lock you up to prevent
you seeing him again, then I will do so."

Richard Hamilton's normal kindly expression and patient,
genial manner had fled with the strength of his fear for his
child. She *was* a child, no more and knew no better and if
she couldn't see the impossibility of it herself then he would
be forced to make her do it for her.

"You will stay in this house with your sister, going no
further than the garden wall until I am convinced you are over
this . . . folly. If you go to the village Alice will accompany you
and if I hear . . ."

Suddenly his grey, elderly face crumpled and he put his
hand to his mouth. "Dear sweet Lord . . . oh dear God, will you
listen to me? If Elly were to hear me she would be horrified, as
I am horrified to be saying these things to you." He blinked
rapidly, clearing his throat, then rubbed his shaking hand over
his face.

"But don't you see, child, it won't do? Your mama would
haunt me from the grave if I let you associate with this
man."

"I know you mean well, Papa, but you and she loved each
other. She left her home to marry you so why cannot— "

"It was not the same, Sara. She was older than you are by
five years or so. I had a home to bring her to. A job, the means
to support her, but this man . . ."

"If he provided me with a home and had the means to
support me, would you allow it?" Her face was stiff with
antagonism.

There was a long silence. Richard Hamilton stared blindly

through the window and out to the bleak winter landscape beyond it. The snow had turned to rain as it so often did in these parts, a steady drizzle which drifted across the garden and lane, the drenched fields, shading the line between grey earth and grey sky. It was bleak, colourless, lifeless as, at the moment, his heart was. He sighed deeply before turning back to his daughter.

"No."

She lifted her head mutinously, the colour in her cheeks a deep flag of defiance and he wondered how two women, his wife and his younger daughter, could be so alike and yet so different. Eleanor, beautiful, fine, frail, gentle, submissive to his kindly will. Sara, beautiful, fine but not frail and certainly no longer submissive to the will of her father.

"Then I will disobey you, Papa."

She whirled on her heel, her mother's scented shawl drifting about her like a delicate fan. She opened the door, her hand fumbling on the handle in her agitation then, without another word or backward glance, banged it to behind her.

Her letter to Jack was desolate, filled with her young love for him, her frustration at being ordered about like a child but also with her challenging belief that given time her papa would come round. After all, he liked Jack and surely that must count for something? She couldn't believe, and she was sure Jack felt the same, that a man as progressive – was that the word? – and so little concerned with convention as her papa could not fail to see eventually how silly and old-fashioned his ideas were. Anyway, she concluded blithely, it really made no difference, did it, for when Jack went up north to work on the proposed Kendal and Windermere line which had been authorised six months ago and where Jack meant to find work as soon as the Lytham line was completed, she would simply go with him. They could be married wherever they could find a preacher and Jack could rent a little house in Kendal, or thereabouts, she wrote artlessly, knowing nothing of Jack's finances, and they would start their life from there.

The letter was posted after midnight on the same day as the quarrel with her father and Sara prayed that she would not have to go through the experience again. The waiting for the house to quieten; for Alice to fall deeply asleep in the bed next to hers. The creak of the stairs as she crept down them and the astonished expression on the face of the marmalade cat as Sara let herself out of the kitchen door. The scurrying run on the track from Lane End, past the spot where Racer and Billyo had caught her and Alice, shuddering away from the memory, and into Wray Green and the tiny postbox. Dark as black ink the night had been, so that though she knew the route as well as her own face she twice fell into the ditch beside the track.

In the letter she suggested that they no longer used the postal services since any letter from Jack to her would be delivered to her papa's door, but that they should exchange letters by the old method, the one which had been used for centuries, and that was to hand them to a tradesman, in this case the brewers' drayman who passed the end of the lane each week with his delivery to the ale-house in Wray Green. He stopped at the camp to sell it to the women there, those who traded it to the men and for the price of a jug of ale would pass on any messages Sara and Jack might have for one another. There was a certain loose stone in the wall and with a bit of thought and goodwill on the draymans' part they could continue to correspond.

Jack didn't know whether to be thrilled or horrified when he received her letter. Bloody hell, she had no idea, none, of the financial provisions he must make before he could begin to think of taking a wife. She was so young, not only in years but in her ignorance of the world outside Wray Green. She had never known want, hardship, hunger. Her family by some standards was poor, living from day to day on what the doctor could manage to extract from patients even poorer than himself but she had always been warm, sheltered, clothed and fed. Now she was proposing to give it all up and follow him wherever he led her, knowing nothing of what she might be forced to endure if he could not provide for her. He was determined he would succeed in the plans which fermented in his head but he could not do it with Sara beside him. He would be hampered, too afraid to dare that bold chance he might take were he alone and she must be made to see that until he had, even in a small way, assured them of some stability in their future together, she must remain where she was.

It was six weeks before they were to meet again, a mild February morning and still almost dark as Sara slipped from the house and along the muddy track towards Wray Green.

They were all still asleep, her papa, Alice, Dolly and even the marmalade cat but, as arranged, the brewers' dray was waiting at the crossroads by the pond in the village. It was nearly five miles to Lytham along meandering lanes cutting through wide fields which had been ploughed in December and January in readiness for the planting of oats and other mixed crops. Already, though it was barely light, labourers were plodding along the muddy tracks towards their day's work for which they would be paid an average of three shillings a week. They would spend the next twelve or so hours, or as long as daylight lasted, planting, or broadcasting by hand the seeds the farmer would fetch on his waggon.

The men wore smock frocks and gaiters and a battered hat jammed down over each face, even the young ones, weathered by their outdoor life. The women were in calf-length, shapeless skirts with rough bodices, sacking over their shoulders to keep out the drizzle which was bound to fall at some time during this winter day, and cotton bonnets. Many were pregnant. There were several children amongst them, more frisky than their elders, who would be put to stone-picking, earning a few coppers with the buckets and buckets of stones they gathered.

"Good morning," Sara called out to them, her luminous gaze enfolding each and every one of them in her own joy. "A beautiful morning, isn't it?" she went on, but no one answered. The women bobbed a curtsey and the men touched their caps and in each face was bewildered amazement. It asked what she was doing here and what the devil was beautiful about this drear February morning? Where was she going dressed in that lovely gown of a blue the colour of hyacinths? She wore the sweetest straw bonnet with flowers beneath its brim, flowers that looked just like tiny sprigs of a hyacinth itself and about her shoulders was a slipping, pastel-tinted shawl. They watched her go by perched like a brightly coloured bird on the seat of the dray, goggle-eyed and open-mouthed, nudging one another and murmuring amongst themselves. What was she doing out here alone and her such a well-brought-up young lass? What was her pa, the good Doctor Hamilton, thinking of and why wasn't that stuck-up sister of hers with her, wherever she was off to?

"'Appen she's away ter Lytham ter see't openin' o't rail-way station," one said, evidently in possession of more wordly news than the rest. "They do say it'll be a grand affair."

"Nay, all't way ter Lytham on 'er own. Doctor'd never allow it."

"Well, she be goin' somewhere an' it's not ter chuck seed on ter't fields like us."

Sara turned to wave at them, her face flushed with happiness and yet saddened by the sight. They were so drab, many of them bent with their labour before their time, their expressions resigned, patient and unthinking as the cattle which stood knee deep in the churned-up mud inside the gate which led from their pasture. The land round here was given to mixed farming, crops and dairy and the dray passed the fellow who would lead them off for milking. A dog slunk at his heels, eyes constantly turning, keeping its pace to the cowman's, ears laid back for his command, for it was the animal's job when the gate was opened to nip at the heels of the cows on their way back to the farmyard.

A hedger was at work on one of the quickthorn hedges which lay neatly about the chequerwork of the fields, repairing patches where cattle, seeking the best grass, had pushed through.

"Good morning," Sara sang out, including him in this perfect day, this day on which she and Jack were to be togther again after almost seven weeks apart. The drayman beside her had to smile at the countrymen's faces, really he did, though he was normally a dour man, used to being alone on his solitary journeying. She was a right perky one, this lass who was off to meet her sweetheart and she'd made a few folk's day a bit brighter with her great shining eyes and rosy face, himself an' all.

He leaned forward, slapping the reins against the supple, coal black rumps of his two fine Shire horses, though of course, strictly speaking, they weren't really his.

"Come up, Champion, come up, Major," he clucked to them and beside him Sara peered excitedly ahead for a sign of Jack who had promised to meet her on the lane where the railway track crossed it at Silcotes. From there they would walk together into Lytham where the ceremony was to take place.

The nearer they got to the small resort the more crowded became the lane. It was evident that not only were the people of Lytham going to enjoy this great day, this auspicious occasion, this splendid moment in the history of their village, but that folk from elsewhere were determined to enjoy it as well. The drayman had to watch Champion and Major for fear they might step on a darting child or a barking dog and Sara heard him curse softly under his breath as his great patient, plodding beasts were jostled by the ever increasing crowds of men, women and children in their best Sunday-go-to-church finery. The working man on his day off wore a wide-cut shirt, freshly laundered for the event, breeches and stockings, many with gaiters over them and a serviceable waistcoat and jacket. Most had a "Wellington" hat, the crown of which curved outwards at the top and a narrow brim curled up at the sides, a style popular twenty years ago and probably first worn by the fathers of these men. Hats were made to last and frequently did so for generations!

The women, too, were dressed in the fashion of years ago, those which endured for decades, since Sunday clothes were worn only once a week or on a special day such as this. Dark colours, of course, since they were practical. An ankle-length gown beneath which a white, lace-trimmed petticoat was allowed to peep. A kerchief at the neck, the point hanging down the wearer's back and the ends tied at the front and tucked into the plain bodice. Some had straw hats which had seen better days, others a sun bonnet with a stiffened brim with lines of ruching across the crown and a frill, or curtain, over the back of the neck. They all, men and women, wore stout black boots.

He was there with his heart-stopping smile, waiting, as he had said he would be, by the side of the railway and her heart jumped with joy, with love and pride, for beside the other men he was like a young and flamboyant god in his striking navvie's dress. His moleskin trousers were immaculate and she wondered how he had managed in the conditions her father had described to get them into so splendid a condition. His double canvas shirt was a soft and delicate cream and over it he wore the rainbow waistcoat she had made for him in shades of vivid blues and greens. In his neck was a bright neckerchief and his white felt hat had the brim jauntily turned up. His hobnailed boots were polished to perfection, reflecting the light from the fitful sun which was trying to shine, and across his arm was a velveteen, square-tailed coat in midnight blue. He looked quite magnificent, outshining every man of every station in life who passed him by, drawing looks of disgust and envy from them and sly admiring glances from their women. The joy in his copper brown eyes, shrouded by thick, brown, gold-tipped lashes, weakened her at the knees and she was thankful she was seated or she surely would have fallen, she told herself. His smooth brown face, his eager smiling mouth, the freshly cut crop of his tumbled chestnut curls, revealed when he snatched his hat from his head when he saw her, were as dear to her as . . . the dearest, most precious thing she knew. Her heart swelled with wondering love and she could hardly wait to jump down into his wide-stretched arms. The broadness of his shoulders, the lean grace of his waist and flank and long legs, his height which was six inches above other men, drew every eye to him but his were only for her. She was his, they said, and, proudly, she acknowledged it for he was hers!

She didn't remember flinging herself from the still moving dray, nor the clamour of people she and Jack pushed through to get to one another. She didn't hear the grumbles, nor the shout of the drayman to watch what she was doing. All she could see was Jack's handsome – for he *was* handsome – laughing face, the blaze of love in his eyes, the whiteness of his even teeth in his brown face and his arms as they reached out for her. They took hold of her, gripping her forearms just above the elbow and his eyes devoured every section of her face bit by bit as though to check that it was just as he remembered it then, thankfully, for it was, he drew her against his straining body, for Jack Andrews had never quite believed this wonderful day would come.

They didn't speak. He bowed his tall frame and buried his face in the soft curve of her neck, pulling her lips up to his throat just beneath his chin. His hands were hard, urgent as they pressed her to him and the crowd gawped as it divided around them.

"Aye up," the drayman bellowed, "tha're blockin' t'road," then grinned his rare grin for neither of them heard him. It was like that for several long moments then, aware of the growing clamour and the stares and murmurs – for what decent girl would embrace a navvieman, or *any* man for that matter in public – they reluctantly parted, looking deeply into one another's eyes, looking and looking but still not speaking for they could not. Their hearts were too full, their thoughts too enchanted and confused like flocks of lovely humming birds which could not settle and yet as clear as crystal in the certainty of their love for one another. It was enough now to clasp hands, eyes still chained, and join the crowds who were making their way to Station Road in the centre of Lytham where the small but magnificent new railway station was to be opened by Squire Clifton and his lady.

There were about two thousand pepole living in Lytham in this year of 1846 and it seemed every one was out on the streets that day and as Sara had already seen on her journey, not only the residents of Lytham but those from every village within walking distance. There were flags and banners decorating every church and house, bunting flying across streets which were jammed from wall to wall with folk doing their best to get to the station. The directors of the railway and a large party of the gentry, including, so Sara had heard, Mr and Mrs Alfred Bentham and their son Anthony, were to take luncheon at Lytham Hall, the home of the Clifton family. They were then to be transported to the station where the decorated "opening train" was to take Squire and Mrs Clifton, plus their distinguished guests, to Kirkham and back, or at least to Lytham Hall junction which was just west of the village.

There were bands playing, a grand procession doing its best to force a way through the crowded streets, tumblers and clowns, troupes of Morris dancers, straggling lines of Sunday school children, dazed and dazzled by the sheer enormity of it all and Sara and Jack, still with scarcely a word spoken between them, clung rapturously to one another, exhilarated not only by the occasion but by the sheer joy of being together again after so long. Their eyes sent sweet and loving messages to one another as they pushed their way down one of the side streets to the new pier which had been erected at the same time as the station, strolling in the quieter area of the branch line which had been added to take freight down to the docks.

"Your pa's still . . . against me then, lass?" Jack said at last, holding her hand tightly in the crook of his arm.

"Yes, Jack." Her voice was low and sad then it brightened with the enduring optimism of the young. "But he'll come round, you'll see."

"Aye, that he will," but at the back of Jack's mind was the spiteful face of Alice Hamilton who, if it took the last breath of her body, would stop her sister having anything to do with Jack Andrews.

"I shall be sixteen soon, Jack." Sara's face was flushed and her eyes cast down shyly as though the adding of one year was to make all the difference to their situation.

"An old lady indeed, my darling."

She looked up sharply then smiled, as much from his teasing as from the use of his endearment.

"I like you to say that, Jack."

"What? An old lady?"

"No . . . oh Jack, say it again."

"My darling . . . my darling . . . I love you."

"My darling . . ."

"Sara . . . lass . . ."

They were lost for words, their emotions like a runaway horse, out of control and going so fast and so furiously they were in danger of being thrown off by the sheer speed of it. He wanted to stop and put his arms about her, hold her against him, kiss her until she was breathless, take her away from the crowds and the noise and the damned railway station which no longer mattered to him now, but he was caught fast in the necessity for behaviour which was circumspect, the behaviour a man must adopt with the woman he means to marry. Doctor Hamilton would get to know of today's jaunt and Jack's name would be further vilified, at least if Alice Hamilton had anything to do with it, but if Doctor Hamilton was not aware of Jack's exemplary manner, Jack himself knew that Sara Hamilton had been treated this day with honour and respect.

But Jesus God, how he wanted her sweetness in his arms!

"We must go now, lass, or we'll miss the ceremony," he said softly, blessing her with the love in his face.

There were spectators of all classes mingling joyously together that day, prepared to tolerate one another, for what did it matter if a landed gentleman rubbed shoulders with his tenant when their small town was being so honoured, not only by the squire and his lady but by the grand future the railway would bring to them all.

A volley of cheers and a discharge of cannon heralded the setting off of the train from the handsome edifice which was Lytham Station. A central octagonal booking hall of lofty splendour, spacious waiting rooms for all classes of traveller, wide platforms one hundred and forty feet long and the whole protected with a roof held up by twelve massive wooden arches made up of segments screwed and bolted together. Quite, quite magnificent, the squire's lady was heard to remark, and thank goodness for the clement weather, she added, as she was handed into the open railway carriage, the only lady to be so honoured amongst the gentlemen.

"Walk down to't sands wi' me, lass," Jack said quietly when it was all over and Sara, still intoxicated by the magic of being with Jack on this wonderful day, turned to look at him, suddenly beset with unease since his manner was so strange. She was unaware of how exquisitely lovely she looked. She was beautiful in repose but the excitement, the joy of being with Jack, her awareness of his love and the anticipation of the bright future they were to share had transformed her beauty to something men stared at in wonder. Her skin was like cream, flushed beneath its surface with rose. Her eyes, long and slanted and green as a cat's, were brilliant, set in a sweep of golden brown lashes and her soft coral mouth, full and silky, still retaining some of its childish curve, widened in an enchanted smile of joy. She had discarded her bonnet which, in the crowd, would keep tipping over her eyes and her tawny hair, of similar hue to Jack's but more golden, tumbled in charming disarray about her proudly set head, curls drifting in wayward tendrils over her forehead and ears. She walked, back straight, small breasts high and peaked, her sweetness young and fresh but with a promise of a womanly maturity which would be quite breathtaking.

They sat on the fine, pale sand and he held her hand as he explained to her why he could not take her with him to Kendal and when she wept, he felt his own tears scald the back of his throat. He held her to him, oblivious of the curious stares of the passers-by, those who themselves had come to get away from the rowdy events in the centre of the town.

"I can't do it with thee beside me, my darlin'."

"Why, why? Oh please, Jack, you promised . . ."

"No, my lass, I didn't. Your letters were full of it but I never agreed."

"But, Jack, why not . . . why not?"

"I've got ter have money," he said brutally, knowing he

must hurt her to make her understand. "Tha' know I mean ter be a ganger, not workin' for a subcontractor but with me own gang. When the company see I'm ter be trusted, that I do what I say I can do, then I can take on subcontracting and later, as contractor and when a railway company invites tenders, you know what I mean . . ." continuing as she nodded, "well, when a railway company invites tender for a job, I can make me bid wi't rest. But I need cash, Sara and the only way I can do it is ter work me ba . . . messen till I drop an' save every penny I earn. For a couple of years at least. I've got together some good men from't camp, ten of 'em. Whistler, o' course, an' others who trust me an' who I trust. A 'butty gang' it's called an' I've struck a bargain wi' a subcontractor to do a certain length o' track on the line from Kendal, for a certain sum. The pay's shared equally among the gang. That's why they've ter be good an' why I've to have men I know'll work an' be trustworthy. Men wi' women an' bairns who want to mekk summat o' themselves an' not go on the randy every pay day. It'll be my responsibility ter collect wages an' pay the men, an' as leader and the one what's struck bargain, I'll get a bit extra. It's a good way of goin' about things, Sara, since it gives men a personal interest in doin' a decent amount o' work, finishin' a contract on time an' movin' on to 't next. If we get a good name we'll have no trouble findin' another. The pay's good, sweetheart, but the work'll be hard for a while."

His enthusiasm cut through her childlike dreams and at last she saw truly what must be. She was a woman, well, almost a woman and Jack's strength, his determination, his freedom to achieve his goal must not be undermined by childish things. She must not take it from him. He was working for her, for them, she told herself, though the tears continued to drip inconsolably across her cheeks and on to the soft wool of her gown. He held her in the crook of his arm, uncomfortable as men are when their womenfolk weep and she made a great effort to control herself.

"It'll be hard, like I said, demanding," he went on softly, "an' I'll have no time for . . ."

"For me."

"Oh lass, I love thi' so but I can't be . . . distracted." His voice broke on the last word.

"Is Whistler's Mary to go?"

"Aye."

"Then . . .?"

"She can fend fer herself, Sara. Tha' can't."

"I could try, Jack, really."

"No, Sara, no," he said emphatically. He lifted her chin, anguished at the sight of her wet cheeks and tear-starred lashes. "Don't tha' see, I can only do it if tha' help me an' th' only way tha' can help is by stayin' at home wi' tha' pa where I know tha're safe. I must know tha're safe, lass, or I can't do it. Do this fer me, my lovely lass. If you love me do it for me."

Their parting at Silcotes was the worst moment either had ever suffered in their young lives and Sara wept as the distance between them widened and even the drayman who had arranged to pick Sara up at four o'clock felt his own eyes prick, thanking God his old woman and him were past such things.

8

The days were dreary and repetitious, only relieved by Jack's letters. She wrote and posted hers quite openly now and received Jack's the same way, defying her papa, swearing to him that if he tried to stop them she would run off to Kendal and look for Jack, live with him "over the brush" as Jack had described the traditional ceremony which united navvieman and their women to one another.

"It's thanks to Jack that I'm here at all, Papa, though I don't expect you to believe me. If I'd had my way I would have gone with him on the day of the opening," both of them wincing away from the memory of the cataclysm of tearing rage which had exploded from Alice on Sara's return from Lytham. Sara had left a note, of course, telling Papa that she was going to visit Jack, though not where, and that she would be home before dark, but even as she had written it she had half hoped, half believed that she and Jack would be on their way to Kendal by nightfall with a letter in the post to her papa telling him of it.

"I wanted him to take me with him, Papa." Her voice was quiet as she spoke for she could see the suffering in his face. "But he wouldn't. He's to start what he calls a 'butty gang' which is the first step to him becoming a contractor."

"I've never heard such rubbish in my life. Jack Andrews a contractor. Why the man can barely write his name . . ."

"Be quiet, Alice," Richard Hamilton said wearily, for had he not had her in his ear ever since they had discovered Sara was not in the house. Sara continued as though her sister had not spoken which infuriated Alice the more.

"A contractor is a man who will— "

"Yes, child, I know what a contractor is and I'm sure I admire Jack's enterprise— "

"Papa! How can you— "

"Alice, please allow me to say what I have to say. I repeat, I admire Jack's enterprise and determination but the chances that he will succeed are slim which is why, among other things, I want you to put all thoughts of marrying him from your mind."

"I absolutely agree and if it was up to me— "

Cutting through her sister's declaration Sara began again.

"Papa," she sighed, as though she were doing her patient best to explain some simple thing to an equally simple child and Richard Hamilton was sadly aware that she had grown up overnight. She was no longer his little girl. "Papa, I love Jack and he loves me. We are committed to one another and there is nothing surer in this world than that one day we will marry. We may have to wait if you won't give your permission but we are both prepared to do it. Jack is making his way in the world, saving his money, bettering his position so that our plans might be accomplished. One day he will be able to provide for me and until that day I am to remain here with you. Could any father ask more of a prospective son-in-law? If he was the feckless philanderer Alice believes he is, would he act as he has done?"

"Really, Sara, you know nothing of the world." There was derisory scorn in Alice's voice. "You know nothing of men like Jack Andrews who seduce women into doing, into giving what— "

"Alice, I will not have this constant interrupting. I know you mean well and have only the best interest of your sister at heart but that does not mean you should talk to her as you are doing."

"Papa, this man, recognising Sara's innocence and inexperience and knowing that his hopes in that direction must come to nothing, has gone tramping off with the other navvies, looking for adventures, looking for other women . . ."

"That's not true." Sara was scarlet-faced with indignation but Alice continued without pausing.

". . . to dangle, searching for whatever might turn up which could be to his advantage, as he did in our home. He will find other women and I for one can only breathe a sigh of relief. Sara will forget him as he has already forgotten her, I am sure."

Alice had barely been able to contain her fury, informing Sara that if one word of this "escapade", as she called it, should get out, if it should get back to her that Sara had been seen with "that man" at the opening of the railway station in Lytham, she would never, never forgive her as long as she lived. She seemed more concerned with the "look of things" and what her equals would say about them than with Sara's actual meeting with Jack. She shook quite visibly with outrage on Sara's return and had been shocked and horrified when her papa refused to lock her sister up on a diet of bread and water. Sara needed a strap to her, Alice told her papa and she for one would be only too willing to apply it.

But still the letters came. At least one a week and each time Sara's eyes would glow with some great emotion as she ran upstairs to the bedroom to read what Jack poured out to her. She no longer read passages out to them at the kitchen table and when she answered them she did so in private.

"Are you to allow this, Papa?" Alice demanded icily, since she firmly believed her father was remiss in his handling of the affair and if she was not to point it out to him she would be as much to blame as he should the outcome be disastrous. "Are you to allow your daughter to correspond with this vagabond after all that has happened? You cannot possibly mean to let her continue this association. It is downright underhand and she should be punished for it. She is a wicked girl. She has disobeyed you and gone against all our wishes, ignored the advice I, as the elder, have given her and I am amazed that you do not confiscate the letters he sends. Let *me* discipline her, Papa," Alice beseeched him. "Let me have the handling of her if you feel you cannot or . . . Papa, we shall be the laughing stock . . ." and on and on and on and in the midst of it all Sara sat serenely opposite Dolly who kept her own counsel, in the kitchen, defying Alice again, sewing what looked suspiciously like a wedding gown.

March and April came with the lovely miracle of spring and the promise of new life, with a curiously warm wind and then soft rain. There was sunshine and skylarks up and singing in the vast arch of blue and in the ditch where Sara and Alice had first met Jack and Racer and Billyo, coltsfoot and speedwell grew. Primroses lifted their yellow faces to the sun and daffodil buds stood up above the grass.

"If you imagine I shall stand by and let you marry that yokel then you must be out of your mind," Alice said venomously to her sister at the end of May. Alice was having a great deal of trouble furthering her own cause with the Bentham and Armitage families and indeed, the last two times she had called on Charlotte Armitage she had been informed that Miss Armitage was not at home. Somehow, Alice was not sure how, the worst had happened and it had got about that the doctor's younger daughter had been seen consorting with that navvie fellow the doctor had mended last back end and though no details had been passed on to her, for who in the village would mention it to the transgressor's sister, she was in no doubt that someone had seen Sara on that dreadful day in February. There had been people there from all over this corner of Lancashire and had not Mr and Mrs Bentham and Anthony been guests of the squire and his lady? What Sara did, what Sara was, by inference rubbed off on Alice and she was devastated by it for it was not her fault. She wanted nothing from life but to be accepted by the "best" families and how could she do that if Sara persisted in this folly? She was convinced that she had been making headway before it happened but now it was all to no avail, for how could she get herself a decent husband if she were, even once removed, to be associated with a rough and uneducated navvie? She would never forgive Sara for her wayward, perverse fancy for this hobbledehoy, this labouring man, nor for her wanton determination to continue with it, indeed flaunt it before what Alice longed to think of as her friends, thereby forfeiting not only her own social position, frail as it was, but Alice's. How could Alice ever hope to enter the world of the Benthams and the Armitages – where the only husband Alice wanted was to be found – when her own sister was so depraved as to show her preference for a man of a rank so far beneath her own, so far beneath that of their dead mother, that most decent folk, of all stations in life, abhorred them? Navviemen! The name stank in nostrils up and down the land and yet Sara was proud of him, proud that he loved her, disgusting as that was, vociferous in her declaration of her love for him and how could Alice hold up her head amongst the people she admired if Sara continued with this . . . this farce?

"What are you talking about, Ally?" Sara said quietly, scarcely glancing up from her needlework. She did hope Alice was not going to continue in this vein for much longer. It was becoming very tiresome and surely Alice must know by now that it did not the slightest bit of good. She and Jack would be married one day, not soon, but one day and if Ally thought that by going on day after day about what a worthless man Jack was she would get Sara to give him up then she was in for a big disappointment.

"You know what I mean. Everyone turning to stare when we walk by and every person of any worth closing their doors to us."

"By worth I suppose you mean the Benthams and the Armitages? You can hardly blame me, or Jack, for that. The Benthams think themselves far too grand for the likes of a doctor's daughter and if you imagine otherwise you are fooling yourself, Alice."

"Anthony Bentham was very pleasant to me when we met on the green several weeks ago."

"Ally, you know Anthony Bentham will marry a girl with money or a title. I know you are longing to be a part of— "

"Really, Sara, you do talk nonsense. It has nothing to do with money. If you hadn't taken up with that . . . that lout . . ."

Sara's face, which had been filled with compassion for her sister since she had always been aware of Alice's desire to "get into" society, hardened and her soft mouth tightened ominously.

"Let me remind you that that 'lout' saved us from what I believe is known as a fate worse than death."

"How can you be so crude? I suppose you learned that disgusting phrase from him."

Alice's tone was as vicious as her disappointed yearnings.

"You thought him perfectly acceptable when he defended you against those men."

"He was not a prospect as a brother-in-law then."

"Well, Ally, I can only say you had better get used to the idea for that is what he is to be to you. As soon as he sends for me I shall go. Perhaps with me out of the way you can resume your 'friendship' with the splendid Benthams and Armitages."

Summer came upon them, hot and sultry, as early as June

when morning roses which had sparkled with dew became burned and limp as noon approached.

"When will it rain?" Doctor Hamilton mourned, studying his wilting garden, breathless in the heat as June passed into July, the atmosphere airless, the skies a burned orange yellow. The heat seemed to gather itself about them, crushing them, making every movement a terrible effort.

Jack's letters came at least once a week and though he was not as eloquent with his pen as he was with his tongue they satisfied her, for it was plain that he had one goal in view and that was to be successful with his "butty gang" and return to Wray Green and claim Sara as his bride. He was longing for the day when they would meet again, he wrote, and looked all the time for an opportunity to come and see her. It was a long way to tramp and he had been sorely tempted to use some of his precious savings on the train fare from Oxenholme to Preston but he knew she would understand when he said that every farthing he put away was another second closer to the day they would be together for good. The weather was pretty bad, he admitted to her, for the heat was a trial to the men but she was not to worry for he himself remained well.

For a second or two the last few words meant nothing to her except a gladness that he was in good health but as she read them again she began to feel a trickle of unease, for did they not imply that though Jack was in good health, other men were not? A slip of the pen perhaps and no cause for anxiety but all the same she was anxious. There had been cases of fever in the district about Wray Green and her father, always busy in the service of his impoverished patients, had scarcely been to bed for a week. There were households in outlying areas where women were not particular where they threw their rubbish, nor the contents of their chamber pots, nor did they care that their children played on rotting garbage heaps. Instead of walking to the source of clean water they were happy to scoop up from a puddle a panful of whatever lay nearest to their back door. Papa deplored it, bullying the women into scrubbing their pots and pans and infants; into at least boiling the foul water they used for every purpose the household needed – except that of washing! – and they promised faithfully they would, which they did until he had climbed up on to the back of his old mare and ambled out of their sight. Most lived in a hovel, sharing the roof space with rats, their kitchens with cockroaches and their beds with fleas. Their homes were built without foundations on the bare earth and the damp rose as the earthen floor sweated and the walls ran with moisture. They were dark and insanitary. The windows were boarded up to keep out the cold and there would be one privy, an earth closet, for a row of six cottages. Papa pestered the owners to mend the leaking roofs and repair the ceilings on which moss grew but the only response he got was that when the tenants paid their rent regularly, the owners would repair the cottages. The children who lived in them were undernourished and poorly clad, constantly streaming with colds and cut in two with coughs, many already in the first stages of consumption. There was always fever of some sort racing from cottage to cottage: typhus, typhoid, scarlet fever, epidemics of debilitating diarrhoea and it happened not only amongst Doctor Hamilton's patients, but in the length and breadth of the land where the poor collected.

Was this the condition in the navvie camp where Jack and his butty gang lived? The hot, sultry weather, the kind of weather which bred these diseases and caused them to run out of control like a moorland fire, was as devastating up north as it was here, apparently. There was some advantage to the fine weather, he wrote, for it had allowed the contractors to push on with the work and the Kendal and Lancaster line was to be opened in September. They would then begin on the Kendal to Windermere branch.

Her father came into the kitchen later that afternoon, his jacket off and draped across one arm and as Sara went to take it from him he flinched away from her.

"What is it, Papa?"

His voice was curt. "Nothing, child, nothing. Only the usual. Let me go and have a wash and then we'll eat. Where is Alice?"

"In the garden reading. It's cooler there."

"Good. I want to talk to you both."

"Is there trouble, sir?" Dolly asked uneasily.

"No . . . well, er, I hope not but I must go out again so I would be obliged if we could eat at once, Dolly."

They ate in silence but for the grumbling voice of Alice who told them incessantly that she longed for the heat to ease since she really must walk over to Charlotte's tomorrow, just as though she was in the habit of doing so several times a week and should she miss, Charlotte would be nothing short of devastated.

"Alice, if I may, that is what I wanted to speak to you about."

"About Charlotte, Papa?" Alice was clearly amazed but ready to be delighted for did this mean her father had at last made it his business to become acquainted with the Armitages? If so it could only be a short step to an invitation, not only from them but from their closest friends, the Benthams!

"No, not about Charlotte, Alice, but about leaving this house."

"Leaving this house? What do you mean, Papa?" Alice's prim mouth popped open. They were, contrary to her wishes, eating in the kitchen since her father said he had no time for the tiny table in the parlour to be set up and though Alice had not been pleased she had not argued. He was tired, she could see that and though it had gone against all she believed in, she had allowed it. The back door stood open to let in any slight breath of air that might be about and the marmalade cat, the only one to enjoy the suffocating heat, lay sunning itself on the doorstep.

Sara laid her knife and fork carefully on her plate as though it was imperative she made no sound and Dolly, who had been about to clear away the used plates, slowly eased herself into her chair, her face watchful, already guessing. It was plain something was up. The doctor had hardly been in his bed for a week, up and down them stairs and off out at all hours of the day and night. Barely a minute to draw breath, let alone eat a decent meal and if her memory served her right, and it usually did, this was the first time he had sat down to dine with his daughters for days. There was trouble, Dolly could scent it in the heavy air, and it could only be to do with these "fevers" that were beginning to grow to such alarming proportions.

"I'm afraid I must ask you not to go out of the house, girls, except into the garden, of course. It may be nothing, it probably is but I would feel happier if I knew you were both . . . at home."

He passed his hand across his face which was suddenly old, gaunt, strained with overwork and Sara felt her heart miss a beat.

"What is it, Papa?" Her voice was light, fearful, and for a moment Richard Hamilton saw his little girl return.

"There is . . . fever."

"But there is always fever, Papa."

"I did not mean of the usual sort but . . . cholera, I think."

Alice put a hand to her mouth in distaste, looking from one face to the other. She had heard of cholera, naturally, as who had not but it was not something that entered a dwelling such as theirs. It was not a disease with which she need concern herself for it did not come amongst people like Alice Hamilton, like Sara Hamilton, like the Armitages and the Benthams. Not nice people, not clean people.

"Cholera? But that is not something which need concern us, is it, Papa?" Despite her certainty she looked over her shoulder as though it might be lurking amongst Dolly's pots and pans, or beneath the cushion on the rocking chair.

"I'm not even sure that it is cholera, Alice. It's over twenty years since I saw it, long before I met your mother. There was an epidemic in one of the cotton towns where I was working. It spread . . . so fast. I was only young then, and strong, but I saw many who were not succumb."

"Then you must not go out either." Alice's voice was firm and her father tutted in exasperation.

"I'm a doctor, Alice. I cannot sit at home and hide."

"But what if you should bring it back here, Papa? It is hardly fair."

"Now stop that at once, Alice. There is no need to be afraid. Sara is not afraid, are you, Sara?"

But Sara was afraid, deathly afraid, not only for her papa but for Jack. Was this the illness of which he spoke, or at least did not speak, which was ravaging the camp, the illness which he had intimated had up until now missed Jack Andrews? Cholera! The very word was enough to frighten the strongest and yet so little was known about it, she had heard her papa say. "The Plague" they used to call it, for it spread so quickly, just as the Black Death had done in the Middle Ages, first flourishing among soldiers in faraway India. It had moved across continents into eastern Europe until every city of every size, including London, was overcome with it and only a decade or so ago in 1831 it had killed many thousands, so many they could not be counted. No one knew what caused it or how to treat it, even now, fifteen years later.

They knew it lived in dirt, she had heard her father say so, in which case it would not thrive in this house where Dolly was such a termagant against any sort of muck but there were many who were not, as her father could testify.

"Can I do anything to help, Papa?" she asked anxiously, while on the other side of the table Alice gasped in horror.

"Do? You can do nothing but what Papa tells you to do, Sara Hamilton, and that is to stay at home where you belong." Her tone was bitter, telling them all quite plainly that the excursion her sister had taken to Lytham would never be forgotten.

"Alice is right, my dear."

"But surely I can help?"

"There are women to help me, Sara. Women who are experienced in nursing and anyway, we are looking on the black side. It might not be cholera but just another case of fever." But Dolly could see he did not really believe it.

Sara remained at home, fretting from room to room and then out into the stifling heat of the garden, hurting herself and Dolly with her nervous anxiety, not just for her father but for Jack. His letters, delivered by the postman every few days, were cheerful and optimistic and she kept hers the same, making no mention of the growing number of cholera cases in the district. The postman obligingly took hers to the postbox when he brought Jack's though Dolly would not allow him beyond the garden gate, making him stand in the deep shade of the oak trees in the lane to drink a glass of her lemonade while he waited. She washed the glass he used with the greatest of care when he had gone since you never could tell what he had picked up, besides his letters, on his travels.

The disease, her father explained to Sara one night when Dolly and Alice had gone to their beds, struck swiftly and savagely and just as swiftly and savagely was over. A child could be playing hopscotch outside its own front door in the morning and be dead by nightfall. Ezra Wilkins, the cowman Sara had passed in February on her way to Lytham, had walked, whistling, to the fields, his dog beside him and by the time he came to sit down to his "noon-piece" was heaving up in agony what he had eaten for his breakfast.

Richard Hamilton knew full well he should not be alarming his child with tales such as these but his tiredness and despair made him careless. She was so sympathetic, not like Alice who covered her ears and ran screeching from the room at the very sound of the word cholera. Sara was so like Elly, so sensitively aware of every emotion, whether it be joyful or uneasy, that a man might feel and it was a great temptation to unburden oneself to such a person.

The days and weeks passed into August. The sky continued a sulphurous, sickly yellow from which struck the harsh and pitiless rays of the sun and in the church by the almost empty pond in Wray Green men and women sank to their knees to pray for rain for surely, *surely*, the clean untainted moisture which fell from God's heaven would wash away this horror, this terrible scourge which, having carried off the old, the young and the undernourished, was now making inroads on those who were, at least to the naked eye, healthy, strong and invincible.

Charlotte Armitage was one and Alice would never get over it, she said, as though Charlotte had been her lifelong and dearest friend. She sent flowers to the family, intimating as much, flowers hand-picked from her papa's garden and a note to tell them of her sorrow but there was no reply.

Fanny Suthurst's grandson, Willy, was another and him six feet tall and as big and strong and lusty as a bullock. Fanny was deeply affronted, for surely the good Lord could have taken her instead since she had let it be known at great length that she was ready to go.

"I believe we can see the end of it, thank God," Doctor Hamilton said to them all one evening. "There have been no new cases for three days and no deaths for a week."

The following day Richard Hamilton did not come home. Just as it was getting dark enough to light a candle there was a knock at the door. When Dolly opened it, it was to reveal the angular figure of Miss Gilchrist, a spinster lady much given to good works who had been helping the doctor in the makeshift hospital set up in the church hall. After all he was a widower and Miss Gilchrist considered she would make a splendid doctor's wife.

Miss Gilchrist's expression was indecisive which was not like her at all, a mixture of emotions ranging from shock to awkwardness to a genuine sorrow chasing one another across her plain, unvarnished face.

"I'm so sorry," she faltered. "To be the bearer of such news . . . there was no one else . . . it was so sudden . . . he didn't suffer," she lied. "He spoke of you and . . . well, I felt it was my duty to come." A great one for "duty", was Miss Gilchrist.

Dolly was the first to realise the nature of Miss Gilchrist's visit and was ready to catch Miss Sara in her strong arms when, after a dreadful moment, she understood.

Sara lay in her bed and stared blindly up into the raftered ceiling of the bedroom she shared with Alice. Even now her sister slept, deep in the state to which the draught Dolly, well acquainted with many of the contents of Doctor Hamilton's dispensary, had made her drink. She had been hysterical, in sharp contrast to Sara's deep and numbing shock. She had, in fact, refused to believe it, almost calling Miss Gilchrist, who was herself bitterly disappointed, a liar when she informed them soberly that their father was dead. Alice had screamed, a child afraid of the unknown, for how was Alice Hamilton, who had still not cracked the well-nigh impregnable barrier which surrounded the Benthams and the Armitages, to do it now? A lady needed a gentleman to protect her as young ladies were meant to be protected until they became wives and passed into their husbands' shelter. How were she and Sara to survive with no male protector? They had no male relative upon whom to call. They could not live here alone, two unmarried ladies, it would not be proper. No, it was not possible and she could not believe it. Miss Gilchrist must be mistaken. Alice's papa had left the house in good health as usual this morning so how could he be dead? And it was not until Dolly had forced the draught between her chattering teeth, that she had become quiet, allowing herself to be undressed and put to bed.

Sara could not believe it either. She knew, of course, for hadn't Papa told her so himself how quickly the disease struck, how quickly it killed but only the other day he had been hopeful it had been on the wane. Papa, dear Papa, if only she could cry for him but somehow she seemed to be held in a chilling state of paralysis which she didn't really want to shatter just now for it would hurt when she did. She seemed incapable of collecting her thoughts. They wandered in her frozen mind, trailing like wisps of cloud, rain-filled and desolate but going nowhere and with nowhere to empty their burden. There would be the funeral, of course. Who would see to that? In the small churchyard beside her mother, his wife, the only woman he had ever loved and even now, three years after her mother's death, she could remember that special link, that reaching out to one another her mother and father had known. You could see it in the looks which passed between them, the hand one or the other would put out which was instantly grasped. A warmth, a giving and receiving which had been lovely to see and Papa had never quite recovered from its loss. He had gone on, naturally, but there had been something lacking in him after that, something Sara could not define, nor name but which she could only describe as an emptiness. Had it been like the emptiness she now felt hollowed out inside her? The numbness which held her like a corpse frozen in ice but if Papa was with her again, his beloved Elly, should she, Sara, be sorry? His beloved Elly. That's what he had called her always, Elly beloved, and her mother had flowered because of it. How had he managed without her, that delicate, elegant lady on whom he had, unknowingly, always leaned? How had it been for him without the love and support of the woman he loved? And the only way she could imagine it was to picture life without Jack in it, and that was unimaginable.

Instead she resolutely studied images of her father, her mother and father together, the peace and security she and Alice had been blessed with in the childhood Richard and Eleanor Hamilton had created for them. Sara had known nothing but love, a merry and joyful love of which she knew her mother had been the chief creator, awakening it in her papa, multiplying what was in him so that he gave it not just to his wife but to his daughters. A reserved man who had been winkled out of his shell by Sara's mother, a good man, a respected man loved by those who had cause to be thankful for what he had given them.

So why could she not cry for him? Why were her tears frozen in her sorrowing heart? She must write to Jack . . . Jack . . . she wished he was here with her, for she was badly in need of the comfort only he could give her. Strong, warm arms to hold her in her grieving for the good man, the kind man who had been her father.

The funeral was well attended, a swift affair, for those who die of cholera are swiftly disposed of. The minister, run off his feet these last few weeks and beginning seriously to wonder in what bit of ground all these coffins were to fit, was tired and the service and interment in the solid ground were brief.

Dozens of hands held Sara's for a moment, sharing their grief with her, for how were they to manage without him, their sad eyes begged her to tell them, but Sara could not answer since she herself did not know. They gazed sadly into her pale young face, into the depths of her clouded green eyes which looked at them but saw nothing. Aye, in a state of dreadful shock was Miss Sara, being held by the hand of that sister of hers who had always been the dominant one, looking as though she would not get through the day without her. They were inclined to think that was the impression Miss Alice wanted to give. As though Miss Sara depended on her at this moment of grief. They were both in black as was their servant, their light cotton gowns hastily dyed for the occasion, their bonnets covered in black crepe. They themselves, though they were impoverished labourers, shepherds, cowmen, hedgers and thatchers had, in respect for Richard Hamilton, tied a bit of black about their upper arms.

It did not go unnoticed by Dolly that the Benthams and Armitages were absent, nor indeed that not one member of what was called "polite society" attended Richard Hamilton's funeral, nor did anyone, bar the vicar, Miss Gilchrist and a few of the women who had helped Richard Hamilton in the nursing of the sick, return to the house for the refreshments Dolly had provided. Dolly knew their absence was a source of bitter disappointment to Miss Alice but perhaps now she would come to realise that, as she herself had muttered, only to herself, of course, that no matter how you flogged a dead horse with a stick it just would not get up!

She must write to Jack, Sara remembered saying to herself time and time again during that long day, for not until she had told him would she truly come to accept that her father was dead. Perhaps when she put the words down on paper she would finally feel the pain of her loss and with the pain would come belief and with belief, acceptance. She still looked for him and listened for the sound of his mare's hooves on the cobbles by the back door and in the days that followed the funeral Dolly watched her anxiously for it was not like Miss Sara to burrow within herself. Always she had shown her emotions whether they be sad or happy. Now she was like a slender ghost restlessly moving from room to room as though she was searching for something, her face quite blank, her feelings buried deep, her eyes wide and unseeing.

Dolly almost wished that lad would turn up if it would fetch Miss Eleanor's girl back from the dark and shocked state into which her papa's death had thrown her. Miss Alice had taken it bad at first, carrying on like a creature demented but she'd pulled herself together, as Dolly had known she would and got on with what she did best, what she enjoyed most, which was being Miss Alice Hamilton, a lady, a daughter grieving for the loss of a beloved father as it was her duty to do. She would make the most of it, hoping for some sign of sympathy and perhaps a way to a warmer acquaintanceship with those who had so far ignored all her efforts to be their friend. Aye, that would keep Miss Alice going but what about Miss Sara?

The letter came a week after the funeral. It was from a firm of solicitors in Preston who, having been informed of the death of Doctor Richard Hamilton, were instructed by the owner of the house which Doctor Hamilton had rented to request that it be vacated by the end of the month.

9

Jack and his gang had been working on the last piece of the cutting that day, not a very deep one but difficult since the blue slaty rock which they hewed through was hard and awkward.

They had done well, the best gang on the railway it was being said of them and the reward for their perseverance, their conscientious application to their work, their efficiency under Jack's management and the sheer weight of their own hard and bloody labour had been the contract, amongst others, to complete this small section of the line. They were to be paid not a fixed day rate, nor piece-work, but a sum agreed by Jack who was shrewd and clear-headed in his bargaining, knowing just what his men could do, and the incentive to get their 'parcel' finished and paid for made them cohese together, working as a well-trained team. They were steady men, men with family responsibilities who, like Jack, were aiming for something more than a hovel by the track, their children barefoot and uneducated, their wives living from month to month bound by the truck system. They were men who had not been consciously aware of what they wanted from life nor, if they did, how to get it, not until Jack Andrews, instinctively recognising the right men for the job, had told them.

Though most of them were, like Whistler, older than Jack, they seemed to sense the resolve in him, the single-minded drive which would carry him from labouring navvieman to contractor, the prize he strove for, and if they were to hang on to Jack Andrews's coat tails would they not improve their own and their families' lot in this brutally hard life they all led? So far Jack had steered them right and in the past six months, ever since they had tramped from Lytham up to Oxenholme where the Lancaster and Carlisle was to join the new Kendal to Windermere line, Jack had struck three bargains with the subcontractor to complete a parcel of the line for a certain sum, in effect becoming himself a sub-subcontractor and it was said he was earning himself a tidy sum, which was reflected in their pay packets. A good lad was Jack who, ever since he'd come back from the "dead", so to speak, after Racer and Billyo had beaten him to bloody pulp, had never once gone on the randy. They said he was courting a girl back in Wray Green and indeed, Whistler told them, swaggering as though the wonder of it brushed off on him, received a letter every week from her which was a marvel to these men who could neither read nor write.

They would be moving on soon, making their way from Kendal further north towards their destination at Bowness in Windermere where the railway station was to be. First level meadowland which would be easily traversed, then there was a large timber viaduct to be built crossing the River Kent and another over the race at Dockray Hall. It was beyond Burneside that the incline began, a considerable incline as the track ran into the foothills of south Lakeland. Deep cuttings which Jack was hoping to bargain for, a high summit from where the line would descend into the Vale of Windermere. Bleak moorland to be got through in a Lakeland winter for it was hoped that the line would be completed by spring.

There had been setbacks, of course. Cholera had struck the settlement a few weeks back and Jack's gang had been depleted by the death of Sam Medcalf, a reliable fellow they had all missed. After a whip-round for Sam's woman and child, a gangling youth by the name of Algie-One-Step on account of Algie having one leg shorter by two inches than the other, had offered his services in Sam's place. He had been taken on and had proved trustworthy and hardworking despite his slight handicap.

There were many landowners in the Lake District who had opposed bitterly the coming of the railway line to their part of the country, saying they feared the "cheap trippers" who would flock there and who were in any case incapable of appreciating the grandeur of the scenery. They would destroy the solitude of their betters and not only that but undermine the morals of the local inhabitants. Droves of working people would be brought in who would benefit neither morally nor mentally from the beauty about them, which the educated classes already, and rightly so, enjoyed and it must be stopped.

They had been shouted down, these campaigners, since progress could not be halted. Far from being wasted on the working-class man, would not such splendour, once accessible to him, draw him away from haunts of vice and intemperance and open up to him the wonders of nature, the peace and tranquillity which could only hearten him?

Jack cared nothing for the rights and wrongs of it as he surveyed with great satisfaction the completed stretch of track, the last rail of which Alfie-Bob and Whistler had just manhandled into place. It was almost dark and in the clear summer sky towards the east a cluster of stars appeared. They seemed to twinkle, to sparkle like sequins on blue velvet but Jack knew it was an illusion caused by a wavering in the air as the heat of the day rose from the baking earth.

Turning away, he jumped down on to the track and studied the rail then put his heavy booted foot on it, and the men, who leaned tiredly on their picks, waited for his approval. He was their "boss" now, the one who made the decisions, at least for them and so far under his guidance it had brought nothing but good to them all.

"Awreet, Jack?" Whistler asked.

"Aye, awreet, Whistler, we can knock off now." He turned to grin at the circle of men, his white teeth gleaming in the dusk and they all relaxed. "Aye, that's the lot, lads an' not a day too soon. We're ahead of oursen by more than a week an' contractor'll be well pleased. That's the twenty miles o' track from Lancaster completed, but fer a bit o' work near Kendal, but that don't concern us."

They all leaned towards him expectantly for they could tell by Jack's face that he had good news for them. Picks were shifted to brawny shoulders and booted feet disturbed the dry grit which rose lazily, invading their mouths and irritating their already inflamed eyelids.

"We're off beyond Kendal, lads . . . aye, I thought that'd please thee, Alfie-Bob. We all know which way't wind blows wi' thee an' that farmer's lass up by Burneside. Reckon that'll not 'ave so far to go ter do tha' courtin' now, will tha'?"

Amidst the laughter, an expression, wistfully sad, crossed

Jack's strong, uncompromising face, making it appear vulnerable for a second or two, more boyish, more like the lad these men had known a year ago before Racer and Billyo had put their mark on him. He was no longer a lad, a carelessly light-hearted, endearingly good-humoured youth who was always ready to laugh, to carouse, to fight and join in whatever passed for entertainment in the camp. He was still good-humoured, unless crossed, and enjoyed a joke with the rest of them but he was the "gaffer" now and was treated with the respectful regard he had earned and which separated him from the comradeship of the navvies and put him into a lonely world of his own. They admired him for what he had done, of course. He was fair, so long as they worked exactly as he wanted them to work, which was as skilfully, as efficiently, as quickly and as hard as he did himself. There was nothing they did that Jack did not do. No task was too difficult, too brutal, too demanding for Jack Andrews and therefore for his gang and he was not slow to tell them so. Aye, a harder man, but not oppressively so and the wages he commanded for them more than made up for the pitiless hours he expected of them, and himself.

But now there was something about him, in his shadowed eyes and grim mouth which disconcerted them, all except Whistler who knew about Sara Hamilton.

Sara! In that moment, as he spoke of Alfie-Bob's fancy for the girl up by Burneside, Jack saw Sara as she had been that day in Lytham. The lovely blue of her gown, the soft colours and the fragrance of her scented shawl. Her small bonnet framing her face with flowers and he felt his loss, for that was how it had been these last six months, strike him savagely. Even now he could feel her body as it melted bonelessly into his, her sweet breath on his chin, the softness of her breasts against his chest, the fragrance of her glossy hair beneath his hands. He had known, over and over again since he last saw her, masculine feelings of joy, pride, wonder, relief that she loved him and yet he was deep in a sweet sadness he could hardly bear. Six months since he had seen his love, her beautiful face smiling and true as he bent to kiss her. She was not really beautiful in the classical sense, he knew that. Her mouth was too wide, and her chin too square. Her cheekbones were high and her nose turned up at the end but it was in herself that her true beauty lay. In the sweet and funny way she expressed her feelings, in her warmth and joy and vivacity of spirit which she gave freely without meanness. She was generous and loyal; look how she made excuses for that damned sister of hers, kind-hearted herself so that she saw no fault in others. Easily hurt, she would be, and that would not do for Jack Andrews who would give his life to save her from the smallest pain. She turned his heart over with her lovely innocence, with the vividness of her expression, the green brilliance of her eyes, her soft tranquillity, her every mood and movement a magical thing to him. Had it not been for her letters he knew he could not have stood the parting from her and only them, and the belief that what he did on the railway would one day bring them together again, and for good, kept him from jumping on the first train to Preston. His blood raced through his veins at the very thought of her and his heart beat like a drum. He could barely speak, for his tongue tripped on the simplest phrase and while the men waited patiently for him to go on Whistler took up the badinage.

"Aye, an' tha'd best not let that pa of 'ers see tha' winkin' at 'er, Alfie-Bob, or 'e'll do thee some damage in a part of thi' what's longin' ter be put ter some good use."

"'Ere, less o' that dirty talk, Whistler, or I'll 'ave ter get tha' Mary ter wash out thy mouth wi' soap an' water," Alfie-Bob reproached him amiably enough. His intentions towards May Wilkinson, the young lady in question, were honourable and now that he had a few bob to jingle in his pocket he had every hope of having them taken seriously by her father.

"Well, what's the plan then, Jack?" an enormous giant of a man by the name of "Little Tom" asked. "'Ast tha' struck us a bargain then?"

"That I have, Tom, an' a right good 'un it is an' all. There's a stretch across the meadowland north o' Kendal, flat as me hand just before where the two viaducts are bein' put in, one over the river an' one over the race. If we can guarantee to 'ave that completed by the end of October, ready for both viaducts then it's ours. There'll be an embankment of earth joining the viaducts an' I've put in a tender fer that an' all."

Jack brushed the dusty earth from his trousers, hitching at the belt which held them up. He had become even leaner in the past six months, the enormous amount of hard labour he did fining his body almost to thinness. Yet his shoulders were broad and powerful and his strength was formidable. His hair, uncut since his stay at Doctor Hamilton's, was a shaggy mane of dusty chestnut curls over his ears and into his neck and the flesh of his face, his neck and throat, his hands and forearms, working in the blazing sun as he did, was a deep coppery brown. He was strong, handsome, aggressive beneath the dust which coated him, a full man now and there was no one in the camp who interfered with him, not even Racer and Billyo.

The men turned to one another grinning, ready to jostle and play like boys. There was no doubt about it, Jack had a way with him when it came to finding and getting them work and they could hardly wait to get home and tell their women. Aye, it had been a stroke of luck for all of them when Racer and Billyo did for Jack Andrews, for had it not been for that brush with death would Jack now be the hard-bargaining, hardworking, ambitious man he had become?

"Tha'll be ready ter move on at first light, lads." It was a statement not a question and they nodded, for they knew he meant not just them but their women, their children, their livestock if they had any, and everything else they might own. They would cut across from Castle Green where the camp was, past Castle Meadows north of Kendal itself, set up a new camp close to where they would put down the track and, by seven in the morning, be ready to start laying it where he instructed them. The womenfolk would be left to fend for themselves as the first set was laid and the race would be on then, for Jack meant to have his share of the best, the finest sections of the railway line between Kendal and Windermere for his gang. By spring, when it ended, he would move on to the next, and the next, until he had enough money to bring his love to live in the house he meant to build for her.

He walked back along the track, Whistler beside him, making for the small stone hut which he had shared for nine long crowded months with Whistler and Mary and their children. His thoughts softened his face. Though he watched his footing his eyes were sightless as he dreamed of the lovely young girl who, of all the women he had known, had been the only one truly to stir his male senses, to intrigue his male sensibilities, capturing his imagination with her glowing warmth, her bright and lively humour, the quality of her nature which answered something in his own.

Though she was only just on the threshold of womanhood she was all that he wanted in a woman. She was clever, having very definite opinions on everything from the right of their little Queen to marry the man of her choice six years ago, even if he was German, to the affairs of Ireland which were in a sorry state indeed. Richard and Eleanor Hamilton, lacking a son, saw no reason to deprive their daughters of the conversation which usually took place amongst educated men and Jack had been astounded by her knowledge. He himself read every newspaper he could get his hands on and knew more than many men better educated than he was and he dreamed of the future, picturing evenings spent in the company of a woman whose mind would stimulate his own. A room, a gracious room with a woman in it of wit and charm and intelligence, and upstairs a bed where . . . Jesus, the nights when he would take her there, undress her in the candlelight, worship the lovely cream-tinted curves of her body, the rosy-tipped peaks and dark shadows of her and teach her to be as lusty, as passionate, as loving as all men dream of their woman being. The dark warmth of the tumbled bed where he and Sara would match one another in the rapturous love they already knew. A physical love that he would show her, give to her, take from her, a love he would enfold her in as no woman before. She was sixteen, he knew, for she had told him so in June and he had become twenty-two in the same month and in a year or two, perhaps when she was eighteen, they would be man and wife. Almost two years and could Jack Andrews, who had no trouble finding a pretty wench to make love to, remain celibate for so long? It would be hard, for just thinking of Sara twisted his guts and awoke a pain in his groin which made it tricky to walk upright. But he meant to have a damn good try. He meant to be a better man than he was. A man worthy of Sara's love. She made him better. Dear God but he loved her.

Tonight, when supper was over and the children in their beds, he would sit down and write to her, tell her what he had achieved since his last letter, of the move to the north of Kendal and the new address to where her letters must be sent. He had been so involved in the complexities of the hard bargaining he had finally executed he had not written to her for a week or two but she would understand, his Sara, his lovely lass, knowing how hard he was working for them both.

Unusually he had not heard from her either for . . . how long was it, ten days, a fortnight? Time got away from him in his race to succeed and make enough money, enough to marry her and bring her to live with him as his wife, and yet at the same time it dragged interminably from day to day, to weeks and months without her love in it.

Alice went mad at first, raving for hour after hour at the injustice of the sudden and dreadful upheaval which had come to topple her and Sara's small but stable world. She had not been completely satisfied with it, she would have been the first to admit, but given time, her own perseverance, good looks and charm, would have ingratiated herself with Mrs Bentham or Mrs Armitage, particularly the latter as she had just lost her only daughter and might have been persuaded to see Alice as a substitute. But now, with Papa gone and her home to be taken from her it seemed to her that the past had been heaven on earth compared to the present, and the dreadful spectre of the future. She just couldn't understand it, she lamented over and over again. This was papa's house and now that he was dead surely it belonged to her and Sara.

"It must have been rented, Ally," Sara suggested tentatively, her own mind clogged and scarcely able to cope with the anxiety of what was to happen to them now.

"I realise that, Sara. I realise it now and can only wonder at Papa's . . . thoughtlessness in leaving us placed as we are."

"Oh Ally, don't." Sara cried easily now and had done ever since the letter from the solicitor had arrived. Great fat tears of desolation and misery which flowed and flowed unchecked and were barely noticed by her though Alice was intensely irritated by them.

"Oh, for heaven's sake, Sara, don't start again. It helps no one to carry on as you are doing."

"I'm sorry, Ally." Sara gulped convulsively, doing her best to stem her weeping. A week ago she had longed to cry, hoping it would relieve her heartache, now she couldn't stop and relief was still far away. "It's just that Papa, if he had known he . . . well, he would never have left us as we are. Oh dear, Ally, I'm sorry, but I miss him so much."

"And I don't, I suppose."

"Of course you do, but you're so much braver than me."

"Rubbish. I have more self-control, that's all. Something you should try to achieve. It is the mark of a lady."

"Yes, Alice," Sara sniffed dolefully.

But the question was still unanswered, the question of where she, Alice and Dolly were to go, and by the end of the month which was next Wednesday. What about the furniture? Was that still theirs or did it now belong to this mysterious gentleman who had, for the past twenty years, rented the house to Papa? A hasty letter to the solicitor had revealed nothing for he could not divulge the identity of a client, he wrote, and no, unfortunately his client would not allow them any more time to find other accommodation. He was sure the Misses Hamilton had relatives or friends with whom they might stay temporarily. The contents of the house were of no interest to his client and must be removed when the house was vacated or they would be sold to pay off the debt Doctor Hamilton had owed but which his client was willing to waive under the circumstances.

"I don't understand," Sara wept, clinging to Dolly as the only unchanging presence in her madly rocking world, but Dolly was suddenly old and just as frightened as Sara, for if these two young women were thrown out of the house where was Dolly Watson to end up? The answer was something she could not bear to contemplate.

It appeared that Alice had been doing nothing else but contemplate in the last few days and it appeared she had found an answer, too, one which gave her a great deal of pleasure. "It's quite simple, Sara, and why you say you do not understand it is beyond me. We have to have a roof over our heads and the only roof which seems appropriate, at least to me, is the one from where our mama came in the first place." Alice had a look of what appeared to be satisfaction about her, satisfaction and triumph.

"I don't understand, Ally," Sara said again.

"Perhaps you don't for your nature has always been somewhat ... lackadaisical but if you don't I'm sure Dolly does, don't you, Dolly?"

Dolly sighed deeply and wiped the moisture from beneath her eyes where it had come to rest in the deeply embedded wrinkles. She nodded her head in sad assent, then, putting Sara from her, sank down into the rocker before the kitchen fire.

"Aye, Miss Alice, tha're right though I can't guarantee tha'll . . ." Dolly hesitated.

"Speak up, Dolly, say what you have to say."

Sara looked from one face to the other, her own forlorn and bewildered. "I wish I knew what . . ."

"Be quiet, Sara, and let Dolly speak."

"Speak about what, Alice? I don't understand."

"Miss Alice is talkin' about yer mama's folk, Miss Sara." The old woman shook her head and her gnarled hands, which had grown that way in the service of these two girls and their mother, twisted in her spotless apron, for even in the midst of trial and tribulation standards were not lowered.

"What do you think, Dolly?" Alice's voice was eager.

"Mrs Kingsley was dead set against tha' pa, Miss Alice." Dolly looked dubious. "He's not good enough for thi', she said, even though he were a doctor an' all but she wanted yer mama ter marry the son of 'er best friend. He were a lot older than yer mama but that didn't concern yer grandmama. He were a good catch, as they say, and I reckon his mama an' yer grandmama 'ad got it all worked out to their own satisfaction an' when yer mama ses she's ter marry yer papa, well, it fair set the cat among the pigeons an' no mistake. 'Don't think I'll ever receive him, 'cos I shan't,' yer grandmama ses, but it medd no difference to yer mama. She just upped an' left an' . . . well, tha' knows t'rest." Dolly's chest heaved in remembered sadness.

"Yes, yes, but I think it only right that we tell our grandmama that . . . that we are . . . that Papa is dead."

"Oh, Ally, don't . . ." Sara moaned.

"That's enough, Sara. I shall slap you if you start again. Now then, Dolly" – Alice was briskly businesslike – "the address, if you please, and perhaps you might inform me of some of the . . . the details of Mama's family. Relatives and so on so that I might speak of them in my letter to . . . to Grandmama."

"She didn't answer when yer papa wrote to tell 'er when yer mama died, Miss Alice. Her own daughter and she never— "

"It doesn't matter, Dolly. I'm sure when I explain our circumstances she will . . . relent. After all, we are her own flesh and blood."

Without another word Alice sat down to write to her mama's mama and as she did so a small smile of pleased anticipation wreathed her rosy lips. There was nothing she would like better than to go and live in what she was certain would be great splendour, for had not Mama's uncle, her grandmama's brother, been a baronet? The estate in Cheshire, the name of which Dolly had reluctantly divulged, not because she was opposed to seeing her lambs returned to the bosom of their family but because she was certain they would be refused it, sounded very grand and from the moment the letter was posted Alice went about with what could only be described as a look of ardent expectation on her face.

The letter came in the first post on the Monday morning.

Dear Miss Hamilton, it said, I have been requested by my client, Mrs Archibald Kingsley, to inform you that she has no daughter by the name of Eleanor Hamilton and that if you continue to importune her she will be forced to take legal action against you. I trust this is completely understood.

It was from a firm of lawyers in Cheshire.

She wept then, wept and raged until Sara and Dolly were frightened for her and for themselves. She ran, like a creature possessed, to the room she shared with Sara, locking the door and, when Sara hesitantly knocked, ordering her to spend the night with Dolly.

Alice was herself again the next day, her face bone white and expressionless and it was as if the incident had not taken place as she put on her hat and squared her shoulders.

She tried Mrs Bentham first, taking Sara with her since Sara, with her tears and her helpless frailty, would surely soften the hardest heart. They dressed in their newly made-over mourning, two slight and woebegone figures, pale and doing their best to be composed, as ladies should.

"I'll do all the talking, Sara," Alice had told her briskly. "I think I know how to address a lady such as Mrs Bentham. Appeal to her better nature, you understand, but if you should feel the need to shed a tear or two then go ahead. It can do no harm. She will offer us tea, I'm sure, so remember your manners. Sit up as Mama taught us and speak when you're spoken to but not unless."

Mrs Bentham did not offer them tea but Alice did not let it deter her.

"You will have heard of our loss and misfortune, Mrs Bentham," she began, speaking as though she and Mrs Bentham were well known to one another.

Mrs Bentham said she had, waiting.

"I thought so. That is why we are turning to you and casting ourselves on your mercy. We must have a roof over our heads by next Wednesday and . . . well . . . I suppose you would call it . . . employment." Alice's face was stiff and without expression as she sat beside her wilting sister on the sofa in Mrs Bentham's over-furnished drawing-room and Sara knew that this mission was costing Alice a great deal. Begging it was, she had said through gritted teeth as she dragged Sara along the lane towards Laurel House, but what else were they to do? Mama would turn over in her grave if she could see the desperate state of affairs Papa's . . . carelessness had thrust on her daughters. But they must eat and have shelter and to achieve that they must have money and surely Mrs Bentham could not fail to help them find some way to acquire it. Alice, being a lady, was doing what any lady would by turning to another for support.

"We can both sew and play the piano," she went on, "and are accomplished in French. Sara is— "

"Yes, yes, I do understand that, Miss Hamilton, but Rosalie and Harriet have their own governess and Lilian is very talented. Her fine sewing is admired by everyone who sees it and she is not in need of piano lessons. We do, of course, have our own sewing woman who comes to us from Kirkham."

"Oh, I'm sure that is so, Mrs Bentham, about Lilian, I mean, and naturally I am not speaking of . . . well, we thought perhaps Mr Bentham might know of a cottage . . ." Alice gritted her teeth. "We have no money and would have to take in sewing to earn it but if Mr Bentham knew of such a place and would wait until . . ."

Mrs Bentham wondered what she meant by "until". Surely the girl did not imagine she and her sister would be drawn into her own exclusive circle where the sort of husband they might wish for could be found. Alice Hamilton had already done her best to infiltrate Mrs Bentham's society, and with what Mrs Bentham thought of as a most unladylike fervour, and this alone was enough to turn her against her, even now.

Alice saw the stiff disapproval on Mrs Bentham's face and her heart shrivelled in her breast for there would be no help offered here. Beside her Sara stirred, folding her trembling hands about her reticule. Her eyes were enormous in her white, strained face. She bit her lip and did her best to keep back the incessant tears which she knew annoyed Alice, praying to the God her mama had believed in but whom she herself was seriously beginning to doubt existed, that Jack would come soon.

"Well, I will ask him, Miss Hamilton." Mrs Bentham swallowed distastefully. "But I can promise nothing." Her already thin mouth closed like a trap over her prominent teeth. "Now, if you will excuse me I have so much to do," implying that really, they had been fortunate in the few minutes she had already spared them in her busy day. "I'm sure something will turn up— "

"By next Wednesday, Mrs Bentham," Alice interrupted harshly, her longing to be accepted by this woman overturned by her very real fear. What did it matter if she spoiled any chance she might have had of being accepted into her circle? If she hadn't managed it as the well-bred daughter of Eleanor and Richard Hamilton, how would she fare now as Alice Hamilton, working seamstress?

Mrs Bentham was not moved nor did she care for Alice Hamilton's tone. You could see it in her expression and manner that she wondered at the temerity of these two young women in coming into her home to ask for help. They were not of her class and, but for the circumstances of their father's death and her reluctance therefore to turn them away, she would have told her maidservant to say she was not at home.

"You must have relatives, surely?"

"None."

"Then . . . perhaps a change of scene," for if this hard-faced young woman thought she was getting a toe inside Dorothea Bentham's door, with access to Dorothea's splendid son, she was mistaken.

"A change of scene?" Alice's voice was coldly polite.

"Perhaps Preston . . . or Liverpool?" Dorothea Bentham stood up, her face rigid with animosity since this was nothing to do with her. The interview was at an end.

They did not get into Mrs Armitage's house since it was deep in mourning for Charlotte Armitage. The family were receiving no callers, the wide-eyed maidservant who answered the door told them, sniffing dolefully, though she had not particularly cared for Miss Charlotte who was, or had been, a spiteful little madam in her opinion.

Miss Gilchrist was sorry, exceedingly so, but her small house had only two bedrooms, one occupied by herself and the other by her elderly servant. She was sure Alice would understand and had she tried Mrs Bentham whose husband had a great deal of influence in the district and would be sure to help? They had tried Mrs Bentham! Oh dear, she wished she could think of something, she added, her expression and demeanour telling them quite plainly that the idea that she could take in two young women and their family servant, not only take them in but support them on her small income which only just fed her and her Phyllis, was quite out of the question.

The vicar could only direct them to poor relief. A temporary measure, of course, while he made enquiries in the parish to see if there was someone who would employ them, perhaps as housekeeper – they could cook and sew – or even nursemaid.

"We cannot be separated, sir," Alice said firmly. "My sister, well, you can see for yourself, she cannot manage without me," for Sara stood, trembling and ready to weep again, her head bowed, her shoulders slumped.

"But even if I could find something you must understand that it would not be together, Miss Hamilton. Your father . . ."

"My father would not have turned us away, sir." For the first time there was a tremble in Alice Hamilton's voice. "My father turned no one away, ever. He was a good man," her attitude telling the reverend gentleman that in her opinion, he was not.

It was the same wherever they went. To the more prosperous farmhouses where the farmer and his wife stared in open-mouthed amazement at the sight of two, pretty, well-dressed young women asking for work as sewing ladies, as piano teachers, perhaps for their daughters, or indeed anything the farmer might care to put them to so long as they could be together and bring their servant. A cottage, no matter how tumbledown, they had their own furniture, even one room, but they must have work.

Until Jack came, Sara whispered to herself as she waited blindly with Alice for whatever was to be. She was still whispering it as Wednesday, the last day in August, dawned.

Alice Hamilton had sat up all night, quite alone but for

the marmalade cat, her eyes unfocused and staring blankly into the candle-lit, fire-lit corners of the kitchen, no longer concerned with the proprieties, it seemed, which said that a lady would not dream of relaxing anywhere but in her own drawing-room. She gazed into the fire and beyond to the terrifying blackness, the unknown and remote future which lay ahead of her. The awful truth that tomorrow she and Sara and Dolly were, quite simply, to be thrown out on to the street. Or, more literally, into the narrow rustic lane which lay at the front of the house. A man was to come, she had been told, and Alice was to hand over the key to him. He expected the house to be empty, for the new tenants had expressed a desire to move in on the following day.

Sara kept on insisting that that navvie she wrote to would come for them, expecting him by the hour she was, or if not him, a letter to say what they were to do. There would be money in it to tide them over and though it was all very worrying Alice was not to concern herself for Jack would put it all right. Jack! Put it all right! Alice had never heard such rubbish in her life and the only puzzle was why the man kept on corresponding with her sister when they had not met since last February. But it didn't matter. He wouldn't come, of course, and if he did Alice Hamilton certainly would accept no help from him. Not from a common labourer. No, this was Alice Hamilton's problem and she would solve it to her own satisfaction. Besides which, devastating as it had been this last week or so, at least it had one advantage and that was it would nip in the bud the alliance between Sara and this man, which was, and always had been, completely unsuitable. There were things to do, to think of, plans to be made and while Sara and Dolly slept she would make them. There was the furniture, china, her mother's piano and pictures and ornaments which must be moved to a safe place. A waggon would be needed, and a man to drive it to wherever Alice decided it would go, and that man would not be Jack Andrews.

She smiled, a cold smile, as she remembered her sister's reiteration that it would all be put right when Jack came. Sara imagined that Jack would take her by the hand, kiss her and hold her, comfort her and tell her not to worry for he would make it all come right. Good God, the man was probably sitting in his tent, or wherever it was he resided, at this very moment thanking the fates for rescuing him from the mess he would have been sucked into with not only Sara to support but Alice and Dolly as well!

Alice smoothed the glossy coat of the marmalade cat which purred on her lap, her thoughts dwelling ironically on the further problem of what was to become of the spoiled animal. Another dilemma, another creature to get settled, or would Jack place them somewhere, all of them, where the cat could be fitted in as well? Herself, Sara, Dolly and the cat, not forgetting their possessions, of course, sneering to herself, snug in a sanctuary hand-picked by Jack Andrews.

She did not move a bodily muscle as she set her mind, which was churning like Dolly's butter-maker, to the days ahead. That was all she could see but it was enough for now. Her thoughts went to the man who had been her father, the man who had forced this catastrophe on them and as they did so a change came over her face which was not pleasant to see. She would never forgive him, never, nor would she forget those people who had, in this extremity, refused to help her. She had deluded herself in the past into believing that one day she would find her rightful place amongst them but she knew different now. And Papa! What an irresponsible, feckless man he had been, drifting through life, pouring his concern, his protective care, not on his daughters and their future as it had been his duty to do, but on worthless trash who hadn't even the few coppers to pay him his due. A fool! That was what he had been and she for one would bear the scars of what he had done to her for the rest of her life.

She smiled then, a smile in which there was no humour, a smile which was to become very familiar to many people. She stood up briskly, tipping the protesting cat to the floor. She gave herself a little shake as though to throw off some slight but oppressive reminder of the past then began the simple task of brewing herself a cup of tea. She was tired but that must be overcome for there was a lot to do. She had wearied her brain down to the bone since the day her father had died in her effort to make some sense, some reason in the treacherous tangle he had left behind, some plan for the future. Today was the last day of the month. Today they, she and Sara, Dolly and the cat, were to be made homeless. They were penniless with nothing but the clothes on their back to take with them wherever they went. If she and Sara had the money to hire a waggon for their things, there was no place to take them, or was there?

If there was a solution to this dilemma, Alice Hamilton would find it, and find it today!

She would start with Dolly.

10

"I don't want to go to Liverpool, Alice," Sara moaned, "really I don't and surely there is no need for such a drastic step. There must be work nearer than that. We have only to find somewhere to live. Please, Ally, don't do this . . . Papa would not agree."

"Papa is not making the decisions, Sara, I am."

Alice studied her sister's flushed and tear-stained face, her own cold and implacable and she felt her hand tingle and her arm twitch in a great longing to slap her sister as hard as she could. Sara had been petted and indulged for the whole of her life, just as Alice had, and yet Alice was at least prepared to face the enormity of their predicament and to do something constructive about it.

Sara, on the other hand, continued to believe that if she remained somewhere in the area and waited patiently, that . . . that ill-bred lout would come and whisk her off to a sweet little villa and boldly solve the problem, not only of Sara's homelessness but that of herself and Dolly as well and they would all live happily ever after. Jack, Jack, Jack, that was all she could drivel on about, her eyes huge and terrified, her hands clutching at Alice like some demented child who is about to lose the only security it has ever known

d there was no time for it. Time had run out for Sara and ice Hamilton and their life here at Wray Green was ended. s Bentham had made that plain and Alice Hamilton would stay a moment longer to be scorned or pitied, which was as bad. She had sidled in the shadow of the Benthams and itages long enough and now, with no other choice open em, she and Sara would make a fresh start elsewhere. anks to Dolly!

"Sara, the man will be here before long to take over the house and I'm afraid we have no choice but to go. Now Dolly has— "

"I'm not going and that is that," Sara said firmly, turning her back on Alice and twitching the hem of her white nightdress. Her mind was just too stunned, too pulverised by what had happened in the last few days to accept what Alice was telling her. Poor Alice was as desolate as she was, what with the letter from the solicitors, both of them, and must have misunderstood, she said firmly.

The idea that "the man", whoever he might be, had the power manually to dislodge them from their home had not even entered her head so if they were stoutly to stay put what could he do? She had never known anyone who had been evicted and was not awfully sure she knew exactly what it entailed but she did not mean to let it happen to her. This was her home and this was where she meant to stay, at least until Jack came for her.

Alice continued as though Sara had not spoken, since she had become aware that her sister had not the faintest inkling of what was happening to them. In the circumstances there was only one way to treat her and that was to act as though Sara was no more than a child who had no option but to go where she was taken.

"I have sent for a waggon to remove our things . . ."

"Remove our things! Oh Ally, how can you say such a thing? Remove our things to where?"

". . . and when they are packed and on the waggon they are to go to the saleroom at Kirkham where they will be sold for as much as the proprietor can get for them."

"Sold! Mama's things . . . her lovely satinwood piano and . . ."

"Dolly is to . . . to . . ." Alice faltered for the first time since she had persuaded Dolly to the course which was the only one open to them. To them all. She knew she would have trouble with Sara. Well, trouble was something she was getting quite good at overcoming, one way or another, and she'd do the same with this.

Sara looked wildly about her, her hair which she had not yet brushed swinging in an arc of rippling fire about her. Her shawl which she had thrown over her nightdress slipped from her shoulders and she clutched it to her in a shiver of cold fear.

Jack had not come, for whatever reason, though her heart, which could not believe otherwise, told her he had obviously not received her letters. There was not the slightest doubt in her mind about it. Jack loved her, she knew it deep in the bones of her, deep in her heart which beat to the same rhythm as his and she had only to wait, be patient and he would be here to draw her thankfully into his protective arms. No one would hurt her while Jack was with her, and he would be soon. She had absolute faith in him. She trusted him beyond reason, beyond her sister who had been there all Sara's life. He would be here. She would wait, but Alice was speaking, saying something . . . something . . .

"Dolly is to go to Wesham," her brisk voice informed Sara, setting herself ready for the outburst.

"Wesham?" Sara looked at her blankly.

"Yes, they will give her a home there until we can send for her."

"Where?" Sara quavered, dread growing in her.

"She is to go, temporarily, into the workhouse— "

"The workhouse!" Sara's face contorted with horror. "Ally, you can't mean it. The workhouse is for the homeless and— "

"Exactly. That is what Dolly is. That is what we all are."

"How can you be so cruel?"

"Would you rather she slept in a field?"

"No, but there is . . ."

"There is nowhere else. And Dolly herself suggested it, didn't you, Dolly?" The lie came easily.

Dolly, who was seated quietly by the fire, raised her suddenly frail head and sighed, then put out a hand to Sara, drawing her by her soft shawl towards her, then pulling her down until she knelt at her feet. She cupped her wet face with gentle hands, brushing away the tears with misshapen thumbs.

"Now stop it, Miss Sara, there's a good lass. This is my decision an' nowt' ter do wi' Miss Alice," which again was not strictly true, though she had seen the sorry advantage to it all the same. "If tha' just tekk tha' head from't sand fer a minute tha'll see there's no other choice."

"Fiddlesticks, Dolly."

"Fiddlesticks or no, I've to 'ave a roof over me head by't time it gets dark an' there's nowt' else but yon. I can't walk streets wi' thee an' Miss Alice."

"We won't be walking the streets, Dolly," Sara cried tremulously. "Jack will surely come today and will find us somewhere and where we are, you will be too and if Alice persists in this foolishness I shall . . ."

"Yes, Sara, what will you do? Give me an alternative and I will consider it. Tell me where else Dolly can go."

"She will stay here with us."

Alice tutted impatiently, doing her best to hold her icy temper in check.

"Sara, listen to me, no, don't say another word, just listen. There is nothing more certain than that we must leave this house, and before dark. We must fend for ourselves. Now Dolly has some small savings which she has offered to us." She turned and bowed graciously towards the old woman but Dolly waved her away irritably. "It is the only way, Sara, to get back on our feet and when— "

"Then we can take a house here and wait for Jack."

Alice gritted her teeth and once again felt an urgent need to smack her sister across her silly face. If she mentioned that man's name again, she would do it, God help her.

"No, we cannot. Our things are to go to Kirkham and the waggon must be paid for."

"Not Mama's piano, please, Alice, not her china . . ."

"We will have our fare to Liverpool."

"No . . . *no*! Ally, what if Jack . . .?"

"And enough to keep us, if we live frugally, for a few weeks until we find work. Perhaps with a seamstress or . . ."

"Oh God, Alice, please, I cannot bear it."

"You *must* bear it, Sara, for we have no choice." Alice's voice had the hardness of flint in it, and the inexorability. "It seems everyone in Wray Green, including the vicar, has set their faces against us, so we must leave."

"But not to Liverpool, Ally . . . please, not to Liverpool. It is so far away," Sara mumbled, bowing her head until her chin rested on her chest. Her shoulders heaved and she sobbed as though her heart was broken. She continued to weep, her tears falling in total silence by then as her mother's piano was manhandled by two of Fanny Suthurst's remaining grandsons on to the waggon. There were dainty rosewood occasional tables, a chaise-longue upholstered in fine silk damask, boxes of books and lovely ornaments, the kitchen furniture, three narrow brass beds with pretty rosettes on the spindles and brass finials on the corner-posts, and the double bed in which Eleanor and Richard Hamilton had begun their married life.

"Tell the man at the saleroom to hold any monies . . ."

". . . any monies . . ." Albert repeated dutifully.

". . . that are due me and I will get in touch . . ."

". . . in touch . . ."

". . . telling him where to send it."

". . . send it. Yes, Miss Hamilton," expecting no tip and getting none.

"I will also send my address to Dolly and she will inform you of it should it be necessary," Alice told him briskly, knowing nothing of the routine, the rules, the oppressive nature of the new Poor Law and the workhouses which had been built since the law had been reformed in 1834. It said that all poor relief should be given only in the workhouse and not in the non-institutional forms of relief previously used. The union workhouse was a grim establishment where the comfort and diet were of the sparsest and the discipline of the harshest. Families were split up in an effort to deter all but the most desperate from seeking relief and the novel idea that Dolly, or any of its inmates, could receive and send out messages to anyone she fancied would have caused a great deal of hilarity among the ex-sergeant-majors who were the workhouse masters.

"Right you are, Miss Hamilton," Albert said sympathetically, his gaze moving round the empty kitchen, coming to rest on the hearth where a fire still burned and the cat sprawled indignantly before it on the bare stone floor.

"Do you think you could find a home for the cat, Albert?" Alice asked, calm as a lily on a pond, and just as pale, but when Albert went to pick it up, meaning to pass it on to his old granny who was fond of cats, the animal spat viciously, fur and tail rising, then cut to the door through which it disappeared.

"Never tha' mind, Miss Hamilton. Yon'll find a home somewhere. They allus do."

But shall we? Sara agonised as she penned a last swift note to Jack. One last desperate plea to come and save her from Alice's determination to find them a new life. She would give it to Albert and when Jack got here, which he would eventually, Albert promised to hand it over to him but where would she be by then and how would Jack find her in Liverpool? But it was a link. Albert was a link, a kindly, well-meaning connection between her and Jack.

She watched numbly from the window as he and Alice made some last-minute adjustment to the ropes which bound her mother's piano to the waggon then turned away blindly to fall into the arms of the old woman who had been her loving, irascible comfort ever since she was born. They could not speak, either of them, and when Alice came to lead Dolly out to Albert, who had cheerfully offered to drop her off at the workhouse, Sara did not see it, nor the note which, at her command, the bewildered Albert passed back to Alice.

Alice handed over the keys to the man who came for them at noon. She did not glance back at the small house which had been her home all her life, for she was too concerned with guiding her half-blind sister along the route which led up to the railway station at Kirkham where they would board the next train to Preston and so to Liverpool.

Jack removed his felt hat and scratched his head, his face so creased with worry the pretty young woman behind the counter of the general store in Burneside, which acted as post office, felt a great urge to put out a hand to comfort him. He was a navvie, his outlandish dress told her that, but he was as immaculately turned out as the squire himself, perhaps more so, and certainly strikingly attractive. A shaft of sunlight from the window glinted off his glossy chestnut curls and coloured his already sun-browned face to a rich, healthy glow. His brown eyes were soft with some deep-felt emotion and his wide mouth quirked at each corner as he did his best to manage a polite smile. His teeth were white, big and even, except for one to the side which was slightly crooked

"Are tha' sure, lassie?" he asked her anxiously. "Jack Andrews, care of the navvie settlement beyond the village."

"Theers nowt, Mr Andrews, I'm that sorry," sweeping her hand in a full arc to display her empty pigeonholes. She did her best to console him with a great show of dimples and her plump, high breasts but he was busy fixing the penny postage stamp to the envelope in his hand. This was the fourth or fifth time he had been in to her pa's shop, each time asking for a letter and each time handing one over for posting to a Miss Sara Hamilton, Lane End, Wray Green, near Kirkham, wherever that might be. Not a relative by the look on his face and the desperation in his lovely, toffee-coloured eyes, but she was certainly a lucky girl to have such a splendid upstanding chap as this chasing after her. Just look at that fine, silk waistcoat, unbuttoned across his cream cambric shirt, which was itself unbuttoned at the neck to reveal a spring of fine curls at the base of his throat. He was tall, towering above the counter, and her, so that she was forced to peer up into his face. Gawd, she wished some chap would look like that at her, his whole body in despair because she hadn't written!

"Is there another delivery today, miss?" he went on, leaning towards her so that she could smell the mixture of tobacco, of some lemon-scented soap and a faint but not unpleasant hint of male sweat. She could feel her own excitement and the pink flush of longing stain her skin but she could have been her own pa for all the notice he took.

"No." Her voice was husky and slightly petulant since most chaps responded to her overt female invitation with dash and alacrity.

Jack sighed, turning away, forgetting to buy the ounce of tobacco Whistler had asked him to get, for it was cheaper here than at the Truck shop at the camp. Leaving the small shop, he walked back down the quiet village street, skirting the paper mill which thrived beside the River Kent. Opposite to Tolson Hall, built by a tobacco merchant, Jack had heard, was the hill on which, thirty or more years ago, had been erected the monument to William Pitt, and to commemorate the British victory at Waterloo.

Jack noticed none of these things as he strode despondently east and slightly northwards along lanes deep in autumn colours towards the camp. This was the second time this week, and it was only Wednesday, that he had slipped away from the camp and walked the short distance to Burneside in the ever more desperate hope that there would be a letter from Sara. He had written several times, telling her to send her letters to the new posting office in the nearby village but it was almost four weeks now since he had received her last one. It had been as it always was, full of love and longing, humorous anecdotes about her father, Alice and Dolly, all the figures who peopled her world; her sewing which was turning now to such practical matters as sheets and pillowcases instead of gowns and bonnets.

The garden, which the summer heat had almost destroyed, and her father's vegetables which had somehow survived. A chatty letter through which the thread of her love was embroidered with nothing to point to any disaster to come. They were all well, that's what it had said, and in that case, why hadn't she written, answered his own frantic pleas to hear from her? Jesus Christ, if anything had happened to her . . .

"Any luck, Jack?" Whistler murmured in an aside as Jack took his place beside him. He had changed from his decent clothes to the rough ones he wore for the shovelling of the tons of earth needed for the embankment between the two viaducts.

"Nay, no luck, Whistler, an' I'll tell thi' this. If I don't get a letter tomorrow I'm off down south ter find out what's up."

Whistler was shocked.

"Tha' can't do that, lad. What about contract?"

"Bugger contract."

Whistler's unease made him brave. "That's all well an' good, Jack Andrews, but tha's more than thee an' that lass ter consider."

"Not ter me there's not, Whistler." Jack levelled an enormous weight of earth on to his long-handled shovel and with the grace and ease of long practice aimed it expertly at the growing pile of the embankment. A line of waggons, drawn by horses and come from a cutting further back on the track, was high above his head, standing on the temporary line of rails which extended as the earthworks grew. Each waggon had been filled by two men at the cutting and held two and a quarter cubic yards of "muck", the name by which the navvies called all kinds of earth and rock. Each man would lift nearly twenty tons of earth a day, chucking it on his shovel over his own head into the waggon. The navvies' principal work was banking, cutting and tunnelling. At this moment Jack and his men were banking and the waggon on the light tram road from the cutting to the edge of the embankment was to be tipped on to its side at the track's highest point, a stout piece of timber preventing the waggon from toppling over the edge. It was Jack's job to decide if and when the waggon was to be emptied and it was perhaps his worried preoccupation with Sara and the absence of her letters that took his attention, which should have been total, from what Algie-One-Step was doing at the top of the embankment.

"Shall I tip 'em, Jack?" he was yelling, no more than a blurred outline in the sun-hazed dust which rose in clouds about them all. It had not rained for weeks and the earth was dry, like sand, getting in the men's eyes and under their eyelids, up their noses and in their ears where it clogged and made them deaf. It drifted into their mouths and between their teeth so that they were constantly thirsty. A gallon of beer a day they were allowed and it was needed when each man sweated that much out of himself in the hard work and heat.

Jack lifted his arm, signalling to Algie-One-Step that he was to hang on, that he himself would climb up and check the embankment. He raised his head to shout, moving his hand so that the shadow of it fell across his eyes, shading them from the overhead sun. Algie yelled back and returned the wave, making some signal Jack was not sure he understood, then, as he watched and waited, Algie stepped back and the waggon began to tip.

"God almighty," Jack whispered, staring in horrified disbelief, paralysed for a brief tick in time as the muck began slowly to leak from the waggon, then, urged on by its own momentum, gathered speed and hurtled down the slope towards him and Whistler.

Whistler had his back to it. He held his shovel in an outraged grip, his face red and sweated beneath its coating of pale dust. His eyes were unusually grim and his mouth was open as he got ready to give Jack Andrews a piece of his mind. An amiable man was Whistler, with no enemies. A man who loved his Mary and his children and was made up with the relatively small but very welcome prosperity they had moved into with Jack. His children had shoes to their feet and had lost that big-eyed scarecrow look vagrant children take on when they haven't quite enough to eat. His Mary had a warm shawl and a bit put by for a rainy day, should it come. Now Jack Andrews, who had made it all possible, was telling him he was off chasing a lass who Whistler was pretty certain would not take Jack in the end. Well, she was the doctor's girl, a lady by all accounts and not for the likes of a navvieman. She'd probably taken up with some nob and had no more time for Jack, who should have known better in the first place. Chalk and cheese, Jack and this lass were, though Jack couldn't seem to see it. Whistler'd tell him so an' all and Jack had no right to jeopardise all their jobs on some wild-goose chase. If they didn't complete on time they'd be fined and the fine would come out of . . .

As Whistler disappeared under two and a quarter cubic yards of muck and rubble and slate and earth, his indignant thoughts were snapped off as sharply and as cleanly as his neck.

Jack flung himself to one side. He had been working a couple of feet away from Whistler towards the front of the first waggon which tipped over and the worst weight of its load missed him. It clutched at his legs as he dived away, though, trapping him for a matter of frantic seconds. He wanted to yell in horror, scrabbling to escape its deadly grip and all about him men stood, frozen in the postures of raising a pick, lifting a shovelful of earth, mopping a sweating brow, taking a gulp of beer, each one paralysed for a moment by the calamity which had overtaken Whistler. They were used to accidents. They happened a dozen times a day but this one seemed indecent somehow. One minute there was old Whistler leaning on his shovel having a jaw with Jack, next he was gone, vanished completely beneath a waggonload of muck.

"Oh Jesus . . . Jesus," whispered Jack, his face yellow-pale and drenched with sweat. "Oh Jesus, help 'im . . ." and flinging himself on to the settling pile of muck he began to dig with his bare hands, like a dog would dig a hole in which to bury a bone, fast and furious and unmindful of the injuries he was inflicting on his own flesh. Within seconds he was surrounded by others as men sprang to help him.

"Not wi' tha' bloody picks, tha' fools," he thundered, "dost tha' want ter kill 'im? Use tha' hands, fer God's sake an' be quick about it," but even then it was too late.

Whistler had been dead for five minutes when they finally freed him. He had an expression of indignation on his face as though he could scarce credit his own bad luck. They cleaned him up before they sent for Mary, removing the muck from his open mouth and eyes which they closed, his nostrils and ears, even using some of their precious ale to wash his face. He was nearly forty, was Whistler, a good age for a navvie since his expectation of life was not long. They died as boys, run over by the waggons they were leading to the tip-heads. They lived riotously, poaching women and game in the immediate vicinity of the line, daring the shotguns of the men to whom they belonged. But though they were brutalised by constant risk and death, the men were careful of their dress and manner when in mourning and made a funeral, particularly for a well-liked chap, into a special occasion. Whistler had been popular and would be missed. In sympathy for him and his family every man on the site, to the astonishment and annoyance of the engineer, downed tools and refused to work for the rest of that day though it was hardly past midday when Whistler died.

It was unlikely that there would be an inquest, Jack was well aware, for railway engineers were a hard lot and did not value their men, indeed did not even keep count of those who were killed. A navvie was no more than another tool, like a waggon or a pick or a shovel, and as easily replaced.

They wore their best to bury Whistler on the next day, each man wearing a white favour in his coat as he followed the body to the grave, each man contributing a penny or two to pay for the service of the reverend gentleman from Burneside. They were solicitous with Mary, some of them offering to take her and her children on since she had no one to support her now. She had "jumped the brush" with Whistler years ago and in due course it was more than likely she would accept one of the offers the men had made. She was a good woman, a good manager and in a month or two, when the sharp edges of her grieving had blunted, being a practical woman and knowing no other life than this, would take the only course open to her and begin again with a new "husband".

It was after the funeral that Jack took Alfie-Bob to one side. Alfie-Bob, after Whistler, was in Jack's opinion the most dependable and intelligent of the gang. They were all hard workers and, providing they were supervised, did well but they needed to be guided, told what to do next and without Whistler to act as his temporary deputy, Alfie-Bob was the only one with the wit and the motivation to see that the work continued, and continued as Jack ordered it. He was courting May Wilkinson, the farm lass from beyond Burneside, his suit being seriously considered by her father. He had to prove to May's pa his worth and endeavour, his ability to provide a decent home nearby in which to shelter the farmer's only daughter and raise the children she and Alfie-Bob would have, so it was in his own interest to keep the work flowing and both he and Jack knew it.

"What's up, Jack?" he asked. The men, as was usual after a funeral, were drinking. At the moment, in deference to Whistler's Mary, they were quiet as they made toast after toast to Whistler. Soon it would become more excessive as the drink took hold and they began to forget the purpose of the randy. Tomorrow though, by sun-up, they must all be at their allotted tasks and Alfie-Bob was the only man, after Jack, who had the capability to get them there.

"This is between thee an' me, Alfie-Bob an' if I find tha's blabbed I'll 'ave thi' off my gang that fast tha'll not know what time o' day it is."

"Aye up, Jack . . ." Alfie began to protest, indignant at the affront to his honour. He could keep his trap shut with the best. With Whistler gone, poor sod, there was a good chance for Alfie-Bob to "get on" with Jack who, all the men admitted, was going somewhere in the world of railway building and with May's pa watching him like some grizzled old hawk, it would be worth something to be on the right side of the man who was Alfie-Bob's boss!

"I'm serious, Alfie-Bob. This is the most important . . . well, let's say it means a lot ter me an' wi' Whistler gone, there's nobbut you left I can trust."

Alfie-Bob puffed out his broad chest and looked Jack directly in the eye.

"Wi' me life, Jack," he announced dramatically. Alfie-Bob was a year younger than Jack, not yet twenty-one, and still inclined to be boyishly theatrical.

"Nay, it'll not come ter that, lad, but tha'll need ter use tha' noddle."

"I'm tha' man, Jack." Again Alfie-Bob preened.

"All tha' need ter do is keep tha' wits about thi' an' tha' trap shut. Think tha' can do it?"

"I can that, Jack."

"Tha' don't even know what it is yet, lad. Dost tha' not think tha'd best hear me out?"

Alfie-Bob became serious then, a cloak of sudden maturity falling across his powerful young shoulders.

"Jack, tha' knows me hopes in . . . well, May an' me, we want ter be wed. Proper wed, not just over't brush. Her pa an' me, we 'ad a chat . . . well" – he grinned endearingly –

"he did all the talkin' an' unless I shape up I can forget May. So I've ter gerron, Jack. I *am* gerrin on, thanks ter thi'. If tha' want me ter do owt', owt' that's legal, that is," he added hastily, for he'd be no good to May in gaol, "then I'm tha' man."

"Thanks, Alfie-Bob. Now, here's what tha're ter do."

11

Sara had not stopped trembling, jumping at every strange sound, and there were many, since she and Alice had arrived in Liverpool by train on the circuitous route from Preston to Parkside and thence on the Manchester and Liverpool Railway to Lime Street Station.

There had been delays, hold-ups for no apparent reason and to the two young country girls, neither of whom had travelled on a train before, it had been a terrifying experience. Alice had, naturally, wanted to take a first-class ticket at a cost of six shillings each, travelling with people who were, like themselves, well bred, but when she discovered that for a cost of three shillings and threepence, six shillings and sixpence for the two of them, they could make the journey third class, she did not hesitate. She was tight-lipped and white-faced with mortification but could not afford to ignore such considerations now since all she had in her reticule was sixteen pounds three shillings and sixpence which had been the sum total of Dolly's savings.

She was in such a taking, every move Sara made, whatever it might be, rattled her into a seething maelstrom of temper.

"I don't know what's the matter with you, Sara Hamilton," she hissed, as they waited on the crowded platform at the top end of Fishergate where her sister clutched her arm and almost pushed her on to the track as a train engine shrieked piercingly. "Pull yourself together, if you please," though she herself found it very alarming.

The railway station was a mixture of styles, from the early dark and clumsy wooden shed which had first served the travelling public, to the high, iron and glass roofing beneath which, it was said, without exaggeration, more trains and passengers passed than in any other in the country. One hundred and thirty-three trains in one day, Preston boasted, of which fifty were baggage and coal trains, and eighty-three for the carrying of passengers. There were twelve leaving on this day for Liverpool alone so they would not have long to wait, the busy clerk at the booking office told them.

It was quite a manoeuvre getting from one platform to another since there was no footbridge to carry passengers and Alice and Sara were forced to walk across the shining, dangerous-looking rails. Seeing the apprehension on the faces of the two pretty and extremely elegant young ladies who hovered hesitantly among the rough crowd, a kindly railway servant escorted them and several other lady passengers across for, as he told them importantly, a stopping train was due and their safety was his dutiful concern.

When they finally boarded the train they were the subject of much astonished scrutiny from their fellow passengers. It was a "stand-up" carriage, or box, with no place to sit except on the floor where, had they done so, they would have been in danger of being trodden on. Whenever the train stopped they and the other passengers were jostled together in a way so embarrassing and intimate, though the men were good-natured and respectful enough, Alice wished a dozen times she had purchased first-class seats. But she had so little money and would it be enough to keep her and Sara until they found work? As soon as they stepped from the train they must find a room and she hadn't the faintest notion how even that was to be achieved. Where did one start? How did one go about it? How big was Liverpool? What price would be asked and when it was how did she know it was fair? Dear God, a hundred questions to which she had no answers as she and Sara, who had retreated into a state of total shock, jostled and jerked their way from Preston to Parkside to Edgehill and then on to the hustle and bustle which was Lime Street Station in Liverpool. During it all she kept one thought firmly in her mind, the one good thing which would come out of the shambles her father's death had thrown them into, and that was the severing of the attachment Sara had formed for the navvie who, if he came looking for her would find no trace. Not even the pathetic letter Sara had left in the hand of the willing Albert Suthurst!

If they had thought Preston to be a turbulent upheaval of

people, of hissing, terrifying steam, acrid smoke, of shrieking voices and piercing whistles, of clatter and clamour above which they could barely think, let alone hear one another speak, it was nothing to the uproar, the cacophony, the mind-numbing tumult of the railway station which, it was reported, was the gateway, in and out, of the busiest port in the north of England.

It gave the appearance of a great cathedral, Sara thought as she gazed fearfully about her in awe, though she had never actually been in one. Splendid it was, with fancy columns and winging roofs, great carvings and delicate tracery, soaring pillars and vast stretches of glass which put the station at Lytham, which she had thought to be magnificent, firmly in the shade, and within it and through it poured thousands upon thousands of travelling people, and, or so she thought, all at this precise moment! Some on small journeys to the markets in the city from nearby Broad Green or Huyton, others moving from one side of the world to the other. From Europe and the Scandinavian countries of Norway and Sweden to the Americas and even further to the continent of Australia. Though Sara had no knowledge of it as her wide-eyed gaze passed from one strange sight to another, the emigrant trade was beginning to grow, taking from the shores of England those who sought a better life than the one they knew here, many of them Irish for there was death and famine and disease there beyond describing.

There were advertisements, posters in bold letters on the walls of the station, inviting those who were to sail to their new life to observe that the American and Colonial Packet Office in Waterloo Road had fast packets sailing weekly to New York, to Philadelphia, to New Orleans and Quebec and for the first time Sara felt her misery ebb slightly and a twinge of excitement tripped her heart. Quebec! New Orleans! Names she had read in books and newspapers and now they were here on a poster, so grand-sounding, so available as though anyone with the will and nerve to do it had only to apply themselves and they could make a success of anything they put their mind to in this busy, thriving metropolis which was the flowing highway to the rest of the world. Perhaps she and Jack, when he came, which he would, of course, when he read the last letter she had left for him, might even . . . what? . . . start a new life together on the other side of the world. They were young and strong and together – oh, together. With Jack beside her Sara Hamilton would be afraid of nothing.

The two girls stood uncertainly at the top of the commanding steps which led down from the station façade to the broad stretch of Lime Street. They had discarded mourning since their fine cotton mourning gowns would not be warm enough for the coming winter and they must travel light. Sara was in her blue, the blue of heaven, Jack had called it, the glow of happiness in his eyes, tenderness curling his lips into a smile which told her he was longing to place it against hers. Her smile had answered his. Knowing his thoughts, knowing him, loving him, wanting to nurture him somehow, shaking her head as she told him on that last day that the colour was that of a hyacinth. As she and Alice hesitated, unwilling to plunge into the maelstrom of traffic and people below, she pulled her mother's scented shawl more closely about her shoulders as though it might protect her from what was to come. A talisman, perhaps, a magic charm which would protect her and keep her safe until Jack came. She could not stop her thoughts from wheeling like the swallows which had lived in Holme Chase, wheeling always back to him, wherever he was. Where was he? Why hadn't he come? Was he ill, dead of the cholera? No, no, she would know . . . she would . . . Even here in the great clamorous hubbub of this city where she should have her wits about her, her mind would just not turn away from the anguish of not knowing and the scene before her became no more than a blur of movement and sound, so fast and furious she found it hard to distinguish one shape from another.

She carried what was known as a carpetbag and she passed it nervously from one hand to the other. It was soft and light and roomy with a metal frame and in it was her warm winter cloak along with all the clothing Alice had told her to bring. A change of underwear, a serviceable working dress, a couple of nightgowns, stockings and her toilet things. The rest of her lovely gowns were packed in the boxes Fanny Suthurst's grandson had promised to store for them in his bit of a shed!

Alice was in the softest jade green, her gown and bonnet almost identical to Sara's, with touches of cream about it, at the neck and sleeves and hem, and beneath the brim of her bonnet. Her shawl was in colours of jade and willow and pearl grey, elegant and eye-catching, as the startled male glances which fell about her testified. Her carpetbag was a match to the one Sara carried.

"Where shall we start?" she murmured to herself, obviously expecting no help nor answer from Sara. Though Alice Hamilton was more than a match for anybody, including these rude men who ran their eyes over her in a way to which she was not accustomed, she did not quite know how to go about putting a stop to it. A haughty stare would have sufficed in Wray Green but it seemed to have little effect here.

"Perhaps we could ask someone?" Sara faltered, her eyes doing their best to follow the moving, endless, crowded flow of carriages, waggons, drays and horse-drawn vehicles of all sorts which coursed densely past the railway entrance, turning left at the corner where a magnificent building, rearing in lofty splendour, proclaimed itself to be St George's Hall.

Alice looked about her, doing her best to avoid the glances of the male population whose gaze continued to plague and annoy her but who else was she to turn to in her search for a decent lodging house? She must approach someone and there appeared to be no respectable women about and if there were, what would they think if they were accosted by a person such as herself. Dear Lord in heaven but it was difficult being a lone woman in this male-dominated world.

A porter was passing, young, solid and reliable-looking in his neat uniform and cap. He was trundling a trolley of sorts on which a mound of luggage was piled. A well-dressed gentleman followed him languidly, watching as the porter hefted it, with the help of the cabbie, on to the back of a hansom cab. When it was all safely stowed away, the man carelessly threw him a tip, climbed in himself and ordered the cabbie to take him to the Pier Head.

Alice took a deep breath and stepped forward, dragging Sara with her.

"Excuse me," she said grandly, putting out a hand to draw the porters attention to her but she had no need. It was, like all the other fellows about her, already drawn.

"Yes, miss?" He grinned, his expression implying that she had only to ask and he would drag the very moon from the sky for her. Alice did not like it and her expression told him so. Alice was not used to being looked at as this . . . this employee of the railway was looking at her. Alice required courtesy, deference from those who were beneath her. Her mouth thinned and her deportment became even more stiff-necked, a bearing which was increasingly to develop as the weeks and months passed. She was annoyed and she saw no reason to hide it.

"We wish to be directed to . . . accommodation," she said frigidly.

"Yes, miss? What sort?"

"We are looking for lodgings, my good man, and being strangers to Liverpool we are in some quandary as to where to start. Perhaps you might direct us?" Her voice rose questioningly.

"Well, there's the Adelphi," eyeing the cut and quality of her beautifully made gown.

"Is than an . . . hotel?"

"It is that, queen, best in town."

For a moment both girls were diverted by the oddness of being called "queen", then Alice's face became momentarily uncertain. Best in town! Expensive!

"We were looking for . . . just a room." She lifted her head regally, her eyes snapping with some emotion the porter did not recognise though Sara did. "A lodging house," then in a rush before she lost her courage, "as cheap as we can find. Respectable, of course, and in a decent part of town but . . . inexpensive." She glared. It was out. She had told this man she was poor, despite her good clothes and he could make of it what he cared to. False pride would not shelter them, nor feed them until they had found work and though he was merely a labouring man of no consequence to Alice Hamilton she found it hard to admit that she and her sister had fallen on hard times.

"There's norra lorra them about, queen, not what'd suit you, any road," looking her up and down knowingly. He saw a lot of queer folk in his line of work and he had long since lost the capacity for surprise, but these two were slightly out of the ordinary.

"Whether they would suit us or not is none of your concern," Alice snapped. "Kindly direct us to them at once."

The porter was not put out by her rudeness.

"Well, there's places down by't docks, like. Fer seamen an' such . . ."

Alice reared up like a horse stung by a wasp. "They would

hardly be suitable for myself and my sister. Surely there is somewhere more . . . more . . ."

"Aye, yer right, chuck." He brightened. "Tell yer what, though. Me Aunty Lil takes in lodgers when she's short of a bob or two. 'Er old man goes ter sea an' 'e's a boozer an' all."

Seeing their look of incomprehension he began to explain. "A drinker, see. 'E gets legless an' when 'e's 'ome 'e knocks 'er about so she likes ter mekk a bit on't side. That way she's allus got a few quid fer a rainy day, like, an' there's a few o' them about wi' me Uncle George. She might tekk yerrin, that's if 'e's not 'ome."

"Where . . .?"

"Abercromby Square, off Oxford Street."

Alice looked gratified. That sounded nice, picturing a quiet sanctuary, tree-lined, tall and respectable houses with a decent respectable landlady who would at once recognise their needs.

"Tell 'er Reggie sent yer," he went on. "Yer go left 'ere," waving a vague hand in the direction of the heaving street, "foller yer noses along Mount Pleasant . . ."

Better and better. Mount Pleasant sounded delightful.

". . . straight on up ter Oxford Street an' Abercromby Square's just off it. Yer can't miss it."

"Thank you, you have been most helpful. Abercromby Square, you said?" Alice braced her shoulders and moved her bag from her left hand to her right.

"That's right, queen. Now 'ave yer gorrit?" Alice said she had, repeating his instructions and Reggie grinned, revealing the poor state of his teeth. Alice looked away hastily. "I might gerrup ter see yer on me day off. Right fond of me Aunty Lil I am," he added. He would not ordinarily have been so familiar with what were obviously ladies of a better class but if these two were so down on their luck they were forced to stay at his Aunty Lil's place then there was no harm in chancing his arm with one of them. Either would do. He winked suggestively, not at all put out by Alice's frozen-faced indignation, before hurrying away to the call of a heavily laden passenger who had just drawn up in a hansom cab.

"Oh Alice, do you think we should?" Sara asked tearfully as she watched Reggie dart away.

"It seems to me we have little choice, Sara. At least we shall be off the streets."

Jack's heart was pumping so hard and so loudly he could hardly hear his own knock on the door at the back of the house. He had debated with himself whether he should go to the front door or the back but after much thought, as he clattered along the rail he himself had helped to build from Preston to Kirkham, the drizzle blowing directly into his face through the glassless opening which served third-class passengers as a window, he had chosen the less formal kitchen. Dolly usually answered the front as it was more correct that a maidservant and not the mistress of the house should do so, but Sara often opened the back.

He had trembled, actually trembled, him, big Jack Andrews, at the thought of Sara standing there, rosy with surprise, her eyes wide and incredulous, then when she saw who it was, the burst of glorious light which would surge from her, the glow, the joy, the leap of love and gladness. He knew exactly how it would be. Like a lovely vision, one he had dreamed of for the past . . . was it really almost eight months? She would be there, filling his eyes and his heart, a reality and not the fantasy he had idealised for so long. Flesh and blood instead of shadow and light. He had wondered deep in the night as he lay in the small space allocated him by Whistler's Mary what he would do when it happened, when she stood before him and now she was about to and he still didn't know. He knew what he wanted to do, by God, but it was eight months and he had not had a letter from her for several weeks so how would she be with him?

He hovered, his mouth dry, his pulses racing in eager and yet anxious anticipation, the benign, still warm autumn sun which had come out as he walked, on his back and when the door opened he thought he would stop breathing.

It was not Sara. It was a woman he did not know and a woman who did not know him. A woman of about forty-five with iron grey hair dragged back from a bony forehead beneath which was a sallow face in which a thin-lipped mouth made no attempt to smile.

"Yes?" she snapped, her eyes running suspiciously up and down his crumpled, navvieman's outfit. She evidently did not like what she saw. Navvies were unwelcome wherever they went, he knew that, no matter how tidy or polite they might be and it was to his disadvantage to dress like one. But he was not ashamed of who he was and saw no reason to hide his identity.

He made a great effort to calm himself, to contain the darting shafts of fear which pierced him, for though he told himself that there was nothing sinister in another woman opening Doctor Hamilton's back door, he could not quell the dreadful panic which did its best to overwhelm him. Perhaps Dolly was ill – not Sara, Dear God, not his Sara – and this woman, from the village no doubt, had been brought in to nurse her. She looked the kind of woman who would do well in a sickroom, bullying the patient into a return to health or incur her wrath.

"Yes?" she said again, her voice and manner impatient. He had not realised he had been staring, awkward and totally silent as his thoughts darted from one alarming possibility to another. He cleared his throat and shifted his feet, hoping with all his heart that Sara, or even Alice, would appear at the woman's black-clad shoulder but neither did.

"Excuse me, but I'm looking for . . ."

"Yes," she said for the third time, her patience wearing extremely thin, ready to shut the door in his face if he didn't speak up soon. She had no time to squander even if he did.

"Sara," he managed to stammer, "Miss Hamilton, please, or Doctor Hamilton if she's not in."

"They're not here." Her mouth closed cruelly on the last word and Jack had time to wonder how she managed to speak without hurting herself, then her words struck him a mortal blow and he felt his knees weaken.

"Not . . . here?"

"That's right and if that is all I'll bid you good-day." She moved to shut the door in his face but he put out a hand to stop her, an action she did not care for as her narrowing, flint-like eyes told him. She was not afraid, oh no, not her, just affronted that this . . . this vagrant should interfere with her door.

"But where are they?"

"I'll thank you to take your hand off that door. My brother's in the back garden and I have only to call out— "

"Your . . . brother?" Jack could feel the blood leave his head and in it began a buzzing, an angry sound like a hive being stirred with a stick. Dear God, dear God in heaven, what was happening? What had happened? Who was this woman who held Doctor Hamilton's door with such proprietorial command? Her brother . . . in Doctor Hamilton's garden? Where was Doctor Hamilton, and where was Sara?

She saw his face change and then she began to be afraid. She saw the blood which had drained away begin to flood back beneath his unshaven skin. His brown eyes, so beseechingly glowing with deep emotion a moment ago, became a flat, muddy, menacing brown and the toe of his dusty, hobnailed boot clamped itself in the space between door and frame.

"Stop that at once," she squeaked, her own face losing even more colour, but the man at the door took no notice. He leaned towards her, his teeth a slashing white snarl in the blood red darkness of his face and his voice dropped to a sibilant whisper. He gave the impression of a man barely in control of himself, a man who, if crossed, might do untold damage.

"Where is she?" he hissed.

"Who . . . who?"

"Tha' know who I mean. Bloody hell, she lives here. Who the devil are thee an' who gave thi' the right to bar the door to her friends?"

"Who for pity's sake? Tell me who it is you want and I'll— "

"Sara. Sara Hamilton, o'course, or Alice, or even Dolly. Any one of 'em will do."

"There is no one here of that name, any of those names. I believe a doctor *did* reside in this house . . ."

"Where the bloody hell is he, then?"

"Young man" the woman was beginning to get her dander up – "if you swear at me again I shall call the constable and have you arrested. You have no right to— "

"By God, if I don't get an answer from tha' soon he'll have to arrest me fer bloody murder."

"Gone . . . they're gone. I didn't know their name," she added hastily. "My brother and I moved in two weeks ago."

"Two weeks!" He fell back, his shoulders sagging, his eyes deep and almost black in their sockets. His hat, which he had removed politely as the woman opened the door, dropped to the path and from the shrubbery, as though at a signal, a marmalade cat darted, twining herself ecstatically between Jack's legs.

"Well!" the woman said, clearly startled. "That animal's been hanging about my garden ever since we moved in, wild as wild. Wouldn't even come for a saucer of milk. I like cats," she announced surprisingly, "but it would have nothing to do with me."

"She was theirs." His voice was hollow and he looked down at the cat as though she were a creature from a nightmare, one into which he had just been submerged. He was out of his depth, floundering to understand what had happened to him, drowning in a sea of fear which threatened to overwhelm him.

"I thought she must be. Well, I'm sorry I can't be of further help," she declared sharply, the softness she had shown for the cat hardening up again.

Another expression crossed her face as something else occurred to her.

"Sara Hamilton, you say?"

"Yes, yes," Jack answered eagerly, hope flooding him and lighting his eyes. "You know where she is?"

"No, but there were letters for her. Several of them. I burned them since I didn't know where to send them."

Jack slumped back against the door frame, the last glimmer of hope dying in his face.

"They were from me," he said bleakly.

"Well, I'm sorry but there's nothing else I can tell you."

"Doctor Hamilton . . . he . . . the previous tenants . . . where did they . . ?" Jack felt as though he were trying to speak with a blanket in his mouth.

"I know nothing about them, young man. My brother rented this house when he retired, from an acquaintance of his. We were reluctant at first, because of the epidemic . . ."

"Epidemic?" He felt the nightmare deepen about him, become even more cloying, its tentacles dragging him slowly to destruction and he seemed unable to do more than repeat the words she uttered.

"Yes, cholera."

"Oh God . . . oh sweet Jesus . . ."

"That will be enough of that, young man. I do not like to hear the Lord's name taken in vain. My brother was a preacher before he retired. Now I really must get on. Oh, there is one thing I seem to remember hearing from my brother's friend . . ."

"Yes?" Jack surged towards her eagerly, almost falling as the cat twisted about his boots.

"The doctor died."

Oh yes, the reverend gentleman said, he knew the family, having been summoned to his back door by the agitated maidservant who knew it would be more than her job was worth if she allowed the rough, unshaven navvie into the sanctum of the vicarage itself. Wait there, she had said, pointing to her clean doorstep, closing the door in his face, hoping he wouldn't deposit any of the muck on his boots on to its pristine perfection, since she was the one who would have to scrub it again.

Oh yes, he knew the family, the vicar repeated, and yes, the doctor did die in the epidemic but what had happened to the girls and their old maidservant he really couldn't say. He made no mention of his own lack of Christian spirit in regard to Alice and Sara Hamilton's search for shelter, saying merely that he had heard that they had been seen boarding a train at Kirkham. Going in which direction? Well, perhaps if he was to ask at the station someone might remember, though since it was several weeks ago it scarcely seemed likely. And really, young man, there was no need to catch hold of his jacket like that since he was doing his best to be helpful. The vicar had frowned, keeping a good distance from the frantic, barely controlled tension in the young navvie on his doorstep. The old lady? Now then, again he couldn't say . . . perhaps someone had taken her in. Again, if he were to ask about the village someone might . . .

For a week he was the talk of Wray Green and its environs, sleeping rough under any handy hedge, tramping from house to house, knocking impertinently on every door, almost forcing his way in as though he suspected the householder of hiding Sara Hamilton against her will, or at least of withholding information as to her whereabouts.

Even further afield he went, tramping up the immaculate gravelled driveways of Laurel House where the Benthams lived and Yew Tree Villa, the residence of the recently bereaved Mr and Mrs Armitage. He got short shrift at both places, being thrown off forcibly by two gardeners, an odd job man and the boot boy from the latter.

The villagers, simple labouring men and women who had been Doctor Hamilton's patients, were so sorry they couldn't help him, the women in tears, some of them, for not only did they sorely miss the good doctor, they were dreadfully sorry for the distraught young man who searched for one of his daughters. They remembered him, of course they did, though they had not known him personally, for hadn't the doctor spoken of him? He'd been beaten by navvies, though he was a navvie himself, eyeing his flamboyant waistcoat and jaunty felt hat.

He looked none too jaunty now, poor sod, his face like that of a man dead for twenty-four hours, his shadowed eyes bleak with suffering staring into something he scarce seemed able to contemplate. If they heard anything, oh yes, they would certainly try to get word to him at – where was it? – but it seemed Miss Sara and Miss Alice and the old woman who had lived with them had vanished as though the earth had swallowed them up. They had heard, as who had not, of the doctor's girls boarding the train but they had imagined they were off on some excursion to do with the doctor's untimely death and were as flabbergasted as he was when they did not return.

The only one who might have led Jack in the right direction, seeing that it had been her grandson who had been involved on the day the doctor's daughters vanished, had died quietly in her sleep a week ago. Her grandson, too grief-stricken and too drunk to contribute what he knew since he had been right fond of his old granny, was unaware of the stranger's presence until he had left and it was too late by then.

Alfie-Bob had never been so glad to see anyone in his whole life, he gasped, almost weeping in his relief as Jack strode into the shanty where Alfie-Bob lived.

"Sweet Jesus, Jack, wheer in 'ell astha' bin? Engineer's bin lookin' fer thi' for days, hangin' about Whistler's Mary's place as though she were keepin' you 'idden from 'im on purpose. Bloody 'ell, the lies I've told fer thee . . ."

"Thanks, Alfie-Bob, tha'll not regret it." Jack barely glanced at his thankfully liberated deputy, his eyes quite blank, Alfie-Bob thought, unfocused almost, like those of a new born infant. Not that Alfie-Bob had had much to do with newborn infants but May's sister had one and its unblinking, unseeing gaze was very much like the one Jack cast about him.

"Wheer's tha' bin, lad? It's a bloody week an' more an' 'ow I kept that bloody lot goin' tha'll never know . . ."

"I said thanks, Alfie-Bob, an' I'll not forget it."

"Bloody 'ell, is that all tha've ter say after what— "

"I'll see thi' right, Alfie-Bob, so let's say no more."

The room was filled with navvies, for this was what was known as their "knock-off" Sunday, the one Sunday in perhaps three or four when they did not work. They sprawled about on rough benches watching as others played cards on the dirt floor, hooting and shouting as money changed hands. A boy near one of the windows was using the light in an attempt to mend a pair of boots and, clustered about several large barrels of beer, half a dozen men waited impatiently for the old woman who tended to the hut to serve them their ale.

On the far wall of the shanty were rows of bunks, one on top of the other with barely enough room between for a man to slither in to sleep. Navvies dozed in them, a few smoked peaceful pipes, the scene so placid it was hard to believe that it needed only one word, or a glance from one to another the recipient did not care for and the whole room would explode into uproar. There were dogs, muzzles resting on paws, eyes and ears restlessly twitching, almost purring as cats might, while rough, tender hands smoothed their coats, for the navvieman loved his dog which he kept for fighting or poaching. More than one of the animals were bitches and their casual coupling produced litters of puppies, most of which squeaked and skylarked in the general confusion.

There was a rough dresser of sorts and an enormous table, cupboards and pots and pans, and a fireplace where the old woman cooked each man's grub. A vast pot simmered on it with several strings hanging from the sides into the liquid it contained and on the end of each string would be Brown Punch's bacon, Little Tom's pound of beef, or Tar Sailor's "taters and cabbage", all cooking in the same greasy water. The woman knew exactly which belonged to who and if she didn't, she'd soon learn!

Half a dozen guns hung on the wall and only the men to whom they belonged would dare to touch them.

"That's all very well, Jack," Alfie-Bob ventured, not recognising the danger he was in, "but this is my job as well as thine an' I reckon I'm owed some bloody explanation."

Jack sprang to his feet, the tension in him so tight and explosive several of the dogs lifted their heads and growled warningly.

"I owe thee nowt', lad, so best get off me back," he snarled, his fists clenched, his stance that of a prize fighter. His lips curled back from his bared teeth and the men in the room grew silent and drew themselves in carefully, ready for what was shaping up to be a fight. Jack Andrews was not a brawler, not now, not since Racer and Billyo had put him off the line for a couple of months last back end. He kept himself pretty much to himself and was left alone but it was known that he could look after himself nevertheless. He avoided any situation which might develop into fisticuffs, barely drank his allotted beer and had never been seen drunk, but now it seemed something had made him madder than a maddened bull and Alfie-Bob was cowering away from him like a frightened babby!

"Nay, Jack, I meant nowt, lad," they heard him babble and they all began to relax, disappointed, for it would have livened up their tedious Sunday no end, but at that moment a voice from the doorway snapped all heads in that direction, including Jack's.

"Well now, will yer look at young Jack an' with 'is fists up an' all. Tis a sight ter warm the cockles of me heart, so tis, but sure an' what does he mean ter do wi' 'em, I'd like ter know. Wipe 'is bum, or p'raps the snot in 'is nose?"

Racer strutted into the shanty, his little eyes gleaming, the flesh on his massive belly shaking as he laughed, winking at several men, but before he could say another word or even raise his own fists in self-defence, Jack was across the earth floor like a dancer, graceful, light, lethal and overjoyed to have some objective, some target on which to purge himself, at least for tonight, of his pain, his grief, his harrowing sense of loss.

He didn't know what to do to find her, that was the worst of it. He didn't know where to start. Tell him what town, what city she was in and he would comb it street by street until he found her. Give him the tiniest clue on which direction to take and if it cost him the rest of his life he would search until it ended. He had been up to the post office in Burneside before he returned to the camp. It was Sunday and the small shop where letters might be delivered and collected was closed but he had hammered on the door until the shopkeeper opened it. He had alarmed the man and badly frightened his pretty daughter with his feverish demand for a letter, *any* letter it seemed to her, and when there was none ready to land one on her pa in his mindless anguish.

Jack's fist struck Racer in the exact centre of his grinning face, smashing his nose to bloody pulp and lifting him a foot from the floor, all eighteen stone of him, before laying him flat on his back.

They roared like animals. The dogs barked, the puppies howled and the old woman scuttled as fast as she could towards the door and safety. She knew what havoc these fights caused and the best place was out of it until their blood cooled, or they were all knocked senseless.

Jack Andrews was like a machine, a machine put together for the sole purpose of doing as much damage to Irish Racer as it could, his own defences impregnable. It was not particularly Racer who was his prey, his mark. Anyone would do really and if Alfie-Bob had not had the sense to back off it could have been him. Jack needed someone into whom he could sink his unassailable fists, his threshing feet, his teeth in the kind of brawling in which no rule counted and no blow was too foul.

Anyone who would take from Jack the despairing fear and sheer bloody frustration Sara's disappearance had caused in him. Any man who would receive and give back the powerful force of Jack's painful sense of futility, of defeat and panic and terror at what might have befallen her.

But Racer happened to be there. Racer it was who had deftly touched the nerve which had released Jack's killing rage and way back in the far reaches of his mind was the picture of Racer putting out a filthy hand to the girl Jack worshipped. Though he had sworn it was over; that he, that day, had done his best in his defence of her and would put the incident from which he still bore scars behind him and move on, with Sara, he was male, a male animal whose mate had been threatened and now the memory of it came back with the explosive power of a howling hurricane.

Jack knocked Racer down again and again. Every time he

got up he knocked him down again. Every time he was hauled up, or was goaded up by the men whose own bloodlust was raised to fever pitch by Jack's deadly and cold demolition of the man not one of them in the camp had ever beaten. Racer was over thirty, but strong, strong as one of the Shire horses which pulled the waggons. In fact Racer had himself pulled a waggon up a sharp incline for a bet once and the waggon had been loaded with muck at the time!

"Kill 'im . . . kill 'im . . . kill 'im," they chanted in unison, swaying as one man, guffaws of senseless laughter each time Racer was put down again, an avid hush as he once again struggled to his feet. There were hoarse yells of triumph as one of Racer's fists skidded off Jack's cheekbone, removing the flesh, the blood from it whipping them up to a crescendo where they themselves longed to be in on the mutilation and murder. They cried out in unison, one single throaty roar.

"Gerrim, Jack . . . hang on, boy . . . that's it, Racer . . . good lad, Jack . . ." depending on where their loyalties lay, the sick excitement of blood-letting, of one man slowly beating to death another setting them to howling and swaying as one being.

They were dragging an almost unconscious Racer to his feet, ready to fling him back at Jack. Both of them were covered in blood, most from Racer when, for no reason they could see, Jack Andrews turned away. Simply turned away. Racer hung like a man crucified, a "mate" on each arm and another at his back. His eyes were almost closed in the pulpy mass of his face and he moaned feebly, his brain battered to the mindless stupor of a wounded animal. Had the men let go of him he would have sunk to his knees.

"Jack . . . what's up, Jack?" they howled. "Tha've finished 'im, lad, all but anyroad. Come on, Jack, kill 'im . . . kill 'im . . . kill 'im."

But it had gone now, that murderous, senseless need to beat his fists against something. To hurt, not Racer but himself in an attempt to alleviate the devastating events of the past week. It had all been emptied out of him for the moment, that hatred of the fates which had separated him from his love. Empty. He was empty and would remain so until Sara was found. There was nothing in him now but a desire to lie down and fall into a state of unconsciousness so deep he would think of nothing, suffer nothing, remember nothing.

He needed oblivion, a black hole into which he would fall and drag about himself; a hole in which he might for a few hours erase his torment.

Where was she, Sara?

Part Two

12

Sara bent her head to her sewing and bit the thread neatly with her small white teeth. She replaced her needle in the pincushion beside her, removed her thimble, placing it with the pincushion in the tidy way her mother had taught her, then laid the length of velvet flat on the table. She smoothed the finished seam, studying it for flaws. When she was satisfied that there were none she put on her thimble again, took up another length of velvet and began to tack it with even stitches, no longer than a quarter of an inch, to the first. She used a special soft thread so that when the time came to pull it out, since it was a temporary stitch, it would not break the fabric in the process. Every stitch she took, every draw of the thread, every movement of her needle was done as her mother had shown her, for though tacking was not permanent she knew the final appearance of the garment depended on the care with which it had been prepared and tacked.

She was making a skirt, not for herself, of course, and not a separate skirt to be worn with a separate bodice but one which would, when she and Alice returned it to Miss Brewer in Concert Street, be attached to its own bodice, that which Miss Brewer and her handmaidens would make on the premises of Miss Brewer's dressmaking establishment. Skirt-making involved a great many long, straight seams which demanded little skill and could be run up without reference to the wearer and so they were given out to freelance needlewomen who made them up at a fraction of the cost it would take Miss Brewer's girls to do. Freelance needlewomen were ten a penny, not just in Liverpool but in every part of the country, hard pressed to find enough work to support themselves and it was only because there were two of them living as cheaply, almost, as one, that Alice and Sara managed.

Sara arched her supple young back, lifting her arms above her head and stretching, then stood up to move slowly across the room. She stared without interest from the window into the square below, watching as a lone sandwich-board man, a placard on his back and another on his front, plodded round the perimeter of the square. The message he gave to its inhabitants was too far away for Sara to read but she continued to watch him apathetically.

It was bitterly cold, a January cold with a thin film of white hoar frost coating the pavement, the cobbled roadway, the worn grass in the centre of the square, every branch of the denuded trees and the rusted iron railings which enclosed it all. There was no one else about, not even one of the feral cats which roamed the area, foraging when they could from the rubbish which festered in gutters and down every back alley. Those who lived in Abercromby Square, mostly in "rooms" or merely in one room, since most of the houses had been given over to lodgings, were decent, hardworking clerks and shop assistants, needlewomen like themselves and even one or two professional gentlemen but none was to be seen today as they went about their business in town.

Sara's eyes, unfocused and lustreless, continued to watch the weary progress of the sandwich-board man as she cast her mind back to that day in August when they had come here. She had followed without question when Alice had led her where Reggie's finger had pointed, past the rows of hansom cabs which lined the roadway outside the station and left into Mount Pleasant. She remembered the small rising of her spirits as she had studied the advertisements on the railway station walls, and the feeling as they rose even higher when they moved into the busy thoroughfare, though it had not lasted for longer than it took to walk the street's length. But coming from the rural peace of Wray Green, the walk along Mount Pleasant had been a novelty which, despite her grieving anxiety for Jack, brought a flickering smile to her pale lips, for she was only young. There were street musicians, hawkers, flower-sellers, knife-sharpeners, dark-skinned men with dancing bears from which she hastily averted her pitying gaze. There were gibbering, grimacing monkeys in velvet suits, and performing dogs. A blind man played a penny whistle, a piercingly sweet tune Sara recognised as "Greensleeves" and memory had knifed her as Jack's face swam into her vision, cutting out all others. Jack singing lustily, slightly off key but sweet and deep, his eyes holding hers, his hand hidden in the folds of her full skirt, holding hers, the lovely crackle and snap of the fire, the melodious tinkle of the highly polished piano in which the flames from the candles had been reflected. Papa's face somewhat shadowed as memories plagued him, Dolly beating time on the arms of the chair, the marmalade cat bouncing indignantly on her lap to the same rhythm.

Jack . . . Papa . . . Dolly . . . all three gone, her own heart ready to break with the pain of it. She had been hurt and lonely and frightened but Alice had plucked at her sleeve, drawing her on, her own face bleak and expressionless. There was a hurdy-gurdy man, she remembered, and about him were a group of barefoot, pitifully thin scarecrows, children with enormous eyes in pinched faces, shuffling in a parody of a dance, but when she had put her hand to her reticule with the intention of throwing a coin or two into the man's hat, for surely these people were in worse straits than she and Alice, Alice had snatched her away quite violently.

"Don't be silly, Sara. We haven't money to be giving away to every beggar who asks us, for heaven's sake. We might be beggars ourselves soon. And keep a firm grip on your bag for there are some very shifty-looking people about in this crowd. You don't want to be wearing just what you have on for the next few months, do you, which you will if you lose it. And stay close to me."

"Ally, please, Ally . . ." but Alice grabbed her savagely by the arm, unconcerned with Sara's shock and confusion, her alarm at the drastic change which had torn apart her safe world, her fear for Jack and Dolly, her panic at the stampede with which Alice had got them away from Wray Green.

"It's no good dawdling about, Sara," she snapped. "We have to find Abercromby Square and if it's not suitable . . . well, we shall just have to keep on looking. Now then, there's the end of Mount Pleasant so that must be Oxford Street."

The noise was deafening. The scrape and ring of iron-rimmed wheels on cobbles, shouts and cries which made the two girls flinch nervously together since they had no idea what they meant. The further away from the town centre they got, more children screamed in play down every street and poorly clad women lolled in doorways, staring in some astonishment at the two elegant ladies who stepped so daintily past their narrow, tiny-windowed homes.

There were several fine buildings on Mount Pleasant, one at the corner of Oxford Street proclaiming itself to be the Medical Institution, its stone front consisting of six Ionic columns and pilasters. In it was a lecture room, a library and a museum. It would be a splendid place in which to spend any free time they might have, Alice declared in satisfaction.

Sara did not care. She barely glanced at the sign advertising its wonders, trudging wearily, blindly behind the upright figure of her sister.

Abercromby Square had seen better days but the houses were superior to those they had observed, row upon row of them, every one identical to its neighbour, which cut away on each side of the main road. Spreading from the centre of the town like a fan, these streets contained a dense mass of houses over which hung a low, broad pall of dun-coloured smoke. Dull, monotonous ugly streets in which dwelled the poor, but Abercromby Square had managed somehow to cling to its late eighteenth-century respectability. The houses were tall and symmetrical, what were known as "town houses", terraced but well built by their previous prosperous owners and were meant to last. The kitchens were placed in the narrow semi-basement and lit only by an area light and the main floor was raised some feet above the level of the pavement. There was a short flight of steps up to the front door, to the right of which was a narrow sash window. Above this window was another with a tiny, wrought-iron balcony and above this two more on different floors, the top one in the steep roof. Every house round the square was exactly the same except in its degree of disrepair, but number seven, which they found after enquiring at several doors, was comparatively well kept and Alice viewed it with approval. It would do for now. She lifted the hem of her jade green skirt and climbed the steps.

There was no door knocker so she hammered with her gloved fist on the panel of the door, turning to look about the square as she waited, signalling brusquely to Sara to keep her eye on the carpetbags since there were more than a few curious passers-by.

Reggie's Aunty Lil was considerably startled when she opened her front door, the one her George did his best to kick down from time to time, to find two beautifully dressed young ladies on the other side of it. She was usually quick witted – well, she had to be with a chap like George, whose temper was uncertain, for a husband – quick tongued as well, but both her wit and tongue deserted her at that moment for, as she was to say later to her next-door neighbour, Mrs Green, she'd never been so flabbergasted in her life.

Well, who wouldn't be, but she was vastly intrigued. She had been letting her rooms for years now, to anyone who could pay the rent, and on time, but she did draw the line somewhere so what was she to make of these two? They wouldn't have looked out of place in one of the fashionable shops in Bold Street, she told Mrs Green. It was not that her rooms were in any way unsuitable, even for these two. They were clean and respectable, just as she was, but she was not used to ladies. Mrs Green would know what she meant. Not ladies like these, at any rate. Now and again, when she was really on her uppers, when her George was off on the other side of the world on some sailing ship or other and her money had run out, she'd been forced a time or two to let her rooms to ladies of a certain profession but the minute George was home she turned them out. For one thing, he'd have been dipping his wick wherever it was available to him and for another she didn't like whores, not really. She'd rather have gentlemen any day of the week but these two . . . well!

For a moment it crossed her mind that perhaps these two were whores, of the highest rank, of course, but then if that were the case what were they doing on the doorstep of her establishment? The moment the woman, the older, frosty-faced one, opened her mouth she established her status.

"I believe you have rooms to let," she said icily, her manner implying that she was doing Lily Canon a favour by asking.

Lily could be icy when she wanted. She was not taking any lodgers, she said, since her George had left her with a few bob and she only let her rooms when she was skint, though she did not voice this last out loud. Sorry, she added, still eyeing them both in amazement, then, her curiosity overcoming her, went on, "How did yer gerrup this far?" since she was a fair way out of town.

"Reggie sent us," Alice answered haughtily, though she

badly wanted to put out a hand to prevent this woman from closing the door in her face. She looked beyond her into the long, clean, linoleum-covered hallway which led to what appeared to be a cosy sitting-room in which a good fire could be heard crackling.

"Reggie? Reggie 'Oo?" Lily Canon asked suspiciously, peering through the half-opened door.

"I'm afraid he didn't give us his surname, did he, Sara?" Sara stared blindly at nothing and did not answer and it was perhaps at that moment that Lily Canon began to weaken. She was such a lovely child, defenceless somehow, pale and exhausted, Lily could see that and how would she fare with only this shrew to comfort her? They were obviously sisters but what a difference there was between them, not just in expression but in manner. One so bold and haughty, the other, the little one, like a whipped child. She didn't know why she described her as the "little one" for they were much of a height but the one who did all the talking gave the appearance of being the taller.

"Reggie did say you were his aunt," Alice went on, lifting her head and thinning her mouth to show she did not care for being kept standing on the doorstep.

"Oh, that Reggie." Lily Canon allowed the door to open a fraction. She crossed her arms on her full bosom, narrowing her eyes as she studied the girl at the bottom of the steps.

"Well, I might just have a room and then I might not. It depends."

"On what?"

"On whether you're in work and can pay me rent."

"Now listen to me, Mrs . . . er . . ."

"Canon."

"Mrs Canon. My sister and I have enough money to give you a . . ."

At that moment the little one raised a weary head and looked directly into Lily Canon's shrewd eyes and though Alice was always sincerely to believe that it was her own persuasive, firm approach that made Lily Canon change her mind, it was not that at all, but the expression in the cloudy sea green eyes of her young sister.

Sara felt it, felt the lessening of the chill. Mrs Canon had a look about her that Sara liked and which gave her a glimmer of hope in this hopeless mess her life had become. Mrs Canon, though she was not Dolly, had a look of . . . well, not exactly warmth but something close which cheered Sara as nothing had on this long and dreadful day. The filthy tortuous train journey, the nerve-wracking moment on the railway steps when they had not known in which direction to go, the sights and sounds and smells – which were nothing like country smells – which had been inflicted on her. Was this to be her new home then? Was this it and was this woman to be . . . perhaps a new friend?

But Mrs Canon, it seemed, was not yet completely satisfied. There was some mystery attached to these two and she wanted to know more about them before she let them over her doorstep despite the sudden touching of her heart by the little one. She was fussy who she took in. Liverpool was a city of enormous contrasts, on one hand great wealth and on the other even greater poverty. There were merchants who, trading to every port that was accessible to them in their sailing ships, had garnered untold riches to themselves, their wealth creating more wealth. They lived in enormous mansions on Everton Brow with fine views over the river and the Cheshire hills, or in Toxteth amid the rural beauty of meadows and pastureland. They possessed beautifully dressed women, fine horses and carriages which carried them about the city like princes.

Then there were the poor, the indigent poor who lacked all means to avail themselves of a comfortable existence. They were, for the most part, unemployed, depraved drunkards and the decent folk of Liverpool were ashamed of their city's reputation for the worst crime rate in Britain. When work was to be had it was ill paid. Poverty and idleness bred crime and the "butty", the Nelson cake or "wet nelly", which was no more than a stale bun loaf soaked in treacle and hard as rock, and "taties" were the poor's staple diet. There was one ginshop to every forty persons and it was a common sight to see brutal men and black-shawled, bedraggled women fighting or fornicating in the very gutters.

There were lodging houses by the score, dozens in every poor street, where a foul bed might be had for a penny a night or where as many as thirty slept in the straw on a cellar floor.

Lily Canon's place was not like these. Lily Canon, or Lily Hall as she had been then, had been brought up in the spanking clean kitchen of her old granny's tiny cottage in Walton on the Hill. She had never known her own ma and pa and Granny hadn't said, but when burly George Canon came sniffing round – her granny's words – she had been unable to withstand his bull-like, amiable assault on her virginity.

Her granny's teaching had never been forgotten. Her and George, for all their enthusiastic coupling, had no children. With George at sea and herself at a loose end, she had taken in a lodger or two but not the sort who expected to pay a penny a night and sleep in straw. No, she was fussy. She wanted no whores. She wanted no trouble, renting her decent rooms to decent folk where possible, so what was she to make of these two, one like a pretty broken doll, going where she was taken, the other watching Lily with the bright-eyed sharpness of a pigeon which hopes for a crumb or two to fall at its feet?

"You say our Reggie sent yer?" she said at last, more to give herself time to study the pair of them than for any particular desire to know.

"That is correct, Mrs Canon."

"Great daft lummox he is, an' all." There was no animosity in her voice.

"He was very kind to us, Mrs Canon," the little one said right out of the blue and Lily Canon turned to stare at her. She'd a good heart at any rate, she thought, even if she was a bit mazed. The girl was looking over Lily's shoulder to the well-scrubbed linoleum on the hall floor, to the grimly polished wood of the banister rail and the heavily framed pictures on the wall which were Lily's pride and joy.

There was a striped tabby curled up on a rug in the sitting-room doorway. It raised its head to look at them indifferently, its own place assured, and in a cage out of sight a canary sang its heart out. Sara thought it sounded lovely, warm and inviting and homely, not grand but something like the kitchen in the house in Wray Green. Her eyes turned appealingly to Mrs Canon and though Mrs Canon's cautious expression did not alter she knew she could not resist this lovely, suffering young girl. She did not know why she suffered but it was enough that she did. To hell with the hoity-toity one. Lily Canon would soon put her in her place but the child . . .

"Well, 'appen he were," was all she said, never taking her eyes from Sara's. "He allus had an eye fer a pretty face."

"Mrs Canon, my sister and I have come a long way today"

– from one world to another, the little one's eyes said quite plainly – "and if you cannot take us in then we must look elsewhere." Alice lifted her arrogant shoulders and her cool green eyes crossed swords with the blackcurrant depths of Lily Canon's.

"Oh aye, an' where's that then?" still holding the little one's gaze.

"From Wray Green."

"Never heard of it."

"Are you to let us in or not?"

"Keep yer hair on, madam, an' wipe yer feet, if yer don't mind. I just scrubbed that step."

To Alice's confoundment Lily Canon swung wide the door, standing back to let them in, watching closely the dragging footsteps of the little one as she lugged the two carpetbags up the steps.

"'Appen yer'd like a cup o' tea before I show yer to yer room?"

It had taken almost three months to find a dressmaker who would give them even the poorly paid and undemanding work of sewing skirt seams and had it not been the Christmas season, one of the busiest times in the dressmaker's calendar, it is doubtful Miss Brewer would have considered them. She didn't like them. She didn't like them from the start. They were too elegant. Too attractive. Too well bred and far too stiff-necked, as she called it, meaning above themselves, to bow their shining heads beneath her repressive boot.

She had viewed them with suspicion from the start, her own neck stiff and unbending, her own chin raised as she studied them through the lorgnettes she affected. Her thoughts, which she prided herself on being able to keep hidden, were revealed quite plainly. Not that she had any need to hide them from these two for they were here seeking employment and their opinions meant nothing to her. Disapproval was written on her face and a certain amount of cool amazement, for never in all the years since she had set herself up in business as a milliner and dressmaker, and before that as an apprentice, had Miss Brewer seen such astonishing applicants for work.

Alice knew at once that they had made a mistake.

"We must wear our best winter outfits, Sara," she had said, "so that the dressmaker can see at once what we are capable of." But this woman was gazing at them as if she would dearly like to show them the door, and might have done so if she had not been on the lookout for a couple of temporary seamstresses, to see her over Christmas, though Alice was not to know this. Who did they think they were? her cold eyes asked them. They were dressed far above their station as would-be employees of hers, apeing their betters in a way their betters would not like. As she did not like. Sewing girls were the lowest of the low, only a couple of degrees above prostitutes, and they should know how to conduct themselves properly or they would soon find themselves without work, that's if they could get it in the first place. That meant being properly dressed in a circumspect gown of a dark colour, not flaunting oneself in vivid blues and greens and bonnets decorated with expensive silk roses. Who were they and how had they come by such outfits? Her expression said she feared the worst as she asked the question.

"We made them, madam."

"Miss Brewer, if you please."

"I apologise, Miss Brewer." Alice spoke through gritted teeth. Alice found it very hard to be subservient to these vulgar women who, because they were in business and therefore providers of employment, thought they could speak to Alice Hamilton as though she were a maidservant. She did not like it and she showed it, which was probably why they had been turned away from the doors of so many dressmaking establishments. If they could not obtain "piece-work" of some sort soon they would be forced to make the rounds of the factories where flannel jackets, trousers, buttonholing, shirt-making could be had through a "middleman" who took his cut of all that the seamstress earned. Low work, rough work with rough people, so now Alice did her best to smile politely and bow her head. She and Sara were already registered in what was known as the Distressed Needlewoman's Society, only just formed and which Alice had seen advertised in an old copy of the *Lady's Newspaper*. The society's aims were to retain a register of efficient hands in order to afford the trade, and others, seamstresses when required without expense to either party and it was through the society that the idea to make up skirts at home had been presented to them.

"Sara and I have always made our own clothes, Miss Brewer," she went on.

"You made them?" Miss Brewer clearly did not believe her.

"Oh, yes, Miss Brewer. Indeed everything my sister and I have on, except our boots, of course" – laughing, hoping Miss Brewer would do the same, which she didn't – "we made ourselves. Gloves, bonnets, the roses on our— "

"I find that hard to believe, miss," Miss Brewer snorted.

"It is the truth, Miss Brewer. Our mama taught us."

"Us?"

"My sister and I."

"Cannot your sister speak, Miss?"

"Oh yes, can't you, Sara?"

Alice was a bit worried about Sara. She stood or sat or was led wherever Alice took her, only coming to life to write long letters to that navvie. She took no interest in Alice's search for work, finding everything but the loss of Jack Andrews of little importance. But this was important right now and she did wish Sara would make some effort to please Miss Brewer since she could be charming when she chose. Elderly ladies liked Sara as she was sweet and good-natured, merry too, though not lately, but now she merely stared at a spot somewhere over Miss Brewer's shoulder as though waiting for the next horror to descend on her.

"Well, I supposed it is to be preferred to a chatterbox," Miss Brewer said reluctantly.

There were many dressmakers in Liverpool. At the top of the profession were the first-rate houses of fashion which catered to the well-to-do, the gentry, even the nobility. Business was conducted in some large detached house in a good part of town. Somewhere a client would be assured of having her horses and her carriage accommodated. She would call at the house to inspect their materials. She would be met at her carriage steps by a "showroom woman" who would lead her to one of five or six showrooms which would be lined from floor to ceiling with mirrors on its four walls. There would be expensive carpet on the floor and equally expensive curtains at the windows. An assortment of magnificent silks and satins and velvets would be displayed for her in every light and after much deliberation she would choose a gown or two in a colour she liked and would then be shown, with much fawning and fussing, to her carriage.

The moment she arrived at her own home a "first hand", the

élite of the dressmaking world, would follow on her heels to measure her for her gowns, bringing with her the materials she had chosen and from then on the customer would be waited on in the privacy and comfort of her own boudoir.

That was the world of the first-rate fashion house.

Miss Brewer was not of this order, nor was she at the opposite end of the scale where thousands of women fought to support themselves on any scrap of sewing they could find, but was somewhere in between, catering to the wives of the city's tradesmen, prominent gentlemen in their field but not of the "best" society. She had a small salon just around the corner from Bold Street in Concert Street, not a good address but near enough and Miss Brewer made a nice living out of it. Her women did most of the sewing on the premises, the intricate work which needed to be constantly supervised, but she followed the practice of many dressmakers of putting out the plain work to outworkers.

"What are you doing at the moment?" Miss Brewer asked haughtily.

"Nothing, miss— " She did not allow Alice to finish.

"And what experience have you had?"

"Well, none, as— "

"None! I'm afraid I only take on experienced sewers, or indentured apprentices who pay me a premium."

"But surely these gowns we are wearing will allow you to judge what we are capable of?"

"How can I be sure that you made them?"

Sara's colour flared as she realised the implication of Miss Brewer's word then she subsided again into the lethargy she had known for weeks now. She found she really didn't care if Miss Brewer thought them to be cheats and liars and it was only later as she walked back to Abercromby Square with Alice that she realised that the dressmaker had condescended to let her and Ally "try out" as skirt-makers.

She seemed to live in a world of shadows now. From the moment she got out of bed in the morning until she got back into it again she was wound up like a tight spring, her youthful stamina almost at its end and she felt as though her body were cruelly afflicted, as if the flesh of her face, her arms, her chest, her back, even the soles of her feet had been severely beaten. Her body ached with some strange malady and she was not to know that she was still deep in the shocked state her father's death, Jack's continued absence and the loss of her home had thrust her into. All the time at the back of her mind, in her heart where it sat like a stone, was her longing for Jack. What had happened to him? The catastrophic events which had occurred since she had received his last letter were ready to overwhelm her and she knew if she did not find some comfort soon she would go under. What was she to do without Jack? How did she come to be here in this nightmare without him? She would rather have gone into the workhouse with Dolly . . . Dolly who should not have been allowed to go there in the first place. Please, someone, please help me, help me, she prayed to a faceless, voiceless deity who seemed indifferent to her anguish, as Alice was indifferent. Alice cared only about their physical needs which were for sustenance and warmth and shelter and there was no one in Sara Hamilton's world to give her what she needed.

It was at that moment perhaps, as she began to realise that she was, to all intents and purposes, alone and unloved, that Sara began to throw off the mantle of shocked terror, though it would be some time before it became apparent. As Alice said to her a dozen times a day, they were among the lucky ones. They had the roof over their heads Alice craved, food in their bellies and a warm bed to sleep in at night.

As the weeks passed Sara told herself it would not be long. It would not be long, she promised silently to Dolly, to herself and to Jack. The moment she had some money she would take the train back to Wesham, whether Alice agreed or not, and fetch Dolly out of the workhouse, bring her to Liverpool. As soon as they had a proper job, she and Ally, with a decent wage they could save a penny or two; when they had a cosy place in which Dolly might live out her days in peace and comfort with those who loved her. Until Jack came.

Until Jack came! The three words were a litany, a supplication she chanted a hundred times a day. She was lost and bewildered without him, doing her best to make some sense of this dreadful muddle her simple life had become and on the fringes of it there was Jack, like a ghost, a lovely, dreamlike ghost which hovered just on the edge of her vision and she longed to indulge herself by drawing it in and weeping over it, studying it, holding it in her arms and warming herself with it. Jack, her man, her love, her heart. Why had he not yet come? What had happened to his letters? What had happened to her letters to him? Had they somehow gone astray, drifting aimlessly between Wray Green and the railway line to Kendal, lost in a vacuum, never to be read? Had they reached the post office in Oxenholme from where Jack told her he picked them up? Were they even now collecting dust in the postbox, the person who dealt with them pondering on the mystery of why they were not collected? Had Jack had an accident? Was he lying ill, perhaps already dead? Oh, dear God in heaven, no! no! She would feel it if . . . It was long weeks, she couldn't even remember how many, since she had heard from him and each day her heart broke a little more but she must not give up hope. Without hope she would die. He would come. He would come soon. But when?

She gazed stonily down at the sandwich-board man, watching until he disappeared from sight into Cambridge Street. She sighed, resting her forehead on the cold windowpane, then turned, drifting across the room to crouch by the small fire, warming her chilled hands. Ally would be back soon with some skirts they had been promised from Madame Hawkins in Bold Street but before that she must write to Jack. Tell him she loved him and waited for him and would never give up hope that he would come to her. She would tell him of all the letters she had written, not just to him but to strangers like the Benthams and the Armitages in Wray Green, influential people who might help her to find him, for she would never believe that he was truly lost to her. One day, when she had the money and had seen Dolly safely out of the workhouse, she would take the train to Oxenholme and look for him, she promised him in her letter but until then she prayed to some compassionate being to keep him safe. She loved him. She would always love him.

In a faraway place beyond Kendal Jack lay on the stony ground staring unblinkingly into the crumbling sod roof of a lean-to, his arms crossed beneath his head. There were sleeping forms about him, a woman and several children. It was cold. His own breath steamed about his head before dissipating into the black night and beneath his blankets he shivered slightly though it was not the cold that caused it.

Why hadn't Sara written? Why were there no letters from her? In *his* letters to her he had told her that she was in future to write to the general store in Burneside instead of

Oxenholme so why hadn't she done so? It was only a short time since he and his men had moved beyond Kendal from Oxenholme to Burneside but time enough for her to have received his new address and write to him there. Why had she not done so? Why had she not sent *her* new address to *him*? Where was she? *Where was she?*

A whisper escaped from between his lips, barely more than a sigh. A woman's name. A woman by the name of Sara and from his wide staring eyes tears ran into his hair.

Miles away in the small village of Oxenholme a man tutted irritably as he shuffled a pile of letters, more than two dozen and all addressed to the same man. The bloody things were getting on his nerves and surely he couldn't be expected to hang on to them for ever, could he? This was a post office not a storage place. He'd ask the post office official the next time he came round and if he said it was allowed he'd destroy the damn things and any more that came. Postmark Liverpool and the writing was that of an educated lady by the look of it but that was nowt to do with him. If folk couldn't be bothered to pick up their mail that was their lookout, wasn't it?

13

"An d'yer reckon you could still hear from him after all these months, my lamb?" Lily Canon's voice was warm with compassion, her face soft with her fondness for the little one, as she still called her privately, but her strong arms and hands thumped at the dough she was kneading as though it were the bugger who had deserted young Sara Hamilton.

Sara sighed, her head bent, the long shining braid of her hair lifting as her young breasts rose. She played idly with Lily's baking spoon, twisting it in nervous fingers, making patterns in the flour which Lily had spilled on the table.

"I can't give up, Lily. I just can't say to myself, 'Sara, you'll never see Jack again so forget him and get on with your life,' so I do the only thing I can and that is to write every now and again to people in Wray Green where he might still be looking for me and to the last postal address Jack gave me and hope he'll go back there. I shall have to give that up soon though, since he'll be a long way north of Kendal by now, almost to Windermere, I shouldn't wonder. That is . . ." She hesitated, her fingers gripping the spoon so tightly her knuckles turned white.

"That is . . .?" Lily prompted gently.

"That is if he's still alive, Lily. It's a dangerous job, being a railway builder and there are many accidents. My father was a doctor and was often called to the navvie site to patch up injured men." Sara's voice was softly despairing. "Oh Lily, I love him so much and I know he loved me the same way. I know it, so I just cannot understand why he has not written to me. I left a note with the people who took over our house."

"I know, lamb, yer told me."

"And I have written since to them asking them to give

him this address if he came to look for me. I've sent word to Dolly."

"I know, I know." Though Lily's voice was gentle her fist was not as she thumped it into the centre of the dough, making flour jump a foot into the air before it settled again. Men were bastards!

"But I've had no reply from her either and that worries me. She lent us her money to come here and I've begged and begged Alice to let me have a few shillings for the train fare so that I can go and fetch her since I know she'd be welcome and happy here with you. In one of your rooms, I mean."

"She would, queen."

"But Alice says we are still not settled enough, that's the word she used, to support Dolly as well as ourselves and Dolly is safe and comfortable where she is until we can fetch her. She, Dolly I mean, would be far happier here with us, don't you think so, Lily?"

"She would, queen," but of course Madam Hoity-Toity would be bound to have some good reason why her little sister could not have the few bob needed to bring the old lady out of the workhouse where she was costing Alice Hamilton nothing! Lily cordially detested Alice Hamilton and, if it were not for the lovely young girl who spent more and more time in Lily's cosy basement kitchen, would have turned her out months ago. Miss Hamilton didn't like it one bit, her sister wasting her time, as she put it, with Lily, and Lily had heard her say so deliberately to Sara in Lily's hearing, the rotten cow. A great one for the social graces was Miss Hamilton, as she insisted Lily call her, and for social divisions and though she and her sister had fallen on hard times that did not mean they should lower their standards by mixing with people who were beneath them. She made it plain to Lily exactly what her place was in their lives though this was Lily's house and they were Lily's lodgers who could be evicted at a moment's notice. Alice Hamilton paid her rent on time. She was quiet and respectable. She and the little one cooked their own food in the big room at the top of the house and ate it there as well, but the minute Miss Hoity-Toity left the house to deliver the beautifully made skirts, the lace-trimmed lawn camisoles, the white silk shawls embroidered with gold thread, the quilted silk petticoats, the frilled muslin underskirts and all the other exquisite garments Miss Brewer now allowed them to make for her, the big, cotton-lined basket she used to transport them on her arm, Sara was down the stairs quick as greased lightning, her sewing in one hand, her treasured sewing box in the other, curling up like a velvet-eyed kitten in Lily Canon's rocking chair by the fire.

Lily was of the opinion that Sara was starved of affection, of the warmth her father and the old woman she called Dolly had shown her. Her sister took care of her, told her where they were to go, what they should wear and eat. She was sharp with Sara though, prickly somehow, as though the child had something which Miss Alice coveted, though what it could be was beyond Lily for Alice was as pretty as a picture, fashionable, and turned heads wherever she went. Perhaps it was the gift her sister had for attracting people, men and women, to her with a sweet smile and a friendly word, a willingness to listen and with obvious interest when they spoke. Lily's friend Mrs Green said so, and when the coalman or the milkman caught Sara in Lily's kitchen, Lily couldn't get shut of them and it wasn't only her fair face which captivated them. They vied with one another to catch her eye, tickled pink when they got her to smile, like great overgrown schoolboys they were, and Lily often had to hide her own laughter behind her hand.

Yes, Sara Hamilton spent a great deal of her time in Lily's kitchen.

"It's warmer here," or, in the summer when the sun struck the roof directly above the big room at the top of the house, "it's cooler here," she would say, her smile shining hopefully, just as though she needed an excuse and Lily had got into the habit of making a few biscuits, gingerbread men, coconut macaroons, almond crunch for the sheer pleasure of watching Sara bite into them like a child and with the same relish. And she called her Lily, just as Lily called her Sara and Lily loved Sara just as though she were the child she herself had never had, though she wouldn't let madam know, of course. Madam was out now, gone to some place up near West Derby which was quite a walk with what she called "samples". Dozens of beautifully stitched garments, not to mention bonnets, the like of which Lily had never seen in her life. She and Sara had made them all, sewing for hour after hour when they had finished their "piece-work". They bought scraps of material from the market, lovely glowing silks and satins and velvets, fashioning flowers and gossamer decorations for hats, garments of lace which looked too delicate to be worn, dainty scraps of this and that, exquisite embroidery like cobwebs, gloves of lace and all placed in the big basket which had become Alice Hamilton's stock-in-trade.

Lily reached for a cloth and threw it over the dough. "There, that'll do for now, chuck. I'll let it rise until it swells an' in't meantime you an' me'll have a nice cuppa tea."

Sara sighed again, a sigh even deeper than the last, turning away from the table to watch Lily as she brewed the tea. Two heaped teaspoons in the big brown pot then a third for the pot itself, for Lily liked a good brew and saw no reason to stint herself. Her George had been home twice since the Hamilton sisters had moved in a year ago and like everyone else who met her he had taken a great fancy to the little one. So much so, instead of boozing most of it away in the Dog and Whistle on Walnut Street, he'd parted with enough money to keep Lily well provided for for months to come. She'd also rented two of her rooms to a couple of decent working girls. One, Abigail Mitchell, a twenty-four-year-old shop assistant at Anne Hillyard's Millinery and Baby Linen Warehouse in Bold Street, the second Matty Hutchinson, a nineteen-year-old seamstress, living "out" but who worked at the respectable establishment of the Misses Yeoland, again in Bold Street. With what George had left her and her three rents Lily Canon found herself well able to afford a fresh pot of tea, strong and sweet as she liked it, whenever she fancied it, instead of making the leaves do twice or even three times before they were thrown out.

Both Miss Mitchell, who was inclined to be reserved, and Matty who was not, cooked for themselves, leaving the house at what seemed the crack of dawn, for they both worked long hours, not returning, particularly Matty who Lily sometimes suspected of having two jobs, until well after dark. Miss Mitchell who, unlike Matty Hutchinson, had never begged Lily and Sara to call her by her first name, kept pretty much to her room, only walking out on a Sunday to Broad Green where her father had a small farm. Matty, on the other hand, was an orphan. Apprenticed to the Misses Yeoland at the age of fourteen, she had left the Blue Coat Hospital, or Blue Coat School as it was now called, with an education which many young females of good family might have envied. In 1709 when it was first opened Blue Coats was a charity school in which forty boys and ten girls were brought up and educated, but in almost one hundred and fifty years the number of orphaned pupils had grown to two hundred and fifty boys and one hundred girls. The girls, in their own wing built in 1817, were taught reading and writing and numbers, needlework, knitting and housewifery but, unlike most of the girls who were put out to service Matty, who was clever with her needle and had an eye for fashion, had been indentured to the Misses Yeoland and now, five years later, was almost a "first hand". She was pert, that's what Lily called her, but you couldn't help but like her. Tough as an old boot, though you'd not think so to look at her with her dark glossy curls and vivid, laughing blue eyes, and sharp as a tack. Cheeky in a likeable way which was why Lily said she was pert but she'd a good heart. She and Sara got on like a house on fire which didn't go down well with Miss Hoity Toity but over the last few months, ever since Matty came to live in Abercromby Square, bringing her bright and cheerful chatter, her unique and irrepressible belief that despite her poor beginnings life was meant to be lived to the full and damn the consequences, Sara had slowly emerged from the silence and stillness her father's death and that sod's desertion of her had thrust her into. It was only at times like this when she and Lily were alone, when the postman had once again gone by without a letter for Sara, that the little 'un slipped back into the melancholy state she had been in a year ago.

A year! Aye, just a year, Lily pondered as she and Sara sipped their tea, since Alice Hamilton had hammered so peremptorily on Lily Canon's door and would you look where her and Sara had got to since then, and, credit where it was due, it was all down to Alice Hamilton, and the long hours the pair of them had put in. That Miss Brewer, who Sara had once described as having a face on her like she'd swallowed vinegar, couldn't do enough for them now, for, though she hadn't told Alice, of course, her clientèle had grown considerably since the Hamilton sisters had begun working for her. The sheer artistry with which they produced exquisite garment after exquisite garment, each one as faultless as its predecessor, had brought a class of customer Miss Brewer had never known before and her worst nightmare was that the sisters might take their genius elsewhere. Tight-lipped and straight-backed, a bit like Miss Hoity-Toity herself by all accounts, now she not only allowed the two sisters to sew the straight seams on her skirts but, when she had realised the treasure of talent she had in her grasp and the efficiency and punctuality with which it was returned to her each day, had started them on the more intricate work her first hands did at the top of her tall, hot in summer, cold in winter house in Concert Street. She had begged them to move in, live in and had offered them quarters of their own, which was absolutely unheard of, but Alice, astute, shrewd and knowing her own worth, had refused. She wanted the freedom to sew for whom she liked, when she liked, though she did not tell Miss Brewer this. She had not forgotten Miss Brewer's contemptuous treatment of them last Christmas. She had plans which she divulged to no one, not even her own sister, and every penny they earned, apart from what was needed to house and feed them, was put carefully in the Union Bank, on the corner of Bold Street and Hanover Street, in *her* name.

Lily wondered what she was up to this cool September afternoon as she and Sara sat companionably before the fire, the tabby curled between them, the yellow canary singing its heart out in its cage by the scullery window. All dressed up she had been in a new autumn outfit the colour of a sunflower. Very simple as all the sisters' gowns were, but striking, especially with that coppery gold hair of hers. She had on a tiny bonnet in chocolate brown, the brim lined in the same colour and material as the gown, the crown swathed with rich chocolate ribbons of silk which tied beneath her small chin in a bow. She had looked quite ravishing, her slender figure swaying gracefully as she set off, basket on her arm, up towards Oxford Street where she turned in the direction of West Derby.

"I shall be home by five, Sara," Lily had heard her say briskly as she came down the stairs, drawing on her brown kid gloves, "and I shall expect to see that green fringed shawl well on its way to being finished when I return."

"Yes, Ally," Sara had answered dutifully, handing her the basket which she had carried downstairs for her and Lily wondered why it was the girl let her sister order her about as though she were a child. Because she acted like one, she supposed and yet she was seventeen now and surely must be considered a young woman? This business with the chap had damaged Sara Hamilton in some way and until she got over it, put it behind her and moved on she would never recover, in Lily's opinion. She needed another man to court her, someone to put the bloom of love in her cheeks, a glow to her clouded, sea green eyes, laughter in her voice but here she was, still brooding after all this time over some bloody navvie – *her* with a navvie – who probably never gave her a moment's thought. She was loyal, give her that and it seemed when her loyalties were offered she never withdrew them. Look how she was over this Dolly.

"I could lend yer t'money, queen," she said casually, just as though the thought had not been simmering in her mind for weeks now.

Sara looked up sharply, almost spilling her tea. Her rosy mouth fell open and she blinked.

"Pardon," she said, though Lily knew she had understood.

"You heard me, chuck. If yer want ter go up to wherever it is an' fetch the old lady here then I'll lend yer t'cash fer yer railway fare. In fact, I've a good mind ter come with yer. I've never bin on one of them railway trains an' I've a fancy ter try one before I die. What d'yer say? Shall we have us a ride up ter . . . where was it?"

"Wray Green," Sara answered automatically, her mind still floundering in the first joyful unsteadiness Lily's words had thrust on her. She couldn't take it in, not all at once and she needed a moment or two to analyse the implication of what Lily was offering her.

The painful memory of that last day, a year ago now, when Dolly had been carted off – yes, that was the word, carted off – with the boxes and the furniture which were to be sold, treated as though she were no more than they were, to be placed in the workhouse until Sara and Alice went back to retrieve her, was a painful one. Dolly whom she had loved and trusted. Dolly who had loved and trusted her and it had been an abrasive sore in Sara's flesh, one which had constantly had its scab knocked off each time she thought of her, which was every day. How could she have allowed it, was her perpetual thought, allowed Alice to do such an awful thing and her only excuse was that she really had not known what she was doing at that time. Her mind had been filled with guilt and her heart with grief. The two had warred with one another, striving for her attention and grief for Jack, for Papa, had won. Grief had stunned her, forcing her into a cold and silent place where only heartache existed.

But that was a year ago and though she still longed constantly, enduringly for Jack, time had dulled her pain, letting in anxiety and guilty shame for what had been done to Dolly. She had allowed Alice to have the upper hand, obeying her, believing her when she said they could not afford even the railway fare, let alone to support Dolly and yet she and Alice worked a twelve-hour day, seven days a week so where was the money they earned? She knew how much rent they paid and she accompanied Alice when they went to St John's Market for provisions. She had heard Alice ask "How much?" and had heard the stallholders answer. She herself had run downstairs to pay the man who delivered the coal and yet not once had she questioned their financial arrangements, leaving it all to Alice.

And yet surely Alice would not ... would not ... what? Lie to her? Cheat her? Keep from her the true state of their finances? Delude Sara into believing that they could not bring Dolly here because of shortage of money when it was not true?

And if she did could Alice be blamed for had she, Sara Hamilton, showed the slightest interest in it all? The answer was no!

She looked up into the shrewd, blackcurrant eyes of the woman opposite, the woman on whom, she realised now, she had come so much to depend over the last few months. She had found warmth, affection, a sense of security she had lost a year ago, even laughter, for when Lily and Matty, both Liverpool born and bred with the Liverpudlians' strong sense of the comic, got together with their wisecracks, who could help but laugh at them? Not that Ally knew, of course, she admitted, then wondered why she felt the need to add "of course". Why shouldn't she make friends with Lily and Matty? They were both decent women. Not ladies she knew Ally would be the first to point out, but big-hearted and generous, as Lily was proving with this offer of a loan.

But Alice wouldn't like it. Borrowing money from ... from an inferior, as she would see it, but then if Ally wouldn't or couldn't loan her the train fare, yes, loan it, then surely she had the right to take advantage of what a friend offered? A friend! Lily!

It was like watching a chick emerge from a shell, Lily decided. Her old gran had kept hens and Lily had often seen their offspring hatch. The shell beginning to shiver into fine, hairline cracks. Slowly at first then more quickly as the hatching chick gathered the strength to peck its way out. A tiny hole no bigger than the nail on her little finger, the shell first then the membrane within it. The hole growing bigger until, with a triumphant flourish, the head of the chick emerged. Peck, peck, peck and in even greater triumph the shell broke in two and out staggered the bedraggled chick.

Sara sat up and in her eyes was illuminated a flare which Lily could only describe as intense excitement. Yes, that was what it was, though Lily had never seen it before, not in the little one, at least. She made some small movement as though, having been held still for so long, her neck was stiff, then she squared her shoulders, pushing out the lovely swell of her young breasts and Lily had time to be thankful that the coalman or the man who delivered the milk were not present.

"Go to Wray Green?" Sara said unbelievingly, loudly, defiantly even, as though Lily had suggested a trip to the moon but she looked so alive Lily felt the joy of it flood through her veins.

"An' why not, queen?" she answered, pretending unconcern. "We could go up to that last place your Jack worked at, I forget the name though yer've told me a dozen times. Ask around a bit, like, an' then, on't way back pick up the old lady an' fetch— "

"Lily, oh Lily, do you mean it?" Sara's face flamed like the sky at the rising of the sun, a glow as deep and lovely and vivid as the sun itself and Lily marvelled at the outburst of sheer unadulterated ecstasy which poured from her. "Go to Oxenholme? Speak to the person in the post office? Find out what happened to my letters . . . were they picked up and if so, when?"

"We could even follow't railway line ter where it fetched up if yer— "

"Lily, dear God in heaven, Lily." Without allowing Lily to finish, Sara sprang to her feet, erupting from her chair like a cork coming from a bottle. "You mean travel on the line – the Kendal to Windermere – where Jack was working when he last wrote?" She stormed from her chair to the door and back again, seriously upsetting the tabby who swished her tail indignantly. She was like an explosion about to happen, emotions seething inside her, emotions of wonderment, of awe, exhilaration, a great upheaval of rapture and gladness which threatened to propel her into a convulsion of either tears or laughter. Backwards and forwards she went, her hands clutching at one another, her head first bent in deep thought, then uplifted in a transport of delight. She talked to herself, words without meaning except to her, in which the name of Jack Andrews was repeated again and again, clapping her hand to her brow as thoughts occurred to her, cupping her flaming cheeks with trembling hands as others came to chase the first.

Lily watched her and said nothing. Indeed for once she was incapable of speech. They stuck in her throat, the words she would have spoken to Sara, words of care, words of caution, words of a love that was deep and wordless, as strong feeling often is. Jesus Christ, she wanted to make this lass happy but was she building up her expectations, giving her something false to cling to, to hope for? She had spoken on an impulse. Not about Dolly who could easily be transported to Lily's house in Abercromby Square, but about the lad Sara loved and was she about to stir up a bloody hornets' nest and all for nothing?

Alice Hamilton thought so and said so in no uncertain terms when she returned, but then had Lily expected anything else? Sara didn't even allow her sister to put a foot on the bottom tread of the stairs to their room before she danced on light feet out of Lily's kitchen, up the stairs and into the narrow passage which led to the front door, casting about her sister like a net, an excited jumble of words, words in no order, words which made no immediate sense.

"I've something to ask you, Ally. No! Tell you and I hope it won't upset our working arrangements too much. A couple of days that's all, I should think, no more, three at the most. After all I haven't had a day off since we started with Miss Brewer, except Christmas Day which everyone has. I'm not claiming that I should have one and not you, of course, but surely it's not too much to ask, though I hardly think it fair to expect Lily to pay for it, do you? We must have some spare cash after all this time . . ."

Alice stared, open-mouthed and speechless.

". . . and though Lily offered . . ."

Alice turned her bewildered gaze to Lily who had come to stand at the top of the stairs.

". . . so I felt in all fairness, since I have worked as hard as you and without any wage— "

"Wage!" Alice's voice came out like the croak of a frog.

"Mmm, so we thought tomorrow, or at least I did and then, after we have been to Windermere if there is no . . . oh, for pity's sake, Ally, what I'm trying to say is if we can find no trace of Jack . . ." She blinked rapidly to clear the crystal droplets which hung on her lashes before splashing to the bodice of her plain grey working dress.

"Jack?"

"Yes, Lily thought that there might be some message, some word at Windermere." Lily had thought no such thing but she merely shifted her weight from one foot to the other, like a prize fighter expecting a swing to the jaw.

"Although the Kendal to Windermere must be finished by now, of course, and then there is Dolly, you see. Surely we earn enough to bring her here where Lily says she can have the room at the front of the house. She could sit on that little balcony and watch the people go by. On a nice day, naturally, and I wouldn't mind running downstairs to bring her food but the . . . oh dear, I don't mean to sound selfish, Ally, really I don't but the . . . this journey . . . if it led to Jack and I . . ."

Alice Hamilton came to cold, rock-like life then, turning her terrifying, glittering gaze from Sara to Lily and back again, her eyes narrowing like those of a fighting cat caught in an alley by another. Her face had lost every vestige of its colour in her icy rage. She lifted her imperious head, her only sign of lost control the force with which she flung the basket of samples to the floor where its contents spilled in brilliant disarray all over Lily's clean linoleum. Alice didn't seem to care.

"Sara Hamilton and you, Mrs Canon" – her overpowering gaze turned in Lily's direction – "I've never heard anything so ludicrous in all my days, really I haven't and I can only lay the blame for it at your door, since my sister would not have thought of it by herself. The idea of throwing good money away on that . . . that clod who has probably had a dozen girls since he left Wray Green."

Sara turned whiter than the snowy apron about Lily's waist

and made a small distressed sound in the back of her throat but she kept steady.

"Chasing after him like some common, low-bred strumpet. I'm quite appalled and Mama and Papa would be the same. We have more work than we can manage and you chatter on about journeys like a child who has no conception . . . Really, you must be out of your mind, or influenced by this woman and it's high time we moved away to a better and more respectable place."

Lily stood stolidly beside Sara and willed her own considerable strength into her, entreating her wordlessly to stand up to this frigid, cold-blooded bitch who was doing her best to drain every drop of life from her. To make her into a carbon copy of herself, unfeeling, unloving, detached from any warmth or friendship, relying only on Alice Hamilton and if she did, if she forced Sara, through her own determined will power, to retreat into that calm shell she had languished in for the past year it would be the end of her.

"Alice, you cannot mean to— " Sara still tried to make herself heard.

"Whatever I mean to do it is for your own good, Sara. And mine too, naturally. Only this afternoon I spoke to— "

"But what about Dolly? We promised her . . ."

"And we will when the time is right, Sara." Alice smiled, relaxing as she perceived the familiar hesitation in her sister who had always been obedient and dutiful. "When we are better established in our own place."

"But . . ."

"Don't make things more difficult for us, my dear, by trying to do too much too soon. We just cannot afford it, not right at this moment. All in good time and then you and I will take the train to Wray Green and bring Dolly back to live with us. This will not be our permanent home, Sara. Surely you know that? Mama's daughters living like this?" Her smile widened and she waved a contemptuous hand to indicate the inferior state of Lily Canon's spotless and respectable hallway and it was this, this slur on the home, on the habits of the woman who had shown Sara more affection in a year than Alice had in a lifetime, that abruptly checked Sara from stepping back defeated from her sister's reasonable logic.

She straightened up and her face moved from uncertainty

to coldness and beside her Lily felt the thankful relief flood through her.

She'd done it! Sara Hamilton had done it, or was about to. The first time was the hardest and this would be hard, a violent clash of wills which Sara would find almost impossible to withstand. There was no doubt who was the stronger, at the moment, and Alice Hamilton, though Lily found it hard to admit, genuinely thought she was doing the best for her little sister and herself, and those who firmly believe they are in the right are the most difficult to defeat but Sara was going to have a stab at it. Pray God she could manage it.

"I'm sorry, Ally" – her voice was high, like that of a frightened child who is defying an adult – "but I must disagree with you. I cannot bear to think of Dolly in that . . . that place a moment longer. I am ashamed."

"Don't be silly, Sara. She is well and comfortable."

"How do you know? Have you heard from her?"

"You know I have not and I would be obliged if you would pick up those garments, put them in the basket and bring them upstairs. We will continue this discussion in private."

Ice froze every word Alice spoke and her face was as sharp as winter, carved from hoar frost and Lily saw Sara shiver.

"There is nothing to discuss, Alice, really there isn't. You see I cannot go on with my life until I have – what is the word? I don't know – but I must satisfy myself that Dolly is happy and that Jack is gone . . . for ever. I cannot rest or even function properly until I have done that. I promise you that if Dolly is content where she is I will leave her there though I would much rather bring her home. As for Jack, if he's gone from me, if I cannot find him, or any trace of him, I will accept what you say about him, though I will find it terrible. I will do my best to make a life, on my own, without him." Her voice broke and Lily felt her own throat close up. "So if you won't or can't give me the money I need then I will accept Lily's kind offer and borrow it from her. And in future, Ally, I would prefer it if whatever we earned was shared between us. I will pay my half of the expenses out of *my* wage. Now then, shall we take the basket upstairs?"

14

Jack Andrews jumped lightly from the still-moving train, his tall, well-muscled body carrying him at a half run towards the ticket collector on Oxenholme railway station.

He no longer wore the traditional dress of the navvie but had on a good quality navy cloth overcoat with a black velvet collar, light grey trousers, narrow in the leg and strapped beneath highly polished black boots. In his hand he carried a tall beaver hat and stuffed in the pocket of his topcoat was a pair of kid gloves which he could not quite bring himself to put on. He looked like a young gentleman of breeding, his chestnut hair neatly trimmed and brushed to a smooth gleam. He was clean-shaven, his flesh sun-tinted still, though he no longer worked in it for fourteen hours at a stretch.

It was a pleasant autumn day and Jack had his coat open and thrown back to reveal his jacket which was the same shade of grey as his trousers. Beneath that, perhaps as a legacy from his days as a navvie, was a vivid peacock blue and green waistcoat. Swathed about the strong column of his brown throat was a snowy cravat which frothed down his shirt front.

The street outside the railway station was lined with yellow beech and the broad spread boughs of sturdy oak. There was a hansom cab, drawn by a droop-headed hack just outside the station entrance, the cabbie appearing to be half asleep but with an eye still on the prospect of a fare. A dog barked frantically further up the street, the cat it had treed hissing venomously above its head. Sunshine dappled the forecourt, turning Jack's hair to dark, burnished copper but he did not put on his hat.

He handed his ticket to the collector at the gate then

stepped out into the forecourt, turning to watch the train he had just left being whistled off by the stationmaster who held his flag in readiness. Jack paused, even now still oddly elated by the fact that the train was to run, as so many trains did, on track he himself had helped to lay. Only last year he and Whistler, Alfie-Bob and Algie-One-Step had laboured on this very spot, levelling the ground, blasting through rock, working in constant danger from explosions, from runaway waggons, from rockfall which buried men alive, from careless handling of trucks such as the one which had finished off poor old Whistler. A year ago, or a little over, they had finished this parcel and marched jubilantly off beyond Kendal, he and his gang, to the meadowland there, and then on to where the first considerable incline of the hills of south Lakeland began. To the parcel he had successfully bargained for and where deep cuttings were to be made. Hell's teeth, that had been bloody hard work, he mused, an expression of remembered adversity on his face.

Posts and rails were erected by the engineers, marking the intended line of the railway and Jack's men had carted away the upper surface of the earth until the hill was laid open and a "gullet" dug, a little cutting just large enough to take the row of waggons which were to carry the earth away. The "muck" excavated was to be used to build an embankment further along the line.

Deeper and deeper the cutting grew, and more and more dangerous became the work. At intervals along its length planks were laid almost vertically up the steep sides, with a horse and pulley at the top of each one, hauling the barrows of muck from the depths. "Making the running", as it was called, was the most spectacular of navvie work and Jack had done his share in his years as a navvieman. You had to be strong. A rope was attached to the barrow and to the navvie's belt, running up the cutting at the side of the plank of wood and then round the pulley at the top where it was fastened to the horse. When the barrow was filled to capacity a signal was given to the man in charge of the horse and the navvie making the running was drawn up, balancing the barrow in front of him.

The success of the venture depended on the steady pulling of the horse and the strength and balance of the navvie, for when he reached the top and tipped his muck he had to reverse the process with the empty barrow but going down backwards. Sometimes the horse slipped or faltered. Sometimes the plank was slicked with wet mud and the navvie fell off, throwing his barrow frantically away from him.

Jack smiled reminiscently at the images which came to him of men who were thrown down the slope but became used to it, himself included, springing up after each tumble, more sure-footed, grinning with relief to find no damage done. Only one man on the track had been killed.

Jack's stern young face softened and the blunt angle of his jaw relaxed. He had reached full manhood now at the age of twenty-three with a wide back and muscular forearms which strained the seams of his good coat. He was large, powerful and dark, his hair a deep shade of chestnut, his body shaped by the physical adversity of his work, well over six feet tall, broad in proportion and striking of feature. His face was strong, determined, unsmiling for the most part and the men who had known him as "merry" Jack Andrews often wondered why they had called him that.

He had done well and they said it was because of his single-minded application to the building of his career. He had no other interest, no other concern beyond becoming a successful railway contractor and he was well on his way to being that. He was no longer one of the vagabonds who roamed wherever the job demanded, but the man who worked directly under the contractor. A large contract was taken and a chief agent was appointed by the contractor to supervise the work and through the agent all the contractor's orders would pass. Jack Andrews was that agent and he had four sub-agents under him, each of whom was responsible for a length of line, and working for them was a timekeeper who kept a record of the time worked by every man in the section. The work was let to "gangers" as Jack had once been, who then employed the labourers. Jack was the man who put it all together, the work and the men. He was a man who could no longer call himself a navvie. He was a man of consequence, whose shrewdness, hardness, far-sightedness and perseverance had carried him in two years from one world to another. He it was who arranged the transporting of the men, the tools of their trade, the picks and shovels and wheelbarrows, the iron bars and barrels of gunpowder, the bricks and mortar to build their huts, to the parcel of land he himself was responsible for and it had all been accomplished, it was whispered, very softly, since no one wanted to get on the wrong side of Jack Andrews, because some lass had let him down! They couldn't understand it themselves for one lass was surely like any other, but be that as it may, Jack Andrews was a different man to the good-natured youth who had "randied" with them two years ago. Soon, Alfie-Bob, who had stuck close to Jack, had confided to Algie-One-Step, when Jack had the necessary cash to bargain for a contract himself, he would be the contractor, the top man. He had shares, Alfie-Bob had heard it whispered, in many new railway ventures and was particularly interested in the proposed Liverpool, Ormskirk and Preston Railway which had been incorporated in August of last year. The building of it was expected to begin soon.

The train, which was on its way to Lancaster, began to gather speed, steam pounding rhythmically from its funnel, the great wheels clattering over the points, carriages beginning to sway. At each window of the first-class compartments was the pale blur of a face, some staring with avid interest at the passing scene, for railway travel was still a great wonder to the vast majority of the public.

He saw her at the last moment, just as the rear carriage reverberated out of the station. A girl in blue wearing a pretty straw bonnet with blue flowers beneath its brim, a girl who turned to stare back at him before the train chugged slowly round a bend and disappeared from sight.

For a second or two he could not get his breath. His guts felt as though they were being torn from his body and his strong legs trembled at the knees. The whole world seemed to shake, or at least the bit of ground on which he stood, and the sound of the dog barking faded away to nothing. A man, come from the train like himself, glanced at him curiously and Jack knew he must look like a prize fighter who has received a severe blow to the head which has left him reeling.

It was not her, of course, as all the other women and girls he had seen dressed in blue had not been her. How many times, dozens, crossing the street in Windermere where the railway line terminated; riding by in a carriage in Kendal; looking in a shop window in Southport to where he, the engineer and the contractor had travelled on the survey. In Preston he had made a fool of himself and badly offended a young lady's father when he had caught her arm in a rapturous grip and whirled her to face him.

In Liverpool, near the railway station, when he and Daniel Browne, the contractor, had gone to meet some of the members of the provisional committee which was to raise the capital needed to begin the building of the Liverpool, Ormskirk and Preston Railway. He had been certain it was her that time! She had been accompanied by a well-dressed young woman with dark, glossy curls which bounced on her neck. She was dressed in blue, the one he had thought was his Sara, walking with that familiar swaying grace, that proud tilt of her head which made her appear taller than she was. He had frantically shouted her name and several people had turned to stare in astonishment, but when he had raced after her, turning the corner into Great Charlotte Street where St John's Market lay, both young women had gone. Mr Browne, whom he had left hovering on the steps of the station, had been open-mouthed with annoyance, sceptical at Jack's explanation that he had thought he had seen an old boyhood friend.

His heart felt seriously damaged at times, bruised and ready to give up in despair at the thought of never seeing her again. Of losing her for ever in the great vacuum which had swallowed her up, but he had his life to get on with, his work, his career, the rise of which had been meteoric, due probably to his obsessive attention to its furtherance. With nothing else to occupy him it had become his life, the fulcrum which supported that life, the instrument which gave it meaning. Without Sara what else was there? Today, in one last desperate attempt to trace her he was to go to the post office in Oxenholme. He didn't know why, really. He was passing on his way to Preston from Kendal to meet with Daniel Browne and it had come to him last night that an hour or two could be spared to make a small detour. His meeting with the contractor was not until first thing tomorrow morning.

The cabbie looked disgruntled as Jack set off to walk the short distance to the post office.

The young clerk behind the counter nodded his head respectfully as the large young gentleman entered the shop.

"Good mornin' ter thi, sir. Can I help thi'?" he asked, somewhat surprised to see such a well-dressed chap frequenting a post office. Gentlemen had their post delivered to their homes, four times a day in some towns, and their servants made any necessary purchases in the way of stamps or telegrams to be sent.

He was not a gentleman after all, the clerk realised as soon as he spoke. Jack, though mixing for the past two years, first with Sara and her family, then with men better bred than himself, had lost much of his broad northern accent, cutting out the "thees" and "tha's" of his heritage, but it was still not the drawling speech of the upper classes which came from between his lips.

"My name's Jack Andrews," he said, his voice cool and level though he was still inclined to tremble inside. "Are there any letters for me?"

"Just one moment, sir." The clerk turned away, fiddling in the pigeon holes behind him, most of which were empty, then suddenly, as though a memory had just returned to him, he whirled back, his round, pleasant face alert, his eyes bright with speculation.

"I remember thi', sir. Didn't tha' used ter come in . . . oh, a year or two back?"

"Yes, yes I did." Jack's voice was impatient. He was not here to reminisce about the past, his frowning expression said, nor did he wish to engage the young clerk in idle conversation.

The clerk looked pleased. "I thought I recognised thi'. I never forget a face though I'm not much on names, which doesn't help in my job." He beamed, a look of satisfaction creasing his face, then again some memory came to plague him and the look of satisfaction died, smoothing away like the ripples of a lake as the wind drops. Another expression took its place, one of bewilderment, of disbelief and of uncertainty as though he suspected someone was having a joke at his expense. He pursed his lips, gazing at Jack with suspicious eyes.

"Theer's nowt here fer thi', sir, but . . ."

Jack felt his heart begin to thump for some reason and a cold sweat broke out down the length of his spine. His hand gripped the brim of his top hat, crushing it, breaking the frame so that later he found, to his great surprise, it was unwearable when he came to put it on.

"What is it?" he managed to say.

"Well, sir, it's just come back ter me that thy name's bin

mentioned in here only this week. Now was it Monday or Tuesday? Let me think." He put his hand to his brow in a gesture of deep thought.

Jack swallowed painfully. "My name . . . Jesus Christ, man, mentioned by who? Speak up for God's sake. Don't stand there gawping like a landed trout. Who? Who was it? Who was asking after me?"

He was almost over the counter, leaning forward across it the better to get at the clerk, wanting him in his hands so that he could more easily squeeze the truth out of him. His face was the dead white of freshly fallen snow and his rich, smoothly brushed hair fell over his forehead in a wild tangle. A pulse leaped violently in his throat and there was another at his temple. He was shaking now, unable to control the ripples of fear, of hope, of desperation that threatened to overwhelm him and the clerk was clearly terrified.

"A young lady, sir," he squeaked, doing his best to loosen Jack's hand from his own waistcoat.

"What young lady?" Jack's roar could be heard in the narrow street and there was movement in the depths at the back of the shop as though someone was coming to investigate the commotion.

"Please, sir, please . . . if tha'd let go of me I'd tell thi'."

"Tell me now, for God's sweet sake before I strangle you."

Jack glared into the face he had dragged towards him, panting with emotion, his fingers digging into the clerk's shoulders like spikes.

"I can't remember her name fer the minute . . . a pretty lady. Sir, please, I can't speak if tha' drag me about like that!"

Jack let go then, breathing like a man who has run ten miles, all uphill, doing his best to calm himself. The clerk brushed at his waistcoat and smoothed his disarranged hair before sidling out of Jack's reach until his back was pressed against the pigeonholes.

"Speak," Jack snarled.

"She were askin' if her letters had bin picked up."

"Good God above . . ."

"An' when I said no— "

"There were letters?" Jack's voice rose to a howl of anguish.

"Oh aye, an' I told her they were still here."

"Sweet Jesus Christ."

"Dozens of 'em, addressed to Jack Andrews, that bein' you, sir," he added unnecessarily, "she said could she have 'em? If tha've proof tha' wrote 'em, I said an' when she showed me summat with her name on I give her them back. Now let's see, what was it? Sara something. I see a lot of names," he murmured apologetically. "She was very . . . distressed, sir." His own face took on a look of great sadness.

"Oh Jesus . . . Jesus."

"Sir, will I get you a chair, sir?" the clerk twittered, for he was convinced the man called Jack Andrews was about to faint.

"Where?"

"Where what, sir?"

"Where had she come from? For pity's sake, man, think . . . think."

"Nay, I can't remember her address, sir. I see a lot of letters, as I just said, but I do remember t'postmark."

"Goddammit, man."

"It were Liverpool, sir."

Sara turned blindly away from the carriage window, her eyes meeting the compassionate gaze of Lily Canon who sat opposite her. Lily smiled encouragingly as though to say, "don't give up, don't give in" but it was very hard to keep back the bitter tears of hopelessness which filled her heart and blurred her vision. She was quite well aware that Lily didn't really believe that Jack was a man of integrity, a man worthy of any woman's love, a good man, a sincere man who had sincerely loved Sara Hamilton, Sara would stake her life on it, but a man who had, through some misfortune of timing, become lost to her. She knew Lily secretly thought Jack was a wanderer, a ne'er-do-well, an opportunist, a seducer, a heartbreaker who, as heartbreakers do, had moved on to more convenient pastures. But then Lily had never met Jack so she knew no better.

They hadn't found him, nor any trace of him, unless you could count her letters which had piled up in their dozens at the post office in Oxenholme. Those letters had made it all the more positive somehow, proof that Jack no longer existed for Sara Hamilton and that Sara Hamilton was no longer of interest to Jack Andrews. Lying there on the counter of the post office, unopened, unread, uncared about, and the pain of it overwhelmed her. It was as though those letters were a confirmation of all Sara's worst fears and the worst one of all was that she would never know. Had he simply moved on, as Alice was always telling her he would, no longer concerned about Sara, about their love, about her letters, about her breaking heart, or was he dead, killed in some accident at the navvie camp? She would never know. The railway station at Bowness in Windermere had been opened in April, five months ago and all signs of the navvies had long gone. A fine building, the railway station, serving the branch line from Kendal to Windermere which Jack and his men, she supposed, had built and if he was still alive, where would he go? She had no answer. Anywhere there was railway building. Anywhere track was being laid and that was virtually every corner of the land. It was hopeless, hopeless and it was time to give up.

That man at the station at Oxenholme, the well-dressed gentleman who had stood beneath the trees, the sunshine dappling him in light and shadow, had reminded her of Jack. But then, did not all tall, broad-shouldered young men do that, at least until she looked into their faces. She saw him everywhere, though why she should she didn't know for none of the men who caught her attention wore the distinctive navvie outfit which had made Jack so dashing.

A great emptiness expanded inside her. A hollow feeling which did not ache or hurt her but dragged her down in misery. She felt a fierce reluctance to believe that she would never see Jack again but she must face it and in the meantime, until she did, there would be a waiting, a longing for the pain to go. She felt an enormous yearning to have the weeks and months pass so that, as it was said it did, time would lessen her sorrow. This time next month, next year, she would not miss him as much and even as she whispered it to herself she knew it was not true. She would miss Jack until the day she died.

What a long journey it had been, not made any easier by Alice's icy tirade before Sara and Lily set out on it. She had threatened Sara that when she returned she would find Alice gone, gone to live at the grand mansion in West Derby which was the first-class fashion house of Madame Lovell. Madame Lovell had got her training in a fashion house in Paris and she was prepared to employ and train both Alice and Sara in the ways of a couturier like the genius Charles Frederick

Worth, who had made his name over the past few years in his own splendid fashion house. A great lady was Madame Lovell, descended, it was said, from the barons Lovell who had come to England from Normandy at the time of the conquest. It was a wonderful opportunity for them both, brought about by Madame's approval of the work Alice had taken to show her. She rarely took on seamstresses in this manner, preferring to train a girl from the very start but she had been so impressed, Alice said proudly, that she had been prepared to make an exception in their case. Sara must be out of her mind to jeopardise their chance with this wild scheme, but it might have been the bird twittering of the starlings at twilight for all the notice Sara took of her. Her vision, her goal, her life at this particular moment was channelled into this journey which, if the fates were good to her, would reunite her not only with Jack, but with Dolly. Lily had stood impassively beside her, saying nothing as Alice had bitterly raged, but letting it be known that Sara had a staunch ally and a true friend and, short of locking Sara forcibly in their room at the top of the house, Alice had no option but to give in.

Her expression had not been pleasant as she watched them climb into the hansom cab which was to take them to Lime Street Station.

But in the end it had all come to nothing, at least as far as Jack was concerned and wouldn't Alice crow over that? The slow journey from Liverpool to Preston, first class this time for Lily would not hear of them travelling in "them cattle trucks", quite scandalised at the very idea. Up through the flat farmlands of Lancashire to Lancaster and beyond, running beside the broad stretch of Lancaster Sands on the west coast. Further and further north until they reached Oxenholme and the deadly blow to Sara's hopeful heart at what she found at the post office there.

It was then that she began to feel the eager confidence, the bright expectations she had nurtured ever since Lily had suggested the journey begin to slip away and their quiet enquiries in the small watering place of Bowness in Windermere, which produced absolutely nothing, no clue to Jack's whereabouts, came as no particular surprise.

Now they were to go to Kirkham where they would leave the train and take a hansom cab out to the workhouse at Wesham.

"I'll pay you back every penny," she said fiercely again and again to Lily, each time Lily opened her purse. Rail fares, fares for the hansom cab, the small hotel in Bowness where they had stayed overnight and Lily had smiled and said she knew she would and she had kept an account of everything she had spent, doing her best to make Sara laugh, holding Sara's hand at each bitter disappointment. Lily in her respectable black looking more like the wife of a parson than of a rollicking, bandy-legged, drunken seaman. If she was taken aback by the shrieking of the train and the speed at which it went, she did not say so though her face paled and she held on to the plush seat of the carriage as though afraid she would be flung out. She had never been further than over the water to New Brighton on the ferry. She was used to the city after thirty years of living there, used to the river and the ships, and her first sight of Furness Fells on the far side of Lake Windermere and beyond that the towering magnificence of the Old Man of Coniston quite took her breath away.

Sara and Lily had nothing to say to one another on the bleak and forbidding appearance of the workhouse when the hansom cab drew up outside its sturdy, wrought-iron gates. The new Poor Law allowed no inducement for men and women to live as idle paupers so those without the means to support themselves were consigned to the workhouse where rules were imposed with such strictness and food allocated with such economy no one would go through the gates while hard work was to be had! Men were separated from their wives and mothers from their children, though Sara was not aware of it as she and Lily waited in the chilly hallway for the despot in charge to be fetched.

He proved to be tall, thin, grey and as forbidding as the institution he ran, not at all pleased to be brought away from his important duties and inclined to look down on the young girl, well bred though she obviously was and the woman he could only presume to be her servant.

"Yes?" he hissed menacingly, his missing and rotted teeth impeding his speech to such an extent a fine spray of spittle wafted in Sara's direction. Rudely, and without giving her a chance to answer, he took out a none too clean handkerchief and blew his nose vigorously, inspecting its contents before stuffing it back in his pocket.

Sara felt her stomach heave but she spoke up bravely. "We have come to see— "

"We allow no visiting of the inmates," he interrupted, eyeing her as though she were an impertinent child and had she been in his charge, woe betide her.

"She is not an inmate, well, I suppose after twelve months one could call her that but she was only left on a temporary basis," and if I had cast eyes on you before she came here she would not have been left here at all, her expression told him.

"Really, Miss . . .?"

Sara drew herself up. "Hamilton."

"Really, Miss Hamilton, I am an extremely busy man," and an important one, his manner implied. "I have been elected by the Board of Guardians to look after these people who are thrown on the parish and that is what I am trying to do. The workhouse master must— "

"Do you have a Miss Dolly Watson in your institution?" Sara's voice had become stronger, cold, and in it was that certain tone and manner with which those of the upper classes are born. It was not intentional but generations of belonging to the privileged classes had bred it in her. The man blinked.

"I can hardly carry the names of— "

"You must have a register."

"Indeed we do but— "

"Then I would be obliged if you would look in it." She waved him away as though she were the Queen of England dismissing a subject and when he went, glowering but obedient, Lily realised with a finality about which she had mixed feelings that pliable little Sara Hamilton was gone for ever. Mind, it was a good thing for if she'd continued as she was she'd have amounted to nowt, under the thumb of that sister of hers for the rest of her life.

But she'd been a sweet little thing, vulnerable, an unhappy child who'd wormed her way into Lily's heart. Now, with her hopes dashed of ever seeing that chap again, the one she'd set her heart on, was she to become as sour as Miss Hoity-Toity?

The events that followed relieved Lily's mind and she wondered afterwards how she could have harboured such foolish thoughts. True sweetness does not turn sour, nor does it dry up. A good heart will remain so whatever the adversities of life and Sara Hamilton's heart was good, sound, steady, warm, wanting to be given in love, if not to a man, then to anyone who had need of it.

"Yes," the workhouse master said when he returned, "we do have a Miss Dolly Watson but she is— "

"Take me to her, if you please and have her things made ready." Sara was already moving towards the door through which he had returned.

"I can't do that, Miss Hamilton. I have to get the necessary authority from the Board of Guardians."

"Take me to her or I shall search this place from cellar to attic and if I find anything which is not as it should be I will be in touch with the Board of Guardians myself. If the rest of the house is the same temperature as this hallway then God help the . . . inmates, as you call them. Now, Miss Watson, if you please."

Her small pointed face was the furious pink of a budding rose and her sea green eyes snapped alarmingly, though Lily noticed she was trembling at this, her first defiance of authority. Her straw bonnet bobbed and as though to show her determination – or was it to hide her alarm at her own audacity – she folded her arms across her breast and tapped her foot ominously on the cold flagged floor.

"Yer'd best do as lass ses," Lily remarked idly, folding her arms across her own considerable bosom.

The room they were taken to was up many stairs and had dark brown, serviceable walls to waist height and above that was an equally drab and sensible mustard yellow. There were several pious texts on the walls, one stating that God saw all! There were no curtains at the window and no carpet on the floor. Down the length of the room were what looked like a row of coffins, slightly wider perhaps but with wooden sides and in each lay an old lady. They wore caps, frilled about their faces which rested vacantly on a pillow of striped ticking. None of them turned her head as the workhouse master, followed by Sara and Lily, strode busily into the room.

"Now let me see," he said, consulting a book in his hand. "Miss Watson is in . . ." but Sara was already there, kneeling at the side of the fourth bed along. The face on the pillow, that of an ancient crone with skin so wizened and thin it could have been a bleached prune, turned slowly. The mouth, fallen in and toothless, quivered and a little pink tongue, no bigger than that of an infant, fluttered against the lips. Then, slowly, unbelievingly, the dead eyes in the face lit up, became alive and from beneath the grey blanket a frail hand found its way out to touch Sara's wet cheek wonderingly.

"Miss Sara . . . eeh, Miss Sara," Lily heard her whisper.

"Yes, Dolly it's me, and I've come to take you home."

15

"If you wish to live in at Madame Lovell's then that is up to you, Ally, but I must stay here to look after Dolly. If I decide to go with you I shall find it no hardship to walk to West Derby each morning and if my funds run to it I shall get a cab home in the evening. But it all depends on what Madame Lovell is willing to pay me."

Sara ladled a spoonful of good beef broth from the bowl on the tray and put it carefully to Dolly's mouth which opened like that of a little bird, or that of an infant, Lily often thought. Sara smiled at Dolly, raising a hand to pat the wrinkled cheek which already, after only a week of Sara's plain but wholesome food, was plumping out nicely. Dolly was already talking of "turning out" the cosy room which was hers, itching to get her hands on a duster and a bit of polish, she said. Not that Mrs Canon's parlour – now Dolly's bedroom and sitting-room – was in any way in need of turning out. Far from it but she'd had enough of lolling about in bed. She couldn't abide doing nowt, she added. She'd had more than her share of bed in that place, thank you very much and why Miss Sara found it necessary to feed her when she was perfectly capable of doing it herself she couldn't fathom, she grumbled but Lily noticed her eyes were deep pools of love, brimming for Sara Hamilton. Something like her own, she supposed and how the girl who would do anything for anybody, give her last farthing, if she had one, to a beggar, could be the sister of the cold-hearted cow who stood rigidly by the door was a bloody mystery.

"Madame Lovell is expecting us both to live in, Sara, and our plans cannot be changed now," the "cow" snapped.

"Mrs Canon will not mind looking after Dolly, will you, Mrs Canon, and you, if you wish, can come up each Sunday."

"I'm sorry, Ally," Sara said calmly, "but that won't do. I have no wish to live in. I would, in fact, rather continue with Miss Brewer and I know she would be glad to have at least one of us remain with her. And Matty said she was sure the Misses Yeoland would be glad of a good outdoor seamstress so I can see no reason why we should move to Madame Lovell's. We already earn enough to keep us in some comfort and I'm content with that."

"Oh, so you are content with that, are you?" Alice's voice said sneeringly. "The measly pittance we earn is enough for you, is it? Well, let me tell you, miss, it is not enough for me. Fiddling about for the rest of our lives on a few shillings a week when we could be earning . . . well, I'll say no more except this. When I have finished we shall be earning considerably more than Miss Brewer, or even the Misses Yeoland, of whom you seem to think so highly, and the name of Hamilton will be synonymous with the best in fashion, not only in Liverpool but in the whole of Lancashire. I mean to get on, Sara, and if you have any sense, which I seriously doubt sometimes, you will listen to what I am saying."

"I'm sorry, Alice, I really am. I will do anything to help you in your . . . your ambition but I don't want to be parted from Dolly." Or you and Matty, the smile she bestowed on Lily said. There was laughter and warmth in Lily's kitchen and could she be sure of finding such prizes in the high-class establishment Alice wished to transfer her to, particularly if all she had was her sister for a companion? She loved Ally. Ally was all the family she had but Sara was no longer under any illusion over Ally's need to dominate, to control, not only her own life, but Sara's. Alice had been devastated by what she saw as their loss of status when they had been forced to leave Wray Green and find menial work. Gentlewomen did not seek employment, nor did they live in lodgings unless life's cruelty compelled them to it. They married their own kind and lived the safe, protected lives they had been bred for. But fate, chance, ill luck, call it what you will, had decreed otherwise and so Alice Hamilton, give her her due, had done what was abhorrent to her, what would be abhorrent to any lady of standing, and that was to go out and find work in order not to starve. To earn her bread and butter.

But being Alice, that bread and butter must be of the best quality and, being Alice, she would move in a straight line to the source from where that quality came. Madame Lovell's high-class fashion house seemed to her to be the promise of a decent and favourable life, bright prospects and even renown for her and Sara and so that was where they must go. No arguments! No shilly-shallying on Sara's part and certainly no concern for Dolly who would be well cared for in their absence by Mrs Canon. If she and Sara were to accomplish the highest peak in what was evidently to be their profession then surely the only place to find it, she was telling Sara, was at the best fashion house in Liverpool?

And was she not right in her thinking? Could Sara blame Ally for her single-minded determination to get on, to raise herself from a lowly seamstress to some high position in Madame Lovell's establishment and to take Sara with her? She had only their good at heart, Sara knew that, but she also knew now that what was right for Ally was not necessarily right for herself. She needed more than Ally could give her and what she needed at exactly this moment was what was to be found in Lily Canon's tall house in Abercromby Square. With Lily. With Dolly. With Matty. She was well aware that she was not ambitious. Not like Ally. She had fitted into the job as a seamstress because it was the only course open to her but her true vocation, had it been allowed, was as the wife of Jack Andrews. She would have been good at that, she acknowledged sadly.

It was as though she had gone back in time to over a year ago now when she had first lost Jack. She was grieving badly again though it did not show in the softly smiling face she presented to Dolly each day. The pain in her chest and throat where the unshed tears clogged was with her night and day. She could not weep and she was continually cold with the agony of her loss which she now accepted as final. It was a physical thing, the deep mourning she was enmeshed in and almost overnight she had felt her youth fall away from her, sloughed off like skin. She had been left with a sense of possessing all the suffering and sorrow every woman knows when she has lost the man she loves. Old somehow, wise, sad and she must find some way to escape it. Not to return to her girlhood for she would never do that but, in time, to achieve the fulfilment of a mature woman, a woman who could stand alone, and that meant without Alice. Beautiful had been her dreams, hers and Jack's. Sad was her fate but nevertheless she must get a grip on it, shape it to her own needs and she could not do it with Alice for ever directing her on how she must be!

"I don't think you realise what a wonderful opportunity this is for us, my girl," Alice snapped, moving unsteadily across the room to stand beside Dolly's bed, her own intensity of will making her tremble. The old woman was propped up with several pillows, each one enclosed in a white frilled pillowcase, exquisitely embroidered in what was known as "white-work". Alice recognised them as those Sara had been sewing in the months before their fathers death. For the linen press she would have as a bride, she had dreamily told Alice, probably visualising her and that oaf's head resting side by side on them, a thought which made Alice shudder. She was glad to see that at last Sara had put away all thoughts of him and was using her bedlinen for the old woman instead. At least something had come out of the ill-advised trip up north if it meant Sara had given up her lunatic dream of becoming a navvie's wife!

"Alice, I know this means a lot to you," Sara said, handing a clean, damp napkin to Dolly, smiling affectionately as the old woman wiped her hands and face. She removed the tray and stood up to face her sister, and Lily, from the chair beside the good fire Sara insisted upon, watched with fascination this new, quite formidable young woman whom she had brought back from Windermere. If she was suffering, and Lily knew she was, she gave no sign of it. And Lily also knew that from now on she would no longer call Sara Hamilton "the little one". She even seemed to have grown taller, perhaps because her tawny hair was no longer falling in a tumble of curls, or an unravelling plait down her back, but was firmly held in a head-tilting chignon in the nape of her neck.

"I do know this means a lot to you, Alice," she repeated, balancing the tray on one arm, "and if it will please you I will come to see Madame Lovell with you— "

"I knew you would see sense, Sara," Alice interrupted, a smile of triumph creasing her face. "Madame Lovell is— "

"Please let me finish, Ally." Sara's voice was patient and Dolly and Lily, who were already comrades-in-arms in defence of the girl they loved so dearly, exchanged glances.

"What else is there to say, my dear? You will be as affected as I was myself when you see the lovely house and the conditions in which Madame's staff work. It is absolutely nothing like Miss Brewer's, let me add, and in fact I was very favourably impressed by the class of young woman who work there. Oh, nothing like real ladies, of course, but with our exceptional talent and, well, our appearance, Madame assured me we should have no trouble— "

"I did not say I would work there, Ally, only that I would go and see if I liked the look of it."

"Liked the look of it!" Alice's face was stiff with displeasure. "How can you possibly fail to like it? It is positively . . . positively sumptuous . . ." Something like Mrs Bentham's luxurious drawing-room in Wray Green, she wanted to add, only twice as splendid, but she realised suddenly that Sara would not be moved by such things. "Really, Sara, you amaze me. Do you mean to tell me that you would sooner sew those commonplace gowns and bonnets Miss Brewer turns out when you could be creating real French couture, for that is what Madame does. Her clients come from only the best society, the most fashionable and wealthy— "

"I know that, Ally, you've told me a dozen times."

"There is no need for that tone, Sara."

"And I'm sure it will be a tremendous opportunity for you."

"*And* for you, my girl."

"But unless I can come home each night I cannot come with you."

"*Home!* Do you mean to say that you consider this place to be home?" Alice's arm swept in a contemptuous arc indicating the inferiority of Lily Canon's warmly comfortable and eminently respectable household, and her lip curled in a sneer.

"It is the only home I have, Ally," Sara said quietly. "You brought me here against my will. No, that's not true since I had no will, no inclination but to stay in Wray Green and . . . and wait for . . . well, you made the choice for me. Now, I am my own woman and capable of choosing for myself. I must admit to a deep curiosity about the House of Lovell and a great interest in the clothes that are made there but I will not be dragged— "

"Dragged!"

"Yes, dragged again into a situation I may not care for. I

shall miss you if you go alone. You're my sister, the only family I have, but I simply could not bear to be torn from . . . from another place. As I said, this is my home now, the only one I know and I feel secure in it."

And until I get over this pain, this pain which comes from a part of me I had not known existed, until I recover from the despair of accepting that I will never see Jack again, I must stay where there are loving arms to comfort me and loving eyes to tell me I am of value. I feel inside that everything is in ruin and ashes, without him, as though nothing will ever be the same again though logic tells me I will recover. I have lost faith. I have lost my love. I have lost Jack but I must not lose this warm place in which I will become whole again. I am constantly astounded that one person, a man I knew such a short time, could do this to me. Could cut a huge chunk out of my life and leave it a cold and empty place. And yet it is so. That is what Jack Andrews did to me and until I am healed from the injury his going inflicted upon me I must stay here. With the two, no, three warm-hearted women who will help me to do it. Not you, Ally, for you have a coldness in you that will weaken my already weak will to go on. You are strong and have proved to be invincible. I am not. I am vulnerable and dare not place myself wholly in your hands again.

There was no indication from the outside of its imposing wrought-iron gates that the House of Lovell was anything other than the country residence of a prosperous gentleman. Its smooth green lawns were freshly cut and rolled, stretching away from the wide gravelled drive into the shadows of the centuries-old oak trees which surrounded it. There were flowerbeds packed with jostling autumn flowers, chrysanthemums and hollyhock, delphiniums and dahlia, shrubs of privet sculpted into immaculate shapes and even a small pond glinting in the pale sunlight, ducks cutting across its rippled golden surface.

A footman opened the door to them, his eyes going over their shoulders, no doubt wondering on the absence of a carriage but Alice soon put him in his place by telling him crisply that they were expected and to inform Madame Lovell that the Misses Hamilton were here.

Sara had time to get no more than a quick glimpse of the broad and shining surface of the hallway in which a great log fire burned, gaining an impression of warmth and luxury and comfort she had not known existed, before the footman summoned them to follow him upstairs. He flung open a door and announced them in ringing tones, his eyes fixed on a point somewhere beyond them and at once they were made aware that they were in the presence of a great lady.

If Madame Lovell was stirred in any way by the fragile loveliness of Alice Hamilton's sister it did not show in her face. She was lovely herself and from across the tranquil elegance of her own private sitting-room Sara looked at her in amazed wonder, a wonder that a woman so young could have achieved so much.

It was not until summoned with a wave of her white, long-fingered and ringless hands to come and stand before her that Sara realised that Madame's youth and beauty were due to the skilful application of powder and paint. She had never seen a woman use such aids before and she found herself studying with great interest the white porcelain finish of her skin, the blush of pale peach at her high cheekbones, the wide coral fullness of her mouth, the well-defined arch of her painted eyebrows and the brown pencilled outline about each eye. Her hair was a rich, glossy brown, so rich and glossy Sara wondered if it was a wig, finding herself leaning forward slightly to get a better look. Madame wore a morning gown of rich ivory silk, starkly simple, long-waisted and fitted to her still supple and well-corsetted figure. There were no trimmings of any kind on it, its splendour relying on its magnificent cut. She wore no jewellery except for an exquisite pair of creamy pearl earrings.

Rosalie Lovell was fifty-four years old and it took her and her French maid, Claudine, two full hours to create the lovely, graceful, thirty-year-old fantasy which Madame Lovell's clients expected to see. She had been born Rosie Lorkin, the seventh child of the sixteen sons and daughters of Ned and Emily Lorkin. Born in the dockland area of Liverpool where Ned had now and again found employment loading and unloading the sailing ships which sat at the end of the street in which the Lorkin family lived.

When young Rosie was eleven years old she had suddenly blossomed, almost overnight it seemed, from the skinny, scrawny child who was faceless and nameless amongst all the other skinny and scrawny children who crammed into the tiny, two-roomed tenement in Dutton Street, coming to the attention not only of her father but her four remaining older brothers as well. Her budding, vulnerable sweetness was torn mercilessly apart one night when her mother had gone down to do a late shift at the "dolly-tub" in the local laundry. They took turns on her, her pa, their Fred and Wilf and Ernie and even Percy who was only twelve himself while the other little girls, her younger sisters, watched in terrified silence.

Had it not been for the nightwatchman who sat in his hut at the entrance to Princes Dock she might have thrown herself in the cold waters of the Mersey, so great was her terror and shame. She had been incoherent, running like a wounded rabbit from its tormentors down Dutton Street towards the water and when he caught her she had screamed like one, high and desolate.

"Lass, you get yersen down ter't Magdalen Asylum in Faulkner Street. They'll see ter thi'," he had told her compassionately, for the child was dribbling her own blood on to her fine-boned, bare and filthy feet. There was no mistaking what had been done to her!

She had stayed at the Asylum until she was healed and from there was placed, like so many lucky ones before her – at least by the standards of most orphans which she had told those in authority she was – in the Blue Coats Hospital. She learned to read and write and sew. She grew exceedingly pretty and in a series of moves over the years, from apprentice to first hand, from one wealthy lover to another, from Liverpool to London to Paris, then back to Liverpool, became the most sought-after, the most talented, the richest and most powerful businesswoman and designer of ladies' fashion in Lancashire. She never married and bore no children.

She looked now into the quiet but alert face of Sara Hamilton. She studied the soft, vulnerable mouth, full, apricot-tinted, the long upper lip which promised a sensuality not yet developed. She noticed the small tremor to it but the girl was self-possessed. She was beautifully dressed in a pearl grey voile, so pale it was almost white, with a touch of pale peach at the neck and wrist. There was a gracefully draped shawl of peach and cream about her shoulders and from it Madame thought she could detect the faint fragrance of roses. Her bonnet was charming. Of the same colour and material as her gown, under its brim were sewn delicate peach velvet rosebuds.

But it was her hair and her eyes which drew Rosalie Lovell's gaze to her, as it would draw the gaze of many men, for though she was simply dressed she was quite magnificent. Her hair was like silken fire, shot with cinnamon and gold and copper and her eyes were like those of a cat, pale, green and slanting and full of misted shadows. What was in them, Rosalie Lovell asked herself? What was in those glorious eyes? They were not those of an artless untried young girl and yet they were innocent, shining with candour, and at the same time mysterious.

Jesus God, the men would love her!

"Well, Miss Hamilton, your sister tells me you are seeking employment," Madame began pleasantly, turning to nod at Alice who, though she was obviously a clever seamstress as the work she had brought to the house demonstrated and was as pretty as a picture in her sunflower yellow, had not a thousandfold of the indescribable magnetism her younger sister possessed in abundance. Seamstresses, even one with the talents of Alice Hamilton, were not hard to come by in Liverpool but a young woman with that unique quality of innocence and sexuality which Sara Hamilton had came along once in a decade. She possessed a combination of youthful beauty, an untouched air of shy modesty and yet she had a look about her, almost an earthiness, which sat strangely at odds with her well-bred gentility. A woman, hardly more than a child really, who would appeal to any man with eyes in his head and fire in his loins. Women like her were as rare as gold, as unique and hard to come by as a precious jewel and must be treated as such, for they were beyond worth in her trade. This one she must have and if it meant taking on the sister who would undoubtedly be useful, then so be it.

She was astonished when Sara Hamilton answered.

"Not really, Madame. I already have work." Sara smiled politely, unaware that as the muscles in her face moved a small dimple pierced her cheek just beside her mouth which lifted and parted to show her small perfect teeth. Her eyes narrowed and her long brown lashes tangled and Madame Lovell was enchanted as she knew her male customers would be enchanted. The male customers who paid the bills their womenfolk ran up.

Madame smiled. Though she was surprised by Sara's answer, she smiled. The sister did not. In fact she was furious, turning on Sara with a hissing malice and fury which seemed quite out of proportion to the circumstances.

"How can you compare the trumpery work we are doing at the moment to what Madame Lovell can offer us, you silly girl? It is an honour, a privilege to work in an establishment as well thought of as this and you should be grateful that you are to be given the chance to do so. Think what you can learn here. Consider the opportunities— "

Madame cut Alice's words short with a peremptory wave of her well-kept hand and Sara found herself most impressed by the way Alice instantly obeyed her. There were not many in this world, in fact Sara could think of no one, who could silence Alice Hamilton with one small gesture and it was this which made Sara finally realise how desperately Ally wanted the job. Of course, Alice did not like the fact that she must seek employment to support herself, at least until she found herself a suitable husband, if that was her goal, but while she was compelled to it, she would do her utmost to see that she had the best. That she would work in the most reputable, the most highly thought of fashion house in Liverpool. She would mix with people who were refined, well bred and well mannered like herself. She would put her considerable talents to good use in pleasant surroundings. She would earn, presumably, the highest wages a seamstress could earn and she would get on, move up, be respected and admired, not only for her attractive appearance but for her undeniable talents.

"Yes, Miss Hamilton," Madame was saying impatiently, "I am sure your sister is aware of the advantages of working in the House of Lovell. It is the best in Liverpool, in Lancashire. Indeed, I think I can say quite truthfully, the best in England. I draw my clientèle only from the most prominent families in Lancashire and even further afield. Ladies come from many miles away to be dressed by the House of Lovell. From the nobility and, on occasion, even higher." It was said simply, a statement of fact with no wish to boast. "There is only one designer whose talent is superior to mine. He is young and has been in Paris only a few years but he will go far. I did my best to persuade him to come to the House of Lovell but he refused, saying the House of Worth – that is his name – will one day be synonymous with all that is genius in fashion. However, I digress." She put a slender hand to her hair, smoothing its already faultless perfection, smiling a chilly smile in Alice's direction. It warmed as it turned to Sara.

"Your sister is most eager that I take you both on as beginners, Miss Hamilton, which is where all my girls start until I am confident they can manage more intricate work. Many of them pay me a premium, I might add, for the prestige they gain in learning their craft from me but, seeing the superiority of the work which your sister was kind enough to show me, I shall waive that in your case. If you come to me, you will work hard, my dear, make no mistake, but you will learn all there is to know about haute couture. You and your sister will share a room— "

"Thank you, Madame, you are most kind and I have no wish to interrupt you," Sara said politely, "but though I'm sure I would be happy working for you, I cannot live in, you see."

"Sara, will you hold your tongue," Alice hissed, her eyes like cold slivers of pale green ice in her furious face.

"I cannot, Ally. It is the truth. I have told you time and time again I must live at . . . at home." She turned with a passionate loveliness to Madame Lovell, her serene face suddenly flushed and determined with some deep-felt emotion. She held out her small, gloved hands in desperate entreaty and Rosalie Lovell thought she had never seen anything quite so appealing, so irresistibly captivating as this child/woman who would, if she had her way, grace Rosalie Lovell's showroom one day. She was very young but even now her impact was quite breathtaking, though as yet Rosalie Lovell could not define it. She felt it, she who had known and dressed the most beautiful women in the country and if it was so strong, so warm, so compelling now, how would it be when she matured into the magnificent woman she would undoubtedly become?

Sara took a small step towards the older woman, her booted feet silent in the deep pile of the carpet. She had never seen such a carpet, not even in the overcrowded drawing-room of Mrs Bentham in Wray Green and at any other time would have admired and marvelled at its splendour. But she had no time for it now. She felt Alice twitch irritably at her side and knew she had done something wrong but she could not help that for she must speak out. Her small teeth caught her bottom lip, leaving it moist and rosy, then she raised her head even higher and squared her shoulders in defiance. The movement lifted her small round breasts, thrusting them against the fine pale voile of her bodice. Her nipples were clearly outlined, tiny distended pebbles just as though her emotions, roused by her firmness of purpose not to be overpowered by her sister and by Madame Lovell herself, had brought an almost sexual change to her young body.

"I would willingly work for you, Madame. To tell the truth" – she lowered her eyes shyly, then raised them to smile – "I am excited at the idea of working in such a splendid establishment." She looked about her at the delicate beauty of the room, the thick-piled cream carpet, the eggshell blue of the silk draperies at the windows, the exquisite elegance of the spindle-legged tables and chairs which she knew must be French and the deep comfort of the cushion-piled sofa on which Madame sat. There were dainty figurines, lamps and bowls of flowers, pictures on the cream, damask silk-covered walls and a tray set on a table beside Madame's hand containing a beautifully crafted and engraved silver teapot, jug and sugar basin and one solitary cup and saucer of porcelain china so fine it was translucent where the light shone through it. The room was high, the ceiling set with painted panels in its magnificent plasterwork and in the wide, columned fireplace carved from pure white marble an enormous fire burned halfway up the chimney, for as she grew older Madame felt the cold.

"But?" Madame questioned quietly.

"I have . . . friends and an old servant of my mother's who I cannot leave."

"Sara, Madame does not want to know the details of our family." Alice's voice was harsh.

"On the contrary, Miss Hamilton, I am most intrigued. I would like to know the reason why your sister is to turn down a place that most young seamstresses would give their right arm for. That is if they didn't need it to sew with." She smiled at her own small joke and so did Sara though Alice saw nothing humorous in the remark. "Please go on, Miss Hamilton," she encouraged.

"You see, Madame, Dolly is old and— "

"Dolly?"

"My mother's servant."

"And your mother?"

"Is dead, Madame."

"I am so sorry," Rosalie Lovell was amazed to hear herself say, for since that day forty-three years ago when she had been raped by her father and four brothers she had cared not one iota for anyone's pain or sorrow.

"So you see Dolly is very precious to me."

Alice snorted but was silenced by a withering look from Madame.

"She has spent the last year in the . . . workhouse." Sara hung her head in deep shame, then raised it to reveal the tears she could not weep for Jack. They trembled on her long, childish lashes. "I swore to myself I would make it up to her. Oh, Madame, it's a long story and I'm sure . . ."

"I have all the time in the world, child." To Alice's astonishment and mortification she patted the plump cushions on the sofa, indicating that Sara, her silly, soft-headed sister, was to sit down beside her.

Again Rosalie Lovell marvelled at her own actions. Why was she so deeply interested in this young woman? she asked herself in bewilderment. Oh, the girl would make an excellent "magazinière" in due course and become a valued addition to the House of Lovell but it was more than that, she was well aware, and she meant to find out just what!

"Oh," she said in afterthought, turning to the rigid-backed, wintry-faced figure of Alice Hamilton whose eyes said quite plainly they could hardly believe what they saw. Her little sister, her sweet but suddenly self-willed little sister sitting down beside the great Madame Lovell just as though they were the best of friends while Alice Hamilton, who had put in all the hard work, who had made the long journey out to West Derby, who had gone on her knees almost pleading for an interview with a woman not fit to clean Eleanor Hamilton's boots, was left to stand like some maidservant waiting on her mistress's bidding.

"Do find a seat, Miss Hamilton," she was told vaguely and when she did so and Madame had turned back to Sara the expression on Alice Hamilton's face was not pleasant.

16

It was a constant source of aggravation to Alice and she could not leave it alone. She was like a child with nettle-rash. She knew it did no good and the more she set about it the more it irritated her but she just could not resist scratching it, returning to it over and over again in that first month after she and Sara began work at the House of Lovell.

Madame had been stern, unsmiling and very autocratic as she spelled out exactly what she expected of the girl she privately and amazingly liked to think of as her "protégée".

"I shall give you exactly four weeks, Miss Hamilton," she had told Sara, "and in those four weeks you shall prove to me that not only will you be punctual every morning but that you will not leave your work-table until your work is finished, no matter what the time of night. It is your concern if you wish to walk home in darkness, not mine. And in the hours you are here I want to see nothing but perfection. That is all I ask. Perfection of work. No matter how tired you are. No matter how your back or your eyes ache, or your legs which have walked the two miles from your home to your place of work, you will turn out your allotted share of garments, each one completed to the exact standard I expect of my staff. This, naturally, means on Saturday as well as weekdays and applies to when conditions of work are normal. At other times, during periods of increased business, those which occur at Easter or Christmas, perhaps a fashionable society wedding when my clients will need new gowns and the bride a trousseau, or when there is a ball of some importance in the city, then you and the other hands will remain at your work until it is completed no matter what the time of day. When this happens I shall expect you to stay overnight at the house since it would be inappropriate for you to tramp about between here and your home in the small hours. You could be required to work, sometimes for eighteen hours at a stretch for which, while you train, you will receive no extra wage. Do you understand, Miss Hamilton?"

"Yes, Madame." Sara nodded her head and her bright curls, those which had an endearing tendency to come loose from her neat chignon, trembled on her forehead and about her small ears.

"I have already explained to your sister what those wages will be, which she will have passed on to you, and the terms of your employment. You are the only member of my staff to be allowed to live out and I am putting my trust in you. See that you do not abuse it, Miss Hamilton. Your sister is not pleased, you realise that, don't you?"

"Yes, Madame, but I have already explained."

"I know, Miss Hamilton." Madame's expression was frosty, for the last thing she wanted was to let the other girls see what could only be described as "favouritism" towards the new hand.

"I require my girls to be of good behaviour, Miss Hamilton, and good character. Sometimes you will be leaving here late at night and will no doubt be . . . spoken to by men who will want to be your . . . friend . . ."

She was vastly astonished at the suddenly cold withdrawal which took place behind the shining eyes and glowing face of Sara Hamilton. It was as though a grey veil had been drawn across her countenance, blurring her features, taking the colour from her flesh and turning her eager warmth to frosted enmity.

"You need have no fear of that, Madame," she said icily as though her employer had insulted her.

"I did not mean to imply . . ."

"Quite, then no more need be said. I shall not abuse your trust." Sara Hamilton's soft, full mouth snapped to like a trap, thinning to a white line and her eyes were the cold flinty green of a beryl gem.

"Very well then, Miss Hamilton. Let us see how you fare, but I must impress upon you that if at the end of four weeks I am not satisfied with your time-keeping, your work or your conduct then I will dismiss you at once."

"Indeed. I expect no other treatment, Madame."

They both lifted unconsciously regal heads, the young woman and the old woman and it was as though a challenge had been flung down and accepted though from whom to whom was not clear.

"I cannot understand you, Sara Hamilton," Alice said bitterly on every Sunday she came home to Abercromby Square. Though the sisters saw each other every day, of course, sitting in the same enormous, high-ceilinged, many-windowed sewing-room on the first floor of the house, they were not allowed to speak unless it was to the first hand in whose charge they had been put. The spacious room housed only six seamstresses, with others distributed throughout equally spacious rooms on the first floor, for Madame believed that clutter caused confusion and did not create the exquisite garments her clients expected of her. There was a stand in the corner of the room where the "presser" worked beside the gas stove which heated the irons; and ranged beneath the windows so as to gain the full daylight for as long as possible were three tables with a girl on each side.

Within a week the Hamilton sisters had moved on from the basic hemming, basting and buttonholing Madame had instructed they were to be started on when it became obvious that their talents were being wasted, being far superior to those of the apprentices and improvers who were their companions. There had been several mutinous faces among those who had been employed by the House of Lovell for a lot longer than they had but nothing was said, for jobs as good as theirs were almost non-existent.

"I can't see why you are so upset about it, Ally," for Sara knew exactly what her sister meant and had indeed been expecting it. Anything which undermined Alice's authority over her younger sister was anathema to her. Each day, as she watched Sara fly up the back stairs like a winging dove in her grey cotton gown, her irritation built up in her. Sara's face would be flushed with running and her eyes bright with the excitement of her new employment. It was worse at the end of the day when Sara bundled her cloak about her and donned her bonnet prior to striding out the two-mile walk which began in West Derby Road and ended in Abercromby Square, and it was all Alice could do not to snatch her cloak from her, smack her silly face and send her up the stairs to bed as she had done when she was a child. She had never smacked her face, of course, but the longing to do so now was strong in her. It should be Sara who shared Alice's room not Betty Holden. Betty Holden was quiet, polite, respectful to Alice who she recognised at once as being a lady, since Betty was not, but it was not the same as having her own sister sharing her room and Alice resented it bitterly. Had she not been so adamant from the first that living in at the house was the best, the only course open to both of them, Alice would have been glad to walk the few miles with Sara to and from Abercromby Square. It was becoming increasingly evident that Sara was developing a more and more independent turn of mind, inclined to ignore Alice's sensible advice on many subjects and Alice felt her authority being slowly undermined. She did not care for it. Indeed it worried her, for what did her little sister, not yet eighteen, know about how to conduct herself as a lady should without Alice's constant guidance? She must be made to see that with winter coming on the only way open to her was to live in at the House of Lovell with Alice. Dolly was up and about now and with Mrs Canon to keep an eye on her would fare very well in the cosy room, paid for out of Alice and Sara's hard-earned wage – another source of irritation – at the front of Mrs Canon's house.

"I am upset about it, Sara, because I can see no reason for it. It is unreasonable and I am constantly amazed that Madame allows it. You are not a strong girl, Sara."

"Rubbish, I'm as strong as a horse and the walk doesn't trouble me at all. I know it's four miles— "

"That is another thing, Sara."

"What is?"

"The way you are beginning to speak and I can only conclude that it is the close proximity of the women in that house."

Sara looked astonished. "The way I speak?" she exclaimed.

"Yes. It is not 'can't' or 'doesn't', but 'cannot' and 'does not'. Your standards are slipping and I do not approve. Mama would deplore it and I— "

"Oh, Ally," Sara laughed weakly. "You really are priceless. In the midst of all the problems we have had and overcome you are worrying about the way I speak."

"Of course. Proper articulation is the mark of a lady."

"Well, that may be so, Ally, but it does not alter the fact that I shall continue to walk home to Abercromby Square each evening. When the winter is over I intend to cut across the fields from Mount Vernon to Lovell House. That will almost halve the journey and anyway, now that I have some money of my own I can always take a cab home at night."

"A cab!" Alice was scandalised. "Have you any idea of the cost of a cab? One and eightpence from West Derby Road to Abercromby Square, that is how much. Can you afford such a price? Besides that it would not be proper for you to travel on your own. No young lady rides alone in a cab, Sara, and Mama would turn over in her grave if she knew."

"Ally, please stop it. I'm not a child any more who must constantly be told what Mama or Papa would expect of her. I've grown up recently and, well, I shall be quite safe in a cab on my own, really I shall."

"But there is absolutely no need for it, Sara. Dolly is in good hands if that is what is troubling you."

"No, that is not what troubles me, Ally, now you come to mention it."

Sara's face closed up tight as though there were many thoughts she wished to keep hidden from her sister and she drew herself up to her full height. Even so her face was below the level of Alice's. She had not put her hair up this Sunday morning but had fastened it with vivid green ribbons into a thick and curling knot at the crown of her head. She wore an old dress of cinnamon brown, made over – unpicked and re-sewn several times as she grew – from one her mother had worn. She was rosy and dishevelled, lovely as a tossing, windblown rose and her sister eyed her with distaste. She was turning out the large, attic room she and Alice had once shared and already, Alice noted disapprovingly, she had rearranged the furniture. The scented shawl was draped over a battered screen which now hid the stove, brought from Lily's basement at the back of the kitchen where innumerable treasures, none of value, had been unearthed. Sara had her eye on several of them, thrilled with her first venture into home-making on her own. There were some sketches she had seen on a stall in the market and she meant to hang them on the plain white walls of the room. The young man on the stall had done them himself, he told her eagerly, only too pleased to draw her into conversation since she was an exceedingly pretty girl. The sketches were simple, a seagull drifting against a smudge of cloud, a sailing ship riding the river, no more than a line or two done in charcoal, delicate and timeless and the artist had promised to put them away for her until next Sunday when she would have the money to pay for them.

"What have you done to this room?" Alice glared about her accusingly, putting a reluctant finger on a small round table which had not been there last week.

Sara frowned, moving towards the solid mahogany sideboard which Lily and Matty had helped her to heave upstairs since it was of no further use to her, Lily said. She swished the duster she had in her hand across its already shining surface, then turned back to her sister, drawing the cloth between nervous fingers.

"That is what troubles me, Ally," she said shortly.

"And what does that mean, miss?"

"It means I am able to decide for myself what I wear, what I buy, what I put in my room."

"Your room! May I remind you I pay half the rent for—"

"I know you do and I wish you to stop. You no longer share it with me so why should you pay rent for it?"

"Sara Hamilton, I will not tolerate such . . . such rudeness and obduracy. You have been brought up as a lady and as such . . ."

"I do not mean to be rude or obdurate but it hardly seems fair to you to pay for a room only I occupy. I can pay my own way now with what I earn at Lovell's. You see, times have changed, Ally. Or hadn't you noticed? I'm a working woman and so are you."

"That is no excuse to ignore your upbringing. Mama would—"

"Oh, for heaven's sake, Ally, will you stop throwing Mama in my face. And speaking of Mama I am sure she would applaud the way you . . . we . . . have managed to extricate ourselves from the sad circumstances following Papa's death with no one's help except perhaps Lily's."

"And pray what has Mrs Canon done to improve our lot, Sara Hamilton? She has been paid for all she has given."

"She's . . . she's . . ." Sara stopped and turned away, her arms gripped fiercely at each elbow across her breast. Her face worked and her eyes blinked rapidly, not to keep away the tears for she could shed none, it seemed, but because she was desperate to blank out the flickering images which blinded her. Jack was never far from her thoughts, even now, eighteen months after she had lost him. Even now when she had given up all hope of ever seeing him again, the pain was still raw inside her. His smile shone in the night for her and the voice of his love sang in her heart, devastating her to a grief she could barely control. If she closed her eyes, whenever she closed her eyes, she could see him as he had been on that last day in Lytham at the opening of the railway station. His amber-skinned face set in curves of aching tenderness, a small smile lifting the corners of his strong mouth as he looked down at her. The expression in his deep, copper brown eyes of a love that told her it was unending. He walked in her dreams, splendid in his flamboyant navvie outfit, his white hat tipped jauntily over one eye, his beautiful peacock waistcoat unbuttoned, his neckerchief loosened to reveal the strong brown column of his throat and the fine tuft of hair at the base of it. In her dreams he reached possessively for her, claiming her, for did she not belong to him and though, in the time they were together, he had done no more than kiss her, in her dreams there was a yearning for more, for the act of love which he had described to her so delicately. He loved her in her dreams. He held her hand and walked with her through the hazed sunshine of summer, poppies about their feet. In her dreams they laughed and loved and Jack was the warm centre of it all, strong and true, merry and vitally alive to her. In her dreams they were together, two halves of a whole joined in an emotional and physical fulfilment which, when she awoke, left her sick and shaking with the torment of her loss.

And only in the company of Lily and Matty did it ease; did she manage to erase from her memory the tall, striding figure, the loose-limbed, graceful way he walked, the infectious grin, the way he winked at her from behind Alice's back, the gentleness of his hands, the feel of the thick riot of his chestnut curls in her hands, his quiet peace, his joy . . . Jack . . . it all added up to Jack Andrews who had dropped out of her life like a stone in a lake. Lily understood and though Sara had not discussed it with her she was certain Matty knew there was some great sorrow in her life. She made her laugh, did Matty, made her realise that there were things worth living for, worth striving for and with her Sara felt herself slip back into that state of giggling girlhood she had never known with Alice. From Lily she got comfort, ease, support, an unspoken loving strength and sustenance which held her steady and from Matty a youthful sense of blithe giddiness to balance her between the two.

From Alice she got nothing!

"Ally . . ." Her voice quivered slightly. "Lily is . . . how can I explain it without hurting you? She is my home. There, I knew it would make you cross," as Alice turned away, snorting in disgust.

"I would hardly call what I feel cross, Sara. More a complete lack of understanding."

"I know." Sara reached for the pot of beeswax Lily had lent her and, putting some on her duster, began to attack the sideboard vigorously. Back and forth flashed her arm and as she bounced so did her tumble of curls. She breathed lustily on the surface she was polishing, then resumed her battle with the duster.

Alice tutted irritably, tapping her foot at the same time on the worn carpet. Her face was poppy red with vexation and her eyes snapped dangerously. It was obvious she meant to have her own way, as she always had.

"Then I would be glad if you would explain it to me, please."

"I cannot . . . not really."

"Not really. What does that mean?"

Sara raised her head, using the back of her hand to push up the tangle of fiery, copper-gold curls which flopped over her forehead.

"I don't know what I mean, Ally, except this. In the last few years I have lost everything I hold most dear. Mama—"

"I lost Mama, too, you know."

"Yes, I know, of course you did. Then there was Papa, our home and . . . and Jack."

Alice made a sound of impatience. "Oh, for heaven's sake, Sara. Are you to bring him back?"

"He has never left me, here, Ally." Sara struck her chest passionately, just where her heart lay. "I loved Jack, I *love* Jack and I don't think I will ever stop."

"What extravagant nonsense."

"No, not nonsense, Ally, and that is what Lily understands and that is why I must stay here, where I am . . . loved."

Sara Hamilton's cry was heart-rending but Alice's heart was not rent. Her face lost all vestige of colour and her eyes narrowed in pure venom. She was incensed. She had, to the best of her ability, protected, sustained, guided and given all her affection to her younger sister and she was deeply offended by the implication that she had been derelict in her duties towards her. She had honestly done her utmost to lead her in the ways of a lady, and now to have it flung in her face as worthless was an insult to her pride. But Alice Hamilton did not give up easily. She might have lost this small skirmish but the war was far from over. She knew where her duty lay, as Eleanor and Richard Hamilton's daughter, and if it took her weeks, months, she would prise her sister away from these women who were having such devastating influence over her. She must get her to the House of Lovell where Sara would fall once more beneath Alice's wise and ladylike dominance, where she would learn all there was to know, as Alice meant to, of how to run a great fashion house. Alice had plans for herself and without Sara beside her it would be well nigh impossible to implement them. It was early days yet so let her have her tiny measure of freedom. Let her forget that lout and get tired of these low-class working women and when she did Alice would come into her own again.

"Very well," she said coldly, "but I shall come to Abercromby Square" – Alice could not call it home – "every weekend to see how things are here. You are still under age, you know, Sara, and I am, strictly speaking, your guardian."

Sara stared in consternation.

"Oh yes, I see that surprises you," Alice said grimly, not at all sure it was true. "I will not enforce it but make no mistake, I mean to keep an eye on you and if I am not satisfied with your conduct I shall make it my business to see that you are brought back to my guidance."

It was just a week later when Alice saw the advertisement in the *Liverpool Mercury*. She didn't know where the newspaper had come from, for it was not the sort Madame Lovell or one of her female clients was likely to read. Perhaps one of the footmen, or the housekeeper, had left it lying about and it had been collected to make paper firelighters by one of the parlourmaids. It was on a chair at the back of the hallway, beyond the circle of light cast by the lamps and Alice picked it up without thinking. Betty Holden was a splendid needlewoman of the plain sort, bending hour after tireless hour over the hems of skirts and underskirts, putting in the well-nigh invisible stitches which were her special skill, but she was not well educated, as Alice understood the word. She could read and write but, knowing that Miss Hamilton was a lady born and bred who had come down in the world through no fault of her own, she was overawed by her and her conversation was restricted to "Yes, Miss Hamilton," "No, Miss Hamilton," "Indeed, Miss Hamilton," and "I'm sure you're right, Miss Hamilton."

After weeks of this in the bedroom they shared, and lacking books of the sort she was used to, Alice was glad of anything with which to while away the remainder of the evening before they got into their respective beds and the newspaper, though not the quality of *The Times*, a good liberal newspaper which Papa had favoured, would do as a substitute.

As she turned a page her sister's name leaped out at her and for a moment she thought her heart would never resume its jerky beat so great was her shock. She had read the words right through to the end before they made any sense to her but even as she did her best to untangle them she glanced about her just as though she were afraid she might find Betty hanging over her shoulder. But Betty sat placidly brushing her long fine hair, her face calm and unthinking, her eyes unfocused. She was impressed by the ease with which her well-bred roommate raced through the words in the newspaper but she would not dream of saying so. She knew her place did Betty.

Alice, who had crumpled the pages of the newspaper guiltily together in her instinctive need to hide away the words written there, opened it again carefully and, making sure Betty could not see should she glance in Alice's direction, reread the advertisement.

WILL MISS SARA HAMILTON, LATE OF WRAY GREEN, NR KIRKHAM, LANCASHIRE, OR ANYONE KNOWING OF HER WHEREABOUTS, PLEASE CONTACT JACK ANDREWS, AGENT, AT THE OFFICES OF THE LIVERPOOL, ORMSKIRK AND PRESTON RAILWAY, OR AT THE EAST LANCASHIRE RAILWAY WITH WHICH IT WILL SOON BE AMALGAMATED. THIS MATTER IS VERY URGENT. A REWARD WILL BE GIVEN.

Alice gripped the paper so tightly it tore beneath her frantic fingers and she made a conscious effort to relax. She breathed in and out deeply, afraid she would swoon, then slowly lowered the newspaper to her lap and stared in growing horror into the steady flame of the candle beside her.

Sweet Christ Jesus, he was still after her. All this time with Alice believing quite firmly that he had become tired of Sara. Tired of her inexperience and youth which could offer nothing to a man such as he, and had taken himself off to see what other women he could tempt with his coarse charms. She could never, if she lived to be an old, old lady, understand what Sara had found so attractive in him though she supposed he had a kind of gypsyish good looks. But thank heaven Alice had been able to get Sara away from him, though the manner of it had been somewhat drastic and thank heaven no one appeared to have seen the advertisement, or at least no one had mentioned it to Alice. The names of many of the sewing girls were unknown to the servants, besides which Sara did not come into contact with any, only the maid who brought the food to the communal room where the needlewomen ate their meals and there was no time for idle gossip. The newspaper was already a fortnight old so it looked as though no one had been drawn to the advertisement or they would surely have spoken up.

So, it seemed the navvie had gone up in the world! Agent now, but still not good enough for Eleanor and Richard Hamilton's daughter, nor for Alice Hamilton's sister. Besides which, if he had been Lord Mayor of Liverpool Alice did not mean him to have Sara. Alice had her own plans for Sara and they did not include Jack Andrews.

Carefully folding the pages of the newspaper, Alice placed them on the bed beside her then turned to smile warmly at Betty.

"Do you not think it is cold in here, Betty?" she asked.

Betty, who had always been addressed as Miss Holden by Miss Hamilton, nearly fell off her chair. Her mouth popped open and Alice wondered irritably why Madame had thought to put her with such a bovine creature. Perhaps because this was one of the best and biggest rooms in Madame's establishment and she, recognising Alice's superiority, had realised it was the only one suitable for her. There were two beds each covered in a snowy counterpane. A large wardrobe which they shared, a dressing-table with a mirror which Alice took over as her own and a small fireplace with two easy chairs before it. There was a bit of carpet on the floor, worn but not threadbare and white muslin curtains at the window. Plain, wholesome, clean and comfortable within bounds. Madame, who employed only the most skilful and respectable women, did not treat them as many employers in the dressmaking trade did. They did not labour in small, inadequately ventilated rooms as countless thousands did, nor were they forced to sleep a dozen at a time in crowded dormitories. Madame's seamstresses slept only two in a room, each girl carefully selected so that her personality and nature fitted that of her roommate, as far as this was possible. Madame had known at once that Betty Holden, docile and submissive, would make a perfect partner for Alice Hamilton, and so she had, willing to bow and scrape and run errands at Alice's bidding.

"Well . . ." She hesitated, not quite sure what answer Miss Hamilton required of her.

"Why do you not run down to the kitchen for a scuttle of coal and some firewood. Madame told us we might have a fire in the evening if we were prepared to make it ourselves and I find it quite chilly in here. I'll make some paper firelighters from this old newspaper while you are gone and then we can sit with our toes to the fire and get lovely and warm before we get into our beds. Off you go, Betty, there's a good girl and perhaps we'll have a mug of cocoa, tell Cook."

Astounded to be invited to sit with her toes to the fire with Miss Hamilton and by the way Miss Hamilton spoke as though Cook was in her own personal employ, nevertheless Betty obligingly headed for the back stairs which led down to the kitchens and when she returned, hefting the coal scuttle filled with coal and firewood in one hand, and balancing a tray with two mugs of cocoa on the other, Miss Hamilton had already rolled and coiled the firelighters and laid them in the fireplace.

Miss Hamilton did not speak again except to wish Betty a curt goodnight as she climbed into her bed and Betty refrained from telling her what Cook had said about uppity needlewomen.

She sighed. She never knew where she was with Miss Hamilton.

17

The two exceedingly pretty girls sauntered between the stalls in Pedlars Market in Deane Street, their full skirts dipping and swaying gracefully, their young, high breasts thrusting forward with the erectness of their carriage, their fashionable bonnets nodding and bouncing as they chatted to one another or turned to glance at the contents of each stall.

Pedlars Market, the front of which was actually in Elliott Street, was not so large nor so splendid as St John's Market but then its function was altogether different. Where St John's Market sold game, poultry, meat, fruit, vegetables, eggs and every kind of provision an efficient housewife might require, Pedlars Market was just what the title said it was, displaying all the goods a pedlar might carry from door to door, and more. Hand-woven baskets, earthenware pots, glass, toys, bonnets, bolts of material, cotton and needles, knitting wool, pins, buttons and ribbons, pans and ladles and scrubbing brushes and indeed boasted that if Madame did not see exactly what she wanted amongst its kaleidoscope of gee-gaws and knick-knacks, its trinkets and bric-à-brac, by next market day whatever it was would be in her hand!

"Mornin' girls," a genial voice called out. "Yer out an' about early terday. Lookin' fer summat special, was yer?"

Both girls turned and a beaming red face in which an eye winked impudently reared up over the stall behind them. "Reared" was the applicable word for the stallholder was no more than four feet six inches in height and he was forced to leap up on a box which he kicked adroitly into position wherever it was needed. Spread out on the stall before him was cheap crockery in many patterns and colours, cups and saucers, plates of all sizes, teapots and sugar basins and jugs.

Later, when the market filled up, he would start his patter, drawing the crowds to his stall with his cheeky humour and the "bargains" he begged them to buy, but at this time of a Saturday morning most folk were either at work or, if they were not, having a "lie-in".

"Mornin', Archie." It was Matty Hutchinson who answered, as she usually did, her irrepressible Liverpool wit rising to challenge his and for several minutes they bantered with one another while, beside Matty, Sara smiled shyly, only putting in a word when Archie spoke directly to her. It was not often that Sara and Matty had a Saturday "off" together since it was a working day for both of them, but now and again, if the work in hand allowed, Madame Lovell and the Misses Yeoland, who employed Matty, gave permission for their needlewomen to take turns at being granted not only their usual Sunday, but Saturday as well. It gave them a chance to do some shopping and Madame, at least, found her girls worked all the better the rest of the time for having had this little treat.

"An' where are you two off, then?" Archie continued. "Doin' a birra sparkin' then? If yer don't 'ave any luck gi' me a shout, will yer?"

"Give over! We'd 'ave ter be pretty desperate ter walk out wi' you, Archie Goodwin, wouldn't we, Sara?"

Archie took no offence. "Is that right, queen? Well, let me tell yer there's many a good thing comes outa small package."

He winked again and from across the aisle another stallholder guffawed and took up the repartee.

"Leave off, Archie. What would these two fashionable young ladies want wi' an old rogue like you? Now if it's quality they're after they need ter look no further."

"Yer must be jokin', Tommy Ashworth. Me an' Sara's right perticler 'oo we're seen with, aren't we, chuck? Come on" – Matty took Sara's arm in a pretence of great affront – "let's gerron an' see if we can't find ourselves a couple o' proper gentlemen."

There was much good-natured laughter and chaff, all of it respectful, as the two girls made their way along the narrow aisles which threaded through the stalls, coming to a halt at the one at the far end on the right. It was very evident that they were both a familiar sight in the market for men and women stallholders alike spoke to them as they went by, even if it was only to nod a smiling good morning.

They were both beautifully gowned and bonneted, Sara Hamilton and Matty Hutchinson, which was only to be expected of young ladies who were employed by two of the foremost fashion houses in Liverpool. Of course the Misses Yeoland, where Matty was now a first hand and earning thirty pounds a year, were not of the status of the House of Lovell, but the two spinsters had a wide clientèle of middle-class ladies, wives of wealthy businessmen, and their quality and style was much sought after. Sara was in the palest cream, a rich, unwatered moiré with a gleam to it which shimmered as she walked. It was really not suitable for walking about the market but it was new, it was May and the weather was mild and spring-like with no need of shawls or cloaks and in the dim light of the market she seemed to float with a glowing radiance about her, caused by the reflection from the lovely fabric. The gown was simply but superbly cut, fitting like a second skin to her breasts and waist where the bodice dipped to a point. The sleeves were wrist length, the skirt was wide, full and plain but about her waist was a narrow velvet ribbon of vivid scarlet and hanging from it in a knot of ribbons at the front was a tiny posy of velvet rosebuds of the same colour. The crown of her bonnet was covered with them, all clustered and curled together as though they grew there to the edge of the brim. The brim itself was lined with cream moiré.

Matty, whose bright blue eyes, dark, glossy curls and white skin looked well in bold colours, wore a gown of soft light twilled silk in a shade somewhere between blue and lavender. It had a richness which turned her eyes to a colour which is often seen in wood violets. Her bonnet, like Sara's, matched her gown exactly, for had not both outfits been made by the girls from materials supplied, at cut prices, of course, since they were the end of last year's summer range, by their respective employers. They had sat together on many an evening in Sara's newly refurbished room at the top of the house, sewing and gossiping and laughing at the exploits of Matty's clients whom she mimicked wickedly. Matty, as first hand, was a fitter now, dealing with the ladies themselves and she had many a tale to recount of the conversations she overheard, much of it quite scandalous. Miss Emily would skin her if she knew Matty passed it on but really, what some of the ladies of society got up to was unbelievable and besides, she knew Sara wouldn't tell anyone else.

It was not every night that Sara and Matty spent in one another's company for when business was especially brisk one or the other was often compelled to work late and then there were the nights when Matty had "a bit of business" to attend to, saying no more, and on these nights Sara sewed alone or went downstairs to sit with Lily and Dolly.

Lily and Dolly were close cronies now, despite the twenty years difference in their age for, like Lily, Dolly was a beggar for scrubbing and polishing and giving "what for" to every surface in the house, horizontal or vertical, it was all the same to her, including those in Miss Sara's room when she was not about.

"'Ere, I'll do that, queen," Lily would say to Dolly when she found her on her knees on the basement steps with brush and bucket.

"Yer'll not," Dolly would answer tartly. "When I can't scrub a few steps then yer can put me in me coffin an' screw down't lid. An' don't walk on 'em, yer daft 'apporth. I've just done 'em."

They understood one another perfectly and though, naturally, they didn't voice it, a great respect and affection grew up between them as they stood shoulder to shoulder in their protective love for Sara Hamilton. Dolly had told Lily, in confidence of course, the whole sad story of Eleanor Hamilton, who died so young, and her vague and kindly husband. About Jack and Miss Sara, God love 'er, whose heart had been broken when he failed to return. About Alice Hamilton and her desperate attempt to climb the social ladder which would lead up to the so-called local "gentry" in Wray Green and the sourness which had begun in her when she had failed.

"She'll need watchin', Mrs Canon," Dolly said succinctly, "else she'll swallow up Miss Sara like the whale swallowed Jonah."

Lily knew exactly what Dolly meant.

"Nay, Miss Watson, not wi' you an' me ter see to 'er, she won't," she answered firmly and they smiled at each other over one of their eternal cups of tea. Dolly was as lively and quick-witted as she had ever been, more so now, for with Lily Canon to gossip with and the "goings on" in Abercromby

Square to occupy her she was as content as she had ever been, even in the little house in Wray Green. As long as Miss Sara was safe – and that meant from her predatory, domineering sister – and beginning to recover from her great loss, not only of the man she loved but her dear Papa, Dolly was "made up" with her new life.

On their day off, if the weather allowed, Sara and Matty would take a walk, either to the Zoological Gardens in West Derby Road, the Botanic Gardens in Edge Lane, or the river. Today it was to be the turn of the river. You would have thought she'd have had enough of walking, Sara would laugh, after the miles she trudged to and from the House of Lovell. It had not been easy, that walk along Oxford Street in the cold dark of a winter morning. Cutting through the maze of ill-lit streets up to Mount Vernon, jumping at every sound and shadow, and then on to country roads, past the Zoological Gardens to the turn into Breck Road where the house stood. High, wind-lashed hedges, the bare branches of trees whipping over her head, rutted, rain-filled lanes, clouds racing across a half-lit sky. Snow had fallen and she had been forced to stay two nights at Lovell House, sharing her triumphant sister's bed. There had been frost, stark and rigid, which turned the fields and lanes to fairyland, diamonds in hedges and white velvet along each still and frozen branch. That had been lovely though she had almost twisted her ankle as she sped along the hard-packed, icy ruts of the lanes.

Now it was spring and for the next few months she would tramp across the burgeoning fields in her stout walking boots, skirting the crops which were planted, marching through herds of curious, big-eyed cows, cutting her journey by half, trusted now by Madame to be on time to start her day's work. Madame had been hinting just lately that changes were to be made in the status of the Hamilton sisters and Alice was tickled pink. Not surprised, of course, for had she not suspected all along that Madame had something special up her sleeve for Alice and her sister who were, after all, a cut above the rest of Madame's girls. On this Saturday she had been vexed by Sara's intention to have a day out with that dreadful girl at Abercromby Square, resentful of the fact that Madame couldn't see her way to letting Alice accompany her sister, who was bound to waste her day completely in frivolous activities. But she had a feeling Madame might be going to discuss her plans with her and so it was as well she stayed close at hand. Naturally Alice could speak for Sara in any matter concerning their future.

The stall at the far end of Pedlars Market was given over to paintings. To prints of what what were described as "celebrated masters", to engravings and pictures of all kinds from the tiniest unframed watercolour to enormous, badly executed and framed oil paintings of ladies with bright pink lips and cheeks, and moustachioed gentlemen. There were dozens of them, hanging from frames, jostling against one another in vivid confusion. There were pastoral scenes, cattle knee deep in lush clover, lowering mountains and high crags on which were perched antlered deer. There were kittens and puppies romping in baskets and to one side, evidently not "good sellers", squares of rough white paper on which were sketches done in charcoal. A swathe of grass starred with delicate flowers. A dog lying in a shaft of sunlight, one eyebrow raised questioningly. A slightly blurred group of barefoot children, a sailing ship, sails furled, spars bare against the sky. All simple, no more really than a hazed outline of the subject, a feeling of what the artist wished to convey but done with heart, with immense feeling, with a touch which was breathtaking.

Among them were a dozen or so of Sara and Matty, alone, and together, serious, laughing, Sara shy, Matty bold but capturing them so accurately it was as though they were both about to step out of the paper.

The young man seated behind the stall had his head bent as his hand flew over a rough charcoal sketch of the old woman on the opposite stall. She was not aware that she was being drawn by the young man and she nodded, half asleep as she waited for customers.

"Good mornin', Davey," Matty called out and the old woman woke up with a start. The young man threw Matty a half irritated, half resigned look then rose lazily to his feet, placing the sheet of paper on a pile of others beside him on the cluttered stall. He was a pleasant-faced young man with a mouth which had a perpetual half-smile lifting the corners. A good-humoured face but watchful as though he was ever conscious of an opportunity which must not be missed. His fair skin was sun-browned from the collar of his open shirt to his hairline, for he worked a great deal out of doors with his artist's pad and paints.

He turned from Matty to Sara, his artist's eye studying the fine bones of her face, the delicate turn to her jawline and eyebrows and his fingers itched to be about the business of capturing her once again on paper. She smiled at him, her expression frank and open. She liked David, for though she was aware that he thought women, at least women with money, to be fair game, he treated her as no more than a friend. As he did Matty. Probably because he knew they could not give him what he needed which was the freedom to paint as he wanted to. He was worth smiling at, most women would agree. His nose was slightly crooked, probably from some fight in his tough childhood but his hair fell in pale gold feathers across his high forehead and his eyes, a deep blue-grey, were long-lashed and set wide apart. His expression was boyish. He was twenty-two years old, Matty had told her and she had also told her that he was looking for a patron – raising her eyebrows suggestively since it could only be a woman – to support his talent.

Since September, whenever Sara came to look at his sketches and at the second-rate paintings done by other artists which he sold, he did his best to persuade her to come to his rooms and allow him to paint her, without much hope, he knew. He made a steady living, selling whatever he could from his stall to women with no taste who could not resist his pleasing looks and charming manner. Framing and mounting portraits was enough to keep a roof over his head, a coat on his back and food in his mouth, but that was all it was and he was constantly on the lookout for a rich patron.

"'An' wharr've you bin up to since we last saw yer, Davey Bretherton?" Matty continued, winking suggestively and Davey winked back at her.

He was aware that Matty knew of his careless approach to everything in life except his art. He and Matty were of the same class. They had clawed their way up the ladder of life from a childhood of hardship and want and were both on the first rung upwards. Nothing must get in the way. At least in *his* way. Sometimes Sara came alone, lingering at his stall to admire his work, sometimes buying a sketch he would gladly have given her. She would shake her head guilelessly, wondering out loud to him on why he should want to sketch her, bobbing her head in embarrassment when he told her, as an artist naturally, how beautiful she was. On occasion he had persuaded her to sit at the back of his stall and pose for him and it was then that the customers flocked, drawn to her innocent loveliness and his artistry as he captured it on paper.

"What were you doing just then, David?" she asked him now. "Were you sketching the old lady on the other stall?" nodding across at her, returning her toothless grin. "May I see it?" She held out her hand and he put the sketch in it.

"David, it's wonderful," she breathed. "Very like her and yet there is so little to it. Just a few lines . . ."

He grinned engagingly and his eyes lit up.

"That's about it, Sara. There's nowt to 'em. To any of 'em else I'd be a famous painter an' not a bloody stall holder." His shrug asked her to forgive his swearing.

"Nonsense, I love it and if I may I'll buy it."

"Glory be ter God, Sara, yer've norran inch ter spare on them walls o' yours. Plastered from floor ter ceiling wi' Davey's pickshers they are an' what your Alice'll do when she sees 'em I shudder ter think. She'll be flingin' t'cat about kitchen in temper an' goin' on about you wasting yer money an' a right old ter do there'll be."

"It doesn't matter what Alice says," Sara protested bravely. "It's my room for which I pay the rent and if I want to cover the walls with David's sketches, which I greatly admire, then I shall. When I have enough money I shall have them all framed."

"'Ere, steady on, chuck," Matty laughed as Sara turned glowing, admiring eyes on David Bretherton. He was tall, slender and when he walked out from behind the stall to stand before her Sara's bonnet was somewhere on a level with his chin. Despite his youth David Bretherton had known many women and was at this moment deeply involved with a widow, twenty years older than himself but with – as he put it – a bob or two to spend and he was doing his best with the power and beauty of his young male body to persuade her to part with a few of them. He needed money to support himself while he fulfilled his passion and talent for painting.

"I'm glad you like it, Sara," he murmured softly.

"Oh? I do, David, I do. May I buy it?" she asked him earnestly and Matty watched them both, smiling. She and David had known one another for years, growing up in the same neighbourhood of Scotland Road and it was she who had brought about the introduction between Sara and David.

They said their goodbyes, Sara with the sketch wrapped in a bit of brown paper tucked under one arm and David's eyes followed the retreating figures of both girls until they disappeared from view, then before he lost it he sat down and rapidly sketched them from memory, capturing the delicate bones and tenderly arched eyebrow of Sara, the bold endearing smile of Matty.

When it was completed he placed the sketch in a satchel at the back of his stall. He would give it to Sara on her next visit. It would please her, he knew and if she was pleased perhaps she would let him paint her, do a formal portrait in colour which could only do justice to her loveliness.

The thought pleased him so much his smile was dazzling as he turned to a plump little woman who was interested, she said, and if the price was right, in the one of the kittens, faltering a little under the power of his smile. It'd look grand on her parlour wall, she added, patting her greying hair where it flopped from beneath the brim of her respectable bonnet. The frame was lovely, as well and she'd have that too for it set the whole thing off a treat, didn't he agree?

The tall, broad-shouldered young man peered absently into one of the three windows which made up the frontage of the outfitter's shop in Lord Street. It was a very smart shop and business was brisk. So brisk it had just moved from the poorer quarters of Corinthian Street to this new and fashionable address, a move which had been widely advertised in all the local newspapers as well as in *Lacey's Guide To Liverpool*.

E.S. Tuton was a silk mercer and shawlman, outfitter to those who travelled to China and all other parts of the globe, it said above the three polished windows. Over the shop windows was a broad ledge on which stood four female figures of stone draped in the Grecian style and behind the figures were five long windows, heavily curtained. Woollens, linens, velvets, shawls, cloaks and every conceivable article of clothing, outer and inner, that a lady or gentleman might require was sold within, it advertised, besides having an admirable tailoring service which was second to none.

The man was well dressed in a good-quality black frock-coat and grey striped trousers. His shirt front was snowy and his boots meticulously polished. The only odd thing about him was that he carried his top hat and gloves instead of wearing them. The sunshine burnished his rich, smoothly brushed chestnut hair with gold and copper streaks and put a gleam of light in his deep brown eyes.

He stared morosely into the window, his expression saying quite plainly that he was reluctant to venture into the shop, then, sighing deeply in what appeared to be resignation, he tucked his hat beneath his arm, stuffed his gloves in his pocket and turned away.

"Get it over with, lad," he muttered to himself.

There were two doors to the establishment, one claiming to be the entrance to "Ladies' Ready Made Linen", the second "Gentlemen's Ready Made Linen". It was through the latter that the young man entered.

"You make suits?" he enquired brusquely of the male assistant who hurried forward.

"We do indeed, sir," the assistant replied, "of the very best quality. What kind of suit were you thinking of?" eyeing the hard lines of the customer's body beneath his clothes, the breadth of his shoulders, the tapering waist, the lean hips. His legs were long and even through the material of his trousers the shop assistant could make out the strong muscles of his thighs and calves. A difficult gentleman indeed to fit in ready made clothing!

"Several," the man growled, glaring around him as though to defy anyone even so much as to look in his direction. He was not a gentleman, the assistant decided, not a born gentleman that is, for his rough tongue gave him away, but nevertheless he looked prosperous enough.

"Of course, sir," the assistant added smoothly. "Might I ask for what occasion?"

"Well, day wear, a couple I'd say and . . . an evening suit." For a second or two a whimsical gleam lit the customer's eye just as though he were dwelling on a private joke and the assistant wondered what it could be but it was none of his business.

"Of course, sir. Perhaps you would care to step into one of our fitting rooms to be measured?"

"Aye, but first let's have your price list."

"My price list, sir?"

"Lad, I don't buy something without knowing what I'm to pay for it." The man smiled grimly, revealing his perfect teeth.

"No indeed, sir, but the price depends on the quality of the cloth."

"Let's hear it then."

"Certainly, sir. Now let me see. Dress coats range from £1 6s 6d to £3 8s 6d which, of course, is the very best."

"Aye, go on."

"Frock-coats are from 18s to £1 4s 6d, trousers from 16s 6d to £1 10s. Waistcoats are extra, naturally, from 9s to 15s and our cloth cloaks start at £1 15s and go up to £3 10s . . ."

"Bloody hell," the man muttered, "that's more than I earned in a month onceover."

The assistant looked startled but quickly recovered his composure.

"Now, our shirts of the very finest lawn range from 10s 6d to 18s 6d each. We have evening cloaks and— "

"Aye, righto lad, that'll do. You get me measured up and tell me the full cost of what I want and I'll tell you if I'll pay it. How's that and let's be sharp about it."

The speaker turned away irritably just as though the whole damned business was something he could well do without. His eyes moved from displays of beautifully made shirts, to waistcoats, scarf neckcloths, breeches and what were described as "pantaloons". He made a small derisory sound in the back of his throat and the assistant turned enquiringly.

"Was there something else, sir?" he asked politely.

"What in hell's name are pantaloons?"

"They are for riding and hunting, sir. Perhaps you would like to try a pair on?"

"God in heaven, no. Me and horses don't get on," and he smiled as though at some memory. His rather grim face lit up with the brightness of it and the assistant was quite flabbergasted by the change it wrought in him.

"Very well, sir, if you'd come this way we'll make a start."

Sara and Matty idled down to the bottom of Whitechapel, turning the corner into Lord Street with the intention of making their way down its length, through Derby Square and on to Princes Parade. It was such a lovely day, they both agreed, it would be a shame to spend it in and about the shops and what better way to while away an hour or two than a leisurely stroll along the parade with the rest of the promenaders?

Sara loved the dock area and the gracefully elegant sailing ships moored there and though it was sometimes a bit embarrassing, for the men who worked there were inclined to stop, grow silent and stare as she walked by, not one made a remark or a gesture at which she could take offence. Even alone she felt no fear. They did not threaten her, these cheerfully whistling, industriously labouring dockers, indeed she had noticed a few doff their caps and nod, ready to smile if she did as though they recognised her for what she was. A young girl who needed the wide spaces and the busy bustle, the uncritical detachment of strangers in which to heal the wound Jack's going had left her with. As though they sensed she nursed some deep sorrow and sympathised with her need to be by herself. She was aware that Alice would have a fit if she knew, expounding at length on the impropriety of a young lady of Sara's class going about unescorted but only Lily and Dolly were aware of the times she slipped out of the house by herself and they were not likely to give her secret away, least of all to Miss Hoity-Toity.

She would walk the long parade, stopping to lean on its parapet to stare bleakly down into the heaving grey waters of the Mersey, watching each little ripple as it slapped against the worn stone. Her gaze would rise to the raucous wheeling of the scavenging gulls, admiring their flawless grace and beauty, then travel across the river southwards to the Cheshire woods or north to the Irish Channel, to Bootle Bay and Crosby, the Rock Perch Lighthouse and Fort. At high tide the parade was often lined with spectators, for there was no finer view in the world, the proud citizens of Liverpool thought.

And then of course there were the steamboats. Every half-hour they departed for Seacombe and Egremont and New Brighton and what better way to spend an hour than watching the comings and goings of the men and women, the steam ferries that carried them, the loading and unloading of the great sailing ships, the ships themselves as they lifted their winged sails and flew down the water on the tide.

Now and again, if her memory was particularly anguished

with strong and painful images of Jack, if she could not clear them from her heart and mind with hard work, or a book she borrowed from the Liverpool Circulating Library at the bottom of Bold Street, she would throw on her cloak and stride out of Abercromby Square and along Mount Pleasant, cutting through to Bold Street, Hanover Street, past the Customs House and down to where the clipper ships and barquentines, frigates and schooners lay sleeping at their berths. Past George's Dock and Princes Dock and its basin and on until she reached Marine Parade. From there you could walk the full length of Waterloo, Victoria, Trafalgar and Clarence Docks, across the Salisbury Gates which opened to allow the great ships into Salisbury Dock. On beyond where the cattle ships unloaded their cargo at Bramley More Dock and further and further until she reached the northernmost point of the dockland, and the Fort.

She literally walked her way back, if not to content, then to acceptance, returning to Abercromby Square with peace in her heart where there had been torment.

But today there was an uplifting of her youthful spirits as the sunshine bathed her and Matty in its benevolent glow. It shot her silken hair through with copper, gold and amber, with tawny lights which quivered in a fall of curls against her creamy neck. Heads turned, male and female, to follow the progress of the two young girls as they sauntered along Lord Street, stopping to gaze into shop windows as they went.

"Look at that lovely silver teapot," Matty enthused, "an' all them jugs an' things ter match. An' will yer cast yer peepers on them rings. What wouldn't I give fer a diamond like that."

The window of Thomas Dinsmore, Silversmith and Jeweller, was given their full attention, as was the splendid stock of rich and elegant furs draped artfully behind the glassed front of Henry George Ireland, Furrier, next door but one.

"Oh, do come and look at this panne velvet, Matty," Sara begged, doing her best to drag her friend away from a picture of herself in the magnificent sable in Mr Ireland's window.

"Where?"

"There, in Tuton's window, in that lovely shade of, what would you call it, garnet?"

"Mmmm, an' it'd suit you a treat wi' your hair."

"I wonder how much it is a yard? More than I can afford I should think." Sara sighed.

"Why don't yer go in an' ask? Yer've a tongue in yer head, haven't yer?"

"I don't like to, Matty. It's bound to be expensive."

"D'yer want me ter go?"

"Would you, Matty? Oh, I wish I was as brave as you."

"Don't be daft, chuck. Now I'll not be a minute."

She wasn't. She came out of the shop pulling a face. Threading her arm through Sara's, she led her away in the direction of Derby Square.

"Aye, yer right, queen. It was expensive an' outa our price range for't time being. But there were a lovely chap in there give me the eye." She giggled and Sara turned to smile affectionately at her.

"You're incorrigible, Matty Hutchinson, d'you know that?"

"I don't even know what it means but whatever it is I think that bloke liked it 'cos he didn't half give me a smile as I left shop. If I'd bin on me own, playin' me cards right which I would, o' course, I reckon I could've clicked."

"You can go back if you like," Sara teased her.

"No. Reckon he's like as not gorra wife an' ten kids at 'ome. Like 'em all."

Matty spoke with unusual bitterness but when Sara turned to her questioningly she squeezed her arm and laughed.

"Eeh, tekk no notice o' me, chuck. Now, let's see what's goin' on at docks. 'Appen there's a couple o' sailors want cheerin' up."

Jack Andrews hailed a cab outside Tuton's, directing the cabbie to take him to the offices of Daniel Browne where the business of the Liverpool, Ormskirk and Preston Railway was conducted, wondering as he did so why he felt particularly disagreeable today. After all, it wasn't every day that a man only a year or two away from being a navvie was invited to dine at the home of one of Liverpool's prominent businessmen. Of course it was Daniel Browne, the contractor, who had been invited in the first place and he himself was only going because of Mr Browne but it was a bit of a feather in his cap, just the same.

"Have you got a . . . ahem . . . evening suit, Jack?" Mr Browne had asked him diffidently, knowing, of course, of Jack's circumstances, and it was for this reason he had paid a visit to Tuton's. He often wondered what his mam would make of her son's swift rise in the ranks of railway builders and vowed, when he had the time, to go up to Woodhead and see her. He wrote her the occasional letter but it was years since he had seen her. Poor Mam.

He sighed deeply, his thoughts of his mother making him feel lonelier than ever. The young lady who had smiled at him in the outfitter's had been the only bright spot in this whole miserable day. He hated bloody weekends and wished now he'd taken up the young lady's very obvious invitation. Pretty she'd been, dark and bold and saucy and the complete antithesis of the girl who resided, like a rare and much valued treasure, in the deep recesses of his heart. He had found consolation and release with other women but in the two years since he had last seen her she had not moved from there and never would. His love for Sara Hamilton was locked in the dungeon of his past.

Sitting back in the cab, he gazed moodily out of the window, dwelling in memories for a brief moment, then resolutely turned his mind to the complexities of transporting cartloads of picks and shovels and wheelbarrows and men to the point along the track where the Liverpool, Ormskirk and Preston Railway had now reached.

He had an even greater interest in this particular railway than in any other he had been involved in for when shares had been offered at its proposal, twenty-four thousand of them at twenty-five pounds each, with dividends of seven and a half per cent, Jack had bought ten of them. Somehow he had scraped enough money together, and now, as a shareholder in the line, and in others, in a small way, of course, he was fast becoming what was known in Lancashire as a "warm man". A man with a bit of "brass"!

Turning his mind to profit and loss, to shares and dividends, to the intricacies of the job in hand he forgot the dark girl in the shop and even pushed to the back of his mind the magical moments he had shared with Sara Hamilton, the silken feel of her skin, her irrepressible laughter and the shiver of joy she had once awakened in him.

Sara!

18

It was the following Monday when Madame summoned Alice and Sara to her sitting-room and, though Alice was disgruntled at the waste of her Saturday and Sunday, which she'd spent hanging around waiting for Madame's call, she threw a triumphant look at the four other seamstresses in the room as though to say "there, at last"!

"Sit down, Miss Hamilton," Madame ordered Alice civilly enough.

"Thank you, Madame." Both Alice and Sara wore the well-made but modest dove grey cotton dresses all Madame's girls wore. It was a kind of uniform, neat and trim with sparkling white cuffs and collar and over it they had on a well-fitting apron which covered them from neck to hem. It tied round the waist and had a frilled bib, with a dozen pockets across the skirt in which all the tools of their trade, or "profession" as Alice liked it to be called, were kept. Each sewing girl, first hands, second hands, third hands, improvers and apprentices, had their own thimble, scissors, tape measure, needles of all sizes, thread of the colour of the garment they were sewing and all must be kept easily to hand.

Sara was surprised by the warmth of Madame's smile. She and Alice had been working at the House of Lovell for eight months now. Officially they were known as improvers and in theory they would remain at this level for a year or two and might then be promoted to third, second and after that, first hand, graduating from simple seaming to the intricacies of cutting and fitting. Ultimately it was possible for them to reach the rank of superintendent and instructor. She was well aware, through Matty, who had been in the business for six years, ever since she became apprenticed to the Misses Yeoland, that many girls were often kept in ignorance of whole areas of the business in an effort to keep them from moving up and on and indeed many of the inferior houses were run predominantly on untrained and poorly paid labour.

Not so Madame Lovell. Sara and Alice had been doing the work of first hands for over six months since Rosalie Lovell could see no point in having two such skilful and talented seamstresses under her roof and not using them to their full capacity. The improvers, even the apprentices, could sew a straight and simple seam! The sisters had both been instructed in cutting and fitting though neither of them really needed any training since both had been doing such things from an early age under their mother's guidance.

As yet, though, neither had had any contact with Madame's clientèle.

"Now then, ladies," she said briskly. "I have decided that it is time both of you moved on from the work you have been doing at the House of Lovell since last . . . when was it?"

"September, Madame," Alice answered eagerly, perching forward on the edge of her seat.

"Of course, September." Madame hesitated and glanced momentarily from Alice's expectant face into the fire and Sara wondered at it for Madame Lovell was always decisive, confident of her own judgment and talent, not only in the designing and creating of beautiful garments but in the running of her great house and all the employees in it. Now it seemed she was stuck for words which was most unlike her.

Taking a deep breath as though to plunge in was the only way she began.

"I have been most impressed, both with your work and with your conduct. You are exceptionally clever seamstresses and not only that but I have seen your designs which are original and very promising. I will go further and say I have never, through the whole of my long career, known better."

Alice preened, turning to give Sara a "didn't I tell you" look.

"You remind me of myself when I was your age," Madame went on.

This was praise indeed and Alice sat up even straighter, the expression on her face one of great satisfaction but at the same time it seemed to convey the impression that it was only to be expected. She knew her own worth, did Alice Hamilton, and now it was to be recognised by Madame Lovell in the only way it could be. Promotion! Alice was already doing the work of a first hand and there were only two positions higher than that. She knew which one she wanted!

"Miss Hamilton, I shall call you that from now on and your sister will be Miss Sara since my clientèle must know one Hamilton from the other." Madame smiled.

It was coming, what she had longed for, and was there anyone who deserved it more? My clientèle, Madame had said and that meant the ladies, real ladies who Alice was bound to meet and could they be anything but charmed by the lovely, gracious manners of Alice Hamilton and then, perhaps . . .

She leaned forward expectantly, her face bright and glowing, looking, in her joyous anticipation, very like her young sister.

"Miss Hamilton, I have decided to put your considerable talents to one of the most important jobs in a fashion house. I am getting older . . . no, don't deny it, my dear, though it is kind of you to do so, but I wish to step back a little and consequently I shall need a trustworthy supervisor, one I can be certain will instruct and guide my girls as I have done. You will virtually run my workrooms, a very great responsibility indeed, and will have in your charge . . ."

Madame's voice faded away until it was no more than the droning of a bumble bee as it dashes itself against a window. The bright, joyful colour had drained away from Alice's face in the shock of her disappointment and she heard nothing of what Madame was saying to her. Supervisor! Instructor! Alice Hamilton was to be no more than a glorified overseer, a woman of no particular standing, for there was nothing more certain, despite what she said, than the reality that this was Madame Lovell's business and Madame Lovell would let no one else run it for her. Not for many, many years! She might talk of Alice being in charge but as she said, it would be in charge of no more than the workrooms. She would not be allowed to associate to any great degree, as Madame Lovell did, with her customers, meeting the well-bred ladies who gave their custom to this great house. She would not wear some modest but lovely creation of her own making and glide about the showrooms as Madame did, but would be expected to remain in the background, just like the other sewing girls. True, she had no need ever again to suffer the backache or eyestrain which was the fate of all needlewomen after bending for sixteen hours a day over her work but she would not be the bright star, the prestigious, envied crème de la crème that only four or five women in Madame's establishment achieved.

". . . and so I propose to pay you sixty pounds a year, which is perhaps the highest wage, at least here in Liverpool, that an employee in the dressmaking trade can earn. You are worth it, Miss Hamilton, and I am sure you will not abuse the great confidence I have in you. Naturally, your board and food will be included in your wage so you can see how much esteem I hold you in. You will begin at once. I know you will stand no nonsense from the girls with whom you have worked, since I know you to be a woman of strong will and resolution."

It was only Alice's strong will and resolution which kept her from standing up and throwing Madame Lovell's damned job back in her face; from screaming to the four corners of the house that she was worth more than this, that she deserved the "best" job in this establishment and Madame knew it. Any competent needlewoman who would stand no nonsense from the seamstresses could be what Madame Lovell wanted Alice to be, but Alice was not only a first-class needlewoman but cutter and fitter as well. She was well bred and knew exactly how to deal with ladies like herself. She was pretty and well mannered and she'd wanted that job more than anything she had ever wanted in her life. Now she had to bite her tongue, arrange her face into a pleasant and grateful smile and give thanks for a job she had not even considered. Sixty pounds a year! God, she should be jubilant, for the wage was more than even a chef of many years standing could earn but the bitterness curdled her stomach and brought the sour taste of bile to her mouth.

Alice'e eyes told of her feelings, of course, and Rosalie Lovell, conjecturing on how she would be in a moment or two, marvelled at the strength of her control.

She turned to Sara who was watching her sister anxiously. Sara could see that Alice was in a terrible rage about something, she didn't know what and could think of no reason for it since the job she was being offered was a triumph. Sixty pounds a year and all found and for doing work which would suit Alice down to the ground. Ordering all the other girls about, playing Miss Hoity-Toity to the hilt, conferring importantly with Madame on the day-to-day running of the house and yet Alice was not pleased.

When Madame spoke again Sara knew why!

"Now you, Miss Sara, have all the qualities needed to be a 'magazinière' and that is what I propose to train you for. Magazinières are usually French but I can see no reason why we should not make an exception in your case. Mademoiselle Jeanette is our 'première magazinière' . . . oh, my dear, do you not know what I mean? You are to be a 'showroom woman', in plain English and will be under the supervision of Mademoiselle for some months until you are capable of . . ."

Alice sprang to her feet and Rosalie Lovell sighed.

"Showroom woman! You propose to give the position of showroom woman to this . . . this child who is not yet eighteen and yet I am thought fit to be no more than supervisor. I am to be shut in the back of the house with thirty half-witted girls who can barely read while she parades herself before your clients. Can you not see that I am far more suited than she is . . ."

"No, Miss Hamilton, you are not."

". . . being older, more experienced." Alice continued as though Madame had not spoken. "I am just as . . . as attractive and can converse with a lady in a way she is used to as she chooses her materials. Sara is not fit, believe me, Madame, since she is shy and tongue-tied."

"I do not find her so, Miss Hamilton," Madame said patiently, while Sara sat as if carved from stone, every vestige of colour gone as Alice's venomous rage washed over her, "and if she is modest then that is all to the good. Shyness is a pretty trait and her youthful charm . . ."

Sara, as Alice had done minutes before, lost the thread of what Madame was saying, drifting away into a shadowed place where voices could be heard but not what they said. Of course she knew what a magazinière was. Had she not seen Mademoiselle Jeanette and the other French ladies who were trained, first as dressmakers as Sara was, but, because of their elegance, their chic, their looks, their talent and their ability to please customers, became essentially the representative of the great fashion houses they served. They guided and advised each client, helping her to choose exactly the right fabric and design for any occasion. It must be the right colour and they must know how that colour would look in every light, deliberating at great length on what suited just her. Even the simplest garment to be worn at home, perhaps, in the client's own sitting-room, must be completely appropriate and needed many hours of careful consideration. The magazinière's taste and flair must be flawless for she was trusted implicitly, not only by Madame but by Madame's clients, all of them wealthy but many with no idea of how to dress themselves fashionably. It was in their hands that the reputation of a first-class fashion house, or a court dressmaker, rested and Madame Lovell was offering such a position to Sara Hamilton.

The little knot of warmth began in the middle of her chest, spreading in a shivery but most delightful way down into her stomach and up into her throat so that she could hardly breathe. It flared then, an explosive excitement which threatened to have her off her seat and dancing about Madame's lovely sitting-room and all she wanted to do was dash from here, fling on her cloak and run across the fields to Abercromby Square. To share this wonderful thing with Lily and Dolly. She wasn't frightened of it, not at all. She knew about clothes, she always had. It was a gift she had inherited from, and which had been nurtured by, her mother. She would be nervous at first but she loved talking to people, any people and she had found that as long as she was kind and honest, without being hurtful, of course, sincere and pleasant in her approach, people responded to her. It didn't matter who they were, of what social standing or of none at all, they were all the same and she'd soon . . .

She became aware then of the great commotion Alice was making and of Madame's cold fury and her joy evaporated as quickly as it had come.

"Sit down, Miss Hamilton, if you please," Madame was saying to Alice, her forbearance thrown to the winds, it appeared, "and control yourself or I shall be forced to summon one of the footmen to escort you to the front door. I have never heard such rudeness and lack of gratitude in my life and I certainly do not mean to put up with it. I have offered you a splendid job with a splendid wage, a job I think you are well suited to and all you can say is— "

"And what about her?" Alice flung a demented look at Sara who found she was fastened to her chair by sudden bands of fear. She had never seen her sister so uncontrolled and she knew Alice would be mortified later when she came to her senses. Alice prided herself on her control which was the true mark of a lady.

"What about her, Miss Hamilton? She is to earn no more than you, I can assure you, in view of her age and inexperience."

"I see," Alice spluttered.

"Do you, Miss Hamilton? I hope so for I will put up with no more of your nonsense even if it means I shall lose both of you."

"You may do just that, Madame. My sister and I will not . . . we are in perfect agreement over all aspects of our lives and if I am not happy then— "

"No! Oh no, Alice, if you are not happy then you must go but I will not go with you."

Both women turned to look at her with their mouths open, then Madame smiled.

"Well said, Miss Sara. I am glad to see you have a mind of your own."

Alice could not keep still, jumping to her feet in her acute distress, wringing her hands in a way which was totally unlike her.

"I will deal with you later, Sara Hamilton," she hissed venomously at her sister, then, whirling on her heel, her full skirt spinning like a top about her, she turned on Madame Lovell.

"You as good as promised me this job, Madame," she protested hotly. "For the past few weeks you have been hinting that you meant to promote me to— "

"To the job which I have just offered you, Miss Hamilton," Madame interrupted. "Now calm down and be sensible, if you please, and allow me to decide what is best for my own establishment and who is to be employed where in it. Sit down and listen to me and you will realise just how fortunate you are. Have you the faintest notion of what goes on in the majority of so called 'fashion houses', and in dressmaking establishments all over the country? There are over twenty thousand dressmakers in London alone and almost as many in Liverpool. Perhaps I am exaggerating somewhat but there are a great many and believe me the conditions the seamstresses work in are appalling. Their hours are long, their quarters insanitary and they do not get enough to eat. I can remember sleeping in a room with ten beds in it, two to a bed. There was one washstand with two dirty broken basins which twenty of us had to share and yet we were expected to present ourselves each day as fresh as newly opened daisies. The bedroom walls ran with damp and consumption among the girls was rife. We ate nothing much beyond bread and butter, for after long hours sitting in a stuffy gas-lit room we had no appetite. We suffered from eye strain, headaches, giddiness, fainting, even hysteria when a girl could take no more. Hour after hour in a bent posture brought on dreadful stomach pain and distortion of the spine, though fortunately I was spared. My companions were so often ill nobody took much notice, refusing to call a doctor. Our faces were pale and puffy, our legs and feet swollen and we were constantly thirsty. I earned four shillings and sixpence a week! I can remember a time when I was about seventeen and by this time an improver in a good house in London. The King's youngest daughter, the old King George II, that is, well, she died and as was the custom the whole population, at least those of decent society, wore mourning. Every woman had to have a black mourning dress and we were put to making them. I did not change my clothes for eight days and nights, Miss Hamilton, and was allowed to snatch only the odd hour or two of sleep on a mattress on the floor and was fed by hand by the owner as I sewed. I almost went blind. We all did. Now those conditions still prevail today and if, as you seem inclined to do, you wish to leave my employ and find an alternative, then be warned that it will be inferior to this. Wherever you go it will be inferior to this. So why not take the job, Miss Hamilton? You will be good at it."

"Oh please, Ally, do as Madame asks, please," Sara begged, the dreadful image of Alice in one of those "sweat shops", as they were called, completely unnerving her. She slid from her chair to kneel at her sister's feet, taking her hands between her own. Her skirts ballooned about her and her body and lovely face rose from it like the stem and blossom of a flower. Her cheeks were flushed and in her distress her hair had become loosened, drifting in soft curling tendrils across her face. She blew one vigorously upwards where it floated for a moment before wisping down again.

Rosalie Lovell held her breath, for even now she was not quite certain that Sara Hamilton would remain if her sister left. She watched, quite fascinated by the battle self-willed Alice Hamilton fought with her own pride. The longing to tell her employer to go to the devil and take her job with her was clear in her expression, the haughty expression of Miss Alice Hamilton, a lady late of the parish of Kirkham. Miss Alice Hamilton would never bend her handsome head to a woman inferior to herself in the social order of things, which Rosalie Lovell was, but she was also practical, a realist and knew that an opportunity like this would never happen again. It was not so much that she had been denied the post she had wanted, though that was bad enough, but that her little sister had been offered it instead and the blow to her vanity had damaged her irretrievably. She would never forgive Madame Lovell and she would never forgive Sara. One day, when her plans came to fruition they would both be made to pay but until then she must bite her tongue and accept the inevitable. But she would never bow her head. Never! She would learn every aspect of the running of a great fashion house. She would pick Madame Lovell's brains, suck from them every last detail that would further her own plans for the future. She would save her splendid wage, add it to the small but growing account she had in the Union Bank at the corner of Bold Street and Hanover Street and indeed, if it could be done, extract every penny she could from every transaction the House of Lovell dealt in and when the time came she would do what she had been scheming towards for the past eighteen months. She must not become estranged from Sara, for Sara was a vital part of Alice's future and though her sister was now a backstabber in Alice's opinion, and could no longer be trusted, Alice must keep her thoughts to herself on that score. Alice Hamilton's time would come!

She lifted her head and there was no sign in her pale green eyes of the vicious content of her heart. It was hard but she managed to smile then thrust Sara from her, shaking her head irritably, so like her usual self, Sara smiled back in relief.

"Get up, you foolish girl," she said. "You will crease your skirt lolling about like that and look at your apron. You have a mark on it. You must change it at once. You know my opinions on the lowering of standards."

"Oh Ally, you're right, as always." Sara beamed, rising to her feet with that particular grace Rosalie Lovell had marked from the start. She leaned forward, impulsively planting a kiss on her sister's cheek from which Alice flinched. But then she was not a great one for demonstrations of affection, Madame knew, not like her warm-hearted sister who would have bestowed kisses on anyone who allowed it. Starved she was, of love, at least from this cold-hearted woman who had risen to stand before her.

"Thank you, Madame," Alice was saying, her head high, her colour the same. "I am most grateful for your offer of the post of supervisor and instructor at the House of Lovell and I can assure you that you will not regret your consideration. I shall, naturally, do everything I can to facilitate the smooth running of the workrooms and you will have no cause for complaint in the behaviour of your staff."

Rosalie Lovell felt a small prick of unease. Dear God, were her needlewomen, innocent of any part in this brouhaha to be made to suffer for Alice Hamilton's disappointment? It would take no great effort to cause strife and dissatisfaction among her staff and Alice Hamilton, if she was so inclined, could turn what was a smooth-running and on the whole a contented workforce into chaotic shambles. A word here, an uncalled-for remark there, whispers in one ear about the laziness of another, a show of favouritism, or disapproval that was unfair and Madame's workrooms would be in uproar. Her girls were clever, hardworking and they were aware of their value in Madame's eyes. That was one of the reasons the House of Lovell was such a success, but let one disruptive influence get out of hand and it could spell disaster.

Alice smiled disarmingly. It was as though the previous scene had not taken place. Alice Hamilton's uncharacteristic loss of control was under close confinement and Alice was the gracious, well-bred, well-mannered young woman she had always been. Her smile was cool but pleasant, her eyes hooded so that the expression in them was concealed. She even took Madame's hand courteously.

Rosalie Lovell relaxed and returned her smile, relieved that the woman had come round. She would, if she chose to, make a wonderful supervisor *and* instructor for she had a great deal of skill and knowledge to pass on.

"There is one thing, Madame, that I think you must insist on, though, now that my sister is to be elevated to the position of magazinière." Alice Hamilton even pronounced the word with its correct French intonation Madame noticed as she withdrew her hand. Strangely, she felt a great desire to wipe the hand Alice had held down her skirt.

"And what is that, Miss Hamilton?" she asked coolly, for if Alice Hamilton in her new position of supervisor and instructor thought it gave her the right to alter or have any part in the running of Rosalie Lovell's business, then she was in for a rude awakening.

"I think it is high time Sara gave up this ridiculous tramping about the countryside and the dark roads of Liverpool and lived in at the house as we all do."

Alice's smile deepened triumphantly.

19

Alice Hamilton was not satisfied and when Miss Hamilton, as her staff had been ordered to call her, was not satisfied, it was they who were made to suffer for it. She had been their supervisor and instructor since May when Madame had, incredibly, promoted her to the position over the heads of older, more experienced, longer-serving sewing women. They had not liked it. They did not like her. She was a lady born, with an hauteur to match and did not consider any one of them to be worth befriending and when Betty Holden had been forced to share a bedroom with her they had felt inordinately sorry for poor Betty. Naturally, now that she was in charge of them, and Betty, Miss Hamilton had been given her own room. Thank God, Betty had privately remarked to Cissie Wentworth with whom she now shared. Cissie was a new girl and keen to make herself pleasant.

"I don't know how you stuck it fer all them months, Betty. It's bad enough workin' for her, never mind sharin' a room wi' her. Did she talk to yer? What did she say?" The picture of the grim-faced Miss Hamilton engaging anyone below the rank of Madame in conversation just could not be visualised and Cissie was wide-eyed with awe and admiration that Betty had managed it for nine long months.

"Nothing really, only ter tell me ter 'be quick' or 'close winder' or 'give fire a stir', things like that. Orders she give me, like she give now. She used ter send me down t'ter kitchen fer cocoa. Cook didn't like it, I can tell yer."

"I bet she didn't. I wouldn't neither. Yer should've told 'er ter walk in the Mersey 'til 'er 'at floats."

"Who, Cook!"

"No, yer daft 'apporth, Miss Prim an' Proper. She was only t'same as you."

"Give over, Cissie Wentworth, would you? Sooner take on Madame, me." Betty and Cissie shivered together, the very thought of crossing swords with the martinet who ruled them filling them with superstitious dread. It was not that they could actually put their finger on what it was she did to upset them but it had not been the same since. It was common knowledge that she had coveted the job Miss Sara had been given and her resentment at being passed over appeared to have stiffened her already rock-like bearing. Her tone of voice, her great dignity, her overpowering presence frightened the life out of them all and she knew it. And she used words they had never heard before!

"Miss Wentworth. I cannot condone this tendency you have to be dilatory and if it continues I shall be forced to divulge your transgressions to our employer. I am in charge of you, Miss Wentworth" – Cissie understood that only too well, the only few words she *had* understood – "and it is my responsibility to ensure that Madame receives the services for which she pays you. I know it is only a minute or two but those minutes accrue to become hours and it will not do."

Cissie was left to wonder just what it was that "would not do", though of course she had the feeling that it was something to do with the fact that she had been a minute late in presenting herself at the work-table. Miss Hamilton was a beggar for neatness and Cissie had thick, wiry curls which would not be tamed and it had been her attempts to subdue them that had caused her to be behind the others.

Miss Hamilton was clever, there was no argument about that, with a great gift, a talent she was not unwilling to pass on to the girls and women in the workrooms. Indeed she seemed to find a great deal of satisfaction in "sharing", she called it, "swanking" they called it, everything she knew, going to enormous lengths to demonstrate a stitch, a hem, the correct way to cut and fit. The trouble was, once she had told you, or demonstrated to you how to go about it, woe betide the poor girl who did not get whatever it was exactly right when next she was called upon to do it.

"What on earth do you call this, Miss Lucas?" she would demand of poor Nancy who was only seventeen and had just moved up from apprentice to improver. The skirt Nancy was hemming would be held up at arm's length, gripped delicately between Miss Hamilton's thumb and forefinger just as though the garment had been dragged through a field of cow-pats.

"It's the skirt of Mrs Patterson's morning gown, Miss Hamilton," Nancy would answer fearfully while every other girl in the room held their breath, not stopping their work, of course, thankful it was Nancy and not them who was bearing the brunt of Miss Hamilton's disapproval.

"Did I not tell you only yesterday that your stitches should be invisible to the naked eye, Miss Lucas?"

"Yes, Miss Hamilton. I thought mine were."

"Do not be impertinent, Miss Lucas."

"I didn't mean ter be, I was just saying— "

"And I'd be obliged if you would not argue either."

The other girls bent their heads even lower over their work, careful not to meet one another's eye or, God forbid, that of Miss Hamilton. Nancy was a lovely sewer, hardworking and conscientious but if Miss Hamilton said her work was not good enough, then it was not good enough.

"Unpick it, if you please, Miss Lucas, and do it again. Fairy stitches, I said, and fairy stitches Mrs Patterson shall have."

"Yes, Miss Hamilton."

"There is no need for tears, girl. Don't let me find a mark on that expensive fabric, do you hear, Miss Lucas. Blow your nose and pull yourself together."

"Yes, Miss Hamilton.

Miss Hamilton was always better tempered when she had reduced a girl to tears, they noticed, wondering why. She moved from room to room, the hem of her full black skirt whispering across the wooden floors, the soft soles of her black taffeta slippers making no sound as she approached. Each workroom had a first hand in charge but Miss Hamilton, strictly speaking, was over them in her capacity of supervisor and if she found something she did not care for, like dropped pins on the floor, scraps of material not swept up, what she called a "slovenly" work-table, then not only the girls were in trouble but the first hand as well. First hands were the élite of the dressmaking trade. It was they who were sent in Madame's one-horse brougham, accompanied by a liveried manservant, to a client's house to measure and later to fit her and in between to oversee the garment's making up. They were trusted with the most skilful tasks and it was because of one of them that Miss Hamilton first got into hot water.

She had taken to wearing black despite the fact that it showed every basting thread it picked up and she could be seen brushing the skirt down a dozen times a day. Normally it was the magazinières who dressed in black, which had been another bone of contention for Miss Hamilton to get her teeth into. Not that her sister should wear black but the style of the gown Miss Sara wore. It was a revelation, not at all like the plain dresses worn by the other magazinières but at the same time it was completely modest. Sara chose a rich panne velvet. A wide, sweeping skirt, the hem higher by two inches at the front where it showed the froth of creamy lace on her petticoat. The back of the hem dipped to flow behind her in a small train edged with black satin. She had made a neat-fitting bolero, open at the front, tight-sleeved with a small, upstanding collar, and beneath it was a man's shirt of undyed shantung with a frilled front and a well-tied cravat. Around her waist was a black satin cummerbund, six inches wide, which fined her already slender waist to a mere wisp. She looked quite magnificent, stunning, stylish, the rich black of the velvet enhancing her gleaming, copper gold hair and flawless creamy skin.

Madame had been impressed, you could see that. A great favourite with Madame was Miss Sara and was it any wonder, but Miss Hamilton was another kettle of fish altogether. The girls in the workroom couldn't believe it. Fancy her wearing black! It was as though having been denied the position she had wanted she nevertheless was determined to dress the part! A black silk dress, long-sleeved and severe and the magazinière's demure lace cap with long streamers of ribbons which fell over her shoulder and down her back to the hem of her skirt. She looked well in black, did Miss Hamilton, give her her due. She was so regal, so straight-backed and prideful, like a young queen, but not a patch on her sister, not by a Liverpool mile!

She had been supervisor for no more than a week when she was called to Madame's sitting-room. No one knew what was said to her but she and Dilly Parker, who was a first hand, never spoke to one another again unless it was to do with work. Like a beetroot she had been when she emerged from Madame's room, her head held even higher than usual, so high and far back on her neck, Cissie, who had been on the landing at the time on her way to the water closet, told the others she looked as though she might fall over backwards.

"Get about your work, girl," Miss Hamilton had hissed at Cissie who was only too happy to comply but it was obvious Dilly had made some complaint to Madame, and who could blame her? She was thirty-four and a fine seamstress but, sadly, not as good as Miss Hamilton else Dilly would have been supervisor in her place.

She was careful after that, was Miss Hamilton, picking only on girls like Betty and Cissie and Nancy who were younger than she was and keen to stay on at the House of Lovell, learning their trade in the clever, talented hands of one of the foremost designers and dressmakers in the country. When they had completed their time they would be able to command work in any of the best fashion houses, if they so wished, since Madame was revered and respected in the trade. So, say nothing. Bite your tongue and bend your head and do your best to stay out of Miss Hamilton's line of vision.

Pity Miss Sara couldn't do the same but then she was Miss Hamilton's sister and had no choice but to speak to her. She was coming on a treat was Miss Sara, going each day into the showroom with Mademoiselle Jeanette where it was reported the clients had really taken to her. But then she was such a friendly little thing, all smiles and pleased as punch to be entrusted with such an important commission, you could tell that. There was no "side" to her, not like her sister, and she was just as likely to be found helping the skivvy carry her heavy scrub bucket back to the scullery, asking her was her cold any better, as she was chatting with Madame on the quality of this fabric or that. She often accompanied one of the first hands to a client's home, for as Madame said she must learn every aspect of the dressmaking trade from the time the first bolt of silk was thrown dramatically across the counter in the showroom to that moment when the finished garment was finally worn.

But Miss Hamilton wouldn't leave it alone, of course, treating Miss Sara as though she were a girl in a schoolroom, one who got seriously out of hand and must be chastised because of it. She couldn't abide seeing her look nice, either, always picking and picking, doing her best to sap her sister's confidence. She was easily hurt, was Miss Sara and the way her sister took the smile off her face was a crying shame.

"Sara, what on earth gave you the idea that you suited that particularly unbecoming style?" she would demand scathingly. "It makes you look so ... so ... full-bosomed, my dear," which was not true, of course. "If only you had consulted me about it I could have told you before you made up the gown."

She would sigh dramatically as though her sister's foolishness was a sore trial to her. "But then that is what becomes of not living in, you see. I suppose that ... that girl, who, believe me, has not a scrap of sense nor taste, told you you looked well in it, encouraging you to invite her to sit in your room and sew with her. Oh yes, I know about that, Sara, but you must not let her influence you. Now go and change at once before Madame sees you."

"It was Madame who chose the style, Ally," Sara answered mildly and the girls at their work-tables bent their heads into their sewing so that Miss Hamilton would not see their smiles of jubilation. It was not often anyone "got one over" on Miss Hamilton. "She said it was especially charming for my figure. Those were her very words, Ally."

"Well, that is her opinion, Sara, and she is entitled to it but I am distressed that you no longer consider my advice worth having. Not very long ago you were only too happy to be guided by me and you and I were the most fashionably and tastefully dressed young ladies in Wray Green."

"I was a child then, Ally. I'm eighteen now and able to decide for myself what becomes me."

"Eighteen! That is no age at all, Sara," Miss Hamilton replied loftily and the girls in the workroom watched and listened, trying to appear that they were doing neither, quite enthralled by the sisterly altercation. Miss Hamilton was known to be twenty-two years of age and it seemed she thought this gave her the right to compel her sister to obey her.

Miss Sara did not think so and for five minutes the pair of them went at it hammer and tongs, going so far as to forget themselves, at least Miss Hamilton did, so that someone went to fetch Madame. A man's name was mentioned, Jack somebody or other, which appeared to deliver a mortal stroke to Miss Sara, but, though she went as white as the frilled trousseau petticoat Nancy was embroidering with love knots for Miss Susan Aspinall who was to be married in September, she did not falter. Indeed it seemed to spur her on to a wrath as fierce as her sister's and many matters over which it seemed Miss Hamilton had been harbouring a grudge were aired for all the workroom to hear. Miss Sara's room in Liverpool which Miss Hamilton was determined she must give up and move in with her at the House of Lovell. Miss Sara appeared to shudder at this, almost to shrink in on herself and who could blame her, Betty Holden thought pityingly, for didn't she herself know what it was like to be dominated by the authoritative Miss Hamilton. Someone called Dolly was mentioned and Miss Sara was close to tears, demanding to know when her sister intended paying back the money they had borrowed from Lily and if Alice wouldn't, then Sara would. And what about the books and pictures and the clothes that had belonged to their mama and which someone called Albert was holding for them? And the furniture, their mama's lovely furniture, Miss Sara had cried passionately. Had it been sold because if not she had every intention of going up to Kirkham to fetch it.

It really was terrifying and exhilarating at the same time until Madame, called by the first hand who had become seriously alarmed, came to separate them, taking first Miss Hamilton to her room and when Miss Hamilton had been dealt with, Miss Sara. Miss Hamilton was white-faced and in a murderous rage when she returned and they all wondered what had been said to her. Whatever it was she hadn't liked it, turning on poor Nancy, who was too tender-hearted by far, until she reduced her to tears.

"I can't have this, Sara. You know it and your sister knows it and yet the pair of you almost came to fisticuffs and in front of the other girls. It won't do and if it continues I shall be forced to let one of you go," And it won't be you, Madame Lovell's expression said but Sara's head was bowed and she did not see it. Rosalie Lovell considered Alice Hamilton to be a damned nuisance, nursing her resentments, envious of her sister's popularity, jealous of her success and if she continued with her disruptive measures there could only be one course open and that was the sack. What a fool the woman was. She had one of the best and highest paid jobs in the business. She was attractive and clever and yet she allowed her bitterness to overwhelm her, to compel her to actions which she could only regret. She just could not forget the past. She could not forget that her mama had been a lady, her papa a gentleman which, in her opinion, put Alice Hamilton only slightly lower than the right hand of God. For years, ever since her mother died, she had ruled – guided, she liked to call it – young Sara and now, as Sara matured into a fine young woman, thriving on her success, Alice was eaten up by the realisation that she was no longer of premier importance in Sara's life. And her attempts to drag her sister back into her control were making her untrustworthy, unhinged almost and Rosalie Lovell must come to some decision on what she should do about it.

"I can't have this, Miss Hamilton," she had said icily, using the same words she was to speak to Sara.

"I'm sorry, Madame, but I feel that I am entitled to chastise my sister when it is needed. She— "

"Chastise, Miss Hamilton! She is not a child."

"In her ways she is, Madame. She is very immature and unless— "

"Unless you stop interfering with her progress she will remain so, Miss Hamilton. So be warned that I shall take steps to see that you are removed from your position of authority unless you heed me on this. Sara— "

"*Sara!*"

"Yes, I call her Sara when— "

"I see!"

"Do you, Miss Hamilton? Then I hope you see that your constant bickering with her on where she should sleep, on what she may wear, on who her friends are . . ."

Alice drew herself up to her full height in outraged indignation. "You forget yourself, Madame." She was at her haughtiest. "She is my sister and I may say what I like to her. It is my duty, my sacred responsibility to care for her since my papa died. She would— "

"I never met your papa, Miss Hamilton, so I cannot judge him but I'm sure he would not want to see his daughter stifled."

Alice gasped and her face was washed with a sudden livid colour. The clock on Madame's mantelshelf ticked pleasantly in the absolute silence and from somewhere beyond the open window a cuckoo called to its mate, hoarse chuckling notes which were immediately answered by the bubbling trill of the female. Someone laughed, probably one of the gardening lads and a man's voice, deeper, could be heard remonstrating.

"Stifled! *Stifled!*" Alice's voice was harsh, strangled in the back of her throat. "How dare you say that to me. I care about my sister and want to see her do well— "

"Unless it is in the job you wanted for yourself, is that it?"

"No, it is not. She has always listened to me. She has always minded what I told her. She trusted me and was prepared to be guided by my expertise. Now she is— "

"She is a woman, Miss Hamilton."

"She is a child, Madame Lovell and she depends on me."

"I rather think it is the other way round, Miss Hamilton."

"Fiddlesticks!"

"So you say, Miss Hamilton, but I believe Sara to be a woman who is doing well in the profession she chose and you must not undermine her like this."

"Madame Lovell." Alice stood up and placed both her hands flat on the table behind which Madame sat and despite herself Rosalie Lovell flinched away from her. Alice's expression was malevolent, her eyes pure green slits of outrage, but even as Madame gathered herself in readiness to ring for the footman and have her removed, for surely she was dangerous, Alice Hamilton stood back, her face wiped clean of all expression, her eyes hooded. She even managed a small smile, no more than a twitch of her clamped, colourless lips, but a smile just the same. Her voice was flat and emotionless as she spoke.

"Madame Lovell," she repeated, "I cannot agree with you, I'm afraid, on the character of my sister. We naturally see her from different viewpoints but I really do think, having known her all her life, that I am better able to understand her than you. Of course, as her employer you must do what you think best, and as your employee I must abide by your decision. I am very grateful for my own position in this house and I can assure you I will do nothing to jeopardise it. Your influence on Sara has not been beneficial in my opinion but it seems I can do nothing, at the moment, to make her see where her duty lies."

"And where is that, Miss Hamilton?"

"With her family. I am her sister, her only family and she should be made to realise it. But her head has been turned, Madame, and being the child she is she cannot help but be dazzled by your favour. However it will not be . . . well, I will say no more, Madame. Now, if we are finished I will get back to my work."

She left Rosalie Lovell with the distinct feeling that it was she who had been dismissed. Now she sat with Alice Hamilton's sister occupying the same chair as Alice had done but the expression on her own face, the feeling in her own heart were vastly different to those she had shown to Alice.

"You must do your best to control yourself, my dear," she said briskly. "Your sister has had a great deal of influence over your life but you must not let it continue."

"I know," Sara said glumly. "She dragged me to Liverpool against my will."

"Oh, how was that?" Madame leaned forward.

"When our papa died we were asked to vacate the home he rented. We had no money."

"There were no friends, relatives?" The question was delicately put.

"No, my mother's family lived . . . live still, I suppose, in Cheshire. We never knew them and I believe my father was an only child. He was older than my mother. The villagers, those Alice wanted for friends, were not friendly."

I bet they weren't, Rosalie Lovell thought. It would be like taking a cobra to your bosom, befriending Alice Hamilton. Instinctively those who met her for the first time, herself included, felt the need to guard their backs and it was hard to know why. She was so pretty. Her manners could be charming and yet there was a tenseness about her, a kind of intensity as though she were inside your brain winkling out your thoughts, stealing them from you in order to better her own position. She was studied. She did nothing impulsively. When she was in command of herself, which was at most times, she measured every word but where her sister was concerned she was obsessive. There was something . . . what was it? She could not put her finger on it but she knew as surely as she knew the sun rose in the east and set in the west that Alice Hamilton was up to something. That she had something brewing in her clever, pretty head and whatever it was included her sister.

"Will you take my advice, Sara?" she asked her softly.

Sara raised her head. Her eyes were wet with tears and she brushed the back of her hand across them. Like a child. Alice was right about that. She was still childlike but all she needed was a bloody good chance, a bit of breathing space apart from her overbearing sister and she would become a glorious woman. Rosalie Lovell meant to give her that chance.

"Yes, Madame, of course."

Madame smiled. "Don't be too quick to make promises, Sara, even to me. Listen to what I have to say, and what others have to say before you agree."

Sara leaned back in her chair and the dimple deepened at the corner of her mouth.

"Yes, Madame."

"Good girl. Now then, what I have to say is brief but it is something I learned quite recently. Life is short, Sara. Too short. You find that you are just about to get your teeth into it when suddenly, it's nearly ended. Don't be persuaded into doing what other people want you to do. Do what *you* want to do. Don't waste it. When you are young life stretches out before you, exciting and lots of it! It goes on for ever and ever, you think, but believe me, it doesn't, Sara, so live every minute. Decide how you want to live it and let no one distract you."

"Alice, you mean?"

"Alice."

Alice sat in the low chair beside the glowing fire. Her own chair, her own fireside in her own room and yet she was not happy with it. The room was lit by several candles in pretty candlesticks and by the light from the cheerfully spiralling flames. It was not a large room but Madame Lovell had not stinted in the furnishing of it and it was comfortable, warm and comfortable . . . and lonely.

It was hard for Alice to confess to loneliness, even to herself, but she was and even as she admitted it she felt the sourness burn at the back of her throat. So many people. So many people like her papa who had been so lackadaisical he had made no provision for his gently reared daughters on his death. Even before that, her mama who had given up her birthright, Alice's birthright, when she had abandoned her well-connected family to marry Papa. Like that clod of a man who had been the first to turn Sara away from her. Like them all, Lily Canon, old Dolly, even that Matty person whose company Sara seemed to prefer, and like that old biddy in her splendidly luxurious bedroom two floors below Alice's. They were all doing their best to lead Sara into contrary ways that would not be beneficial to her in the end. Alice had taken care of her, directed her, taught her to be a lady as their mama had taught Alice, but she was still only a child beneath the veneer of maturity working at the House of Lovell had given her. Sara, though again Alice did not like to own up to it, was far cleverer with her fingers than Alice. She had a shrewd grasp of fashion, which way it would develop and what suited who and, dear God, it was hard to say, people liked her better than they did Alice. Alice couldn't see why for she and Sara were equally attractive and charming, but there it was and so Alice must, must keep a firm grip on herself and let no one, not Sara nor Madame or that common Dilly Parker, get under her skin again. It had been close today, really close. She had lost her temper but she had controlled it just in time and drawn back from the confrontation with Madame and if it took all her will and resolution, her unbending resolve, of which she had a great deal, then she must gather it about her like a shield. Protect herself and do her best to tighten that close bond which had existed, and would again, between herself and Sara. Be calm and self-contained until the time came when she could command her sister to her. When they would gather up their belongings and set out on the wonderful path to the united future she and Sara were to share, the future which was Alice's vision and goal.

20

The Liverpool, Ormskirk and Preston line of the East Lancashire Railway was opened to traffic on April 2nd, 1849. Jack Andrews was there for the official opening ceremony along with hundreds of excited spectators, may of them crowding into and around the brand new terminus, Exchange Station in Great Howard Street.

When the line had been proposed in 1844 it was intended to provide a direct communication between the great seaport of Liverpool and the ever growing network of the northern lines, a connection formed with the whole of the manufacturing districts of Yorkshire, by the Blackburn and Preston and the Lancashire and Yorkshire junction. A branch from the main line at Ormskirk would offer cheap and convenient access to the rising and much frequented watering place of Southport, not only to those in the north but to those who travelled from the counties of the Midlands.

Jack had been working on the line as agent to the contractor for two years. With his employer Daniel Browne who, it was rumoured, would have a knighthood by the year's end, among the gentry, Jack was to travel part way on the footplate of the engine. The line proceeded from Exchange Station to the west of Aintree Racecourse, a distance of four and three-quarter miles, where Jack intended to leave it at Aintree Station.

Normally there was a steeplechase and several hurdles run at the course in March, and in July at the Cravens Meeting, a cup race and others were got up over a period of three days. In September another day's sport was held and all these meetings were well attended, but today, with a specially built railway line and station to accommodate the racegoers, who were expected to number thousands, it had been decided to run several special races in honour of the occasion. Many of the local dignitaries, the inhabitants of Liverpool and the gentry were expected to attend, including the family of the late Earl of Derby who had been a keen supporter of the sport.

Jack was not a gambler. His mother's upbringing and the sorry state he had seen his navvie mates get into when they lost their wages on a bet made him uneasy about chancing his hard-earned cash on the fleetness of foot of a horse, the staying power of a pugilist or the ferocity of a particular dog. He would put a few bob on a nag today, for his fortunes had risen since his navvying days. It was a special day and the young lady who was to accompany him, already ensconced in a special seat for the guests of men like himself would expect it. He had the North Countryman's dislike of chucking his money about without surety of a return but today was the end of the line for Jack Andrews in more ways than one. The Liverpool, Ormskirk and Preston line of the East Lancashire Railway was finished and he must decide what he was to do with his future. There were many opportunities open to him.

Railway speculation, railway mania, as it was called by more than a few, had become in many ways a great evil, the fever of the ordinary man to get "in on it" causing desperate hardship when he saw his small savings disappear like smoke. The spirit of gaming was rife in every inn and gaming house in the country and those who frequented such places could not resist the challenge of it. Shares were bought this week to sell the next, sometimes successfully, for as they rose in price those who sold realised a profit. But sadly, this was not always the case and many a shareholder was driven to despair when he lost all he possessed. All classes of people plunged into the frightful whirlpool. Bankers and merchants, bank clerks and haberdashers, old men and young lads chanced their painfully saved guineas but none more successfully than Jack Andrews who was now in a position to contract for a "parcel" of line which, as contractor, he would lay with the labour of "butty gangs". He had found the butty system worked successfully when he himself was a navvie for it was his strong belief, and had he not proved it, that the best way to get things done was to give the men a personal interest in doing a decent amount of work and therefore finishing a contract on time. The East Lancashire and the Lancashire and Yorkshire Railways were to construct several interlacing lines over the next two years but Jack had a fancy to get away from Lancashire. In the Lake District the Furness Railway, incorporated in 1844 to build a line between the sea and the mountains through Cumberland and Westmorland, was asking for tenders and he was half tempted to go up there and make his bid.

He was in a strange, restless mood as he climbed up on to the footplate of the locomotive, shaking the grinning red-faced engine driver by the hand, grinning himself for he could not help being influenced by the sense of excitement. The train was to set out at ten o'clock. It was an uncertain, misty day, not sure in itself whether to be sunny or not. On the railway platform Liverpool's most substantial gentlemen drank champagne and filled the spring air with the fragrant aroma of their expensive cigars, some of them accompanied by their wives and families. Many of the gentlemen, like Jack, were to ride as far as Aintree, meaning to do as he intended and spend the rest of the day at the races, though the most important were to return to Exchange Station for the grand luncheon which awaited them.

The station yard was jammed with the finest carriages and carriage horses and everywhere flew flags and banners and there was even a marquee to contain the massive luncheon the worthies were to consume on their return. There were children swarming everywhere, unsupervised and in danger of being trampled on. Tall silk hats and ostentatiously beflowered bonnets mingled with cloth caps, bowlers, and the more discreetly ornamented and outdated "drawn" bonnets of the lower classes, for this railway era belonged to them all no matter what their status and who could resist the excitement of it?

The platform along which the train was drawn waiting for the "off" was a triumph of noise and colour with even more brightly hued flags draped on either side of the track. At opposite ends of the train two brass bands played stirring martial music in strident competition with one another and small boys marched around them to the irritation of the bandmasters.

The early morning mists lifted and the engine driver fiddled importantly with several levers and knobs, wiping his hands and face on an oily rag. He was evidently eager to be gone, raising his eyebrows in question and Jack shrugged then leaned out of the cab to see what was holding up the grand start. Steam hissed about the engine's great iron wheels and chuffed sedately from its funnel. The pale spring sunshine broke through, glinting on trombone and tuba and, in one sudden heart-wrenching moment, before he could set himself against it, Jack was plunged back in time. Three years in time to a day very much like this one only instead of the sober frock-coat and striped trousers he wore today he was dressed in moleskin, double canvas shirt, velveteen square-tailed coat in a brilliant shade of blue, hobnail boots, a gaudy neckerchief, a white felt hat with the brim turned up and a vivid peacock waistcoat made for him by the girl who walked by his side.

Sara! He was at once engulfed in the pain of it and in his pain he clung desperately to the handrail beside the footplate. It overwhelmed him, the memory, as clear and sharp as a sliver of crystal, her face luminous with love beyond description, her rosy mouth parted as though waiting for his kiss, her green eyes shining into his, filled with her admiration for Jack Andrews who felt ten feet tall because of it. She *had* loved him. He could not have mistaken it, and he had loved her, there had never been any doubt of that and yet some evil thing had parted them, torn them from one another with a force which even now left him weak with the anguish of it.

"You all right, sir?" the engine driver enquired as the gentleman leaned against the side of the cab, narrowly being missed by the heaped shovel of coal which the lad was about to fling into the engine's glowing fire. Drunk probably, the expression on both their faces said as they exchanged glances and was it any wonder the stuff that was being chucked down every man's throat. Except theirs, of course!

Jack straightened up and his bleak eyes came to rest on the awkward face of the driver. God's death, even after all this time she still had the power to strike at him with a strength which frightened him at times. He still looked for her, though by now he had accepted the fact that he would not find her. Even the advertisement he had put in the *Liverpool Mercury* had been inserted without much hope of it being successful and nothing had come of it. He had even considered hiring a private detective but then what could he do that Jack had not already done? Tramping the streets whenever he could.

Hanging about where he thought young, well-bred ladies might likely be. The libraries and art galleries and museums, all the best shops, naturally, in Bold Street and Lord Street but it had all been to no avail. She was in Liverpool, or had been when she wrote, but Liverpool was large, densely packed, teeming with life on every street corner, along every smart thoroughfare and road which led down to the docks. He had walked the length of Marine Parade and Princes Parade a dozen times when he was in town, which was not often as the Liverpool, Ormskirk and Preston line spread away from the city. The trail of Sara Hamilton was two and a half years old, cold and sterile and could Jack spend any more time trying to follow it when the rest of his life lay before him and it must be filled with something other than a lovely ghost. He was twenty-five, a young man still but he would one day want a wife, children, his own home and if it was not to have Sara Hamilton in it he must . . . Dear sweet Jesus, he must find a replacement.

"You all right, sir?" the driver said again and Jack made a great effort to drag himself back from the past, rubbing his hand vigorously across his face as though to dislodge the cobwebs of remembrance which clung there.

"Yes, oh yes, thanks." He did his best to smile. "That champagne's pretty potent stuff."

The driver grinned with relief. "Aye, it is that, sir. Old Jem Gaffney, 'e's relief fireman . . . well, 'appen I shouldn't be tellin' yer this . . ."

"I won't repeat it, if that's what's bothering you."

"Aye, well." The driver narrowed his eyes. This chap who was summat to do with the railway wasn't a gent, a real gent, you could tell that by the way he talked, so perhaps it was safe to tell him about Old Jem. Willie Jenkins, which was himself, wouldn't give a gent, a real gent the time of day, but this chap was one of them, meaning himself and Fred the stoker, so he thought he'd chance it. Passed the time while the nobs decided when they were going to get the bloody train started!

"Pinched a bottle of champagne, Jem did," he declared solemnly.

The young stoker nodded wisely, his grin revealing his high regard for Jem.

"Drank the bloody lot, if you'll pardon me, sir, an' when

Arnie Widdup, 'e's porter, sir, found 'im, Jem were only tryin' ter light 'is pipe at water pump in't station yard. When drinks in brains're out, they do say!"

Again the stoker, a lad of no more than sixteen, nodded wisely.

"Yes, you're right there." Jack smiled pleasantly and Willie was relieved that he appeared to have got over his funny turn.

It seemed the moment of departure was imminent for the Lord Mayor could be seen approaching the engine where it appeared he wished to shake the engine driver by the hand. Favoured guests began climbing aboard the resplendent carriages, accompanied by an ear-splitting crescendo from both bands, each playing a different tune, a great deal of whistling and shrieking from the engine and a surging clamour from the crowds who began furiously to ply their Union Jacks.

"It seems we're about to go," Jack observed to the engine driver.

"Aye, an' about time an' all before t'rest of Liverpool tries to gerron t'train," the engine driver replied, beginning to whistle irritably through his clenched teeth. He took out his watch and glared at it.

"Ten bloody minutes late already," he snapped with the sharpness of a man who takes pride in running on time.

"Just the Lord Mayor to get aboard," Jack murmured soothingly, wondering how the young lady was faring. He couldn't quite remember her name – Maude . . . Madeleine – he only knew she had been the prettiest waitress in the dining-room at the York Hotel last night when he and Daniel Browne and several other gentlemen with interests in the railway had dined there. She had blushed and dimpled when, managing to get her on her own as she was helping to hand the gentlemen their hats, coats and canes at the end of the meal, he had acted on impulse and invited her to come with him today. Perhaps she would like to have a port and lemon with him in his room when she finished her shift in the dining-room, he had politely asked her and was not surprised when she eagerly agreed. Her blushes and dimples had been charming and completely false as he had discovered when, later, she had undressed herself very slowly, very coquettishly, removing the layers of her clothing one by one until, innocence itself, or so she would have him believe, she had lain back on his bed and invited him to admire, not only her pert young breasts but the delightful cleft between her legs. He had spent several hours in her tireless embrace, sending her home in a cab, already regretting his invitation. And it had done nothing to help him make his final decision. North or south, east or west? What did it really matter without Sara? All railway lines were the same. All women were the same but he meant the former to become the means to purchase the latter. To make Jack Andrews into the wealthiest contractor in the business of building railways. There was nothing else for him. He felt quite empty. He neither hurt now, nor felt content but he knew, as the cacophony of noise exploded about him, that he could not spend the rest of his life looking back to the girl who had filled him with laughter, with delight, with love. His own life waited for him and somewhere, surely, there was someone ready to fill his heart as Sara had. Could there exist another woman such as Sara? Could there? He would never know unless he looked.

He sighed and deliberately let go of the memory of the girl called Sara.

The crowds in Bold Street were particularly dense and the two fashionably dressed young ladies found themselves increasingly jostled the further down its length they wandered. The mist had risen, leaving a pale yellow sunshine and above the roof of the Police Court to their left they caught a glimpse of the pale bluebell sky, but still the crowds flocked, growing thicker and even more excited.

"Well, I don't know what the 'ecks goin' on but I've 'ad enough. Come on, Sara, let's go down ter't river an' watch ferries comin' in. It's a grand day fer a walk. Just gerra niff o' that air."

Matty lifted her head and drew in the aromas which pervaded the city, coming from the dock area and which were for the most part unnoticed by those who lived by its side. She eyed the broad shoulders of a young postman resplendent in a scarlet cutaway tailcoat with blue lapels and cuffs. He was so intent on his mail he was not looking where he was going and he cannoned into her, to her delight, almost taking her pretty lace parasol from her hand. He tipped his tall beaver hat and winked, for she was very pretty, steadying her parasol and when she smiled at him, her eyes brilliant in her rosy face, he almost collided into someone else in his confusion.

"Well, all I can smell is fish and the river and do stop winking at that poor postman. How can he be expected to do his job if he is languishing after you?"

"Is that wharr'e's doin'? I thought he were tryin' ter click wi' me."

Sara laughed, unconscious of the admiring looks she was drawing to herself. Matty was pretty but Sara Hamilton had a quality of beauty which most men would be hard pressed to describe but which was a magnet to them just the same. It was like comparing a smart little sail boat to the ethereal elegance of a clipper ship when putting Matty Hutchinson next to Sara Hamilton but then, as Lily had said to Dolly only the night before, some men liked a smart little sail boat and would find a clipper ship too much for them to handle.

The two girls had decided on their parasols as they left Abercromby Square since the sun was bound to shine on this, their first day off together in many weeks. Now that Sara was a magazinière her time off was even more restricted since so many of Madame's clients asked for her personally and though she still had one afternoon off a week and one full day a month she had to take them when it was convenient to Madame. She had often pondered on the strange coincidence of why she and Ally never seemed to have the same day free, unaware that Madame Lovell arranged it this way. Ally was always planning some uplifting excursion, to a library, a museum, an exhibition of antiquities she was sure would benefit Sara's education, bemoaning the fates which forced her to leave her sister to her own devices. Sara had never told her of the jaunts she and Matty enjoyed, leaving her to believe that Sara went about under the chaperonage of Lily, or stayed at home to work on her own sewing. Not that Lily was the person Alice Hamilton would have chosen to chaperone her gently bred sister but she was at least a respectable woman of a decent age.

The days that Sara and Matty shared were very dear to Sara and she looked forward to them with great anticipation. Matty was great fun. She was coarse sometimes in her humour but so good-natured Sara could not take offence. She had a big heart and was generous and loyal. She did not seem to consider the wide gulf which existed between her class and Sara's, but then neither did Sara.

"I know," Matty urged, "instead o' goin' down to't docks an' watchin' t'ferries come in why don't we gerron one an' see where it takes us?"

Sara turned and clutched Matty's arm, her face lighting up with excitement. "Oh Matty, do you think we could?" It might have been a trip to London Matty had suggested.

"Why not? I don't know why we didn't think of it before. It'll not be much, the fare I mean, an' it dunt matter where we go, does it? We've gorrall day. We could 'ave a walk on t'other side ter . . . well, wherever we fancy. What d'yer think, lar?"

Matty tossed her bonneted head dramatically then twirled her parasol for good measure to the delight of several passing young gentlemen. Her eyes were wide and gleeful as she looked into Sara's face.

"Oh Matty, I'd love that."

"Would yer, chuck? Me too. Me boots aren't meant fer country roads but what the hell! Let's do it."

They had almost reached the Town Hall, hesitating on the pavement as they tried to get across the teeming traffic in Moorfield, when they heard the music. It seemed to come along Moorfield from the direction of Tithebarn Street and so great was the press of people moving towards it Sara and Matty had a great deal of trouble remaining where they were. They clung together, their lace parasols twitching this way and that and their full skirts swaying and dipping. Sara held on to her bonnet and Matty did the same as they tried desperately not to be swept along with the multitude.

A road-crossing sweeper, his small feet bare and filthy with the horse manure he constantly tramped about in and which it was his job to remove, ran across the road to them, grinning and gesticulating like a monkey. His legs were thin and bowed. He was plainly ill nourished, his face bleached and skull-like but his grin was endearing.

"Wanner gerra'cross, queen?" he chirped to Matty as though recognising the one with the "mouth". The Liverpool mouth which was never short of a word, or even two.

"Well, we did, but what's goin' on up there? Sounds like a fairground?" Matty tossed her head in the direction from which the sound of the music came and which was drawing the crowds like filings to a magnet.

"Summat ter do wi' toffs, chuck. I seen carriages all goin'
up that way. They say Lord Mayor's there an' all."

"Go on!"

"'Onest. Ladies in bonnets an' such, though norras nice as
yours," he added impishly, hoping for a tip.

"Gerron wi' yer, yer cheeky monkey," slipping him a
farthing which he pocketed with a flourish and a bow.

"Shall we gerrup there an' 'ave a look, queen? It's only five
minutes outa our way. If there's nowt much goin' on we can
still tootle down to't ferry."

"But what is it, d'you think?"

For some unaccountable reason Sara felt a strange reluctance to follow the sound of the music. It reminded her of
something she didn't wish to be reminded of which was silly
because it was only a brass band like the one she and Matty
listened to, toes tapping, in Princes Park.

"I was looking forward to the ferry, Matty," she continued.

"'An we will, chuck. It's only ten o'clock, We've all day to
ourselves so why not go an' 'ave a look at what's 'appenin' in
Tithebarn Street. Eeh, I do 'ope it's a fair. I do love a fair."

It was not in Tithebarn Street but in Great Howard Street
which led off it. The crowds became thicker and the music
became louder as they were swept along, unable to extricate
themselves had they wanted to and it was all Sara could do
to hang on to Matty's arm.

"Put yer parasol down, chuck," Matty shouted in her ear,
"else yer'll lose it an' 'ang on ter yer 'at."

"I am doing but I still can't see what is happening,
can you?"

"No, but we're nearly there."

They were carried along between wide gates and into a vast
cobbled yard which was jammed from wall to wall with fine
carriages pulled by sleek, restless horses, with bad-tempered
coachmen who were doing their best to settle their charges.

The building on the far side of the yard was very grand,
long and well proportioned and it was then that Sara knew
what was happening here today.

At once she tried to turn, to battle her way back through
the crowd which was doing its best to battle its way in the
opposite direction but it was no good. She was trapped in
one of those timeless moments which occur only in dreams. A
feeling that she was walking very slowly, floating almost with

her feet barely touching the ground. She was moving and yet she was going nowhere, fastened like a fly which has alighted on treacle. All around her was a roaring sound, like the one she had heard as a child when she had held Mama's seashell to her ear, the one which Mama said had come from the sands at Rhyl where Mama went for her holidays when she was a child. You could hear the waves crashing and pounding in it and that was all. She heard it now except for the odd whistle and shriek which pierced the muffling fog about her.

Her instinct, every nerve in her body, every inch of her flesh, her heart and anguished soul wanted nothing more than to get her away from this place which was stabbing her – she was sure she must be bleeding – with memories, lovely memories, terrible racking memories of another day like this. She couldn't go into the station, the railway station where today the brand new line from Liverpool to Preston was to be officially opened, not if she was to keep steady her hard-won equanimity, that which she had wrapped about herself, inch by painful inch, to protect her from memories of Jack. This was Jack's world and she wanted none of it. This was what Jack had introduced her to over three years ago. This was where, or a place very like it, he had given her his love, his masculine adoration, his promise to come back for her. He had smiled and kissed her and gone away and she had never seen him again.

She did not know she was weeping desolately as the triumphant crowd swept through the wide and splendid entrance hall and on to the platform. She clung to Matty's arm. Matty waved and clapped and jumped up and down, carried along on the great wave of exultation generated by the crowd and beside her Sara was pushed this way and that like some broken doll. Her bonnet had fallen to the back of her neck where it hung by the ribbons and her hair, freed in the mad rush through the station yard, fell across her shoulders and face, blinding her along with her tears so that she did not see the slow movement of the "special" train as it crawled ponderously from the station

"Damn an' blast it, we missed it." Matty was still absorbed with the train which was beginning to gather speed. The engine was no more than thirty feet ahead of where she and Sara had been propelled on to the northern end of the platform and hanging from it, grinning like a small boy, was a man she recognised.

"Look, will yer look at 'im. It's that chap. 'Im I saw in't shop in Lord Street, d'yer remember? When were it? Must've bin a year ago. Fancy me rememberin' all this time, but then, can yer wonder? Look Sara, d'yer see 'im? There, at front wi' engine driver. A right looker in't 'e?"

Matty turned to jog Sara's arm then all thoughts of the good-looking gentleman she had first seen in Tuton's a year ago were gone, as the train was gone.

"Eeh, love, what's up? Wharris it? D'yer not feel well? Yer as green as a bloody cabbage, 'onest. 'Ere, let's get yer to a seat."

"No, no really, Matty, I'm fine, really I am."

"Well, yer don't look it an' what yer crying for? 'Ere, come an' sit down a minute."

"No." Sara took a deep breath and managed a smile. "Honestly, I think it was just the crowds." She allowed Matty to lead her towards the station entrance, moving along with the spectators who had quietened now that the train had departed. She felt better, calmer, more in control of her silly emotions which had blown up out of all proportion to the event. It was only the inauguration of a new railway for heaven's sake, something which happened all the time in the growing network which was snaking all over the country. She didn't even know now why she had felt so . . . so strange. Why she had begun to weep so foolishly. Of course, memories of Jack were painful to bear but that part of her life was over now and she must move on to the remainder of it. Let Jack go. Ease him out of her heart, Jack, her love.

She held on to Matty's arm as they sauntered down Chapel Street, turning left at St Nicholas Church, the sailors' church, through Back Goree and on to Strand Street. The wind off the river dried the tears on her face which she had explained to Matty were through fear of the excessive crowds, and lifted her hair in a glorious banner of gold and copper about her head.

"I'd best get my bonnet on," she said, laughing with her friend. "If Alice were to see me now she would be convinced I was about to sink into a life of depravity and sin. No lady goes about without a bonnet, you know."

"I know what yer mean, queen. I can just 'ear 'er sayin'

it an' all. Now then, which ferry d'yer fancy? New Brighton? Or 'ow about a trip ter Woodside? We'd just get the eleven o'clock. They're ringin' t'bell now so come on, chuck, look lively. They say t'view from Bidston 'Ill's grand an' then we could 'ave a spot o' tea in the Woodside 'Otel. What d'yer say? Shall we treat ourselves?"

Sara squeezed Matty's arm, thanking the fates which had led her to Abercromby Square and the friends she had found there. She would not have survived without them.

21

She had been a magazinière for almost a full year when she met Paul Travers. He was already in the "premier magazin" or "first showroom" when Sara entered and he stood up at once though he was a gentleman, a customer and she merely an employee of the House of Lovell.

Sara Hamilton would be nineteen in June but she still had no conception of her own beauty nor the impact it had on men, and the expression which crossed the face of the extraordinarily courteous gentleman went unnoticed by her. Her whole attention was on the woman who leaned gracefully in the chair beside the ornate fireplace in which a cheerful fire blazed. It was April and Madame's lawn was a carpet of swaying golden daffodils which clustered thickly beneath the budding branches of the great trees but there was still a chill in the air and a fire was needed.

"Good morning, Miss Damask. A lovely morning, is it not?" Sara inclined her head towards the gentleman who was still on his feet as she spoke to his companion.

"Yes, I suppose it is." The woman with the improbable name of Miss Rose Damask yawned, "Though I find this early rising most tedious. We didn't get to bed until three, did we, Paul?"

"No, my pet, we did not." The man grinned good-humouredly and Sara, who had half turned politely to him as he spoke, caught the full force of it. It was warm, lively, intelligent, whimsical, conveying quite plainly his own tendency to be amused by what he saw as life's absurdities. They had never met before, he and this astonishing young showroom woman, his grin said, and yet within the space of thirty seconds Miss Damask had revealed his relationship to her with no concern for the proprieties which stated that a man and his mistress must at least make a pretence of discretion. Would it shock her? Would she be embarrassed and look away or would she demonstrate her training and retain her cool composure, pretending nothing untoward had been said?

She did the latter, of course, her poise undented but he could swear there was a prick of laughter in her sea green eyes.

God, she was lovely, her loveliness overshadowing Rose's flamboyant beauty which was considered to be quite supreme, as a just opening rosebud will eclipse the ostentation of a decorative but full-blown rose. She was dressed in the usual black of the magazinière but what an outfit! It was almost mannish in its stark simplicity but the body it covered could in no way be described as anything but totally female. She was not tall but her figure was perfectly proportioned and the smoothly gleaming black velvet added a vulnerability, a sensual delicacy which was quite devastating. By God, she devastated him! Young, of course, far too young for Paul Travers, who liked his women mature, experienced, self-assured, at the peak of their womanhood which was why he was fond of Rose Damask and why he had allowed her to drag him here to the House of Lovell this morning. God in heaven, what did he know about fashionable gowns, except, of course, how to divest a lady of one. But Rose had been quite magnificent last night, not only at the theatre but later in the bed they had shared in her hotel room and he had allowed himself to be persuaded. A voluptuous, sensuous woman was Rose, much practised in the arts of seduction and whenever a play she toured in was in Liverpool they resumed their relationship with great enthusiasm.

"Now what can I show you, Miss Damask?" Sara smiled sweetly, doing her best not to let the hilarity she felt be revealed by her expression. Rose Damask! What a comical name, not her own naturally and yet it was absolutely right for the sensationally beautiful actress who was performing at the Theatre Royal in Williamson Square. She and Matty and David had made arrangements to go and see her on Wednesday evening in the play *Honeymoon*, that is if she and Matty managed to get away from their respective employment in time for the second house. David had booked three seats

in the gallery, costing a shilling each and they were lucky to
have them, it was said, since every seat in the theatre, which
held just under two thousand people, was sold out. A very
popular actress was Miss Rose Damask, who had just finished
a run with the play at the most famous theatre in the land, the
Theatre Royal in London, of course.

"What do you think, darling?" Miss Damask said in her
beautifully modulated voice, turning eyes which were so deep
a brown they were almost black on her lover. They narrowed
and her perfect eyebrows dipped ominously when she saw
where he was looking. She tapped his arm peremptorily for
though she did not love Paul Travers – she had never loved
any of her lovers – and was not in the least bit jealous of this
one's affections, she did not care to have his attention drawn
away from her, especially by another woman.

"Whatever you want, my pet. I'll leave it up to you. I
scarcely know a ballgown from a nightgown." He raised
an ironic eyebrow in Sara's direction and his eyes twinkled
wickedly.

"What nonsense, Paul. You know perfectly well as you
have proved many times in the past." Miss Damask threw
him a mischievous look and he smiled lazily.

"Behave yourself, Rose. You will shock this young lady.
See, she is beginning to blush," which was not true for
Sara Hamilton, in the year she had been first showroom
woman, had been privy to many indelicate whisperings when
gentlemen brought their female "friends" to be measured for
a House of Lovell gown. Nevertheless she couldn't help but
smile, bending her head in an attempt to hide it but he caught
it and his eyes narrowed in laughter, sharing her amusement
though he was careful not to let his mistress see it. Reaching
into his waistcoat-pocket he drew out a cigar. With a slight
inclination of his head in Sara's direction, asking for her
permission to light it but not expecting to be refused, he
put a match to it, blowing the fragrant smoke up towards
the ceiling of the quite magnificent room.

The House of Lovell's premier magazin was over a hundred
and forty feet long and seventy feet wide since it had been the
ballroom in what was once a private house before Madame
Lovell bought it fifteen years ago. In every panel around three
of its walls, reaching from the thickly carpeted floor to the
ornately carved ceiling, was a mirror set in a handsome gilt

frame. Down the fourth wall was ranged a row of long French windows which opened on to a broad terrace with steps leading down to the lawn and the wind-blown daffodils. Each window was draped with velvet curtains. The main colours in the room were ivory and the palest green with a hint of raspberry pink here and there, in a cushion or two on the wide velvet sofas and in the bowls of multicoloured roses which stood on small, informal tables. There were balloon-backed, cabriole-legged chairs like the one in which Miss Damask lounged and on the wide mantelshelf was a French clock in ormolu and two exquisite Sèvres vases. From the ceiling hung three enormous chandeliers supporting one hundred candles apiece and which had been lit half an hour ago by the footmen.

In different parts of the room, here in daylight, there in a shadowed, candle-lit corner, were counters of polished ebony, elegantly ornamented with gilding and on each one had been draped an assortment of costly and very beautiful silks and velvets, satins and voile, mousseline-de-laine which resembled muslin in texture and would be popular in the coming summer months, Madame had declared. There was pekin, a silk woven in narrow stripes, and Persian which was silk again but so fine it was transparent. There were shimmering lengths of zephyr and others of surah, soft and brilliantly coloured from India. Rich Genoa velvet which, despite its name, was satin with arabesque figures in velvet.

There were two straight-backed, fine-legged gilt chairs with velvet raspberry pink seats at the corner of each counter. Miss Damask rose gracefully, moved across the room and seated herself at one, indicating to her companion that he should sit beside her.

It took three hours to choose what she wanted, for Miss Damask was most particular, especially as she knew Paul Travers would foot the bill, probably for the last time, she thought sadly. So, if someone other than herself was paying, why not have the very best, she always told herself which was her due after all, in view of who she was. Paul was a skilled lover and a generous man, one of the wealthiest and most influential in Liverpool but Rose was a realist and at thirty-five knew that her beauty was waning. That already, though he was careful not to hurt her, Paul was losing interest, ready to move on to his next conquest, to a more exciting challenge and you had only to see the way he watched the magazinière, hypnotised by her youth and delicate loveliness, to know where that challenge lay. He was hanging about at each counter like a schoolboy in a sweet shop and had it not been for the girl, Rose was well aware, he would have become impatient hours ago. She drank coffee from a tiny, paper-thin china cup and nibbled on ratafia biscuits while Paul, eyes narrowed and speculative, smoked cigar after cigar until one could hardly see across Madame Lovell's elegant room. He scarcely took his eyes from the girl who seemed unaware of it and Rose sighed, for she would have given much to be in her shoes at the beginning and not the end of a love affair with Paul Travers.

They were bowed out to Paul Travers's brougham by two footmen, followed by the poised, still smiling figure of the magazinière.

"The first hand will come to measure you at your hotel as soon as it is convenient to you, Miss Damask," she said politely.

"Perhaps this afternoon then. I am to be here only until the end of the week and I shall need several of the gowns right away. Indeed, you had better let me have them all by tomorrow night." There were a dozen!

"Of course, Miss Damask. There will be no problem about that. Shall we say two thirty?"

Rose Damask did not answer. She took Paul Travers's hand as he sat down in the carriage beside her, a look of regret crossing her still unlined and beautiful face.

Sara smiled up into the carriage, the enormity of the task ahead of her and the seamstresses not revealed in her expression. The man, Paul Travers, had the bluest eyes she had ever seen and they were looking directly down at her. A quite indescribable blue, like hyacinths perhaps or the cornflowers which grew in the lanes she tramped between the House of Lovell in West Derby and Abercromby Square, but brilliant as though there were diamonds in them. He was not, strictly speaking, handsome, for his face was too strong but his features were pleasing with a look of good-natured tolerance about them which she found attractive. And yet besides humour there was keen intelligence there, a tough-fibred shrewdness which said he would be a difficult man to take advantage of. His mouth, smiling now to reveal his good white teeth, was strong, set in the brown smoothness of a freshly shaved face. His hair was cut short, a well-brushed cap of light brown which the April sunshine streaked to a glinting fairness. He was beautifully turned out, of course, in an immaculate black frock-coat and tight grey trousers. To her young eyes he was old, though, as old as her papa, she thought, but she liked the way he smiled at her.

"And you will guarantee the velvet ballgown for no later than Wednesday?" Rose Damask warned, wanting to get Paul away from the girl and the girl's eyes away from Paul.

"Of course, Miss Damask. Everything you have ordered will be ready the moment you require it. I shall measure out the materials at once."

"Thank you for your kindness, Miss . . .?" Paul Travers added. "You have been most attentive and very patient." He turned to grin disarmingly at his companion. "Miss Damask is well known for her . . . discrimination but it can be very trying to her . . . friends."

"Not at all, sir. I was only too happy to assist her."

"I can see that, Miss . . . er . . ." and to do more than that his wry expression seemed to say, for her quiet charm, her infinite care in helping Rose to choose the exact materials and colours which suited her, had been unflagging. Of course, she was an employee of the best fashion house in the county, hand-picked and groomed by the famous Madame Lovell but still she had never faltered in her efforts to please. No more than eighteen or nineteen, he would have said, but her composure, her deportment, her smiling and yet modest bearing had been that of a mature woman. Her behaviour had been exemplary, that of a lady and yet he had caught a hint of fun, almost of levity in her expression when her eyes met his. Just as though, despite the seriousness of the occasion, for what could be more serious to a woman than choosing new gowns, she had found it to be a great amusement. As though it gave her joy. Rose had liked her, he could tell that, and so, by God, had he!

As though reading his thoughts, or perhaps his relaxed dreaming face, she spoke.

"You liked her, didn't you, Paul my darling?" She kept her voice light, almost roguish as though the answer was of little importance to her.

The bland expression he put on for his competitors in business at once fell into place and he smiled ruefully.

"Good God above, Rose, she is young enough to be my daughter."

"What difference does that make? And you have just answered my first question."

"What in hell does that mean?" His tone was truculent.

"You did not deny it, Paul, merely evaded it."

He moved uncomfortably, making the lighting of another cigar an excuse to let go of her hand and Rose Damask knew she had lost him. And to whom!

He saw her at once, picking her flushed face out of the hundreds which surrounded it. She was in the gallery seated between a pretty woman with dark hair and a young man with fair, tousled curls, a man no more than a year or two older than she was. The man spoke to her with the ease of long acquaintanceship, or perhaps that of a lover, Paul thought, and suddenly was horrified at the snarling explosion of what could only be jealousy which hit him. The man leaned across her, resting his arm on the back of her seat as he spoke to her companion, turning to look into – Dear God, he didn't even know her name – into her face and again that feeling of rage surged through him, a rage one male directs towards another who threatens what is his.

He lowered his opera glasses, wondering why he had run them along the rows of seats in the first place. He sat alone in a box, knowing as he had entered it it would be for the last time to watch Rose who was to go on to Leeds on Sunday. He was well aware that he had made love to her for the last time on the night before he had taken her to Madame Lovell's, though he had not known it at the time, and the reason for it sat below him in the gallery on the far side of the theatre. He wanted to laugh, really he did, for the whole bloody thing was ludicrous. Paul Travers, only a few short months off his fortieth birthday, falling arse over apex for a child with a pretty face and charming manners. God above, he had barely exchanged two words with her that were not about frills and hemlines and the quality of the damned velvet and those in the alert presence of his mistress. Ex-mistress, he told himself righteously, then could have laughed out loud for it was as though already he was justifying himself in the eyes of the magazinière. Jesus, he wished he knew her name! The magazinière. Hell's teeth, he had thought of nothing and no one else for the past twenty-four hours. All he could see as he made a pretence of working at his desk in Water Street were her luminous green eyes fringed with drooping brown lashes. Had they been tipped with gold or was it a trick of the light? He had dwelled on them for hours and on the gleam and hue of her hair which reminded him of a ring his mother had once worn which had been ingeniously crafted from gold, from silver and copper and platignum and all these gleaming colours were in her hair. She had walked like a young queen, her back straight and yet gracefully supple. As she moved her hips had swayed and her young breasts had lifted at each step and instantly he had wanted her. Wanted to unbutton that dashing frilled shirt which looked so much like the one he himself wore, push it aside, ease it from her shoulders, expose her breasts, cup them lingeringly with eager, possessive hands, caress and gently nip them until she arched her back and lifted them to his eager lips.

Jesus God, what the hell was the matter with him, for even here in his solitary box as the lights dimmed and the orchestra struck up he could feel the bursting pressure in his crotch. He was thirty-nine, for Christ's sake and had known more women, had more women than he could possibly remember and yet he was mooning about like a half-grown schoolboy over a girl half his age!

There was only one remedy, of course, and it was one he would relish taking. He would start tomorrow. Send her flowers, flatter her, sweep her off her feet, woo her – dear God, didn't he mean seduce her? – which he knew he was very good at and when she was ready, for he was a gentleman and an accomplished lover and would not rush her, he would make her his mistress. When he had – best be forthright – used her, in no time at all she would be out of his blood. He would tire of her then as he had tired of every woman he had ever known. He would make her a handsome gift, more money than she could earn in ten years and move on to the next one.

He sighed, well pleased with his solution to the vexed and puzzling question of his sudden desire for Madame Lovell's magazinière. She was unlike many of the women he had fancied himself in love with, in a light-hearted way, of course. Younger, for one, original, fresh, but after all that was all she was, a woman, no different from any other except in shape and size and colour. He would not harm her. She would suffer no dreadful result from their relationship, he would make damn sure of that and when it was over would be none the worse for it.

He sat up suddenly as though a thought had struck him. Perhaps the fellow beside her had got there first. It was hard to believe when he studied in his mind's eye the sweet innocence of her. She had an untouched look. The look of a girl who has known no man's kisses, let alone his body. The glow young women have that is left over from girlhood but which is lost the moment their virginity is taken from them. She still had it. A softness, a ripe fullness to her mouth, a smoothness to her flesh, a pure and immaculate look which it would be his pleasure to rumple. His mouth became suddenly dry and, raising his opera glasses to his eyes, he trained them again along the gallery below him until he found her.

She was gazing at Rose, whom he had not even noticed come upon the stage, with the rapt wonderment of a child and on either side of her her companions did the same, evidently unused to theatre-going. He felt jaded all of a sudden, like a man who has seen and done everything, with none of the bewitchment the three young people were enjoying and the opera glasses dropped heavily into his lap. He did not look at her again.

The lights went up in the first interval and with a startling buoyancy, an abrupt return of youthfulness he had not felt for years, Paul sprang to his feet as the girl and her two companions rose to theirs. It took him no more than a minute to race round the back of the boxes, down the stairs and be indolently lounging against the wall, one hand in his pocket, the other holding his cigar, when the three young people reached the top step.

"Why, if it isn't Miss . . . Do you know I cannot quite recall your name. Perhaps . . .?" He grinned as though surprised to see her.

She was completely flustered this time, flushed and bright-eyed but shy now that she was away from her place of employment where her composure was supreme.

"Sara, Sara Hamilton," she murmured, her eyes cast down. He was enchanted. Sara, she was called Sara.

"Miss Hamilton, how very pleasant to see you again."

She was in figured ivory, a lovely silken thing over which she wore a vivid green velvet cloak lined with the same material as her gown. The collar was high, framing her flushed cheeks and a disarming cluster of escaping copper curls drifted across it.

"Mr Travers." She bobbed her head again and her curls bobbed with her. His breath was short and hard inside him and his heart wrenched with some unfamiliar emotion but his wide grin remained where it was, warm and infectious.

"Are you enjoying the play, Miss Hamilton?" he asked her and was overwhelmed by the almost unearthly quality of her joy as she answered.

"Oh yes, sir, it is quite superb and so is Miss Damask." Her expression said he must be very proud to be the friend of such a talented and beautiful creature.

"Indeed, and you are with . . .?" He turned courteously to the dark girl who was gazing at him as though he had just stepped down from the place where the gods resided, then to the young man whose face had taken on the slightly bored expression the young assume when faced with the elderly! He was neatly but poorly dressed in a cheap and ill-fitting suit.

"This is my friend Matty Hutchinson, sir. Matty, may I introduce you to Mr Paul Travers," showing her breeding in a way Ally would have been proud of. She almost added, "the lover of Miss Rose Damask", but caught herself in time, biting the inside of her cheek and doing her best not to giggle at her own frivolousness. There was something in Mr Travers's lovely blue eyes which seemed to say he shared her inclination to sudden laughter.

"And this is Mr David Bretherton, another friend of mine and a very clever artist. David, Mr Paul Travers."

"Indeed," Mr Travers said as he shook David Bretherton's hand. "You must let me see some of your work sometime, Mr Bretherton."

David Bretherton sprang to life and his face became respectful. A rich man, as this one obviously was, must be treated with care.

"I'd be delighted, sir. Just tell me where and when."

"Well . . ." It was evident that Mr Travers was somewhat taken aback by David's response. His remark had been merely one made for the sake of politeness but he continued to smile, if somewhat coolly.

"I have a stall in Pedlars Market, sir," David added disarmingly, aware that he had gone too far. "Miss Hamilton and Miss Hutchinson often visit me there and have even been kind enough to allow me to sketch them."

David Bretherton was a man and it had not taken him long to note where Mr Travers's eyes lingered. He might be tempted to come, and when he came, to buy, if sketches of the delicious Miss Hamilton were for sale.

"Perhaps one day you might . . .?" he added, diffident this time.

"Indeed, I might, if these two young ladies cared to show me where it is." He turned to Matty and she giggled, becoming a delightful rosy pink under his scrutiny, for this man was a "toff" and they were the best sort to know. They spent money on a girl, took her to smart places, to plays such as this, to the races at Aintree, to dinner at the Adelphi. They bought her presents, French perfume and jewellery, she had heard and though she had yet to meet such a man this one seemed a likely candidate even if he was a bit old.

Knowing exactly what he was about, Paul Travers made a great show of admiring Matty. Matty's dashing bonnet and her glossy hair which gleamed darkly beneath it, deepening her already deep smile and turning her eyes to vivid stars. He seemed to say he thought her to be quite splendid before he turned back to Sara.

"May I give you two ladies a lift home after the show?" he asked mildly, his eyes a pure, warm blue, innocent of guile. "My carriage is at your disposal. It is a long way to West Derby, Miss Hamilton and cabs are scarce at this time of night."

"We don't live in West Derby, Mr Travers. Madame allows me to live out. Matty and I are in lodgings in Abercromby Square."

Hell and damnation, just when he thought he had found the perfect opportunity, having first dropped off – what was she called for God's sake? – Matty, a quite blameless opportunity to get Miss Hamilton alone, it seemed he was to be saddled with her friend and the chap was looking very eager, not wanting to be left out of a chance for a ride home.

The lights dimmed and the curtain began to rise. People were seating themselves, irritably pushing past the four of them as they stood in the gangway. Paul felt the impatience rise in him then and the sudden awareness of his own foolish behaviour made him stiff, almost cold as he spoke.

"I'll meet you in the foyer at the end of the play," he told them curtly, then turned on his heel and strode back to his own box.

It was the glint, the reflection on the lenses of his opera glasses which gave him away. Though he sat in the shadows of the box his snowy shirt front gleamed whitely and so did the cuffs which showed as he lifted his arms.

She couldn't enjoy the play after Mr Travers left them and she didn't really know why. He had been pleasant and it had been very kind of him to offer them a lift home in his carriage but it had unsettled her for some reason and again she didn't know why. What was it that had spoiled her bright enjoyment of Miss Rose Damask's wonderful performance? She could think of nothing, though Mr Travers had seemed somewhat . . . cross as he turned away to walk back to his seat. Where would that be? she wondered, letting her gaze run round the tiers of boxes on the far side of the auditorium. In a box, of course, one of the most expensive ones near to the stage for he would want to be as close as he could get to Miss Damask.

She saw him then and she was not even sure how she knew it was him. He sat to the side of the box almost with his back to the stage looking out into the audience. He had his opera glasses to his face, held there by both his strong, brown, well-shaped hands – why had she noticed them? she wondered – and the glasses were pointed straight at her. She couldn't see his eyes, of course, but she knew, as she stared blindly at him that he was staring just as blindly at her.

22

He sent her roses, creamy white rosebuds, their furled petals edged with blush pink. The card with them had nothing written on it but his name.

Alice was beside herself with some emotion neither Sara nor Madame, whom Alice had dragged into the turmoil, could recognise, not at first.

"But I don't know why he sent roses to me, Ally. Really I don't," Sara kept on saying, eyeing the exquisite bouquet with a mixture of bewilderment and pleasure, wringing her hands and casting frantic looks at Madame.

"I don't believe you, Sara and nothing you say will make me believe that a man sends flowers to an innocent girl. I blame myself, of course, for not insisting that Madame compel you to live in when you were made magazinière. Heaven only knows who you meet in the showroom and, living as you do with the freedom I have allowed you, it seems you have every opportunity to take advantage of my trust. I suppose whoever it is, Paul Travers" – studying the plain white card with the sneering contempt it deserved – "took a fancy to you and, being no gentleman, made advances which you presumably allowed. Dear God above, what am I to do with you? Your reputation will be in tatters— "

"Miss Hamilton, if I may ..." Madame Lovell did her best to hold her temper in check as she spoke but Alice Hamilton took as much notice of her as she would a troublesome fly. Less, for she would have swatted at a fly.

"Ally, please, let me explain," Sara begged.

"An explanation is certainly needed, miss, and at once, and in the meanwhile kindly ring for one of the maidservants to remove these ... these ... things to some suitable place, preferably the rubbish tip."

"Miss Hamilton, would you— "

"I will brook no interference, Madame." Alice turned to her employer, the full force of her fury breaking over Rosalie Lovell's head. "Not this time. My sister is ignorant of men."

For a moment she hesitated for the statement was not strictly true. But then that navvieman could not be counted, could he? He and Sara were never alone together, were they? Just once, a tiny voice whispered, on the day he and Sara went to Lytham. Dear Lord, oh dear Lord, what was she to do if it happened again?

Taking advantage of the brief silence, Madame Lovell, who had been on her way to the premier magazin when she had been diverted by the commotion on the landing outside the workroom, put her hand on Sara's arm. Sara still held the roses and they glowed softly, a creamy glow which was reflected in her face as she bent her head to their fragrance.

"Sara," she said gently, "have you no explanation as to why Mr Travers should send you flowers? I mean, has anything taken place between you?"

"Taken place?" Sara looked up, her expression even more confused. "What could have taken place? I have only met him once ... well, twice."

"Twice? But he has only been here once that I can recall. With Miss Damask the other day."

"Yes, Madame, but we ... that is Matty and I" – not daring to mention David Bretherton – "met him at the Theatre Royal last night. By accident, of course," she added hastily.

Alice was incensed. "This really is disgraceful, Madame, and I beg you to think again about my sister's accommodation in this house. The theatre! I had no idea."

"Miss Hamilton, I am well aware you are not pleased and neither am I but do let us find out what has happened, if anything, before we ..."

Alice snatched the roses from Sara's arms, her face screwed up distastefully, then turned to the footman who had brought the bouquet from the front door where it had been delivered.

"Dispose of these, my good man."

"Really, Miss Hamilton, will you please allow me to speak and I would be obliged if you would refrain from ordering *my* servants about as though they were your own. Remember your position here, if you please. Thank you," as Alice finally fell silent. "Now, I am as amazed as you that a gentleman . . ."

Aware suddenly of the avid interest of the footman Madame stopped speaking. She knew that within half an hour, less, a report of what had happened and the reason for it would be all over the house but it was too late now. The innocent – and she was undoubtedly that – cause of it stood flushed and dismayed, her eyes on the roses now as though she could not bear to part with them.

"I think we had better go to my room, Sara," she went on sternly.

"But I have a client waiting, Madame." Sara could not seem to drag her eyes away from the flowers which the footman had taken and was holding gingerly in his arms as he waited for his mistress to tell them what he should do with them.

"Mademoiselle Jeanette will see to that, Sara. Come."

"But . . ."

"We must have a talk, you and I. In the meanwhile Roberts can ask one of the parlourmaids to arrange the roses in a vase. I think they would look particularly nice in the workroom where all the girls can enjoy them."

Having reduced Paul Travers's extraordinary floral tribute to Sara Hamilton's young beauty to the ordinary, Madame turned towards the stairs, drawing Sara along behind her like a small boat attached to a larger. At their backs came Alice, not at all pleased to have her orders to the footman countermanded but glad that they were at last to have the contentious issue of Sara's "living in" finally cleared up.

She began to say so. "When you hear what I have to say I am sure you will agree, Madame, that Sara can no longer— "

Madame, who had reached the head of the stairs, stopped suddenly, so suddenly Sara bumped into her.

"Miss Hamilton, I think Sara and I can manage without you. This does not concern you. Sara is a member of my staff and I, as her employer, will deal with it."

"Madame, I think you forget that— "

"Miss Hamilton! Back to the workroom and at once."

Alice had no choice but to obey, slinking off with her bloody tail between her legs, the footman gleefully told the servants in the kitchen and not before time, bossy cow! Giving

him orders. Calling him "my man" and her no more than a
servant herself. Face on her like thunder, she had, and pity
them poor girls in the workroom for they'd be the ones to pay
for it. And Miss Sara, an' all, if the look Miss High and bloody
Mighty threw at her retreating back was anything to go by.

Later, when Sara had gone, her eyr ;hining with the truth
of it, Rosalie Lovell sat back in her chair sipping the hot
chocolate she had ordered, her gaze speculative as she
gazed into the glowing heart of the fire. She wished she
could take her damned corsets off but she was to see a very
influential client in an hour. Besides, smiling to herself, she'd
end up like her old mam if she let her standards slip, flopping
around in a wrapper and comfy slippers by the fire. It was
a great temptation sometimes just to let things go. To relax,
lie in bed, forget about business and clients and fabrics and,
reverting to the speech of her childhood, do sod all. Allow
herself to be the age she was. She was in her fifties. She had
more money than she knew what to do with and sometimes
she wondered why she got out of her bed each day but it was
at moments in the day like this, when she had warmed herself
in Sara Hamilton's glowing admiration and gratitude and in
the vanquishing of Alice Hamilton, that she knew why. She
enjoyed it, the manipulation of others, and especially the likes
of Alice Hamilton who tried so hard to best Rosalie Lovell.
She laughed, snorting into her cup of chocolate. If, no matter
which way she turned, she could trump Miss Hamilton then
Rosalie Lovell's day was the better for it. She wondered why
she let the woman stay on sometimes but she was increasingly
aware that it was because she enjoyed these little encounters.
They fired her blood. They made her feel young. She enjoyed
seeing Alice Hamilton squirm and she used her sister in the
process, she knew that, too, though she was fond of the child.
How Alice twisted and turned to have her own way with her
young sister who, it seemed, had caught the lustful eye of
one of the wealthiest men in Liverpool. Not that the child was
aware of it. Not really, nor of the inevitability, the certainty
that if Paul Travers wanted her, he would have her.

She remembered her own first lover . . . sweet God, nearly
forty years ago now but how he had swept her away with his
passion. What was his name? She couldn't remember but she
could remember how it felt. By God, she could remember
that. Perhaps it was because it was so clear in her mind still

that she had not warned Sara, nor forbidden her to associate with Mr Travers. What had she told her? Nothing really, only to be discreet, which had confused the girl further.

Well, it was Sara Hamilton's life. Hadn't Rosalie Lovell told her only the other day to grasp it by the horns and grapple with it until it was exactly the shape she wanted it to be. To live it to the full because it was short and she was old enough to decide for herself, wasn't she. She'd told her so often enough, and that bloody sister of hers.

Dammit, why in hell's name was she drinking this foul stuff? Where was the brandy, for God's sake? She just felt like a brandy even if it was only eleven o'clock in the morning and if at her time of life she couldn't do what she damn well wanted then she might as well be in her coffin and six feet under. Brandy made her feel good, less old and hadn't she girls by the score who could see to her client? Sara Hamilton was one! Wasn't that what Rosalie Lovell paid them for?

The brougham stood just beyond the gates of the house, drawn there so that anyone at a window of the house, should they glance out, could not see it.

Sara was not alarmed. In fact she scarcely noticed it as she stepped out towards West Derby Lane. It was almost dusk, just gone half past seven and she had worked hard for the past twelve hours, most of them on her feet. Hours spent in consultation and deliberation with several of Madame's clients. A journey out to Alderley in Madame's brougham to the home of one of Madame's most important ladies, Mrs James Wickham, to measure her for an outfit for her daughter's wedding which was to take place in June. Mrs Wickham had already chosen the material and though it was normally the first hand who measured a client Mrs Wickham had particularly asked that Miss Sara accommodate her and who was Madame to argue with Mrs Wickham who spent a fortune at the House of Lovell each year. Mrs Wickham had five daughters, the youngest fourteen!

Every moment of Sara's day had been busy and deeply satisfying. The unpleasantness with Alice and the resultant chat with Madame still simmered quietly at the back of her mind but that's where she intended to leave it until she felt able to get the day's events into some kind of perspective.

Despite her resolve, as she slipped from the workroom,

when no one was looking, she had taken one of the creamy white rosebuds from the bowl, keeping it out of sight until she left the house. It was pinned now to the collar of her long, serviceable cloak, the one she wore for her journey to and from work and she could smell the flower's fragrance as she walked.

It did not distract her though. She had too much on her mind with Mrs Wickham's outfit who, as the mother of the bride was determined it must outshine every other outfit at the wedding, especially that of the mother of the groom and she was depending on Miss Sara, she said, to make sure it did. Powder blue taffeta, she had a fancy for. She was a woman who, as a girl, had been golden-haired and pink-cheeked and white-skinned and still imagined she was. Sara had introduced her to a rich shade of blue, or was it lavender, exactly like the bluebells which hazed the ground beneath the trees which stood about Mr Wickham's extensive property. To be made from lutestring, Sara had recommended, which was a fine corded glossy silk, very expensive, which of course was just what Mrs Wickham wanted to hear. A fitted bodice since Mrs Wickham had a fine bosom. A skirt with an extravagant train edged with ruching of the same material, full and wide, for the narrow skirts of the early years of the decade were definitely out, and a stunning hat which Sara would design for her and which she knew Mrs Wickham would adore.

Not too plain, Mrs Wickham had beseeched her, examining her own reflection anxiously in the mirror, after all she was the mother of the bride!

"Of course not, Mrs Wickham," Sara had reassured her, but speaking firmly, for where fashion was concerned Sara was firm since she knew about it. She loved clothes and she understood them. She knew how to dress other women and she knew how to dress herself. Besides Mrs Wickham's outfit there was the bride's gown which Mademoiselle Jeanette was overseeing, the bride's extensive trousseau which consisted of at least two dozen gowns, one for every occasion from first light until the last candle was blown out. Morning gowns, afternoon gowns, tea gowns, dinner gowns, ballgowns, not to mention the scores of petticoats, the chemises, the frilled and embroidered nightgowns, every article of clothing which a bride would need. Then there were Mrs Wickham's four remaining daughters who must all be dressed according to

Mr Wickham's station in life and every single thing to be finished down to the last stitch by the end of May.

No, Sara had certainly no time to be bothered with Ally's tantrums!

It was as she passed the carriage door and was on a level with the horse's hanging heads that the carriage door opened. At the sound her heart felt as though it had suddenly been squeezed with a fist then, as it was released, it immediately began to hammer at twice its normal pace. She had heard, as all young women had, of the desperate measures the underworld of Liverpool went to – indeed it happened in all the big cities – to lure, or simply abduct unprotected girls, even children, carrying them off to a life of degradation and shame, forcing them, because they were young and innocent, into the oldest profession in the world, as Sara had heard it called. Dear God, why had she not listened to Ally? Taken her advice, obeyed her order to live in at the house? She had been filled with a resolve to be independent, to extract herself from beneath Alice's dominance and if sometimes as she faced this long walk home at the end of the day she wished she was ensconced, as Ally would be, in a cosy room under the Lovell roof, she had only to think of Ally's triumph to set herself striding out into the night. Now look what had happened! She was to be carried off to some place of ill repute to become the . . . the target of . . . of what men did to women in such establishments and nobody would know. Sara Hamilton would just vanish off the face of the earth.

Her frantic thoughts took no more than ten seconds to pass through her head. She whirled to face her attacker, lifting both her fists defensively somewhat in the manner of a prize fighter but the man who had jumped lightly from the brougham laughed. He took a step back from her and the light from the carriage lamps fell across his face.

It was Mr Travers.

"Steady on," he said, grinning with delight at her show of spirit. "I wouldn't care to have my eye blackened and by a young lady half my weight. If it got about my reputation would be in tatters."

His grin became even wider and she could see the gleam of his white teeth. "Good evening, Miss Hamilton," he went on, laughter still rumbling in his voice. "I do apologise for startling you. Perhaps I should have gone about it another way but whichever way I approached you it would have had the same result. But see, take that look of alarm from your face. It is only me. Paul Travers."

He held out his hands disarmingly as though he would take hers between them, his eyes softening imperceptibly but she backed away, open-mouthed still, her eyes wide and glittering in her paper-white face. She caught her foot in the hem of her gown and he leaped forward, ready to steady her, ready to help her, to take her hands and pull her into his protective arms, his expression seemed to say, but the mishap brought her from her shock and even in the half light between night and day he could see the colour flood hectically beneath her skin.

She put out her hands again to ward him off, then, drawing herself up, stamped her foot in fury.

"How dare you give me such a fright. Have you no sense at all? Have you the slightest notion what it is like walking these lanes in the dark with— ?"

"I have, that is why I am here, Miss Hamilton and I, or my carriage, will be waiting here every night to take you home. It is not right that you should go about unprotected. Indeed— "

"Indeed, Mr Travers!" She drew herself up even further, her bonnet still no higher than the point of his chin. "Indeed, what concern is it of yours, may I ask?"

"None, of course, but . . ."

"Exactly, so would you kindly allow me to go about my business while you continue to go about yours."

"When a young woman such as yourself, a defenceless woman, is determined foolishly to put herself at risk then a gentleman has no choice but to protect her whether she likes it or not."

His voice had taken on a grating tone and Sara could see he was offended. But then so was she. He had no right to think he could just casually wait for her right outside her place of employment where any of the servants might see, and think the worst, of course. And if Ally were to witness it God alone knew what might happen! Did he honestly think she would be overjoyed to see him, so much so she would leap into his carriage and accept his offer to drive her home? He had no right to assume it just as he had no right to send her roses, causing her a great deal of embarrassment and no end of conflict with Ally, though Madame hadn't seemed unduly concerned. All young ladies, if they were attractive, had admirers, she had said and Sara must get used to it. She was only surprised it had not occurred sooner since Sara now came into contact with many gentlemen in the showroom. Most of them married, of course, but they were the ones who were interested in girls like Sara, though Rosalie Lovell did not add this last.

But Mr Travers was a bachelor. Sara had been bewildered, for how could Mr Travers, old enough to be her father, surely, be considered as an admirer? Besides which he was in love with Rose Damask. He was her lover, their demeanour in the showroom had said so and yet he had sent flowers to his mistress's dressmaker. It made no sense, none at all and now, after the furore of the roses this morning, here was the man himself begging her to ride home in his carriage!

Her confusion showed in her face and at once Paul stepped back, figuratively and physically. She was young, her face that of a guileless child and his own became warm, gentle and yet at the same time ablaze and urgent. He was not aware that his feelings shone so incandescently from his smiling face though Sara, had she noticed them, would have been ignorant of their meaning. His curving mouth moved and lifted, mobile in its need to be about something which even he was scarcely aware of but he waited patiently.

"I am seriously displeased, Mr Travers," she said sternly and he wanted to smile, to laugh at her delightful earnestness, to sweep her up into his arms and kiss her until she smiled with him.

Instead he did his best to be grave. "I can see that, Miss Hamilton, and I can only apologise again. I should have been more considerate of your feelings." His mouth lifted in a wry smile which begged her indulgence. "But I see you are fond of flowers."

"I beg your pardon?" She was beginning to soften though she held herself defensively, not at all sure how to handle this strange incident. She had no experience of men, only Jack, and that was . . . that had been . . . it was ended. Three years . . . but she must not allow herself to slip back to the past since it only hurt her.

"You are wearing a rosebud," Mr Travers said, his eyes twinkling in the dusky light.

Her hand went to it and she bent her head. "Yes, it is so exquisite."

And so are you! He did not speak out loud.

"But it caused a great deal of embarrassment, Mr Travers. My sister was livid."

"Your sister? Your sister works at the House of Lovell as well?" He moved an inch or two towards her, pleased when she stood her ground.

She was smelling the bud, her nose wrinkling delicately as she enjoyed its fragrance but she looked up at once.

"Oh yes, Alice is four years older than me and is a supervisor and instructor, but she is . . . well . . ." She sighed deeply, enchantingly and he let himself be enchanted. He said nothing though. "She thinks I am still a child and cannot forgive me for living out."

"She is right, Miss Hamilton, and I— "

"Please, Mr Travers, we have already established that I am quite well able to look after myself."

"Have we, Miss Hamilton? If I had had designs on you, and I am sure you know what I mean, how easy it would have been to snatch you away."

"With a coachman and two horses who are all fast asleep?"

He laughed so loudly the coachman woke up with a start and both horses snorted irritably.

"What . . . what?" the coachman muttered, fiddling blindly with the reins still between his fingers, and the horses tossed their heads as though in agreement.

"You see what I mean, Mr Travers?" Sara smiled demurely. "All as lively as crickets and eager to be involved in some daring escapade."

"Yes, you're right, Miss Hamilton, so it is obvious my intentions towards you are strictly honourable else I would have brought a length of rope, my racing curricle and a horse to match." Even as he spoke he knew he lied. This young woman, though she spoke with the cultured tones and had the manners of a well-bred lady, was a seamstress, and seamstresses, actresses, shop assistants, housemaids and other serving classes were fair game to gentlemen who did not have marriage in mind. "So will you allow me to convey you to your home in my carriage? I shall only follow behind if you refuse and that would look even more suspicious. Besides, I am curious about this sister of yours."

"Alice?"

"Alice."

"What can you want to know about Alice? She is very pretty and very clever. So clever I am constantly amazed that she does not take it into her head to live at Abercromby Square just to keep me from . . ." She paused and he bent his head to her downcast face.

"Yes?" he prompted. The brim of her bonnet hid her expression and he wanted to miss nothing, not a smile, not a frown, not a blush nor a blink of her golden-tipped eyelashes, not one nuance of what Sara Hamilton was thinking or feeling.

She still hesitated and, taking advantage of it, moving with that somewhat arrogant sureness which had come with his upbringing, he opened the carriage door.

"Hop up," he said cheerfully, not by a flicker of a muscle showing his true feelings, nor the doubt he felt, right to the last, that she might not obey him, "and on the way home you can tell me all about . . . Look, I can't keep on calling you Miss Hamilton. I realise that we have not been formally introduced but surely we can progress to first names," just as though they had been acquaintances for weeks instead of four days.

"Very well," she answered as she allowed him to hand her into the deep padded comfort of the two-seater brougham.

"Sara then," he said caressingly and the girl whose name it was felt a small frisson of pleasure move through her veins and along the surface of her skin.

There was a rug of soft fur and though the night was mild he tucked it about her with the lingering tenderness of a lover. When it was to his satisfaction he leaned back, reaching into the inside pocket of his coat for his gold cigar case. He was about to light the cigar he withdrew when something, he didn't know what, held him back. It was a certain quality in her manner, her upright carriage even when seated. She reminded him of the way his mama sat in a chair, and his sisters who had all been taught by their nanny and then by a governess that a lady's back never touched the back of the chair. A seamstress she might be but the look she cast in his direction told him no gentleman lit a cigar without first enquiring of the lady with him if he might.

He was taken aback for a moment or two, ready to ignore the strange feeling of diffidence she had roused in him, ready to go ahead and light the cigar anyway, but he found he couldn't.

"Do you mind if I smoke, Sara?" he heard himself ask courteously and at once she smiled, the proprieties observed.

"Oh no, Mr Travers. I like the smell of cigars. My papa always smoked one after dinner."

"Your . . . papa?" He choked on the words, the cigar he was holding suspended from nerveless fingers halfway to his lips which had parted to receive it. Her papa! Bloody hell, he didn't know whether to be dumbfounded by her ladylike manner or wryly amused at the neat way she had bracketed him in the age group of her father. Served him right, of course, for allowing himself to be tempted by a woman half his age and one so innocent it almost broke his courage for how could he tamper with it?

When his cigar was burning to his complete satisfaction he leaned back beside her, crossed his long legs and turned to grin mischievously at her.

"Now then, Miss Sara Hamilton, to while away the boredom of this tedious journey why do not you and I tell one another our life stories? I appreciate that mine will be considerably longer than yours but I pride myself that it is not without interest. Now then, you first." He beamed with great good humour then was quite astounded when she turned away from him, gazing out of the window and across the dark fields towards Everton.

"I'm rather tired now, Mr Travers, so if you do not think it impolite I would prefer not to make conversation."

Her cool young dignity amazed him. He felt like a callow youth who, having made an improper advance to a lady, has been firmly put in his place but he merely bowed briefly in her direction.

"Of course, Miss Hamilton."

At once she turned contritely, having heard the brief flare of hurt in his voice. Her face was a pale creamy white against the dark blue velvet of the carriage seat. Her eyes were enormous and he could have sworn, brilliant with tears. He sat forward and leaned towards her and for a tense, spark-filled moment their faces were so close he could feel her sweet breath on his mouth, then she smiled, a heart-stopping smile, luminous, radiant, joyous. She laid a hand on his leg and he felt the muscles quiver from his knee to his groin and for several appalling moments he was afraid of the reaction of his own male body. He had always, in the twenty-five years since he had his first encounter with a willing parlourmaid, thought it to be a simple matter to lie with a woman. Now he was confounded by his own mixed emotions. He wanted more than anything in the world to take this girl's hand and lift it to his lips, kiss it reverently, treat her like a fine-spun thread of silk which might break. Gently, tenderly to cherish her but at the same time he felt a great need to urge her hand up his thigh, to place it in the increasing heat where his manhood stirred. He wanted to feel the small bones of her neck beneath his strong hands and to kiss her so roughly he bruised her soft lips. To hold her like a bird in the palm of his hand, and yet to part her thighs and impale her with his pounding body. He felt warm, damp with sweat but he could not turn away from her lest she recognise the reason.

"I'm sorry, Mr Travers. That was not only inconsiderate but downright rude after you have been so kind. To go to all this trouble" – she smiled – "and I have done nothing but treat it as an inconvenience. Please forgive me."

She drove spikes into his heart with her candour, evidently seeing him as some elderly contemporary of her own father. Someone to whom she must show respect and courtesy.

As the spikes thudded home there came the soft dawning of his true feelings for Sara Hamilton and with the realisation came the sad knowledge that they were not reciprocated.

23

His carriage met her every night outside the House of Lovell and Sara Hamilton became, within the week, the source of avid gossip, not only among the seamstresses but the servants themselves; the scandalous topic of such speculative muck-raking, Alice Hamilton could never hold up her head again, she said wildly. If their mama and papa were alive it would kill them all over again and the only course open to them both was to resign at once and start again in another part of the country. Somewhere they were not known. She was convinced she and Sara, with a decent reference from Madame and the knowledge and experience they had gained in the three years they had been in Liverpool, would soon find similar employment and if not then she had a plan, a scheme which she wished to discuss with Sara and of which she was sure Sara would approve.

There was a curious gleam in her eyes as she spoke just as though, despite being mortified by her sister's shameful association with Paul Travers, she was secretly glad for some reason known only to herself that this had happened.

The roses came every day until the place looked like a damned flower shop, the parlourmaids told one another, smirking, always the same colour, creamy white tinged with blush pink and Sara could not help but be enchanted with them.

"Alice, it's servants' gossip, nothing more," she protested as another bunch arrived. "Mr Travers has been kind to me, I don't know why . . ."

"Do not be ridiculous, Sara. The man is not just being kind as you so naïvely put it, else he would send flowers to every female in the establishment, including the skivvy who scrubs the scullery floor. And now his carriage waits for you at the gates for anyone to see. You surely cannot be so artless as to believe he has no ulterior motive behind this sudden interest in you. Only last week it was common knowledge that he was the . . . that that actress who brought him to the showroom was his mistress. Now she has left town and he has turned his attentions to you. How do you explain that, I would like to know?"

"It is not at all like that, Ally. He was quite appalled to hear I was walking from Lovell House to Abercromby Square, especially in the dark. He said no woman should be out alone . . ."

"You are not a woman, Sara, you are a lady and he is only saying what I have been telling you for the past two years. Will you not see the sense of it and ask Madame if you may live in? There is a bedroom next to mine which is empty and besides being more suitable, living in, I mean, it will put a stop, not only to this man's attentions but to all this dreadful gossiping about you and him. Everywhere I go they are whispering, stopping suddenly when they catch sight of me and I am ashamed of it. Before it is too late, Sara, I really must insist— "

"I'm sorry, Ally."

"Of course you are not sorry."

On and on it went, to the great delight of the servants and the seamstresses and once again Madame had to call Sara and Alice into her sitting-room. Again no one was privy to what was said but after that Miss Hamilton, if she berated her sister did it in private.

It was two weeks later, as April slipped serenely into May that he was again waiting for her in the carriage. She had grown used to it standing down the lane, the coachman's polite good evening, miss and the lift of his coachman's hat, just as if this was something he did all the time, the horses restlessly rattling the harness, the relief as she sank back in the deep blue padded cushions, for she really was tired. She knew by now, after all she was an intelligent woman, that this was not the action of a man who had no more on his mind than the welfare of one human being for another. No man sent his carriage every night to take home a lowly seamstress, not without purpose he didn't, and even Matty had looked dubious when she had watched Sara alight from it. Lily and

Dolly, of course, had been scandalised, even though they felt relief that she no longer walked the dark and lonely lanes, begging her to be "sensible" and "a good girl like yer mama was" and even to "listen ter yer sister" which, coming from Lily was quite astounding.

They said very much what Ally said but she turned deaf ears on them all. She didn't even know why. Perhaps it was because Mr Travers was a man twice her age and surely didn't expect . . . well, what gentlemen expected from certain ladies, or so she had been warned. An affair, Ally intimated, some nasty intrigue which could only ruin Sara, not only in her career but later, if she were to . . . well, it was not outside the realms of possibility that Sara might marry, she said, ignoring Sara's moué of disagreement. And then there was herself. If Sara insisted upon continuing this association might it not affect Alice's chance of a decent marriage. No man would wish to be related to an unmarried woman who was in a dubious relationship with an unmarried man!

Lily had been more blunt, telling her in no uncertain terms, explicit terms, what Mr Travers had in mind for her. An older man with money and a young woman with looks. Really, Sara was lunatic even to consider it and as for the bloody carriage, Lily would pay for a cab herself to fetch Sara from West Derby each night sooner than let her fall into the hands of that old lecher. Tell him to go to hell, the dirty old devil, she said, but again – Sara didn't know why – she found she didn't want to. He was . . . he made her laugh. On the few occasions they had met he had lightened her heart which had been heavy for so long. Made her feel rare, special, which, after what Jack had done to her, was a salve to her wounded spirit. The roses alone put a glow on each day, starting it with a splendour which gave a spring to her step.

She liked him!

Late snowdrops were pushing their green spears through the earth. The delicacy of wild primroses and violets starred the grass beneath the trees and across the garden the grass changed to the rich hue of the coming summer. Tall soldier tulips were in full bloom, jostling for space among ranunculus, hyacinth and anemones, brilliant with colour in the lovingly tended borders. Buds were beginning to open and blossom exploded on the branches of the apple trees at the back of Lovell House. Blackbirds sang dementedly from every bush and Sara, stepping out into the garden for a breath of fresh air at noon, had felt some strong emotion, some cleansing, reviving emotion fill her heart and her lungs. She had breathed deeply of the soft, wine-like air, drawing it down inside her and she knew she was better. In what way she could not explain, only that something had happened to her and she felt good about it.

That evening she was startled when the coachman, who usually jumped down from his box as she approached, stayed where he was and the carriage door was flung open from the inside. Though she had half expected it several times in the past two weeks she was even more startled when Mr Travers stepped down, bowing ironically, his teeth gleaming in the amber smoothness of his face as he held the door open for her.

"Miss Hamilton . . . Sara," he said lightly, "a lovely evening, is it not?" His eyes were a brilliant blue in the dusky light of the May evening, the reflection of the carriage lamp a more profound brilliance in their depths. She saw the fine lines about them deepen in laughter.

"Mr Travers, sir, you startled me." She could not help but smile back, bowing her own head a little as a lady would to a gentleman acquaintance.

"I apologise, Miss Hamilton . . . Sara," his mouth curving over her name. "I seem to be always springing a surprise on you but then do you not find it makes life so much more exciting to be surprised from time to time?"

"I hadn't thought of it like that, Mr Travers, but yes. One knows one is alive when the unexpected happens."

"Quite! Now, will you allow me to help you up into the carriage? It is still chilly, is it not, despite the onset of spring?" She could tell this polite but sardonic chit-chat amused him.

His eyes were still on her, crinkled in wry humour as though he laughed at something within himself but as he sat down in the carriage beside her she could also see something other than laughter stir in their depths. She could feel his powerful presence an inch from her shoulder. He was a tall man, lean, but with strong muscled shoulders. His hair was thick, mid-brown interlaced with streaks of pale gold. It was inclined to curl over the collar of his coat despite his evident attention to it with a hairbrush. He wore no beard and his dark-complexioned face was slashed with fierce brown eyebrows. Even though he was relaxed, smiling at her with what appeared to be enormous pleasure, his chin thrust forward arrogantly, firm and pugnacious as if he was well accustomed to having his own way. His mouth was strong, hard perhaps, except when he smiled which he did now, the expression on his face curiously gentle.

But his eyes! She had never seen eyes like them, eyes of such a vivid, beautiful blue she could only compare them to the sapphires in the ring her papa had given her mother on their wedding day. Long brown lashes framed their vibrantly smiling depths and in those depths was a watchful amusement, mocking almost, as though he found the world vastly entertaining and not to be taken seriously. Now that she knew him a little better she could sense the vigour in him, his complete masculinity and she wondered in great astonishment why she had considered him to be old. To be like her papa!

He was dressed for evening in a superbly fitting black saxony dress coat, a white waistcoat with embroidered borders, narrow-legged black trousers to match his coat and evening pumps. His shirt front was snowy and finely pin tucked. The collar was high, the points of it just touching his firm jaw and his white cravat was tied in a flat bow under his chin.

"You look very smart, Mr Travers," she said without thinking. "Are you to go to a party?" and was bewildered by his shout of laughter.

"Sara Hamilton, I do believe I have never met anyone quite like you. It is most refreshing to hear a lady say exactly what comes into her mind. Promise me you will never change."

"Well, I'm not sure about that, but is it true?"

"Is what true, Sara?" He turned towards her, leaning forward, and took her hands between his own, doing nothing with them that might alarm her, though he could barely control his desire to carry them to his lips. To turn them over and kiss the soft palm, the fleshy mound at the base of her thumb, the inside of her wrist. To place a light, teasing tongue on the pulse that beat there, to perform, in fact, all the sweet intimacies he had performed with many women in the game of seduction.

"That ladies do not speak their minds to gentlemen?"

"Do you not know any gentlemen, Sara?"

"None at all, Mr Travers."

Oh God, she was so lovely, so trusting and innocent, admitting to him, as no experienced woman would, that she was untouched. That no man had put his hands, or even his lips on her. That she had reached the age of ... what, eighteen? nineteen? working in Madame Lovell's showroom under the lustful eyes of many men, he was certain and yet was still a girl. A maiden, as they said.

He would be the first!

"Why is that, Miss Sara Hamilton? Why is it that a beautiful young woman like yourself . . .?" He meant to tease her a little, no more, but even as he spoke her long, fine lashes drooped, shadowing her eyes as she lowered her head. He gently let go of her hands and leaned back in his seat.

He could not go on. He was quite devastated. She was clearly hiding something, unwilling to meet his eyes with the candour he found so enchanting. There *was* a man in her life. There must be. Before he could stop himself, afterwards ready to throw himself in the Mersey for a half-baked, love-struck fool, he spoke, his voice harsh.

"Is it that Johnny I saw you with at the theatre because if it is I can only say take care. He is looking for one thing only and that is someone to support his talent which, like all artists, he believes to be prodigious. He is a parasite, a sponger and will only— " He bit off the sentence, unable to go on.

She was open-mouthed in astonishment. She blinked rapidly then began to laugh, great peals of merriment which lasted for several long moments, leaving her gasping for breath.

"Mr Travers, you can't mean David?"

"Aye, that's the one," he snarled. "Well, he is no gentleman and certainly has no morals. I bought every damn one of his sketches of you and the other girl and he had the bloody nerve to charge me five guineas apiece for them."

"And are they not worth that, Mr Travers? You are telling me you were swindled?"

"No, I was not swindled, madam, because I wanted them and I am willing to pay the— "

He stopped abruptly. Their eyes met. They began to laugh together, both of them rocking in their seats, their mouths wide, shaking their heads as paroxysms of mirth shook them both. The absurdity of his reaction and her clever response which had disarmed him immediately sent him into further gales of noisy laughter and up on his box the coachman wondered what the hell was tickling the master. He'd never heard him laugh like that before but then he'd never seen him take a fancy to a girl young enough to be his daughter before. Getting into his dotage, poor old fool and like old fools in their dotage they liked them younger and younger. Mind, she was a good looker, but then they all were, Mr Travers's women. He wondered idly as he drove the carriage round the now familiar corner of Chatham Street and into Abercromby Square how long it would take him to get her into bed. Thomas would know, of course. Things would be different then with long waits outside her lodgings in the bloody cold or, as sometimes happened, Thomas not required as Mr Travers took out his light racing curricle to show off his masculine prowess to his latest!

He was there the next night, and the next and when Paul Travers asked Sara Hamilton to take luncheon with him at the Adelphi Hotel on her next day off, Thomas knew the time was almost upon them.

"Be careful, queen. Promise me you'll be careful." Matty's face was creased with worry as she watched Sara carefully tie the ribbons of her bonnet beneath her chin.

There were no words to describe the way Sara Hamilton looked that day, Matty decided. She wore a gown of dove grey broadcloth, so pale it was almost white. The enormous skirt was held out with half a dozen stiffened petticoats and it swayed about her like a graceful bell. The neck of the bodice was square cut and edged with a fine band of pale peach satin, the bodice itself fitting superbly to her high young breasts and narrow waist. Down the back from the neck to the waist was a row of tiny buttons, forty-two in all, covered in dove grey satin. Her bonnet was small and neat, framing her face, the underside of the brim lined with ruched satin in the same pale peach which was repeated in the wide ribbons which tied beneath her small chin. The fabric for the whole outfit had come from Madame's old stock and in three nights, working until the small hours, she and Matty had completed it, putting in the last stitches only the night before. With the resilience of youth, neither showed any sign of weariness.

"Yer know wharr I'm talkin' about, don't yer, Sara?" Matty

adjusted the bow of the bonnet, though it was already perfect, then impulsively reached out and pulled Sara into her arms. She hugged her hard and Sara reciprocated laughingly, careless of any crushing to her gown or displacement of her bonnet.

"Matty, Mr Travers is a gentleman," she protested.

"'E's a man, chuck, an' you look good enough to eat. Listen ter what I'm sayin', love," she pleaded. "I know about men an' they can't be trusted. None of 'em, so think on."

She released Sara abruptly, turning away and flapping her hands as though Sara was to take no notice of Matty Hutchinson's distress as long as she heeded her words. "Now, I'm sayin' no more, not now, anyroad, burrif 'e asks yer to go . . ."

"Where for heaven's sake?"

"Well, to 'is rooms."

"Rooms! He has a house, oh, I don't know where, out beyond West Derby somewhere and he'd hardly . . ."

"E'll 'ave rooms in town, God's 'onour," Matty said grimly. "They always do an' yer've not ter go near 'em, d'yer 'ear."

"Lord, you sound just like Ally."

"Jesus wept!" Matty sounded horrified. "Yer've not told Miss 'Oity-Toity, 'ave yer?"

"Of course I haven't. Now, how do I look?"

"Need yer ask, chuck, that's what frightens me."

Sara turned again to Matty, shy now, to place a kiss on her cheek. "Thank you, Matty. I don't know how I would have managed without you."

"Nay, I only did the 'ems,"

"I don't mean the sewing, Matty."

He told her later he would never forget the grim-faced, gimlet-eyed expressions on the faces of the three women who stood at Sara's back when she opened the door to him. God knows how they would have acted if it had been dinner and not luncheon to which he had invited her, he added, grinning broadly as he handed her into the carriage. He had fully expected the two older ones to demand that Sara "bring in the young man and let's have a look at him", and the younger one hadn't been any more welcoming either! It was awkward for them all, he supposed, but what else did they expect? He and Sara were not two people starting out on the customary courtship, introduced by mutual friends, as was usual, or through either her family or his. Theirs was not the usual relationship although he supposed it was a very common one. He had not meant to go up the steps to the door himself. It had been his intention to send Thomas, his coachman, to fetch her, as he would any other young lady in whom he was interested, most of dubious reputation which were the only kind he consorted with unless it was in the home of friends, of a business acquaintance, or in his own. Of course, Sara did not have a dubious reputation, of that he was positive, but she was a young woman earning her own living and no matter how well bred she was she would never be welcome in the homes which were open to him.

Paul Travers came from an old, respected and very wealthy Liverpool family. He was the only son of Paul Travers, dead now these past fifteen years, who had been a ship owner and merchant like Paul's grandfather and great-grandfather before him, each with the family name of Paul. He had sisters galore and his mother, who had been a good deal younger than his father when they married, was still alive, sprightly, nosey, for ever dragging eligible young ladies into his line of vision, despairing, she scolded him, that he would ever give her a grandson.

"You have grandsons all over Lancashire, Mother, since my sisters have proved most fertile. Why mine should be longed for quite so frantically, I cannot imagine. I am not exactly in the twilight of my years yet, you know," he would drawl, doing his best not to yawn, for the subject was one that was aired each time he dined at home.

"Don't be pert, Paul, it does not become you," as though he were still a boy. "It's high time you married, you know it is. Into your thirties . . ."

"Well into my thirties, Mother, as you well know and when I meet a lady with whom I can contemplate sharing the rest of my life then I shall snap her up and you shall be the first to know, I promise you."

"And what about the business? Your father's business. It has been Travers and Son for over a hundred and fifty years but you have no son and if you don't look sharp you never will have."

"Mother," he said laughingly, "it is a well-known fact that a man can sire a child in his seventies. Look at old what's-his-name, you know, the one who married that fifteen-year-old when he was fifty-four and was a father within nine months."

"Don't be coarse, Paul."

"Sorry, Mother. I really am a trial to you, aren't I, but you see I enjoy my bachelor state too much, for the moment at any rate, to give it up. One day I will, I promise you and you shall have a dozen grandsons in as many years."

"If I live that long," his mother said tartly.

He was beginning to think "old what's-his-name", the one who had married the fifteen-year-old, had the right idea after all. Sara caused a minor sensation when she walked ahead of him into the dining-room at the Adelphi Hotel. It was filled with fashionable and wealthy people, most of the ladies elegantly gowned but somehow Sara in her stylishly simple dress of pale dove grey drew glances from every man and woman in the room. They knew him, of course, and he nodded pleasantly to several acquaintances who, by the expressions on their faces, thought him to be a lucky dog, calling one or two by name, but who was she, they wanted to know.

A sibilant hiss ran from table to table as they speculated about it but even before Sara Hamilton and Paul Travers had decided on their main course it was round the whole dining-room that the lovely young girl he had come in with was none other than a magazinière at the House of Lovell! Some of the ladies present were dressed by Madame Lovell and indeed had spoken to Miss Sara, as she was known, and though she had been perfectly acceptable to them there, she was not here! Paul Travers was going too far, really he was, bringing his little shop girls and seamstresses to a place like this, to sit among people like themselves. He would be fetching his mother's parlourmaid next. That actress a few weeks back had been bad enough but she at least had been able to act the part of a lady. Was this one to make a show of herself, they whispered to one another, watching avidly in case she did, sipping champagne and laughing gaily with a man twice her age, a man who was considered to be the most eligible bachelor in Liverpool.

Paul and Sara did not notice. Sara was too enthralled with her surroundings, by the exquisite furniture, the gleaming crystal and silver, the muted, tasteful colours and textures, the pictures, the flashing chandeliers, the deep pile carpet which, though she had seen them all at the House of Lovell, seemed even grander in this setting. She glanced about her with the open admiration of a child, turning her head this way and that, twisting in her seat the better to see, beaming into every pair of eyes which met hers. Music came from somewhere, soft and tranquil, inviting peace and calm. It was like some splendid dream, she marvelled to herself, an entrance into another world and Mr Travers had opened the door a little to allow her to peep in. Not her world, of course. It could never be that, just as Mr Travers could never be what Matty had hinted at. This was a special day and she would cherish it for it would never come again. It couldn't. Not for her and Mr Travers. Not for her or any man, except one.

The waiters hovered deferentially, ready to leap forward at the slightest movement of the head waiter's hand. Mr Paul Travers was a regular and wealthy customer but even so, though they had seen many beautiful women come in on his arm, none had been like this little one. She was a perfect lady, as well mannered as any, charming and elegant but now and again a small and delightful giggle escaped from her. Her slanting green eyes smiled up at them in thanks as they served her and they vied with one another to wait upon her, bowled over by her sweetness, every last one of them, and could you wonder that Mr Travers couldn't take his eyes off her.

He couldn't, Paul would have been the first to admit it. The way her eyelashes rose and fell, tangling on the soft flesh beneath her eyes. Her mouth as she opened it to spoon ice-cream into it and the way her tongue quivered in anticipation. Her hair escaping in glossy tendrils of molten copper from the back of her bonnet to lie on her creamy neck where a faint and childish blonde down grew. Her absolute absorption in Paul himself when he talked to her, the pause before she answered as though carefully weighing each word, and yet the impulsive way she leaned forward to touch his hand when he made her laugh. His wondering desire for this girl overwhelmed him and he found himself sitting back in his chair, hands and napkin idle, wordlessly watching her. She was not overawed by all this, that was obvious, despite her delight in it and he was amazed at his own joy in her. Even the way the waiters fell over themselves to attend to her pleased him and made him smile. Her confidence astounded him, her poise, her unrestrained and infectious laughter, her readiness to share it without reserve with anyone who glanced at her, no matter what their rank, even those who waited on her, and yet she was never over-familiar and so neither were they. Under her youthful enjoyment and inclination to be amused Sara Hamilton had the bearing of a great lady and if Paul Travers had known Eleanor Hamilton he might not have been surprised, for she lived on in her daughter. He knew if he were to take Sara to his home and introduce her as a young woman of good family his mother would welcome her as the perfect daughter-in-law, but as she was now, to his mother Sara would be less than her own parlourmaid, for she knew her parlourmaid to be respectable!

"Would you care to help me walk off that enormous meal you made me eat, Sara Hamilton? I cannot remember when I last saw anyone with such a good appetite and yours encouraged mine. Do you know, I don't think I have eaten ice-cream since my small nephew had a birthday party at New Park House. I had quite forgotten how delicious it tastes." He grinned down at her, raising two quizzical eyebrows. "But unless I get some exercise I shall be sorry. You realise you are to blame, don't you?" offering her his arm as they stepped out into Ranelagh Street.

"Me? What have I done?" She smiled in return, looking up into his face as she took his arm. All streets led to the docks in Liverpool, like the spokes of an opened fan and they both turned to look down Ranelagh Street towards its hub.

"You infect me with such a sense of youthfulness I find I'm doing things I gave up years ago. Eating things I have not eaten since I was a lad. Chocolate and raspberry surprise, indeed!" He shuddered delicately, continuing to smile down at her.

"Well, I thought it was absolutely delicious. The whole meal was delicious and I adored the champagne." She burped gently, putting her hand to her face, then grinned. "Do you know, Mr Travers, that was the first time I have ever drunk champagne."

"Is that so, Miss Hamilton, but can we just get one thing settled?" He felt as skittish as she apparently was.

"Yes, Mr Travers?" She glowed up into his face, her small hand tucked into the crook of his arm. The champagne fizzed inside her making her want to dance and giggle. She really had

had a lovely day out with Mr Travers and she must remember every detail to tell Matty.

"If you continue to call me Mr Travers I swear I shall never take you out to lunch again."

"I did not know you meant to, Mr . . ."

"Paul. My name is Paul."

"Very well, Paul."

"Thank you, Sara." His own heart and head were beautifully light just as though it was not only Sara's first taste of champagne, but his. "Now, having cleared that up, to my satisfaction at least, since I was beginning to feel like an old but respected family retainer, shall we now decide what we are to do with the rest of this splendid day. Perhaps a walk down to the river," gazing down Ranelagh Street, "or," spinning on his heel and whirling her with him until they looked up Mount Pleasant, "perhaps you would prefer the Botanic Gardens, or the Zoological Gardens. They do say the menagerie is quite spectacular."

She knew he was laughing, not at her but with her, and she squeezed his arm, a gesture which, had she not drunk the champagne, she would have considered most familiar. It was as though this day was some tiny span in time and space, a bubble in which she and Mr . . . er . . . Paul were captured and in which they might do as they pleased, for no one was watching. Not Ally, not Lily who did not like Paul because he was old, foolish woman, not Matty who had tried to warn her of some impending danger, not even Thomas who Paul had dismissed earlier.

Paul looked down into her eyes, floating in their iridescent green depths, drowning in them, knowing he was surely going to make a complete fool of himself over this delightful child, this girl, this young woman who had so completely and so rapidly taken over, not only his thoughts but his life. He wanted to lift her up into his arms, thrust his way down Ranelagh Street, elbowing aside those who got in his way, carry her off to some lovely private place, lay her on a velvet cushion and heap on her every softness, every comfort, every luxury she could possibly desire. Furs, perfumes from France, fabulous jewels worn by the world's most beautiful women . . . dear sweet God . . . himself! Keep her from other men, other people, make her wholly his, a prisoner in his heart to cherish for the rest of his days.

Without a thought for who might be watching, after all he was well known in Liverpool, he lifted her up into his strong arms, one arm about her waist, the other at the back of her knees.

"Which shall it be, Sara Hamilton, the river or the Zoological Gardens? You choose. This is your day." He swung her round and round, her skirts flying up to reveal the mass of lace about her six petticoats. Her head flew back against his shoulder and she put up a hand to her bonnet, her mouth wide in a smile of pure happiness. Her reticule swung out as Paul went round and round and for fifty yards in both directions people stopped to stare in amazement.

"I don't know, really I don't and if we don't control ourselves they will be sending for a constable to lock us up," but he could tell she did not mean it, including not only herself but him in this dizzying joy, just as though they were both no more than children.

"Quickly then, make up your mind," and still he whizzed her round and still people stopped to stare, open-mouthed but beginning to smile with them.

"Oh Lord, I love the river and I love the menagerie but really I think it might be wise to put me down for I fear I shall be sick down your coat."

"Dear God, child, what next? Chocolate and raspberry surprise all over my good melton!"

"I fear so, sir."

"Then let's be off to the menagerie where I swear I shall buy you afternoon tea and cream buns for I'm sure by the time we get there you will be hungry again."

Their heads were close together, their faces rapt, their eyes shining still with the foolish laughter they shared and for the first time in three years Jack Andrews slipped entirely from the mind of Sara Hamilton.

Part Three

Part Three

24

Sara leaned back against the wooden fencing which surrounded the paddock, watching as the groom turned the
pretty mare round in a complete circle. She was a young
sorrel with a beautiful glossy coat of light, reddish brown,
her mane and tail several shades darker. She was skittish,
wanting to baulk at every daisy and buttercup, lifting her
dainty head to jingle her harness but the groom whistled
between his teeth and checked her with the long rein and,
recognising the voice of authority, the animal settled down
into a steady trot.

Along the line of each fence there were walnut trees,
planted one hundred years ago by the first Paul Travers,
their short, pale grey trunks dappled beneath the fresh, olive
green rustling of their leaves. In one of them a chaffinch sang
loudly "chip, chip, chip, cheweeoo" again and again before
taking off into graceful flight, a flickering patch of pure white
on its underside.

The sun was pleasantly warm at its meridian and Sara and
Paul stood in the shade of the trees. She held a parasol over
her bare head. It was white, a lovely thing of lace, fringed and
appliquéd with the palest of pink roses. Her gown was white
muslin, unadorned except for the wide, pale pink taffeta sash
about her waist. Her hair was fastened carelessly with a knot
of white ribbons, tumbling in a glorious cascade of tawny gold
and copper from the back of her head to her waist.

"Well, you know I can't accept it, don't you, Paul," she
protested. "For a start, where would I keep it?"

"Here in my stable and then whenever we feel like it and
you can find time from that job of yours we can ride out
together."

"And what would your mama have to say about that? She already thinks of me as a woman of loose moral fibre with neither the sense nor taste to know where her place is. I am a sewing girl, nothing more."

"Rubbish!"

"You know how they gossip about us already and we have known one another no more than a few months. You cannot give me this expensive animal and expect it to go unnoticed. Besides, you are always giving me presents."

"Perfume and handkerchiefs. Nothing a lady cannot receive from a gentleman. Your mama must have told you a dozen times that it is perfectly correct to accept— "

"Oh Paul, stop it. You turn everything into a joke and this is serious."

He pulled his face into a comically earnest shape, standing to attention as he did so.

"Will this do?" and could she help but laugh, as he always made her laugh.

Paul relaxed and put his immaculately booted foot on the bottom rung of the fence which divided the paddock at the back of New Park House, leaning his forearms on the top rung as he turned to watch Sara. New Park House had been the family home of the Travers family for a hundred years, ever since Paul's great-grandfather, knowing he could now call himself a rich man, had built it and brought his bride here. He had accumulated blocks of property in Liverpool and its neighbourhood and along with the Moores of Bank Hall, the Crosses of Crosse Hall, the Travers of New Park House had prospered. Paul's grandfather had been born at New Park House in 1756 and thirty years later, his own father and, another twenty-three years on, in 1809, Paul himself. The house, strangely, was not far from Lovell House in West Derby, five acres of parkland and gardens which were themselves surrounded by farmland belonging to the family which was let to tenant farmers, and in the exact centre of it all stood a beautiful house of honey-coloured stone draped with ivy. There were a multitude of chimneys, for Paul Travers the first, a man who had spent a great deal of his life in the tropics, felt the chill cold of northern England deep in his bones and had fires roaring in every room into which he was likely to step. The roof of the house was a pale, pale rose, the slates faded with the years. There were big bay windows, for again

Paul's great-grandfather had liked light, airy rooms. All about the house there were trees, pruned carefully each winter by an expert so that they did not encroach on the sunlight he loved. It was a graceful, elegant house and yet it had a look of endurance about it, patient and immovable, like a mother who serenely waits to welcome home a wandering child. It sat on a slight incline, the lawns about it sloping down to a small lake on which swans glided. There were vegetable gardens at the back of the house, set within a high hedge of hawthorn to screen them from the family's view and beyond that were the stables and paddocks, for the Travers men had a great love of horses.

"She's called Storm," Paul murmured persuasively, his blue eyes as clear and innocent as the autumn skies above their heads.

"I don't care what she's called I cannot accept her."

"It was your birthday in June and I gave you nothing but a bracelet which is hardly special. And you cannot deny that Storm is special, can you?"

"Paul Travers, you're a scamp, do you know that?"

"Yes, I do, but a charming one so will you accept that Storm is yours? No one else will ride her."

"I can't ride, Paul."

"Tim will teach you when I'm not here," nodding in the direction of the groom.

"And I have no riding habit."

"You're a seamstress so that will be no problem."

"Paul, oh Paul, you are incorrigible, what am I to do with you?"

"I'm sure I could think of something, my pet." His grin was lazy, his face creased in great good humour but in his eyes a small spark could be seen, a spark Sara had become increasingly aware of as the weeks and months ran on.

Sara had never been inside New Park House, naturally, though Paul had brought her out here several times to watch the training of his thoroughbreds. There was a small gate set in the wall at the back of the estate through which she consented to come, though he would have brought her, had she allowed it, not only to the stable and paddock by the front gate and long winding drive which led to it, but into the house itself. Or so he told himself but deep down even he knew that it would be inconceivable to expect his mother to receive a young woman she would consider no better than the maidservant who served her tea. She would have heard about Sara by now but would not be unduly concerned since all gentlemen had a mistress. She would not care to have his mistress strolling about the paddock looking at his horses but she could do little about that and so, as a lady, she would choose to ignore it.

He and Sara continued to stand in an easy silence as they watched the sorrel being put through her paces. It was unseasonably warm and the drone of midges mingled with the sounds of the horses as their strong teeth tore at the juicy grass. There were four matched greys, carriage horses, keeping close together as though they were so accustomed to it when they took Mrs Travers for her carriage drive they could not get out of the habit, even here in the paddock. There was a handsome hunter, his coat as black and glossy as ebony, his tail and mane held high as he strutted his magnificence for all to admire. Several chestnut mares and their foals edged nervously to the far side of their own paddock, the mothers alarmed for the safety of their offspring and in all four enclosures there grazed pure-bred animals for Paul Travers purchased only the best. They were of every colour, dapple grey, black, chestnut and sorrel and they kicked up their pedigreed heels in the warm September sunshine.

Paul kept his voice smooth and inconsequential, just as though it was his intention to tease her and make her laugh, which he did. Not even this girl whom he had loved for almost six months knew of his true feelings for her. He was only too well aware that if she did she would run for cover like an alarmed doe. In those six months he had squired her about Liverpool, taking her to balls and official dinners at which he needed a partner, forcing them to accept her, at least while she was with him. Liverpool society had been set on its ear, of course, since Miss Sara Hamilton, who had become almost as well known as her employer in the world of fashion, was not marrying material. She was nothing more than a seamstress, a young woman, it seemed, with a mysterious past, for who knew where she came from and what could the wealthy Mr Travers have in mind for her? Liverpool society could not make up its mind on the nature of their relationship, for Paul Travers was seen in the company of other young women, not of the well-bred sort, flashy young women he escorted to gambling houses and gaming clubs. And if Miss Sara Hamilton and Mr Paul Travers were involved, physically and emotionally, as Liverpool believed them to be, would she continue to go about with him as though his extra-curricular attachments meant nothing to her? It was a mystery they could not solve and over the past few months speculation had been rife. Was he to marry her? It would kill his poor mama if he did. Was she his mistress and if so why did she continue to work as magazinière at the House of Lovell? Why had he not set her up in her own establishment since the cost would be nothing to him?

Their curiosity was so intense it led many ladies who had never before frequented the House of Lovell hurrying to Madame Lovell's doorstep to get a look at this young woman, child really, for she was a mere eighteen or nineteen, who seemed to have captivated a man almost twenty years older than herself, a man who was the wealthiest, most eligible bachelor in Liverpool.

Rosalie Lovell was delighted with the increase in business and the new clients who, once they had been dressed by the much talked about Miss Sara Hamilton found they were so enchanted with the gowns which, it was rumoured, were her own design, were reluctant to go back to their previous dressmaker.

"You have become quite the thing, Sara, my dear, did you know? You have brought a lot of custom to my house but I, like everyone else I'll be bound, am very curious about the true nature of your relationship with Mr Travers. Oh, don't get on your high horse with me, miss. I am not about to sit in judgment on you. Many seamstresses, if they have any claim to looks, take a lover."

"Paul Travers is not my lover, Madame. He and I are friends, no more." The coldness in Sara's voice quite shocked Rosalie Lovell and she studied the rigid-backed figure of the young woman who sat opposite her, but Sara returned stare for stare, her eyes daring her employer to say one more word on the subject. Rosalie Lovell sighed and dismissed her.

The bond between Sara Hamilton and her sister Alice became even more fragile in those first weeks after word of Sara's involvement with Paul Travers became common knowledge in Liverpool society.

"You will stop this at once, Sara, do you hear? Do you

hear me? I will not have it. He is, or already has for I fear it is too late, destroyed your reputation, unless he means to marry you, is that it?"

Alice became very still as she spoke the last few words, just as though the thought was something she could not bear to contemplate. It appeared from her frozen expression that she would rather see her sister dishonoured than married to Paul Travers, married to anyone for that matter, and only Alice knew the reason why. If that happened Alice Hamilton's hold on her sister would be finally broken for good and her own life would be in ruins.

"I do not mean to marry him, Alice. Not that he has asked me," Sara added coolly, much as she had done with Madame. "Paul and I are good friends and I can see nothing wrong with that."

"Do you not? You can see no wrong in racketing about Liverpool, completely unchaperoned, with a man old enough to be your father? Really, Sara, you never cease to amaze me. And as for him he should be horsewhipped. I am only thankful that . . . well, that there is to be no marriage. He is not the right man for you, my dear."

"Who is the right man for me, Ally? Does he exist? You did not like . . . Jack" – her voice broke a little on his name and she shook her head as though to dislodge some memory – "because he was not a gentleman and had no money to support me. Now it seems a wealthy gentleman is interested in me but he does not suit either."

"Do not speak to me like that, Sara. I am your sister and have only your welfare at heart."

"Fiddlesticks!"

"I beg your pardon!"

"You do not have my welfare at heart, Alice, I see that now, only your own. You want only what is best for Alice Hamilton. You are self-seeking and self-willed. Now, if you'll excuse me I have work to do."

Sara turned to leave the small parlour at the back of the house where Alice had drawn her to have a quiet word with her. As she moved into the hallway Alice grabbed her arm, whirling her about to face her. Momentarily her fear and fury almost overwhelmed her and her face twisted into a snarling mask. A maidservant opened the door from the kitchen and was so surprised she just stood there, mouth agape, giving the servants in the kitchen a grandstand view of the "set-to" between Miss Hoity-Toity and the House of Lovell's increasingly popular young magazinière. They all, without exception, stopped what they were doing and edged closer so as not to miss the least word or gesture. It was not often that anything came to relieve the tedium of their long day.

"Don't you turn your back on me, Sara Hamilton," Miss Hoity-Toity was saying. "You have done nothing but undermine my authority with my staff and ridicule my position as your sister ever since Madame made you a showroom woman. It has gone to your head and I am ashamed of you. How dare you insult me."

The servants thought Miss Hoity-Toity was about to have an apoplectic fit. Her face went from fiery red to ashen white, her eyes staring in green madness, her mouth a colourless slit from which her words spewed like chips of ice.

"And how dare you insult the good name of Hamilton."

"Please, Ally, leave it. I'm not in the mood for one of your lectures."

"You are not in the mood, miss! Very well, I will make this brief."

The servants crept across the kitchen, crowding at the back of Clara, the maidservant, but Alice and Sara were too absorbed with one another to notice. If the Liverpool Brass Band had marched up the hall playing "God save the Queen" Alice and Sara would not have noticed.

"Please do, Ally. I am expected in the showroom in five minutes."

"Are you indeed, then let me say this and then that is the end of it. If you do not put a stop to this foolish attachment you have formed with this man I shall be forced to exercise my right as your guardian to make sure you do. I have taken legal advice and as you are not yet twenty-one— "

"Oh Ally, please, don't be any more nonsensical than you already are. You cannot force me."

"Can I not? Can I not? We'll see about that, miss. It is high time I got you away from this place and from Liverpool. It so happens I have the means to— "

The servants were enraptured. Miss Sara was not.

"Stop it, stop it, Alice! I am going nowhere with you, now or ever. You have dragged me about the country against my will and because of it I lost . . ." Sara's throat worked and for a moment she was speechless but she made a great effort to recover. "Your authority over me ended a long time ago but you will persist in convincing yourself that you can still treat me as a child. I am not a child, Alice, and you are not my guardian. I can take legal advice myself, you know. Mr Travers will no doubt know of a good man. Now leave me alone. Get on with your life and let me get on with mine, whatever it is to be. I would like us to remain friends, Ally, but that is up to you. Now I really must get to the showroom, if you'll excuse me."

The servants resisted the strong temptation to applaud as Sara turned on her heel and walked away, inclined to tremble but glad that at last she and Ally had had the confrontation which had been threatening for so long. She would never give up seeing Paul, never. Her relationship with him had become very precious to her. His undemanding friendship, his flippant good humour, his unexpected, almost weekly invitations to this function and that, gradually had become an important part of her life.

He took her to a Grande Soirée at the Town Hall given by the Lord Mayor, Mr John Bramley-Moore, at which upwards of fourteen hundred of Liverpool's grandest folk were present. They were amused, both she and Paul, at the sensation they had caused, particularly Paul, as they stood, her arm through his, her head no higher than his shoulder, at the top of the stairs leading into the ballroom.

"Smile, my pet," he had whispered wickedly into her ear. "They are dying to know what can possibly be taking place between an elderly gentleman like myself and a child like you," and when she did so, brilliantly, she could see the startled speculation in their faces as they wondered what Paul Travers had said to Sara Hamilton to make her glow as she did. She wore her very first ballgown that night, an off-the-shoulder white watered silk with no embellishment other than one enormous scarlet rose made from silk at her waist. She looked quite devastatingly stunning in her new-found self-confidence and yet there was an untouched look about her which made more than a few gentlemen wonder on the true relationship between her and Paul Travers. Her hair was dressed low on the nape of her neck in an enormous chignon, the weight of it tipping back her head and giving delicacy to her slender throat. The chignon itself was scattered with tiny seed "pearls", bought only that morning from a stall on Pedlars Market and her hair gleamed like spun copper.

He had danced with no one else, grinning delightedly and whispering nonsense in her ear and she found she enjoyed it. In August he escorted her to a Grand Fancy Fair and Flower Show at Princes Park, again under the auspices of the Lord Mayor. A fearful thunderstorm blew up over their heads halfway through the afternoon and all the hundreds who were there ran for cover to one of the many marquees and tents which stood around the park, but not until many of them got a soaking. Sara's pretty bonnet, on which were sewn real white rosebuds from Madame's garden, drooped and dripped until Paul untied the ribbons and removed it under the fascinated gaze of some of the most prominent persons, and their wives, in Liverpool. He had brushed back her damp curls with a tender gesture, smiling down into her face as though they were alone. The day was not completely wasted, they heard him tell her, for the Mayor with whom Paul was on friendly terms had told him that it had realised the grand sum of £9,593 6s 2d which was to be divided between three public charities.

She had reached up with her dainty handkerchief to wipe his wet cheek, her eyes warm with affection and she was not to know how close Paul Travers had been to breaking then. It took all his self-control to keep from begging her not to be so bloody stubborn and why the hell was she allowing him to waste his life, which was a damn sight shorter than hers, with this bloody nonsense. He was wealthy. He could give her everything she had ever wanted, and many of the things he wanted her to have. He could give her more love than she had ever known – from any man, for he was aware by now that there had been someone in her life though they had not spoken of it. He would float her in love, drown her in it, overwhelm her with it, in his arms and in his bed if she would let him. He would give her his heart, his soul, pluck them from his body for without her he could not survive.

Something of what he felt must have shown in his eyes for she drew back hesitatingly, a shadow turning the green of her eyes to the darkness of winter moss, but from somewhere he had drawn the strength to grin engagingly before dropping a light kiss on the end of her nose, surprising her and the open-mouthed crowd who dripped about them.

He winked. "Close your mouth, Sara Hamilton," he told her solemnly, "or that moth which I swear just flew out of the Lady Mayoress's bosom will flutter into it." He had been rewarded by her infectious chuckle.

He took her to concerts at the Philharmonic Concert Hall, opened at the end of August and where Miss Jenny Lind sang on two occasions for the benefit of the Philharmonic Society.

In early September he walked with her round the stalls in Pedlars Market which was to close down the next day. David Bretherton had been there, emptying his stall, dressed in a suit of decent broadcloth, smart and prosperous-looking.

He greeted her cordially and shook Paul by the hand and when Paul asked him if he would part with the remainder of the sketches he had done, not only of Sara and Matty, but of sail boats and seagulls and playing children, he had grinned and said he would but the price had doubled since last Mr Travers had purchased them.

Paul took them and handed out two hundred guineas as though they had been pennies.

"That young man will go far," he murmured to Sara as he took her arm. "He has a patron now, you do know that, don't you?"

"A patron?" Sara looked mystified.

"Yes, the wife of one of Liverpool's older businessmen."

"What does it mean, a patron?" she asked him curiously, nodding in goodbye at David.

"My sweet, surely you know what a patron does?"

"Tell me."

She looked up into his face, her eyes wide with interest, her lips slightly parted, moist and rosy and, as on so many other occasions, it was all Paul could do not to sweep her into his arms and kiss her until she gasped. How could she not sense it in him, he often wondered, when every beat of his heart, the erratic rhythm of his pulse, the dryness of his mouth when she looked up at him as she was doing now must surely reveal it to her?

He managed a wicked smile. "He is her lover, Sara. She keeps him in return for . . . what he gives her, pays his rent and buys his clothes while he nurtures his talent. She had a small "showing" for him, I believe, which was moderately successful and when she needs him he . . ."

"Yes?"

"Sara I have just said he is her lover." He shrugged his shoulders and raised astonished eyebrows.

"And does her husband not mind?" Her eyes were wide and wondering.

"They are discreet and so her husband, and society, do not mind."

"How appalling," she said hotly, for as yet the gossip about her and Paul had not reached her ears.

Paul had some business to attend to so he had sent her home in the carriage alone and as Thomas drew up at the foot of the steps which led up to Lily's front door he nodded in the direction of the small, wrought-iron balcony on the first floor.

"The old lady no better, Miss Sara?" he asked as he helped her down from the carriage and led her respectfully across the pavement.

Sara paused on the bottom step, holding up the wide hem of her gown to reveal the lace on her petticoat and an inch of black-stockinged ankle. Thomas eyed it appreciatively, then returned his gaze to her face. She lit up in that lovely way she had, just as though Thomas had given her a gift of diamonds. No wonder everyone who knew her thought the world of her, those in the stable at least. Even the young housemaid who was often summoned to fetch a pot of hot coffee or a jug of iced lemonade when Miss Sara was in the paddock had been charmed by her sweetness of manner and great courtesy, even to her, reporting back to Mrs Cherry who was cook at New Park House that she couldn't believe the things that were being said about Mr Paul and the young lady, though of course Mrs Cherry had told her to mind her own business and get on with her work!

"No, Thomas," she said now. "She's never got over that fall she had last June. Even now she can't even get out to sit in the garden." She bit her lip and her face clouded.

"I'm sorry, Miss Sara. Well, I'd best be off. Mrs Travers'll be waitin' for 'er drive. See yer in West Derby termorrer night then."

"Thank you, Thomas."

Dolly greeted her lovingly from the chair by the fire, her wrinkled old face becoming even more deeply meshed as she smiled. She was thinner than she had been two years ago, despite the good food Lily stuffed into her, but on her face was that expression of supreme content which only the old who know they are loved have.

"'Ad a nice day out, chuck?" Dolly had picked up more than a few of the Liverpool "sayings" which she heard on the lips of Lily and Matty, "chuck" being one, "queen" and "lar" being others.

"Yes, thank you, Dolly. You know I always enjoy Mr Travers's company."

"Aye, well." Dolly was not so sure she approved of the way that there Mr Travers took Miss Eleanor's lass about with him unchaperoned. Miss Eleanor wouldn't have cared for it but then Miss Eleanor was dead and Miss Sara had her own hard row to hoe in this world, and all alone for Miss Alice was as much use as two left hands.

"I didn't tell you he'd bought me a horse, did I? He wants to give it to me as a late birthday present." Sara shook her head as though the antics of Paul Travers were exasperating beyond words.

"'An 'orse! Mercy me! What would yer do wi' an' 'orse round 'ere?"

"Exactly, that's what I begged him to tell me, but he only grinned and said I could keep it at New Park House and go out riding with him whenever I wanted to. The fact that I cannot ride . . ."

"Yer mama was a lovely rider." Dolly's face became soft with memory and her boot-button eyes deep in the seams of her face were dewed with fond tears.

Sara, who had spread her length inelegantly in the chair opposite Dolly, her skirts hitched up to her knees in an attempt to find a degree of coolness, for it was warm in the room, leaned forward breathlessly.

"Mama! I didn't know she was a horsewoman."

"Oh aye, a lovely seat it were said she 'ad. I remember 'er in 'er ridin' 'abit. Medd it 'erself, o' course. What a picture she were. Looked a lot like you, Miss Sara an' yer pa loved her just like . . . well, will yer listen ter me bletherin' on an' Matty's upstairs lookin' for yer. In a bit of a state, she were an' all."

"Matty! What's she doing home so early?"

Sara sprang to her feet, smoothing down her skirt with suddenly anxious hands. "Is she ill, Dolly?" Her face creased in a frown, her delicate eyebrows dipping over her small nose.

"Nay, love, yer'd best go up an' see. Lily's wi' 'er."

As though it was nothing out of the ordinary both Lily and Matty were in Sara's room. Just recently she had taken over the whole of the attic floor and with Lily's permission and Lily's nephew's help, the same one who had directed them to her in the first place, had knocked down a couple of partitions so that it was now one large room about thirty feet square. On the floor was a carpet the colour of burnt honey, bought cheaply from Cutter's Furniture Mart in Bold Street where second-hand stuff could be had for next to nothing, or so Reggie, Lily's nephew had told them. The carpet, come from some grand drawing-room where the owners had fallen on hard times, stretched from wall to wall. The room was simply furnished, again either from Cutter's or Lily's cellar, with no more than half a dozen pieces: a couple of deep chairs upholstered in pale apricot velvet, a lovingly polished but slightly lopsided chiffonier leaning against one wall. Velvet again at the two end windows, though the open skylights which were let into the roof were bare of covering. The walls were painted with a touch of warm cream and were unadorned but for a dozen charcoal sketches, all neatly framed and all of herself and Matty. There was a round polished table on which stood a copper bowl filled with cream, pink-tipped rosebuds, a narrow bed in one corner draped with a shawl in shades of honey, apricot and cream and a splendid Chinese screen, torn here and there but very lovely, which hid the stove and cupboard in which she kept her pots and pans.

Matty's head was bent in what looked like deep despair and her glossy curls were tumbled across her face so that Sara could not see it. Lily held her hand, murmuring soothingly but Matty sobbed and sobbed, not even ceasing when she heard Sara's voice.

"Dear sweet Christ," using words she had heard Paul use. "What has happened?" She threw her reticule to the table where it landed in the bowl of roses, before moving swiftly across the room to kneel at Matty's feet. "What is it, Matty? Has someone died, darling? Oh Matty, tell me what is upsetting you."

Taking Matty's hands in hers she chafed them vigorously, at the same time doing her best to see into her face beneath the curtain of Matty's hair but Matty drooped even more, overcome by her desperate misery.

Sara turned to Lily, the expression on her face becoming even more alarmed. "What's the matter with her, Lily? Has she told you?"

"Oh aye, she's told me an' she wants me ter tell you." Lily's laconic answer gave no indication of what the trouble might be, nor her opinion of it but in her eyes was the softness of deep compassion.

"Well, go on then, tell me," Sara snapped impatiently.

Matty moaned, slumping even further into the depths of Sara's velvet chair. Tears splashed from beneath her hair, spotting the bodice of her pretty gown and she wrung her hands, and Sara's, despairingly.

"She's got sack!" Lily's voice was abrupt, her mouth shutting to with a snap as though she would dearly love to give someone a piece of her mind.

Sara turned to Matty for confirmation, her eyes and mouth wide in amazement.

"The sack! What for?"

"Fer 'avin' a baby, that's what for!"

25

Alice Hamilton, for eighteen months supervisor and instructor at the House of Lovell, looked far older than her twenty-three, almost twenty-four years. Her face, which had once been as soft as that of her younger sister, had become rigidly fixed in such an expression of permanent disapproval it appeared to have fallen in on itself, as a face does in death. Her mouth had thinned and her eyes surveyed her domain and those in it, hostile and bitter, from between narrowed lids. She wore nothing but black which seemed to drain her once youthful colour from her flesh and, though it was not known, of course, especially by her sister, she detested Sara Hamilton with a venom which grew with every passing day.

She was a disappointed woman. She had money in the Union Bank at the corner of Hanover and Bold Streets, more money than she knew what to do with and yet she was not satisfied. She had one of the best jobs in the dressmaking trade. She had a comfortable bedroom and sitting-room of her own, since she was one of Madame Lovell's most valued and trusted employees, thought well of by Madame's clients – though not her own staff – and the effort to keep her thoughts and her words to herself continually drained her so that she often felt unwell. It was her nature to say exactly what she thought. To give, even to those who did not want it, her advice and her opinion, since she knew she was right and others were wrong, but she had discovered over the years she had been in Madame Lovell's service that the only way to keep not only her job but Madame's good opinion was to say nothing to anybody about anything.

It was Sara Hamilton's fault, of course. Her own little sister who, for the first fifteen or sixteen years of her life had been guarded and chided by Alice and with such good results. What a lovely, biddable child she had been, sweet-natured and eager to do her best to please Alice in every way she could. She had relied on Alice as an example of all that was proper, believed everything that Alice told her but now, in just a few short months, Sara had become rebellious, challenging Alice's authority on every matter from the way she should dress, the room she continued to live in at that woman's house and, in particular, her choice of friends. For months Alice had urged her – whenever they were alone since Alice did not want a scene to which Madame might be brought – begged her, ordered her to give up her scandalous association with Paul Travers but Sara had merely shrugged her shoulders, saying that she and Paul were friends, no more. She was not his mistress, she added coldly, eyeing Alice with great distaste and, strangely, Alice had believed her. No matter what her faults and the good Lord knew she had many by now, Sara was not a liar. And in this new bold quality she appeared to have acquired it wouldn't have mattered to her what Alice thought, therefore she had no need to lie, her manner seemed to say.

For a while after this Alice still had hopes that her own secret plan to extricate Sara from the influence of these dreadful people with whom she consorted might come to fruition. If she could appeal to Sara's better nature, reveal to her the details of her own plan which was, simply, that she and her sister open their own establishment, might not Sara then turn back to her? Their own business! She had the money, penny after penny garnered from here and there and painstakingly added week after week, month after month, year after year, to her private account at the Union Bank. There were the proceeds from the sale of their mama's things, retrieved in the first year they had been in Liverpool from the man in Kirkham who had sold them for her. She had enough now to rent a smart little shop in Bold Street, furnish it elegantly and, quite simply, steal as many of Madame's customers as would come with her. The same superb service and style but without the House of Lovell's exorbitant prices.

But they would not come without Sara which Alice had accepted with resigned bitterness.

Sara had laughed, laughed when Alice had, with shining

eyes and the stiff pride of her own achievement, placed the gift of it before her.

"But Ally, I can't leave Madame Lovell." Sara had stopped laughing at once when she had recognised Alice's affront, knowing she had deeply offended her. She had been unable to explain to Alice that the laughter had been no more than nerves, a nervous reaction to the idea of living and working alone with Alice, but Alice, who would not have understood anyway, was white-faced and mortified.

"Do you mean to tell me you do not wish us to have our own establishment?" she hissed. "That you have no ambition but to remain here as showroom woman for the rest of your life, or is it that you have hopes of Mr Travers? If that is what you are hoping for then let me assure you that man will never marry you, and neither will any other man. That lout of a navvie could not stomach it when it came to the test— "

"Ally . . ." Sara's voice was high with pain but Alice Hamilton ignored the warning there, reviling Jack Andrews and Paul Travers in equal measure until, her composure completely gone, Sara fled, crashing the door to behind her and crashing the lid closed, for the moment, on Alice's dream.

They were no more than polite with one another from that day.

She had just come out of the bank in Bold Street when she saw them. It was not often she left the house in West Derby except to go to church on Sunday, a practice she had taken up recently. She worshipped at St Luke's in Leece Street since it was the most fashionable in town, a fine new church where the wealthy and pedigreed did their praying. All of white stone, very imposing with windows of cathedral-like proportions and a gallery to house the ambitious choir of which Alice soon hoped to be a member, since it was a door leading to all kinds of opportunities of a social character. Very impressed Alice had been when she had first attended Sunday morning service and was gratified that already several of the upper-class ladies, recognising her own quality, were beginning to nod graciously to her.

She went nowhere else, the reason being she had no one to accompany her on any outing she might care to take but today she had been to see the bank manager at the Union Bank at the corner of Hanover Street and Bold Street. She had conferred with him on where best to place her savings;

on how to invest them to her own advantage and had been pleasantly surprised at the growth of some shares she had purchased in railway stock. The bank manager had been most helpful, suggesting further investments, perhaps a little in shipping or coal mining, small amounts naturally, or even, knowing her profession, leaning forward confidentially as he spoke, in a small but thriving dressmaking business which needed an injection of cash to expand. The owner, a Miss Butler, had premises in Upper Arcade in Leece Street very close to St Luke's Church. A very handsome property and well placed for business. Perhaps Miss Hamilton would like him to arrange a meeting with Miss Butler who was a fine Christian lady and if the project was agreeable to them both, well then . . .!

They were arm in arm, laughing merrily, their faces rosy in the crisp, frost-scented air. Both of them emanated such an air of youthful high spirits and great good humour, those who passed by them could not help but smile as well for it was the season of goodwill, and laughter is infectious.

They stopped to peer into a bow-fronted window where gaily wrapped boxes of bon-bons, chocolate-covered raisins, sugared almonds, home-made chocolates, twisted barley sugar sticks and sticky treacle toffee were heaped cheek by jowl in a glittering Christmas display. There were tinsel and ribbon and coloured candles and the two young women stood, noses pressed to the window, like a couple of wide-eyed children.

One of them was heavily pregnant.

She couldn' stop herself. If Madame Lovell had grasped her by one arm with the bank manager on the other she would have wrestled herself free of them and darted across the road, through the clogged traffic, to confront her sister and her sister's friend who was a whore.

She narrowly missed being run down by an alarmed horse as she darted almost under its hooves but she did not notice, nor hear the outraged shout of the cab driver. She had never been so mortified in her life. Oh yes, she was well aware of the gossip which surrounded her sister but that was all it was and her sister was as untouched as Alice herself, but the trollop beside her who had been dismissed from the dressmaking firm of the Misses Yeoland was no more nor less than a prostitute. Alice had always thought so, right from the beginning and now her present condition confirmed it and she was arm in arm with Alice's sister.

Grabbing Sara by the shoulder she whirled her round to face her, almost dragging her from her feet on the icy pavement. It had snowed lightly two days ago then frozen hard and there were ridged ruts underfoot which were treacherous. The whore, the pregnant whore who was still hanging on to Sara's arm, was pulled round with her, cumbersome and awkward. With a cry she lost her footing and her balance, going down like a sack of coal, landing heavily on her side, her breath knocked from her lungs with a loud gasp.

For a startled moment Sara stared into her sister's face then, shaking her off with an impatient gesture, knelt at once beside Matty, lifting her gently into a sitting position, smoothing her skirts, holding and patting her hands with such a show of devotion and concern, Alice was incensed.

"Let go of that woman at once, Sara," she shrieked, "and come away with me now. How can you call yourself a lady and consort with the likes of her? I never cease to marvel at your lack of judgment, even now after all that has happened, but surely even you must know by now what sort of a person— "

"Stop it, Ally. Let go of me and give me a hand to get Matty to her feet. She is near her time and— "

"Near her time! Sara Hamilton, I never thought I would hear such indelicate words on the lips of my sister. Our mama would— "

"Goddammit to hell, Ally," again using one of Paul's more colourful expressions, "if you can't help then stop hindering me." Sara put a hand gently to Matty's cheek. "Are you all right, darling?" she asked tenderly.

Darling! She called the whore "darling"!

"Does anything hurt?" Alice's sister was saying, "I'd best get someone to call us a cab. Ally, will you take your bloody hands off me and make yourself useful by getting us a cab." She was frightened by Matty's bone-white face and it made her careless of what she said, or to whom, or even of who overheard her.

"Sara, please, don't get involved with . . . with . . . Listen to you, shouting obscenities like a common street-walker-like this woman here who . . ."

Alice's face was twisted into an expression of desperate appeal as though to say this was Sara's and her own last chance.

A crowd had gathered, most of them men who were eager to help the extremely pretty young lady who knelt on the icy pavement, though most were embarrassed by the condition of the other one. Women with child, at least in decent households, did not normally venture out of their homes, especially on a day like this.

Sara evidently had the same thought. Shaking off Alice's increasingly persistent hand, she clutched Matty to her in a passion of remorse.

"We shouldn't have come. I told you we shouldn't have come, Matty Hutchinson. It is far too dangerous underfoot but no, you wanted to see the shops."

"Give over, our Sara."

Our Sara! In the way of many northern working-class families this . . . this awful woman was calling Sara by the affectionate, the possessive 'our'!

"It's th'only day yer've 'ad off in weeks," the woman went on, "an' I weren't gonner miss it 'cos of a birrof ice. Tell yer what, though, me bum's cold! Now get me on me feet."

"Perhaps I can be of assistance?" a smiling voice asked at Alice's back, "that's if I can get through this throng of admirers the pair of you seem to have gathered about you. Not that I blame them, let me hasten to add, for you both look extremely fetching."

Paul Travers squatted down beside them, dislodging the black-garbed woman who, for some reason, was shaking Sara like a terrier with a rat in its mouth.

"Paul, oh thank God. The Lord must have sent you."

"Well, I don't know about that, my pet, since the Lord and I are not on friendly terms but it is very pleasant to be welcomed with such warmth." He grinned down at Matty who managed a tremulous smile.

"Stop that foolishness, Paul, and help me to lift Matty to her feet. She has fallen quite heavily and with the baby due in two weeks . . . I shouldn't have allowed her to persuade me. Now, is your carriage handy?"

"At the kerb as we speak, my sweet, snarling up the traffic so we had better look lively." His amiable grin, his complete inability to treat anything, even this, with the slightest seriousness, took the tension from Sara's face and she relaxed, leaning on his strong, comforting shoulder.

"Oh Paul, have you any idea how wonderful it is to have you around?"

"I shall remind you of that at a later date, my pet. Now then, if we can get rid of this woman . . . who the hell is she?"

"My sister."

"Your sister! God's teeth, what is she trying to do?"

"Kill me if she could but failing that get me back under her authority."

"Sara, will you please explain . . ."

"Later, Paul. See, here's Thomas, now lift her carefully."

"Oh, for God's sake, Sara, I'm not 'urt."

"Do as you're told, Matty, and allow me to know what is best for you. Thomas and Paul will— "

"Sara Hamilton! I order you to leave this . . . this person and come home at once. Have you the slightest notion of how degrading all this is, this spectacle? Your behaviour, this woman, these people. I have never witnessed anything quite so appalling and in such bad taste and really, I blame myself. Come back with me, Sara. Let me talk to you. I have just seen the bank manager. Please, we cannot talk here amongst all these . . ." Alice pulled a face, glancing round her at what she evidently would like to call riff-raff.

Sara turned on her, silencing the murmuring group of people who stood in a loose circle about them, shocking Paul with the ferocity of her attack.

"Leave me alone, Ally, for God's sake, just leave me alone. Take your hands off me and let me be. You can go to the devil and take your daft ideas with you for all I care. I've had enough. Enough! Now let me get by."

"Sara, you will regret this."

"Alice, let me go, *let me go*, for pity's sake. Can't you see it's too late?"

She began to cry then and at once Paul reached for her, folding her in his arms so that only the top of her pretty bonnet could be seen beneath his chin.

"Madame," he said coldly to Alice, "I don't know what you want but if you don't leave Miss Hamilton alone I shall call a police constable and have you arrested."

* * *

Matty's son was born twenty-four hours later, two weeks early but strong and healthy and the "dead spit" of his mam, Lily said fondly as she dandled him on her knee. A whorl of dark silky hair on his neat skull, a rosebud mouth which sucked hopefully even when it was not attached to his mother's nipple, and an unformed blob of a nose.

"I'm gonner call 'im Paul," Matty announced defiantly. But for Mr Travers the babby might have been born in the damned street, she added, so, with his permission she would name her son after him.

"Well, you can ask him, Matty, but I know he'll be horribly embarrassed if you do," Sara said diplomatically. She eyed the boy apprehensively, praying that Lily would not invite her to have a "hold", as they were all doing, even old Dolly, her mouth wide in a toothless smile.

"D'yer reckon? P'raps I'd berra think o' summat else then." Her disappointment was plain.

"I do know Paul's second name is James."

Matty's face lit up. "That's it then, James, an' we'll call 'im Jamie. Jamie 'Utchinson."

No one was ever to know who Jamie Hutchinson's father was, not even Sara. They were all well aware that Matty had been acquainted with several "gentlemen", for she had often gone out after dark on a "bit of business", whatever that might be. They had not questioned her, not even Dolly who had been told fiercely by Sara that it was nothing to do with them and Matty should be left alone to conduct her life as she thought fit, which was what Sara was determined to do. Lily had agreed with her, saying folk must make their own mistakes and pay for them, though she had not meant it unkindly. Both she and Sara were quite passionate on the matter of privacy, going to great lengths not to "poke in their noses where they weren't wanted", taking the view that if Matty, or Lily and Sara for that matter, were to come a cropper, then the others would always be there to pick up the pieces. Lily's George had died at sea the year before, falling to the deck from the rigging and breaking his neck and Lily's financial position had been a bit "dicky" for a while but with Sara and Matty both earning good money, and the quiet but kind-hearted Abby Mitchell introducing her friend, Isabella Knowles, as another paying guest, Lily had come through. That's what they were there for, Sara had declared stoutly, to see one another through, and now there were Matty and Jamie to be considered.

"Well, me an' Miss Watson'll see to 'im, Matty, won't we, Miss Watson?" turning to the almost bedridden old lady. "Whilst yer goes to work, I mean, Matty."

"We will an' all, Mrs Canon, an' glad of it. It's bin a long time since I 'ad me 'ands on a babby."

Lily and Dolly, despite their friendship and deep affection for one another, still clung to the formal Miss Watson and Mrs Canon.

"D'yer reckon I could gerr another job in't dressmakin' trade, our Sara?" Matty asked doubtfully. Sara and Lily had "seen her through" her pregnancy, housing her, feeding her, even giving a hand with the layette which had cost next to nothing, of course, with so many fingers stitching on the cheap materials to be had from St John's Market.

"Matty, you are a wonderfully clever seamstress and anyone would be a fool not to jump at the chance to employ you."

"Even with a bastard at 'ome."

Sara leaned forward angrily. She was sitting on the end of Matty's bed, the skirt of her black velvet magazinière's gown bunched up about her. She had pulled out the pins from the chignon she wore in the showroom and her hair fell in a glowing, rippling curtain of fire down her back. She had brought Matty some roses from the bouquets Paul still sent regularly and she held one to her nose, sniffing its delicate fragrance. There was a good fire in Matty's grate and its glow painted her smooth skin with a golden patina and created dancing shadows on the white walls and ceiling of the room. The curtains at the window were drawn and the room was warm, drowsy with that sweet baby smell of milk and freshly aired napkins.

"Matty! You are not to say that about Jamie. I'm surprised at you."

"It's true, an' you be careful an' all. Learn yer lesson from what 'appened ter me." Matty nodded her head wisely.

"I don't know what you mean."

"Don't yer, then yer must be soft in't head. Mr Travers is mad fer yer, anyone with eyes in their 'eads can see that an' if yer don't marry 'im yer barmy."

"Marry him? He hasn't asked me and you're talking absolute nonsense. We are no more than good friends, loving friends,

if you like but that is all there is between us. We both like it
that way. It suits us."

"Bloody rubbish!"

"Matty!"

"Oh, don't kid me, our Sara, an' listen ter what I'm sayin'.
Don't go gerrin inter't same pickle as me." She looked
down, cradling her "pickle" to her breast, her face soft
and marvelling, the matter of employment forgotten in her
absolute adoration of young Jamie Hutchinson.

"What can I do for you, Sara?" Madame asked her the next
day, smiling pleasantly as she handed her a cup and saucer,
studying the girl who was seated opposite her.

Sara wore what had become her own particular style in the
magazin, a superbly cut and fitted skirt, this time in a rich
barathea with a lustre to it that gleamed in the firelight. It
was black, of course, perfectly plain except for a band of
velvet sewn about twelve inches from the hem. The bolero,
edged with the same black velvet, had what was known as a
"bell-sleeve", narrow at the shoulder insertion but widening to
a bell shape which finished between her elbow and her wrist.
Her blouse was pintucked down the bosom, high-necked
with a narrow frill and the sleeves were full, ending in a
gather at the wrist and showing about six inches of fullness
beneath the bolero sleeve. She had her hair tied up with
black velvet ribbon, not in its usual chignon today but, as
though to contrast with the severity of her outfit, slightly
tumbled, curls bouncing from the top of her head where the
ribbon was fastened reaching to her shoulders. She looked
quite magnificent and Rosalie Lovell wondered how much
longer Paul Travers would wait to get her into his bed. He
had not done so yet. Rosalie Lovell was well versed in the
art and look of loving and as yet Sara Hamilton was familiar
with neither. It was odd really. Everyone believed she was
Paul Travers's mistress and as such she should have been a
pariah, a woman who no other woman would consort with
and yet the fashionable and wealthy of Liverpool flocked to
the House of Lovell to be dressed by her. It was probably Paul
Travers's influence which protected her, of course, which was
a good thing otherwise Rosalie Lovell would have been forced
to get rid of her. A businesswoman first and last was Rosalie
Lovell and a magazinière who did not attract business, in fact

frightened it away, was no good to her. And Sara was no longer just a showroom woman but a designer of great flair and creativity and there was more than one lady in society wearing her creations.

Sara took a sip of her tea then placed the dainty cup and saucer on the small table beside her. She cleared her throat, folding her hands neatly in her lap, something Madame Lovell had seen her do a hundred times. It was a sign she was nervous.

"I have a friend, Madame," she began, and her hands clenched tightly.

"Indeed, Sara?" Madame said encouragingly.

"Yes. She is a very clever seamstress. She was apprenticed to the Misses Yeoland when she was fourteen and for the past nine or ten years has been employed by them, becoming first hand when she was twenty."

"A talented woman then. The Misses Yeoland are very particular."

"Yes, but . . ."

"But, Sara?" Madame leaned forward slightly.

"She got into . . . trouble." Sara glared defiantly into Madame's face and Rosalie Lovell almost laughed out loud. A bear cub defending another, that was what Sara seemed to be and with such vigour it exploded about her like a firework.

"Trouble, Sara? You mean she is to have a child?"

"She's had a child, Madame. The day before yesterday. A son. The Misses Yeoland were forced to let her go . . . that is how they put it, months ago, but now, well, she must have work. She must support her child so she must have work."

"And you want me to give it to her?"

"Oh, Madame, would you?" Sara sat forward in her chair, her face flushed and eager, her eyes brilliant with hope, with a fervour which made Rosalie Lovell wonder if this friend of Sara's, whoever she was, knew how fortunate she was to have Sara Hamilton for a friend.

"I would have to consider it very carefully, Sara. You must know how respectable folk, and I mean our clientèle, would view a situation like this. The mother of a bastard touching their— "

"Madame! What a dreadful thing to say." Sara was appalled.

"That is how they would view it, Sara. They are of the opinion that a woman who has a child out of wedlock is not fit to walk the same earth as themselves, being little more than a common whore. They would not let a whore sew their petticoats and ballgowns. They might catch something dreadful, you see, for it is a well-known fact that women like your friend carry disease and— "

Sara stood up in outrage. "Madame Lovell, I am disappointed in you. How can you speak like that about poor Matty. She is a lovely young woman. Clean and kind and generous."

"Sit down, child. It is not me who is speaking but my clientèle."

"So you are telling me you will not give my friend a job in your— "

"I did not say that at all, Sara."

"But . . ."

"I merely wished to point out the difficulties you . . . er . . . we would have to overcome."

Madame Lovell sat back, a strange weariness showing about her eyes which even the carefully applied powder and paint could not hide. She was dressed in a youthful buttercup silk, an exquisite morning gown which Sara had designed for her and which Alice Hamilton and her girls had made up. It was, like all Sara's designs, simple, the beauty of it in the cut and fit but somehow, for the first time, Rosalie Lovell was conscious that it was too young for her, or, she was too old for it. She really did feel tired today, ready to say to this talented, eager young woman who was at the beginning of her career, "Leave me alone. You get on with it. You decide. Let me relax by my fire. Let me remain here with my memories and put in your hands, and your sister's hands, for no doubt she will find some way to interfere, the life of this great fashion house which is the only child to which I will ever give birth."

"Madame . . .?"

She came to with a start. God, she must be getting old, drifting off in the middle of a conversation, her mind fogged with thoughts, jumbled as the minds of the old are jumbled.

"Yes?"

"Are you not well, Madame? You seem . . ."

"I am quite well, thank you, Sara. Now then, I have an appointment in half an hour. Some legal thing which must be dealt with at once so if you don't mind . . ."

She indicated that the interview was over and Sara rose to her feet, smoothing her hands indecisively down her skirt.

"But, Matty? Will you . . .?"

"I will consider it, Sara, but really the decision is not mine to . . ."

"Pardon?"

"It will all become clear when . . . Now go along, child. Mrs Davenport and her daughter have already arrived and will be waiting for you. I will see you later."

The commotion began just after five o'clock that afternoon and could be heard all over the house. It began with a shriek which froze the very blood in her veins, Cook said, and caused the skivvy to drop half a dozen saucepans which she was about to scour. The clatter was indescribable and it was not until it had all subsided that the turmoil beyond the green baize door, which led from the kitchen into the hallway, become audible again to the cocked ears of the servants.

It was Miss Hoity-Toity! Dear God, they thought she had been put firmly in her place ages ago, told by Madame to keep her nose out of Madame's business, or so Betty Holden and Cissie Wentworth had told Sally Battersby, the parlourmaid, with whom they were on friendly terms.

They crept to the door, even Cook, who should have known better, and opened it a crack.

"I won't do it. I will not do it!" Miss Hoity-Toity was saying, screeching really. Not a bit ladylike, which was what she made herself out to be. It seemed to come from the upstairs landing as though Miss Hoity-Toity, in her determination not to do what was being asked of her, was making for the stairs and the front door.

"If Madame wishes to employ women such as that one, then that is up to her but I will not soil my reputation by remaining in the same house. She is a loose woman, Sara, a trollop, a drab and I cannot, *cannot* work with her. Do not ask it of me."

The words faded away. The servants closed the door, exchanging open-mouthed glances with one another. They were not surprised half an hour later to be told by the equally open-mouthed Betty Holden that Miss Hamilton had packed her bags and gone.

26

"I have a Christmas present for you, my pet," Paul said, holding out his hand to her. "Now it is nothing like Storm so don't pull a face at me. By the way, Tim says to tell you she is as docile as a lamb now and is ready to be ridden by the most inexperienced rider. He wants you to come over on Boxing Day, and so do I. Not too early because it is customary for the servants to receive their gifts from my mother, but any time after eleven he would be happy to give you your first lesson."

"Paul," Sara sighed in resignation, "when are you going to believe me when I say that not only have I not the talent, the inclination to ride with you, but the time. Madame would dismiss me if I took an hour off here and there to gallop all over the countryside. What are you smiling at, you rogue? You are up to something."

"No, no, please go on," but his smile had become deep and mischievous.

"As I was saying, I cannot spare the time. Have you any idea how many hours I have worked this week alone? You know how busy we are just before Christmas and with Alice gone . . ."

Sara bent her head, doing her best to restrain the tears which threatened to spill down her cheeks, tears of remorse, tears of genuine sorrow, tears which remembered all the years which she and Alice had shared and which, before they came to Liverpool, had been contented ones. Alice had never been a great one for hugs and kisses but she had always been dependable, someone for the child Sara to lean on, consistently to be relied on to show Sara how to behave in any given situation. Her very restraint had been a comfort at times, for Sara had always known exactly where she was with Alice.

Now she was gone.

Sara had wept, wept and begged her to stay. She was sorry she had spoken to her as she had done in Bold Street, she moaned. It had been inexcusable but Alice must see that Matty . . .

"Matty! That is all I hear these days, Sara, and since it is obvious that you care more about her welfare than mine, more about your friendship with her than your sisterly duties towards me then there is no more to be said. You have cajoled Madame into giving her a job here, here in the House of Lovell where decent girls live and work and I cannot forgive you. And neither will they. They are not accustomed to being in the company of fallen women and I am quite certain that more than one will follow my example and leave. They have already said so."

"Ally, please, won't you reconsider? There is no need for you to come into contact with Matty in . . ."

Even as she spoke Sara felt a pang of shame. Putting Matty in some back room where she would work alone was not what she had in mind for her and she hoped it was not in Madame's mind either. Matty was gregarious and would wilt if she were isolated from the other girls, made to feel an outcast. Besides, what she had done, though it was not right, had been done with a good, generous heart and should Matty be punished because of it, as the man was certainly not being punished, Sara was sure.

"I am supervisor, Sara," Alice continued coldly, "and cannot help but be involved with her at times. I would be forced to handle her work and quite frankly I cannot bear the thought of it. If she comes here then I shall go."

"Ally, don't do this. I can't bear to think of you all alone."

"Then come with me, Sara." Alice grabbed Sara's hand eagerly. "I am to buy a partnership in a small but very successful dressmaking business in Leece Street. I have signed nothing yet but Miss Butler is a woman I think I could admire," and if she's not then I'll soon lick her into shape, her demeanour said. "Not quite a lady, of course, but respectable. There are rooms over the salon and she has promised me one for my own use. We could share it, you and I. It will be as it was when we were in Wray Green. Just like old times, do you remember?"

Oh yes, she remembered, Sara thought despairingly, pulling her hand roughly from Alice's grasp.

"I can't," she babbled, "I'm settled here now, Ally."

Alice flushed, then her intense face drained of all its colour, leaving her grim-mouthed, hard-eyed, menacing.

"Very well then, Sara Hamilton. As you said to me only last week, to the devil with you and the sooner the better."

"Ally, don't say that. I was upset, I didn't mean it."

"Maybe you didn't, Sara Hamilton, but I do."

Now Paul took her cold hands in his warm ones. "Forget it, Sara. There is nothing you can do about it. You and Alice have both made your decisions and neither one of you can alter it, isn't that right?"

"I suppose so." Sara sniffed dolefully, accepting the handkerchief he held out to her and blowing her nose vigorously.

"You suppose so? Would you change your mind and go and live with Alice, work with Alice in a small salon in Leece Street?"

"Sweet Jesus, no." Sara looked up horrified and he wanted to laugh, for she was using more and more of the oaths and expressions he himself used.

"There you are then, and Alice, from what you've told me of her, will certainly not back down so won't you try to get this thing into perspective. If neither of you can agree with the other . . ."

"God in heaven, the very idea of being under Alice's thumb again appalls me."

"Of course it does, just as staying on at Lovell's and working side by side with Matty appalls Alice, so put it all behind you and get on with your life. You won't lose touch with her, not if you don't want to. You can go and visit her after Christmas which brings me back to my Christmas present to you."

"But I don't want it to end like this. We are sisters."

Paul sighed and sat back in his chair which was as rickety as the rest of the furniture in the room. He almost tipped over backwards.

"Good God above, Sara, when are you going to get some decent furniture for this place," he grumbled. "I'm frightened to move in case I go arse over tip. Now listen to me and then we will say no more on the bloody subject. It's Christmas Eve and I have more important and pleasant things to discuss with you than your sister. In a few weeks, when she has had time to settle down, put her mark, which you tell me she likes to do, on the business, take it over and all those in it, she will be tickled to death to see you. To show off what she has accomplished."

"You don't know Alice," Sara said moodily, staring into the glass of champagne Paul had just poured out for her.

"Listen to me, she'll be as proud as punch to— "

"Oh Paul, do you really think so?" she pleaded pathetically.

"Of course I do." He stood up and moved to the fire which crackled in the grate, took a spill from the container on the mantelpiece, lit it from the flames and put it to his cigar. "Now come here and see what I've got you for Christmas."

He began to smile, a wickedly infectious smile and she returned it, for who could resist Paul when he set out to charm. She rose from her chair and moved slowly across the carpet towards him. She was still in her magazinière's black since she had only just got back from West Derby, brought in Paul's fast little curricle with a great dash and flourish by Paul himself over roads still treacherous with ice. Paul, already dressed in his immaculate evening suit, had grumbled all the way home, asking her did she know how difficult it was to get a table at the Adelphi on Christmas Eve and if they didn't look sharp Armand would let it go to the first man to slip him a guinea or two. How long would it take her to change? While she did so he meant to take a second bottle of champagne down to the ladies, meaning Dolly, Lily and Matty who sat in worshipping contemplation of young Jamie Hutchinson in Lily's cosy room. He did not know them well, having done no more than wish them a polite good evening on occasion but he meant to rectify that this evening, he promised and would she like to make a small side bet that he could get them tiddly in the fifteen minutes it should take her to dress.

But somehow one glass of champagne had led to another and Sara had become more and more maudlin with every one, wondering what "poor Alice" was doing, after all it was Christmas Eve and it *was* the first time they had ever been apart. They were sisters, she said and Paul knew that unless he changed her mood, lifted her from what had been a long, dragging day fitting the last of the ordered Christmas gowns, she would be miserable right through Christmas and Boxing Day.

"What is it?" she asked him, her smile deepening. "Obviously not a carriage for my horse to pull."

"Animals like Storm do not pull carriages, my dear."

"There you are. See how much I know about equine matters, and if it's diamonds they won't suit me."

"No, not diamonds."

He grinned lazily, his strong teeth clamped round his cigar, the smoke wreathing his smoothly brushed head. Paul Travers was forty years old but his masculine beauty was undeniable. He was at his prime, lean, flat-bellied, long-legged. His face was a smooth amber with no more than a few deepening lines about his eyes, a crease between his brows when he frowned and a vertical slash at each side of his strong, smiling mouth.

"Then what?" She stood directly before him. She wore high-heeled boots and her eyes were on a level with his mouth and for some reason she found herself studying it, noting the pleasing shape of his upper lip which was long and upturned at the corners. There was a soft indentation in the lower, which was shorter and as he continued to smile down at her, somewhat puzzled by her own sudden stillness, she placed her finger across them both. A light touch, just as though she were asking him not to speak, for it seemed something inside her had words to say and she really must listen to them.

At once the smile left his face, for Paul Travers was a sophisticated man, a man of experience who knew women and he had recognised immediately what was in Sara Hamilton's bemused expression. He was also not a man to let an opportunity slip by him.

"Sara?" he murmured questioningly against her fingertip, then, throwing his cigar neatly into the fire, he took her hand between his, cupping it like a captured bird. He turned it over, the inside of her wrist uppermost and bent his head, placing his warm lips to the pulse which beat frantically there while she watched with breathless fascination. He went no further. If she took fright he was ready to step back, grin and say something light and nonsensical, make nothing of it, give her time to recover and pretend it had not happened or if it had it was only Paul being his usual whimsical self.

But if she allowed it he would know exactly what to do next. The bed was in the corner, the women would not come up . . .

She allowed it. She seemed to sigh as she leaned towards him, her warm, champagne-scented breath whispering against his hands.

"Sara?" he said again, his eyes a warm, midnight blue in the lamplight, putting out a ·hand to cup her cheek. His thumb caressed her smooth skin, feeling the bloom on it, the warmth of it as she came slowly towards her own blooming as a woman at last.

Letting go of her hands and placing them flat against his chest, he put one hand at the back of her neck beneath her hair as though to prevent her escaping, then with the gentlest, softest touch, a brushing, no more, of their lips, he kissed her. His hands held her steady, one at her neck, the other at her chin, not allowing her mouth to evade his, had it wanted to which it didn't, it seemed, as he continued to kiss her, folding his lips about hers, parting them, taking her lower lip between his, slowly moving one step at a time, pleasing her, loving her, by God!

When he lifted his head for a moment his strong, handsome face was stern and uncompromising but she did not see it as she swayed, eyes closed, in his arms.

"Sara, my sweet love." He bent his head again, his lips travelling along her jawline to find the lobe of her ear then back down the column of her throat to the frill at the neck of her blouse.

Her hands fought to get free and for a despairing moment he thought he had lost her then, as he moved back a fraction, they flew to the back of his head, clinging like small birds in a spread of ivy to the crisp hair on his neck.

"Paul, I'm . . ." Her voice was husky.

"Yes, my darling?"

"What . . .?"

"Hush, my love. You are safe with me. You know that, don't you? No harm will ever come to you while I'm here."

"Paul . . ."

"Yes, sweetheart . . . yes?"

"Are you to make love to me?"

He laughed triumphantly. "I think it is about time, don't you, Sara Hamilton, but do you want me to?"

"I think I do."

"Then yes, I am."

He turned down every lamp and in the light from the dancing, singing flames of the fire he slowly undressed her, sighing over every sweet curve and hollow, his hands gentle on her breasts, which were as rich as cream and tipped in rose. His mouth was warm on her belly, his champagne-scented breath drifting to every part of her arching body. His lips delicately took the rosy peaks of her nipples and his tongue teased them until Sara thought they would burst with pleasure. His own clothes had been discarded, cast away so smoothly she was scarcely aware of it. He lay beside her on the rug, the flames turning his body to a shade of burned honey and polished amber and when she sat up to look at him, her breasts falling forward into his waiting hands he knew it would be unequalled, his loving of Sara Hamilton. She was not shy but her glance was hesitant, for she had never before seen an unclothed male, nor was she overly modest and he rejoiced in it for it seemed she was a true woman, one who would be his equal in what they were about to share. Her eyes ran over him, studying his long legs which were covered in a faint brown fuzz of hair, the smooth line of the muscle from his hip to his knee, the spring of brown curls on his chest, even his nipples which peaked at her touch.

At last her eyes came to rest on the thicket of hair between his legs from which his penis stood proud, a lordly lift and thrust of his loins which soon, she was well aware, must be attended to.

"Are you afraid, little one?" he asked her softly, seeing where her gaze lay.

"I'm not sure . . ." She lay down again beside him, her eyes wide with some emotion he was not sure of, then as he reached to stroke her breasts, to roll her nipples, first one then the other, between his thumb and forefinger, they became unfocused, narrowed, beginning to grow darker and darker as desire was lit in her again. She made a small sound in the back of her throat which he recognised as need.

"Sweet Jesus Christ, I've wanted this," he groaned. His hand ran lightly from her breasts down her flat stomach to the thatch of copper curls between her legs. They were already damp. Swiftly he parted her legs, afraid even now that she might refuse and slowly lowered himself down on her. His head was thrown back and he called her name as he entered her. He felt her flinch but the cleft between her legs was wet and slippery and in a moment it was done. As gently as he could he moved inside her, feeling her body grip his in the close bondage a man and woman know when they are fast on the incoming tide of passion. It mounted, gathering speed, that swell of love mingled with lust, carrying them on its waves, riding higher and higher, wind-tossed, and when she called his name, shatteringly, piercingly sweet he knew he had won her at last. She was his! his!

They made love again later and in between she slept in his arms as trustingly as a child which knows it is safe. He remained awake, watching her sleep, waiting for her, protecting her, cradling her with passionate longing, a longing which was not romantic but a fiercely masculine yearning to keep what was his beside him. He had been amazed by her acceptance of his body and by her response to it. He knew she had been virgin when he took her, the evidence was there between her thighs, but each time they came together she was ready for him, ready to love him in the night with her hair spread out like a fan on the hearth-rug, her skin as lustrous as pearl and fragrant as the roses he still continued to send her.

He knew a great peace, a great sighing peace for at last, at last she belonged to him. For eight months he had wanted her, in every way he had wanted her, waiting patiently which was not his way. Not as a monk, of course, since he was a mature man with needs which must be eased. He would marry her now, he told himself confidently and impregnate her at once, if he had not already done so this night. Sweet God, he had not expected it to happen and when it had the last thing on his mind had been the avoidance of pregnancy. It didn't matter now, of course. Before the spring came they would be man and wife.

He turned his head away from her in sighing contemplation of their future together, his hand not relinquishing its possessive hold on her breast, staring deep into the glowing embers of the fire which needed replenishing. The room was growing cold and he must go soon, though he was aware that the women downstairs would know exactly what had happened up here tonight. Hell's teeth, his horse and curricle still stood at the front of the house, the reins carelessly looped round the railings at the top of the basement steps.

But there were things to be discussed with Sara before he left. This made a difference to the Christmas present he had intended to give her, of course, since it would not do for Mrs Paul Travers to work in, let alone own a fashion house. But that was not an insurmountable object. They would put in some clever woman to run the place. Sara would know how to go about it, perhaps even the redoubtable Miss Alice Hamilton who, he was sure, would give her right arm to get her hands on it. To be in charge! He would have the deed reverted back to his name and buy Sara something else, whatever she had a fancy for. Furs, jewellery, a fine new carriage and four matched horses for as sure as hell his mother would not give up hers! An engagement ring, of course, the best that money could buy. Christ, what an upheaval this would cause: his mother, his family but Sara was a lady born and bred and would fit into her new role as if she had been trained for it. Which, knowing something of her background, she had. They would come to know her, to love her as he did, especially if she gave him a son.

He turned back to her, sliding his hand from her breast until it rested on her flat belly, smoothing the tangle of damp copper curls at its base. A son. Perhaps already she had a son in her womb.

She stirred and smiled in her sleep and his own lips curved upwards at the corner. She moved closer to him, sighing as though in great content. Her lips parted and his arms closed joyously about her.

"Jack," she murmured, turning her face into his shoulder.

27

The thunderbolt hit the House of Lovell on the morning of January 1st and for half an hour Dilly Parker, who had been put in charge of the girls in the sewing rooms until a replacement for Miss Hamilton had been found, could do nothing with them. They couldn't take it in, they told one another disbelievingly and was it really true or just some silly schoolboy prank on the part of the footman? Madame Lovell to retire. It was like saying Her Majesty the Queen was to abdicate, it was so far-fetched and they wouldn't believe it, not until Madame herself told them.

It was the same in the servants hall for what was to happen to them? they asked one another fearfully. Good jobs like theirs were hard to come by, for though Madame Lovell was a bit of a martinet, demanding service second to none at every hour of the day and night, she had been fair and had paid well for that service. Was their new owner, whose name had not yet been revealed, to dismiss the servants he, or she, thought surplus to requirements, for even they admitted there were a lot of them just to look after one old woman.

It was not until the new owner's name was disclosed that they began to understand, to smile and nudge one another as it became clear to them what had happened and under their very noses, too. Miss Hamilton had been a bad beggar, strict, cruel even at times but she had, it appeared, been right about her sister after all. Miss Sara's fancy man, no less, had bought the place and they had no difficulty at all in imagining what Miss Sara had done to achieve what was virtually ownership of the topmost fashion house in Liverpool

Sara herself could not believe it. There were many things she could not believe, nor understand in those last days of

1849. One of them was Paul's flippant attitude to what had been to her a delightful but also meaningful milestone in their relationship. When she had awakened in her bed where he had transferred her during the night, he was already dressed and his manner was exactly as it had always been, engagingly cheerful, smilingly good-humoured, obligingly helpful even, as he searched in her small kitchen behind the Chinese screen for coffee beans, declaring he could not function until he had a cup of piping hot coffee in his hand. It was as though what had happened the night before had been no more to him, or to her, his manner suggested, than a handshake between friends. She might even have described him as suave, urbane as he leaned over to kiss her, making nothing of the phenomenen that she was stark naked under her mama's scented shawl.

"I'd best get this fire going, my pet," he had remarked, ambling about barefoot in his black evening clothes, "or we shall perish of the cold. Not that I'm much of a hand with a fire, you understand, in fact I must confess that I don't think I have ever made one." He grinned wickedly. "Do you think I should ask Mrs Canon to come and— "

"Paul, don't you dare," ready to laugh with him for the idea of the stiff-faced Lily – and she would have a stiff face – marching up the stairs with the coal scuttle was enough to make anyone laugh. She wanted to get out of bed but her clothes were all over the place, flung hither and thither by Paul, she supposed as he had stripped her last night. She felt awkward and she didn't like it, nor did she like the way Paul's vivid blue eyes ran calculatingly down her body as she slipped hastily into her bedgown. It was so casual. She didn't know quite what she had expected, if indeed she had thought about it, which naturally she hadn't since it had been so unexpected. He was always teasing, light-hearted, audacious and irrepressibly unable to be serious for a moment, but, well, last night he had been different, she could have sworn it. There had been about him a sense of vulnerability which was an odd thing to say knowing his strength. A softness, a truth she had never seen before, as though he were revealing to her some side of him which he had always kept hidden. A swell of tenderness which had swamped her, not just emotionally, but physically so that her body had responded naturally to his. She was a woman and had been ready to be loved, she knew that and several times in the past months had found herself wishing, astonishingly, that Paul would . . . Well, wondering what it would be like to, some day, to . . . He was very attractive, masculine, and she was no longer a child.

There was Jack, of course, who was lost to her for ever. Lost in the emptiness of her heart which had once held him safe. Alice had been right about him. He had answered none of her letters, ignored the one she had left with the woman in Wray Green, that's if he had ever gone back to Wray Green, and had proved beyond doubt that his life had no room for Sara Hamilton in it. And because of it Paul's attentions to her had been even more welcome. His obvious pleasure in her company, his obvious pride when he took her about to functions to which she should not really have gone and wouldn't but for him, had been a soothing salve to her badly wounded spirit. She had become increasingly dependent on him, increasingly fond of him and, despite what was locked in her very soul for Jack Andrews, last night had been enchanting. She had found his embrace, his kisses, his frank admiration of her body very welcome. There had been no awkwardness, no embarrassment, no clumsiness but then she supposed he was very experienced with women.

Quite simply she had enjoyed it, which had surprised her for she had been led to believe from what Alice had let drop that nice women merely put up with it for the sake of their husbands and the children they hoped to have. Of course, Paul was not her husband so perhaps that was the reason.

But now she felt embarrassed. Now she felt awkward, for it seemed to her that something should be said by one of them. But who! Surely Paul, as the man, the instigator, Paul, her friend, should not simply ignore it. She was woefully ignorant of such things, but should he merely have the coffee he was clamouring for and simply go home? Dolly and Lily and Matty must be faced . . . Dear God, how was she to do that? Was he to leave her with the daunting task of explaining that . . . that he was now her lover? Was he her lover? Dear God in heaven, she knew so little about it all.

"About your Christmas present, my pet," he had said to her as he knelt by the grate attempting to kindle the firewood while she made the coffee.

Her Christmas present, of course. Perhaps the giving and receiving of that and of hers to him would disperse the constraint which lay about them but he had merely gone on to explain that he had found he had left it at home after all.

Perhaps on his dresser, and if it was convenient he would call back later in the day. There was the family Christmas dinner to be got through, she would understand, he said, smiling winningly over his shoulder, and as he had small gifts for the "ladies" and the infant, he would see her then.

He left soon after, kissing her lightly on the tip of her nose as if she were a child.

The interview, if she could call it that, with Lily, Dolly and Matty, had been perhaps the most horribly embarrassing moment of her life. She had been prepared for recriminations, protestations of horror, of reproach, of sorrow and distress since it was obvious to all but the most obtuse that Paul had spent the night with her. She had made up her mind that she would brazen it out, tell them that she was old enough to make her own decisions about the men . . . man in her life, that it was her business and not theirs. That she was grateful for their concern since naturally they would be concerned. They were her friends but so was Paul. Goddammit, using one of Paul's expressions, it all sounded so . . . bloody ridiculous, using another! They were more than her friends, the women downstairs. They cared for her, about her. They were her family, the only family she had now and deserved an explanation, but how on earth did one go about explaining what had happened last night? How it had come about. She was not even certain herself.

They were in Dolly's sitting-room when she went down. They had evidently been exchanging gifts for there was pretty coloured ribbon and wrapping paper strewn about the room and for just one moment as she entered it there was a dreadful silence.

"Happy Christmas," she said brightly, moving hastily before she lost her nerve to kiss each one in turn. The baby was cradled against Lily's capacious bosom, his plump cheeks and an engaging dark curl all that could be seen of him in the folds of the crocheted shawl Dolly had made for him.

"Happy Christmas, my lamb," Dolly murmured sadly, her old eyes deep and anxious.

"Happy Christmas, chuck." Matty managed a smile and squeezed her hand just as though Sara had been told she had some disease which would soon carry her off.

"Happy Christmas, queen. Come an' sit by't fire an' we'll 'ave us a sherry," was all Lily said.

And that was it. They did not judge her. They were not to reproach her. They loved her. She was their precious child, beloved and rare, but she was also a woman and whatever mistakes she made, as they had all made mistakes, for were they not human, they would be there to help carry her through them. To get her to the other side.

He brought her diamonds! Tiny but exquisite diamonds linked on a fine gold chain which, when her lobes were pierced, he said jauntily, smiling down at her, would swing delightfully from her ears. No more than two inches long or they would have been ostentatious, didn't she think so and he seemed unaware of the cold hollow his words had scraped out inside her. He presented her with the small box in front of the others, who were stiff with him, just as though she was no different to them. Meant no more to him than they did, though the earrings must have cost a small fortune. It was as though he was telling her and in a situation where she could not question him, that men gave diamonds to their mistresses, at least wealthy men and it seemed Paul Travers now considered that was what she was. His mistress!

There was a soft cream shawl of mohair for Dolly, warm and light as a feather, a dress length of silk in a handsome shade of midnight blue for Lily, a dainty parasol for Matty of white muslin and broderie anglaise, dashingly adorned with raspberry pink satin ribbon and a quite extraordinarily beautiful ivory rattle for Jamie decorated with a pair of silver bells. All evidently chosen with great care and thoughtfulness, exactly right for each recipient and they were received with astonishment, for they hardly knew Mr Travers. Matty was quite overcome. His kindness, his generosity in including, not only the ladies but her son in his gift-giving, her son who would, as all bastards did, live with the stigma of his birth for ever hanging about his neck, took her usual chirpy speech away from her and she could only hang her head, studying the obviously expensive present with misted eyes.

"What's this I see, Miss Hutchinson? Not tears on Christmas Day, surely, and you with the handsomest son in Lancashire? Come now, let me see you smile or I shall think my present was not to your liking."

He put his finger gently under her chin, his eyes twinkling

warmly with understanding. He did not condemn her, they said, as others would condemn her and neither did these women who were her friends. She had a place here and so did her son and thanks to Sara – and himself though as yet no one knew of it – she had decent employment to go to in the new year. So what was she crying for, the quizzically humorous smile on his face asked her.

Sara watched him, her heart swelling with an emotion she could barely contain. He was a good man, the sweetness of him buried deep beneath the whimsical, often pungent, sometimes mocking, frequently sardonic exterior he showed the world. He was treating Dolly and Lily as though they were ladies, courteous and with none of his usual impudence, and over the past week or two, ever since he had carried Matty into the house after her fall, he had brought them small gifts, a posy of violets for Dolly from the flower-seller on the corner of Bold Street, a pound of best china tea, the sort Sara said was her favourite, for Lily, and Sara knew that the envelope containing ten guineas which had been slipped beneath Matty's door a couple of days after Jamie's birth could have been from no one but him.

He could not stay long, he said. Christmas Day was a family day, he was sure they would understand. His mama, his four sisters, their husbands and their multitude of children were expecting him home for Christmas tea, sighing, his eyebrows raised in amused resignation. He hoped they would continue to enjoy the rest of the day and no, he would not have sherry, thank you.

"Now look after that infant, Miss Hutchinson. He is going to be a fine boy when he grows and a credit to his mama."

"Oh, I will, sir, and thank you," Matty said fervently.

"And as I just happen to have this bit of mistletoe about me" – his lips curled in an endearing smile, for they knew he had stolen it from the hallway where Matty had hopefully hung it – "I'll have a kiss from all of you. You first, Miss Watson . . ."

He kissed them all in turn, Dolly and Lily ready to giggle like girls as he placed a circumspect peck on their cheek, but Sara could not fail to notice the one he gave the surprised Matty was on her rosy mouth and was of a more robust and lingering nature.

He did not kiss Sara!

"I'll see you to the door," she said politely, wondering where the fine bright sparkle of the night before had gone.

He kissed her then but on the forehead, before turning away to run lightly down the steps to the waiting carriage.

"You look very lovely this morning, my pet," he called for anyone to hear. "Now get those ears pierced as soon as you can. I want you to be wearing my diamonds the next time I see you."

His grin had been wide and charming but in his narrowed blue eyes had been a challenge she did not understand.

She watched the carriage move off towards Oxford Street, Thomas eagerly urging on the horses and as they went she could not fail to realise that Paul had not mentioned the next day when she was to have had her first riding lesson on the sorrel Storm.

It was Madame who broke the news to her, seated in the same chair and the same room where, before Christmas, Sara had begged her to employ Matty Hutchinson.

"I have something to tell you, my dear and as you will be the one most concerned it is only right that you should be the first to know, that is if you don't know already." She smiled brightly.

Sara sat forward in her chair. Was it to do with Matty? Was Madame, after all the furore over Alice who had not been seen nor heard of in nearly two weeks, to go back on her word and explain that after all she could not give Matty a job? That the other girls would not like it and in the circumstances . . .

Madame cut crisply through her thoughts.

"I am to retire, Sara. I don't know quite what I shall do with myself" – beginning to laugh – "but whatever it is I shall do it abroad. Italy perhaps, or the south of France, somewhere warm, at any rate. So you see when you asked me the other day whether I was prepared to employ your friend I was somewhat nonplussed, since the decision was not really mine to make but the new owner's."

Sara could not speak. Her eyes were enormous in her shocked face and her brain seemed to be empty of all thought.

"I see I have surprised you, my dear. I am myself surprised for I thought he would have told you, but never mind. He will soon do so. Perhaps he means it as a new year's gift

though I was under the impression that Christmas had been
... But I digress. Now I will not tell you how old I am, only
that the years that are left to me I wish to spend in pleasant
distraction which I have had no time for in the past. I shall
visit my friend, Mr Worth, in Paris. Perhaps a month or two
in Rome and Naples. I have an ... an acquaintance there, a
dear gentleman ..." Madame smiled archly, the smile making
her seem younger than her years.

"Do I shock you, Sara? You know a woman of mature years
can still find ... well ..." She became brisk. "I am wandering
from the point. I have sold the House of Lovell to Mr Travers
on one condition only and that is he allows you a free hand
in its running. You cannot imagine how relieved I was when
your sister went. I do not mean to be offensive but when she
left I could only look on it as— "

"Mr Travers ... is ..." Sara's voice was no more than a
quaver in the back of her throat.

"Yes, Paul Travers, and I must say I am surprised that he
... I was under the impression, as I said ... Well, Mr Travers
is a businessman first and last and knows his own mind best.
I hope I have not spoken out of turn, my dear, but you had
to be told as my staff are to be told later in the day."

I have a gift for you, my pet, he had said, lounging by her
fireside, so pleased with himself the very air about him had
crackled. His eyes had snapped joyfully and deep in their
depths that light which she had seen on many other occasions
swam lazily to the surface. Not diamonds, she had said to him.
Diamonds won't suit me, she had said to him, teasing him,
since the moment had seemed fraught with a charged emotion
she found took her breath away. No, not diamonds, he had
answered, his mouth quirking in an engaging smile. Then he
had kissed her, made love to her and at the end of it apologised because he had left her Christmas gift on his dresser!

Diamonds. The next day he had brought her diamonds and
she had not seen him since!

"Are you all right, Sara?" Madame asked anxiously, so
alarmed by what she had apparently seen in Sara's face
she had actually risen to her feet. She had never seen colour
leave anyone's face as quickly as it had left Sara Hamilton's
and not just from her skin but from her eyes which changed
to the washed-out green of a duck egg, and from her lovely
tawny hair. She seemed to fade, to shrink somehow, to wilt

back into her chair like a fresh flower will wilt without water. Her hands on the arms of the chair gripped them so fiercely they turned as bone white as her face and she stared with such horror Rosalie Lovell reached out with her own hands to give Sara something to hang on to, should she need it.

"What is it? What has happened? What did I say?"

Sara forced herself to swim towards the light at the surface of the whirlpool which was dragging her down into its depths. She was completely disorientated. Was she in a dream, a nightmare or was it some foolish absurdity of Paul's, some nonsense he had thought up in that intricately clever mind of his? And yet why should he? What was happening? Why was he doing this and the next confused question was, doing what? It had seemed to her, moments ago, that Madame had implied Paul had bought the House of Lovell as a gift for her, for Sara Hamilton, and it also seemed to her that the diamond earrings had been an afterthought, a substitute for something else.

And it could only have happened because she had allowed him to make love to her. Given herself to him, she believed the phrase was. Given him the gift of her virginity, was that how it was described, and which was much prized. And so, having taken it, he had no further use for her. He had bought the House of Lovell . . . to impress her? to bribe her? was that it? But now, having no need of such chicanery since he had got what he wanted for nothing, he had changed his mind and given her diamonds instead. Oh yes, expensive, but so easy, so casually tossed into her lap as though she were no more to him than . . . than a street woman he had picked up and taken to his bed. All these months they had been friends, companions, sharing one another's company, humour, sadness sometimes and in all that time he had never refused her his masculine protection, support, respect! Until now!

She stood up abruptly, her young face almost unrecognisable in its hardness, its unyielding implacability and Rosalie Lovell flinched away from it.

"Sara . . .?"

"Thank you, Madame, I shall do my best to live up to the responsibility and trust both you and Mr Travers have placed in me and to continue in the tradition the House of Lovell has known in the past. Now, if you will excuse me, I have clients expected within the hour and I must see to the materials."

*   *   *

Paul leaned against the grey, one hand caressing its soft muzzle, the other flung across its back. His gaze was unfocused, unseeing, though he appeared to be intently studying a robin as it pecked vigorously at the berries on the branch of a rowan tree. The bird seemed oblivious to him and his horse, not the slightest bit concerned by his proximity. It stopped its busy pecking for a moment, cocking its head on one side then, as though performing just for his benefit, it began to sing, short liquid phrases running together in a most wistful way.

A couple of sparrows alighted on a higher branch and at once, its song discarded, the robin turned on them aggressively.

It was only just daylight and eastwards a flush of apricot outlined the dark oaks, the arrow-straight pine trees, the denuded rhododendrons which grew in such profusion in the woodland which surrounded New Park House. There was a heavy hoar frost, crisp under Paul's booted feet, turning the trees and bushes to brilliant white-diamond beauty where the rays of the sun touched them.

There was a narrow, half-frozen stream to his left and a water rat scrabbled frantically through it, breaking the thin layer of ice as it drank. The horse wickered uneasily and Paul blinked, coming from his reverie with a start.

"There's nothing to be alarmed about, old fellow," he said gently, pulling the animal's ear. "Let's walk on, shall we?"

The grey obeyed, pushing through the winter vegetation, his hooves breaking the thin crust of frost which coated the ground. He moved placidly beside the man with no need of guidance and it was obvious there was a strong bond between them.

They came to a clearing in which fallen trees had been neatly stacked in rows, waiting for the gardener to saw them into manageable logs for the great number of fires kept burning, as was the custom, in New Park House. There was no sound here but the warble of a thrush some way off, and nearer, the thin twitter of several blue tits which roamed the wood in search of food.

As though of one mind both horse and man stopped in the centre of the clearing and the man sat down on a fallen tree.

"I don't know what the bloody hell to do, Troy," Paul

Travers said almost dreamily, just as though he had been hypnotised into speaking his innermost thoughts. "That's the truth of it. I know I've hurt her terribly. Jesus Christ, I've insulted her but . . . God in heaven, when she said his name it nearly killed me. What man wishes to hear the name of another man on the lips of the woman he . . . he has just made love to, tell me that? I was going to ask her to marry me. When we made love, she responded, she turned to me and . . ." His voice broke then, the halting speech of a man trying to find his way through the bleakness which beset his own heart giving way to the thick whispering tone of one who was close to breaking. "Diamonds, bloody diamonds I gave her as though she were a whore who had pleased me. She's the only woman who has ever meant anything to me and I turned my back on her. Oh, Jesus God . . ."

He lifted his face which was wet with tears, the harsh, difficult tears of a strong man who is weakened and his groan was deep and painful. "Jack, she called me Jack and how can any man who loves a woman, who has just lain with her in love, bear the agony of that? Who is he? Who is Jack? Goddammit, what does he mean to her? Surely she is not . . .? Sweet Christ, not another man?"

A woodcock, its nest no more than six feet away behind the neatly stacked timber, burrowed deeper in its sanctuary and several small woodland creatures froze as Paul Travers's cry rose on the hard, cold air. The grey twitched its ears, turning to look apprehensively at his master with large, fringed eyes but Paul was beyond noticing.

"I can't bring myself to go near her, you see, that's the bloody trouble, for I think I might hurt her quite badly, and yet I can't just step out of her life, not now, not with this damned business to see to."

There was silence then for several minutes. He sat on the stack of wood, his knees bent and apart, his hands hanging between them, his head bowed as he stared at the frozen ground. The woodcock eased itself carefully out of its nest, for in this hard weather it must search for food and the other animals were about to move on when he slapped his hands on his thighs, the sound transfixing them all once more into immobility.

"I can't let the bloody thing fall apart. There are dozens of them, servants and . . . and the sewing women . . . and her.

Their jobs depend on it, on me. Oh, goddammit to hell and God rot Jack whoever he is to eternal damnation."

His mood had changed from deep sorrow to a savage snarling anger as he sprang to his feet and the grey, sensing it, backed away from him.

"I've got to go on and that's all there is to it," he rasped harshly, just as though he were in some terrible argument with an adversary. He punched the air with a powerful fist. The peace of the woodland was shattered and gone. "I've got to go on and pretend that . . . that we are . . . Oh Jesus Christ, how am I to do it after what happened? Jesus, oh Jesus!"

For perhaps fifteen minutes he stood silently, his head sunk on his chest and all about him, almost to his very feet, the woodland animals resumed their busy foraging. One even sniffed at his boots, its whiskers twitching, its small eyes wide in bewilderment, then the grey whinnied from the far side of the clearing and Paul Travers came out of his deep musing with a sharp exclamation.

"Bugger it," he snapped, narrowing his eyes perilously, the menace aimed at himself more than anyone else. "I'll let no woman reduce me to this. God's bloody teeth, am I to be destroyed by a pretty face and a comely figure? There are more women on God's earth than leaves on a bloody tree and all willing, for a price, to lie down and open their legs."

But not one like Sara Hamilton, his beleaguered, rebellious heart whispered to him as he strode across the clearing and flung himself on the grey's back.

28

The man stood on the deck of the sailing ship *Shenandoah*, his hands gripping the rail, his eyes piercing the gloom of the coming day. There was a faint smudge of illumination in the eastern sky as the ship waited patiently for the daylight when, on the morning tide, she would move to her berth.

Shenandoah, ten days out of New York, was at anchor in Bootle Bay, just outside the mouth of the River Mersey. It would be dawn soon on New Year's Eve 1849 and in a few hours the man would move down the gangplank and step on to the shores of the land he had left six months ago.

He turned, leaning his elbows on the rail, his shoulders hunched into the warmth of his greatcoat as he looked up into the miles of rigging, the furled sails of the packet ship which had brought him from New York. The ship had been built expressly for the packet service and the carrying of Royal Mails to and from America, though cabins were available to passengers with twenty-five pounds in their pocket. Packet ships were fast and reliable and indeed the crossing would soon be even faster as the very latest steam ships were launched, but this did not concern Jack Andrews as he contemplated his future in his homeland.

He had left it with one purpose in his mind and that was to do his best to put all thoughts of Sara Hamilton out of his mind for ever, though Daniel Browne, with whom he was now in partnership, had believed Jack had gone to explore the growing increase and need for railways in Canada and the United States, which he had. What had been termed the 'railway boom' was over in Britain and the sessions of 1848 had added only eighty-three to the number of Railway Acts, which, when added up in actual mileage, came to a mere three hundred miles. Railways were amalgamating, being leased to others, and in the years 1846, 1847 and 1848 there had been an almost uninterrupted decline in the market value of railway property. With this in mind Jack Andrews and Daniel Browne had turned, as many contractors had, to markets abroad and what more lucrative than the young and burgeoning countries of the 'new world'.

Jack had volunteered to seek them out!

There were still opportunities, of course, in the building of railways in Great Britain. In the north-west, waiting on any man with the right bid, was the Ulverstone and Lancaster Railway, a nineteen-mile line from the Furness Railway at Ulverstone to the Lancaster and Carlisle Railway at Carnforth and there were others in Wales and the south of England, but the biggest challenge to men like himself and Daniel, who were contractors, was on the continents of Europe, of India, of the East and Australia, of the Americas. There was a need for men like himself, men who recognised need, men with no ties who could take ship at a moment's notice, which was why he had gone first to Canada then to the United States instead of Daniel. Men who could travel to assess that need and to satisfy it. Labour, men in their hundreds and thousands were what was wanted and Jack knew how to get his hands on them, persuade them that India, Australia or Canada were the very places they wanted to be for it was there now that the railway boom was to continue. Men knew and trusted Jack Andrews, for when he told them to move a mountain of earth they knew he knew it could be done since he had done it.

The sky was lightening rapidly and Jack felt the ship come alive beneath his feet. Barefoot sailors swarmed across the deck and sprang into the rigging. There were shouts of command, and answer, and in the wheelhouse Jack could see the captain peer ahead into the murk as the helmsman swung the great wheel.

He shoved his hands deep into his pockets, turning to brace himself against the ship's railing. It was cold with a biting wind taking the flesh from his face and slipping like a knife into the bones of him, despite his fur-lined coat. He'd needed the coat's warmth up in the wastes of Canada as he had surveyed the great expanse of land across which what was to be known as the Grand Trunk Railway of Canada was to run. Already a great tubular bridge was being planned to carry the railway across the St Lawrence River at Montreal, a marvel of engineering which would equal any bridge in the world, is was said.

From there he had gone south into the States, travelling through verdant, uninhabited forest, crossed the emptiness of the Great Plains, climbed almost into heaven itself as he traversed the Rocky Mountains, been sucked dry in the barren deserts and had become increasingly aware that it was here that his fortune was to be made.

As the wintry night fell away Jack began to distinguish landmarks which he had last seen six months ago. A fine pearly mist hung above the swelling waters over which the ship now flew and as he watched, his eyes hooded and brooding, a glint of sunlight polished the heaving flatness of the great River Mersey to a pale gold. The sky was an indistinct blue, neither night nor day as yet and above his head a dusting of stars winked and went out. Seagulls wheeled overhead, accompanying the ship on the tide. The south-swinging curve of the coast hid the city for a while and he could detect nothing but a few villas sitting comfortably among the sandhills on his left and the outline of New Brighton emerging on his right.

The houses increased in number. Waterloo and Seaforth shone out from the rising sun and on the other side of the water, as Jack swung about to watch, were the white sea walls snaking up the river to Egremont and Seacombe. He turned again to where mile after mile of dark, grey granite stretched along the docks from Huskisson Dock into the winter mists at the head of the river. There were warehouses and more warehouses storing all the great wealth that was to cross, or had already crossed, the mighty oceans of the world. His eyes rested on the fretted tower of St Nicholas Church, the sailors' church where, for Jack had seen it on one of his many walks in search of Sara, was a sundial on which was the inscription: OUR DAYS ON EARTH ARE BUT A SHADOW.

How would Jack Andrews fill his shadowed days without Sara in them?

The river had become increasingly busy as the *Shenandoah* sailed towards her mooring. The bustling highway which led to, and from, every corner of the globe was alive with ships. A tall frigate swayed gracefully on her way out to sea, bursting into white sail bloom as she went, sea-birds flying in her wake as though at the wake of a plough. The air was salty on Jack's lips and the cries of the birds rang in his head, but the cheerful bustle of the landing stage from where, it seemed, a passenger ship was about to sail, the constant shouting, hooting, whistling and banging did nothing to lift his spirits.

It was a new year tomorrow. A new decade. Where was she now, the girl who had dropped off the edge of his world into nothingness? The woman, for she was that now, whom he still cherished in the deep and hidden recesses of his heart. He had searched for her for years and found nothing so why had he come back? he asked himself, as he made his way to the cabin to collect his bag. There had been work in plenty in America, railways waiting to be built across the vast continent, across prairie and desert and mountain. He could have made a life out there but a phantom had drawn him back to his homeland and could he deny to himself that that phantom was a young and beautiful girl whose infectious laughter had captured his young man's imagination, whose goodness and honesty had captured his soul, whose loveliness had fired his young man's body and whose sweetness had remained in his heart for over four years. She would be almost twenty now, a woman, a woman perhaps married to another man. A woman with children of her own and until he had seen her, discovered the truth of her life and made certain that there was no longer any room in it for Jack Andrews, he could not settle to getting on with his own. First he would travel up to Woodhead to see his mother, immerse himself in her good, sound, practical common sense, listen to the wisdom of the down-to-earth Lancashire woman who could, with a few pithy words, put everything in its true perspective. Go back to his roots, to what had made him, get a grip on what was important to him beyond Sara before he resolved where it should take place.

There would be a delay in berthing, the respectful steward told him, owing to the late sailing of the ship for Philadelphia and the captain sent his compliments and begged his pardon and if Mr Andrews cared to join him in the wheelhouse they might take a noggin together. Jack declined politely and said he would remain where he was and to thank the captain for his offer.

The wind cut through even his warmly lined overcoat. It lifted his thick curling hair, rippling it about his head and he wondered absently where he had left his hat as he watched the confusion on the dock. That was one of the things he disliked about being successful. The damned top hat he was supposed to wear as a man of substance. His jaunty navvie's hat had been so much more to his liking.

The brougham with Thomas at the reins waited for her as usual that evening and the next but on each occasion, with a polite good evening to the astonished coachman, she walked past it, continuing on down the lane towards the main West Derby road and the city. It was mid-winter and cold as the hobs of hell, as Matty had put it succinctly early that morning but she was determined to cut Paul Travers, and the support he held out to her, from her life. Her personal life. She would, naturally, as his employee, be forced to treat with him at the House of Lovell but she would face that when it came.

On the third night his face appeared in the lighted window of the carriage, startling her, but she gave him the courteous greeting she had extended to Thomas, indeed, she included Thomas in it just as though there was no difference between Mr Paul Travers and his servant.

His face hardened but she maintained her aloof expression and steady pace until she was well past the carriage.

"Sara." The sound of the carriage door being flung open and her own name called did not stop her, though she could not help the leap of gladness nor the way in which her heart had lightened at the sight of him.

"Sara, goddammit, will you stop this nonsense at once and get into the carriage," he called after her. His voice was heavy with peril and it was directed at her. He was plainly furious at her headstrong refusal to do as she was told and when he grabbed her by the arm, swinging her about to face him she could feel the angry steel of his fingers digging into her flesh.

"Sara, what in hell's name do you think you're doing? Get into the carriage, woman. This is not the night for a two-mile walk to Abercromby Square. Bloody hell, it's going to snow soon, or so my gardener who knows about such things reliably informed me." He made a determined effort to smile and his teeth gleamed white in the darkness but she did not return it.

"Will you let go of my arm please. You are hurting me." She used a tone so cutting and so contemptuous she could see, even in the dark, the fierce prick of fury in his eyes but she did not weaken. She had made her decision over the last few days, a hard decision but one she meant to stick by, that she would continue to work at the House of Lovell since she would be a fool not to, running it as Madame had run it but with some added ideas of her own to attract the fashion-conscious ladies of Lancashire. She would become Madame Lovell, to all intents and purposes, since it seemed that was what Madame and Paul Travers had agreed but she'd not let this man believe that, along with the fashion house, he owned Sara Hamilton.

"This is bloody ridiculous, Sara, and you know it. Why won't you let me take you home? You can't walk all that way by yourself in the dark."

"I can, and I did. Last night and the night before that. Besides, I shall have Matty with me from tomorrow." Her voice was icily detached.

"But there is no need, tonight or tomorrow, whether you are with Matty or alone. The carriage is here at your disposal. Come, Thomas is chilled to the bone sitting . . ."

"Then tell him to go home. Now if you don't mind I must be on my way as I have a long walk ahead of me."

She turned on her heel, striding out into the darkness beyond the carriage lights despite the hampering weight of her long woollen gown and cloak but he would not let her go. When Thomas had told him only this morning that Miss Hamilton had rejected, for the first time in almost nine months, the offer of the carriage to take her home he had been appalled. In the past few days, ever since the one on which he had made his decision to do his best to free himself from the sweet coils of this stubborn but captivating young woman, this young woman who had murmured another man's name as she slept in his arms, it had not once occurred to him that she would now despise his help, particularly the use of his carriage. That she would prefer to trudge the long miles to Liverpool rather than be beholden to a man who had, or so it would appear to her, made love to her, used her body, then laughingly thrown diamonds in her lap as payment. Good Christ, it was no wonder she was acting as she was. She had obviously been told of his purchase of the House of Lovell which, let's face it, he had meant to give to her as a gift. But, hurting her again despite their friendship, he had not told her himself but only because he had wanted to surprise her, to savour the pleasure of her delight, he told himself, which was true but a man's name had come between them and Paul Travers shared nothing of his with another man.

He did his best to be patient.

"Come back to the carriage, Sara. We must talk," he heard himself say amazingly. "There are things to be said between us and we cannot do it here."

He was almost walking backwards, shuffling along in a ludicrous fashion, slightly in front of her which he did not find to his liking. Paul Travers had never begged for anything in his life and his arrogant nature did not care for it. Nor did he know why he persisted really, for was this not the perfect way to end a relationship which he could not control as he always had in the past? Yet he could not see her tramp the miles to the city in the pitchy dark of a December evening. No matter what had happened it was not in him to allow a woman, any woman to walk the dark hours unprotected.

"If you will not come back to the carriage," which had begun to follow them towards West Derby Road, "then I shall walk home with you," he told her quietly, stepping in beside her, "and if you persist in this foolishness in the future then I shall simply wait for you each night at the gate and accompany you to Abercromby Square. You can refuse to ride in the carriage, Sara, but you cannot prevent me from walking with you."

She stopped abruptly, her breath exploding from her with a violence which spoke of her anger. She whirled to face him, her cloak spinning out like a fan before settling again in graceful folds about her. It had a wide hood edged with a pale fur, he did not know what sort, for though the cloak was heavy and serviceable, it was her nature to add some small but elegant touch which lifted it from the ordinary. The brougham with the bewildered Thomas on the seat above the rump of the horse had drawn up beside them and the light from the carriage lamps fell on her framed face. It was drawn into lines of implacable fury, a fury which Paul should have welcomed, for again it would have made it that much easier to leave her. Instead he could feel the weakening of his bones, the surging rush of his blood through his veins, the foolish leaping of his heart. He could not go and he could not stay, that was his dilemma and all because of a man called Jack.

"Who is Jack?" he heard himself saying before she could speak, then leaped forward to catch her as she swayed into his arms. Even in the faint light of the carriage lamps he had seen the shock drain her face, seen her eyes darken and go blank, her lips part in what seemed to him to be a cry of anguish though no sound came from between them.

"Sara . . . Dear God, Sara," he cried hoarsely, swinging her limp body up into his arms. Her head lolled back against his arm and her hood fell away from her bleached face. He cradled her against him in an agony of remorse then turned to shout up at the open-mouthed coachman.

"Don't just sit there, you bloody fool. Get down and open the carriage door and be quick about it."

Dolly had cried out in terror and even Lily had fallen back, her hand to her mouth, when Mr Travers carried the huddled form of their Sara into the narrow hallway. Matty, her son in her arms, shrieked and nearly dropped him but Paul merely brushed past them on his way to the stairs which led up to Sara's room.

"She's all right, Mrs Canon, really she is. She's had a shock and . . ."

"I'll put t'kettle on then, or p'raps a brandy . . .?"

"There's no need for either, Mrs Canon, I'll attend to her. Is the fire lit in her room?"

"Yes, sir. I did it meself an 'our since."

"Good, then thank you, Mrs Canon, that will be all," just as though she was one of his bloody servants, Lily thought indignantly and she'd be damned if she'd let him carry their Sara up the stairs, her stairs, mind, sweeping aside all those who loved her and worried over her as though it were nowt to do with them!

"I'll come up wi' yer, sir. She'll need— "

He turned on her, heavy with menace, ready to tell her to mind her own bloody business, she could see, his brows dipped in fierce anger, his face strained into deep lines from some violent emotion he evidently felt, but before he could speak Sara's voice drifted weakly from somewhere in the region of his collarbone where her face was buried.

"It's all right, Lily, I'm all right, really I am. I'll be down to see you all shortly but Mr Travers and I . . . we have something to discuss."

"But why's 'e carryin' yer, lamb? 'Ave yer 'urt yerself? See, let me come up an' . . ."

"No, please, Lily. I just . . . twisted my ankle getting into the carriage, that is all. Clumsy of me but there it is."

"'Appen it needs a compress then."

You could tell Lily Canon didn't believe a word of it. Dolly was old and bewildered and Matty young and foolish and ready to be taken in by anything any man told her – hence the baby in her arms! – but Lily wasn't daft, nor was she blind. There was something more here than a twisted ankle. This man was . . . well, not to put too fine a point on it, their Sara's lover. He'd stayed the night on Christmas Eve and they'd all kept their gobs shut but that didn't mean they liked it, or him, charming as he was. Anyone who hurt Sara Hamilton would have to answer to Lily Canon for it and she was none too happy with the way things were going.

He was halfway up the stairs by now and short of treading on his heels and risk being shoved down again Lily had no option but to remain where she was.

"I'll be up directly," she called warningly.

"There's no need, Lily," Sara's voice floated down to her. "Put the kettle on and I'll come down to you shortly."

He placed her gently in the chair, pulling up the footstool and resting her feet on it just as though she really had injured her ankle. He eased her cloak from about her shoulders, brushed back the tangled curls from her forehead with a tender hand, smiled at her then knelt to give the fire a vigorous stir. He heaped on more coal, placing it as carefully as he had seen his mother's parlourmaid do, then straightened up, reached into his pocket for his handkerchief and destroyed its immaculately ironed whiteness as he wiped the coal dust from his fingers.

"Shall I make tea?" he asked diffidently, hovering on the hearth-rug, his size, his virility, his obvious prosperity out of place in this room which, though clean and warm, was not of the order to which he was accustomed.

"No, thank you." Sara leaned back in the chair and sighed, staring into the leaping flames of the fire then looked up at him, holding his gaze for several moments, her eyes filled with a clear light he did not recognise.

"How did you know about Jack?" she said.

"You . . . spoke his name."

She looked surprised. "Spoke his name? When?"

He was restless, moving from the fireside to the door, then back again, touching her cloak which he had flung on the chair before he answered.

"The other night. The night we made love."

"Aah . . ." She looked hastily down at her hands which began pleating folds in her skirt, her face flushing a lovely rosy pink.

"You remember that night, Sara?" His voice was quite neutral. He returned to the fireplace and leaned one elbow on the mantelshelf above it, affecting a casualness he did not feel. Reaching into his waistcoat pocket he withdrew a cigar, smelled the aroma of it for a moment then placed it between his teeth. He did not light it. She found herself watching him, watching the reflections and shadows which chased one another across his stern face, watching his hands, strong, long-fingered, his hands which a few nights ago had brought to life the tiny fuse Jack had lit in her as a girl. She had not known it was there, nor that it had been burning slowly all these years waiting for the explosion of pleasure Paul had fired in her.

At the memory of what they had done together, what she had allowed to be done to her she felt herself blush hotly. Not with shame but with shy delight.

"I see you do," he went on, smiling a little, in his blue eyes a vivid starry brilliance that told of his own keen sense of gratification, "but when you fell asleep and I held you . . ." He turned away then, making a small, tight sound in his throat, "I . . . you were so . . ." Again he cleared his throat then, in a rush as though to get it said before he lost his nerve, "You spoke his name, Jack."

"I'm sorry. I can understand why . . . how you . . . why you should feel insulted, but it is not what you think."

"What do I think, Sara?" His voice was again expressionless, though from beneath her lowered lids she could see the tremble of his fingers which held the unlit cigar.

"That I, that Jack and I were . . ."

"Yes? You and Jack . . .?"

"We were never lovers, Paul. I was . . . we were too young." She looked up at him then and the clear, honest truth shone from her eyes. They brimmed with tears which did not fall.

"Tell me, Sara. Tell me all of it. I know nothing much of

your life before we met. You are still young, too young to
... dear God in heaven." For a moment he lost control of
the iron will which held him. "You were a child, a beautiful
child when we met and cannot have ..."

He bowed his head, his distress so great she stood up and
went to him, putting a hand on his arm, feeling the muscles
tense beneath his sleeve.

"Paul," she said softly. He looked at her hand, then at her.

"Tell me about Jack, Sara."

"What do you want to know?"

"Everything. Who he was, everything."

"He was a ... navvie."

"A navvie!" Had it not been himself who was involved he
might have laughed it was so bloody preposterous.

"Yes."

"Do you mean to tell me you formed an attachment with
a common working man? You who are so fine, so lovely. A
navvieman! One of those who ..."

She stiffened, drawing away from him, pictures of Jack
in his immaculate navvieman's outfit, pictures so clear and
beloved the man before her fell away into the shadows Jack's
brightness created. Jack, brown eyes, deep, warm, filled with
his honest love. Jack laughing, impish, Jack serious, dedicated
to his work and their future together. Worthy of any woman's
love had been Jack Andrews and she would not let this man
tarnish his memory.

"He was a good man, a brave man and what his work was
made no difference to me. He was honestly employed." Her
voice had grown cool. "He worked on the railway near Wray
Green."

"Tell me about him." Her coolness alarmed him for it meant
the man had been something to her but he kept his face
expressionless.

She became quiet, still, as though she were caught in some
timeless moment in which he had no part, even her breathing
slowing and he knew she had gone from him, gone back into
the past ... with Jack.

"We were picking blackberries, Alice and I. September it
was, a hot day and I had washed my hair. Alice was cross,
saying I was ... oh, I don't remember her words but she did
not approve of it hanging down my back."

Her eyes became soft and shadowy, dark as woodland

moss as memory took her back to that day and Paul wanted to throw himself across the room and shake her until she came back to him but he had asked for the truth and so he must listen to it.

"They came out of nowhere, a gang of men and . . . and with them was Jack."

Paul flinched at the softness in her voice as she spoke the man's name, turning away from her, staring blindly at the sketches on the wall, for could he bear what she was going to tell him?

"Alice stood up to them. She had a stick . . ." She laughed brokenly and put her hand to her mouth. "She was always brave, braver than me, but they were . . . offensive. They wanted to . . ."

"Dear sweet Christ." He would have gone to her but she put out a hand to stop him.

". . . I was fifteen and had never . . . They said things . . ." Her voice died away to nothing and his heart constricted with pain, hers and his own. Tears like great fat raindrops dripped across her pale cheeks.

"Sara . . ."

"No, let me go on. They were rough and there was no-one to help us, except Jack. I didn't see him at the back of the gang. I was so frightened . . ."

"Sara, darling, don't go on if . . ."

"But he fought them. Jack stood up and fought them, at least a dozen. Run, he said. Run like the wind, he said to me and Alice and when my father brought him home I thought he was . . . was dead. They beat him, broke his body. He was so badly injured my father . . . he might not walk again, he told me. I helped to nurse him."

"He was a courageous man," he said simply.

She smiled brilliantly. "Oh he was, Paul, he was."

Paul straightened up and the expression of anguish on his face began to fade a little. It was not what he had expected, dreaded and the relief began to sing through him like some lovely melody, filling his heart with wonder, wonder and astonishment that he could have been so insane. She had been a child, fifteen, and like a fifteen-year-old girl she had formed a romantic attachment for the knight in shining armour who had slain the dragon. It was just like her to make no difference between a rough-spoken navvieman and . . . well, her own father who had been a doctor and had taught her his own convictions. This man, whoever he was, had saved her, and thank God for it, from a terrifying experience and so she had believed herself in love with him. It had been no more than that.

"My father restored him to health. He was with us, Dolly and Alice, Papa and me for two months then . . . then he went up north, to find work and . . ."

"I'm sorry, dear God, I'm so sorry. Will you ever forgive me?" His voice broke as he moved to take her hands. "I thought . . ."

She freed one of her hands and laid it on his own pale cheek.

"Paul, what is it, Paul?"

"I thought . . . I'm a jealous bastard, Sara. I thought he was . . . that there was another man. Forgive me."

"I haven't seen Jack in almost four years. I don't even know where he is. You are the only man who . . ." She bobbed her head and colour flooded her face.

He could feel himself unfold inside, just as though everything that had been tied tightly had loosened, everything that had been clamped shut had opened, everything that had been gripped in a fetter of madness had been released and had moved thankfully into its own place.

He took her hand, the one that rested gently against his cheek, turning it so that his lips were warm in its palm, then in a great exultation of joy drew her fiercely into his arms and held her tightly against him.

"Sara, my lovely girl, oh my love." His arms cradled her and his hands stroked her hair and he rocked her, not to ease her pain, but his own. The jealous pain he had suffered during the past week and for nothing.

"You're tired," he said at last, reluctantly. "I'll go but I'll be here first thing in the morning. There is much I want to say to you, Sara Hamilton. To ask you . . ."

She put her hands behind his head and, sighing delicately into his mouth, drew it down until it rested on her own. Her kiss was warm and moist.

"Don't go," she murmured. "Send Thomas home and stay with me."

* * *

Her hand rested in the crook of his arm and his right hand held it as they sauntered past St Nicholas Church. It was barely nine thirty, the first day of the new year, the first day of the new decade and the first day of their new life and they were like children, made up with it, enchanted with each other and with the world. Paul talked, talked to her as though he could not contain all he had to tell her, though he would save the best until later, he told her, his eyes deep with the knowledge of what else they would do later. They were at ease with one another for they had been friends before they became lovers and heads turned to look at them for they emanated the joy that only lovers display. He spoke of his family, of his business, his love of ships and the sea. He even told her how old he was and she didn't seem to mind. He had no conception of how his love for her had affected him so that though he told her forty in his boyish delight, he could have passed for fifteen years younger.

She spoke of Wray Green and Dolly, of her dead mama whom she still missed and of her papa whom she had loved dearly. Of Alice who had looked after her for many years and who, despite their differences, she still looked out for. Of the House of Lovell and her plans for its future, that is if he would allow it, she added shyly, wondering why he grinned so hugely in answer. Of Matty who was to be such a help to her, of Jamie who she was still afraid to hold and of her belief that she and Matty would have to live in at Lovell House, again if it was all right with him.

They had decided on a walk along the Marine Parade but George's Dock was so crowded they could barely get through. There were hundreds of people milling about in great confusion, men and women and children, some soberly dressed and quietly respectable with a good box between them, others in shawls, men in worn, mended trouser and jackets, scarves and a cap and no more than a bundle apiece tied up in a bit of cloth. Though there was evidently a great gulf between them, socially and financially, the expression on every face was the same. Fear, fear of the unknown and sadness, a deep despairing sadness as though they were to part with the dearest thing they possessed. They were, many of them, for to leave the shores of a beloved homeland, no matter for what cause, is hard.

"What is happening?" Sara murmured, leaning closer to Paul who put a protective arm about her.

"They are emigrating. Sailing for Philadelphia, I believe, on the packet ship. Irish, a lot of them. There is famine. You will have read of it?"

"Yes, oh yes."

"See." Paul pointed to a hollow-cheeked man and woman nearby with half a dozen wizened children clinging to the woman's skirt. A dazed old grandmother held a baby, dreadfully silent, and beyond the dock lay the ship which was to carry them to their hope for the future. The packet ship *Independence*, bound for Philadelphia on the next tide.

Everywhere people wept and hung about one another's neck and Sara felt the great swell of happiness she had known this day ebb away, dashed on the rocks of her heart as she compared it to the misery which was all about her.

"I'll try and get through, hang on to my arm," Paul said grimly as he began to push his way towards Princes Dock, though that seemed equally crowded as a second ship was being brought to her mooring.

An officer was shouting commands from the deck of the second ship, the *Shenandoah*, she was called, and men scampered up masts and spars. Sails were furled and seamen juggled with ropes and along the rail those who were about to disembark watched impatiently. Men mostly, in top hats and warm overcoats for the wind was cutting off the river.

Except one! He was hatless and the wind ruffled his curling hair, lifting it and tossing it across his forehead. He reached up a hand to push it back and when his eyes met hers it was as though someone had driven a nail into her heart, a nail which twisted and turned, doing untold damage to flesh and muscle. Her heart recoiled, bucking away from the pain, and the memory of pain, but it did no good, it would not let go, hammering and hammering until it was unbearable. She could not breathe. Her frame shook as though it was buffeted by a great storm and she cried out so loudly Paul turned to her in alarm.

"What is it, my love, what is it?" He drew her into the shelter of a stack of boxes, holding her by the shoulders as he peered anxiously into her face, his own spasming in concern, for she continued to shudder as though with a chill. He put his arms about her, pressing her face into the solid comfort of his chest, his back to the docking ship.

"What is it, my darling?" he asked her again, holding her away from him for a moment to look into her face.

Making a great effort, one that took every atom of strength she possessed, she looked beyond Paul's broad shoulder, across the seething activity which precedes the docking of a sailing ship, beyond the rail of the ship and across the years which had divided them, into the unbelieving face of Jack Andrews.

For an eternity their eyes clung and for an exquisite moment in that eternity she felt the empty place inside her that only he could fill ease gently, thankfully, with joy. She saw his lips form her name. He drew himself up, his face lit with his incredulous love, ready, she was convinced, to do away with gangplanks and such and leap the rail directly on to the landing stage.

"What is it, my little love?" she heard Paul say with such a wealth of love and tenderness in his voice she wanted to look up at him, to smile and . . . and . . . but Jack's eyes would not let her.

Paul put an arm about her and she watched as the physical shape of Jack's face changed. It was as though a fist had smashed into it. As though he had been poleaxed as the beasts at the slaughterhouse are poleaxed and the result was much the same.

His eyes died. They simply died then he turned away, the sight of her in the arms of another man too much for him to bear.

She did not see him again as the tears came to blind her.

29

She and Matty, with Jamie tucked up warmly in a wicker basket, moved into Lovell House on January 4th.

"I shall sleep in the bedroom at the corner of the house, the one at the front overlooking the rose garden," she told the cook-housekeeper who had been summoned to the sitting-room which had once been Madame Lovell's. Mrs Atkins did not like being summoned. Mrs Atkins had not been across the threshold since the day, many years ago now, when Madame had told her she had no wish to be consulted on such things as what Mrs Atkins was to prepare for dinner, who Mrs Atkins hired and fired, what provisions she bought and who did what in the house, as long as Madame found everything to her liking. Rules had been laid down on that first day, rules Madame Lovell wished to see enforced and if one of them was broken, if a fire was left unlit, a sideboard undusted, a spoon unpolished, a carpet unbrushed or a meal not to her liking, then Mrs Atkins would be held to blame. In other words Madame wanted perfection. She didn't want to know how Mrs Atkins achieved it, she just wanted it!

Now here was this little upstart – who was well liked, Mrs Atkins admitted, but who was no better than she should be for why else would Mr Travers have put her in charge? – telling her which bedroom she would require. It'd be the girl who sat beside her next, the one who dandled a handsome baby on her knee and had the brazen effrontery not only to meet Mrs Atkins's eye, but to stare her out. No shame, none of them, girls of today and these two seemed to be thriving on their sinful ways. If this hadn't been such a comfortable and easy place and had she herself been twenty years younger, she'd hand in her notice on the spot.

"D'yer not fancy Madame's bedroom then?" she asked insolently and was glad to see Miss Sara Hamilton flinch as though she had hit her, but she lifted her head just like she was mistress of the house and the girl who sat beside her smirked for some reason.

"I'm glad you brought that up, Mrs Atkins."

"Oh aye?" Lady Muck might be in charge of the business but Mrs Atkins ran the kitchen, the servants and the house and if anything was said about it she'd go straight to Mr Travers and tell him. She'd have no slip of a girl who didn't know when to keep her hand on her halfpenny meddling in *her* domain.

"Yes, I might as well tell you now, then you can pass it on to the other servants."

Mrs Atkins waited, her hands crossed warningly over her immaculately starched and ironed apron. Her white frilled bobcap was drawn down to cover every last wisp of her iron grey hair and her eyes stared unblinkingly at the flibbertigibbet who was the master's mistress! Her face was mutinous but somehow she could not quite bring herself to open and contemptuous defiance.

"Well?" she asked resentfully.

"You are probably not aware of who owns this house, Mrs Atkins, this house and this business. This property to the very walls of its boundaries. If you were you would not be taking this recalcitrant attitude."

"Pardon?" Mrs Atkins looked confused.

"I will overlook your . . . awkwardness this time, since I want us to get on."

"I beg your pardon!"

"Now look 'ere, yer stupid old cow. Yer'd best watch yer mouth or— "

Lady Muck put out a restraining hand, placing it on the other one's arm and for the first time Mrs Atkins took a good look at her. At Lady Muck, that is. She was beautifully dressed as always in the black velvet magazinière's outfit of skirt, bolero and cream ruffled shirt which was so dashing and which suited her so well. Her vibrant copper hair was brushed back into an enormous bun which was enclosed in a black velvet net at the back of her head. She was as smart as she always was but she had not that glowing, polished look of youth, that tawny gloss of health, that delicate bloom of fresh loveliness which they had all grown used to. In fact, she looked bloody awful, Mrs Atkins was inclined to think, her eyes seeming to stare off at something only she could see and her head cocked as though she were listening for something only she could hear. Perhaps she was breeding and if she was, what was to happen to the House of Lovell?

Mrs Atkins straightened up, narrowing her eyes as they ran speculatively over Sara Hamilton's figure.

"Please, Matty, leave this to me," Miss Hamilton said to the girl who had just spoken.

"Well, she's no right ter talk ter yer like that, silly old sod. Doesn't know which side 'er bread's buttered, obviously."

"Mrs Atkins, what Miss Hutchinson is trying to tell you is that I am the owner of this house, this property, this fashion business, in fact everything that once belonged to Madame Lovell is now mine, so you see I am your employer. You are my servant, my cook-housekeeper and I am quite happy to keep it that way, if you are. Madame Lovell was satisfied with your work and with the way you ran the house and supervised the other servants. That is reference enough for me. Your wages will remain the same until I am satisfied that the service I require and which you gave to Madame Lovell is to continue, then I shall consider giving you all a rise. Now, have you anything to say, Mrs Atkins?"

Miss Hamilton raised an imperious head and Mrs Atkins was struck by her likeness to her sister. Miss Hoity-Toity they had called Alice Hamilton and dear God, don't let this one be going the same way or it would be hell on earth for the lot of them.

Then Miss Hamilton smiled, a smile of such sweetness despite her ravaged face, Freda Atkins felt the breath sigh out of her thankfully. Miss Hamilton'd let no one mess her about, that was evident from the tilt of her well-bred head but she'd be fair, even good to them if they shaped, her smile told her.

"Yes, mum."

"Go on, Mrs Atkins."

"Will yer be wantin' a fire in your bedroom? Madame liked one in the winter."

"Thank you, Mrs Atkins, that would be lovely, and" – she turned to the other one, Miss Hutchinson— "which room would you like, Matty? Perhaps the one with the smaller one off it? It would make a convenient nursery for Jamie."

"That'd be grand, queen, which reminds me. I'd best be givin' 'im 'is dinner else 'e'll be shoutin' th'odds," though her son was gazing contentedly into the dancing flames of the fire with no sign of any "odds shouting". "I'll slip inter't little parlour what's at the end of th'all. Is that all right?"

"Ycs, of course. You could make it your own sitting-room, just for you and Jamie when you want to be alone," leaving no doubt in the minds of both women that should Mr Travers call he would want a place to sit with her without interruption. "Of course," she added hastily, "you are more than welcome to share . . . well, I suppose I had better get used to calling it *my* room, when I am alone."

She glanced about the lovely room which Rosalie Lovell had decorated and furnished to her own elegant taste, but her expression was one of indifference as though however it was decorated and furnished it was all the same to her and Mrs Atkins wondered what had happened to her since Christmas.

"Right, queen, ta. I'll not be long."

Miss Hutchinson hoisted her son to her shoulder, smiled at Miss Hamilton and left the room, presumably in the direction of the small back parlour.

"And that is another thing, Mrs Atkins."

"Yes, mum?"

"Miss Hutchinson will be needing a nursemaid for Jamie. Could you help us there?"

Mrs Atkins ran her mind past several of her nieces of whom she had many, two already working at the house.

"I can, mum. I know the very girl."

"Good, then that will be all, Mrs Atkins. Will you see to the bedrooms right away, please and have Roberts take up the boxes which are at the front door. They are clearly marked. I shall leave it all in your capable hands. I'm sure you and I understand one another now and will get along well."

"Yes, mum, thank you, mum."

She couldn't wait to get back to the kitchen where the reception of her news was most gratifying. Mrs Atkins was in charge, the dispenser of discipline, the giver of orders which she expected to be obeyed, an autocrat and a perfectionist but she was so overcome by their new situation, the bombshell of their new mistress, she was as excited as the scullery maid who was only twelve. She let them all get into such a state that for several minutes there was bedlam with maidservants milling about like sheep escaped from a pen with no sheep dog to guide them.

"I don't believe it."

"Eeh, an' 'er no more 'n nineteen."

"Course, we know 'ow she gorrit, don't we?"

"Madame'd turn over in 'er grave."

"Madame's not dead, yer fool, an' she sold it to 'im what give it to 'er."

"What about our jobs?"

"Reckon she'll fall flat on 'er face," and so on and so on for at least five long chaotic minutes until Mrs Atkins, suddenly growing alarmed at the turmoil her news had caused, called them all to order in a voice which they recognised at once.

"Now then, you lot, that's enough. What d'yer think this is, a party? It don't matter who owns the place we've our work ter see to an' there's plenty o' that so let's get at it. You, Sally, take Clara an' the pair of you set to on the front corner bedroom. What? Yes, the yellow one," since Madame had decorated each bedroom in a different colour scheme, "an' then you can start on the pink. Yes, I know Madame called it rose but it's pink ter me. Turn both rooms out, air the beds, clean bedlinen an' a fire ter be lit in both rooms. And that dressing-room off the pink room's ter be for't babby. That's enough, that's enough!" as commotion exploded once more at the reference to the "babby" for not one of them, decent folk all, had ever been exposed to an illegitimate child before. "Now scoot, the pair of you, an' Freddy . . ." She turned majestically, beckoning to the boot boy who was not awfully sure what was happening, only that it made a nice change from working the knife-cleaning machine which the footman, Roberts, had set him to.

"I want yer to dash over to Old Meadow Farm, yer know where I mean?"

"Yes, Cook."

"Tell me then." She fixed him with a stern look and he drew himself up bravely.

"It's where yer sister lives, Cook."

"An' what's 'er name?"

"Mrs Watson, Cook."

"Right then. I'm goin' ter write 'er a note an' yer ter purrit in 'er 'and. Understand?"

"Yes, Cook."

"Tell 'er it's very urgent. What've yer ter tell 'er?"

"That it's very urgent, Cook."

"Good lad. Now before yer go 'elp yerself to one 'o them biscuits what Mary's just gorrout of the oven."

The soft black numbness which she had managed to gather about her began to tremble in panic as soon as Mrs Atkins shut the door behind her. She closed her eyes and at once Jack's face sprang vividly into the space behind her eyelids. She watched it, as she had watched it when Paul put his arms about her on the landing stage and she began to moan silently behind her clenched teeth. She had seen it alter from disbelief, to incredulous love and joy, then, as the awareness of what he saw struck him, to the swift, downward spiral of horror and despair. So many years between them, so much pain and loneliness and when at last they looked on one another again she had been in the arms of another man. It was not to be borne but somehow she must bear it.

It was making her ill though, and those who loved her were concerned about her, asking what was wrong. Had she pain? Could they call the doctor? Was it something she had eaten, or perhaps picked up at the docks where many strange people, meaning foreigners, hung about? She could neither sleep nor eat, despite the egg custards Lily made for her since they were "light and nourishing", the broths and soups, even the ice-cream Paul brought round from the ice-house at New Park House. She had lost so much weight in four days her gowns were already beginning to hang on her and for the first time in her life she had used a touch of rouge to disguise the hollow pallor of her cheeks. She found her mind had a tendency to drift, wanting to probe at memories then shying away from them when they hurt her. She dreamed, when she did finally fall into a light doze, in an explosion of colour. Jack in his multi-hued navvie's outfit, his white teeth gleaming in his sun-browned face, his white felt hat pushed to the back of his chestnut curls. The bright golden yellow of the field at the far side of the blackberry hedge on the day the gang found her and Alice and the crimson of the poppies they had stepped on as they backed into the ditch. Bright blue skies and a purple-red stain of blackberry juice on her own fingers.

Her face would be wet with tears when she awoke and she knew if she was to recover from this second mortal blow she must find some way to forget it. To shroud it in a mist of forgetfulness and go on in the life she had built for herself since she and Alice had moved to Liverpool.

Paul had been distraught when, for the second time in two days she had fallen against him, lifting her up into his arms, shouting savagely to those about them to "make way there" and as he hurried with her towards the cab rank at the back of George's Dock she had known with every shrinking, shrieking nerve end in her body that Jack was watching them.

Lily had screeched in terror and Dolly fell back in her chair and had one of her turns when Paul carried her up the steps and into the house and this time he let Lily take her, put her in a chair opposite Dolly, chafe her hands and gaze frantically into her blank and ashen face. Surely this time, his incoherent mind babbled, it must be some "woman's thing" which had struck her. Perhaps it was her time of the month and how was he, a helpless male, to deal with that, allowing himself to be pushed to the back of the room while the women fussed round her.

But she had wanted him. She had turned great dark eyes to him and begged him to take her upstairs. In her room he had sat down in her chair beside the fire and gathered her firmly into his lap. With his arms about her he had rocked her gently, murmuring soft, unintelligible words in her ear, smoothing her hair back from her face, kissing her brow. She had wept and though he had not understood why he had not pressed her to tell him. He stroked her back and her neck and offered her the only comfort he had and which she seemed to need, the comfort of his broad, warm chest.

After a while she calmed, leaning tiredly into the curve of his shoulder and even then he did not question her. He did not know why she wept, nor what had changed her from the laughing, enchanting young woman of this morning to the grief-stricken child she had become. Some male instinct in him seemed to say it was to do with the man called Jack. The man she had cherished since she was fifteen years old as her knight in shining armour. Perhaps the telling of his tale last night had awakened her memories of him. Women were such strange, romantic creatures, their imaginations thrilling to sentimental images of men's stoicism in the face of danger. She had carried this man's courage about with her for over four years and now, now that she had become his, Paul Travers's mistress, she was, or so he told himself, saying farewell to the fantasy and, with a woman's frailty, it was distressing her.

"Don't leave me, Paul," she had begged him fiercely and he knew this time it was his comfort she wanted, not his body. When, later, he had undressed her and put her in her nightgown she had clung to him so desperately he had shed his own clothes and, climbing into her narrow bed where last night he had brought her to ecstatic climax after climax of love, he had held her gently, making no attempt to do more than tenderly stroke her back and face.

Except to slip back to his rooms for a change of clothing and to his office to check that his "fellow" was carrying on in his absence he had not left her. He did not make love to her. He did not question her, merely watching her, holding her hand, smiling at her in a way which would have astounded those who knew him. Tender as a mother with a child, he was as he waited, knowing she would be his again. Loving her, patient, ready for her when she needed him.

Last night he had slept beside her in the bed in the attic room at Abercromby Square and tonight he was to share her bed in the front corner room at Lovell House.

She felt a small stirring of amusement inside her, for what would they make of that, these women of her household who she knew called her "whore" behind her back. She had yet to speak to the seamstresses though she was pretty certain that by now the servants' grapevine would have passed on the incredible news that Sara Hamilton, who four days ago had been magazinière at the House of Lovell, now owned the bloody lot. She had been in and out of the sewing-rooms this morning, pretending an interest in Dilly Parker's reports, thanking God that Madame Lovell seemed to have had the gift of picking exactly the right kind of woman to work in her fashion house. Dilly was no genius but during these past four days, while Madame sailed off to a life of idleness in Italy or France or wherever her fancy took her and Sara Hamilton nursed her badly injured heart and spirit, Dilly had been like a rock, keeping it all together. Set the sewing girls in her care to tasks which had fallen behind in the Christmas rush.

Christening robes and petticoats which needed smocking and embroidering, the sorting of materials and sewing threads; the making up of six nightgowns ordered by Sara before Christmas as a present for the women with whom she lodged. She would pay Madame the full price for them, she had said laughingly. Before Christmas. Before Paul. Before Jack.

She bent her head into her hands, then straightened up again sharply, willing herself not to drift away again. Thank God it was January. Christmas and new year over and the ladies of Liverpool not yet thinking of their spring outfits but they would be soon and would they order them at the House of Lovell now that Madame Lovell no longer owned it?

She stood up awkwardly. The ache in her heart seemed to spread to every other part of her body, making her joints hurt and her head throb but she knew that if she sat about and contemplated them she would lose herself for ever.

She moved slowly towards the window, drawing aside the velvet drapes to look out on to the garden. Her garden. It was bare, cold and grim, covered still by the thick hoar frost which had continued since before Christmas. A wintry sun hung almost colourless behind the black fretwork of the giant oaks and smoke drifted from the chimneys to obscure it further. From one of the tree's spread roots rabbits bobbed and nibbled, searching for food, and rooks rose in the sky above them in an explosive trail. It was all so desolate, so exactly matching what was in her heart she wanted simply to drift back to the fire, huddle over it, do nothing, fade away, die!

She was about to turn away from the window when something caught her eye. Something small and unassuming, a delicate touch of colour at the base of an oak tree, yellow and blue and white, barely revealed in the hollow made by the tree's roots.

All thought left her as she opened the long French window and stepped out on to the terrace. Her mind was blank like a page which is not yet written on, waiting for the hand which was to put words, or pictures, on to it. It was bitterly cold and the air was hard as she drew it into her lungs.

Leaving the window standing wide open, she moved slowly across the terrace and down the steps to the crisp lawn. Where her skirt brushed it as she drifted across the frozen ground she left a ruffled trail and Clara and Sally, who were cleaning her bedroom windows, stared, wide-eyed and slack-jawed as their new mistress, without coat or bonnet and who must have lost her mind, trailed off in the direction of the stand of trees at the front of the house.

They were crocus, and mixed with them were snowdrops. Only just sprung from the leaf mould which had collected in the roots of the trees, they grew, shyly tender and new and full of the promise of the spring to come and the picture of them was at once printed delicately on to her empty mind.

She sank to her knees, unaware that the maids were nudging one another at the upstairs window, nor that Paul Travers was moving slowly across the grass towards her. She put out a hand and gently placed a forefinger, first on one fragile spear and then on another, mesmerised by something which whispered within her and by the frail beauty of the flowers which, despite the hardness about them, were living and growing in hope.

"Sara."

She turned and smiled up at him, then held out her hands. He took them and wonderingly lifted her to her feet for there was colour in her face and her eyes were a lovely vivid green.

"Paul, I was looking at the crocus and the snowdrops."

"So I see, my darling."

"And there were rabbits."

"There usually are, sweetheart." His expression was one of such tenderness, such a great and unquestioning love, she found herself unable to look away from him. Not that she wanted to for he was good to look at. She blinked, then, reaching up, she kissed him gently. They stood facing one another, hands still linked and at the window the goggle-eyed maids giggled, watching in amazement.

"Do you know how much you mean to me?" she asked simply.

"Tell me, but first let's go inside."

"No, I'd rather stay here. It's winter, cold, bleak midwinter but the spring is to come. Good things are to come and I must be ready for them."

She was telling him she was to recover from what it was that ailed her.

He let go of one of her hands and touched her cheek fleetingly, his eyes moving across her face, then he sighed.

"Tell me," he said at last.

"I don't really know where to begin. I don't really know where it began, or when, but I know how much you mean to me. You are the dearest man in the world, Paul, in my world and I want to be with you. Is it foolish to say . . . how funny you are?"

"Funny! I'm not sure I like the sound of that," but he was grinning in that wry, lopsided way he had.

"I mean you make me laugh."

"That's better and I'm glad. Laughter is very serious."

"There, you see. That's what I mean."

"You're a funny little thing yourself, my love."

"We suit each other then."

"It seems we do, my precious."

"I'm safe with you, Paul, and yet life is exciting, if you know what I mean."

"And it will be even more exciting in the future, my pet. I intend taking you to magical places you have never even heard of. You shall come with me on my ships to . . ."

He stopped for she had retreated from him a little, beginning to shiver as though the cold had just struck her. The bright flush left her cheek but her eyes still shone with an incandescence which he knew was the light of her feelings for him, feelings she was allowing him to see for the first time.

But she was still not herself. She was still frail and vulnerable to something in her past and he was not to know, as he drew her under his cloak and led her across the lawn towards the open French window that though Sara Hamilton depended on him, leaned on him, allowed him to love her body, thought him the dearest man in the world, she had not said the words, "I love you" for she could not ignore the terrifying, the glorious, the sweetness of the emotion she had just reinterred in her heart for Jack Andrews.

30

The carriage containing Jack Andrews, Daniel Browne and Daniel's daughter Margaret drew up in front of the house, the faces of all three registering the extent of their wondering approval.

Jack whistled in admiration, turning to pull a face at Daniel.

"Jesus, Dan, you never told me you had such influential friends. Oh, I'm sorry, Miss Browne, I really do apologise. I am in the company of men so much I forget my manners sometimes." He smiled disarmingly, reaching out through the open window of the carriage to open the door but he was forestalled by a liveried footman in a wig.

"Dear God, will you look at the flunkey," he murmured in Miss Browne's ear but she turned to frown at him and he sighed, allowing himself to be handed down on to the gravelled driveway. Miss Browne followed, fluffing out the wide skirt of her evening gown, patting her hair and arranging her cloak. She was obviously nervous, for though Daniel Browne, whose only chick she was, was a wealthy man, she had never before moved in such illustrious circles as these.

Lights spilled out from every uncurtained window at the front of the house, and from the opened front door where menservants stood unobtrusively to help the guests. There were maidservants to assist the ladies, guiding them to a room where they might leave their wraps and where another maid, a ladies maid, was ready to do repairs to a hair arrangement should it be needed.

The hallway was luminous with candlelight and fragrant with hothouse blooms and from somewhere came the faint but tantalising aroma of the meal they were to eat.

"Are you sure it's all right, Dan?" Jack muttered as a poker-faced butler divested him of his evening cape. Miss Browne had vanished for the moment, to the ladies room, he supposed, so he could speak as he wanted. "Me coming along at the last minute like this, I mean. Bloody hell, won't it upset the seating arrangements or something? Not that I know much about it since me mam wasn't one for dinner parties but I've heard there has to be equal numbers of each sex."

"Don't worry, lad." Daniel was a Yorkshireman and spoke as broadly as Jack. "When I told Mr Travers you were here overnight he said to fetch you along. Some chap'd been taken ill so his mother'd be glad of someone to make up the numbers."

"Well, if you say so."

"I do . . . aah, here's Margaret," offering his daughter his arm.

Carriages continued to roll up the drive behind them as they were ushered up the wide, richly panelled hallway. They were offered sherry as soon as they entered the drawing-room where they were looked over by a dozen pairs of well-bred eyes but at once their host was there, extending his hand first to Miss Browne, to her father and then to Jack.

"It's good of you to invite me, sir," Jack said politely, sipping his sherry which was much too sweet for his liking.

"You are most welcome, Mr Andrews and for God's sake don't drink that bloody stuff if you don't want to. My mother serves it for the ladies. How about a whisky?"

He snapped his fingers and at once a manservant materialised, making Jack blink, but he found himself warming to this man who, though he was a good deal older than himself and came from an old Liverpool family of much influence, had a smile which seemed to mock everything, just as though none of this meant anything really. He had been brought up in this world of ease and luxury where other men jumped silently to do his bidding and therefore was so used to it he took it for granted but he had a look of humour about him that Jack liked.

They sipped their whiskies companionably together, making idle conversation, Mr Travers bemoaning the fact that they could not smoke but Jack noticed that, despite his apparent boredom with the life which forced him to give dinner parties such as these, his eyes were everywhere, making sure there was no gentleman without a drink and no lady without a partner. The perfect host, in fact.

"Excuse me, Mr Andrews, but I must speak to a friend of mine. Browne and his daughter are by the piano, I see. Will you join them and I will see you at dinner?"

Jack had no desire to hover about the piano with Dan who, though he was a man not much older than their host and bloody good at anything to do with railways or money, was a widower and somewhat dour. Miss Browne who, he suspected, was his own age and seemed destined to be that sad thing, an old maid, was too determinedly arch and hard going at the best of times.

He shoved one hand in his pocket and leaned indolently against the wall by the doorway, sipping his whisky, then another, wondering when in hell they were going to get some grub. They were all chattering away like a flock of starlings, saying nothing that interested him and he wished now that he'd gone to that gaming house in Mount Pleasant as he had intended. He didn't like being in Liverpool and the sooner he was away up north again to Lancaster where he and Daniel had made a bid for a "parcel" of line on the Furness Railway, the better he would like it. He was always afraid he might see her, see them, and it made him . . . well, not exactly nervous but jumpy as a cat. He spent as little time as he could here, leaving most of the "office work", as he called it, to Daniel while he "mucked in" with the navvies on the lines. He was the organiser at the site, getting together and keeping together all the paraphernalia which included the men, until the parcel was finished and Dan was the organiser in all else. Dan was getting ready to retire since he had done his share, making a fortune while he did it, and wanted a bit of peace after a life of dashing from one end of the country to the other, he said, and when he did it was all to pass into the hands of Jack Andrews who, although he was already worth a bob or two, would come out of it a wealthy man like Dan.

They were all in evening dress, of course, and even he had to admit it was a dazzling spectacle. Under the soft radiance of candle-lit chandeliers, diamond tiaras winked and glittered, and bare, white shoulders gleamed enticingly. There were several pretty young ladies and he noticed that most of them were eyeing him furtively from behind their fans. Not that he was interested since he liked his women to be married, or at least experienced enough to know that he was a bachelor and intended to remain so. Nevertheless he winked at a couple and was amused when they ducked blushingly behind their frantically beating fans.

Mr Travers tapped him on the shoulder, saying he would like to introduce him to the hostess, his mother who, when the introduction was made and she heard Jack's broad Lancashire vowels, threw a look of outrage at her son as though to say what was the world coming to when a lady of good society was forced to entertain a man in her home who was not.

Mr Travers exchanged an unruffled grin with him then turned to draw forward a young lady who was to be his partner at dinner which was about to be served.

If the enormous drawing-room with its marble fireplace and gilt-framed mirrors, its French ormolu clock and Sèvres vases, its wide velvet sofas and dainty, balloon-backed, cabriole-legged chairs, its deep carpets and delicate, linen-fold panelling had been impressive, then the dining-room was even more so. It was high-ceilinged and had carved wooden walls on which were portraits of Mrs Travers as a girl and four others Jack took to be her daughters, since they were of the same blue-eyed, golden-haired prettiness. The dining table was long and highly polished, its silver and cutlery reflected like diamonds in the darkness of the mahogany, easily seating the thirty guests behind whose chairs a footman stood.

Miss Drusilla Page proved to be as vapid, as dull, as tiresome as she was pretty, believing she had no need of conversation since her smile was so exquisite a gentleman would want nothing more than to gaze at it, and her.

"And what d'you think of Miss Jenny Lind, Miss Page?" he asked desperately, for surely a lady would be interested in the singer and the concerts at which she performed at the Philharmonic Hall.

"I don't think I am acquainted with her, Mr Andrews," she answered. "Does she live in Liverpool?"

When the ladies had gone, leaving the gentlemen to their port and cigars, Mr Travers drew him to one side, saying there was to be a game of cards in his study, winking conspiratorially as though he knew full well what his guest had suffered at the hands of Miss Page and was glad to be able to offer some alternative entertainment. Miss Page and her sister were to sing in the drawing-room, raising his eyebrows whimsically and of course, Mr Andrews was more than welcome to sit with the other guests and listen to them if he wished but having overheard the remark about Jenny Lind and Miss Page's answer – though he was polite enough not to say so – he thought Mr Andrews might find the cards more to his taste.

Jack grinned, liking this flippantly good-humoured chap more and more, and said he thought the cards would be fine.

"My study is at the end of the hallway, just down there," indicating a door to the side of the wide staircase. "There's whisky and brandy and cigars so help yourself. I'll round up a few more chaps and see you in a moment or two."

It was as though someone with a fist on him like Racer had sprung out from behind the door and driven it directly into Jack's midriff. He actually felt himself fold over as the breath was knocked from his body. He had fought Racer and beaten him, making himself "Cock of the camp", for no one had downed Racer before. Now he was down, down and bloody out and how in hell was he to get himself up again? Jesus, oh sweet Jesus, do I deserve this? his mind babbled frantically. Am I such a sinner that whenever I think I might recover, whenever I get my life sorted into some kind of . . . of calm, not happiness but bearable calm, something comes along and kicks me down again.

She was there, in the well-furnished room with him, her face laughing at him from the panelled walls. A dozen pictures, at least, no more than sketches really, with no colour in them, just black and white, but so vivid, so lifelike, so absolutely bloody beautiful he felt the tears start to his eyes. Sara looking over her shoulder, her lips parted in the beginnings of a smile. Sara, her face serious as she studied something in her hand. Sara with a pigeon on her shoulder, her eyes wide as a child's in wonderment. Sara laughing at another girl . . . did he know her? Oh Christ, sweet bleeding Christ, he must get out, he must leave. Was she here in this house? This man, Paul Travers, was he . . .?

His heart pounded so furiously he could feel it behind his eyes, at his wrists and below his jawline and he thought it was about to burst from his chest. It frightened him, his own frenzy, and when Mr Travers walked into the room, smiling and apologising for the delay it was all he could do not to snarl and spring at him, hit him in the face, grapple with him and demand to know what the bloody hell it meant. What was Sara, his own lovely Sara who had never, not once, left his heart in nearly five years, doing on this man's bloody wall?

But life had taught Jack Andrews the wisdom of control, the holding in of his own smashing need sometimes to slam his way through obstacles; the benefit of words rather than fists and he shoved his own deep into his trouser pockets where none of the men who had entered with Mr Travers could see them. Where he stood was in shadow and his face was dark and expressionless as was his voice as he spoke.

"I was admiring your sketches, sir." No one, not one of them who were gathering about the card table, knew what an effort it cost him to remain calm.

"Aah, yes, they are lovely, are they not?" Mr Travers's face underwent an instant transformation, flooding with a tenderness so deep Jack saw several of the gentlemen exchange furtive glances.

"She . . . is . . . your wife?" The underlying harshness in his throat was struggling to get free and Jack clenched his fists so fiercely he felt his own fingernails cut into the flesh of his palms, drawing blood.

Mr Travers looked embarrassed for a moment, glancing about him at the "chaps" who seemed unable to meet his eye. One reached for the cards and began to shuffle them while another stared deeply into his glass as he swirled it round and round.

Then, his eyes the most vivid and startling blue Jack had ever seen in a man's face, or indeed in any face, blue and proud and brilliant with what looked like tears, his host spoke softly.

"No, not yet, Mr Andrews, but she will be on her twentieth birthday which is at the end of the month."

He ran out into the darkness, his face a mask of harrowed pain, ignoring Mr Travers who, completely dismayed by his guest's reaction, had followed him to the wide steps at the front of the house. Jack left him there, left his good evening cloak and, he realised later, his own sanity for a while as he strode off down Mr Travers's broad driveway.

The gravel crunched beneath his evening pumps and his breath laboured in his throat and chest as though he had been running. He could feel the sweat slide down his face to his stiff shirt front. It gathered in the small of his back and in his armpits but though the June night was mild he felt cold.

He came to some gates and without stopping or even conscious thought he turned to his left, striking off along the narrow road which was unlit and completely deserted. There was no sound but for the murmuring rustle of a small night wind in the trees and his own footsteps in the road.

He followed the high wall which surrounded New Park House until he came to its perimeter, almost running by now as though in an attempt to escape the wild pain and fury which pursued him.

There were woods and a field or two on his left and from one of them, bursting through the hedge in a silent explosion, a dog fox ran. Some small creature hung from its mouth and, startled, it stopped for a second to glare at Jack, its muzzle raised, then it hurried across the road and slipped into the hedge on the opposite side.

There was a smell of hawthorn in the air and some blossom Jack could not recognise: an aroma of snowberry and dogwood, the fragrance brought out by the warmth of the sun that day.

He stumbled at one point, falling headlong into the ditch at the side of the road, crushing the meadowsweet and willowherb which grew in its bottom and wetting his evening suit in the trickle of water that ran in it.

Lights began to shine now on his right and though he did not consciously think the thought, he realised it was no more than ten thirty and people in the houses were not yet in their beds. There were villas with long front gardens filled with the shapes, and sounds of trees, rustling leaves and a dog barked frantically from behind a closed gate. Someone played a piano and there was laughter but Jack Andrews staggered on, wondering where in hell he could lie down and die. He knew, with the rational part of his brain which still faltered on, that sometime, tomorrow, next week, a year from now he would be, not cured, not restored to full health, but functioning again and that all he had to do was get through the night, the week, the year until that time came, but he was, at this moment, unsteady with the sensation that something had come loose inside him, as if his heart had become detached and was thumping and shaking until he felt sick. He must find a bolt-hole, a place to gather what strength he

could. He needed a drink, one of those whiskies Travers –
aah, don't . . . Sweet Jesus, don't – had offered him. A bottle,
something to help him to fall into oblivion.

He turned blindly to his right, a wider road this time, again
with fields on both sides and he was startled to hear what
sounded like the roar of a wild beast. He stopped, turning
his head this way and that, completely disorientated, sick and
confused. He was fighting, God above, he was fighting not to
think of her, not to see her in a white . . . a white dress . . .
a veil . . . and later in . . . please, please, don't let me, help
me to switch off my mind, switch off the pictures of her, with
him . . . in . . . on . . . Oh, Jesus . . .

He threw back his head and howled into the night.

"S . . . A . . . R . . . A . . ."

She was restless, wandering from the chair by the fire where
she had settled to read Charles Dickens's latest book, *David
Copperfield*, a copy of which Paul had brought her. She moved
to the open French window, then back again, fingering this
and that on the way.

"Oh, fer God's sake, queen, will yer sit down or go inter't
garden an' 'ave a stroll. I can't concentrate on this beadwork
on Mrs Whatsit's bodice wi' you prowlin' round like a caged
animal. What's up wi' yer?"

Matty cast an impatient glance at Sara, her sewing held in
careful hands, for it was delicate, intricate work, her needle
poised ready for the next tiny stitch. Hundreds of beads
glittered in a box on the table beside her, cream and silver
and gold, ivory and glass, all of different shapes and sizes
but tiny and fragile as spun sugar, and as difficult to sew.
Matty did all the beadwork now, sewing for hours on end
until, only last week, she had purchased a pair of spectacles.
They didn't do much for her looks, she said ruefully, for
they made her look like a bloody schoolmarm but Thomas,
Mr Paul's young coachman, with whom Matty had struck up
a friendship, didn't seem to mind. Privately, in one of their
rare moments alone he had told her he could always take
them off to kiss her, and anything else she would allow him
for that matter.

"Cheeky bugger," she'd told him, "yer can tekk a walk in't
Mersey 'til yer 'at floats, so yer can," but she hadn't meant it
and he knew it, for she and Thomas had an understanding,

unspoken at the moment, that was budding nicely. Thomas
didn't mind about Jamie, in fact on the couple of occasions they'd "walked out" together, Jamie'd gone too. Matty
Hutchinson was a happy woman now and she only wished
she could say the same about Sara Hamilton.

Sara was talked about all over Liverpool, which didn't
seem to bother her and her liaison with Paul Travers hadn't
damaged her business either. Just the opposite, Matty would
have said, for the ladies flocked to get a look at this young
woman who had captured the heart, the attention, the good
name and, supposedly, the wealth of the man who had
avoided the coils of marriage for twenty years now. A
handsome, devil-may-care sort of a man, an intelligent,
audaciously witty and endearingly droll sort of a man who
was so besotted with her he had abandoned all pretence of
discretion. He stayed openly at the house he had given her.
He took her about with him on his arm as though she were
a young queen and, it was rumoured, intended to marry her
as soon as she would have him.

All true, Matty knew that, for Lovell House was her home
now, hers and Jamie's, though she and Sara often took the
brougham, Sara's brougham, down to Abercromby Square to
see Lily and Dolly. Like two little birds in a nest was how Lily
described her and Dolly, though the simile was not very apt
for Lily was more like a large, good-natured bear cossetting a
crumpled old tabby cat. Dolly was getting very frail and, the
doctor said privately, would not get through another winter of
Liverpool's damp and chill. Her heart was not what it once had
been and her old joints "gave her gyp", she said but she was
happy in the protective, affectionate care of Lily. Matty knew
Sara slipped Lily a few quid every week, just to make sure
they wanted for nothing and with at least one visit a week so
that Dolly could "have a hold" of the squirming, good-natured
boy who was Matty's son, that was exactly how it was! They
wanted for nothing.

But what about Sara? Matty didn't know what ailed her but
something did. Oh, she was fine when Mr Paul came to make
her laugh, to hold her on his knee and kiss her until she
gasped, not caring who saw them; to sweep her off to the
lovely bedroom they shared on most nights and where a fire
always burned; to take her in the carriage to some smart place
in her beautiful clothes, making her shine and sparkle and

glow, not seeing that really she was as fragilely empty as a broken eggshell. She thought the world of him, you could see that. Anyone with eyes in their heads could see that, clinging to him as tenaciously as the lovely blue wisteria clung to the front wall of Lovell House, and for the same reason, Matty secretly thought. Take away Lovell House and the wisteria would collapse, shrivel and die!

She worked hard, harder than anyone else in the house, often, when Mr Paul was not there, getting up before the skivvy who lit the kitchen fire and not falling into her bed until long after Roberts had locked up. She was, quite simply, the leader of fashion in Lancashire and every female within ten miles rushed to have made copies of what she wore and when they did she moved on to something else. In the house she dressed in black still, but what style, what daring, what nerve! A skirt and blouse with a red silk cravat, with full sleeves gathered into a wristband and over it a wicked little Zouave jacket. A black silk dress with a broad scarlet sash tied in an enormous bow at the back, the ends hanging down to her hem and her hair in a net made of strands of silver. Sleeveless waistcoats, scarlet stockings and a dashing military cap with gold tassels. Light summer dresses with sleeves of puffed muslin and tulle with waistbands of coral and pearl. Plain pastel-tinted gowns of delicate cream and ivory with richly exotic shawls of patterned crimson. Black military boots of kid with tasselled tops and rosettes on the instep, a sable muff, a coffee-coloured walking outfit trimmed with black satin, a black lace evening gown over sequined taffeta and another which was no more than a froth of amethyst gauze like sea foam over six rustling taffeta petticoats.

She was a sensation wherever she went, always with Paul Travers so that no one could snub her and, having shaken her hand once could they refuse to do so a second time?

Everyone, that is, except Paul Travers's mama! He was with her tonight at a dinner party at New Park House, swearing to Sara that it would be the last time he would do it without her. When they were married, he told her gravely, his mother must receive her, or lose her son.

Perhaps it was this which made Sara pad about the room as she was doing now, fiddling with the latest marvel, a photographic portrait in an elaborate silver frame taken at the photographic establishment at the top of Duke Street.

Matty intended having one made of Jamie since the likeness was remarkable, though Sara and Mr Paul looked very stiff and serious and not at all like their usual selves.

Sara turned from the photograph she had been studying to a slender glass vase in which a solitary stem of freesia stood, lifting it to her nose to sniff its fragrance before putting it down again and moving back to the chair by the fire. She picked up her book and opened it but, watching her from beneath lowered lids, Matty could see she wasn't really reading it. She looked up several times, glancing about her and once she shivered though it was not cold. It was as though some uneasy, unseen presence was haunting her peace, roaming about in her subconscious mind, distracting her and once again she snapped the book shut, jumped up and moved feverishly to the open window.

"Jesus wept, what's up wi' yer? Yer like a cat on 'ot bricks . . ."

"I don't know. I don't know, Matty. Something . . ."

"What, fer 'eavens sake? Yer mekkin me as bad as you, fidgetin' an' flutterin' about room . . ."

"I'm sorry, but I can't seem to settle. It's as though something . . . someone is out there . . ."

"Eeh, give over, chuck, yer givin' me't creeps."

". . . calling . . ."

"Callin'? Bloody 'ell."

". . . or asking me to . . ."

"What? Christ, our kid, I'm all goose bumps, God's honour! Shut winder an' come away, there's a good lass. Why don't yer read yer book ter me. That way we'll both enjoy it. Yer know 'ow I liked that other one. What were it?"

"*Dombey and Son*," Sara replied absently, fingering the curtain at the window, peering out into the summer night which had fallen completely in the past half-hour.

"That's the one. Come on, lar, sit yer down."

The peace of the candle-lit room was suddenly shattered by the roar of some animal, a wild animal and Matty jumped to her feet, squeaking in alarm.

"Bloody 'ell, what were that?"

"Only one of the lions at the Zoological Gardens. You know how close it is."

"Aye, burrit sounded as if it were in't damn garden."

"It depends on which way the wind is blowing. When it comes from— "

She stopped speaking abruptly, cocking her head to one side in a listening attitude. She put one hand to her mouth, covering it and a small moan escaped from her. She began to shake and the curtain she held rattled frantically on its pole.

"Oh dear God," she whispered and Matty felt the hairs at the back of her neck and on her forearms rise and grow stiff.

"What, Sara, lovey, wharris it? Wharris it?"

"I don't know, Matty . . . I don't know but whatever it is it's breaking my heart."

31

Alice Hamilton glared at the burly porter who plodded towards her on Strand Street. He had a cask balanced across the back of his neck, supporting it easily enough, despite its weight, with one hand and he moved forward confidently as though expecting all those in his way to get out of it, which they did. Except Alice. She continued to walk doggedly towards him, her head and her parasol held high, her eyes conveying the message that he'd best not obstruct her. The porter, he couldn't have said why himself, meekly stepped aside into the gutter though the awkward movement almost unbalanced his cask.

Alice glided on, barely noticing him really except as an obstacle which had, rightly so, removed itself from her path. She had been down to one of the warehouses on Back Goree to inspect a roll of bleached cotton which, if the quality was right, she intended to purchase for Hamilton and Butler. She was on her way back to the salon now to give Evadne her opinion. Evadne deferred to her on most things, naturally, since Alice was so much more experienced, perhaps not in the actual making up of a garment, but certainly in how to run a business.

The cotton had been of the best quality, fine, but hard-wearing and would be ideal for the making up of petticoats which would then be embroidered and smothered with broderie anglaise as Alice's clients liked them to be. Her clients – how she loved the sound of those words – though they were not of the standing of those who had patronised the House of Lovell, were of the prosperous middle class, wives and daughters of self-made men and they liked to display their standing in the world with plenty of expensive adornment which, of course, made Alice a handsome profit, particularly if the cotton she purchased could be got cheaply.

"I don't sell cotton by the roll, madame," the warehouse manager had said, mistakenly as it happened since he was not aware of the character of the lady to whom he addressed his remark. "This is a warehouse, not a shop, and besides— "

"Then I will speak to whoever is in charge, if you please," Alice had said, turning away disdainfully.

"It's no use you speaking to anyone, madame. This lot's bound for India and will be aboard the— "

"Are you the owner of this . . . this lot?"

"No, but I am the manager and— "

"Then kindly fetch your master and be quick about it. I have no time to stand about arguing." Alice tapped her foot menacingly and for reasons only the docker carting the cask could have sympathised with, the man felt a great compulsion to do as he was told.

"Mr Grimshaw is on board the— "

"Well, you had best fetch him if you do not want to miss a sale."

"But this lot's already sold, madame."

"Fiddlesticks! A couple of rolls will make little difference to wherever they are going. Now please, fetch Mr . . .?"

"Grimshaw, madame." The man sighed resignedly.

"Grimshaw, and it is miss!"

They had been no match for her, of course, and not only had a bargain been struck but Mr Grimshaw had agreed to deliver the two rolls of cotton she had decided upon – after opening several bales until she was satisfied – within the hour.

It was a mild day, the pale blue veil of the sky striped with hazed layers of drifting cloud, the sunshine slipping in and out of them, but Alice kept her parasol up, for a pale complexion was the mark of a lady and she was very conscious that she was one. She felt well and content, for the small business she had put her money in was thriving and already she and Evadne were talking of expanding into the shop next door in Upper Arcade, the lease of which would be available at the end of the year.

The only irritation in Alice's pleasant musings on her own successes of the past nine months was the irritating, not to say maddening news that the House of Lovell had been sold to Mr Paul Travers who had made the lot over to Sara. Of course it was all over Liverpool how her sister had earned *that* plum and Alice had been mortified at first, hardly able to hold up her head amongst her clients for the shame of it.

But strangely, the scandalous gossip had brought her nothing but sympathy and an increase in custom from those, she suspected, who were eager to get first-hand news from the sister of a fallen woman. She and Evadne, though Evadne had been reluctant, had taken every advantage of it in any way they could and Alice, at least, had played the distressed – and innocent – gentlewoman to the hilt.

It had scourged her though, knowing what she had missed. Dear God, how she would have loved to get her hands on such a renowned and high-class fashion house. Without Madame to hinder her she would have swept Sara aside as only she knew how, clearing out what she called the "dead wood", engaging young improvers who need be paid very little to do the tedious work, with herself and Sara to act as first hands for the more intricate; for the cutting and fitting, overseeing it all, making sure it ran like clockwork but also making sure she made a handsome profit from it. As she did now in her own establishment. Not that she produced shoddy work, far from it, she just produced it more economically. She did not "mollycoddle" her sewing girls as Madame Lovell had done. There were four of them sharing a room in the roof space above Alice and Evadne's quarters on the second floor of the salon in Upper Arcade and though it was a little cramped they were young and fresh from homes where they had known no better. Daughters of farmers and tradesmen come from large families would find it an improvement after sleeping six to a bed, she told herself smugly. And the premium of twenty-five pounds she and Evadne asked was very low considering it was quite usual to demand fifty to sixty pounds in London.

Alice Hamilton thought herself to be a fair woman. She wanted no flibbertigibbets working in her household so it seemed to her that to prevent one appearing her girls must be kept close confined. For twelve hours a day, unless of course they were excessively busy when the period would be extended, they worked from six in the morning until six at night, including Saturdays and from nine at night until six in the morning they were expected to regain their strength in their narrow beds.

Alice required "her" girls to be of good character and good
behaviour which was why she insisted they sleep on the
premises. She had only to remember her own sister to be
warned of the dangers of being too lenient and on Sunday
she expected them to go to church with her. She was well
aware of the splendid impression she made on the female
congregation – who knew her and, naturally, who her sister
was – when she glided up the aisle with her four bobbing,
demurely gowned and bonneted young ladies behind her. It
was a well-known fact that needlewomen, in what was known
as the "off season", were inclined to supplement their incomes
by means of . . . well, she was too much of a lady to speak the
words but that harlot who now lived with Sara at Lovell House,
Alice had heard, was an example of that. Nobody was going
to accuse Alice Hamilton of letting such immorality take place
amongst her girls, on or off the premises. She fed them good
substantial meals, filling meals in which the honest potato
was the main ingredient, with meat and fish now and again,
plenty of bread and they thrived on it, even putting on a little
weight.

They were "bound" to her for a period of three years and
at the end of it, when they became improvers she would
persuade Evadne to get rid of them, send them to find work
elsewhere, which they would easily do having been trained
by the best, and begin again with younger girls who would
pay a further premium but who were unpaid themselves. She
and Evadne were well able to manage all the intricate work
in the sewing-room and with the girls to do the plain sewing,
which was most of it and under supervision, it all worked out
splendidly.

It was not often that she got out of the salon, as she liked
to call it, though Evadne, who was not as well bred as Alice,
was inclined still to call it the "shop". She glanced about her,
apparently looking into shop windows, holding her skirt a
scant inch or two above the pavement with her left hand to
prevent the dirt which was scattered there from staining the
hem, while her right balanced her parasol. She was in a smart
blue-grey walking outfit consisting of a wide skirt and fitted
jacket which she had, naturally, made herself from a length of
valencia, a woollen cloth, the warp of which was of a cotton
and silk mixture, the weft of worsted. It was light enough for
a summer day and yet warm enough for autumn and with

a good mantle would probably see her through into the winter. Her bonnet was made of the same material, the brim stiffened and she had added touches of cream: the ribbons of the bonnet; the collar on her jacket and at her wrists. Her parasol was cream silk and her boots cream kid. She knew she looked very fetching, attractive even, for since she had left the frustrations she had suffered at the House of Lovell to become her own mistress at Hamilton and Butler, her looks had returned. She did not dwell on them, of course, since a lady didn't but she was gratified by the admiring glances which were accorded her by passing gentlemen.

She continued along Church Street, pausing at the junction of Hanover Street and Ranelagh Street to let the traffic thin. There were dozens of four-wheeled broughams, each drawn by one horse, their coachmen flicking their whips adroitly over the animal's back and doing their best to move on, for the street was choked with a straining, stamping, neighing mass of horseflesh. There were two wheeled hansom cabs whose cabbies only got themselves further entangled as they tried to force their way through the four-wheelers. Coal waggons, brewer's drays, dock waggons and timber waggons which threatened to drive their load directly into the plate glass of shop windows. Fishmonger's carts and private carriages, the windows of which were firmly fastened against the smell. Sunlight glinted on the brightly polished metal of the leather harness and on the panels of doors but Alice was in no mood to admire them as she did her best to get herself from one side of the road to the other without being trampled on.

There was a brougham ahead drawn up to the pavement, its presence there responsible for much of the chaos in the street, and a man and a woman were alighting, the man turning back to speak to the coachman. He was a tall man, handsome, distinguished. His hat was held in his right hand and his hair, which was of a mid-brown colour, was turning grey at the temples. There were lines furrowing his brow but he was smiling, his teeth white in his dark-complexioned face as he turned back to the woman. Alice hissed through her teeth as she recognised the woman as her sister. The man was her sister's lover, Paul Travers.

They were both expensively and fashionably dressed, the man in a well-cut morning coat of rich blue broadcloth with wide tails, cut back from his lean waist to reveal tight, dove grey trousers strapped beneath the foot. His waistcoat was the same colour as his trousers and his top hat was black.

The woman was in a hue which Alice could only describe as sand-coloured, a rich silk which gleamed in the pale sunshine. Her jacket was fitted, fluting out below her waist in a peplum. The skirt was not particularly wide but it was ruched from the waist and flounced from the knee, the flounces caught up at the back to reveal kid boots which were the exact shade of the gown. Her bonnet, which sat at the back of her head, was of cream straw, decorated with loops of coffee-coloured ribbons which tied under her chin. Her hair glowed like fiery copper shot with gold and her skin was fine and creamy with a touch of rose at each cheekbone. She looked quite glorious but at the same time ethereal, fragile and the man held her arm protectively.

Draped from her shoulders was the shawl Alice had always coveted and which Alice's mama had given to Alice's sister. Alice had never forgotten how she had felt then and even now it brought a taste of bile to her mouth. She had loved that shawl, the scented shawl, Sara had always called it since on it lingered the delicate fragrance of the pot-pourri their mama had made, and as she watched her sister, her sister who had everything Alice Hamilton should have had, she hated her with a hatred which burned a pain inside her.

The brougham moved off with much whip-cracking and an offensive word or two and when Alice got across the road, the woman – somehow Alice couldn't seem able to call her "sister" any more – and the man, arm in arm and laughing as bold as you please, were gazing into the window of a jeweller's.

"No, Paul, no!" she heard the woman say. "I could open my own jeweller's shop with what you have already given me."

"Just a simple gold wedding ring was what I had in mind, Sara."

"No." The woman's voice was harsh and Alice was quite diverted, hanging about without appearing to, in the doorway of the shop next door but one. She kept her parasol partially lowered, hiding her face behind it. It seemed the man and the woman were arguing right here in the street for all to hear and see and Alice did her best to edge nearer without them noticing, of course, which wasn't hard the way they were carrying on.

"Don't spoil the day, Paul, please," she heard the woman

plead, keeping her voice so low Alice could hardly hear her but Alice had had years of practice of moving about quietly, discreetly hovering in hallways and doorways in order to overhear what other people – particularly the girls – were whispering about. Her ears had become attuned to the murmured word, to the sentence left half finished, even the expression on the speaker's face and the way their lips moved.

"We have been over this so often now," the woman Sara was saying. "Over it and over it and my answer is still the same and if it does not please you then you must separate yourself from me. I can't marry you."

"Won't, you mean, don't you? There is absolutely no logical reason why we shouldn't be married, Sara, none." The man's voice was painfully urgent. "You had agreed, even to the date which was to be on your birthday in June. You had promised and then, suddenly, you said you wanted a postponement and without any kind of reasonable explanation or— "

"Paul, I did explain . . ." The woman was close to tears, Alice could see that, still staring blindly at the glittering display in the jeweller's window and inside Alice a bubble of thrilling satisfaction rose. It served her right, the little hussy. Alice was glad that she was unhappy for she deserved it, though why she should refuse this handsome, wealthy man was a mystery to her. It had been rumoured in Liverpool that they were to have been married several months ago and it had not happened and everyone had assumed, Alice among them, that Paul Travers had changed his mind for why, Liverpool society had wanted to know, should the man marry Sara Hamilton, the new owner of the House of Lovell, when she was available to him whenever he felt the need? He'd already paid for that privilege, hadn't he? But it seemed from this frantically whispered argument which was taking place only a few feet away from Alice that the boot had been on the other foot!

"Yes, Sara, but your explanations don't satisfy me." He became eager suddenly, bending his head close to hers, apparently pleading with her and Alice could not hear what he said. The woman's head was bent, her face hidden by the curve of the man's shoulder but Alice could see by the movement of her bonnet brim that she was shaking it slowly from side to side and finally, sighing, the man took her arm and led her away from the shop and along Bold Street in the direction of Leece Street.

Alice followed them at a discreet distance but halfway along it they turned into Ireland's, the furrier, and she could hardly follow them in there, could she? She and Sara were completely estranged now, though Sara had been to Alice's premises a couple of times to plead with her, to beg her to resume their sisterly ties. Alice had refused, of course, on one occasion telling her in a voice loud enough for her clients to overhear that she did not consort with common prostitutes.

She had thought Sara would faint she went so white but she had merely said, in a sad voice, "Oh, Alice . . ." then, lifting her head and squaring her shoulders, walked with great dignity from Alice's salon.

It was strange really, she was often to think later. It was as though God was directing Alice, placing her and all the players in exactly the right position at exactly the moment they were required to be there. It must be the hand of God, Alice decided. It was too great a coincidence and to convince her further, the second encounter took place right outside the beautifully carved door of Alice's own church, St Luke's, just as Alice was to cross Berry Street and into Leece Street.

She had been wishing, as she walked along, that she was on more intimate terms with Evadne so that she could gloat with her over the scene she had just witnessed in front of the jeweller's shop, when she saw him and for a second or two she felt the blood drain from her head and she knew a great need to lean on the church door. Even to go inside to the cool dimness and sit down but a voice in her head was whispering, "This is it, this is it, the moment for which you have waited ever since Sara Hamilton turned her back on Alice Hamilton and told her to go to the devil. Even before that when you were forced to watch her preen in your mama's scented shawl. This is it!"

Many of Alice and Sara's ills could be placed at the door of the big man who was walking towards her. She wasn't quite sure how she arrived at that conclusion, she only knew that from the day she and Sara had met him and his gang in Wray Green, things had not been right for Alice Hamilton and now here was her chance to reap the justice she deserved. God had put him here, in Alice's path and retribution was meant, surely, swift retribution, straight from God, and Alice Hamilton. It had been he who had sparked the first rebellion in Sara. He who had led her astray when he took her to Lytham on the occasion of the opening of the new railway line and station. He who had kept that defiance alive with his letters which, thankfully, Alice had managed to divert.

Perhaps it would all be for nothing. Perhaps he. had forgotten about the fifteen-year-old girl he had charmed so many years ago. Perhaps he was married with a family of his own and would not care particularly what Sara Hamilton was up to. Or perhaps not and there was no harm in trying, was there? He certainly looked very prosperous, even attractive in a coarse way, she supposed. He was dressed as a gentleman dresses in an olive green morning coat with trousers in a discreet check of olive green and brown and his brown top hat was tipped rakishly over his brow.

He stopped dead when his eyes came to rest on her, causing a small flurry of activity and exclamations as several people at his back did their best to avoid collision. His sun-browned face paled, becoming a strange murky colour that was not unlike that of his coat. His mouth opened and closed, like a fish out of water, Alice thought triumphantly but at last he spoke her name.

"Alice . . . Alice?" he croaked and Alice thrilled to the pain which was in his voice.

"Miss Hamilton, yes, Mr Andrews." She twirled her parasol in an ecstasy of joy and she was not to know how like her sister she looked as her green eyes danced and a lovely rosy flush of anticipation dyed her cheeks.

"This is a surprise, Mr Andrews. I had thought you still to be . . . well, working on the railway. Up north somewhere I believe you said when last we met."

"I am, Alice . . . Miss Hamilton." His eyes were almost black with the depth of his shock and though Jack Andrews dealt with men at all levels of society now, a self-confident, self-assured man, he seemed tongue-tied and ill at ease and Alice revelled in it.

"Really! Your style of dress has altered since then it seems," running her eyes rudely up and down his smartly tailored figure.

"I'm a contractor now," he answered shortly, beginning to regain his composure. "I have a partner in Liverpool whom

I consult with now and again but yes, I am working on the Furness Railway."

"How very interesting," though plainly she was not interested at all.

"And you, Miss Hamilton?" he asked politely, beginning to edge on his way now that the shock of their meeting was passing, eager to get on, to get away from whatever pained him and Alice felt the surge of elation rush through her veins for it was plain that Jack Andrews was frightened of something.

"Oh, I have my own small business, Mr Andrews, just over the road in Upper Arcade in Leece Street. A fashion salon. It is becoming very successful, I am happy to say."

"Good, very good, I'm very pleased for you."

She could see it now in his face. The longing to say her name, to ask after her, to find out what had happened five years ago when he and Sara had become separated. She rejoiced, her heart singing inside her as she drew her sword and began to sharpen it in preparation for cutting Jack Andrews's heart from his body.

"I myself have a partner, Mr Andrews," she said prettily, watching as he flinched away from her in readiness for whatever it was she was to tell him.

"Really . . ."

"Yes, a Miss Evadne Butler. We make a good team."

"Splendid. Now I'm afraid I . . ."

"Since, of course, Sara is Mrs Paul Travers now, as I'm sure you know. As a matter of fact I have just seen the pair of them going into the furrier. He cannot resist buying her the most expensive gifts and it is to be a sable cloak, they told me, for the coming winter. Really, it seems he can deny her nothing."

He swallowed agonisingly, continuing to look into her smiling face as though hypnotised. His eyes watched her mouth and in them was an anguish so deep she felt a thrill of awe. Surely no man could feel about a woman as this man apparently felt about Sara Hamilton and survive the loss of her? They were blank and empty and yet harrowed, reminding her of something . . . aah, yes, she had it, they reminded her of Sara's, years ago, when she had mourned the loss of this very man. How very strange!

"I must get on," but he did not move.

"Such a lovely wedding they had in this very church." He turned his head obediently to follow her pointing finger. "A splendid affair with the cream of Liverpool Society there, of course. I was myself a bridesmaid and the reception . . . I have never seen anything quite like the wedding cake. He is such a generous man, Paul, and absolutely adores her, as she does him."

He made a sound in his throat and his eyes beseeched her to stop but he continued to stand, paralysed and mute, as Alice Hamilton stripped him of his love, his dignity, his manhood, his strength, his future.

"A honeymoon in Venice and though I am not . . . well, as you are an old friend" – which should have warned him but did not – "they have reason to believe . . ." She blushed girlishly. "I am to be an aunt, Mr Andrews, what do you think of that? Such happiness. Well, I must get on. I have so many things to see to, as I'm sure you do so I'll bid you good-day. So pleasant to renew our acquaintance."

When she turned for a moment on the corner of Leece Street, looking back over her shoulder, he was just where she had left him, the tide of pedestrians on the pavement washing round him like the waters of a river washing round a rock. They stared curiously at the well-dressed young man who stood, his eyes and face blank, looking, and yet not looking, at the door of the church, wondering what ailed him. Surely he was not drunk? He was too respectable for that and yet what other explanation could there be for his strange behaviour?

Alice continued to watch him. It had been satisfying beyond all her wildest dreams, the sweetness of the revenge she had extracted from the navvie. From the man who had first separated Alice and her sister and the only disappointment was that Sara would never know and suffer as he did. That would have been splendid. If the meeting with the navvie could have taken place outside the furrier she could have kept him there until the man and woman came out. Let him see them together. Rubbed even more salt into the open and, surely, soon to be festering wound she had inflicted on him.

But perhaps, on second thoughts, it was as well it had happened as it did. Something might have been said, by the navvie, or by Sara, which would have revealed Alice's lies and only God knew what might have happened then.

No! God did know what should happen and had arranged it perfectly for Alice to carry it out. She turned away, sighing in contentment as Jack Andrews began to shuffle slowly along the pavement in the direction of Renshaw Street.

32

They had been arguing about it for three months now and Paul began to be afraid that it would sour their relationship. They were as close as ever, as loving as ever, as tempestuous in her wide bed in her lovely room as ever, but whenever he brought up the question of marriage she froze in his arms, pulling out of them, once even striking him across the face as though in reaction to desperate fear.

He knew he must be patient, give her time; why, he didn't really know, he often thought irritably and time was not something of which he had a lot to give. Not that he was an old man, or even middle-aged, he told himself, but he was a damn sight older than she was. He wanted a son, children, and though he was well aware that he had argued with his mother that a man could father a child until he was in his dotage, and it was true, he wanted to see his children grow up, to be there when the next generation of Travers and Son took over.

He loved her. God, he never stopped loving her. She was like a drug to which he was hopelessly addicted. When, the night following the dinner party at New Park House, she had told him as gently as she could, he knew that, that she could not marry him on her twentieth birthday as she had promised him he had been stunned. He had simply stared at her for what seemed a long time wanting to shout and bluster like a child which has been denied a toy but he was a man, not a child and so he had remained calm.

"Why not?"

"It's . . . too soon, Paul."

"Too soon after what, my darling? We have been lovers for six months now and I can see no reason to wait. God almighty,

Sara, I'm asking you to marry me not commit murder, you know. An honourable estate, so they tell me," doing his best to smile his touchingly lopsided smile, "and one which I'm eager to enter. Only with you, of course. I'm what is known as a 'catch', my love, so snap me up and put the rest of the female population out of its misery."

She had no conception of the effort it took to speak so lightly, so flippantly and he was relieved to see her relax, to smile at him in exasperation.

"Darling," he went on, "I want to give you a child. All women want a child, Sara, so I've been told, and I want you to give me a child and though we can just about get away with this unholy alliance we have at the moment Liverpool would throw up its collective arms in horror if it were to bear fruit. Besides which, I must have a . . . well, you know . . ."

"Yes, I know, a legitimate son to carry on the family business." She grimaced, not with distaste but with impatience.

"Is that too much to ask for, my darling?" He took her hand, carrying it to his lips, brushing them across her knuckles.

"No, it's not, Paul, and I can understand exactly what you mean but . . ."

"But what? There are no buts. There is nothing standing in our way that I can see and if there is I would like you to tell me about it."

His face grew stern as if daring her to produce any objection which could be of the slightest relevance. "Surely you're not afraid of the awkwardness you will come across amongst my family and friends. You know my mother will be stubborn at first but as soon as . . ."

"No, it's not that."

"Then what? Tell me." Again he did his best to smile, though his stiff cheek muscles twitched with the effort.

There was a sweetness about her, a candour which was so endearing he leaned towards her, convinced she was about to confide in him.

She was exquisitely dressed that day in a rich, gleaming silk gown the colour of saffron, trimmed with contrasting velvet bands in claret. The sleeves were cut wide at the wrist to reveal white lace undersleeves and her hair was tied up carelessly with saffron-coloured ribbon falling about her head and slender shoulders like living flame. He felt a great desire to plunge his hands into it, fancying if he did, though, that he might burn himself. Instead he put up a hand and tenderly tucked a stray curl behind her ear.

It was Sunday and the house was quiet. Matty had gone off on some secret jaunt which, because Paul Travers had driven himself over in his curricle, involved Thomas who had not then been needed, though neither Paul nor Sara, as yet, were aware of it.

They were in her bedroom, totally alone on the upstairs floor, for even the needlewomen on this lovely June day were taking the air in the garden or, those who had family or friends nearby, out visiting them.

"I'm not ready for marriage yet, Paul," was all Sara would say, still holding his hand in hers. "I'm learning to run the business which takes up all my time and if I married you and had a child I would be tied down."

"No, you wouldn't, my love," he lied passionately, not consciously aware that he did. "There would be a nursemaid."

"Where would we live?"

He was caught off guard. "Why, at New Park House, of course. Four generations of Travers have been born there and my son— "

"There, you see! How could I run this business living at New Park House, where your mother would resent me and your friends ignore me?"

He was growing angry in his disappointment.

"You are simply making excuses and I would like to know why. Do you not care for me?"

"Oh Paul, of course I care about you. Come to bed and I'll show you how much." She began to smile and undo the buttons down the front of her bodice, hoping to divert him, he knew, as she revealed the soft, creamy tops of her breasts, but he frowned.

"I don't mean that, Sara. If a man and woman love one another and they are free to do so the next natural step is to marriage."

"Oh, don't be so pompous, Paul. We have managed without marriage up to now. Cannot we go on as we are? Please don't let us quarrel. Come and kiss me and then . . . well . . ." She smiled, her eyes widening as a child's would when it knows it is about to be naughty and hopes it will not be punished. "I know it is wicked to make love on a Sunday morning," she twinkled, "but won't you help me with these buttons," deliberately pulling at her gown so that one rosy nippled breast popped from its lacy covering, followed by the second. Her gown fell off her shoulders, the sleeves still holding her arms so that she was helpless, his captive, or so she was telling him.

Paul felt himself swell and harden as she stood, eyes cast down, demure as a child about to recite a nursery rhyme, her lovely breasts flaunting themselves proudly as her own breath deepened. He knew what she was doing, just as he knew she was doing it deliberately to get him away from the vexed question of their marriage, but she was so damned lovely, so exciting, so inviting, how could any man resist her invitation, even though he felt like bloody well strangling her. After he had made love to her, of course.

She sank to her knees on to the low stool before the empty grate, her skirts ballooning up about her, looking at him from under the long tangle of her lashes.

"Make love to me, Paul," she said huskily.

He couldn't resist her. He moved across the room, kneeling as she did but on the floor so that her breasts were on a level with his face. He put his parted lips between them, licking the fragrant divide, feeling her shiver, then took each one in turn into his mouth, sucking strongly, feeling the nipples come up against his tongue.

His hands moved to the hem of her gown then up her legs, lingering on the naked flesh which was like silk to his touch, parting them at her thighs, spreading them roughly, his fingers finding the hot, wet cleft between them, probing until she gasped. With a moan she freed her arms and wrapped them about his head, clutching him to her, her own thrown back until her freed hair reached the floor.

He lifted her, then with a harsh cry threw her on her back to the carpet, flung up her skirts over her head and took her at once. He was deliberately ruthless, cruel even, trying to hurt her, to degrade her but she held on to him, calling out his name again and again.

He stripped her then. He did not undress her as he had always done, slowly and lingeringly, or even with urgent love. He simply stripped her, then himself and for an hour treated her as he might some bought whore, doing things he had never done before in his pain at her rejection of him.

But she was generous, loving, so bloody responsive, just as though she knew exactly what was in his head and was sorry for it. She would not marry him but she would give him this which was all she had to give, she was telling him, but was it enough for him? He did not know, he only knew he could not harm her, hurt her more, humiliate her more for he loved her. When he put his hand on her breast she purred like a cat and though she had the sweet freshness of a child she was not one. Her buttocks were tight and round with the sheen of a pearl on them and her breasts bounced joyfully, swinging in his face as she moved over him. She was glorious as she explored his body from his eyebrows to his toenails, as he had taught her and he anguished on how he could give her up. How, how could he? Surely he could convince her that they should marry. He must, he must. Dear sweet Christ, he must.

But three months had gone by since that June day and still she would not have it. He knew she was beginning to enjoy the power and influence she had at Lovell's. She was not overbearing but she quietly demanded her own way in its complete running, in the direction it was to take, listening to no one, not even him. She knew best, her manner said, in every aspect of fashion, in the inspiration and creation of every garment which went from the house. She was clever and charming and knew exactly what every client wanted and how to give it to them. Calculating, she had become, manipulating men and women alike, from the small boot boy in the footman's pantry who doted on her since she always spoke to him, to the wealthiest, most influential lady in Liverpool who was her latest customer and eager to be dressed in whatever style Miss Hamilton told her she was to put on. Her designs were eagerly sought after. She was famous, infamous, he supposed. She was a marvel, in business and in his bed, or rather hers, and he knew, if he were honest with himself, she was exactly what he, Paul Travers, had made her.

Another month went by and Sara sat on the wide-cushioned window seat of her bedroom, her face drawn, her eyes shuttered, her gaze unfocused as she looked out over the dying glory of her garden. Its autumn colours were the exact same shades as her hair which rippled down her back, gold and russet leaves of tawny brown dancing on the branches and twigs in the slight wind and flying like homing birds in the air before coming to rest in the thickening carpet across the lawn.

Her body felt bruised, for she had just spent another afternoon in Paul's arms, playing the whore, she privately and sorrowfully called it now, since it was the only way she could divert him from the everlasting, ever-increasing arguments they had on the subject of when she was prepared to marry him. It was October and winter was fast approaching and she should be down in the room she had made over into what she called her workroom.

There were designs she was producing for Mrs Edward Williams whose husband was brother to a baronet and who wanted, no, demanded that Miss Hamilton create her complete winter wardrobe before the month's end. Mrs Richard Clarke had need of seven new ballgowns for the Christmas season since she had seven engagements in one week and could hardly wear the same gown more than once, and Mrs James Wickham, whose daughter Miss Hamilton had dressed so stunningly for her marriage early last year, had confided that her second daughter was to have a spring wedding and could Miss Hamilton begin at once with the inspiration which would make it the most talked-about wedding of the year?

And they were only three of the dozens who expected Miss Hamilton to give them and their wardrobes her undivided attention.

Her workroom contained an enormous table on which was piled a sample of every fabric in her storeroom, and an equally enormous drawing board where were pinned dozens of sketches. Sketches and ideas and notes which referred to each client's design and requirement, though Sara did not take a great deal of notice of these last. She knew she was often considered high-handed as she brushed aside some tentative suggestion one of her ladies might make on the possibility of a bow here or a frill there but she knew what was right, what suited them and she told them so. Politely, of course, but firmly, smiling as she did so and they were always enchanted with the finished product, but she knew she was gaining a reputation for being . . . difficult, and she knew, as she knew the colour of her own hair, that it was the constant upheaval with Paul that was causing it. She could not imagine life without him in it, but she could not manage it when he was . . .

Take this afternoon, for instance. He had come thundering up the gravel drive in his curricle, barely in control of the wild-eyed, thoroughbred beast which pulled it, or so the gardener had seemed to think as he leaped for safety over a pile of autumn leaves. Fortunately she had been alone in her workroom when he invaded it with his restlessly pacing, vigorously tense masculinity, sweeping her into his arms and up the stairs as though he had been denied her body for six weeks instead of six hours. That was how long it was since he had climbed out of her bed at dawn, going first to his rooms to change before taking a cab to his office. He had been tender then, holding her half-awakened body to him possessively as he kissed her goodbye, smoothing back the tangle of her hair which he had himself tangled the night before, whispering to her that he would be back later and she was to stay just where she was, laughing softly, his male virility appeased by her drowsy-eyed submission.

It was as if a demon had entered his soul during the morning, a demon brought on perhaps by some chance remark. A man in his employ whose wife had given birth to a son? A nursemaid pushing a baby carriage down towards the Marine Parade, something to remind him that time was marching on and Paul Travers wanted to be doing the same. Not exactly pushing a baby carriage although Sara thought, smiling a little, she could just imagine him doing precisely that. His wife on his arm, his son in the baby carriage, the sun shining benevolently on his own pride and satisfaction and it was she, Sara Hamilton, who was preventing it from happening.

Why couldn't she marry him? Why? Why? It was not as if she didn't care for him, love him really, she supposed, in a way which was honest and true. She did. He was her friend and lover and she was happy in his company. He made her laugh. He excited her. He calmed her. He protected her. She was safe with him. Safe from the memories which still haunted her. Memories such as the day when she had seen Jack on the deck of the ship. It was on that day that she had decided to marry Paul. She had panicked, she knew that now, believing that, to erase Jack completely and finally from her heart, her thoughts, her life, she must change who she was. It had seemed logical to assume that if she were a different person, not Sara Hamilton but Mrs Paul Travers, her heart, her thoughts, her life would be different and the person she had been, the one who loved Jack Andrews, would no longer exist.

She had been wrong, she had soon learned that, but it had taken her until the night of the dinner party at New Park House, the one to which Paul Travers's future wife had not been invited, to do something about it. To tell Paul she could not marry him. It was not that she had been hurt, or offended by Paul's failure to introduce her to his family, though she would have respected him more had he done so. She had told herself that when they were married Paul's circle would be forced to accept her and did it really matter that she was excluded until then from these unimportant functions? The answer, which was no, seemed further to indicate that her relationship with Paul was very fragile.

But none of these things counted for anything beside the strange and frightening feelings which had plagued her on that same summer evening as she and Matty sat in what was still called Madame's sitting-room. She had felt as though there were something bursting inside her; as though something violent had escaped from its usual calm sanctuary and was going at breakneck speed through her veins and arteries; crawling beneath her skin until she could not sit still, or even stand in one place for longer than a minute or two. She had been . . . not precisely frightened but intensely distressed. It was as though some . . . as though there was something beyond her and her thoughts, beyond the house and garden, that suffered so intensely, its pain had transferred itself to her, foolish as it sounded, even to herself and of course she had not tried to explain to anyone else. Not even Paul.

It was on that night, as she lay alone in the bed she usually shared with him that she had known, sadly, that she could not marry him. She could not marry any man, she supposed. If, caring about Paul as she did, she could not bring herself to tie herself to him – is that how she thought of it, appalled – then how could she possibly marry anyone? He was so good to her, so patient and loving and yet beginning to resent her, to resent the fact that the son he wanted, the children he wanted, the wife he wanted were to be denied him if he continued to be the lover of Sara Hamilton.

Naturally it had occurred to her, and she supposed, to him, that instead of her he could marry some eager young virgin of good family and breed himself ten children before he was fifty but could she continue to be the mistress of a man who had a wife? Many women did. Paul loved her and would make it perfectly clear to her, and to his wife, she assumed, that he would continue to do so. That Sara was first in his heart but would their relationship survive that?

She sighed deeply, her face unutterably sad since she knew it wouldn't. She stood up and pulled together the wisp of lace, ribbons and tulle Paul liked her to wear in the bedroom. A negligee of the palest dove grey which shaded to deeper blue-grey in its folds as she moved and so fine and light the outline of her body, her rose-tipped breasts and the coppery curls between her legs were plainly visible. She threw it off and reached for her undergarments and a serviceable dress of warm russet which matched her hair. It was almost over, the afternoon, not wasted, of course, since she enjoyed the hours of pleasure she shared with Paul but it was too late to go down to her workroom and take up where she had left off when Paul came. Tomorrow the House of Lovell would be closed since Her Majesty the Queen was to visit the city, along with her husband, Prince Albert and her four children, the Prince of Wales, a handsome boy of ten by all accounts, the Princess Royal, Princess Alice and Princess Helena. Like most employers Sara had given her seamstresses the day off to go down to the river to see the royal family embark on the steamer which was to take them on a tour of the dockland and to watch the festivities which would come later. They were all excited and praying for a fine day, particularly as there were to be two magnificent firework displays in the evening at the north and south end of the docks.

But now she'd go and see Dolly, that's what she would do. Have a good old gossip with Lily, a cup of tea, a laugh, make sure her two beloved friends were in good health and perhaps see if she could persuade the pair of them to come with her and Paul to watch the crowds, the procession, gaze at the decorations with which the town was bedecked, and listen to the bands. It was said that Her Majesty was to show herself at the windows of the Town Hall and Sara knew that Dolly, who

loved and admired Queen Victoria for her qualities, not just as
Dolly's sovereign but as a wife and mother, would be, in her
own words, "made up" if she could catch a glimpse of her.

It might be awkward, of course, for neither Dolly nor Lily
could be said to be at ease with Paul. He was charming to
them, courteous, kind and thoughtful, bringing them small
gifts over which he took great care in the choosing. Gifts
he knew they would appreciate but the two ladies did not
like the way Mr Travers treated their Sara, nor for her ruined
reputation which was all down to him, of course. Despite the
fact that he had asked Sara to marry him and it was not his
fault that she was not Mrs Paul Travers, they were suspicious
of him, wary with him, uneasy, so perhaps they might not care
to sit beside him in his carriage, even to see the Queen.

Paul had said he would be back – he never used the word
"home" – for dinner at about seven, kissing her fondly for
she had pleased him this afternoon so she just had time to
drive down to Abercromby Square and back before then.

They were overjoyed to see her as though it was months
and not just a week since last she had called. It had been a
decent summer, mild and dry and Dolly was "fettling well"
she said and though she and Lily exchanged glances which
made Sara smile, just as though she had asked them to share
the carriage with John Wilson who had been tried and hanged
for the murder of a Mrs Hinrichson, her two children and
her servant earlier in the year, they agreed they would be
delighted to see the Queen the next day.

They chatted for an hour and drank Lily's strong, sweet tea,
discussing Matty and her fine son who was now the apple of
Dolly's old eye, and the pleasing but astonishing news that
Miss Mitchell, lodger at Lily's these past several years and, Lily
had been convinced, well past such things, was to be married
and had diffidently requested that the House of Lovell should
make her wedding gown!

No, the arrangements for the next day were not too early,
bearing in mind it took Lily a fair while to get Miss Watson
to her feet and together, as Sara rose to go, they hoped the
weather would remain fine for their dear Queen.

"Yer look thin, Miss Eleanor," Dolly remarked as Sara
reached for her mantle, putting out an old, brown spotted
hand to pat Sara's arm. Sara and Lily showed no surprise for
Dolly was in that pleasant twilight which old people reach

when their present is often peopled with their past and had
recently begun to call Sara by her mother's name.

"Yer work too 'ard, that's your trouble." Her old eyes ran
speculatively over Sara's slender figure. "Time thi' 'ad a bairn,
I'm thinkin'." She shook her head as though "Miss Eleanor's"
failure to produce a bairn was something that worried her
greatly. Lily and Sara exchanged startled glances.

"But I'm not even married, Dolly." Sara smiled, patting the
old hand on her arm.

"Aye, I'm well aware o' that, lamb, an' what I want ter know
is when's that lad comin' for thi'? Nice lad, 'e were, an' didn't
'e love my coconut macaroons?"

33

"I can't stay, Dan, and that's the truth of it. I thought if I lived up north, kept away from Liverpool I could cope with it but I can't. When her sister told me the other day – about the wedding – it was more than I could stand. It finished me."

Jack Andrews stood, his back to Daniel Browne as he stared moodily from the window of the office in New Quay. His eyes were dulled, not really seeing the seething activity which was taking place beyond it in the steadily falling rain.

"I'm sorry, Jack. God, I'd no idea you were . . . romantically involved with a young lady. You gave no indication of it when you went off to Canada earlier in the year," and if you had I doubt I would have been quite so open-handed with my friendship and patronage, Daniel Browne almost added, for he had had hopes of an alliance between his Margaret and this young partner of his. They were not in the legal sense of the word true partners, he and Jack. There were no documents drawn up or papers signed to bind them together but the older man, for whom Jack had once worked as subcontractor, had been more and more relieved to let Jack take over what was the dirty, the tiring, the less pleasant part of Daniel's work out on site. Daniel was getting older. He had taught Jack all there was to know, all that he knew, on how to grab a contract, how to raise money and how to distribute it in the building of a railway. It needed great speed, good organisation, a proper division of labour to become a successful contractor, to know precisely how much to quote a mile for a whole line and when you had learned these things it was possible to amass a fortune as he had done, or, on the other hand, collapse into bankruptcy as so many others had.

There was only his Margaret now and though she was to

inherit all that Daniel Browne had accumulated, somehow there had been no suitors. Jack Andrews was not a gentleman in the proper sense of the word but he was a decent man. He was clever, shrewd even, intelligent, not afraid to gamble when necessary, worked hard and would be kind to Margaret when Daniel was gone.

But now, it seemed, Jack had become involved with some woman and, having lost her to another man, was intent not only on getting out of Liverpool but out of the bloody country, or so he said, as soon as he could find a passage.

He couldn't help himself. "Don't be a bloody fool, Jack," he blurted out. "You can't mean to give up" he almost said "all I can offer you" but stopped himself in time, continuing "all you have built up here. You're well thought of in the business of railway building and to go off across the world just to avoid some woman seems a bit drastic. There's opportunities . . ."

"Not many now, Dan. It's over here, the big rush. The opportunities are abroad now and I can do just as well, better, in North America."

"God forbid I should speak out of turn, Jack, but there are more fish in the sea than came out of it."

"What?"

"There are other women, for God's sake. What's so bloody special about this one?"

Jack didn't appear to have heard the irritable question.

"I hadn't seen her for years, Dan, four or five. I'd worked up north, as you know, and in Lancashire and though I still thought of her I'd long since given up imagining I would find her again."

Jack sighed, leaning his forehead on one of the small panes of glass in the window, his eyes following without interest what looked to be a uniformed brass band marching smartly along New Quay towards George's Landing Stage where an enormous tent appeared to have been erected. There was a great crowd of people about, many of them lining the street, poised on the edge of the pavements and belligerently hanging on to what they obviously considered to be their bit of territory, turning to glare at anyone who challenged them for it.

Others surged along New Quay, following the band which was not yet playing, waving small Union Jacks, children skipping beside their parents, all somewhat bedraggled in the almost solid sheet of water which fell from the leaden sky.

The weather matched his mood exactly. He shoved his hands deep in his pockets, wondering what the hell was happening and at the same time not really caring. There was a magnificent arch further down New Quay, stretching from one side of the road to the other made up of a triumphal display of entwined flowers and greenery with the slogan "God save our Queen" in vivid colours across the top.

Gradually he began to notice that there were devices, flags, bunting and banners strung from building to building, that every ship he could see was dressed all over and that there was an air of general excitement in the street.

"What's going on?" he asked irritably, turning to glare at Dan as though the whole bloody thing had been contrived to exacerbate further his own deep and despairing depression.

"Lord, Jack, where in hell have you been? Have you not heard that the Queen and her family are to visit the town on their way back from Scotland?"

"Bloody fine day they've picked, and I've only just got into Liverpool myself, Dan. I came straight here but" – he pushed a hand through his thick hair— "I was in no mood to notice the . . . jollifications."

"So it seems. So what is it you have to tell me that I don't already know?"

Jack grimaced turning away to glare out of the window again. "I'm off with Brassey, Dan. He's undertaken to build the Grand Trunk of Canada, had you heard, the whole five hundred and thirty-nine bloody miles of it from Quebec to Lake Huron. It'll take years, you know what the terrain's like, and the climate."

"Only what you've told me."

"It gets to forty degrees below freezing and God knows how the men, three thousand of them he's to take, will stand it."

"But you mean to try?"

"Aye." The long despairing sigh trembled out of Jack's lungs and Daniel marvelled that any man could be so affected by a woman. She must have qualities which were unique, whoever she was, to so weaken a man, especially a man such as Jack Andrews who, years ago, had been "Cock of the camp" when he was a navvie.

"Well, Jack, I'll be sorry to see you go but I can't stop you.

I'm ready to retire, as you know, and Margaret and I will probably do a bit of travelling on the continent. Spend the winter in France or Italy."

"Oh aye."

"Yes, well, I'd best get down to join the rest in welcoming Her Majesty. She and the Prince spent last night with the Earl of Sefton at Croxteth Hall. His Worship the Mayor is to meet them at the boundary of the borough at ten thirty and there's a procession to come through the town. The Chairman of the Dock Committee and others, I believe, are to present congratulatory addresses to the Queen after which they're all to board the steamer *Fairy* and cruise on the river. Margaret wanted to see it and I promised her I would take her." He shrugged. "She'll be here in a moment or two."

"Aye, right, I'd best be off then."

"You're to go soon?"

"As soon as I can get a passage. The end of the week, happen. I've agreed to see to some of the navvies, make sure they get aboard, you know," for Daniel was as well acquainted as Jack with the wild ways of navviemen.

Daniel stood up and they shook hands awkwardly, raising their eyebrows and shrugging their shoulders in embarrassment as men who have formed a friendship often do at parting.

"Can I say something, Jack?"

"Depends what it is."

"This woman . . . sorry, I didn't mean to pry," as Jack winced away from him.

"It's . . ." Jack swallowed painfully. "No offence, Dan, and yes, I know what you're going to say. She must be something bloody special to . . . well, she is."

"Does she live in Liverpool?"

"Aye, why d'you think I'm leaving?"

"Of course."

"We met her husband, you and me and Miss Browne a while back."

Daniel looked surprised. "We did?"

"Aye, at that dinner party, oh, last June or July. I forget the name of the house but it was set in a bloody great park."

"You don't mean Paul Travers?"

"Yes." Jack's strong mouth firmed and thinned and he ran his hand through his hair again in what seemed to be only barely controlled menace, directed at he knew not what.

"But Paul Travers isn't married," Daniel protested. "There was a rumour a while back but, well, as they said" – forgetting for a moment Jack's feelings on the matter— "why should he marry his mistress? You don't buy the cow to get a jug of milk."

The silence was so deep and appalling Daniel Browne thought Jack had not heard him, hoped he had not heard him, for what he had just said about Paul Travers's mistress, especially to the man who loved her so desperately, was inexcusable.

"God above, Jack, I'm sorry," he blustered, taking a step away from the pillar of frozen bone and muscle, flesh and sinew that was Jack Andrews. He raised his hands, palm outwards for though he himself had never encountered it, Jack's strength and ferocity were well known in railway building circles.

Still Jack stood, his hand almost on the door knob, his sleeved cape over his arm, his face turned away from Daniel so that whatever expression was on it was hidden.

"Jack . . ." Daniel faltered for he could feel some emotion pulsating through Jack Andrews which was threatening to explode from him with a force which might destroy them both. Jack was twenty-odd years younger than he was. He was stronger and could, with one hand alone, slowly choke the life out of Daniel, or just as quickly and easily beat him to pulp.

When Jack finally spoke it was like nails being drawn across glass, setting the teeth on edge. He did not turn round.

"Are we talking about the same lady, Daniel?" Daniel did not fail to notice the use of the word "lady".

"I . . . well, I suppose so."

"Tell me her name, if you please."

"She is . . . her name is Sara Hamilton. She owns a fashion house – well, he bought it for her – the House of Lovell in West Derby."

Again, and for at least sixty seconds there was that long and terrifying silence. From outside the crescendo of noise grew, evidently heralding the arrival of some personage of importance, presumably Her Majesty, Prince Albert, and their four children, and at the same time the door burst open and

449

the aggrieved face of Margaret Browne appeared in the doorway. Jack stood so close to it she cannoned into him and Daniel breathed out a long slow sigh of relief. He'd never been so glad to see anyone in his life as his homely daughter.

It brought Jack Andrews back from the shadowy world in which he had existed ever since Alice Hamilton had hammered in the last nail of his crucifixion nearly a month ago. It brought him back from the mists of oblivion which a full bottle of whisky a day wreathed about him, brought him to savage, searing flames of pure agony, but it brought him back and he was alive!

With a thunder of boots on the uncarpeted stairs he flung himself out of Daniel Browne's office and into the crowds on New Quay.

"Why don't you come with us, Matty? Bring Jamie. He'd love to see the bands and the ships," Sara said, smiling at Matty who was seeing them off. The big carriage stood just beyond the front door, the rain slicking the horses' backs to polished pewter. Thomas, water dripping stoically from his chin, held the carriage door open.

"Yes, come with us, Matty. There's plenty of room in the carriage for all of us even with Miss Watson and Mrs Canon and then you and Thomas can go off by yourselves. Oh yes." Paul Travers grinned wickedly. "Do you think I am blind, or just getting too old to notice what's going on under my very nose? I have seen the way you and my coachman exchange glances." He winked and Matty almost winked back he was so taking. Matty had noticed Mr Paul was always referring to his age these days, wondering why, for he looked so handsomely dashing today as he and Sara prepared to climb into the carriage and drive down to the river to see the "fun" as he called Her Majesty's visit. Perhaps it was because Sara was so hesitant about marrying him; after all he was over forty though no one would think so to look at him now.

They were under the porch which protected the steps and front door of Lovell House, glad of its shelter too, for the rain was coming down in buckets, when the man was first noticed.

Sara was laughing at Paul who was struggling with what was known as an "en-tout-cas", a waterproof parasol which was very popular with ladies in inclement weather. It was dainty, made of heavy cream cotton and had a turned rosewood handle with a silver collar.

"This damned thing must be broken," he was grumbling, giving it a fierce shake and peering under the cream lace trimming at the catch before turning impatiently to the footman who held open the front door. "Is this the only umbrella in the house?" he demanded.

"No, sir, there is the one kept in the hall. The one I use to protect the ladies who come to the house. It's large and . . ."

"Bring it out, man. It sounds ideal. Better than this bit of nonsense."

It was then he saw the man who stood beneath the trees and his spluttering ceased abruptly as he narrowed his eyes and craned his neck to see him better.

They all turned to see what had caught his eye and Sara became, for some reason, very still.

"Who the devil's that?" Paul growled menacingly. He handed the en-tout-cas to Roberts and strode forward to the edge of the steps, and behind him Matty stared curiously at Sara. Matty was not afraid of the man, whoever he was, for they had Mr Paul, Roberts and Thomas to protect them should the man turn awkward but who was he and what was he doing there and why should his appearance turn Sara to a frozen pillar of marble?

He made no move to come forward, simply stood in the downpour, his sleeved cloak dark and heavy with rain. He wore no hat and his hair was plastered to his head, limp strands sticking to his forehead and over his ears. He was too far away to make out his features but even from this distance his general air of being soaked through to his very skin was evident. Rain dripped from him, from his chin and his ears and the hem of his cloak but he appeared to be oblivious to it.

Still he did not move. The sound of the rain pattering on what was left of the autumn leaves and plopping in the puddles which had formed in the drive was all that could be heard, for even Paul, who had seemed ready to stride down the drive and accost the fellow, was mesmerised by his strange behaviour. Roberts had moved to stand at his shoulder, his jaw becoming truculent, ready to give Thomas the wink should the intruder turn nasty but the man made no move that could be described as threatening.

They might have stood there until night fell, Matty was beginning to think, when suddenly and surprisingly Sara took her arm in a grip so fierce and painful it brought tears to Matty's eyes then just as suddenly she let go of her and began to walk jerkily towards the steps which led down to the drive. She wore a gown in a shade of the palest almond with a lovely bonnet to match decorated with ribbons and flowers of bronze satin but as she stepped out from beneath the shelter of the porch the outfit immediately became spotted with drops as big as a guinea piece. Within a couple of seconds it began to darken with rain.

They all turned to stare at her now, bewildered by this sudden turn of events and though they did not know what the feeling they felt was, nor what had caused it, they were overwhelmed by it, and by Sara's expression.

She put a hand to her throat, clutching at it as if it were torn with pain and the pulse beneath her chin throbbed violently. Her face was paper white and her green eyes were dilated so that they seemed to be black.

"Sara?" Paul said in astonishment, putting out a hand to restrain her, or to support her, for surely she was going to faint but she threw it off, beginning to move, slowly at first but gathering speed, skimming lightly as a bird down the drive, the darkening material of her wide skirt tipping crazily about her as she ran. Her arms lifted and reached out as she ran and so did the man's.

"What . . .?" Paul's voice creaked like a rusty hinge.

"Bloody 'ell . . ." Roberts was not much clearer and Matty reeled back, unable to speak at all for surely Sara had lost her mind? They could hear her voice, small incoherent cries which told them nothing but they made sense to the man, it seemed for his arms took her and folded her against the length of him, lifting her from her feet. His head bent into the curve of her neck, burying his face there and they stood, locked together as one flesh, while those on the steps could do nothing but gape, even Paul Travers who loved her.

But not for long.

"Jesus Christ, what the bloody hell's going on here?" he snarled savagely, the rampant masculine fury a man feels to see his woman in another's arms causing such havoc within him it threatened to have him off his feet. His face was black with jealous rage and he began to run, his boots flinging up gravel with the force of his passage.

Matty watched, unaware that she was clutching at the footman's arm, her eyes wide and incredulous, her hand to her mouth in shocked horror. There was going to be murder done here was her only thought and God help them all when it happened. Who was to murder whom she was not sure but Sara Hamilton was Paul Travers's woman and this man, whoever he was, was in mortal danger.

"Sara," Paul was shouting, "Sara, what in hell's name d'you think you're doing? Let go of her, let go of her, you bastard." His voice rose almost to a scream in his sudden terror, just as though Sara were being held against her will, which obviously she was not. Perhaps it was this which terrified him!

They took no notice of him; indeed, Matty was inclined to think, they clung even more tightly to one another. Sara had her hands at the man's wet face, cupping it wonderingly as she looked up into it. Their eyes were locked tight, deep copper brown glaring down into luminous green as though in savage anger but in them was a glow, a look of heartfelt relief, a warmth, a sense of life which Paul Travers could not bear to see.

"Jack," he heard Sara whisper, oblivious to him, to the rain, to the amazement of Roberts who had shaken off Matty's hand and had followed in case there should be trouble. "Jack . . ."

There was a thrill of exaltation in her voice as though she spoke the name of God.

"Yes." The man's throat closed on the word and as Paul reached them he could see, despite the rain which drenched them, that they were both weeping.

"Take your bloody hands off her," he thundered, unable to bear it, unable to understand it, unable to do anything at all except give in to the savage need he felt to kill the man, then, just as suddenly, as he was about to drag them apart, he recognised him. His mind took him back to that evening when Dan Browne had brought an unexpected guest to New Park House. A nice chap, pleasant, and though a bit of a rough diamond, courteous and very attractive to the ladies. He had – oh Jesus Christ – he had admired Paul's sketches of Sara, then simply walked out of the house and off into the night, not even stopping to retrieve his cloak.

"Why, it's Jack Andrews," he faltered, the recognition

startling him, halting his madness, but only for a second. "Take your bloody hands off her," he roared again, "and you, Sara, get up to the house. Matty," he shouted, "come and fetch her and you," snarling in the direction of the open-mouthed footman, "send the boy for the constable. You'll be in gaol before the day's out, laddie buck."

They were coming out of the soft, private, painfully sweet circle of love in which they had been enfolded, eyes still desperately clinging, for it was such a long time since they had looked at one another, hands still reluctant to part, their expressions speaking of the immeasurable depth and strength of their love which had survived five years of separation. Sara leaned against him, her face pressed into the wet cloth of his cloak.

His voice was no more than a whisper, meant only for her but Paul heard it and felt his vision blur as his grieving started.

"I've waited five years for this, my Sara," he heard Jack Andrews say. "I thought I'd lost you for good. I've searched."

"Hush, I know," she soothed him. "I've looked for you too . . . up north in . . . but you're here now . . . I'm here."

He put a big hand to her chin and lifted her face and again there was a sense of them drowning in one another's eyes.

"My own, you are mine."

"Yes, always."

"I lost you but I never stopped loving you, never."

"I know, my love, I know." She touched his face, then her fingers twined in his wet hair, bringing his lips down to hers, offering their sweetness as she had done five years ago, but his hands became urgent on her arms, unwilling to let her go but sensing the menace of the man behind her. He himself could not be hurt, not now, not ever again, since he had what he had come for but Paul Travers was out of control and Sara must be led away from the danger.

Matty took her and Paul motioned the footman to leave them. He wanted no assistance in his annihilation of Jack Andrews. Jack Andrews! Jack, the man who had been between him and Sara right from the start. Oh yes, he knew he had lost her, her own words had just told him. Had he ever had her in the true, spiritual sense of the word, his agonised soul begged to know but he could only find release from his agony by slowly and systematically beating to pulp the man who had taken her from him.

"You are treading on dangerous ground here, friend," Jack began placatingly, not wanting to hurt this man who was already hurting beyond endurance, this man who, having lost the woman he loved, the woman Jack loved, was now losing his mind.

"You are no friend of mine, you bastard and I'd advise you to leave this property at once. Sara is to marry me."

"I don't think so."

"You don't think so? You know nothing about her. Nothing! She is my mistress."

"I know." The two words sighed painfully out of Jack's mouth and just beyond the two men, still held on one side by Matty and on the other by Roberts, Sara moaned, struggling to get free.

"Then leave us alone, damn you. And if you won't, then fight me for her. Go on, hit me, damn you, hit me."

"I don't want to hit you, Mr Travers, but I will if you make me. You see there's no point to it. Sara is mine. Even though she has been . . . even though you and she . . ." Jack swallowed agonisingly, almost at breaking point, and Sara wept out loud. "She has always been mine and I'll not let her go again. We were parted when we were both barely more than children but I am a man now and she is my woman. Ask her."

"Oh, for Christ's sake, man, put your bloody fist in my face and let's get on with it."

"Let her go."

"Are you to do nothing but talk, you bastard?"

She screamed then, a high piercing scream which sent the rooks nesting in the branches of an oak tree high into the sky. In the kitchen heads turned towards the front of the house and on the drive the horses reared, almost dragging Thomas, who was still at their heads, from his feet.

"Stop it, stop it. Dear God, I can stand no more. If you are to fight over me like two dogs over a bone, the winner presumably to claim me for his own, then you may do so but I warn you neither of you will see me again if you do. I won't have it, d'you hear? I won't have it!"

They turned, both of them with expressions which were strangely alike. They loved her, she could see that but she could also see the indecision in Paul's eyes. He knew, even if she sent Jack away, that she would never marry him. He would never have his son from Sara Hamilton, nor the conventional marriage which, despite his flaunting of the rules of society, he secretly craved. He was forty one years old now, middle-aged and she was twenty and, should she consent to marry him, would he ever have a moment's peace wondering if she still loved Jack Andrews? It was all there in his face and, though she could not have sworn to it, could she detect a fleeting expression of relief as though to ask was this a way to escape his obsession for her? At this precise moment he wanted to batter through the obstacles which stood in his way, as he had always battered through any obstacles which stood in his way. He was a man who, since his father died, had followed his own road in the world of business, made his own life to fit him exactly as he wanted it. Until he had met her he had snapped his fingers and not been surprised when whatever it was he wanted had fallen into his lap. Women, expensive horses and wine, the best that money could buy, but he had not been able to buy her and the thought came to her that perhaps that was why he had not let her go. Why he had persisted and persisted since he knew no other way. She had loved him. She still loved him. Not in the way she loved Jack, for that was something deep and instinctive, another sense, like hearing, or seeing, one that she had carried about with her as she did her ears, or her eyes.

Now she must hurt one of them. She could not let them fight, for if they did they would tarnish what had been bright and lovely between them. Between the three of them. Between her and Jack and between her and Paul.

She saw it in Jack's eyes and knew he understood. Though they had been apart for five years he knew her well. He was as much a part of her as she was of him, one flesh though they had never loved one another in the physical sense as she and Paul had. One mind, indivisible, the rhythm of life coursing through them both at the same sweet pace. A fragile link which had never broken. His face was at peace. It was a bold face, strong-boned, his unsmiling mouth forming her name, his brown eyes deep and fathomless with his love which had waited for her and would go on waiting for her until she was ready. Even beyond the grave if that was her choice. He knew of her relationship with Paul Travers but it did not alter Jack Andrews's love for Sara Hamilton. Paul Travers had known what Jack Andrews had not but Jack Andrews had what Paul Travers did not. He had the heart, the sweet soul, the very essence of Sara Hamilton. She was his as she had never been Paul Travers's.

He squared his shoulders, the rain still falling heavily on him, sliding across his face, dripping from his chin. He blinked rapidly, his eyes not leaving hers.

"I sail for Canada at the end of the week on the *Hibernia*," he said tonelessly, then he turned on his heel and strode off into the dim, wet passage between the trees towards the gate.

There was utter silence for several moments. Sara watched Paul's throat work as if he wished to speak, then, finding himself unable to do so, he bowed his head in submission. He moved slowly towards the carriage, stepped heavily into it, not looking back at Sara Hamilton as Thomas climbed up on to the box and drove away.

He was on the deck of the Royal Mail steamship *Hibernia* when he saw her, just as he had seen her on the last occasion on the landing stage when she had been on the arm of Paul Travers. This time she was alone. She carried nothing but a carpetbag, soft and light and roomy with a metal frame and though Jack was not aware of it, the very one which had come with her from Wray Green to Liverpool. She was in a simple, serviceable gown of dark blue with a bonnet to match, just as though she knew she must come to him with none of the finery she had known in her previous life. About her shoulders was the gracefully slipping shawl she had worn on that first night at her father's house five years ago when he had regained consciousness to find her watching over him. Her mother's shawl, she had told him. Her mother's scented shawl which was beyond value to her.

Jack rested his arms on the rail. He was smoking a cigar as he waited for her but he flipped it into the grey surging waters of the river as he saw her approach through the jostling crowd of passengers who were all trying to get on to the gangway at the same time. He wanted to plunge through those who were already aboard and lining the rail, sweep them all aside and leap the gangway to the landing stage. Reach out for her, hold her to him in a passion of relief, then carry her up to the double cabin he had booked and make love to her before the ship even left the dockside. He wanted to vault over the ship's rail, jump that narrow span of water which separated the ship from the land and, taking her by the hand, proclaim to the wondering crowd that she was his and was she not rare, the woman he loved and who loved him. And he wanted just to stand where he was and watch her coming towards him as he had dreamed of her doing, coming through the years that had been denied them, through the pain that they had suffered, the loneliness, the fear, the need to deny the past in order to cope with the present. To revel in her slow, but determined approach, to see her smile as she spoke to a beaming docker, the set of her slender shoulders as she squared them in preparation for the climb up the steep gangway.

She looked up and saw him and her eyes glowed with love, with courage, with excitement, with the sheer joy of being alive in a world which she was to share with him. It was as though a candle had been lit beneath the shining surface of the green waters of a lake. It shimmered, its steady flame unquenched, unquenchable and he began to move towards the head of the gangway to meet her.

They reached it together.

"I'm here, Jack," she said, the candle in her eyes exploding into a sunburst as he held out his arms for her.

THE SHADOWED HILLS

If I'd known grandchildren were so much fun I'd have had them first! This book is for mine. Daniel and Adam Pitt.

1

The letter was brought to Cloudberry End just as they were sitting down to lunch, conveyed by the second of the three deliveries which the postal service of the nearby town of Crossclough provided. It was brought, with others, on the silver tray by Freda, the head parlourmaid, as was the custom, and placed beside the master who was tapping his fingers in an impatient tattoo on the shining surface of the table.

He took out his watch and glared at it.

"Where in hell are they?" he demanded of his wife. "I ask very little of them except that they be on time for meals but it seems they can't even do that. At one o'clock precisely we eat lunch in this house and they bloody well know it."

Though Jack Andrews was married to a lady he did not call himself a gentleman and saw no reason to curb his own inclination to curse whenever he he felt like it. They were all used to it, his wife, his children, his servants and showed no surprise nor offence when he did.

"Jack, darling, it *is* only a little after one and I'm sure they'll be here any moment," his wife said soothingly, and, as though their children had overheard the exchange between their parents, and to their mother's evident relief, the door was flung open with a great flourish and a good-looking young couple were revealed in the doorway. A small, brown, rough-haired bitch ran ahead of them, settling herself at once in a square of sunshine which lay across the carpet where she immediately fell into a light doze.

The two youngest children of Jack and Sara Andrews did not so much enter the room as make an entrance, lounging for a moment in the doorway, sure of themselves and their privileged place in this household, their matching smiles winning, their demeanour unabashed, the son's expression at least telling them that though he was late he was sure they would forgive him since he was so irresistible.

His father evidently did not agree with him.

"And what time d'you call this then? You both know what time we eat."

"Good morning to you, sir. Good morning, Mother, or is it afternoon?" their son said sweetly, kissing his mother on the cheek before seating himself on his father's left. His sister did the same, placing her rosy lips to her father's cheek as well as her mother's, in the absolute certainty that neither of them could stay cross with her for long. She shook her bright red mop of curls which rioted in a wild explosion about her head, extended her artificially sweet smile to the maidservants to indicate that they might begin to serve and threw herself – her mother could think of no other way to describe it – into the chair opposite her brother.

Christopher Andrews shook out his napkin, placing it across his knee and nodded to Lottie, the under parlourmaid who was helping Freda to serve, indicating that he would have a little soup. "Very little, thank you," he added, wincing away from the very smell of food and his sister Katy knew, despite his cheerful manner and impeccable appearance, that her brother was suffering from a monumental hangover, even at this late hour of the day. His voice was somewhat hoarse as though he had smoked too many cigars the night before and his green eyes were narrowed against the daylight which, though muted, seemed to hurt them.

Chris Andrews was the youngest son of Jack and Sara Andrews, named for his paternal grandfather of whom it was said in the village of Woodhead where his widow, Jack's mother, still lived, that he could idle his way through the day with nothing at the end to show for it with more success than any man in the district. His grandson had the attractive auburn look of his mother, lean and graceful and with eyes the colour of woodland moss but his nature came from the man who had fathered his own father. His mouth was thin, hard, tilted by a somewhat cruel humour as though there was nothing and no one in this life who could possibly make Chris Andrews believe it was meant to be taken seriously and he was the proverbial thorn in his father's flesh. He was twenty years old and had never performed, at school or at the university where he was supposed to be studying law and from where he had just come, what his father considered a hard day's work in his life. Jack Andrews was a wealthy man and there was no necessity for Chris Andrews to work, in Chris Andrews's opinion, not one shared by his father, and the mighty bellowing which echoed about the house when Master Chris was at home was legendary in the Longdendale Valley.

His sister, Katherine, was very like him in looks apart from the colour of her eyes which were a rich, clear amber, like whisky, her father used to say; but where Chris was languid, indolent, his attitude one of anything for a quiet life, Katy Andrews was inclined towards downright and undisguised rebellion, a wilful determination to have her own way, becoming truculent, even aggressive when it was denied her. This seldom happened, at least when her father was away from home which, during her childhood, had been often, for it was easier to let her do as she pleased, within reason, of course, than face the awesome might of her hot temper.

They ate in silence for several minutes. Jack Andrews, who in his early days had eaten food his cook wouldn't care to put in a pig swill bucket, relished a decent meal. He didn't feel "right" unless he had a good breakfast inside him of bacon, kidneys, sausage, mushrooms, fried tomatoes and at least two thick slices of fried bread done just as Mrs Tiplady, his cook, knew how to do them.

He was the same at midday, stoking himself up for the afternoon's labour with Mrs Tiplady's vermicelli soup, salmon trout with parsley, butter and new potatoes, followed by gooseberry tart with custard. He did full justice to his heaped plate from which, Katy was amused to notice, her brother studiously kept his gaze averted. He himself toyed with a forkful of this and a spoonful of that, going through the motions of eating lunch with his family while her mother cast anxious glances at her father, well aware that the previous little exchange was by no means over. Jack Andrews was known throughout the world of railway building as a hard man, an authoritative man who had worked a full fourteen hours, sometimes more, out of every twenty-four and he fully expected his sons to do the same. He disliked failure and, since he himself had never failed despite the poor start he had had in life, he could see no reason why his sons, who had known every advantage he had lacked, should not achieve even greater heights in the world of business, or in any profession they chose to take up for that matter.

Unfortunately, the authority he showed in his working life did not produce the same results in his own home and his two youngest children were known for their lack of discipline and definite inclination to defy his direction, which was a pity, for his two eldest were a credit to him.

He sat back in his chair, indicating to Freda that she might remove his plate. Yes, he'd have another cup of coffee, he said, and then he'd best be off.

"And what do *you* propose to do with yourself this afternoon, lad?" he continued as he sipped his coffee, eyeing his son's sartorial splendour with evident displeasure. Chris wore a well-cut pair of doeskin breeches and a high-cut, single-breasted tweed country jacket and waistcoat in shades of brown and fawn. The jacket had a vent at the back, an outside breast pocket and a slit cuff on each sleeve. His knee-length riding boots were of the finest leather, a highly polished brown, and his small, octagonal tie sported a tiepin fashioned in gold in his initials. He looked every inch the favoured son of a wealthy father, which he indubitably was, the impish smile he cast in his mother's direction seemed to say as he lounged at his ease at his father's table.

"I have not had the pleasure of your company since you came home," his father went on, "so I assume you've been keeping out of my way which is wise of you. Where the hell you get to is a question I'd like answered, though I don't suppose you'll oblige me and why that damned university has to close its doors for weeks on end is beyond me. Hell's teeth, if they kept you at it for fifty-two weeks in the year, as every other damned working man is kept at it you'd be a bloody lawyer by now. And how much longer am I expected to support you while you skylark about in the so-called 'halls of learning', tell me that?"

Katy could see with something approaching horrified laughter that her brother was doing his best not to yawn. He failed, his jaw cracking with the strain.

"You bone-idle young pup," his father roared. "If you're so bloody worn out with junketing about the district in the pursuit of pleasure, happen a day or two in my company wouldn't go amiss. Perhaps I'll take you with me to Manchester this afternoon. I've a bit of business to see to there, legal business which needs attention. Your training might come in handy."

"Well, sir, as it happens I was going to talk to you about that." His son did his best to look serious.

"Were you now?"

"Perhaps after lunch, before you ... we ... set off for Manchester we could have a chat?"

"A chat! A chat about what? I haven't time to be sitting about like one of your mother's callers, drinking tea and gossiping over the latest doings in the valley. I'm to be in Manchester by three and the train won't wait on my pleasure, lad, nor yours, so you'd best say what you've got to say right now."

The two maidservants exchanged resigned glances. They'd be here all day at this rate, if they were any judge of it, which they were for they'd worked at Cloudberry End long enough to recognise the signs; the master and his son were settling themselves for a rare old ding-dong.

"Go on then, I'm listening," the master said, signalling to Freda to refill his coffee cup.

"Well, sir ..." His son leaned forward, smiling with that infectious humour which most thought so endearing but which was totally lost on his father. It cost him a great effort for his constitution was exceedingly fragile today. He had been up no more than half an hour, having spent the morning with his head beneath the bedclothes, shielding his eyes from the light. His head was painful and his stomach sour and as she watched him his sister was aware, for had she not heard the thunder of his horse's hooves beneath her bedroom window last night, that he had not come home until well past three. He would have been out with his wild-riding, wild-drinking and spending friends, those whose fathers were not of the industrial middle classes as his father was. Young squireens from the landed gentry beyond Hollingsworth on the Lancashire side of the Pennines. Johnny Ashwell from Ashwell Hall, Tim Warren of Dunsford Manor and others of the same breeding who had nothing to do with their time but lark about the countryside, getting themselves and any willing dairymaid they could lay their hands on into trouble while they waited to step into the shoes their pedigreed fathers would vacate in due course.

"Well, sir," Chris said again, evidently at a loss as to where he should begin since his head ached abominably and he had

had very little sleep. "It occurs to me that I am not exactly cut out to be . . . a lawyer"

His father continued to sip his coffee, giving every indication that he had nothing to say on the matter though they all knew better, even the parlourmaids who drew closer together as though to prop one another up in the blast which was surely coming. They didn't know why Mr Andrews bothered, quite honestly, since there was nothing more certain than that Master Chris would do exactly as he pleased and why he had stayed so long at that university was a mystery to them.

"Oh aye," his father said at last and with amazing mildness.

"Indeed, I find I cannot make head nor tail of what is being taught me and I also find . . . well, I am not particularly interested in it in the first place. It needs a man with a . . . a . . . serious turn of mind, you see, to concern himself with legal matters and so I thought . . . well, I have my allowance."

Sara Andrews sighed so heavily and at such length they all turned to look at her, even Lottie and Freda. She nodded at the maids to indicate that she would take more coffee and Lottie sprang forward with the pot, glad, it seemed, as they all were, of the diversion.

Sara thanked the maidservant then turned back to her husband, her softly clouded green eyes imploring. Please, be gentle with him, her eyes begged him. He is young and thoughtless and surely he is what we have made him? He is not industrious like the other two. He is not ambitious either but his good humour is so engaging how could anyone, least of all his mother, bear to see him chastised? She failed to realise that it was her own indulgence, which her husband was not able to withstand, that was the root cause of the problems her two youngest children caused him. Don't be too hard on him, her expression pleaded. He will fit in somewhere if his father would just be patient . . . and kind. A place would be found for him and until then . . .

Her husband was a man who had clawed his way to his present position, snatching what he wanted, for the past thirty or so years, from all rivals in the construction of the railways, fighting, she was certain, hard and dirty, for it was a competitive business. He had bid for contracts as far north as Scotland and as far south as Cornwall, and won them too, travelling for weeks on end and for thousands of miles, driving his men as hard as he drove himself, coming home like a whirlwind to disturb the routine of the home he had built for her at the base of the brooding peak of Black Hill in the Dark Peak district of north Derbyshire. He was a man who had laboured to get where he was, and what he wanted from life, and he expected his sons to do the same. His two eldest boys had not disappointed him but this one, this audaciously charming and far from unintelligent son of theirs seemed to possess a restlessness, a reluctance to settle to anything which smacked of time-keeping, of routine, of responsibility, in fact of what other men described as work, preferring to shoot grouse and partridge up on Bleaklow, drink brandy, play cards and spend his time in the company of low women, his mother feared.

Jack Andrews's face softened as he looked at his wife. He was still a handsome man despite his fifty-one years, massive of build with dark, curling hair only recently touched with grey. A man whose devotion to his wife was as well known in the valley as his disagreements with his youngest son. They had been married for twenty-five years and wherever they went showed an open delight in one another which was as diverting to those who found themselves in their company, as it was unusual. He loved her and was loved by her and neither of them saw any reason to hide it. Of course their family and servants were used to their utter devotion, their tendency to touch one another's hand, to smile a secret but what was very evidently a private smile at one another, which could be very disconcerting at times, particularly when it happened across the dinner table when they were dining with friends.

Sara, even at forty-five, was a vividly beautiful woman, graceful, elegant and sweet-natured, inclined to laughter and sometimes even mischief. Because of the nature of her husband's work she had often been alone bringing up their four children and she had been lenient with them, soft some called it, so that they had grown up out of hand, or at least the two youngest. The eldest boy, Richard, who was a clever engineer, had gone off a year or two back to make his fortune in the business of railway construction as his father had, and was at this moment on the other side of the world in Japan. The Tokyo to Yokohama line was to open in September and Richie Andrews, who had promised his mother most faithfully that he would write at least once a month, had also promised her he would come home when the line was completed before setting out on another adventure. China needed railways, Canada, South Africa, South America but Sara had given up so much of her life to the laying of those shining steel rails, first with her husband and now with her eldest boy, she was sometimes inclined to be tearful about it as she leaned on her husband's broad chest in the privacy of their bedroom at Cloudberry End.

Why couldn't Richie build his railways in his homeland, she had sighed, so that his mother could see more of him? But the truth of it was that the building of railways which had been so abundant in her husband's younger days was virtually finished now in Britain. In Jack's day thousands of miles of track had been laid from one end of the land to the other. A legion of navvies, her husband among them, had blasted their way through obstacles which had seemed insurmountable, until the network of rails spread north, south, east and west like the threads of a giant cobweb. The railway age, begun in Stockton exactly fifty years ago, carrying on through five decades was, but for the odd branch line here and there, effectively finished. By 1860 all the main lines were completed and Sara Andrews's son, her first-born, had been forced to look elsewhere in the profession first his father and then he had chosen.

Now they all waited for the explosion of displeasure which must surely come from the master of the house. Young Chris Andrews would not be allowed to skylark about the countryside with Johnny Ashwell and Tim Warren, surely, but to what occupation other than the seeking of pleasure was he suited? For the past year Jack Andrews had been retired from railway building, at the entreaty of his wife. His investments, his shares in the railway, in coal mining, shipping, in several cotton mills in Lancashire and woollen mills in Yorkshire brought him in great wealth, and the paper mill he had recently purchased beside Topside Reservoir kept him fully occupied, and at home, which pleased his wife. But what was to be done with his youngest son who, it seemed, did not care to go into the legal profession as his father intended, since a lawyer in the family would have come in right handy.

"So, my son, you are to give up your studies at the university, or is it that the university has given up on you? The latter seems more likely, I would say."

His son shrugged deprecatingly and grinned, though his eyes were wary.

"That's about the size of it, sir."

"Oh, Chris darling, now what have you done?" his mother wailed and Katy sighed and raised her eyes in the direction of the ceiling. Good God, hadn't they all been expecting this ever since her brother had gone, with great reluctance, to begin his training in the legal profession? He was no more suited to it than the dog who dozed, one eye opening occasionally to check on her whose dog she was, in the square of sunshine by the window. Chris was a pest, a menace, an aggravating nuisance who, as a boy, and even now, had teased her, fought her, coaxed her into wild escapades – not that she needed much coaxing, she remembered – the pair of them getting into so much trouble her father had threatened to send them both off to boarding school. Life had been, she freely admitted it, unendurably boring since he had left for the university. He was four years older than she was and had always harboured the belief that he was the best looking, the most winning of their mother's children, not only her favourite, which was probably true, but that of every maidservant in the house. He was never defeated, never dismayed, carefree and smiling when he got his way, strutting through life like the young lordling he thought himself to be.

But then wasn't she exactly the same? The thought made her smile.

"Really, Mother, does it matter what he's done?" she protested, "since it was bound to happen sooner or later. He was never cut out for the academic life, was he, so whatever it was, probably to do with a girl, or gambling, would have come about— "

"Katherine, that's enough from you," her father snapped.

"Well, it's true and you both know it. Does he ever show interest in anything other than playing the fool with those half-witted friends of his?"

"This is nothing to do with you, Katy Andrews, so I'll thank you to keep your mouth shut and your nose out of my business. This is between Father and me— "

"Be quiet, lad," his father interrupted him, "or I swear I'll take a strap to you" – which they all knew was an idle threat since it would distress his wife – "and as for you, Katherine, I fail to see— "

"Please, Jack, don't upset yourself, darling," which again meant don't upset *me*.

"Upset myself. *Upset myself!* God above, Sara, what am I to do with the pair of them? Chris is twenty and shows no aptitude for anything other than gaming and . . . and other things, and as for Katy she conducts herself with a lack of decorum which would not look out of place on a girl who has been brought up in the back streets of Liverpool. Jesus Christ . . ." His frustration contorted his face into a deep, ferocious frown. "I am forever being told that she has been seen somewhere she has no right to be. Oh, hell and damnation, Sara . . ."

Jack pushed his hand savagely through his thick hair, making it stand on end and his deep brown eyes, darker than his daughter's, were lit with fires of outrage. The splendidly cut black frock-coat he wore strained across his broad shoulders. He was very evidently doing his best to contain his thwarted anger, for the sake of his wife only, but his daughter did not see, or refused to see, the signs of danger.

"Father, you know there is always someone who delights in tattling about others. What I do is perfectly harmless."

"Oh, it is, is it?"

"Yes, and why you listen to such gossip is beyond me."

"Katy, I'm warning you."

"Why don't you tell them, whoever they are, to mind their own business?"

"Katherine, for your own safety's sake, either go to your room or be quiet until I have finished with this . . . this workshy young devil here. And when I have done so I shall have a word or two to say about your harmless behaviour."

"Surely you are to take no heed of some busybody who has seen me racing my mare up towards Bleaklow Head."

"There are dangerous bogs up there, girl, which— "

"Which I know about, Father, and so avoid them. I have been on the moors all my life, you know that."

"That's just it and from now on I insist you stay in the valley or, if that don't suit, in your mother's drawing room where you belong."

Her father, for once ignoring his wife's imploring expression, leaped to his feet, his face outraged. He had two sons who were a blessing to him, one an engineer and one up in Edinburgh training to be a medical doctor. Clever was David Andrews, like his older brother Richard, hardworking and assiduous in his studies, but these two wild ones, his son Christopher and his daughter Katherine, were a sore trial to him.

He glared at them both. His daughter had fallen into a frowning silence, her mouth set in a mutinous line, her jaw tight clenched, while his son appeared to have sunk into a light doze similar to that of the animal on the carpet.

His wife watched them all anxiously, her arched eyebrows dipping in a frown. Jack looked as though he would like nothing better than to give both his son and his daughter a good hiding, or, failing that, lock them in their rooms on bread and water, and Sara wondered why it was that either one of these two caused more trouble, more ructions, more downright aggravation than her other two put together. Their father turned, ready to explode with frustration, looking for something on which to vent it.

"And what's that bloody animal doing in here? I've told you a hundred times, Katy, to keep the thing out of the house. Are you incapable of obeying even the simplest order?"

"Yes, Father. I mean, no, Father."

"Well see to it in future."

"She's doing no harm, Father," and as though she knew she was being discussed the scruffy-looking little bitch raised her head, seeming almost to smile in supplication, thumping her short stubby tail on the carpet in an ecstasy of devotion.

"Katherine." Her father's voice had an ominous sound to it.

"Darling," his wife interrupted smoothly, "do sit down and see if there is any mail for me. It's time I had a letter from Richie."

It was a diversion and they all knew it. The only person who could calm Jack Andrews when his two youngest children threw him into a rage was his wife and though the matter of what was to be done with her youngest son was not yet dealt with, and the question of her daughter's wild riding on the moor was one which cropped up almost daily, it could all be left until another time, surely?

Her husband sat down, somewhat calmer, and his children exchanged relieved glances. He riffled through the post, still irritable, then handed a letter to his daughter.

"Aye, lass, there's one here but it's not from Richie. Pass it to your mother, Katy, and take that look off your face, for I mean to have my way in this. You should not be riding alone and especially not up on the moor. You know how dangerous it is. You are sixteen years old and if you want to ride then take Dicken with you," he was saying but a strange sound from the end of the table, a sound somewhere between a moan and a hiss of agony brought him instantly to his feet again and cut off his flow of exasperated words.

"Sara . . . darling?" he questioned, his voice aggressive, for what hurt his wife hurt Jack Andrews a hundredfold. In fact he wouldn't have it at any cost. His sole purpose in life was her happiness and whoever had written her the opened letter which was trembling in her hand had better have a bloody good reason for doing so.

His chair fell backwards with a crash. The dog leaped to her feet and began to bark and Lottie dropped the laden tray, scattering soiled dishes all over the rich pile of Mrs Andrews's beautiful sand-coloured carpet. Both Chris and Katy pushed their chairs back and stood up uncertainly, still clutching their napkins, watching as their large father scooped up their dainty little mother, holding her to him in an agony of remorse just as though whatever ailed her was his fault.

"Sweetheart, what is it? Tell me, darling, is it bad news?" Though he could think of nothing and no one who would dare upset his precious and half-fainting wife. "What is it?"

"Jack, oh Jack," she was moaning into his shirt front and both Chris and Katy exchanged appalled glances. What on earth could there be in the letter clenched in their mother's hand and who was it from? Whatever it was it had badly upset her and if their mother was upset their father would lash out at the first person who came to hand, namely them and hadn't they had enough for one day? Should they make a run for it? their eyes asked one another, since the one thing they had learned early in life was that for Jack and Sara Andrews no one existed but each other. Something that had happened in their past before their children were born, though they knew none of the details. Oh, they knew their parents cared about them and their upbringing had been safe and protected, a perfectly happy childhood, but they knew they came second in their parents' affections.

Their exchanged glances asked the same question. Did their mother and father want to be alone or should they stay in case . . . well, something might be required of them?

It seemed unfeeling simply to drift away as though they were not in the least concerned about what was happening.

"Who's the letter from, my darling?" their father was pleading. "Won't you let me see it?" For their mother was still clutching it, all crumpled up, in her hand.

"It's from . . . someone called . . . Henry Taylor."

"Henry Taylor?" Their father looked bewildered.

"Henry . . . Oh God, Jack, it seems he is . . . *Alice's* husband."

Sara Andrews choked on the last two words. She burrowed like a small animal against her husband, incoherent sounds coming from her and Katy could feel the cold run through her veins and small frozen feathers of ice trail across her flesh. The hairs on the back of her neck rose stiffly, for the total disbelief and repudiation in her mother's voice were quite indescribable. She wanted to go to her, to hold her protectively in her own strong arms, for Katy Andrews was almost a head taller than her mother, but of course her father wouldn't allow it. He would let no one comfort his wife, not when he was there to do it and Katy accepted it, as they all did, even her brothers, at Cloudberry End.

"Let me see it, sweetheart," Katy's father said gently. "Let me have the letter. Don't cry, my love," for his wife had begun to weep with the inconsolable intensity of a whipped child.

"Father . . . Dear sweet Jesus . . . father." Chris's voice was ragged, his face white, his distress so great Katy moved round the table to take his hand. Fight like two cats in a sack they might, but in adversity Chris and Katy Andrews had always stood shoulder to shoulder.

"Oh, mum," Lottie moaned for she could not bear another moment of the overwhelming disaster which had come upon them all.

It must be Master Richie in that heathen land he'd gone to, or Master Davy up north in his grand medical college. One or the other of them must be dead to make the mistress carry on so, though she had no idea who Mr Taylor or Alice might be.

Freda led her away, murmuring soothingly, her own heart heavy, closing the door quietly behind them, for the family would want privacy at this moment of sorrow.

Jack and Sara might have been alone for all the notice they took of their bewildered children.

"I'm going to throw it in the fire, my darling," Jack said

firmly. "That's the best place for it. I don't give a bugger what it says. Give it to me, Sara, please. I have no interest in that woman. None. After what she did to us . . ."

Chris and Katy were astonished to see their father, who had never been other than strong, contained, tempered, clutch their mother to him as though in fear, his face contorted with some emotion they could not even begin to describe. Loathing, perhaps, a revulsion so great it was ready to tear him apart with some dreadful memory, a strange reluctance to take hold of the letter and yet an urgency to have it out of his wife's hands and disposed of at the back of the fire. Clear, tawny brown eyes stared incredulously into vivid green then, mouths agape, jaws slack, returned to goggle at the scene which was being enacted at the foot of the table.

"Jack," their mother whispered, "you must read it." Her voice was muffled and yet stronger. "We can't just throw it in the fire and then . . . forget it ever came."

"Damn it to hell, Sara, why not? Why not, dammit? How can you bear to . . . she nearly killed me . . . not physically, I know that, but . . ."

Jack Andrews threw back his head and glared at the ceiling, his gaze so menacing, so perilous, Katy felt her brother start forward as though afraid for someone's safety but she held him back, for this was between their parents, whatever it was, and must not be interfered with by outsiders.

"I know, beloved." Her mother's voice was filled with infinite tenderness. "Oh, I know, and I will never forgive her myself but we . . . oh please, Jack, you must read what her husband has written."

"No, Sara, I can't. I won't let her tamper with our lives again. We have had twenty-five years of . . . of . . . and I cannot risk it. Please, darling, let me put it to the back of the fire . . . please."

"I can't, Jack, I can't. After all, Alice is my sister and her daughter is my niece."

"Daughter! Dear God, what are you talking about, Sara? You're not making any sense. Come, won't you let me send for Matty? If you were to lie down . . ."

"No, Jack, oh no, please listen to me. Alice is dead and her husband is sending her daughter to us!"

2

Madge Andrews leaned forward in the small bow window of the cottage, relishing for a moment the warmth of the sunshine streaming through it as she watched her granddaughter gallop her little sorrel mare up the steep track which led to Madge's front door.

Madge sighed in resigned exasperation, for the girl was dressed as no girl should be. Oh, she was in the decent riding habit her mother had had made for her, and insisted she wore, a rich, blue boxcloth with a jacket bodice and a neat white cravat at the neck but under the long, trained skirt she wore trousers. Again, it was quite acceptable for a lady to wear trousers beneath her riding habit, Madge knew that, but not in the style Katy had adopted. Tight they were, clinging as though they had been painted on her shapely legs, which were clearly visible since the skirt, all five yards of it, was bunched up above her thighs. The top hat she was supposed to wear but rarely did, at least out of sight of her parents, was attached in some way to her saddle and her vivid red hair swirled about her head like a newly opened chrysanthemum. As though it had a life of its own it snapped in the wind which blew even on the mildest day in the high moorlands, snatched back from her white, strained face and Madge sighed again since she knew that face well and it boded ill for Madge's peace.

Madge, whose mother had been a Yorkshire woman and a great one for what she called "fettling", had just finished her own. Since seven thirty that morning she had been in a frenzy of polishing and deep scouring. Nothing in the cottage had escaped her watchful eye. She had yellow-stoned her front doorstep, cleaned her windows, turned out her bedrooms and banished from every nook and corner what had always

offended her the most and that was muck. She had emptied
the drawers in her kitchen dresser and relined them with clean
paper and she had just been about to start on the cupboards,
relishing the scrubbing of her already spotless crockery, when
the sound of horse's hooves on the cobbles had brought her
to the window.

She tutted irritably. "I'd best mash t'tea," she told the tabby
cat in the chimney corner, which had raised its own irritated
head at the commotion beyond the door.

Madge talked to the cat all the time for, as those who live
alone do, she liked to address her remarks to someone. "An'
I suppose I'd best get out t'gingerbreads an' all. She love my
gingerbread, do Katy. Now don't tha' look at me like that,
Tab," as the animal continued to show signs of annoyance,
for where Katy went so did her dog and Tab and Muffy were
old adversaries, "but I know what tha' mean," Madge went
on, just as though the animal had spoken. "'Tis the end of our
peace, for wherever she go she causes nowt but bother an'
vexation. An' that animal of hers is no better, fetchin' muck
all over my clean flags an' do the lass say 'sorry,' or even
notice? No, she don't. I know she's me granddaughter, Tab
and I'm right fond of 'er fer she's a good heart but she's worse
than that there basket of kittens with her mischief, an' just as
thoughtless."

Madge Andrews sighed deeply for the words were true. She
had been uttering them to the cat and to herself for the past ten
years, ever since the then six-year-old Katherine had evaded
her governess, or whatever the woman who had charge of
her education was called, finding her way, not along the
road which ran beside the reservoirs from Crossclough to
Woodhead, but riding her little pony up through the oak and
rowan and birch woodlands which clustered on the lower
slopes of Tintwistle Knarr, Round Hill and Butterley Moss. She
had somehow leaped the tumbling waters of Crowden Brook,
skirted the quarries, guided her small mount up gritstone
slopes and down sliding shale, unafraid, unaware even that
what she did was anything out of the ordinary.

Before that day she had travelled once a week with her
mother in the carriage as far as it could be taken by the
horses, struggling on foot up the last few cobbled yards to
visit her grandmother.

But once a week was not enough for young Miss Katherine

Andrews who loved her grandmother dearly and so, having decided she had no further use for the simple sums, the French verbs, the singing lessons, the learning of the neat copperplate handwriting her governess insisted upon, and the sewing lessons her mother insisted upon, she had simply – somehow – saddled her own pony and raced off in the direction of Woodhead, which she found without the slightest trouble and had been doing so ever since.

They had tried, or rather Sara had tried, for Jack was so often away, to curb her but it was like trying to put a halter on some legendary winged creature, a wild Arabian steed which would fade away, droop and die if it were tethered. At first, with Dicken, her father's conscientious stable lad always a few paces behind her, she had been given the freedom to go where she pleased. Or where Dicken pleased, for the young man had been born and bred in these parts and knew every clough and waterfall, every black reef of gritstone, every quaking morass of bog. He knew where to find stretches of rough moorland where the horses could safely gallop, how to cross steep ravines without breaking the horses' fragile legs, how to find his way home when the weather turned nasty and, more importantly, to recognise when it was about to, and when he had divulged all he knew to his young charge she simply discarded him, galloping off on her own.

What a hue and cry that had caused, her poor mother white and silent, her brothers frantic, for their father would kill them all if he came home to find his only daughter vanished beneath the innocent-looking sphagnum moss which covered the lethal boggy ground.

Just as it was getting dark and her mother about to get out her mourning gown, Katherine had ridden casually into the stable yard of Cloudberry End, slipped from her tired mare's back and professed herself astonished by all the fuss. Dicken knew she was perfectly well able to climb to the top of Bleaklow – or at least as far as the peat bogs allowed – on her own, she said. She had crossed the road which led between Valehouse and Torside Reservoirs where it turned at the village of Hollins, and then over the railway track which her own father had helped to lay nearly forty years ago. There were pastures and woodland by Rollick Stones and then straight up by the side of Wildboar Clough with the Shining Cloud Hills on her left until she reached the dizzy heights of Bleaklow Head.

She had to walk her pony in several places, as Dicken had showed her and yes, she was aware it was an inhospitable wilderness as her brothers said, or rather shouted, ready to throttle her, over two thousand feet high, but she had been very careful, as Dicken had taught her to be. Yes, she knew lives had been lost on Bleaklow but not hers since here she was to prove it, and no, she couldn't promise her mother never to go again because that would be dishonest since she would be forced to break her word.

Yes, they had tried. Dear God, they'd tried, Madge Andrews knew that, especially her son who, in turn, found his daughter lovable, exasperating, defiant, good-humoured – if not crossed – honest, maddening, shocking and even terrifying with her complete lack of fear. She had been locked up, starved for two whole days once, her saddle hidden, her riding clothes and boots removed from her wardrobe, her father ready to flog her with his leather belt, but in the end he did the only thing he could do. Told Dicken to follow her the moment her pony was saddled, which was all well and good, said the mortified Dicken but Miss Katherine could ride rings round him, God knows how, but she could. She was trickier than a cartload of monkeys and she and her mount could vanish without a trace the minute he took his bloody eyes off her, he complained bitterly to his master, who understood and sympathised with him enormously, and Dicken didn't care if he got the bloody sack for saying so.

Now, here she was, labouring under some bitter and vexatious problem if her manner and the expression on her face were anything to go by as she flung herself vigorously out of the saddle. Not that she wasn't careful with her pretty little mare which appropriately she had named Storm. It was her mother who had suggested it, it was said, which Madge thought made sense since Sara Andrews's life was stormy with this girl of hers, not to mention the lad who had been named after Madge's own beloved husband.

Madge shrugged ruefully, her wrinkled face uneasy beneath her lace and ribbon cap. She was a strong, plain woman, born in Manchester to a comfortably-off family who were in cotton, ready to settle in a respectable marriage to a man her father approved of until handsome, merry, irresponsible Chris Andrews came into her life and swept her off her sensible, well-shod feet. That was over fifty years ago but she was still able to look after herself, thank the good Lord. She had most of her own teeth and though her once dark, glossy hair was now a pure, shining white, she was upright, in good health and as determined as it was her nature to be to remain that way. The only part of her that had let her down was her eyes and she wore wire-rimmed spectacles which clung precariously to the end of her nose.

Katy slashed her riding whip dangerously against her full skirt as she strode across the cobbles, bending her head beneath the low lintel of the cottage door and it was apparent from the tenseness in her face that her mood was just as savage as her whip.

"Come in, Katy lamb," her grandmother said mildly enough. "But should that there horse be left standin' like that? Are tha' not goin' to tie it up or summat?"

"No, she'll not go far," Katy answered absently.

"Happen she won't but she seems to 'ave tekken a fancy to Annie Lennox's primroses an' Annie'll not be best pleased to find 'er window box all eaten up."

"Oh, never mind Annie Lennox's primroses. I'll fetch her some more from Cloudberry next time I'm over."

Madge sighed deeply before lifting her cheek for her grand-daughter's kiss then began to bustle about the kitchen, Katy at her heels, pouring boiling water into the teapot, warming it in readiness for the tea, swilling it round and round, for Madge was very particular about her frequent "brews" and warming the pot was an essential part of the procedure. Three heaped teaspoons of tea were placed in the pot, one for her, one for Katy and one for the pot itself, before the second lot of water was poured in and the tea was left to mash. A tray was laid with a pretty, drawn-thread tray cloth and two of Madge's best, rose-painted china cups and saucers, a sugar basin and milk jug to match, and on a plate she arranged the gingerbreads and an almond slice or two of which Katy was equally fond.

Madge liked to do a bit of baking every day, keeping her hand in, she called it, making sure her biscuit tin and her cake tin were well stocked since she had a great many grandchildren, even great-grandchildren, any or all of whom were inclined to descend on her without a moment's notice.

Stepping over the dog with an irritable "tcch-tcch", she placed the tray on the plush tablecloth which covered the kitchen table when it was not in use, poured out the tea and handed a cup to Katy who took it absently and began to sip.

"Sit thi' down, lass, an' give over frowning. There's summat up so why don't tha' tell me what it is? What's brought thi' over here at such a lick an'in such a state tha's lettin' that animal o' thine make free wi' Annie Lennox's window box? Nay, don't argue. Tha's in a flummox over summat, that's plain to see but best calm down first afore thi' fly off t'handle."

"Grandmother, I can't calm down. I'm . . ."

"Tha' can lass, an' tha' will."

"Oh, Grandmother . . ."

"Don't tha' 'oh, grandmother' me, Katy Andrews, for I'm too old for your shenanigans an' I'll not put up with 'em."

"It's not my shenanigans this time, Grandmother," but nevertheless Katy settled herself, sighing wearily, in the chair opposite her grandmother, soothed by her grandmother's refusal to be anything other than calm as she always was, watching as, her tea drunk, she took up her knitting which was always to hand. Katy had never, in all her life, seen her grandmother sit and do nothing. If it wasn't mending or darning, it was knitting for one of her innumerable grandchildren or great-grandchildren, this time a tiny matinee coat for Violet's latest. Violet was George's eldest girl and George was Madge's eldest boy and Violet already had eight little 'uns about her feet in the tiny, dark cottage along the lane. They all lived close by, Madge's sons and their wives, her grandchildren and their spouses, and to tell the truth she often wondered what on earth had possessed their Jack to bring his lovely, ladylike bride to this desolate place where nothing much grew but broom, heather, bracken and sheep.

The Dark Peak it was called, composed of gritstone, black reefs of it, wave upon wave of it as though it were a sea which had solidified; and interspersed with these seas of rock was a quaking morass of bogland. The land of the gritstone uplands was a fierce and treacherous land which soaked up the rain like a sponge and a horseman unfamiliar with the terrain, careless with it, could be sucked into it, horse and all, before he had time to say "whoa", which was why Jack was so afraid for his girl.

Below the line of the peatland there were wide patches of rough moorland covered with tussocky mat-grass, and hawthorn grew on the edges, with rowan and broom, with sessile oak and swathes of birch. Tumbling waters fled down ravines where fern clung, and grouse flapped from under the heather as men approached with guns. Sheep wandered, gnawing at the poor crop, rough, wild sheep with names such as Gritstones and Lonks, the only sort that could survive in this bitter land. The area was carved by running water as streams ran from the inexhaustible reservoirs of the grits, setting out from the crest of the peaks on their journey to the lowlands. The water cut narrow but deep gorges, joining forces with other streams, increasing its power as it excavated cloughs ranging from mere notches down the face of steep scarps to the narrow, wild and impressive valleys below, filling the reservoirs of Valehouse, Torside, Rhodeswood, Woodhead and Bottoms which provided the city of Manchester with clean water.

A rough land, a hard land where a man must be hard to endure it, and a woman harder, but when the sun shone, as it did today, the sky was filled with a pure blue light which seemed to shimmer on the edge of the horizon and it took on a rugged beauty. Skylarks, barely discernible to man's eye in the sky to the back of Madge's cottage, sang their hearts out and the hare's-tail cotton grass was covered with burgeoning fruit, the whiteness of it giving the impression of a recent snowstorm.

"Grandmother," her granddaughter began, replacing her cup and saucer on the table and helping herself to another almond slice.

"Yes, lass?" Madge answered serenely, since she believed nothing her granddaughter could say or do was likely to alarm her, not at her age.

"Did you know Mother had a sister?"

Madge felt her old heart lurch perilously and knew that her earlier belief was wrong. Her still nimble fingers became a jumble of thumbs and stiff joints and she was aware with that part of her brain which dealt with everyday, basic things that she would have to pull at least two rows back and start again since she'd dropped several stitches.

The startled expression on her face must have given her away, for Katy straightened up from her usual pose of sprawling indolence to one of sudden interest.

"You did know, didn't you?" Her tone was accusing,

implying that she took it hard her grandmother had failed to confide in her.

"Aye, I did, but I never met 'er, lass."

"Did anyone? Meet her, I mean."

"Nay, not that I know of, anyroad."

"Well, it's a bit of a facer to learn you've family you didn't even know existed."

"Aye, lass, I suppose it is."

Silence fell as Katy brooded on this last, her unseeing gaze fixed on the crackling coals in the fire, the familiar objects of her grandmother's kitchen which she had known all her life, fading to the edge of her conscious mind.

Madge Andrews's boxframe cottage, which stood with a dozen or so others in the small hamlet of Woodhead, was built of local stone and had a rose-coloured clay tile roof over which, during the years, lichen had grown. There was ivy climbing the wall and partly covering the roof and in the summer it was joined by a thriving eruption of pink sweetbriar roses.

But despite its air of well-kept prettiness the walls of the cottage were poorly insulated, the upstairs windows, made of cylinder glass, were draughty and though the doors at the back and front of the cottage were sturdy and well fitted and much had been done to restore the old building, for Jack was a wealthy man and a good son, the only really warm place was before the enormous fireplace on the end wall. All the cooking was done in the fireplace, for Madge had resisted all Jack's efforts to put in one of the new-fangled cast-iron ranges which had become so popular. She liked the place just as it had been when her Chris had brought her here as a bride nearly sixty years ago, she protested sharply, and saw no reason for change. She was attached to her high-backed rocking chair, her hand-made rugs, her old dresser, and with a canary singing in a cage, with her Tab and Tab's everlasting litter of kittens which resided in a basket in the chimney corner, a water butt – her only concession to modernity since Jack said she was past plodding down the track to the stream – at her back door, she was as snug as Tab and her kittens themselves. She would be seventy-five this year, a great age for any woman but despite this she resisted fiercely any suggestion of giving up her independence.

Jack had wanted her to go and live in style and comfort at Cloudberry End but Madge, fond as she was of the sweet girl her son had married, couldn't quite picture herself in the overwhelming luxury and grandeur of Jack's brand new house which perched on the gentle lower slope of the valley looking out over the reservoir. A lovely house, to be sure, built of stone with a long, low front, standing solitary and alone, exposed to the fierce storms which swept over the moorland at its back. Five acres of garden it stood in, with terraces dug out of the sloping land, gardens full of old-fashioned flowers, with clipped hedges and paved walks sheltered from the cold winds. Laurel hedges edged the drive which led to a round gravel court for the easy turning of Jack's fine carriages and inside the house it was even grander. A wide hall three times as big as Madge's cottage, a parlour, a drawing room, a dining room, a breakfast room, all shining and glowing with lovely polished furniture; above these were bedrooms by the score and even a couple of bathrooms with flush "lavvies" and constant hot running water.

It was beautiful: the setting, the comfort, the velvet lawns all about the house, the colourful flowerbeds, rose beds filled with sweetbriar, with cabbage roses, moss roses, old white damask and maiden's blush and a fragrance too incredible to be described. Sweet Williams crowding against iris and peonies, pinks, carnations, wallflower and Canterbury bell, an invasion of the senses which was almost too much to be borne. An arbour spread with honeysuckle and roses, a terrace with steps leading down to it all, balustrades and sundials and benches under trees and at the end of her first visit Madge couldn't wait to get back to the simplicity of her own small home.

Cloudberry End was only a mile or so out of the busy little country town of Crossclough where a railway station on the Manchester to Sheffield line made it convenient for Jack to get about on business and for Sara to travel to Manchester and the splendid shops there. What had worried Madge more than anything when Jack begged her to come and live with them was the unimaginable situation of having her family, George's, Will's and Harry's families drop in on her at Cloudberry End in the easy and familar way they did at Woodhead. Jack had "got on" and it was rumoured he might even be a millionaire and George and Will and Harry had remained exactly what they had started out as, which was farm labourers. Jack had acquired polish, a "posh" way of talking, or so Harry said sneeringly, and Jack's wife, there were no two ways about it, was a lady and could no more sit and gossip with Madge's other daughters-in-law than Jack's elegant carriage horse could be put in tandem with the one which pulled old Arkwright's plough. A proper lady she was, though she never threw it in your face but it was there just the same. They might have been born in a different class and culture, George's lot, Will's lot, Harry's lot, so far apart had Jack grown from them. Jack had travelled all over the world and the furthest her other sons had been from Woodhead was to Penistone to see the fair.

As for Jack's children, they were the children of a lady and could find no common ground on which to meet their cousins. There was already bad feeling between Chris Andrews and George's Paddy, who were the same age, and with Will's twin sons, Josh and Jake, who often hung about with Paddy. They were outspoken in their rough contempt – and envy, Madge suspected – of their fine cousins at Cloudberry End.

"Do you know anything about her, Grandmother?" Katy went on, leaning forward to peer into Madge's face. "For some reason Mother and Father have kept her existence a secret from us. She's called Alice Taylor, apparently, and all these years, twenty-five, ever since they married, they've spoken not one word about her and what I'd like to know is why? What possible reason can they have had for keeping her hidden? Not that I'm particularly concerned about that, you understand" – since I already have more relatives than I know what to do with, her expression seemed to be saying – "but it's all such a damned mystery and now Mother's shut up in her room with Matty, and Father's dashed off God knows where and nobody will tell us a thing. Chris, who's in trouble again, by the way, and should have gone to Manchester with Father, galloped off in great relief and Father didn't even notice, he's so upset. But nobody will tell us so I came to you."

The room was still but for the crackle and splutter of the fire, the plaintive mewing of the kittens whose mother had sauntered off in the direction of the open back door and the canary which was going through its repertoire in the window bottom.

"Grandmother?" Katy urged. "Do you know what's been going on?"

Madge lifted her head and looked into the flushed, intense

face of her granddaughter. "The child of my child is twice my child," the old proverb went and though it was not true of her other grandchildren, it was about this one. Twenty-seven grandchildren she had had and she'd lost count of her great-grandchildren but this one, this unpredictable, self-willed, rebellious, hot-tempered daughter of her youngest son was the one special in her heart. She was strong, flaunting what she liked to call her independence in the face of anyone who tried to restrain her, which Madge could sympathise with since she herself was the same. But inside she was sweet, as the kernel of a walnut is sweet though the shell is hard. And though she was not yet seventeen, in Madge Andrews's opinion, she was ready for marriage, which meant for loving. She held her own mother and father in deep affection, of course, but who can lavish love on a couple who are obsessed only with one another? Who share a strange single-minded rapture which, because of its sad beginnings made the two involved so tightly welded together they were as close as two sides of a sovereign?

But was Jack and Sara's story hers to tell? Madge Andrews asked herself. Was it up to her to reveal to their daughter why Sara had not spoken to her own sister for twenty-five years? It was not much of a story really. Nothing dramatic or sensational though it had seemed tragic to Jack and Sara at the time, and the outcome had been a happy one. But perhaps it was now to be resolved, that strange estrangement, if Sara's sister had been in touch with her as Katherine's questions seemed to indicate.

"Aye, my lass," she said hesitantly, "I seem to remember thy pa telling me some tale years ago about a falling out."

"A falling out? Over what? I can't imagine Mother falling out with anyone."

"Well, my lamb, tha' must ask tha' ma what happened. I do know when tha' pa brought her back to live 'ere I were dumbfounded for there's nowt up here for someone like tha' ma but she made friends wi' . . . well, with her own sort. Mrs Ashwell an' the like and seemed content enough. Tha' pa did say as how he wanted to fetch her away from . . . memories what might hurt her, I suppose, and him an' all, from what I gathered. Summat happened in Liverpool . . . well," she went on briskly, "it's not for me to say but he wanted to mekk a fresh start."

"But why?"

"Nay, lass, that's for them to tell thi'. But why should tha' ma speak of her sister now?"

"She had a letter this morning from her sister's husband. He said Alice was dead."

"Eeh, never!" Madge put a hand to her mouth, inclined to be tearful, for the loss of a sister must be a terrible wrench.

"Yes, so he said and it seems he means to send Alice's daughter up here to stay with us. Damned cheek, I call it, after all this time." Katy's face became pink with indignation. "The thought of some squalling brat demanding everyone's attention from morning till night doesn't bear thinking about," meaning the disturbance of the smooth rhythm of Cloudberry End which revolved carefully around herself. "I have no intention of spending my days in the company of another girl which they will probably try to make me do." She shuddered visibly. "Can you imagine it? 'Take her with you, Katy,' they will say but I refuse absolutely to be bothered with her, Grandmother, and that is that."

Katy's golden tawny eyes snapped dangerously and her full mouth, the ripe colour of a hedgeberry, thinned to a white and mutinous line. She tossed her head and Madge was startled, as she always was by the movement of Katy's short halo of hair which swirled about her skull, reminding Madge of a field of corn when the wind ripples through it. Not that her granddaughter's hair was anything like the colour of corn, far from it. It was rich and glowing, like the leaves of a copper beech but with streaks of gold shot through it, a crop of softly bouncing curls. It had been the talk of the valley from the day Katy first brazenly displayed it, for how could Sara Andrews allow her daughter to wear it so short? It tumbled over her forehead and ears, curling against her creamy white neck, a declaration that Katy Andrews was like no other girl any of them knew. Delicately shaped copper eyebrows arched, or scowled fiercely more often than not, above slanted eyes which were fringed with long, copper lashes and her presence was so taut with tension, with a need to be about something, anything which did not smack of the tedious, of boredom and routine, it was positively painful to be in her company for longer than half an hour.

The rough-haired bitch who had been dozing in a patch of sunshine which lay across the scrubbed flags stood up and stretched her back legs, first one then the other, giving herself a good shake. She sauntered across the kitchen, grinning in that amiable way a good-natured dog has, her short tail moving in small circles. The kittens in the basket began to spit and claw, recognising an enemy which they appeared to think threatened them, defenceless as they were without their mother but they were beneath the bitch's notice as she laid a loving muzzle on Katy's knee. Katy stroked her head absently, her gaze still fixed on her grandmother.

"Chloe," she announced. "Did you ever hear the like? Biblical, Mother said. Something to do with Puritans, God help us."

"Chloe?" Madge murmured. "'Tis a right pretty name."

"D'you think so? Well, Chloe is to be here by the end of the week and if Mother thinks I am to make a little sister of her then she's sadly mistaken."

Katy was prevented from further speculation about the girl who was her lost cousin by a sharp rat-tat at the door which, without waiting for an answer from within, opened immediately, much to the consternation of Katy's dog. She began to bark frantically, for the animal which lumbered in ahead of the man who had opened the door could only be described as the worst canine nightmare any dog could have the misfortune to suffer. He was squat, a cross between a bulldog and some other breed which, though Katy could not immediately bring his antecedents to mind, had obviously been strong, broad-backed, thick-necked and vicious. He was a dirty white in colour, his legs short and splayed, his deep chest and neck supporting a huge head with a broad, square skull. His muzzle was short with an upturned lower jaw. His eyes were deep and dark, ringed with pink and in them was a venom which brought Katy to her feet since his intention was obvious. It was written in his snarling mouth and lowering brow. He meant to take hold of her own brave little dog by the scruff of her neck and snap the life out of her which he could do with a shake of his massive head.

The next two minutes were no more than a whirling, deafening blur to Madge, a blur which contained flashing images of snapping jaws and vicious teeth, of savage, furious eyes blood red with rage, of flying, crashing china as her precious cups and saucers were flung from the tray when the bigger dog crashed against the table. There were howls of animal pain and howls of human fury, of curses, both male and female, of shouted commands, of brawny male arms and dangerously fragile female hands as Katy Andrews and Paddy Andrews, who was her cousin and the owner of the mauling dog, did their best to separate him from Katy's defiant little terrier. The kittens mewed piteously but not even to defend her family would Tab venture into the fighting arena, cowering by the back door of the scullery and Madge found herself lifting the heaving basket on to her lap, for it seemed likely to her that its howling contents might be reduced to bleeding scraps of fur and flesh in the savagery of the turmoil.

At last Paddy had his dog by the collar, almost strangling the thing as he heaved him towards the door, still turning his head to snap and snarl at the terrier and even, Madge was inclined to think, at his master's hand in its bloodlust.

Somehow her grandson opened the door without help, for both Katy and her grandmother were fully occupied in calming their respective charges. He flung the animal on to the cobbled track where, instead of subsiding since his foe was out of reach, he threw himself against the closed door again and again, much to the alarm of Katy's sorrel mare who, since it seemed to her she was in mortal danger, took off at the full gallop in the direction of her stable at Cloudberry End.

"Dear God in heaven," Katy shrieked, and in her arms and pressed to her heaving breasts her dog shivered and moaned. "I hope you're bloody well satisfied, Paddy Andrews. That dog of your is a menace and should not be allowed out of your cottage yard without a chain on it. In fact I've a good mind to ask my father to see the magistrate and get an order to have him put down. It might have . . ."

Paddy only laughed. "Nay, lass, don't tha' speak ter me of vicious dogs. That thing tha've got clutched ter thi' is as lively as a bloody rat an' tha' knows what 'appens ter rats, don't tha'?" He appeared to be completely unruffled by the commotion, even finding it a source of amusement. There was no harm done, was there, except to his gran's cups and saucers so what was Katy Andrews, who really was growing into a very tasty piece of female flesh – and Paddy was a man who appreciated a pretty woman – making such a bloody fuss about? Her animal had a torn ear – he could see the blood on Katy's dress – but that was all. He admitted his dog was hard to handle where other dogs were concerned, since he had trained him to be a fighter but he was harmless, even docile in the presence of humans. Normally, when he was to go where he knew there would be other dogs he would keep him on a chain, but though he had taken note of the sorrel placidly eating her way through Annie Lennox's window box and had even known she belonged to Jack Andrews's lass, he had given no thought to what might be inside his grandmother's kitchen. Obviously his cousin Katy, but he had forgotten that bloody little excuse for a dog which trailed at her heels.

Paddy, Patrick George Andrews to give him his correct name, was the youngest son of Madge Andrews's oldest, George. Big he was and though it was not mentioned, nor even acknowledged, was the spit of his uncle Jack, Katy's father. He was broad of shoulder, narrow of waist and hip with long graceful legs which could stride out for hours on end, carrying him for miles across barren hillside and moor as he took his dog, and himself, to the fights which were arranged at the back of isolated inns and where prize money might be had. Since he was a lad of fifteen, enormous even then, he had fought in over a hundred bouts. He had never been marked and his good looks, dark and gypsy-like, ensured that he was never short of female company. A rebel was Paddy, working casually when he was in need of a bob or two – which was not very often since he won many purses in the ring – in the quarries which abounded in and above the Longdendale valley. Gritstone and sandstone and limestone quarries which the accessibility of the railway had made available to the industries of south Lancashire, Cheshire and the West Riding of Yorkshire. He had the dark curling hair and deep-set brown eyes of the Andrews men. His mouth was wide and inclined to smile more often than not since life was pleasant for Paddy Andrews, but his short temper and hard fists were legend in the valley, should any man attempt to cross him which few did. He was dressed casually in an open-necked checked shirt, corduroy breeches, gaiters and heavy working boots. The dark stubble on his sun-bronzed face and jaw testified to the fact that he had not shaved for several days and where it dipped beneath his chin to his throat it met a bloom of coarse chest hair which sprang from the open neck of his shirt.

Katy eyed it with distaste, her nostrils flaring. Her arms were wrapped protectively about Muffy's still quivering body and she breathed heavily with outrage.

"What the hell is there to smile about, you clod? That vicious brute of yours might have killed Muffy."

Paddy shouted with laughter. "Muffy! Muffy. What sort of a bloody name is that ter give a dog? Muffy."

"What's wrong with it? What, may I ask, do you call that devil which is howling outside my grandmother's door? Satan, I shouldn't wonder! You do realise that he has so terrified my sorrel that she has taken to her heels."

"Well, his name's not bloody Muffy, I can tell you. Jesus . . ." Paddy's laughter became even more pronounced as he lounged by the door with every appearance of great good humour, his hands on his hips, his teeth a startling white slash in his sun-tinted face.

"You realise that I shall have to walk home now, don't you?" Katy hissed, infuriated by his laughter. She advanced towards him, her intention of marking him in some way, as his opponents in the ring had never been able to do, very obvious. "And if my mare damages herself between here and Cloudberry End then you will have not only me but my father to answer to."

Paddy's grin widened. "Oh ho, you really must not frighten me, like that, cousin. I'll not be able ter sleep at night fer worrying about it." He was enjoying himself immensely for there was nothing he liked more than a good fight, particularly if that fight was with a woman, for who knew where it might lead? He allowed his gaze to roam admiringly over Katy, from her head to her well-polished boots, then up again to her flaming halo of glorious hair beneath which the furious pink of her face glowed. It lingered for several impudent moments at her breasts which still heaved against Muffy. Her eyes were the colour of the cat's in the doorway, a deep, golden amber, narrowed and snapping with flecks of outrage, glowing brown and her wide mouth was as red as a poppy, howling her affront. She turned and placed the dog carefully in the chair where she had been sitting before he arrived and, turning again, placed her hands on her hips and glared at him and as she did so Paddy was surprised by a sudden and quite incredible flow of something which began in his chest and travelled to the pit of his belly. A feeling very familiar but one he did not associate with girls like Katy Andrews, by God, and one which had something in it he did not recognise. She was a young girl to him, no more than sixteen or seventeen, he supposed, though her full-breasted figure, which was heaving threateningly in his direction, said otherwise. She'd need taming by some man and wouldn't he like to be the one to do it? A spitting, scratching she-cat who was asking for a bloody good hiding with that wicked mouth of hers but afterwards . . . aah . . . afterwards!

"Well, well." He grinned impertinently. "So Miss Andrews of Cloudberry End can't walk a couple o' miles wi'out gettin' a blister or two on her delicate little feet, is that it? An' as fer yer pa bein' a threat ter me, lass, well, that remains ter be seen. Can't manage 'is own lad, so the talk goes."

His smile gone, he turned away contemptuously. Paddy Andrews answered to no man, not even his own pa. He'd only called on his grandmother because he happened to be passing and she brewed a glass of ale which was to his liking, and he was fond of the old girl. So sod Katy Andrews and sod the lot of them at Cloudberry End. He despised them all and if he could do them a bad turn he would.

"I can walk as far and for as long as you can, Paddy Andrews, and still arrive without a blister. I'm not one of those pampered girls who can't go about without a parasol or their smelling salts."

She was beginning to annoy him with her persistence, her determination to have the last word, her absolute certainty that she was in the right and Paddy Andrews was no more than a lout who must be put in his place.

"Listen, lass, I don't give a damn what you, that prick of a brother of yours, nor that— "

They had both, in their strange absorption with one another, forgotten the existence of their grandmother and when she spoke they both turned to her with what looked like bewilderment.

"Patrick, that is enough, an' as fer thee, Katherine, I'd like ter remind thi' that this is my house and I'll have no more bad language in it. You'd best go, grandson, an' tekk that dratted dog with thi'. If tha' was half a gentleman . . ."

"A gentleman! Him!" Katy spluttered, almost in tears with temper.

". . . I'd ask thi' ter walk tha' cousin home."

"Ha! Walk home with him. I'd sooner walk home with his damned dog."

"Now then, Gran, she's just told us she can outwalk anybody

in't district so let her bloody do it, an' wi'out my help. An' remind me ter mekk damn sure there's none o' them fools from Cloudberry End visitin' thi' next time I'm over or there'll be skin an' hair flyin'. An' that means you, lady," glaring at Katy. "Yer nowt but a jumped-up load o' nobodies, the lot o' you. Yer pa came from workin' stock, like me an' me brothers an' cousins but the way tha' carries on yer'd think tha' were related ter't bloody queen. None of 'em, especially that son of a bitch who rides about wi't gentry, 'ad better cross my path, I'm warnin' yer."

He turned to glare, his contempt for Chris Andrews plain to see and Katy fell back before it, wondering what it was that had made Paddy Andrews, who had been good-humoured enough five minutes ago, turn so sour.

3

The train had laboured its way up the incline which had begun in Hadfield, climbing steadily as it rattled towards the Longdendale valley and the railway station at Crossclough which stood at fifteen hundred feet above sea level. On either side of the track were the lifting moorlands and craggy tops of the Dark Peak, bleak and inhospitable on this colourless day even to someone who was familiar with them as Jamie Hutchinson was. Crossclough, which was no more than a mile or two from Woodhead where the train would pass into the tunnel, was on the narrow peninsula of land which reached out through Lancashire and Derbyshire and into Yorkshire where the tunnel emerged at Dunford Bridge. Woodhead Tunnel, just over three miles long and on which so many men had been crippled or killed, was really two single-track tunnels running side by side beneath the dark, rolling moorlands, the upland deserts of peat and heather which were the hallmark of this land. High, wild moorland where, at this time of the year, indeed at most times of the year, the air was filled with the sound of the water which tumbled unceasingly down dozens of cloughs and into the reservoirs beside which the railway track ran.

The valley was wide and shallow, its lowest point defined by the narrow road which meandered on to Penistone; by the railway, and the string of reservoirs which lay along its bottom. There were fields on either side of the ruffled waters, dissected by dry stone walls. There were woodlands, and scattered cottages dropped down into a sea of bilberry, of wavy-hair grass and the strong and yet delicate grace of fern, and about them rose the multi-hued lift of new heather, bracken and crowberry. But higher still the moors were featureless, rolling on as far as the eye could see, which wasn't far today for the cloud was down.

Jamie did his best not to be too obvious about it but he just could not take his eyes off the delicately lovely creature who sat opposite him in the first-class carriage of the Manchester to Sheffield train. He himself had travelled from Liverpool, changing at Manchester and had only at the last minute decided to travel first class. He was careful with his money, particularly now when only God knew how far it was to stretch, but somehow his return to what he called "home" had seemed a special occasion and needed an appropriate precedent to mark its importance and what better way to travel, and arrive, than in style? It was the ending of his old, hard way of life and the beginning of his new, which would probably be just as hard though in a different way. The impetuous decision to spend his hard-earned money had manifested itself in a cushioned seat in the luxury and well-lit comfort of a first-class carriage instead of the tiny windows, the foetid atmosphere, the bare boards, the dingy, smoky oil lamps which barely illuminated the conditions third-class passengers must endure.

She was dressed completely in black, the lovely, drooping young woman who stared fixedly out of the window, and he was amazed that someone of her youth and quality should be travelling alone. The males of the middle and upper classes guarded their females as though they were made of jewelled gold, protecting them from other males like himself and would certainly not believe that any woman, at least of theirs, was capable of travelling from one town to another unchaperoned, and not only arrive, but arrive safely. Women, or at least ladies, were incapable of getting from their own drawing room to that of a friend without some male to guide them there, even if it was only a servant!

The young woman's clothing was very evidently of the best, even he who knew nothing of ladies' fashions could see that, and though it was drab, as mourning is meant to be, it was . . . well, he could only think of the word stylish, which sounded a bit fanciful. Her gown, revealed when her black, fringed shawl slipped from her slender shoulders, fitted her superbly, hugging her breasts and the smallness of her waist in a way which drew his eyes to them no matter how hard he tried not to. Her hands were small and white, the nails a perfect, pearly oval but they were not at ease, as she was not, twisting anxiously around one another, or clutching fiercely at the small, black reticule in her lap. Her bonnet was small in the style of the day, almost the shape and size of an inverted flowerpot, completely unadorned but for a small veil which she had turned back from her face, inadvisably he was inclined to think. The narrow brim allowed the muted daylight to touch her hair which was like nothing he had ever seen before, and yet at the back of his mind where distant memories lay he seemed to think he had seen hair that colour and texture somewhere. It had a gloss on it like silk and its hue was somewhere between gold and copper and pale chestnut and yet it was none of these since the three melted together into a living flame of glory.

Suddenly she turned her gaze from the drab scene she was studying beyond the carriage window and before he had time to look away their eyes met. Again they were an incredible colour. Blue-green, vivid, like the seas he had sailed across south of the equator, turquoise almost and fringed with long, curling brown lashes and again he had the strangest feeling of having seen them before. They were unfathomable, unreadable, deep and still and for a fraction of a second they stared, startled, into his before her lashes dropped in confusion. She bit her lip; the blood ran pink beneath her white skin and she turned her head away as though in deepest embarrassment, presenting him with the delicate arch of one copper eyebrow and the perfection of her profile.

Christ Almighty, but she was lovely, and where in hell was she going all alone on this murky May morning? The train would reach Crossclough soon, then on to Penistone before dropping down to Sheffield and when he alighted at Crossclough, as he was about to do, she would be left to the mercy of the fashionably dressed young dandy who, like himself he supposed irritably, had done nothing but stare at her ever since she had boarded the train in Manchester. She was very young, no more than sixteen or seventeen, he would have said and would she be safe from any advances the leering young gentleman might press on her?

Damnation, why in hell hadn't she got into a carriage with another woman in it, or at least several passengers so that the chances of her being left alone with some man who would think any woman travelling by herself was fair game would be lessened? Perhaps he might suggest to her that when the train reached Crossclough, which it should in the next five minutes, he himself could escort her to a first-class carriage where the protection of another female might be available.

Or would that alarm her even more? Would she shrink away and tremble as he had seen her do several times on the twelve-mile journey from Manchester; look at him with those amazing blue-green eyes, the expression in them telling him she was convinced he meant her no good?

Jamie sighed deeply, shrugging his broad shoulders more comfortably into his rough reefer jacket, working the collar more snugly up about his neck. Though it was May the temperature was more like January and even here in the enclosed carriage the damp seemed to slither inside his warm jacket and woollen gansey, feathering his flesh which was used to more tropical elements than these. God alone knew what those in third class suffered, he thought, travelling as they did in what was virtually a wooden box with only one small window which frequently would not close. He knew because he had travelled in one.

He shoved his hands more deeply into his pockets and clenched his blunt-angled jaw as the dilemma of the girl opposite gnawed at him and yet it wasn't his bloody dilemma, for God's sake, so why should he feel it was? He was coming home, if he could call it home; about to see his mother for the first time in five years, about to start a new way of life and before he'd even got off the blasted train he had taken upon himself a tricky problem which was not his problem to solve.

Jamie Hutchinson stood six feet four inches in his stockinged feet and had a frame to match his height. His shoulders strained at the seams of his navy blue reefer jacket and his thigh and calf muscles, which were clearly defined beneath the durable woollen fabric of his trousers, were as hard and tensile as a coiled spring. He was dark, his over-long hair tumbling in rough waves about his head and falling over his brow to his fiercely scowling eyebrows. His skin was as brown as his mother's prized walnut dining table, a rich, warm brown which had been achieved in more southerly climes than those of the Dark Peak. His eyes were blue, brilliant and penetrating, long-lashed, narrowed with fine lines radiating outwards from each corner as though he were accustomed to squinting over shimmering seas in which the sun's rays were caught. A strong man with a pleasant face, good-humoured, with a mouth which seemed inclined towards laughter, but there was something in the set of it which said he was not a man to be trifled with.

The train began to slow, the rhythm of its wheels altering and from the engine a piercing whistle warned those who stood on the platform ahead to beware. The young woman stared fearfully from the window, her hands knotting together in what appeared to be real fear and Jamie's face softened. She was nought but a young lass, a little bit of a thing who seemed to be trapped in some fearful predicament and could he, in all conscience, get off the train without doing something, saying something which might alleviate her alarm? Her eyes were wide, almost blank with some distress and her small teeth worried her full bottom lip.

He couldn't help himself. He leaned forward and when he spoke both the girl and the chap by the opposite window who still stared avidly in their direction jumped slightly.

"Are you all right, miss?" was all he said but he might have made some indecent remark to her the way she shrank back in her corner. Her skin paled even further, and her eyes widened even further, if that were possible, so that they were enormous and glittering in her face, but her answer, when it came, was quite composed.

She lifted her head haughtily. "I beg your pardon?" Her tone was icy and she recovered her balance as if by magic, her young face set in a mask of cool rebuff.

"I just thought you seemed . . . disturbed." He shrugged deprecatingly, letting her know he meant her no harm nor offence, sitting back again in his seat.

"Not at all, thank you." Her voice was polite, nipping any familiarity firmly in the bud, giving him the level stare young ladies gave to gentlemen who were making a nuisance of themselves.

"I'm sorry, I didn't mean to intrude." He smiled and the smile lit his face, giving it an endearing, boyish quality. He pushed his big hand through his unruly hair so that it fell in even more tumbled disarray on to his forehead and somehow the natural gesture seemed to reassure her, for she relaxed and her mouth did its best to smile back.

"The next stop is Crossclough," he went on gently. "I am to

get off there," and in his voice was the message that if she did need help he would be only too glad to supply it. His blue eyes had melted from the vivid brilliance of the hot skies of India and Africa where he had journeyed to the gentle serenity of those above his own homeland and the girl sensed he was no threat to her.

"So am I," she answered in a low voice, once again turning to look fearfully out of the window.

"Really. Then perhaps I can help you with your luggage," glancing at the rack above her head.

"Thank you, that would be most kind."

"You are to be met?" he asked politely and was startled by the sudden shadow which darkened her eyes.

"I'm . . . I'm not sure. A letter was sent but . . ." She bent her head, again biting her lips. "I'm not sure."

"Then perhaps I might . . ."

"Oh no." She looked up at him hastily, that careful mask of a lady dealing with the unwanted advances of a gentleman settling again over her face. "I have the address. I . . . I shall take a cab and find my own way there."

"Of course."

There was silence again apart from the slowing clack and clatter of the train's wheels and in his corner the young dandy cast furtive glances, fewer now he knew that the young woman was to alight at Crossclough, his own hopes in that direction dashed but reluctant to miss any further exchange.

Jamie stood up with a courteous inclination of his head towards the girl, lifting down his sea bag and several other packages from the rack above him, placing them on the seat he had just vacated. He looked down at her, an expression of smiling enquiry on his face, asking her permission to place her luggage beside his own, noticing the way she shrank away again in alarm as his size became apparent. He had that effect on people, some finding it reassuring, others threatening. It could be a drawback and an advantage, he had found, particularly the latter in his years at sea. Twelve years he had sailed before the mast, enduring great hardship at first, since he had been a lad of only fourteen on the day he set sail. Scrubbing decks, coiling ropes until his hands bled, climbing spars and the dangerous, dizzying heights of rigging to furl and unfurl sails, constantly seasick on a diet of pork, beef and maggoty biscuits. He had been at every man's beck and call in the first months, evading those wanting only to use his young boy's body as they might a woman's until, at the age of sixteen, he had suddenly grown upwards and outwards, fourteen stone of hard muscle, large, powerful, his body toughened by the physical adversity of his life on a sailing ship.

He had often wondered why he had elected to go to sea in the first place, for he had been brought up forty or so miles from its ocean-going call, and he supposed that was why. It was the unknown. It would be exciting, an adventure, a chance to see the world which a boy brought up in the shadow of the Dark Peak would never see. He had been born in Liverpool, his mother had told him, though he remembered none of it, for she and her husband, who was not Jamie's father, had moved to Crossclough with the family who employed them twenty-five years ago. So, he thought, if he were to call anywhere by that name, Crossclough was his home. He had come back to it to settle, to leave behind the wandering ways of the sailor, to find himself a wife, start a family and, if hard work was the key, to be successful in his new employment.

Having received her shy nod of thanks he lifted down the young lady's bags, then, lowering the window, leaned out to open the door. He stepped down on to the platform, placing her box and a somewhat worn carpetbag beside his own luggage before turning back to her, holding out his big hand.

She was still fixed in her seat, her eyes almost blind in her panic, or so it seemed to him, her glance flitting over his shoulder to what was beyond it. She pressed even further back into her seat and for a moment he felt a spurt of irritation. For God's sake, what was there to be afraid of in this quiet little country station which catered to barely more than a dozen or so passengers in a day? The picket fence which stood between it and the road was sheltered by hawthorn trees planted thirty years ago to cover the ravages the laying of the railway track had caused, and against the fence were white-painted, wrought-iron benches, placed there for the comfort and convenience of those who waited for a train. There was a little waiting room and a ticket office beside which a uniformed railway servant stood to collect tickets. It was as peaceful a scene as any to be found in a community the size of Crossclough, which was scarcely any larger than a village and yet it appeared to appall her.

"Will you take my hand?" he asked her encouragingly, watching with fascination as she drew in her breath and clenched her small jaw with such savage determination it was as though she were about to be dragged into a cage of wild beasts. Putting her small, gloved hand in his, where it vanished in its vastness, she stepped down on to the platform.

"Thank you, you are most kind," she said in that automatic response she had been taught, probably by her governess, he thought and why the bloody woman wasn't here with her now was a mystery since she was so obviously not able to take care of herself. She stood uncertainly, staring about her, scarcely aware of him, he could tell that, and he stood beside her, reluctant to leave her on her own, looking like an enormous and kindly bear protecting a dainty kitten. She was so bloody helpless, he reflected exasperatedly, like a woman marooned on a strange island where the natives were bound to be savage and how was she to cope with it, and them, her manner seemed to ask. And yet she held herself bravely and as tall as she could, which was no higher than his collar button, her head erect, her chin rigid to stop its trembling, her wide, frightened eyes suddenly fixed on a small group of people who had come through the gate from the road and were hesitating by the ticket office.

At once Jamie was aware of who it was she reminded him. The same colouring. The same air of delicate loveliness, of fragile vulnerability, dainty and soft as gossamer, slender as a willow, a scrap of swansdown to be blown willy-nilly by any chance breeze; the woman who stood by the gate and whom she resembled so accurately was none other than his mother's employer, Mrs Jack Andrews.

They did not seem to see him, Mrs Jack Andrews, her daughter Katy and her youngest son Christopher, for all three pairs of eyes were fixed on the girl beside him, as hers were on them. The family likeness was striking, for in different shades of auburn, he supposed you would call it, they were all of the same colouring. Only Katy's deep brown eyes had come from her father's side of the family and as they all stood rooted to the spot, himself included, though he didn't know why, Katy's turned away from the girl and came to rest on him.

It was as though a candle had been lit at the back of her eyes. Katherine Andrews seemed to explode, to ignite with joy, to blind all those about her with her glowing excitement.

She was dressed in some outfit of tawny silk, unadorned with the flounces and bows which were the rage, very rich and gleaming but simple, and a small hat of the same colour and material, the brim of which was turned up all round, something in the style of a child's sailor hat but worn on the back of her head. Again it was unadorned, but Katherine Andrews needed no embellishment with hair as vivid and wilful as hers. It burst from beneath the brim of the hat in a truly awesome cloud of springing curls, tumbling about her ears and neck and over her forehead to her eyebrows.

"It's Jamie," she shrieked for all of Crossclough to hear and though Jamie felt the urge to sigh in exasperation, for it seemed Katherine Andrews had not changed in five years, he could not help the sudden tug of his lips in a smile.

She began to run towards him, her hat flying off and bowling along the platform to the delight of boarding and alighting passengers, and those who stared from the train in surprise at the young woman who ran like a fleet-footed deer past their windows. Her skirt flew up to reveal several inches of lace-trimmed petticoat and even more of stockinged leg above her dainty kid shoes. She flung wide her arms as she ran, oblivious to the open-mouthed stares of those about her, her face ecstatic and on it was drawn the lodestar, the driving force, the mainspring, the very reason for living which coloured Katherine Andrews's existence. It was written as plain as words on a page what she felt, as it had always done and Jamie's heart, which had moved in pleasure at the sight of her, dropped like a stone.

Jesus God, he had forgotten how she was. The childish adoration. What might even be called fanatical worship, the intense, narrow-eyed determination of eleven-year-old Katherine Andrews who had formed such a passionate attachment for him she had refused to be parted from him, doing her best to clamp herself to his side, to go exactly where he went when he was home five years ago.

She had been a child then, easy to elude, easy to placate and please and promise as one would a child. Now she was a woman, but Christ Almighty, it seemed her feelings towards him had not changed.

Her body met his with a force so strong it nearly had him off his feet. She was not small, nor was she light. Though her waist was slender she was deep-bosomed and her hips were what he could only call womanly. She topped the girl beside him by at least half a head and the contrast between them, despite their similar colouring, was quite incredible.

"Jamie, Jamie, Jamie, you're home . . . Dear God, you've come home at last," she was babbling, her rosy face pressed into his shoulder, the sweet, wholesome smell of her enveloping him, her arms a stranglehold about his neck and for the life of him he could not prevent his own from lifting to hold her, to fold her against him.

"Katherine," he managed to gasp, doing his best now to put her from him, to dislodge her from round his neck, to avoid her kisses which she seemed intent on placing wherever her lips could reach, preferably on his own, while the girl beside him watched in bemusement.

"Oh, Jamie . . . Jamie, you're home . . . home."

Over her head Jamie could see the perilous, tight-lipped outrage on the face of the young man who stood by the gate. What the hell was going on, his green slitted eyes demanded and Chris Andrews, galvanised into sudden furious action at the sight of his sister clasped in the arms of a brawny man of the working classes, strode out along the platform, his face compressed into lines of fury. His mother was not far behind him, her face like paper, her clear blue-green eyes, so like those of the girl with whom Jamie had just travelled from Manchester, wide with shock.

"Jamie . . . oh, Jamie, if you knew how I'd missed you. All these years and not one letter, you devil. Not one. You promised to write and all I had was news of you from Matty about places . . . but it doesn't matter now. You're home and— "

"Katherine, that's enough. You are making a spectacle of yourself," her brother said icily. "Take your hands off— "

"It's Jamie, you fool," she breathed, her face and voice enchanted. She patted his chest, ready to snuggle up to him again, unconcerned with the delighted stares of Fred Beardsall, the ticket collector, who would have something to tell his old woman tonight, and of Archie Bagshaw, the postman, who was collecting some parcels at the back of the train and would have the scene in every detail all over Crossclough within the hour.

"We know who it is, Katherine" – her mother nodded graciously at Jamie – "and would be obliged if you would be a little more circumspect in your behaviour. You are not a child."

"Oh, Mother . . ."

"Katherine! Go and get your hat before it rolls beneath the train." Her mother's voice had chips of ice in it. The voice of a lady, a lady born to be obeyed as her upbringing and breeding had taught her and there were not a few about who were of the opinion she should have used it more often in the past, particularly on this rebellious girl.

"Mother . . ."

"Katherine, do as I say."

Reluctantly Katherine stood away from Jamie, then turned and hurried up the platform to retrieve her hat which Fred Beardsall had rescued for her and it was then that the mother and her son turned to look again at the girl beside Jamie, as he did himself. What an ethereal creature she was, a snowdrop beside the tall, colourful sunflower who was Katherine Andrews and whether it was because of the journey they had just travelled together or the raw antagonism in Sara Andrews's face, she drew closer to him as though seeking his protection and Chris Andrews's eyes gleamed in sudden speculation.

"You are . . . . Chloe Taylor?" Mrs Andrews asked distantly and Jamie noticed that for some reason she gazed slightly to one side of the girl's face as though reluctant to look into it. He was astonished and, if he were truthful, strangely angry, for Mrs Andrews was acting as though the girl was some kind of low person who had accosted them without provocation and must be dispatched with the contempt she deserved.

"Yes, ma'am." The answer was so low it was barely more than a whisper.

"We had your father's letter."

"Yes, ma'am." The girl's head rose, a delicate blossom on a slender stalk, but proud, unbowed, as though to say, frail as she was, she would not be frightened by Sara Andrews's evident hostility. She was frightened, Jamie had seen it in the train and as she stepped down on to the platform, but she would not let this woman know it, her erect carriage said.

Chris Andrews stared at her appreciatively, as bowled over by her delicate beauty as Jamie had been, with nothing to say for himself now that his sister had been removed from the embarrassing spectacle she had made of herself with one of his mother's servants. That was who he was, and he'd best remember it, Chris Andrews's green, flinty-eyed expression had said, and now another expression had come to replace it. Jamie recognised it, for was he not a man and had he not seen it in other men's eyes when they were presented with a pretty and perhaps available young woman.

"Well . . ." To Jamie's amazement it seemed Jack Andrews's ladylike wife had nothing further to say to the girl who must surely be a kinswoman of hers and whose existence Jamie had not been aware of and who, it was very apparent, was an unwelcome guest at Cloudberry End.

Mrs Andrews turned to him. Her eyes warmed and at once she was as he had always known her. Kind, sweet-natured, gracious, affectionate even, for she and his mother had been close friends for years despite the difference in their rank.

"Jamie, it is good to see you. We had no idea . . . your mother never mentioned you were coming home."

"She didn't know, Mrs Andrews. I thought that by the time a letter was posted in Liverpool I would be here before it so I decided to give her a surprise. She is well, I hope."

"Oh, of course, and just as irrepressible. You know how she is."

He smiled. "Indeed. She will never change. And my stepfather?"

"Vigorous as ever. Still driving my carriage as you will see in a moment."

"Mother."

"Yes, dear?" Sara turned to her son who had become restive under the pleasantries his mother and Jamie were exchanging. Her gaze passed over the girl – Chloe Taylor, was that what she had said? – as though she did not exist and again Jamie was mortified for her.

"I had better get Fred to send up the luggage in the station trap," Chris said smoothly. "We shall be hard pressed all to get into the carriage as it is," his insolent tone implying that Jamie Hutchinson's enormous bulk would take up more than his fair share of the seating.

"There is no need, Chris," Jamie ventured politely and at the use of his Christian name Chris Andrews frowned. Though he and his brothers, with a young Jamie Hutchinson, had roamed the moorland together when they were boys it was evident that that boyhood friendship, now that they were grown men, was ended and he did not care for the use of his Christian name without the obligatory "master" before it.

But be damned to him, Jamie thought savagely. He'd call no man master, not now. Jack Andrews he'd address as Mr Andrews as was only courteous with an older man, but if this young puppy thought he'd bow his head humbly to the son of the man who owned Cloudberry End, even if Jamie's mother and stepfather worked for him, then he was sadly mistaken.

"I shall walk up to Cloudberry," he continued coolly, "since I'm sure you and . . . Miss Taylor?" with a warm smile at the silent girl beside him, "will have much to talk about."

"I'll walk with you, Jamie." Katherine took his arm proprietorially, ready to stride off in the direction of the gate, but Jamie felt a strange reluctance to leave the young woman to the cold, dreadful and amazing hostility of Mrs Andrews. She remained still and frozen by his side, awakening a gentle pity in him, a need to protect, to defend. She reminded him of a doe he had once seen cornered by a group of hunters. The beautiful animal had been transfixed, her coat rippling in terror, her eyes sightless, stunned, as though in stillness and silence she might avoid the awful fate which was to be hers. They had shot her just the same.

"No, Katherine, go with your mother and with Miss Taylor," for somehow, though why he should think so since a more careless, unthinking creature than Katherine Andrews did not exist, he had the feeling she might stand as a bulwark between her mother and the girl. Again, why a bulwark should be needed he couldn't imagine, but for all her faults Katherine was warm-hearted, there was no doubt about that, and perhaps with her casual approach to anything which did not directly affect her she might be kind to the girl.

"I don't want to, Jamie. I want to walk with you. There is so much to talk about and I want to know what you think of me now that I'm grown up." She smiled impishly. "What d'you think? Am I— "

"Oh, for God's sake, Katherine, go and get in the bloody carriage," her brother snapped. "You do nothing but talk nonsense and anyway, how in hell's name can you walk up to Cloudberry dressed like that? Look at your shoes."

"Mind your own damned business, Chris." Katherine's face was furious. "If I want to walk with Jamie then I shall. We have so much to say to one another, haven't we, Jamie?" She turned to glow up into Jamie's face, her own telling the world what was in her heart.

"Katherine, take your . . . take Miss Taylor to the carriage while Chris sees to the luggage."

"Mother, please."

It was not often that Sara Andrews could withstand her stubborn daughter. It was not often that she even tried, but she seemed to have about her today a grim air of coldness, of fixed and unbending resolution that would not be denied. It was so unlike her Jamie could only wonder what had happened to alter her so. It was obviously something to do with this young woman whom she seemed unable to bear to contemplate, but whatever it was put steel in her and her daughter recognised it.

She tried one more time, her mouth set in a tight line of pleading.

"Mother, it will be crowded in the carriage and— "

"Do as you are told, Katherine, and take Miss Taylor with you."

The last Jamie saw of them as he shouldered his sea bag and gathered his packages about him was the bone white face of Chloe Taylor as she stared in what looked to be despair from the carriage window.

4

Chloe Taylor stared sightlessly from the window of the room they had put her in, shivering though it was not cold. Far from it. An enormously extravagant fire roared up the chimney, a fire the likes of which she had never before seen since Mama had not cared for lavishness. In the fireplace behind the brass fender stood a brass coal scuttle, polished to mirror-like gloss, filled to its brim with even more coal, evidence that if she cared to she might build the fire even higher.

She had been here for two hours. A neatly uniformed and obviously excited young housemaid had unpacked her bags, her face crimson with bursting curiosity, her eyes bright with speculation, hanging her gowns, two of them, both black, away in the wardrobe, neatly folding her immaculate, exquisitely made underwear into the top drawer of the chest. Her silver-backed hairbrush and mirror, an unexpectedly extravagant gift on her sixteenth birthday from Mama, and her tortoiseshell comb, now resided in perfect alignment on the dressing-table and her clean nightgown, again fashioned and embroidered with consummate skill by herself and Mama, had been tucked away beneath the frilled pillow on the enormous canopied bed. The maid had fidgeted about the room, straightening the lace runner on the chest of drawers, twitching the curtains into a more pleasing line, giving the fire an unnecessary stir until, unable to find anything further which might need her attention, she had bobbed a curtsey, asking if there was "anything else, miss?"

"No, thank you," Chloe had answered, standing awkwardly by the fire, since she was not used to being waited on, her hand resting on the back of the low, comfortably padded chair which was evidently hers to lounge in if she so desired.

"Rightio, miss," the maid said cheerfully. "I'll get on then."

"Thank you – er . . .?"

"Ivy, miss."

"Thank you, Ivy."

"Lunch is at one, miss, madame said ter tell yer."

"Aah . . ."

"Ring if yer want anythin', miss. Bells by't fireplace," and with another dipping bob and one last wide-eyed, fascinated glance, Ivy left the room, hurrying off back to the kitchen to give a full report to the rest of the eager servants on the looks, the demeanour, the state of the guest's wardrobe and the exquisite colour of her hair which had been revealed when she removed her bonnet. Of course, Freda and Thomas had already seen her, Thomas on the journey from the station and Freda when she opened the front door which was part of her duties as head parlourmaid. It was Freda who had given Ivy instructions on the transfer of the visitor's luggage from the hall to the front corner bedroom on the first floor. One of the best guest bedrooms which surely must indicate the importance of the young lady.

Yes, a fine bedroom, a luxurious bedroom even, Chloe admitted miserably, with two long windows at the front and one at the side in which there was a padded seat, and with a sigh she slowly sank into it. She leaned back against the wooden frame, bending her knees and clasping her arms about them. She lowered her head, resting her forehead on her hands, longing to burst into noisy tears and cry out her pain and grief and heartache, her very real fear and her homesickness for the tall, narrow house in Upper Parliament Street which she had shared with Mama and Papa until Mama's death. She longed to give way, to let go, to shout and bluster as she was sure that tall, red-headed lump of a girl downstairs would do, the one she supposed was her cousin. Let them all be in no doubt that she wanted to be here as little as they wanted her here but she had no choice, as Papa had awkwardly explained to her. The new Mrs Taylor, only a year or two older than Chloe and already pregnant with her first child, had thought it best that a young, unmarried girl like herself should not be exposed to the tribulations and embarrassment of pregnancy and childbirth, she had told Chloe's papa. Indeed, it was not at all "proper" and therefore they both agreed, he and the second Mrs Taylor, that it was best that she go and stay with her relatives for a while.

He had written to Mama's sister, the one Mama had loathed and, she had said, pitied for her disagreeable nature and Chloe was to go and stay with her in some God-forsaken spot in the wilds of the Pennine country, just until the baby was born, Papa had added placatingly.

She had pleaded and begged but it had done no good and so here she was, for where could a girl of her age and social class go but where she was sent, obedient to her father's wishes and making the best of it as her mama had taught her.

But it was worse, far worse than Mama had said it would be. Not that Mama had been up here or seen her sister for over twenty-five years but she had described her to Chloe, painting her in such grasping, self-centred, greedy and Godless colours, Chloe had been hard pressed to believe that such a monster could be related to her own God-fearing Mama. A liar and a cheat who had swindled Mama out of a great deal of money over the sale of a fashion house in Liverpool, though she had revealed none of the sordid details to her innocent daughter. She had run off with some rough man in the building trade, sailing away with him to Canada and them not even married. A woman not fit to lick Mama's boots and Chloe had been appalled and terrified when Papa had told her what was to become of her.

"May I come back home and help to care for the baby when it is born?" she had pleaded, ignoring her stepmama's horror-stricken pretence at a faint since no young, unmarried woman spoke of such things in the presence of a gentleman, even her own papa. "I will take on the duties of nursemaid willingly, Papa, if you would allow it, and would keep out of the way," meaning her stepmama's way, of course. "I like children, you know I do and would not mind at all if you would give your permission and . . ."

"Henry, really! A man in your position allowing your own daughter to play at nursemaid. What would your business acquaintances and friends think if it should get out? No, far better to send her for a while to her relatives where I'm sure she will be kindly treated and, who knows, where eligible young bachelors will be guests. They are well placed, I believe. Mrs Cartwright's husband is connected in some way with the railway and says Jack Andrews is well thought of, apart from his . . . other advantages. So you must put all thoughts of acting as nursemaid quite out of your head, my dear. Your papa has a position to keep up and if it became known that— "

"I wouldn't tell anyone, Papa. I would just stay in the nursery and look after the baby. Oh, please, Papa, you know how Mama felt about her sister. She will not want me, Papa. She will have children of her own, I'm sure, and if she is wicked, as Mama said she was, then . . ."

"Your mama was inclined to . . . to exaggerate somewhat, Chloe," Papa had said distantly.

"Indeed she was—" her stepmama began but Chloe had rounded on her, her white face flooding with outraged colour.

"How do you know what my mama was like? You never met her since she would not have a woman like you in her home. She would be turning in her grave this very minute if she knew you were here, sleeping in her bed, using her things."

"Henry!" the second Mrs Taylor shrieked. "The baby . . ." And Henry Taylor, a chandler in Water Street, who desperately wanted a son, a son who would in time help him in the successful business which, with the injection of his first wife's money after her death and the sale of her own dressmaking establishment, was growing beyond his wildest imaginings.

He half carried his fainting wife from the dining room and the slightly apologetic look he gave his daughter said quite plainly that she could see how he was placed and must surely understand. A man's duty was to his wife, it said, especially if that wife was with child and that child might be a son.

So, here she was, and but for the large gentleman who had helped her from the train, oh, and the smiling housemaid, she had received not one kind word, nor even a friendly glance from a soul this day. Her aunt – she supposed she must admit to her being that – after a cold stare and a brief nod had totally ignored her, treating her like some new servant who was to work in the kitchens. Worse, for most mistresses would find a comforting word or two for a homesick kitchenmaid on her first day of duty. Her cousin, the girl called Katherine, had been in such a taking over her mama's refusal to allow her to walk back with the big man, she had sulked and tapped her foot all the way to Cloudberry End where the man also seemed to live and Chris, as his mama had addressed him, had eyed her with a look on his face Chloe did not care for at all. She'd seen it before on men's faces, of course, even on that of the big man in the train though he'd done his best to hide it. To be polite and careful with her. She was a lady and deserved respect, no matter how pretty she was, the look in his brilliant blue eyes had said, and how could she not be aware that she was pretty? It had been the cross she bore ever since she had moved from childhood to girlhood, causing no end of trouble to her mama who had made her wear her hair dragged back from her face in heavy braids, but it had done no good, for men continued to stare at her in fascinated awe, and in other ways which she did not like to mention.

She turned again to the window, leaning the back of her head against the frame. There were two men working at the far end of the garden. Well, a man and a boy, industriously turning over the soil, their backs bending and straightening in unison, their spades biting into the dark earth at precisely the same moment. A row of plant pots, at least two dozen of them, stood on the path, the plants obviously waiting to be put in the ground and as she watched another man came round from the back of the house pushing a wheelbarrow. On it was a further load of pots, wobbling a bit as he manhandled it, in a short cut, across the grass. Behind him pranced a small dog.

The first man stopped work, leaning on his spade, his face irate, Chloe could see even from the bedroom. His free hand rose and formed a fist, his head nodded angrily and though she could not hear the words he spoke she knew he was giving the newcomer a piece of his mind for crossing the lawn and leaving imprints in its shaved perfection. The man with the wheelbarrow, looking abashed, carefully trundled it on to the footpath, almost carrying it. The dog wagged its tail frantically. Its tongue lolled from its mouth and its ears pricked in anticipation.

Chloe leaned forward for a better look, wondering who it belonged to and as if in answer to her pondering the tall, red-headed girl came skidding full pelt round the opposite corner of the house. Her hair was all over the place. Chloe had never seen anything like it since it seemed to be cut as short as a man's and if Chloe's own mama had been in charge of her the girl would have been in dire peril. It bounced and swirled about her head, glowing like a beacon in the small gleam of fitful sunshine which had decided to peep out, completely unbound by anything at all, even a bit of ribbon. She had discarded her silk gown and now wore what looked like a riding habit in a rich shade of blue. The skirt was long, trained and full and she held it bunched up above her knees and, horror of horrors, showing beneath it were a pair of trousers and glossy riding boots!

"Muffy, come here at once, you devil, or I swear I'll take my whip to you," she was shouting loud enough for Chloe to hear even though the bedroom windows were shut. "Catch him, Billy," and the boy sprang forward eagerly. "Shut him in the stable, will you? I'm off to Woodhead so will you go and saddle Storm for me, Noah?" this to the man with the wheelbarrow. "I can't find Dicken or Jimmy. God alone knows where they get to when they're needed, and if anyone asks you haven't seen me."

The second voice seemed to come from nowhere. "But I've seen you, Katherine, and I'd be obliged if you'd come indoors at once and change back into your gown. Your mother and Chris are about to sit down to lunch and you are to go upstairs and fetch . . . fetch our guest."

Katherine came to such an abrupt halt she made heel marks in the gardener's obviously prized lawn and a look of resigned horror came over his face. The dog had raced over to her, the boy in unsuccessful pursuit, jumping up at her in ecstasy and leaving muddy paw marks all over her skirt, since he had been rummaging in the soil at the back of the flowerbed where the gardener and his boy were digging. Katherine clapped her hand to her forehead in exasperation. Chloe was not sure whether it was at the dog or the male voice which seemed to come from just beneath her window. She stamped her foot fretfully and Chloe held her breath.

"Oh, Father, really! Do I need to? I did my duty this morning, you must agree and I promised Grandmother I would be over to give her a full description of the girl. I'll have my lunch there so . . ."

"No, you will not, Katherine. You will have your lunch with your family. You know how difficult this is going to be for your mother, and for me, so kindly do as I say."

"Father, please don't make me. Oh, damn that bloody animal."

Chloe gasped in horror, clapping her hand to her mouth.

"Watch your language, my girl," for though it appeared

Jack Andrews was at perfect liberty to curse whenever he felt the need for it, a young lady such as his badly brought-up daughter was not.

"If he had been shut up as he was supposed to be I wouldn't have had to chase him all over the bloody garden."

"Dammit, Katherine!"

"But I knew the minute I was up on Storm he'd be after me and I didn't want to take him today." A secretive expression flitted across her face, gone in a moment, but Chloe had seen it even if the man below had not. "Oh, damn and blast . . ."

"Katherine, come inside at once," and Katherine, it seemed, had no choice, vanishing disconsolately from Chloe's view. The two men and the boy huddled together for several minutes, evidently exchanging opinions on the scene they had just witnessed and the dog lay down in a patch of weak sunshine.

Chloe put her feet to the carpet. She was shocked and amazed and she knew her mouth hung open in a most foolish way. She wanted to turn to someone, though of course she had no one to turn to, and ask them if they had ever seen or heard anything like it in their life because she certainly hadn't. The language and bald-faced defiance of the man who must be her cousin's father, and as for that outfit, the indecency of the trousered legs, and the hair, well, she could hardly believe her own eyes. For a young woman to act like that, to look like that and to speak like that, especially to her own father, was scarcely believable and if she hadn't witnessed it she wouldn't have believed it. And in what was supposedly a decent family. They were evidently people who had no respect for one another, she decided, nor even affection and certainly no regard for the niceties of social behaviour. If she had spoken to her papa like that, let alone the cursing, Mama would have locked her in her room on bread and water for a week. She had never heard a man speak as Katherine Andrews had, let alone a woman and the thought of spending even an hour in the company of such uncouth and probably uneducated persons as these, even if they were as enormously wealthy as this room, this house seemed to say they were, filled her with appalled horror. Oh, Mama, you were strict and sometimes harsh, I suppose, but why did you have to die when you did? Why did you have to die at all? It is not even a year yet and barely three months since Papa married that woman who has driven me out, but for all your severity I know you loved me and I miss you.

She stood up, clamping her soft lips together to suppress the wail of misery which wanted to escape. She glanced about the room apathetically, noticing with a part of her mind which, without being consciously aware of it, gloated over its elegance and comfort, the thickness of the rich-piled, buttercup yellow carpet, the lacy white frills about the canopy of the bed, the glowing polish on the satinwood wardrobe, the chest of drawers and the dainty, kidney-shaped dressing-table on which a triple mirror stood. The walls were papered in a pale yellow and silver striped wallpaper. The quilt on the bed, a patchwork quilt, was made up of every shade of lemon, ivory, bold yellow, daffodil and buttercup banded with white and on the low table by the long window an enormous copper bowl was filled with yellow and white roses. Where would they get roses at this time of the year? she wondered, sighing deeply. She smoothed the rich golden yellow velvet of the curtains at the window, marvelling that though the sun did not enter the room, at least at this time of the day, it seemed to be filled with it, deep and glowing. There were pictures on the wall, pastoral scenes done in watercolours, a field rippling with poppies, another of buttercups and daisies with cattle standing knee deep in grasses.

She walked across the room to look at them more closely and was amazed to see that the signature on them was of the famous and talented artist David Bretherton who had been born in Liverpool. If they were original, and they appeared to be, they must be worth a fortune.

On the mantelpiece above the fire was a pretty brass clock set between two pale and pirouetting ballet dancers. She picked one up and smoothed its graceful form with a careful finger. So many lovely things. It was all enchanting and in any other circumstance she would have been enchanted. Though she had not offered the knowledge to Mama she had always been drawn to beauty. She could stand for an hour, and had when she was let, and absorb into herself, through her eyes and the pores of her skin, the glorious, furious, sometimes delicate colours of a sunset. The sky first turning yellow, merging to green as the golden sun vanished and when the sun had gone, dropping gracefully, slowly, below the horizon, the heart-stopping glory of fiery brown, crimson and orange, spreading upwards as the orb of the sun sank to its next day. An arch of rose on rose-pink, lingering as night crept overhead until the pink turned to violet and plum purple.

Enraptured she had watched it happen across the River Mersey, the waters mirroring the sky, until Mama, who liked a brisk evening walk before prayer meeting, pulled at her arm to fetch her from what she called her daughter's "daydreaming".

The moon, mistress of the night, seen from her bedroom window, the earth shine lighting up its surface, the silver stitching about it pulling at her heart in its loveliness. March sunshine filled with the fluttering wings of the first Brimstone butterflies, yellow and blue, blush red and chocolate brown. Bluebells in April, a hazy carpet beneath the close-packed trees of Mill Wood beyond West Derby where Papa took her as a child, and primroses, the first flower of the year. The song of the thrush, the bird looping up in low graceful flight from the garden at the back of the house . . . oh, she could go on and on and on, remembering not only the rich beauty she loved but the unthinking content she had known as a child. She had not, of course, divulged her thoughts to Mama simply because Mama would have thought her "fanciful". She would not have approved, nor understood. Mama had been practical, down to earth, believing in the performing of one's duty and responsibility to others, as the Church taught; in hard work and decency and had certainly not had time in her busy life simply to stand and stare at what she would have called trivialities.

Her own room at home had been a plain, no-nonsense sort of a room with everything in it Mama considered suitable for a young girl. A narrow white bed and a table beside it on which her Bible rested. A wardrobe in which her exquisitely made dresses and mantles hung, the cut and colour of the garments again picked by Mama who knew best, naturally. A square of carpet on the floor and . . . Oh dear Lord above, give me strength, if it is Thy will, but I would exchange the deep-piled comfort and luxury of this room for the plainness and sparseness of my own, and with all my heart if it could only be made possible.

The knock on the door was peremptory and it was flung open without waiting for her to answer. Chloe clenched her jaw even tighter, so tight she feared she would be unable to open it again when the time came, but it was the only way she could keep her composure from shredding away in tatters about her. She had not changed since she had nothing to change into except another black dress but she had unbraided her hair, brushed it vigorously and braided it again, even tighter, if that were possible, coiling it up into an enormous bun at the back of her head. Though she was not aware of it, since she had done it that way because it would have pleased her mama, the style gave her a strange, exotic look, lengthening her blue-green eyes, heightening her already high cheekbones and accentuating the faint hollow beneath them. Her mouth was a rich, ripe coral against the black of her gown which, because of its plainness and absolute lack of colour, emphasised her startling and delicate young beauty. She would have been mortified if she had known.

"Lunch is ready," the girl in the doorway said curtly. "They sent me to fetch you."

Chloe had argued with herself for the past ten minutes, ever since she had known Katherine was to come up for her, warned by the unseen man's voice, telling herself she didn't want any lunch. She didn't want to eat at all, ever again; in fact she was convinced she would just heave it all up again if she did. Or it would stick in her throat and refuse to go down. But it had to be done sometime or they would only come to the conclusion that she was afraid of them and that would never do. She was afraid of them but she'd be damned . . . Oh God, forgive me, I'm already picking up their profane language. But she'd not let them know she was afraid.

"Thank you," was all she said, lifting her chin which was already high, a little higher.

"Are you going down like that?" her cousin asked curiously, just as though Chloe had on some strange and outlandish costume. She herself was in the tawny silk she had worn that morning.

"Like what?" Chloe heard herself say defensively.

"Well, in that black dress."

"I am in mourning for my mama." She tried her best to keep the tears from her voice but it trembled badly.

Amazingly Katherine softened. "Oh, of course, I'm sorry."

Chloe felt a tiny feather of warmth touch her skin and her back relaxed a fraction from its aching stiffness.

"When did she die?" Katherine went on, holding open

the door for her to go through. She eyed the scraped-back braids, the high-necked severity of the mourning gown with faint disapproval as though she couldn't understand why anyone would voluntarily trick herself out in such drabness, her expression saying that she certainly wouldn't, no matter who had died.

"Last August."

"Last August!"

They were halfway down the length of the landing along which most of the doors stood open to reveal bedrooms as delightful as the one Chloe had been put in but Katherine's hand on her arm halted her and swung her back to face her.

"D'you mean to say your mother has been dead since last August and yet your father has left it until now to . . ." she almost said "discard" you, ". . . to send you to us?"

"I don't know what you mean."

"Well, he has managed to look after you himself all these months so why has he suddenly decided that you'd be best off with us?"

Chloe had an instant picture of her stepmama's triumphant face as she had waved to her from the window of the house in Upper Parliament Street but she made her own stay calm and expressionless as her cousin blundered on.

"And how did he know we would take you in, anyway? Your mother and mine were not, apparently, on the best of terms."

Chloe could not help it. "And is it any wonder?" she said furiously.

"What is that supposed to mean?" Katherine's chin took on a truculent angle and Chloe felt a great desire to strike it. Dear Lord, she had only been in this house a couple of hours and already she had been incited to swearing and seized by the desire to hit another human being. Her voice rose to an angry squeak though she did her level best to remain calm.

"How can you ask that after what happened between them? Mama was devastated." Her voice rose even higher in remembered pain and Katherine began to look alarmed.

"Oh, for God's sake, be quiet. You'll have Mother and Father up here in a minute and I'm supposed to be bringing you down to the dining-room. They'll want to know, of course. Why your father sent you here, I mean, so you'd best save your explanations until then. Come on, and do try to look as though you are going down to lunch and not to your own hanging."

Again Chloe clamped her teeth together since it seemed there was no avoiding the confrontation with this girl's family. Best get it over and done with and then she could retire to what she supposed she must call her room and howl herself into oblivion.

Katherine opened the door to the left of the staircase and ushered her into the room. As she had upstairs, Chloe was at once aware of a sense of warmth, of comfort, of polished surfaces, a gleaming and a glittering which was ready to dazzle her until she looked into the bone white face of the woman who was her mother's sister. She did not speak.

The two gentlemen present rose to their feet politely, the older one indicating brusquely that she was to sit on his right with Katherine between her and his wife, holding her chair until she was seated. She had no more than a brief glimpse of a face which would be good-humoured under other circumstances, she was sure, and of deep brown eyes beneath fiercely dipping brows. The younger man, the one called Chris, remained standing until the other man – it must be his father – sat down again.

"I'm Jack Andrews," the older man said shortly, "as you will no doubt have guessed."

Somehow she unclamped her jaw.

"Yes, sir." Her voice was low but steady. There were two women at the back of the room and she was conscious of their curious glances. One of them was the maid who had opened the door to them earlier in the day, the other an older woman, steady, nudging the younger as though to tell her to stop gawping and get on with her job.

"You have met my son and daughter?"

"Yes, sir."

"And my wife?"

"Indeed," though she did not look at her aunt.

"Have you anything you would like to say to us?"

Chloe raised her head to look at him in some astonishment. What on earth had she to say to these strangers who had, as Christians should, taken her in but who were treating her as though she had done them some grievous harm for which they could never forgive her. Even the man, her aunt's husband, seemed to have the greatest difficulty in looking at her, carefully keeping his eyes on his plate, or his wife, or the wallpaper, rather than meet hers.

She cleared her throat and the maidservants who were just about to serve soup, paused uncertainly.

"Only that it is most generous of you to allow me to stay with you, sir." What else could she say beyond the polite response anyone in her position would make? Even those few words stuck in her throat but she supposed, in one way, it was generous of them to give shelter to a complete stranger, for that was what she was.

"You are comfortable?"

She nodded her head. He was doing his duty as a host but she was also aware that he was setting guidelines, letting her know what her position was here in this house. She was not to think of herself as a member of the family. She was a guest, one his wife had obligingly accommodated for as short a time as possible, but no more. Polite they would be with one another, since one was polite to a guest in one's home, but anything warmer, more cordial, more personal was out of the question.

She understood, though she did not know why.

It was the girl, of course, not knowing, nor caring, what the past had held for her parents, who broke away from the icy courtesies which were being exchanged. The maids had served the soup, a deliciously rich soup in which fine slices of leek floated, and they had begun to eat when she broke the silence.

"Do you ride?" she asked, turning to look at Chloe and her dreadful black dress as though assessing what might be needed to smarten her up a bit.

"Ride?" Chloe was clearly startled and Katherine raised her eyebrows.

"Yes, on a horse."

"A horse?"

Katy sighed in exasperation. "You do know what a horse is, surely, even if you have lived in the city. I presume they have them in Liverpool though one wonders how one could possibly get a good gallop in those congested streets."

Her brother spoke for the first time, leaning back indolently in his chair despite his father's frown. "I suppose there are bridle trails and paths in the woods and fields about the city,

Katy." Chloe might not have been there. "Johnny Ashwell has some cousins who live in . . . oh, somewhere on the outskirts and I'm sure they have stables. I have a feeling they ride to hounds in Cheshire which, if my geography serves me, is somewhere over that way."

"Well, they would, wouldn't they? The great and glorious Ashwells and what surprises me is that Johnny manages to stay on his animal at all, his seat is so appalling. I saw him the other day going hell for leather up towards Tintwistle Knarr with that imbecile Tim What's-his-name in tow and he was all over the place. He reminded me of nothing so much as a sack of coal, lolling from side to side, his head going ten to the dozen and his mount baulking at every blade of grass."

"Rubbish, he is as good a rider as I am."

Katherine shrugged and rolled her eyes as though to say, "Well, there you are then," then lost interest and the matter was closed, it seemed.

Chris glanced languidly at Chloe and in his eyes was a spark of something which could have been admiration, the look a man allows a woman whom he might just be interested in, a secret look since he knew his father's eye was on him. His eyelids drooped as though he had not had much sleep the night before and he yawned several times behind his hand.

"I hope those yawns are not meant to indicate that you are too exhausted to accompany me this afternoon, lad," Jack Andrews said crisply to his son, pausing in the act of lifting a spoonful of soup to his lips, "because if they are it cuts no ice with me, for I mean you to come along just the same."

"Accompany you, sir?" Chris assumed an injured air and Chloe noticed the two maids exchange glances. Trouble brewing, those glances said and for the first time since she had entered this house she was diverted from her own heartache. This was them as they were when she was not present and she found it intrigued her. For the moment they had forgotten her as their own affairs, the daily and presumably important concerns of the Andrews family took precedence over all else.

"Aye," her uncle continued. "I've a mind to try you out in the paper mill."

"The paper mill! Christ Almighty, Father, surely you cannot mean me to spend my days in that appalling hell-hole? I'd go out of my mind."

"Really! Then how are you to spend your days, lad? It is honest labour," his father began to thunder and at the end of the table Sara Andrews made a small sound in the back of her throat.

"Oh God," she mumbled, staring into her soup and they all turned to look at her, even the maids, and on all their faces, except Chloe's, was an expression of awful dread.

"Sara, sweetheart," her husband began, rising from his seat and Chloe was bemused by the emotion, total and consuming, which lit his face. She didn't know what it was since she had never seen it before. It was tender, gentle, cherishing, all in one, and yet there was a passion in it which was quite embarrassing to watch. It said that he would gladly give his life if it would save his wife a moment's anguish and it was then that she began to have some intimation of what joined Sara and Jack Andrews together. And perhaps an understanding, when it was finally made clear to her, of the past in which her mother had played a part.

She was badly startled by it but at the same time completely fascinated.

"It's all right, darling," her aunt said, the look she bestowed on him identical to the one he had just given her. "No, really, it's just that . . . it's just as though she has come back to remind me."

Lifting her head her aunt looked down the table to where Chloe sat and in her face was such a depth of sadness Chloe felt her own heart squeeze, though she didn't know why.

"It's her, Jack. If I didn't know Alice was dead I would swear it was her."

5

Matty Jenkins smiled at her son or rather at his profile which was outlined, strong and bold and serious, against the flames of the brightly burning kitchen fire. He was sitting in her husband's comfortable chair, his leg bent, his right foot resting on his left knee, reading the newspaper which came across daily from the house when Mr Andrews had finished with it. Not that Thomas was particularly interested in the sort of newspaper his employer read. *The Times* was not really his cup of tea, he had said to her cheerfully, since Thomas was an unfailingly cheerful man, thank the good God, but the paper rolled up into decent firelighters for when the front parlour fire was lit on special occasions, so it wasn't wasted.

Matty was making bread. There was a fine film of flour coating most surfaces of the warm kitchen: the plain deal table where she worked, the stone-flagged floor about the table, her own apron and face and hair, and some had even come to rest, featherlike, in her son's dark curls. Matty was inclined to fling things about a bit when she was enjoying herself and she enjoyed making bread. It gave her a great sense of who she was, and how far she had come from what she had once been, though she didn't dwell on that now. Her Jamie, her illegitimate son Jamie, was living proof of who she had once been, though she didn't dwell on that, neither. Life had been good to her. Life and Sara Andrews whom she'd die for, God's honour, and she gave thanks every day to some faceless, nameless deity, whom she was reluctant to call God, for what she had. This tidy little cottage, for instance, nestling in a dip at the front of Cloudberry End, screened from the house by a well-kept hedge of holly and a dozen or so mature beech trees. For her Thomas who had come with her from Liverpool since she'd not be parted from Sara, even for him, she'd told him, and for the children he'd given her, Dulcie who was a mother herself now and, late in life when they had both thought themselves to be past such things, their Tommy, a scamp of a lad at fourteen but with the warm heart of his mother.

Matty was getting on for fifty and her Thomas fifty-three but they could both still do a hard day's work with the best, though it was seldom they were called upon to do so. Thomas was coachman to Mr Andrews, and to Mrs Andrews whom Matty called Sara. She and Sara had been friends for thirty years nearly and a day never went by when they didn't see one another. They shared their troubles, always had, though thank God there'd not been many of those in recent years at least not until this last one had come along and it was a facer all right.

She glanced again at the dark bulk of her strapping son, watching him frown, wondering what it was in the newspaper that put that expression on his normally even-tempered face. Lord, she couldn't get over how big he was. You forgot in five years the size and shape of even the most beloved son, but then his life at sea had formed him, and, though she could barely remember him after twenty-seven years, his pa had been a big chap an' all.

She gave the dough a last hearty slap then, folding it in a clean cloth, placed it in the hearth to rise.

"Mind yer feet in that there dough when yer gerrup, our Jamie," she said, the nasal lilt of Liverpool still in her voice despite her twenty-five years' exile from the place of her birth.

"Aye, Ma." Jamie continued to read, the toes of his stockinged feet wriggling pleasurably in the warmth from the fire. He had on a pair of corduroy breeches and a rough woollen gansey, the sort sailors wore, and his hair stood up in a mass of tousled curls about his head as though he were in the habit of running his hand through it.

"What yer readin', son? 'Owt interestin'?"

"Mmmm?" Jamie's voice was vague, giving the impression that he had barely heard his mother and if he had he was too engrossed in the newspaper to give her an answer.

Matty was not offended. She rummaged through a basket of washing she had just brought in from the washing line in the garden, lifting out several shirts and flinging them energetically on to a chair. Like a great white sail a flannel sheet was lifted into the air, then allowed to settle across the table. She smoothed it carefully with hands which were worn in the service of others, hands which had once done the most delicate embroidery in Liverpool, though it was many years now since she had taken up a needle and thread to do more than darn the socks of her menfolk, mend a rip in Tommy's shirt, which happened every day for he was a real lad, run up a shirt or a plain gown for herself or put up a hem on an over-long skirt for one of the maidservants at the house.

Bending over her son she withdrew the "sad" iron, "sad" come from the word solid, which the iron was, from the heat of the fire, one of a pair, and with a great deal of spitting and hissing and banging, the first to test the iron's heat, the latter to remove a certain amount of soot which clung to it from the flames, she began vigorously to dash it up and down the first shirt.

"I asked yer what were so interestin' in that there paper, our Jamie? Yer've 'ad yer nose stuck in it this past hour wi'out a word ter say fer yerself. After five years wi'out a sight of yer I'd be glad of a word or two about what yer've bin up to. Yer'll 'ave seen sights yer pa an' me'll never see, or our Tommy fer that matter. Mind you . . ." she brooded pensively, ". . . Tommy's bin that restless lately I'd not be surprised if he didn't tekk off like you did. He's finished school an' Mr Andrews 'as offered ter tekk 'im on in that there paper mill he's just bought but that don't suit our Tommy. Oh no, he ses, I'm not workin' in no mill, though what he do want he can't say. Summat oudoors, likely, but there's nowt round 'ere for a lad, Jamie. Not unless he wants ter get set on in one o't quarries or go fer a farm labourer like them Andrews lads and where's that gonner fetch him up? I said to 'is pa . . ."

Her voice rambled on and her iron hissed and glided in harmony with it. Though his mother had begged him to tell her of what he'd been "up to" in the five years he had been away, her mind had veered back from his travels to the worrying one his boisterous young half-brother was to take in the future.

And could you blame her? Jamie had been out of her life for the best part of thirteen years, ever since Tommy was born, practically, and it was natural that her maternal pride and anxiety should be fixed on her last-born.

He watched her for a minute or two, then smiled, more to himself than at her, his good white teeth a startling slash in his deeply sunbrowned face. He rustled the newspaper and the cat on the hearth-rug at his feet glared up at him irritably, miaowed in a plaintive voice since her place had been partially usurped by the newcomer's feet, curled her tail about her body and did her best to resume her interrupted sleep. Jamie studied his mother, suddenly noticing the dashes of grey in what had been her glossy dark curls. There were wrinkles seaming her lively face, about her mouth and eyes, wrinkles which had not been there when he went away. A shaft of pale May sunlight from the side window caught her as she leaned across him to retrieve the second iron, putting the first in its place to reheat, and it tinted her skin to gold. She was still a handsome woman despite her years but with eyes which were a paler blue than once they had been and her trim figure had thickened at the waist and hips and her bosom was deep and motherly.

"I've told 'im an' told 'im he must settle on summat," she was saying, "but he just laughs an' ses he will soon enough but I'm that feared he might get in with that lot up by Woodhead."

Jamie's indulgent smile died away and he let the newspaper fall to his lap.

"What lot's that then?"

His mother banged her sad iron viciously over her husband's inoffensive shirt, her face falling into a worried frown.

"Them lads o' George an' Will Andrews. Yer know, Jack Andrews's brothers. There's Paddy, he's George's youngest an' at twenty they say he's wilder 'n a caged animal in a zoo. An' the other two're just as bad. Twins, they are, Josh an' Jake an' if Paddy ordered 'em ter jump off Lud's Leap in ter Combes Clough they'd not 'ave ter be told twice. I'm only surprised yer've not come across 'em in yer wanderings, wherever it is yer get to. Anyroad, they're always in trouble, drinkin' an' mekkin' a nuisance o' theirselves with girls hereabouts. Woe betide any lass what finds 'erself on 'er own wi' them three. Oh, no, there's nowt happened yet," seeing the look of consternation on her son's face, "but Ivy Arkwright what's parlourmaid ter Sara, Mrs Andrews, said they didn't half give her some cheek t'other evenin' when she were walking back along t'road from her pa's farm at Thornley Clough. T'weren't even dark. A decent girl on her afternoon off! Well, her pa were all fer goin' over to George's place an' givin' the lot of 'em a good hidin', tekkin' his lads an' all, but Mr Andrews said leave it to him an' he'd sort it out an' I suppose he'd have words with 'em, though what good that'll do I don't know. Anyroad, it's the thought of our Tommy tekkin up wi' 'em what frightens me, our Jamie. He's bin seen wi' the twins, seventeen they are an' far too old fer him ter be goin' about with, an' all of 'em with a shotgun apiece, though where our Tommy got hold of such a thing I couldn't say, and he won't. Shootin' rabbits they were up on Hankeith Hill an' where's it all goin' ter lead to, that's what frightens me. Shotguns an' him only fourteen. His pa's spoken to him but you know how soft he is. Ses the boy's not bad, which is true, an' he doesn't want ter break his spirit."

Matty shook her head and thumped the iron on the table just as though she'd like nothing better than to clout it round the ears of the Andrews lads who were doing their best to lead her Tommy astray. Her face was creased with some dread which her mother's heart did not care to contemplate. Her Tommy was a good lad, sweet-natured but rough and cheerfully rumbustious as lads are. He'd not hurt a lass, or any living thing deliberately but that Paddy Andrews had the charm and devilment of Old Scratch himself and his influence could fling boys like her Tommy and the Andrews twins into trouble before they even knew they were approaching it.

She sighed heavily, still shaking her head as though to clear the cobwebs of alarm from her mind. She looked up and smiled at Jamie, her usual blithe optimism, which had got her through many a rough patch in her life, lifting the corners of her mouth and narrowing her faded blue eyes. Once they had been as brilliant as those of her eldest son, twinkling wickedly at any man with a claim to looks who smiled at her but now, with the disquieting images still lurking at the back of them, they were clouded and flat.

She did her best. "Will yer listen ter me goin' on about what'll probably never 'appen an' you only 'ome a few weeks. We've not seen a lot of yer, lad, an' me an' yer pa were only wonderin' t'other night where yer get to. Saul Gibbon told yer pa he saw yer up on Pikenose Moor, t'other day. Said you was standin' gawpin' at Philcox's farm, that's 'ow he purrit, an' when he spoke yer jumped a foot in th'air. What you up to? Yer've not said a word about what yer mean ter do, son, now that yer've left the sea. Yer *have* left it, haven't yer?" she asked anxiously, since she had a warm feeling that this big lad of hers would be a great comfort to her as she got older. "Yer not goin' back, are yer?"

"No, Mam, I'm not going back. I've finished with the sea and not before time an' all. I'm getting too old to be climbing rigging in a force eight gale."

He stood up slowly and stretched his tall frame – as far as he could in the low-ceilinged room – and his mother admired the long and beautiful length of him. And he *was* beautiful. A strong masculine beauty which had nothing of softness in it, magnificently put together with each part of his body in perfect symmetry with the rest. Long, graceful bones with flat muscles which glided smoothly from the deep curve of his broad chest and shoulders to the concavity of his lean belly which, as he stretched, flattened even further above the belt which held up his breeches. His body, beneath his clothes, was hard and powerful, shaped by the manual adversity of the work he had performed since he was a boy, and he was attractive too, his mother thought proudly. Far from handsome since his face was too rugged for that, but his dark hair curled pleasingly over his well-shaped skull, his mouth was wide and generous, his lips soft and his teeth good.

Aye, a face to please some woman to be sure but it was his eyes which were his most compelling feature, being of an incredible blue, deep and magnetic. A cobalt blue which could change, with his emotions, to the serenity and softness of pale azure; eyes heavily lashed, dark at the roots but tipped with gold. Aye, a good-looking lad, well, man really, was her Jamie and she'd not be surprised to see the lasses come flocking when word got around that he was home. As for being too old to climb rigging in a force eight gale, whatever that was, he was talking through his seaman's woollen hat, so he was. He was in his prime, was her Jamie, and she was right glad he was home to stay.

"Don't you worry about Tommy neither, Mam," he said, as he made his way towards the front door of the cottage, dropping a light kiss on her hair which was still filmed with flour. He had to bend his head to avoid the blackened beams and as she watched him go his mother wondered where her enormous son would fetch up in this working man's world of poky cottages and cramped farmhouses, of low doorways and tiny windows, of minute patches of garden scarcely bigger than a pocket handkerchief, or none at all, which was the fate of frailer men than himself. He needed a great deal of space to accommodate the splendid size of him since he filled any room he entered, overwhelming the more ordinary mortals who shared it with him. A house the size of Cloudberry End, for instance, with its grand proportions, its high ceilings, its vast, meandering acres of garden, not to mention the equally vast acres of woodland and moorland and tumbling cloughs which surrounded it, land owned by the wealthiest man in the district, Mr Jack Andrews.

"Hold on, my lad, don't you tell me not to worry about our Tommy," she said sharply. "A mother can't help worrying about her children no more than she can avoid givin' birth to 'em once they're inside her. D'yer think I never bothered me head over you, not ter mention me heart, when you were away? There wasn't a day went by when I didn't wonder where the devil you were, or even if you were still in the land o't livin." She almost choked on her indignation.

"Well, I'm home now, Mam. Home to stay. I've plans in my head, things I've been thinking on for the past five years and if everything goes as I mean it to, and he shapes himself, there's no reason why our Tommy can't be included in them."

Matty Jenkins's face lit up and she dropped her sad iron to the table with little or no concern for the fate of her husband's shirt which she was just about to tackle. Ignoring the ominous smell of singeing wool, if she even noticed it, she followed on her son's heels to the opened door, her hands plucking at the sleeve of the reefer jacket he had just put on.

"What d'yer mean, our Jamie? What plans? What yer goin' ter do, fer God's sake, an' how does our Tommy fit?"

"Now then, Mam. I'm only right at the very beginning so I can tell you nowt' because the whole bloody scheme depends on someone else and could easily come to nothing. I've someone to see."

"Who, tell me who?"

"I can't. Not until things are more settled. That's if they do settle. Now be patient, Mam, and I promise as soon as I've anything to say you'll be the first one I'll say it to."

"Oh, lad, how can I set meself to . . ."

"You'd better, Mam, or me pa'll have no shirt."

"What?"

"Me pa's shirt. It's burning."

"Oh, my dear Lord, an' it's his best."

Flinging herself nimbly across the kitchen, she picked up the sad iron and placed it in the fire next to its twin then turned back to her son, ready to insist that he tell his mother what he was up to but he'd already gone, in which direction she could not say, for when she got to the door he was nowhere in sight.

"Mr Hutchinson's here, sir." The maidservant bobbed a curtsey. "Ses he's an appointment," which seemed highly unlikely to her, since when did a grand gentleman like Mr Andrews entertain a rough seaman like Matty Jenkins's lad? Not that he wasn't a fine figure of a man and she'd be willing to spend an hour or two in his company, or even more, any day of the week; polite too, with a lovely grin but that still didn't put him on the same footing as Mr Andrews.

"That's right, Ivy. I'm expecting him. Show him in, will you?" the master said, standing up, if you please, just as though Jamie Hutchinson was as good as him.

"Rightio, sir." Ivy was not quite the professional Freda was, inclined to be less "formal", but it was Freda's day off so Ivy had answered the door and right glad she was about it, for it meant she could have a real good look at the enormous young man who strode so confidently into the master's study, holding out his hand to him as though they were equals and him with a pa, well, step-pa, who was Mr Andrews's coachman!

"Will that be all, sir?" she asked, her eyes out on stalks.

"Well, perhaps a drink, Jamie? What can I offer you? I know sailors are said to prefer rum but . . .?"

Jamie smiled engagingly, at least Ivy thought so.

"No, I'd prefer a brandy, sir. Besides which I'm no longer a sailor."

Ivy hung about, hoping to hear what he meant to be.

"Is that so?" the master said. "Well, sit down, lad, sit down, and tell me what you want to see me about." Ivy did her best to make herself invisible, for she would be made up if she could carry the news back to the kitchen. The master moved towards the small table where the silver tray on which several silver-topped diamond-cut crystal decanters stood. He poured out two generous measures and, to Ivy's disappointment, noticed her hovering discreetly by the door, waving her away irritably, the wave indicating that she was no longer needed.

She was tempted to linger outside the study door in the hope of overhearing a word or two but at that moment Miss Katherine clattered down the stairs with a face on her which Ivy and the other servants knew only too well. There had been more rows since Miss Chloe had come to stay at Cloudberry End than could be counted in the days of the month, and the girl in the house no more than a few weeks. Miss Katherine was expected to entertain her cousin, or at least keep her out of madame's way, rumour had it. Go about with her, make a friend of her, it was implied, since they were much of an age but Miss Katherine didn't care for that at all, objecting strenuously, loudly and with no thought for Miss Chloe's feelings who sat beside her each morning at the breakfast table as she did so. Miss Katherine wanted to leap on to her horse's back and go galloping off as she had for the past few years, not wet-nurse some city-bred mouse who had never been on a horse's back in her life, she said rudely.

Miss Chloe had stated coldly that she had absolutely no need of her cousin's company since she could entertain herself and, it being Sunday, she would be obliged if someone would direct her to the nearest church. Anglican, of course. That brought the lot of them to a standstill, particularly Miss Katherine who, as far as Ivy knew, had never been inside a church since the day she was christened.

Now, by the look on her face she was about to make someone's life a misery.

"Who was that, Ivy?" she asked peevishly, turning in the direction of the drawing room where her father had ordered her to sit and sew with her cousin.

"Jamie Hutchinson, Miss Katherine, come ter see yer pa."

If she hadn't seen it herself Ivy wouldn't have believed the transformation that took place in the master's daughter. From a drooping, woebegone, mutinous figure who gave the distinct impression the hangman's noose awaited her, she blazed with a sudden fiery intensity which made Ivy take a startled step backwards in case she herself was burned in the flames. Her head came up and her wilting back straightened to its normal long and graceful curve. Her eyes flooded with a glowing tawny light, a clear transparent brown in which gold flecks danced with joyous anticipation, and before Ivy could stop her, which she wouldn't have tried if she could, Miss Katherine was across the hall and without knocking had flung open the door of her father's study.

"Father," Ivy heard her cry in a voice in which nightingales sang, "why didn't you tell me Jamie was coming?" then the door was banged to behind her and Ivy heard nothing more.

Jamie sprang to his feet as Katherine swept into the room and his first reaction, fond as he was of her, was one of sharp irritation. Damn and blast the girl, why in hell's name couldn't she stay in her place for once? It was not that he was one of those men who believed women were meant for bedding and breeding but this meeting with her father was one of the most important moments in his life. He needed her father's complete attention. He needed time and a degree of calm in which to lay out his plans to the man he fervently hoped would agree with them, his proposition scrutinised and approved, in fact his whole bloody future, and it could hardly be done in the atmosphere of explosive fireworks with which Katherine treated every aspect of her life. He had glanced appreciatively about the room as he had entered it, noting the well-polished beauty of mahogany, the rich-piled luxury of expensive carpets, the fine prints of country scenes on the panelled walls, the smell of leather and good cigars, all speaking not only of great wealth but of good taste. He could not say he aspired to a room such as this for himself but he overwhelmingly wanted the chance to try for it. He couldn't honestly say he wanted to be as rich as Jack Andrews but he wanted to be as successful and if this girl who was flaunting herself so gloriously for his inspection ruined it he would never forgive her.

Jack Andrews sighed. He had no idea why Matty Jenkins's lad should have asked to speak to him, though he suspected that money might be involved. That's what most men wanted from him these days, knowing him to have an abundance of it. Schemes for this or that, wild ideas which needed an injection of ready cash, his, and which they were sure he would be only too eager to provide once they had presented their daft plans to him. Crackpot inventions, most of them, ill-thought-out businesses which would go under in six months or less, but which their innovator was convinced with a hundred guineas, again Jack's, would turn them into millionaires. He was also none too pleased at Katherine's very obvious delight in Jamie Hutchinson's presence in his study, wondering as he took another sip of his fine brandy how she had learned he was here. Not from Sara who was the only one to know of this meeting since both he and his wife were already a trifle alarmed at their daughter's lunatic attachment to the man who was their coachman's stepson. Five years ago at the age of eleven it had not unduly concerned them when she had clung passionately to his twenty-year-old coat tails, weeping and wailing when she was detached from them, but she was sixteen now and must be made to see that her position, and Jamie's, were very far apart. She was a young lady, her mother's daughter and would, in the fullness of time, marry some suitable young gentleman of her own sort. He himself had a working-class background but he didn't want to see this headstrong lass of his consigned to a labourer's cottage, living on a labourer's wage which must provide for her and the children she would undoubtedly produce on an annual basis. She would be a gentleman's wife, living the life her own mother lived, the life for which Sara had raised her. This . . . this attachment she seemed to have developed for Matty Jenkins's lad, her illegitimate lad, must be firmly nipped in the bud.

He reached out to a box on his desk and, offering it politely to Jamie, who refused just as politely, took a cigar from it and lit it, blowing fragrant smoke to the ceiling.

"I didn't tell you, Katherine," he said wearily, "because it does not concern you."

She glided, there was no other word for it, in a way which would have pleased her erstwhile governess, graceful as a lady should be, until she stood directly in front of Jamie, her flushed face smiling radiantly up into his. Her father might not have spoken – or even been there.

"I've tried to get over, Jamie, really I have," she said softly, positive that he had been as frustrated as she was at her failure to call, "but you know we have my cousin Chloe with us and it has made it very difficult but I promise— "

"Really, Katherine, it is of no consequence."

"Oh, but it is. I am being made to . . . to be with her every minute of the day. I don't know why since she does not want me but my mother insists."

"Katherine, I would be greatly obliged if you would go and join your cousin in the drawing room. Jamie and I have something to talk over and— "

"Really!" She whirled from her ardent contemplation of Jamie's embarrassed face to her father, then back to Jamie again who, like Ivy a few minutes ago, had the distinct urge to step back from her, from the overwhelming impact of her appeal which could threaten and, at the same time, bewitch any man. Her face became even more animated. Her eyes widened in excitement and she put her hand on his arm, waiting, he could see, to be enlightened.

"Well?" she demanded.

"It is a private matter, Katherine," her father said brusquely. "Jamie . . ."

"I wouldn't tell anyone, Jamie." She was enchanted to be part of anything which included him. "You can trust me, you know you can," she cried joyfully, longing for him to share whatever it was with her, her young, self-absorbed soul yearning towards him in a way her father did not like. There was a strange fervour in her eyes, a moistness to her parted lips, an unconsciously sensual lift to her full breasts which arched in the direction of Jamie Hutchinson.

Jack Andrews's face darkened and his eyes narrowed dangerously, but the man towards whom she was leaning was not responding to Katherine's wilful charm. In fact his face was grim and in it his eyes were a cold ice blue. His blunt-angled jaw was set in a purposeful way and aimed straight at Jack's daughter and, astonishingly, she faltered, even dropping her over-familiar hand from his arm.

"I'm sorry, Jamie," she said demurely, amazing her father with her sudden restraint. "I didn't mean to be a nuisance, really I didn't. I'll go now and leave you and Father to your business and perhaps later, when you're ready, if I may, I'll come down to Matty's and you can tell me about it, that's if you want to." She smiled repentantly.

"Oh . . . of course," Jamie faltered, as flabbergasted as Jack Andrews by the abrupt about-face of this girl who had never, to his knowledge, been humble, decorous, or sorry about anything in her life. She was a young princess, or so she believed, who could do as she liked with her father's subjects, taking what she wanted when she wanted it and kicking up such a hell of a fuss until she got it no one, except now and again this father of hers, had tried to curb her. She said the first thing that came into her head with little or no regard for anyone's feelings but now, with a quiet smile at her father and a last innocent look at himself, she moved gracefully across the room and went out, closing the door noiselessly behind her. The gleam in her eyes was hidden from them both.

"Well," her father gasped, "that's the first time I've ever seen her back down from a confrontation without a fight. What in hell got into her, d'you think?" raising amazed eyebrows, asking Jamie's opinion since he knew Katherine as well as any of them. "She's been a hellion since her cousin arrived and that's God's truth, fighting like a navviewoman, and I've met a few, against the constraint her mother is . . ."

He stopped speaking abruptly, clamping his teeth about his cigar, for though this lad's mother was almost one of the family it did not do to be gossiping about what was really none of his business. Matty would know all about it, of course, but still, it was not the kind of conversation which two men involved themselves in.

He "humphed-humphed" a time or two, clearing his throat awkwardly before leaning back in his chair as though to indicate that they might continue. He studied the man who stood before him, taking note of his strong, decisive face, his fiercely dipping eyebrows, the resolution in his firmly held mouth, his clear, direct gaze which did not falter from his own. Jack Andrews had dealt all his working life with men, navviemen who were the hardest, most intractable men in the world. He knew men. He could read a man's character from so many things. The easy way he stood before him, or otherwise. What he did with his hands, or his feet as Jack looked him over. His eyes, of course, which were the clearest indication of a man's temper and what he saw in Jamie Hutchinson's he found he liked. He had noticed him, at a distance, naturally, about Cloudberry End from time to time. As a young boy larking with his own sons, and, at Sara's request, sending him, again with his own sons, to the grammar school in Crossclough. The lad had had a good education, particularly for one whose mother and stepfather aspired to be no more than servants, but at fourteen he'd given it all up and gone away to sea, foolishly in Jack's opinion, who could have used him in his own business, or at least found him something more fitted to his learning and with more future in it. He hadn't even tried for promotion in his chosen employment, or if he had he hadn't got it. A man with his brains and education would have had more than a fair chance of gaining his master's ticket, but Jamie had remained no more than a common seaman, a deck-hand on a sailing ship for the past eleven or twelve years. Now he was home and for good, it seemed, and what did he want from Jack Andrews?

"Sit down, lad. Will you have another brandy?" he asked genially, testing him right from the start.

Jack lowered himself into the handsome leather chair on the other side of the desk.

"No, thank you, sir. I'm not much of a drinker though I've had my share in the past few years. Sailors are not known for their temperance, as you can imagine. Besides, I need a clear head for what I want to discuss with you." He grinned engagingly and Jack found himself returning it. Jamie had passed the first test, it seemed.

"Oh aye, and what might that be?" Jack asked. He drew deeply on his cigar, one hand in his pocket as he leaned back nonchalantly in his chair, at ease with himself, with his state in life and not particularly concerned or so he would have him believe, with the proposition – that's what it would be – that this enormous young man was about to put to him. Sara had begged him this morning for Matty's sake, she said, to give Matty's son whatever he might need in the way of cash for whatever he might have in mind, and Jack supposed he would, in the end, if only to please Sara, but he'd be damned if he'd just hand it over without a bloody murmur.

Jamie Hutchinson took a deep breath.

"Valley Bottom Farm, sir. It's on your land and I want to rent it from you. I've saved every penny I could, even invested some of it in . . . well, when I was home last you spoke of shares you had. D'you remember?"

By God, he did. He and the lad had met up on the path to Tintwistle Knarr and had walked back together. He had been surprised by Jamie's interest in the market, pleasantly surprised and quite willing to talk about it.

"Well, sir, I took your advice."

Advice! He didn't know he'd been giving any!

"It's taken me five years but I've enough to set myself up as a farmer."

"Have you now?"

"Yes, sir. I don't want anything from you but to rent the farm and some land."

"Do you now?"

"Yes, a small dairy herd, perhaps, sheep up on the high ground, some crops, whatever will grow up here. I'm no farmer, sir, but by God, I can learn. I've been studying farm journals for years."

"As long as that?"

"Yes, sir. I made up my mind when I was last home and if hope and optimism and bloody hard work are the ingredients needed to be successful then I'll be the most successful farmer in the valley and when I am I propose to buy your farm from you and if you won't sell it then I shall look elsewhere."

"By God, lad, I believe you would." Jack began to laugh and Jamie was astounded by his merriment and by the expression on his good-humoured face which Jamie failed to realise was recognition. Recognition by Jack Andrews of himself thirty years ago.

"Then . . .?" Jamie asked carefully

"Let's have a chat, shall we, lad, about your financial position. Always remember, should I agree to your . . . er . . . offer, that the financial position of any man, combined with his bloody and absolute determination to get what he wants from life, is the key to either success, or failure. Now then . . ."

6

Jack Andrews had bought and made extensive improvements to Waterway Paper Mill primarily as an investment and as an interest to fill his days after he retired from railroad building, but with his usual enthusiasm he had become so involved in its day-to-day running it had turned into what was essentially a new career for him and well worth the five thousand pounds he had spent to regenerate it.

There had been a paper mill on the site for one hundred and fifty years or more, driven by water power, of which there was a plentiful supply tumbling down a dozen cloughs into the valley. Paper-making by hand, sheet by laborious sheet, producing only a few hundredweight a week, each sheet as it came out of the vat laid by the "coucher", alternated with a sheet of woollen felt, into a pile. The owner, who had died penniless, unable to compete with the new mechanism for which he could not find the cash, had simply let the small business and the buildings which housed it fall into a state of tumbledown disrepair.

Jack soon put that right.

Of the one hundred and ten paper mills established in England after 1861, thirty-four had a short life: twenty-five less than five years and no more than one-third were still in business after ten years. There was a great increase in the demand for paper, of all sorts, due to the growth in industry, in trade, in the reading of newspapers and books, and with the enlarging of the supply of materials, again of all sorts, how could a paper manufacturer fail? was Jack's astonished question and he proceeded to show them, those who failed, where they went wrong.

Audrey Howard

He began by chucking out the old vat method of paper-making in which for generations the water-driven mill had produced the hand-made sheets of quality paper. He was a man who had done things on a grand scale all his working life, being involved in the sheer immensity of the Grand Trunk Railway in Canada and the Victoria Tubular Bridge which carried it across the St Lawrence River at Montreal.

Before that, and closer to home, he had shared the heroic savagery, the bloody determination and punishing labour which went into the building of the three-mile-long Woodhead Tunnel under the Pennine range. No one had kept an account of how many men died there, blasting through the millstone of those ferocious hills, though not a few of them were buried in unmarked graves in the graveyard at Woodhead Chapel, no more than a mile or so from Jack's home.

"I'm not fooling around with machines which were out of date before I was born," he told his family, none of whom, at the time, were particularly concerned. "I've ordered a couple of Fourdriniers – paper-making machines, darling – which, with the beating machines, should employ getting on for ninety people, something that will be welcomed by those in the district who are desperate for work."

"Beating machines, darling?" his wife asked vaguely, doing her best to show some interest.

"Aye, that's where it all starts, in the beater."

"But what is it?" She smiled encouragingly and Jack needed no second asking.

"It's a big oval tub with a revolving horizontal roll set with knives," doing his best to make his explanation as simple as possible. "Something like a paddle wheel. You put in your china clay, your sulphate of ammonia and other chemicals and mix it all together with the pulp."

"What pulp is that, my love?"

Jack was never less than unfailingly patient with his beautiful and much loved wife even though he was well aware that she was asking these questions to please him.

"It is the pulp made from the esparto grass that has been treated in the digester. That's the first process. The next is on the Fourdrinier, called that after the chap who designed it. Well, sweetheart" – smiling at her tolerantly, seeing that she was doing her best to understand, which was more than could be said of his children, Chris and Katy – "it's a bit complicated

542

but when it's all ticking over to my satisfaction perhaps I'll take you round and let you see how it works for yourself."

"Thank you, darling, that would be nice," returning his smile for they both knew she would never set foot in any place Jack considered to be dangerous, or even the slightest bit uncomfortable for his well-bred wife to endure.

Jack had not the same compunction about his youngest son. When his factory was running smoothly in the efficient way he liked and since his son still showed no sign of buckling down to anything beyond enjoying himself – at Jack's expense – he had let it be known that they were both to be at the gates of the paper mill, the Waterway Paper Mill, as the grand, newly painted sign proclaimed it to be, by seven thirty each morning.

"If the hands know you're on time, lad, then they will be," referring to the punctuality of his journeymen paper-makers, the men who worked on the digesters, the beaters, the women who sorted the esparto grass which came from Tunisia; those who worked in the drying and pressing rooms, the cutting rooms and the men who tended to and fed his two steam engines with the endless tons of coal on which the whole thing depended. And naturally, an eye must be firmly kept on his manager and his foremen since it was on their honesty and efficiency his profit depended.

"Get yourself down here," he would roar at the foot of the wide staircase at Cloudberry End, "for we've a business to run. Aye, I'm sorry you've had no breakfast but that's your fault, not mine, for I'm sure Freda called you at the same time she called me. So you can take that look off your face and make an effort not to look so pingling, lad. I heard you come in last night but it makes no difference to me if your head's rolling about on your shoulders like a bloody cannonball. You've still a day's work to do and the carriage is at the door. I take it you'd like to continue to receive that generous allowance I give you? Aye, I thought so."

Chris would follow his father, scowling fiercely against the light which hurt his eyes and the thundering movement of his lean body which hurt his head, hastily shrugging his way into his jacket, ramming his curly-brimmed bowler on to his auburn curls which seemed to ache as well.

For almost four months now he and his father had made this journey, sharing the carriage, crunching down the smoothly raked gravel driveway to the ornate, wrought-iron gates of Cloudberry End, turning left towards Crossclough and the factory which stood on the edge of Torside Reservoir.

The drive along the reservoir was a pleasant one, at least his father thought so, and said so almost every morning. When they entered the gates, promptly at seven thirty, or sometimes before since Jack liked to keep his workmen "on their toes", they were greeted by bobbing heads, the touching of a respectful finger to a peaked cap, even a dipping bob here and there from a grateful woman since Jack Andrews was known as a fair employer and, though he did not do so, could boast he knew the name of every man and woman in his employ. It was something he had learned in his years on the railway.

But, on this particular day neither father nor son received more than a surly glance from beneath the fiercely scowling eyebrows of a broad-backed labourer who was shouldering an enormous sack of china clay from a waggon. There were several other men working alongside him and it was noticeable that, in so far as the job they were doing would allow, they were giving him a wide berth. The yard, even at this time of the morning, was as busy as an ants' nest. There were other waggons loading and unloading, all pulled by the enduring patience and indomitable strength of handsome Clydesdale horses. Their harnesses were jingling as they tossed their heads up and down; their broad backs and flanks glistened with spit and polish, for they were much loved and fawned over by the men who drove them. Their gigantic hooves were garlanded with a smoky cream fringe of hair and their tails, of the same colour, swished constantly against the attack of troublesome flies. In their cream-coloured manes were tied a multitude of bright ribbons.

The men grunted as the heavy sacks were placed on their shoulders, sagging slightly as they took the load, all except the tall and powerful man who accepted his as though it were a sack of feathers. He kept his gaze on the two men who were alighting from the carriage, his head, on which sprang a mass of dark brown curls, held high. The angle at which it was carried might even have been described as disdainful, though his rough, working man's garb of trousers tied below the knee with twine, his stout, unpolished boots and faded, collarless shirt were exactly the same as every other man's in the yard.

Waterway Paper Mill was built around three sides of a large mill yard. There were two storeys, the upper storey housing the offices and other administrative workrooms where once the waste cotton material, from which paper had previously been made, had been stored.

On the far side of the yard a waggon loaded with esparto grass had just drawn up to the wide open doors of the sorting shed where the new material would be separated ready to be directed to the various treatment sheds. There the esparto grass, or alfa, would be cleaned and bleached with solvents, its uniform length of fibres and its free-draining qualities making it particularly suitable to be converted into the pulp which in turn would be manufactured through several processes into close-textured, resilient, porous and clear paper.

Up until a decade ago most of the pulp from which paper was fabricated had been made from the waste materials, cotton and linen rags, of the mills which abounded throughout Lancashire and which gave the county its lead in the production of paper. There was a variety of the necessary chemical products immediately available. There was a constant supply of industrial labour, for Lancashire had a long-standing tradition of skilled work in its mills, but the most important factors were the proximity of coalfields, an abundance of soft, pure water and the availability of transport, in the early days by canal, then by rail, to take its finished products to market.

Though Crossclough was, strictly speaking, in Cheshire, placed as it was on the narrow peninsula of land which reached out eastwards through Lancashire and Derbyshire and into Yorkshire, it had the same favourable factors which operated in the paper-making industry in Lancashire. Esparto grass was easily and swiftly transported from the port of Liverpool forty miles away by the fast trains which hurtled almost on the hour every day of the week through Crossclough, the finished product taking the same swift journey back again, mainly to Manchester which was by far the largest market for Jack Andrews's product. Esparto grass imports had risen from fifty-one thousand tons in 1863 to almost one hundred and fifty thousand tons annually in 1876 but the possibility of the large-scale use of the timber resources of the world was opening up with the invention of a chemical process for producing good quality cellulose from wood, and already Jack was talking of importing wood pulp. You had to keep up with the times, he told his family when they met at mealtime, frowning in the direction of his son who, as usual, looked glassy-eyed with boredom, since he heard it a dozen times a day at the mill.

It was going to be a hot day. It was mid-August and even at this early hour the men were sweating with the strength of their exertions, their muscled backs and shoulders, their brawny forearms rippling in the mist-hazed sunshine. Jack Andrews employed over ninety people in his mill. He had installed two steam engines to drive eight beating machines and two paper machines and it was on these that the skilled men worked while the women sorted and prepared the esparto grass. The men in the yard were unskilled labourers, rough and ready men, somewhat like the navviemen he had once directed, using their muscles not just in the carting of bales of grass and rolls of finished paper wherever they were told, but on one another in the fist fights which broke out on pay day. Some of them, those who were family men, not only loaded and unloaded the waggons, but drove them to and fro between Crossclough railway station and the paper mill. They were decent men with wives and children to support and because of it could be trusted to convey their loads to the waiting railway trains without succumbing to the temptation of the inns which lay along the way. Sometimes, when a delivery was urgently needed and was within driving distance they could be trusted to convey it directly to the buyer by what was now considered the somewhat old-fashioned method of horse-power. They looked after their animals as though they were their own, trustworthy reliable men, which could not be said of Paddy Andrews.

"Good morning," Jack called out to them, nodding civilly to the man who was, after all, his nephew. It was two months since Jack's older brother George had approached him somewhat sheepishly, not liking to ask a favour, but asking it just the same, for he was of the opinion that if his lad could just get himself set up in some decent, permanent work it would be the making of him. With Jack to see he kept at it, perhaps he might give over this shilly shallying from job to job, this liking he had for fighting in the boxing ring and make something of himself. George and Will and Harry, who were also Jack's brothers, were labourers on other men's farms and had lost most of their sons and even a couple of daughters to that promised land across the seas known as the New World, since there was little to keep them in the Longdendale Valley. The brothers were sadly aware, though they did not admit as much to their children's mothers, that they would never see their offspring again. America, where it was said the streets were paved with gold and if, when the seekers after a new life found it was not true, then an enterprising chap could buy himself a mule and a pick and go and dig it out of the ground for himself. George had only this one lad left, he said disconsolately to Jack, and if he were ever to have a grandchild or two at his knee then his only hope was Paddy. So, if Jack could find him summat in that there mill of his – and if Paddy could be persuaded to it – George would be eternally grateful. There was only him and Paddy living in the muck and muddle of the crumbling and untidy cottage since his Ethel had died a year or two back. If Paddy could be kept occupied happen he wouldn't be as wild and daft as he was. Fights and the like, drinking, a bit of poaching, not only game but other men's wives but a bit of steady work might settle him, didn't Jack think so?

"I'll try him out, George." Jack always felt slightly uneasy in the presence of his poorly educated, poorly placed brothers and for that reason was often inclined to allow them to persuade him to something he did not always care for. "Just in the yard at first but if he shapes . . . well, I can't promise anything. It's up to him. Send him down tomorrow."

Paddy had given no trouble, indeed he worked hard, was punctual and if not exactly civil at least he was not blatantly defiant with the foreman. He had a tendency to let thirty seconds or so go by when given an order, a curious smile on his lips which could be unnerving, or so the foreman, who knew his reputation, said. You were never sure whether he was going to obey, he told the manager.

"And does he?"

"Oh aye, eventually, but it's a bloody long thirty seconds while yer wait ter see what he'll do."

The other men seemed inclined to keep their distance from him, which was again a bit awkward, for they had their jobs to do as he did, grinning nervously when Paddy addressed some remark to them, and Jack could see why. Paddy was a big lad, there was no doubt of it and his talents with his fists were legendary.

Men moved purposefully or languidly, according to their nature, about the yard. They seemed to have the inconsequence of mechanical figures to Chris Andrews, set in motion by the order of his father to perform inconsequential tasks and he was constantly amazed that these men could accept their lot so tamely. Chained to the two huge steam engines which in turn bound them to the beating machines and the paper-making machines which moved like great undulating slugs across the length of the machine shed. The pulp flowed out through a strainer into what was known as a head box. From there it spread out on the endless copper screens which lay across the machines, the screens so finely woven the fibres in the pulp remained on them while the moisture was drained off.

The screen moved on and on, travelling remorselessly forward, but with a sly, side-to-side motion which settled the fibres and knitted them together until they reached the suction roller where any excess water was finally extracted. The pressed fibres then ran on in a continuous sheet of paper almost one hundred inches wide, ready for the next mechanical process.

Chris loathed it. His flesh crawled every time he entered any of the sheds. For one thing he felt as though the ammonia and other chemicals with which the esparto was incorporated was coating his skin and not only on the outside but within him as well. It seemed to slide down his throat the moment he took a deep breath, making his eyes sting, catching at his lungs until he thought he might choke. His stomach which, the night before, had been saturated with an enormous amount of brandy, and nothing since, for his father's voice at the foot of the stairs did not allow him time for breakfast, rolled over uneasily and he was forced to clamp his mouth tightly shut, only opening it to deliver a shouted message from his father to the manager, to the man in charge of one of the sheds, to a brawny labourer on the matter of his careless handling of a roll of paper. That's what he was, a messenger boy and nothing else and he was painfully aware that every man in the factory knew it. He had to shout because of the noise which was quite deafening, the clatter and crash of the machinery, the rhythmic bang of the head box as it took on another load of pulp, the hiss and swish of the live pulp as it snaked along the copper screen. They watched him, the men in the yard and the sheds, nudging one another as he went by, smirking, since they knew he was only employed because he was the owner's son, a young man pretending to be about something important but what he actually did at the factory not one of them could really say. He was a man trapped between his own belief that as the son of a wealthy father he had no need to work, and his father's belief that, as a man of the working classes, it was dishonest not to be gainfully and decently employed.

"Reckons 'iself too fine a gentleman ter dirty 'is 'ands in trade," they whispered behind his back, since he made no attempt to hide his distaste for factory life and indeed for all those involved in it. He was fit only to do what gentlemen did, which was to shoot grouse in season up on his father's grouse moor beyond Arnfield, drink brandy and claret until he fell insensible into his bed, play cards and other more dangerous games with the sons of the gentry. The men his father employed were forced to toil for twelve hours a day, six days a week, a total of seventy-two hours for a wage of just twenty-five shillings and threepence, and their womenfolk who laboured just as strenuously were rewarded with ten shillings less than that. They lived in tiny cottages in and around Crossclough, mostly four-roomed, two up and two down, each one crammed with the children which came with tenacious regularity every year, paying rents which varied from three shillings and sixpence to five shillings and sixpence each week. There was no such thing as running water and only the most basic pretence of sanitation. Cooking was done in the front room and the weekly washing in the one behind it and on wet days the family wash, and sometimes others people's wash if a woman took in washing to make ends meet, hung flapping damply about the cottage for days. Their homes were cheaply furnished and their families were cheaply fed and the sight of the master's son all tricked out in his silk waistcoats and expensively tailored suits taking a job which might have gone to a more deserving and needy man caused a great deal of resentment. Strangely, though Jack Andrews was just as immaculately tailored as his son the men had no such thoughts about him since he did as hard a day's work as they did and had done since he was a lad.

And none knew this better than Chris Andrews as he dragged himself, or at least that's how it appeared to his reluctant body, across the yard in the direction of the beating shed where he

549

was to tell Mr Harrop, the factory manager, that Mr Andrews, senior, of course, would be glad of a word with him at his earliest convenience.

At his earliest bloody convenience, Chris repeated through gritted teeth. He felt like some half-grown schoolboy entrusted with a message from the headmaster to a lesser teacher. It was a wonder his father didn't make him write it down so that he wouldn't forget it, or better yet, write it himself, telling his son to be a good boy and deliver it as quickly as he could.

A dog was snapping and snarling over something in the corner of the yard, his fur bristling, his ears laid back as his vicious jaw closed about a rough brown object which squealed in terror and pain. The dog threw back his head and the squealing stopped immediately but, not quite satisfied that his victim was properly subdued, the beast shook it savagely.

It was the ugliest dog Chris had ever seen. His muzzle, from which the dead rat swung, was short, wide, his lower jaw protruding beyond his upper. His eyes had such a look of vicious malevolence in them Chris came to an abrupt halt. The dog studied him intently, not making a sound, his whole body tensely still just as though, should Chris consider taking his prize from him he had better be prepared to lose a hand, or perhaps his life.

There came a short, sharp whistle from the direction of the waggon which was still being unloaded of its cargo of china clay. Was it the same waggon, or a second one? Chris wondered mindlessly, since time had no meaning in this place. A minute ticked on endlessly for an hour, an hour dragged like a day and at the end of each day he felt as though he had been incarcerated for a week in the Waterway Paper Mill.

The dog pricked his ears and with a speed and fluidity astonishing in one of his clumsy-looking bulk, swerved away, racing across the yard on his short legs as though he were a greyhound fresh from the trap. He skidded to a halt at the feet of the man who had whistled, lowered his rear end to a sitting position on the cobbles, every inch of him quivering in ecstasy-ridden adoration, his tiny eyes fixed slavishly on the man's face as he offered him the dead rat.

"Good lad, there's a good lad," the man said, in what could only be described as doting fondness, placing his big hand on the animal's broad head, rubbing it and his slavering muzzle with obvious signs of devotion. He took the rat from the dog's mouth whilst he watched him anxiously as though in some doubt that his offering might not suit and when the man threw it back to him with a "Good lad", falling on it joyously before waddling off into a corner to enjoy his kill.

The man was Paddy Andrews.

Those about him who had all stopped work to watch did not smile or joke with him on the skill of his dog as a ratter. They did not indulge in light banter, nor nudge one another in amusement at his unbelievable and what, in another, would have been called a fatuous display of affection. They did not move nor speak, not to him or each other until, with a growl at the two men who stood on the waggon placing the sacks of china clay on the labourers' shoulders, Paddy indicated that he was ready for another. They obliged quickly and the men resumed work.

Chris didn't know why he did it. The dog had not menaced a soul in the yard except for the rat and was now lying placidly in a square of sunshine tearing it to bloody pieces. The incident had held up the work for no longer than two minutes and yet something about the man, about the dog and the former's perfect belief that the animal had as much right to be there as the horses, as the men themselves, set his teeth and his nerves, which were stretched to breaking point anyway, on edge and before he had given himself time to consider the consequences he was across the yard tapping on Paddy's shoulder.

"Just a minute," he said to him as he was about to enter the shed. "I'd like a word with you."

Paddy turned and from his bit of space by the wall the dog lifted a suspicious head, ready to lumber to its feet should an order be given. Paddy didn't speak, just waited for his cousin to do so, one brawny arm lifted to balance his burden, the other flexing in readiness for a move he might not care for, which could be anything he considered to be insulting, every man in the yard knew that. An affront to Paddy Andrews which could take the form of a sidelong glance, a lift of the eyebrows, an innocent frown, even a smile which just did not suit him.

"It seems to me that dog of yours is somewhat dangerous," Chris went on, narrowing his green eyes in an unconsciously menacing manner. "He should not be hanging about the yard where there are women and possibly their children. He looks vicious to me and though he has undoubted talents as a ratter

I think it would be wise to keep him at home in the future. Besides which, if every man we employ brought his dog to work we would be inundated with them. See to it, if you please."

The fact that he was talking to his own cousin did not seem to occur to him and if it did it made no difference. They had never been friends, even as youngsters, though they were of the same age, for the difference in their upbringing, their education, their standing in the community – since Paddy's family had none – was quite unbridgeable.

Paddy's few years at school had not made him familiar with words such as "inundated" though he knew exactly what his cousin meant.

"We employ," he returned contemptuously. "Who dost tha' mean by we? I don't work fer thee, lad, not a pipsqueak what can't do nowt but run messages so tha'd best scamper back ter tha' pa afore tha' ends up in all sorts o' trouble tha' might not like."

Chris Andrews was not a coward but nor had he the size and strength of his cousin who was known to go in for the art, if you could call it that, of bare knuckle prize fighting for the entertainment of the gentry, who liked to see one working man batter another senseless over twenty or thirty bloody rounds. Indeed Chris had been present when Paddy had done so and had won money on him. Paddy was famous for it, as his dog was famous for its prowess in mauling and mangling other animals in the illegal dog fights which took place after dark in secret places on the moor.

"You'd best watch your mouth if you want to keep your job," Chris answered hotly, ready, despite the three or four stones in weight and six inches in height his cousin could give him, to bristle up to him. He himself was lean, fine-boned, a whippet challenging a bulldog and Paddy's face creased in a satisfied smile. He dropped the heavy bag of china clay, which hit the ground with a noise like a clap of thunder and, bending his knees and back, lifted his fists and began to weave a graceful circle about his employer's son.

The men in the yard, open-mouthed in amazement, for surely not even Paddy would take on Jack Andrews's lad, Jack Andrews who was a man of power and influence in these parts, closed their mouths and, gesturing to others who had not heard the exchange, scurried to get a good spot in the crowd which quickly gathered about the two young men.

It might have become dangerous. There was no doubt in the minds of the men who watched that Paddy Andrews could batter their employer's son with one hand tied behind his back and it was evident that Paddy thought so too, and relished the idea. He grinned, the grin itself like a slap in the face to the lighter man. Paddy jabbed at him playfully, making no move as yet to mark him with a fist the size of a horse's hoof, his grin deepening as Chris whipped back hastily.

"What was it tha' wanted ter say, lad?" Paddy asked pleasantly. "Summat about my dog, were it? Come on, speak up . . ."

"What the bloody hell's going on here?" a voice thundered, before Paddy had managed to land even one serious blow on the dancing, shifting, light-footed grace of his cousin's person. Chris, who had done some boxing at school, had at least learned how to avoid a blow if not to land one, though how long that state of affairs would have lasted was uncertain since Paddy was just as sure-footed and just as determined to knock him senseless.

"Clear a way there and you men, get back to your jobs, that's if you want to have one by the end of the day. Andrews, pick up that bag and take it to wherever it's meant to be, now, yes now, I said and look lively and as for you . . ." turning to his red-faced son, ". . . you'd best follow me into the office. I've a word or two to say about— "

"I don't think so, sir," Chris Andrews retaliated, his face draining of its inflamed colour, of his fury, his bloodlust, his frustration and his disenchantment with the life he was being forced to lead.

"Don't you answer me back, you young limb," his father bellowed. "Get up to my office . . ."

"Not while that man works in this mill," his son said quietly then, to his father's astonishment and that of the watching men, including Paddy Andrews, he calmly turned on his heel and strode from the yard, his red hair gleaming in the bright sunshine, his head high, his back tall and straight.

They did not see him that evening at dinner and his bed had not been slept in, Ivy said fearfully the next morning to Mrs Tiplady who reported it to her mistress, but after all he was a man of twenty, nearly twenty-one years and though his father despaired of him, short of tying the lad to his coat tails, what could he do about it? The slightest thing seemed to unsettle the lad. Oh aye, they'd all heard of the scuffle down at Waterway and the sacking of Paddy Andrews because of it, but what had become of the master's son? Probably in some tavern, drinking off his ill humour or senseless in some floozie's bed. He'd come home when he ran out of money, no doubt.

He did, unrepentant. Cocky, Freda was inclined to think, she told Mrs Tiplady after she had served the family their evening meal, not sorry for what he'd done, for fighting and drinking and staying out all night and his pa spoke sharply to him, Freda reported, though not sharply enough in her opinion, for he worried his ma no end and his pa told him so.

"Well, Father," he had said flippantly, "it's heartening to know that someone cares about my welfare but then a child's mother is bound to be concerned about her child, wouldn't you say, even if that child is worthless."

7

He was standing on the cobbled track which divided the
farm from its outbuildings when she saw him. His hands
were pushed deep into the pockets of his corduroy breeches.
He wore no jacket and his shirt sleeves were rolled up for
it was a mild day and his smoothly muscled forearms were
as brown as a gypsy's. He was utterly relaxed, his manner
one of dreaming contemplation since he thought himself to
be unobserved, like a man whose mind has gone drifting off
somewhere pleasing, leaving his physical self behind.

To the right of the track was the farmhouse, surrounded
by a broken-down drystone wall and crowded up against it,
its foliage casting a shadow over him and the track, was a
somewhat stunted horse chestnut tree in still gloriously red
flower, which was surprising since the fierce winds which
raged over these stark hills and through the valley bottom
did not allow for a profusion of growth.

She almost turned back. It was several months since she
had last seen him on the Manchester to Sheffield train and in
that time she had barely given him a thought as she wrestled
with her own unhappiness and the tribulation of how she could
escape it. She still harboured in her sorely tried heart, foolishly
she knew, the hope that she might find some employment
which would suit her and her talent for dressmaking, taught
her by Mama, and perhaps some little place of her own she
might make into a home. She didn't know where. She had, of
course, given up completely the idea that she might live again
with Papa and his new wife. Indeed she had had no word from
Papa since she left Liverpool, though she had written regularly
every week since she had arrived at Cloudberry End. She was
lonely, she admitted it and it was perhaps this which made

her hesitate, which made her study the man on the path for a moment or two longer, unseen.

She felt she knew him, for his name and what he was up to were for ever on her cousin's lips. Jamie this and Jamie that was her sole topic of conversation and there had been many arguments between her and her father, since Mr Andrews did not care to have Jamie Hutchinson's activities discussed at every meal, he thundered, and if Katherine did not stop dwelling on it morning, noon and bloody night he would begin to regret he had ever let the man have the damned farm in the first place. Katherine had been threatened with the most horrible punishments if she didn't let Jamie alone, since apparently she had been seen at Valley Bottom, her mare tied to the wall of the farm, on several occasions and her poor mother's nerves were in tatters just as her daughter's reputation would be if she did not learn to be more circumspect. She seemed determined to be included in every detail of Jamie Hutchinson's new career as a farmer and from her conversation it seemed the man could not make a decision or take a step without her supervision, from the purchasing of his small dairy herd, the seeds for his crops, the farm machinery he had bought second-hand at a farm sale, even a puppy given him by some chap or other Katherine had known and which was to make Jamie a splendid sheepdog. Katherine was his right-hand man, his mentor, his inspiration, to hear her speak, which Chloe was sure was not true, not from what she had seen of him and his quiet air of resolution which he had displayed on the journey from Manchester.

She looked at him now, the man who, or so she would have everyone believe, belonged exclusively to Katherine Andrews. He was very still, at ease, Chloe thought and in the most curious way something in his demeanour touched a chord in her. Something which spoke of tranquillity, of a man of peace and perfect content, of which she herself was in short supply these days and it was this which drew her towards him up the track and even gave her the courage to speak to him cautiously

"So this is it?" she said, quietly enough not to disturb him, to shatter his deep reverie but loud enough to announce what she hoped was her unthreatening, uncritical presence.

He turned sharply, still caught fast in his brooding contemplation of the land sloping upwards from the farm in a patchwork of browns and greens, fields divided by grey, stone walls, most of them urgently in need of repair. The wind, coming straight from the moor above them brought the fragrance of heather and bracken and the coarse, damp smell of hare's-tail cotton grass.

He seemed to feel no surprise at seeing her there. He smiled at her and again she felt that faint pull of something pleasurable inside her, something which drew her on until they stood almost shoulder to shoulder on the track looking up at the rough moorland together.

"Aye, this is it," he said simply, almost dreamily, his eyes following the track which led away gradually before disappearing towards Round Hill and Spond Moor. The drystone wall beside it meandered like a bit of abandoned grey ribbon, threatening to collapse in many places, its stones scattered beside the track where no one, for many years, had bothered to pick them up.

"When are you to begin?" she asked him, following his gaze up to the ridged outline of the hill at the back of the farm. Though it was high summer and the sky was a cloudless blue, it was grim nevertheless and she shivered inside her light summer cloak, wondering at the folly and bravery of those who lived up here wresting a livelihood of sorts from its poor ground.

"I've begun," he answered, turning back to her, smiling, still in perfect harmony with the elements about him and with her, it seemed, though they had met only once before. "I'm living in the farmhouse already."

Now that he had pointed it out to her she could see a thread of grey smoke whipping from the one chimneypot sagging at the apex of the roof. She turned from her bemused perusal of Valley Bottom Farmhouse, this man's farmhouse now from all accounts, and smiled back at him.

"So you have."

There seemed to be no more he wished to say and they remained in what appeared to her to be a rather pleasant and companionable silence. She leaned her back against the crumbling stone wall and so did he, his arms folded now across his broad chest. She could hear the sound of running water, a sound which was becoming very familiar to her, and from the shelter of the tussocky grass where it had built its nest a skylark rose on the air, going up and up until it was no more than a tiny dot in the blue arch of the sky. They both watched it in that silence which did not seem to be strange to them and when he spoke it was softly as though the great peace on the hill must not be shattered.

"You've found a place for yourself then, at Cloudberry, I mean?" His voice was hesitant with no intention to pry.

"Not really, though I find I have taken to country life."

"Does that surprise you?"

"Oh yes. I was born and brought up in Liverpool, you see. I am used to bustle and noise and the absence of both up here alarmed me at first."

"And now?"

"I have grown used to it. I walk a lot and then there is my sewing. It's something I enjoy."

"So I see." He smiled down at her, indicating the pale dove grey gown she wore.

She smiled back at him, relaxed and astonished that she was. "I decided to discard my mourning black. My aunt and uncle are surprisingly generous with their money and my allowance, as my uncle calls it, is quite enormous."

Silence fell again, and again it was an easy one, then, "Would you like to take a cup of tea with me?" he asked her, his eyes clear and steady as he smiled down at her, untroubled by her beauty, by her unexpected arrival, by the strangeness of a tough-fibred farmer like himself – he hoped he was that – inviting this elfin-like creature to take tea with him. It seemed natural somehow, with none of the complexities of Male and Female in it, merely two people who might be friends taking another small step towards that easy relationship.

To her own surprise, since she was often shy with strangers, she found herself agreeing.

"Yes, I would, thank you."

"The kettle will be on the boil. It always is so it shouldn't take long," he told her as he led her through the ramshackle gate which would one day keep his livestock out of his bit of garden. "Mind the cobbles. They need relaying but I'm afraid the job is a long way down my list of what needs doing. Yes, I can tell you know what I mean," as she smiled widely at him in what he realised was sympathetic humour. "My cattle are to be delivered tomorrow."

"So I believe."

"Pardon?" He looked bewildered.

"Mr Hutchinson, I do assure you there is no part of your life, nor your plans for it which I do not know. My cousin is most enthusiastic."

"Oh God," he groaned, "that girl will be the death of me, really she will. She means well but she cannot believe I can manage this new life of mine without her at my elbow."

"I know, so she implies." Chloe dimpled in the most delightful and amazing way and he realised she was teasing him. He grinned at her ruefully, wondering how to explain the relationship between himself and the wayward Katherine Andrews but she did not seem to care about it, merely saying, "Do go on, Mr Hutchinson. You were talking about your livestock?"

"Yes, so I was. Well, my sheep, what I could afford, are up on Spond Moor and I must hire a man to mend the walls before the foolish creatures all vanish into another farmer's flock. There are crops to sow but my brother is to give me a hand."

"So we heard," laughing again. "You are going to be busy," she continued in her gracious, ladylike way, though her laughter was warm and friendly. "I only wish I could help," she added, "since I would be glad of something to do, something useful. Of course, I could make curtains . . . or the bedlinen, pillow cases, things like that," she went on breathlessly as the idea grew in her mind. "I must be honest with you, Mr Hutchinson, I'd be hopeless at cobble laying, or wall building and as for sheep and cows I should be terrified if I came face to face with either one." She began to laugh unrestrainedly and so did he. "But a bit of sewing, I could manage that." Her face brightened even more, just as though a lamp had been lit behind it, the very thought of doing something specific, even for this man who was really a stranger, filling her with pleasure.

He was astounded. "That's a most generous offer but I couldn't possibly ask you to do it, Miss . . .?" He could not recall her surname and he raised his eyebrows enquiringly. He knew he sounded pompous but he was so bowled over by her offer he couldn't think of anything else to say.

"Why not? It's one thing I'm good at and my name is Taylor, but I would like it if . . . if you . . . my name is Chloe." She knew it was forward of her and her mama would have had a fit since a well-bred lady did not invite a gentleman to call her by her given name on almost first acquaintance. Except for the occasional conversations she had with Katherine and the somewhat furtive exchanges Chris Andrews tried to draw her into when they found themselves alone together, no one had called her by her Christian name in three months. Her aunt and uncle demanded nothing of her and gave nothing to her beyond a distant politeness. They met only at mealtimes, and after a while, as the weeks passed, it seemed they had grown used to her quiet presence at the table, barely noticing her, as they would barely notice a chair or a salt-cellar or a fork. They had long given up attempting to force Katherine into taking Chloe about with her, for which she at least was truly thankful and so, for the most part, Chloe was free to do as she pleased. This walk was one of her favourites. The track led from the woodland at the side of her uncle's property, across an easily traversed hillside meadow and on up to Valley Bottom Farm, which, though it didn't actually rest in the valley, did so in comparison to the high peaks of Black Hill and Bleaklow. The track went nowhere else, petering out beyond the farm and up until today she had met no one in her solitary meandering.

"I know," Jamie said, a small smile playing round his mouth.

"Pardon?"

"I know your name is Chloe."

She began to laugh. "Katherine?"

"Katherine."

There was a puppy just inside the kitchen door, his body wriggling in ecstasy as Mr Hutchinson held it open for her, yapping and nipping at her boots, and then at her hesitantly outstretched hand as she knelt down to him. His huge paws reared up against her, planting themselves on her shoulders. She scratched his ears in some trepidation and he turned his head to attack her hands with a rough, over-exuberant, scratchy tongue.

"Careful, he'll have you over if you don't watch him. He's supposed to be a sheepdog, or will be when I've finished with him," his owner said cheerfully. "Get down, Captain. I call him Captain after the many masters I've sailed under. Now mind your manners, lad," but it was too late and as Chloe landed on her backside, her pale grey cotton skirts up about her knees, revealing not only her white stockings, her many white frilled petticoats but her white, lace-trimmed drawers, the puppy leaped into her lap and turned his attentions to her face.

"Oh my," she squealed, her breath gone, her gold-shot russet hair tumbling about her laughing face, her cloak coming undone and slipping from her shoulders, her long, white slender neck arching in a lovely line as she attempted to avoid the puppy's avid tongue. "Oh my, Mr Hutchinson, I'm afraid it's too late for manners. Will you please rescue me from this rough scamp before he eats me alive."

Jamie Hutchinson turned from his host's duties at the glowing coals of the fire where the kettle had rested, the expression on his face one of good-humoured exasperation but it slipped away as his eyes came to rest on the girl who sprawled in his doorway. Her severely dragged-back hair was gone in an eruption of glorious, tangled curls about her shoulders and down her back to where it swept the old stone flags of the kitchen. Her legs, slender but shapely, were revealed to the knees and as the puppy redoubled his efforts to get at her flesh, any bit of flesh would do, her skirt rose even higher until it was about her waist. Her heels scrabbled frantically on the flagged floor as she tried to escape but her efforts only excited the puppy further in what he evidently considered to be a game she was devising for his enjoyment. She was giggling helplessly, her cool young dignity completely gone, her composure, which no one at Cloudberry had ever broken through, or if they had she had not allowed them to see it, flung to the winds in her joy in the puppy.

Jamie was spellbound. He had the kettle in one hand, the teapot in the other, just standing there, he realised later, with his mouth foolishly open, his heart violently thumping and the sudden thrusting ache in his loins hurting him quite intolerably. She was the most enchanting thing he had ever seen, her eyes sparkling like turquoise through the curtain of her hair, her mouth wide as she laughed, her small tongue pink and quivering between her perfect white teeth. Perfect! That's what she was, he told himself as he fell mindlessly and irrevocably under her spell. But what the bloody hell was he doing, gawping at her like some ignorant farm lad who had never before seen a pair of drawers except on his ma's washing line.

Oh God!

"Please ... Mr Hutchinson ... rescue me ..." she was pleading between squeaks of laughter.

"Right," he said, continuing to stare at those slender white calves and the expanse of white frilly drawers above them.

"Mr Hutchinson ... I beg of you ..." and as a note of something he did not quite recognise as awareness sharpened her voice he hastily placed the kettle and the teapot on the table, realising with that part of his brain which still functioned logically that the soot on the kettle's base would leave a mark on the chenille cloth his mam had given him for his kitchen table.

"Captain," he managed to bellow, but the dog, not yet recognising his name, nor the authority in his master's voice, continued to lavish his young devotion on Chloe and it was not until Jamie had picked him up by the scruff of his neck and flung him outside the door, where he howled plaintively, that peace was restored, at least inside.

When Jamie turned back to her Chloe had arranged her skirt to a more decorous length, though she still sprawled somewhat awkwardly on the floor. He held out his hand to her and she took it, aware of the sharp tension in it, in the hard palm and the strong brown fingers, for though she did not know what it was that had happened between them she knew something had.

He pulled her to her feet, then, unable to bear the lovely closeness of her, the dishevelment of her spectacular hair, her fragrance, her softness, her brilliance which he wanted more than he had ever wanted anything in his life before, even this farm, he stamped back to the fireplace, giving the strange impression that she had seriously offended him in his determination not to let her see the effect she had had on him. He rattled about with spoons and tea-caddies, with cups and saucers and milk jugs, giving her time to recapture the profusion of her hair and himself his badly strained peace of mind.

"I think I'd better get back," she said hesitantly behind him and he whirled to face her, his face stern and paler than usual.

"No, please don't go. Stay and have your tea," and he at least was well aware that he was saying something else. Stay, yes. Don't go, yes, but nothing to do with cups of tea.

She was bewildered. "Mr Hutchinson . . ." She was about to

trot out the platitudes her mama had taught her which were meant to rebuff, politely, of course, any gentleman who was becoming a nuisance but the words just seemed to die in her throat in a way which had never happened before. Even before life was breathed into them they withered away and she found herself moving, trancelike, towards him.

"Mr Hutchinson . . ." Her voice was husky with something she did not recognise as her awakening sexuality.

"Jamie, please," he heard himself murmur, studying her mouth, waiting for her to say his name for the first time.

"Jamie . . ." It thrilled him. He watched her helplessly as she drifted even closer to him and he knew she was hypnotised by something he was directing at her and he was acutely aware that it must be he who put a stop to it. Christ Almighty, what in hell was happening to him? he asked himself, knowing what it was even as he denied it. He'd known many women since he'd become a man but in ten years no one had ever touched his heart. He had thought her lovely, enchanting even, on the train and had been surprised by the enormous urge he had felt to protect her, which he had put down to her defenceless fragility. Her face at the carriage window as the Andrews drove away had awakened a strong feeling of pity in him but he had not once considered her as a woman on that train journey. A young, frightened girl she had been and that was what his maleness had responded to.

But now he wanted her. Sweet Jesus, how he wanted her but she'd not thank him if he made advances to her here on the old rag rug his mam had given him and on which countless dogs and kittens and children had rolled in play. She was too fine for that, too . . . special. Yes, that was the word and though it surprised him, for he had always been a man to take an opportunity when it presented itself to him, he was reluctant to do so now.

"Sit down, Chloe," he managed to say, "and let me pour you a cup of tea to hearten you on your journey." He knew he sounded bloody ridiculous. It was one of those trite remarks a hostess might make to a guest but it was the best he could think of at that precise moment.

She did as she was told, her manner still dream-like, her eyes a soft, clouded, greeny blue, her lashes drooping, her lips still moistly parted, a flush of apricot in each cheek. Jesus, but she was beautiful, with some physical thing her mama had not taught her, nor even thought to warn her about, but by Christ, he'd not take advantage of it, nor of her ignorance, her innocence, no matter how she damn well looked at him.

"I'm to rent this farm from Jack Andrews, did I tell you?" he heard himself babble, glad of anything to dissipate the languorous warmth which still had a hold of them. "I saved enough and invested money . . . Mr Andrews helped me."

"Really." Her voice was low and still thready but he could see reality touch her gently.

"Yes. I intend buying it one day when I've the money. Here's your tea . . . sugar? And perhaps some milk? It's fresh . . . well, as I was saying . . ." His own voice was almost his own again. "I can't buy yet or I would have nothing left for beasts and machinery, you see."

"Of course." She sipped her tea obediently though it was strong, not what she was accustomed to drinking, and the mug was thick and sturdy, again not what she was used to, never taking her eyes from his face, mesmerised, it seemed, by the sound of his voice which was murmuring of everyday things, but which appeared to electrify her.

"You'll have heard of the Agricultural Holdings Bill which was passed in March?"

"No, I don't believe so." The personification of exquisite politeness.

"It gives tenants rights which they didn't have before."

"Really."

"Yes," taking a sip of his own tea, wishing it had a shot of whisky in it to steady his overstretched nerves.

"If a tenant makes an improvement to a farm, like this one, say, then he is entitled to compensation from the owner. And of course I shall be improving it."

"What will you do?" It was with great relief Jamie could see she was taking a genuine interest now, coming out of her trance, out of the bewildering web he and she had blundered into.

They both turned to look round the comfortless room. The farmhouse was in poor repair, since it had been unlived in for many years. He and his mother had done what they could, scrubbing the floors, the windows, even the walls but there were none of the homely appointments to be found in Matty's cottage. A solid table left by the previous owner since it could not be got through the doorway, a couple of rush-seated, spindle-backed chairs made from cherrywood, and a lopsided dresser on which several pieces of serviceable pottery stood. No more than a plate or two and half a dozen knives, forks and spoons. The enormous hearth, characteristic of farmhouses and cottages of the previous century, sported a huge, crackling log fire, the kettle and what appeared to be an all-purpose iron pot. There was nothing else. Nothing that was not strictly practical, not even a jar of flowers which after all could be gathered for nothing. The walls had suspicious patches of what looked like damp and the woodwork about the windows was crumbling with age and neglect.

"Well . . ." Jamie sighed somewhat helplessly, seeing it for the first time as it would appear to a woman such as her, but knowing there was nothing to be done about it. "The drystone walling for a start."

"And the cobbles up to the farmhouse door." She smiled, a natural smile which he returned.

"Yes, and then visitors will not fall and damage themselves, and of course," he went on hastily since it seemed she knew exactly who one of those visitors would be, "there is the farmhouse itself. It is barely fit for the mice to live in let alone humans."

"Mice!" She shuddered and looked about her apprehensively and he wondered, fast in the throes of helpless fascination, why it was women were so afraid of mice, at the same time enchanted with her because she was.

"Oh, they'll be long gone soon," he soothed her. "There's a fine litter of kittens in the stable at Cloudberry, all looking for good homes so I'll fetch a couple up here and they'll soon be rid of them."

"What about Captain? Won't they fight? I thought cats and dogs were mortal enemies. Not that I know much about it since I'm familiar with neither." She leaned forward confidentially, putting her elbows on the table, cupping her chin in her hands, and he wondered at the sad echo of – was it loss? – in her voice. What had she known in her young life? What was she doing here? Even his mother seemed reluctant to talk about her and why had her father, who surely could not help but love this beautiful young woman, sent her here to a house where she was very evidently not welcome?

"How old are you, Chloe?" he heard himself ask abruptly.

She did not seem surprised or offended by his question which was not one a gentleman asked a lady.

"I'm eighteen, nineteen in September."

"I shall be twenty-six in December."

"I see," she breathed and though she was not exactly certain what she meant by that it seemed to satisfy him.

"I think you had better get home now, don't you?" he asked softly.

"Where is that, Jamie?" It was said with no appeal for sympathy.

His insides wrenched at the sadness in her voice but he resisted the temptation to take her hand and bring it to his lips. God Almighty, he had got up from his narrow truckle bed this morning, his first night spent in this new home of his, his first day of his new life ahead of him and like a thunderbolt, striking at him with ferocity and yet at the same time exquisite tenderness, this girl had walked into his farmyard, into his farmhouse, into his heart even, and settled herself in it, whether she knew it or not, with the serenity of a cat curling itself before a good fire on its own hearth. His thoughts were wild and foolish for how could he believe that this would be her hearth one day, an easily broken creature like Chloe Taylor who should by rights be adorning some rich man's home where she would have need to do no more than take a stitch or two of fine embroidery each day. Jamie Hutchinson should be looking about him for a brave-hearted, strong-shouldered, wide-hipped young woman – like Katy Andrews, his bemused mind whispered, who would scrub and scour, plant seeds and plough furrows and give him a dozen healthy children while she did so.

Of course he should, but could he? Now?

"I'll walk you to the edge of the wood," he told her, already expecting her to do what he thought best for her.

"Can we take Captain? Poor puppy shut outside and it wasn't his fault. I shouldn't have knelt down beside him."

"He knew exactly what he was doing, the young devil. And he must learn to live outside, Chloe. He's not a pet but a working dog."

She looked quite horrified. "Outside! By himself? How could you? He's only a baby even though he is so big. Oh, Jamie, I couldn't bear to have him fretting in one of those awful outbuildings on the other side of the track. Surely he could be allowed to sleep on this mat before the fire? It must be damp and cold out there, particularly in the winter and I'm sure it will do him no good. Oh, please, Mr Hutchinson . . . Jamie, let him come inside now and I'm sure he will behave for you when he is properly trained. I could make him a blanket of his own."

He was helpless before the appeal in her voice, in her body which surged towards his in desperate defence of the dog. He was left without resources as the natural barricades which a man puts up about himself in order to get through life without mishap shattered and came crashing down about him. Jesus Christ, how could he possibly deny her whatever she asked of him when her little flower face, which had paled with the strength of her outrage over the dog, swam inches below his own. She was up on her tiptoes, her nose on a level with his chin and he had only to reach out and pull her to him, press her face into the curve beneath his chin, fold his arms across her back and simply hold her. Assure her that he would do anything she wanted, with the bloody dog, with this farm, himself, his life. Oh, Jesus God, if he could . . . if he could . . .

He held up his hands as though in submission, palms towards her and with a great effort he managed to smile.

"I give in, I give in, really I do. The animal shall sleep in my bed if that's what you think's best for him and shall eat the best steak the butcher in Crossclough can supply."

Her face broke into a smile of huge delight.

"Oh, Jamie, do you mean it? You don't, do you, not about the meat, but you will let him sleep in the house?"

He sighed, defeated. "Very well, but next time you come bring that blanket, for I'll not have him upstairs."

"Oh, I will, I promise, I promise."

She collapsed into the chair, her face rosy again, her laughter bubbling up, high and lovely to hear and the girl who was just about to tie her mare to the iron ring at the gate lifted her head in shocked surprise. Her fingers became still for a moment and then clumsy as she did her best to loop the reins through the ring and the mare, sensing her mistress's flaring unease, backed off, eyes rolling, ears pricking.

"Stand still, you fool, for God's sake, and not a sound," she hissed, her face turning in bewilderment towards the farmhouse, but it was too late as the puppy, who had flopped disconsolately in a bit of sunshine by the doorstep, sprang to his feet and galloped frantically towards her. He began to bark, knowing already that this was his domain and that inside the house were his people whom he must guard, but at the same time, since he was still very young, he could not resist greeting with great affection this new human he vaguely recognised.

"Oh, God alive," Katherine Andrews moaned as several pounds of ecstatic dog flesh leaped up against the skirt of her blue riding habit. Her mare reared and whinnied in alarm and from a rotting pile of wood in which she had cornered what she was positive was an enemy, her small terrier flew to defend her. The puppy, who had meant no harm, began to howl as Muffy showed him her teeth in a savage snarl though she was half his size, backing off in great haste towards the safety of the door. When it opened he thundered inside and cowered behind Chloe's skirts.

When Jamie, who had opened the door, saw who his visitor was, his heart sank like a stone to his boots but he did his best to smile.

"Katy, what a commotion. I thought a pack of wolves was attacking us. I'm afraid my brave hound has not yet learned any manners and I'm sorry if he has damaged your gown. He was the same with Chloe, jumping up and almost taking her off her feet. In fact he did take her off her feet, didn't he, Chloe?"

Katherine's eyes narrowed suspiciously. The sight of her cousin lurking in Jamie's kitchen was not one she had expected and she did not like it. This was her territory. It belonged to her, with Jamie, for had they not brought it to its present state which was one of being ready to begin. To plant and . . . and all the other things Jamie meant to do which, as yet, she herself was not too clear about. Sheep and cows and hens and . . . and things. For weeks she had been coming up here and standing, hands on hips, feet apart, as a man might stand, gazing with proprietorial pride over the land which Jamie was to farm. As Jamie did. Side by side they had discussed what Jamie and his brother were to do. Sometimes Tommy would come with them which was a bit of a nuisance but as he was to work for Jamie it couldn't be helped. The joy of being alone with Jamie was indescribable. She had never been happier. She and Jamie were going to do this together, though neither of them had said so in so many words. There was no need. It was understood. She loved him and when he had a moment to turn round and see her, really see her, he would know he loved her. She only had to be there when he did.

So what was her cousin Chloe doing in his kitchen, smiling, almost purring, Katherine would have said, like the cat who has just had the last saucer of cream?

She felt the confusion press around her heart. She didn't really know what to do, how to feel or even how to behave at this precise moment, which was unlike her since she had always said and done the first thing that came into her head but something, some instinct, some female sense begged her to be careful, to watch her mouth, to guard her tongue, even to hide the expression in her eyes since, her senses told her, she was in great danger.

"Really," was all she said, clamping her lips firmly about her teeth.

"It seems I am to be honoured with visitors today which is just as well for I shall be up to my eyes in work as soon as the herd arrive. Tomorrow, they said, and I am to collect the plough at the end of the week. Tommy is coming up later to give me a hand so I shall have no time for entertaining. Chloe and I have just had . . . there's tea in the pot, Katherine, if you fancy a cup. Come in . . . do come in."

He knew he was saying more than was needed and so did Katherine and she felt the first stirring, not just of alarm but of real fear. Why should Jamie, a man, not a callow youth, be in such a taking, such a state of jabbering foolishness, like a husband who has just been found in awkward circumstances with his wife's maid?

She walked towards them, aware that Chloe, whether on purpose or not, had moved to stand beside Jamie in the doorway. Her face was composed, pale, and her eyes were clear and untroubled. She looked as she had always looked, unapproachable, detached from those about her, her dove grey gown falling, unwrinkled, in soft folds to her feet, not a button awry, not a hem out of place. Yes, just as she always did except for several tendrils of red-gold hair which fell about her ears, drifting to her neck and to her placid white forehead as Katherine had never seen it do before.

Their eyes met and held and though Chloe Taylor, until this moment, had been only vaguely aware of the empathy which had blossomed, the warmth which had been kindled today between herself and Jamie Hutchinson, perhaps of no more than friendship since she had no experience of men, nor of need, she did recognise the challenge in her cousin's eyes for were they not both women? Jamie was an extraordinary man. They had met only twice but each time he had given her something, something unrecognised but which had made her feel . . . what? Safe, comforted, at ease and she had liked it. And him! Something unusual had happened between them today. As yet she had had no time to study it, to mull over its contents, to examine it in depth, to visualise what she would do with it when she knew what it might be. She would go back to Cloudberry and her room there, sit in the window seat overlooking the garden and call up every moment, bring each one forth and listen to what Jamie had said to her and how he had said it. Remember the expressions on his face and what had been softly inherent in his voice.

And she knew something else she would do as well. She would come again to Valley Bottom Farm to visit him, as she sensed he wanted her to and that brooding look in Katherine's eyes, which she had been allowed to see, would not stop her!

8

Chris Andrews watched his cousin come towards him in that straightbacked and yet supple way she had of walking, placing each foot on the rough path with sure grace, one before the other as a cat does. Even though she was making her way uphill it did not hinder her. Her head was up. She wore no bonnet and despite the dullness of the day there appeared to be a gleam, a gloss about her hair, as though the sun touched it. It was held at the crown of her head with a froth of peacock blue satin ribbons, a small unconscious rebellion, he thought, surprised, against the pale grey sombreness of her half mourning. She was a young girl who should have been in pretty colours, defying convention with a touch of frivolity though there was none to see it and none to care if they did. Her hair hung in an enormously thick, curling cable, giving the impression it longed to be free, strands of it falling across her breasts, the rest hanging down her back from the confining ribbon to just below her waist. The damp in the air had wound her hair into tight ringlets at her forehead and neck and put spangles of mist in it, like tiny diamonds which, again, though there was no sun to reflect in them, sparkled like dew on early morning roses.

He saw all this from beneath the overhang of the enormous rock which formed part of a tumbled group lying at the side of the clough. The water accelerated past him, hurtling white drifts dividing on either side of grey rocks which, blackened by the moisture, resembled enormous lumps of coal, shiny and polished to ebony. It thundered down to each level in a skirt of misted gauze edged with lace, floundering and hissing, leaping from rock to rock so that there was nothing but the sound of its frantic race to reach the reservoir in the valley. When he stepped out on to the path up which Chloe climbed she recoiled savagely, almost overbalancing into the demented stream.

"Whoops," he said, laughing, reaching out to take her fine-boned arm in his strong, horseman's hand, steadying her but at the same time drawing her closer to him. "Careful, or we'll both be in the clough, though I must say I have often wondered how long it would take to get to the bottom by water instead of the more conventional way. Not long, I shouldn't wonder, though in what state one would arrive . . . well . . ."

He grinned engagingly into her startled face which was very close to his own, leaning even closer in a way which she recognised, for it was not the first time he had accosted her this way. His smile had in it the impudence of a young gentleman who knows he is flirting with a female who is not a lady, at least in his opinion, and she felt her anger erupt.

With a violence which astonished him – she could see it in his transparent green eyes – she snatched her arm away from his over-friendly hand and, brushing past him, continued up the path without speaking, her face taut and furious.

He had lain in wait for her on many occasions since she had been sent to Cloudberry End and though she would not let him see it, since she despised him for his weak character, his belief that no woman could resist him and what she saw – or what her mama would have seen – as a most immoral determination to avoid doing a hand's turn if he could help it, she was beginning to be somewhat nervous of him. Well, perhaps not exactly nervous of him since that implied she could not control him, had no power to stop the silly games he played with her, but she did wish he would accept she had no interest in what he called "being friendly".

There was the time in the wood when she had gone to sit in a patch of sunlight to read a book she had taken from her uncle's library. *Far from the Madding Crowd* by Thomas Hardy, it was, published only a year or two back, and she had been deeply immersed in the passionate exchanges between Bathsheba and Captain Troy when a shadow had fallen over her, blotting out the sunshine, blotting out her pleasant hour of forgetfulness from her own dispiriting life. He had laughed and chattered and done his best to draw her into his own, what she saw as facetious nonsense, talking about how pretty she was and how lonely she must be and if ever she needed a friend she had only to turn to him. She would sooner befriend Katherine's little dog.

Then there had been the incident in the back parlour where he had done more than try to be her "friend". A little kiss, he had said, which naturally she wouldn't miss and would certainly enjoy sharing with Chris Andrews. His face had been so serious when he had drawn her into the room she had been completely fooled and had allowed herself to be enticed from the narrow passage but when his true purpose had been revealed it was all she could do not to strike him.

He had stepped into her path in Crossclough, bowing and doffing his hat, asking her where she was going and did she mind if he accompanied her and perhaps, afterwards, they might . . .

She had not allowed him to finish but had swept up her skirt and continued on her way to the haberdasher's where she meant to purchase velvet ribbons to match a new gown she was planning for the winter.

There had been other times when he had been more determined and she had almost had to struggle with him to avoid the delights of what he called "being friendly" and so she had learned to watch for him, note where he was going and with whom and when he was gone to slip away across Cloudberry End wood like some stealthy intruder. When she knew he was at the paper mill she could relax but even then, sent on some errand or other by his father, he would sometimes pop up in the most unexpected places, his grey cropping the vegetation behind some handy huddle of rocks, his grin engaging, pretending to be apologetic for alarming her but leaving her in no doubt that he was not at all sorry, not really.

She climbed steadily away from him, moving through the undergrowth which, nourished by the spray from the fall of water, grew in great abundance. Ferns fringed the water, beautiful in their display of misted droplets which slid from frond to frond and then to the ground, turning last year's leaf mould into a quagmire. There was a path of sorts, with rocky outcrops and from every bit of ground where sustenance might be had grew saplings of rowan and sycamore in their full summer glory. Chloe had, on Katy's advice, bought herself from the generous allowance her uncle gave her some sturdy leather boots which gripped her about the ankle, supporting their tendency to turn on the uneven ground and their serrated soles gripped the wet stones and were impervious to the boggy ground. She had been out walking almost every day since she had come to Cloudberry End and had become strong, able to stride out for hours. Chris, in the well-polished boots he wore to the office at Waterway Paper Mill, had a job to keep up.

"Chloe, wait, don't run off like that," he gasped, his predilection for good brandy and good cigars, hours at the gaming table and other, more punishing pastimes, leaving him out of breath. "I'm not used to this, cousin," he heaved. "I'm not a great one for the outdoors unless I'm on horseback. Please, have mercy," laughing, "take pity on me and let's have a breather. Why don't we stop and admire the view? Can you honestly tell me that it's not worth looking at, even on a day like this?"

They had reached about halfway up the Black Hill from where the watercourse flowed. The gritstone cliffs which formed the clough were about twenty feet high on either side at this level, the water which flowed through it gentler now, just a mild froth and dither, with miles of boggy moorland beyond where the bog-cotton grew and curlews piped a tune. Just heather and broom and rough stone, a rabbit or two flirting their scuts and high, high above, a hawk lay on the air with nothing more than an occasional flicker of its wings to keep it there.

The moorland stretched on and on to the murky horizons, vast wastes of hazed purple and golden explosions of gorse, the tawny brown of bracken, all divided by the narrow paths where sheep trod.

Chloe emerged from the tangle of vegetation, sparser now, striding out across the springy turf, skirting tumbled projections of half-buried rocks from behind which sheep got clumsily to their feet and leaped away in alarm.

"Chloe, dammit, won't you stand still for a bloody minute? Anyone would think you were afraid of me."

It was perhaps this which stopped her. The idea that he might think he frightened her; even if he did she had no intention of letting him see it. He was a boy, a silly boy playing silly games, dangerous games, for should she tell his father it might be awkward for him. The Andrews family might regard her as an unwanted visitor who must be put up with until the time came for her to leave, but she was a relative, a defenceless young woman and she was sure Jack Andrews would be mortified if he knew what his son was up to.

She turned, looking back to where he struggled in what she recognised as his "city" shoes to get a foothold on the rocky, tussocky ground. His face was aflame with his exertions of the last ten minutes but when he saw she had stopped, so did he, his hand dramatically to his heart, grinning in that imbecile way which he thought so irresistible. He was a handsome young man, she could not deny it, and neither would he if she told him so. There was no doubt he would have girlish hearts atwitter up and down the valley and there was talk that eighteen-year-old Miss Diana Ashwell of Ashwell Hall, where Chris was on good terms with her brother Johnny and where Aunt Sara called at least once a week, was very taken with him. It would be considered a good match. His money and her breeding but it seemed Chris Andrews had other things on his mind at the moment and if his relentless pursuit of herself over the last weeks was anything to go by, Diana might have a long wait for her trip up the aisle with Chloe's cousin. Not that she suspected his intentions towards herself were anything but dishonourable. The narrowed gleam in his eye distinctly told her so.

"What do you want?" she asked sharply, hoping to put him off with her icy rudeness.

Though it was midsummer the air had no warmth. Indeed it might even be said to be what her uncle called "hearty", giving one the inclination to walk briskly, not stand about admiring the view, spectacular as it was. She pulled her warm cloak more closely about her, clasping her arms across her breasts beneath its folds so that she looked like a dark finger of flinty stone, only her hair bright and lively as a flame in a grate.

"I can't say I want anything, cousin."

"Then why do you keep following me around?" she asked accusingly. "Every time I go out I can guarantee I shall meet you somewhere along the way. I swear I don't know how you do it since I am sure your papa does not allow you to spend a lot of time away from the mill."

He shrugged, a shadow darkening his discontented face. "True. My father would chain me to the damn paper machine if he could but even he knows better than to do that. He sends me to collect parcels from the station and to deliver notes. They are tasks with little or no responsibility, for which he believes, by the way, I am not yet ready, but I am perfectly happy to perform them. They get me away from clanking machines, spinning wheels, pulleys and rollers, pipes and straps and wires and the everlasting "stuff" which pours from one end of the bloody place to the other. And it gives my father a reason to justify the allowance he makes me, to pretend I'm working, d'you see. But whatever am I thinking of? I came up here to get away from it, not to talk to you about it. I'm sure you and I can find more pleasing subjects to discuss without a great deal of trouble."

For a moment, as he spoke of the paper mill he had regained that strained, strung-up look he wore to the mill every day, a little pale, a transparency in his eyes which spoke of his aversion to manufacturing and his own seemingly inescapable burden of being involved in it. But now he changed, his face deepening into a curving smile, his eyes narrowing in that way which had become so familiar to her. An acquisitive face, she called it, since he did not try to hide the very obvious fact that he would like something from her.

He strolled indolently up the last bit of slope towards her then, with a courtly gesture, he swept his arm across his chest inviting her to rest on a lichen-covered rock beside the path.

"Do sit down, Chloe and if *you* are not out of breath, then at least allow me to catch mine."

"Catch your breath by all means but I shall get on. No doubt I shall see you at dinner."

Her contemptuous rejection of him and his attempt to be "friendly" hardened his face and, taking her by surprise and before she had time to turn away or even free her arms to defend herself, he sprang forward and caught her to him, all pretence at being "civilised" cast on the wind which blew across the tops. Their faces were so close she could see the tiny golden brown flecks in the depths of his green eyes and the long droop of the copper-coloured lashes which surrounded them. His skin was flushed, so much so she could feel the heat of it against her hastily averted cheek and when his lips laid themselves on the line of her straining jaw she was not surprised to find them on fire.

"Let me go . . . let me go, Chris."

"Now don't be silly, sweetheart," he gasped. "You know I won't hurt you."

"Take your hands off me, you fool." She jerked herself away from him, no more than an inch or two, but her wriggling body seemed to fan the flames of his male excitement.

"You don't mean that, my love. You have been telling me for weeks with those cast-down eyes of yours that you would not be averse to . . ."

"Don't be so bloody ridiculous," she gasped, suddenly realising why it was her uncle and Katy seemed to find such satisfaction in swearing. "Really, if I were to tell your papa . . ."

"Tell my papa!" His voice was clipped, his own jaw stiff as he did his best to reach her mouth with his. "It would be your word against mine, sweet Chloe, and who do you think will be believed? The son of the house or the unwanted cousin whose character and morals are known to no one. We met you only three months ago so how are my parents to know what kind of girl you are or what you got up to before you came to Crossclough? Come now, don't struggle, my pet. You know you want this as much as I do."

Dear God, where did men get their bloated sense of their own desirability to women, any woman, and how could this fool seriously believe that her frantic struggles were a sign of her own willingness? she agonised, as she did her best, if she could not escape his mouth, at least to sink her teeth into his lower lip. It seemed to please him. He began to laugh.

"Spirited as well, eeh? Well, that's all to the better. I've been wanting to do this to you ever since you stepped down from that train. Eyes on you like a startled deer and a mouth as luscious as a ripe peach . . ."

"Oh, for heaven's sake, get away from me, you idiot." Strangely, now that he had caught her she was no longer afraid. It was all so silly, even his words seeming to come from some cheap melodrama. "Let me go and I promise I'll say no more about it. I know this is the sort of thing young gentlemen get up to but . . ."

"I see, so you *do* know more than that innocent face and those great wide eyes imply you do."

"No, of course not . . . please, Chris."

"Give me a kiss then. I promise you'll enjoy it. I'll let you go at once if you'll allow me just one kiss. I know Mother and Father treat you as though you didn't exist and Katy is too concerned with involving herself with Jamie Hutchinson to befriend you but I'm more than willing to make up for their— "

"I have no wish to be your friend, can't you see that?" She snorted derisively, doing her best to get her arms out of her enveloping cloak, to bring her knee up into what she believed was the most vulnerable part of a man's body. Even if she didn't hurt him, which she wanted to do most savagely now, at least it might force him away from her, but he bore her back relentlessly until she felt the damp and rigid hardness of stone behind her. Her head swung frantically from side to side as she did her best to avoid his burning mouth, her face screwed up with deep revulsion, when, suddenly, so suddenly she almost fell over, he let her go, stepping back from her, straightening his jacket, smoothing down the alarming bulge in his breeches, then pushing both hands through the dishevelment of his auburn hair.

"I'll force no woman," he spat out. "I've no need, for Chris Andrews can take his bloody pick."

"Then why pick me?" she panted, doing her best to draw a deep breath into her lungs, putting up shaking hands to her own hair from which the ribbon had come loose, lying in a vivid splash across one grey-clad shoulder.

"Oh come on, stop playing the innocent with me. I've seen the way you look . . ."

"*At you!*" Her voice was incredulous and not only that, but scathing.

There had been, though neither of these two young people knew it, way back in the dark generations of the Andrews family, a labouring man by the name of Bartholomew Andrews whose temper was so short and vicious those who lived and worked in his vicinity walked about him on tiptoes lest they disturb the uncertain equilibrium of his nature. A word, a look, even the lift of an eyebrow, it was said, could set him off and his first wife, who had died young and rather mysteriously, might have told a tale or two had she lived. Black Bart's temper was a legend up in the wild dales of Yorkshire where the family then lived and every now and again, as the generations came and went, it flared up, sometimes in a female but more often than not in a male descendant of Black Bart Andrews.

Though it had not yet manifested itself in Jack and Sara

Andrews's youngest boy, who had never as yet been seriously crossed, it lay dormant in Christopher Andrews.

At Chloe's cutting words it exploded into life, surprising not only her but him, and before she could lift her hands to defend herself or even steady her back against the rock, the palm of his lean hard hand lashed her across the cheek, rocking her head and neck with such force she thought she heard a bone click somewhere and an agonising pain rippled through her body. She felt her senses begin to slip away, not just with the torment of her ricked neck but by the sheer horror of being struck by another human being. Never in her life had anyone offered violence to her and the shock of it flung her giddily into reeling blackness which threatened to bring her to her knees.

At once Chris Andrews was filled with remorse. Unlike his rough ancestor, Chris had a veneer of the civilised, cultured upbringing a woman such as his well-bred mother thought fit for her sons and though the violent flash of uncontrollable rage had been real enough, the sight of his cousin fainting against the rock where his blow had knocked her brought him instantly back to the realisation of who he was, of who she was, of what he had done. He was amazed at himself, stunned as to where that explosive white light of passion had come from, even wondering if it had actually happened it was so incredible.

But his cousin's cheek, which had the fiery red imprint of his hand upon it, her rapidly puffing eye and a small bleeding cut by her mouth where his signet ring had caught it were enough confirmation, if he needed it.

"Dear sweet Jesus . . . Oh, Christ, Chloe, I'm sorry. Hell's teeth, I'm sorry . . . there, let me . . . won't you sit down? I honestly don't know where that came from, really I don't."

His demeanour was anguished, bewildered, his own dreadful action so completely out of his own range of what he believed himself to be, which was a gentleman, of course, he could only stammer like a child. He would never forgive himself, his manner said and if she would just allow it he would, if necessary, carry her home on his own back, or at least to where his grey was tethered.

The pain, and the man who had inflicted it were too much for Chloe and she began to shake in great rippling tremors, putting up her hands in horror to him when he would have helped her.

"Don't . . . please," she mumbled. Her mouth was numbed and inclined to be unmanageable so that she could not speak properly. Her head lolled on her neck as though something had snapped and she could see the rocks and trees, the clouds and other, quite unrecognisable objects, flying round and round, going past her blurred eyes in the most dizzying way. Her stomach heaved and she had the greatest difficulty in keeping within it the last meal she had eaten which, for the life of her, she couldn't recall. Was it breakfast or lunch? And her face was beginning to burn with a pain which was unbearable.

"No . . . of course not," Chris was stuttering. "I'm sorry . . . so sorry but . . . will you ever forgive me?"

"No."

"Jesus, I deserved that."

"Go away." Her eye was already so swollen she could barely see out of it and Chris knew and was appalled, since he had knowledge of such things at school, that she would have a livid bruise about it by this evening. God in heaven, what would she tell them at home? He had meant her no harm, none at all. She had intrigued him from the first day she had come to stay in his home since, not only was she exceedingly pretty but she was unknown, a mystery, a challenge which he would enjoy conquering, and though he had been told she was his cousin, his young unmarried cousin and therefore untouchable, he had not quite believed it. She was very like his mother, of course, and would not have been accepted if his parents had the slightest doubts as to her ancestry, but his male curiosity and desire only knew that she was a young, beautiful woman whose body his lusted after. He would not, naturally, he told himself, have gone further than a kiss or two, had she been willing, for the consequences of such actions would have been disastrous for them both, particularly him! A bit of harmless fun, that was all, a kiss that no one would know about and now, through his own amazing loss of control, he had put a mark on her that could not be missed, or explained. If only she hadn't fought him. If only she hadn't been so bloody scornful, sneering, none of this would have happened. Oh God, women were the bloody limit.

"I can't . . . well . . . just leave you here, Chloe," he said helplessly, moving from anxious foot to anxious foot and on his face, though he was not aware of it, was a growing look of exasperation that said he wished to God he had never clapped eyes on her.

"Please leave me alone," she mumbled, hiding her face in the fall of her hair.

"But . . ."

"You have injured my . . . my face, not my legs. I can walk back."

"Well, if you're sure . . ." relieved, it seemed, to be rid of her. "Only Father will be . . . you know how he is and then there's Zack."

"Zack?"

"My grey."

"Of course."

"Then I'll go." He hesitated, his handsome young face creased with concern, not for her now, she realised, but for himself. "Er . . . what will you say . . ." He cleared his throat and pulled at his cravat. "I mean, how will you explain . . ."

"Don't worry, I won't tell them what happened. As you said a few minutes ago, a girl who leads on a gentleman deserves all she gets."

"Chloe . . ."

"Oh, for goodness sake, go." Her tone was bitter. "But I have this to say. If you touch me again I shall go, not to your father but to the local constabulary. I shall make such an outcry no man will trust you about his daughter ever again. Even if, like you, they wonder about me, they will say there is no smoke without fire."

"Chloe, I promise, honest to God . . ."

"Don't bring God into this, please. I'm beginning to wonder if He has the slightest concern for . . ." Her voice from beneath her curtain of hair broke and she turned away.

When, several moments later, she turned back, he was gone.

The sky was beginning to lose its light, changing slowly to that deep shade of damson which heralds a summer thunderstorm when Jamie found her. He had been up to Browden Meadow where his small flock of sheep were grazing, checking on the state of the pasture and the nourishment his Lonks might get out of it. It was poor and there were flocks from several small farms like his own to share it but Lonks were hardy beasts and those he had found with his own brand on them seemed to be thriving. There was a storm brewing, a vivid lightning storm which would have the moorland creatures, including the sheep, cowering under any cover they could find and he meant to do the same when he got home. His young dog, Captain, who slunk uneasily at his heels, was already turning his head this way and that and pricking his ears, his coat beginning to ripple in alarm.

He could not at first put a name to the dark huddle of something which crouched at the base of the rock beside the path. Captain was not inclined, as he normally would be, to bound madly forward and investigate, his fear of the coming storm keeping him fastened as though by a rope to Jamie's ankle.

Jamie hesitated, his heavily booted feet sending several small pieces of stone clinking into a narrow crevice and at the sound the huddle moved. The head . . . yes, it was a head, lifted and reared back and a small gasp escaped from the whiteness of what Jamie now recognised as a woman's face. And not just any face, but the face of the woman who had been in Jamie's mind and thoughts for weeks now, in the very heart of him, like the thrilling notes of a songbird, or the perfection of that songbird in flight across the evening sky. An exquisite flower which cannot be forgotten, a bright star in the firmament, an image of all the dreaming thoughts men have when they contemplate the woman they will love.

Chloe! Chloe!

Throwing off his perplexity on what the hell she was doing up here alone and more to the point why she was crumpled up like some child's discarded toy at the base of the rock, he leaped down the path towards her. She had seen him come to a halt higher up the path and even in the deepening gloom he could not fail to notice the way she drew herself into her cloak as though she would dearly love to slip quietly under the rock and hide away from him, as though she were afraid of him, as though his presence was something she did not care for.

"Chloe . . .?" His voice was uncertain though he knew without doubt it was she, hoarse with his fear since it was very evident she was deeply distressed.

He slithered wildly on loose stones and wet grass, scrambling to her side, sinking to his knees and bending his head to peer into her face. His heart was pounding with something he recognised as fear and his voice was rough with it as he spoke.

"What is it? What's happened? Have you fallen? Where are you hurt? Here, let me lift you a little," reaching out with strong, yearning arms but not as yet touching her, since he did not know where she was injured. Her hair hung in a tangled mass of curls about her head, falling across her face, over her shoulders and down her back, darkened by the damp, and through it her clouded blue-green eyes peered up at him.

Well, one did. The other seemed to be half shut, sunk in folds of swollen flesh, shadowed by something he could not as yet recognise. As he put out a hand to her she shrank away from him and he was left in no doubt that his touch, perhaps even his presence was unwelcome to her. That indeed she was frightened of it.

"Chloe, it's me, Jamie. Don't be afraid. Won't you tell me what's happened to you, my dove?" Neither of them noticed his use of the endearment. "You have obviously hurt yourself . . . well, your face," for as he looked even closer there was no question Chloe Taylor had a spanker of a black eye and a livid weal down one side of her dazed face. Neither injury was consistent with a fall. More like a fist . . . a clenched fist, or perhaps . . .

She was in a state of shock. He had seen it before when a man had an accident at sea. A sort of a daze, stunned, not senseless but in such a deep well of distress all thought and feeling and speech are impossible. He didn't know what or who had done this to her and in any case that could wait until later. What she needed was warmth and comfort, a compress, perhaps some sort of lotion, though he didn't know what, for her face. Cherishing was what Chloe Taylor needed and he, who loved her, was the one to give it to her.

Murmuring gently, the soft, incomprehensible sounds with which a mother would soothe a hurt child, he persuaded her to allow his arms about her, to be lifted from the damp, cold ground, to be wrapped against his chest in his own warm jacket, to be held tenderly, her face hidden in the curve of his shoulder. She was light, insubstantial, as tiny and breakable as a bird, as the dove he had likened her to in her plain, pale grey gown which was revealed as her cloak fell open.

"Come, my little dove, let me take you home," he whispered, his mouth against her damp hair, and strangely, they both knew he did not mean Cloudberry End.

9

No one missed her until the next morning which, later, Chloe though wryly, was an indication of her importance in the household of Cloudberry End.

Chris Andrews was relieved when he entered the dining room that same evening to find that his cousin Chloe had not put in an appearance. He knew it was only a matter of time before Chloe's face, which he was sure was a sorry sight by now, was noticed and remarked on, but he had been worried all day on how she would explain it to his family. A fall, perhaps, or that old adage that she had walked into something, but her non-appearance was a relief. Though she was treated with cool politeness, no more, by his mother and father, somewhat in the manner of hosts who are too well bred to question an unwelcome guest on when she might be expected to leave, and with casual indifference by Katy who saw no benefit to her in her city-bred cousin, surely her absence would be noticed and something said. They could hardly start dinner, at which she was usually present, without a well-mannered murmur of curiosity on where she could be and, sure enough, his father raised his eyebrows at her empty chair.

"Aah, if you're looking for Chloe, sir," Chris said smoothly, "when last I saw her she spoke of feeling unwell."

"Did she now? Well, she might have sent a message to inform your mother she wouldn't be down."

Jack Andrews glowered at the place where his niece's quiet presence normally hovered, for that is how she appeared to him who was used to his own daughter's noisy and colourful occupancy of the space about her. "Surely it is only good manners to let your hostess know you will not be dining, I should have thought. I don't know, the ways of the young never cease to amaze me, and if I were to treat my mother that way— "

"Never mind, dearest," his wife interrupted him gently, taking up her spoon in readiness for the fragrant bowl of soup Freda had just placed before her, her smiling expression saying quite clearly that, as she was not here, that cuckoo which had invaded their nest, why did they not enjoy her absence while they could. Not that the girl was any trouble and to tell the truth Sara had become quite used to having her about the place. If she had not been so uncannily like Alice, indeed it was just like having her dead sister sitting at her table, she might have made more effort to be civil to Alice's daughter. She was not an unkind woman and often felt guilty that she could not find it in her heart to be warmer towards her niece but each time she did so what had happened would come back and haunt her. Those years when . . . well, she was not going to dig up the past, nor bring Alice's ghost into the present but, being a woman who in her young days had known what it was like to be desired by more than one man she had not failed to recognise what was in her son's eyes when he looked at his new-found cousin, which wouldn't do at all! In fact she fully intended writing to her brother-in-law at the earliest opportunity demanding that he remove his daughter as soon as possible. They had given her a home for almost four months now and surely that was long enough for him to have resolved whatever difficulties he might be having with his new young wife?

"Shall I send Ivy to see how she is, mum?" Freda asked her mistress when the family were all served and tucking into Mrs Tiplady's splendid soup.

"No, I don't think so, Freda. If she is unwell then a good night's sleep will do her good."

"Very well, mum." Freda exchanged a glance with Ivy, for none of them ceased to be amazed at the cold-hearted way Miss Chloe was treated. A nice little thing, she was, with a kind word or a smile if she met you on the stairs and no trouble at all, not like the headstrong daughter of their master and mistress. Right sorry they were for her at times but then it was nowt to do with them, was it?

Jamie Hutchinson's small farmhouse had undergone a quite startling transformation in the four weeks since he had moved into it. He had returned to Crossclough on the first day of May and now it was the last day of August and thanks to his mother and the girl who was curled up like a terrified child in the chair before the glowing embers of the fire, the interior was as snug and comfortable as any you could find and a perfectly acceptable home to bring any bride to, which, he had acknowledged subconsciously, was what he had been working towards. Once his flock were out on the grazing moor and his small dairy herd contentedly browsing belly deep in the fenced pasture he and Tommy had prepared; once his fields in which he was to plant his first attempt at crops were ploughed, again with young Tommy's assistance and the plough horse he now owned, he and his brother had turned their attention to the actual farmhouse. The cows had to be milked daily, of course, a task he and Tommy shared, and when that was done they had set about repairing the drystone walls, the loose stones on the cobbled path, the gates and the roof and the rattling window panes, while inside his mother had a lovely time arranging his few bits of furniture to her own satisfaction.

The girl, as his mother called her somewhat suspiciously, since Chloe was not the sort of female Matty Jenkins could see as a farmer's wife, had brought up red plush curtains for the windows, both kitchen and bedroom. She had made them herself, after a great deal of measuring, from some stuff she had found in the attic, she said simply, the ethics of removing what was not hers to remove of no concern to her, it appeared. They were warm and bright and sturdy enough to keep out the most searching of the winds which blew up on the bleak winter moorland, with brass curtain rings which ran on a brass pole.

She had sewn plain pillow cases and sheets since, she explained regretfully, she had not had time for the exquisite embroidery with which she would normally decorate such things. Jamie needed bedlinen at once, and blankets, and then there was the quite incredibly lovely bed quilt she had "thrown together", again racing against the clock, and if Mrs Jenkins would give her permission she would go upstairs at once and make up the enormous brass bed she knew Mrs Andrews had sent up earlier in the week. Hadn't they all been driven to distraction by Katy's constant reminder to her mother that it was needed up at Valley Bottom Farm? The folding truckle bed would do for Tommy when he stayed over, as Chloe knew he sometimes did. Oh dear, her hand to her mouth, she did hope Mrs Jenkins did not think she was interfering, really . . . please forgive her, but it was so lovely to have something useful to do at last.

The kitchen glowed as the fire Jamie had replenished roared up the chimney and Captain hutched himself a bit closer to it, his eyes rolling in ecstasy. The hooked rug he lay on had been a gift from Madge Andrews, brought up by Katy who had no talent for such things, worked in rich colours of red and yellow and orange which made a bright splash against the grey, well-scrubbed stone floor. The ovens on either side of the fire winked and twinkled in the reflected glory of the flames, blackleaded by Matty to a gleaming ebony and kept that way by Jamie who had a sailor's passion for cleanliness and neatness. Along the mantel above the fire stood a row of copper pans of varying sizes. Beside them were candlestick holders, a couple of enormous seashells Jamie had brought back from some exotic beach, a tea caddy and a bunch of hardy wild flowers which had survived on the high peak and which Jamie had picked and arranged, for some reason known only to himself, in a glass jar.

There was a highly polished dresser, a settle at right angles to the fire, its back to the door to avoid the draught, and an elaborately carved child's chair with the initials TH and the date 1788 set in its back.

The chair in which Chloe had been placed was a rocker, a man's chair, big and deep, lined with bright cushions at its back and seat. There was a clock tick-tocking against the whitewashed wall, its face colourful with paintings of the moon, the sun and a sprinkling of stars and in the centre of the room was a plain deal table covered with a red chenille cloth. In its exact centre was a bowl filled with red polished apples. Hanging on hooks from the beams, so low that Jamie had to bend his tall frame to avoid them, were several iron pots, left, like the child's chair, by the previous owners.

It was delightfully warm in the kitchen, tranquil, quiet, and when Jamie turned to look at her as he lifted the kettle from the fire to make the tea, Chloe had fallen asleep. Her head was to one side resting on the back of the chair and her hair, which had rippled concealingly about her, had fallen back to reveal her pale, defenceless face. Pale, yes, pale as bleached bone, except where the bruise lay, the livid outline of a hand, the small cut which had bled and dribbled to dry down her face, the deep, purple plum of the socket about the eye and the eye itself which though closed in sleep was deeply embedded in her swollen flesh. All he could see was the pathetic coppery brown tips of her lashes protruding slightly from the slit of the injury.

Someone had hit her!

He felt it begin to rise in him then, the slow, deep, moving tremors of a rage so terrible he wanted to sweep to the floor all the homely things he and his mother had arranged so carefully in this, his first home. To smash and savage everything, anything he could lay his hands on since it was the only way to let it out of him. To do something, even if it destroyed his own place, to release the explosion of hatred, of venomous, perilous, terrifying rage – it terrified *him* – which needed, since it could not reach the man who had done this to her, to destroy what lay readily to hand. His hands clenched into fists, so tight he could feel his fingernails cut into his palms. He wanted to crash them against the walls, the table, to howl dementedly at the hurt which had been done her. His mouth twisted back on his teeth in a snarl like that of an enraged leopard and he felt his blood run hot and fast in a need to kill . . . to maim . . . to hurt . . . really hurt . . . but then to kill the man who had lifted his hand to this fragile girl, to the delicacy, the sweet vulnerability of this young woman whom Jamie Hutchinson loved and lived to die for. He would die for her if he could find the bastard who had struck her, die for her and bloody swing for him, whoever he was and if it was the last thing he did he would find him.

He knelt at her knee for over an hour, pushing aside the reluctant dog in order to be closer to her, slowly, slowly beating down the hating rage inside him, bringing it under control so that he might be as she needed him to be when she awoke. Chloe had her feet tucked up under the skirt of her gown and he was able to lean gently on the arms of the chair, his face no more than six inches from hers as he studied her. The hot rage had gone, leaving what was worse, a cold thirst for revenge but at that moment, until she awoke, he was content to kneel on the hard stone and drown himself in the beauty of his sleeping love. To protect her sleep which was nature's way of curing, and which Chloe had entrusted with him, to defend her innocent belief that no harm could come to her while she was in his care. In all the times she had been up to Valley Bottom Farm, no more than half a dozen, he supposed, if that, there had been no reawakening of the strange feelings which had linked them on that first occasion. She had been friendly, glad to be of help, eager to be doing what she was so good at, sewing something to make his home more comfortable, even making, as she had promised, a cosy blanket bed for the dog. She had drunk his tea, chatted shyly with his mother, had a word or two to say to Tommy who had been struck unusually dumb by her exquisitely tinted loveliness, and listened attentively while he himself told her of his plans for the future. She never spoke of the Andrews family, who, he heard from his mother, treated her shabbily, though was it any wonder after the suffering Chloe's own mother had caused Jack and Sara Andrews? She would not say what form that took since it was not her tale to tell, she said, but it must have been devastating to make Sara so bitter against her sister's daughter.

She began to stir, making small mewing sounds in the back of her throat, stretching a little, then catching her breath as she moved her neck too hastily. Her eyes opened, at least one did, and as he eased back a little so as not to alarm her by his closeness, smiling his slightly lopsided, good-humoured smile, she opened her mouth on a wide yawn.

"Ouch." She winced, lifting a hand to her cheek, looking into his face as though there was nothing untoward in waking in Jamie Hutchinson's kitchen with Jamie Hutchinson at her feet.

He grimaced in sympathy. "It would be daft to ask does it hurt, wouldn't it?"

"Yes, it would, and yes it hurts but I imagine it looks worse than it feels." She did her best to smile and his heart lurched.

"That's good," he managed to answer.

"You think so? I must admit to a great reluctance to look in a mirror."

"Wise, I think, at least for a day or two. In the meanwhile no one need see you if you don't want it. Only me, and I'm quite ... I don't count seeing that— " He stopped abruptly. He felt the hot blood rush to his face in embarrassment. Him, a grown man blushing and awkward and yet her eyes ...

oh bloody hell . . . her one good eye was clear and steady, as though she had already acknowledged and accepted the strangeness of their situation.

"What are you trying to say, Jamie?" She had become very still, holding her breath almost, for there was no doubt that this moment, this moment of pain and awkwardness and bewilderment at what was taking place, was very important. She was no longer alarmed for she had no fear of this enormous man who gave her shelter when she needed refuge from the storms and tempests of the Andrews family. Who gave her his company when her heart was weary with loneliness. Who gave her laughter when she was despondent. She had found tranquillity in this small farmhouse, a certain peace and content, a place of serenity away from the alarums and excursions of Cloudberry End. She had come to like Mrs Jenkins, despite knowing Jamie's mother was suspicious of her and her motives in coming here, and young Tommy, so full of boyish, boisterous good humour, made her feel as though she were no older than him. Though she had come up to the farm no more than half a dozen times in the last few weeks – timing it when she knew Katy was at her grandmother's – she was strangely at ease here.

"What am I trying to say?" he repeated, his voice low and sweet and deep as only a lover's voice can be. "I think it might be that I love you, Chloe Taylor. That I have loved you from that moment at Crossclough Station when I saw your face at the window of the carriage taking you to Cloudberry End. I love you, my dove, and I want you to feel the same way about me, if you could. That is what I am trying to say."

He bent his head as though afraid her answer might be too much for him and his wide shoulders trembled briefly, then he looked up at her. He lifted a hand and almost dreamily ran a tender finger down the curve of her chin. "I love you, Chloe, and I want nothing more than to serve you but if you could . . . feel just a little of what I feel for you I would be eternally grateful." He smiled. "My life is yours, sweet Chloe. I am yours. Yes, that is what I'm trying to say and though I am sorry about your face, the slight . . . rearrangement does not offend me. There, will that do for now?"

"Oh, Jamie . . . Jamie . . ." She smiled back at him a smile of lilting sweetness, though it turned into a moue of pain which had her gasping. "I don't know what to say to you."

"I love you, Jamie, would do admirably." He grinned but there was a depth of seriousness in his eyes.

She hesitated. There was no one she trusted or liked or admired or respected more than this big, quiet, dependable man but did she love him? She knew nothing of love in its romantic form. Her mother and father had not shown love, to each other, or to her, and what she would have described as the excess of passion her aunt and uncle shared seemed too extreme, too frantic to be quite real. She was aware that Katy Andrews was devoted to Jamie, indeed she probably loved him in her young and ardent way. Chloe would like to be in love with him, for what would be more glorious than to leave Cloudberry End and its unwelcoming occupants for good and have a home, a home of her own? To depend on no one, not her Aunt Sara and Uncle Jack, not her papa and stepmama, and put herself in the strong, protective, loving hands of this man in whose face, as she hesitated, was dying the hope of his love.

It took no longer than thirty seconds to decide the course of her future but, just to make sure, to make sure she could not go back she must begin it at once.

She leaned forward with perfect trust and placed one small hand on the flat plane of his brown cheek.

"I do love you, Jamie," she said, meaning it, though not in the way he wanted her to mean it and as she said it she swore he would never know the difference.

She watched his blue eyes come brilliantly alive and the wide mouth open and stretch in a smile of triumph. The colour surged again beneath his skin so great was his emotion and he seemed incapable of speech. Turning his mouth into the palm of her hand he kissed it reverently and she knew with a certainty she wondered about, since she was no more than an innocent girl, that this man idolised her, idealised her and it was going to be difficult arranging matters without distressing or offending him. Marriage he would need. Marriage he would have, and naturally so would she, but marriages took time to arrange and she wanted no time in which to think, to have people think for her, to be argued at, screamed at – by Katy, there was no doubt of that – to be the subject of gossip which might, or might not, rage about Cloudberry End. In fact, she never wanted to see Cloudberry End again.

Lifting her gently to her feet Jamie stood her on the colourful mat and her cloak which had been wrapped about her fell to the ground. Holding her by both arms above the elbow he bent his head and placed his mouth on hers in her first kiss, then, with the tenderness of a mother, moved his lips to her ravaged cheek and eye, gently, so lightly she could barely feel it.

"Jesus God, if you knew how much I love you," he breathed. She could feel his heart pound beneath her cheek as he pressed her tenderly into his arms and his body quivered with his effort to hold himself back from her. In his eyes she was an innocent, inexperienced girl who, one day, or night, she supposed, he would gently, slowly teach the ways of physical love. The act which would unite them, the technicalities of which she was only vaguely aware, but that would not do. It must be now, tonight, not as was usually the case the seduction of an ignorant girl, though she was that, but of this man who loved her with the devotion and respect a man shows to the woman he truly loves. How to begin? How? What must she do to get him to . . . to make love to her?

Afterwards she was to realise that two healthy, normal young bodies have no need of thought, or planning, or indeed of anything but where they can lay themselves down together in the act of love. Male and female, a certain interest and attraction, desire she supposed it was called and before her untried body and mind could jib at it, perhaps become awkward with shyness, she was in his arms, her toes barely touching the ground, her arms twined about his neck in a way that amazed her. His mouth was firm and warm, sweet and soft at the same time, parting her lips, his tongue hesitating enquiringly as it caressed the soft, moist inner flesh of her opening mouth. He moved his head from side to side, and so did she, she found, his lips taking hers, first the top then the bottom, then letting them travel along her jawline and down her throat to the breathlessly leaping pulse at its base.

She found it . . . not unpleasing! Her body had a sudden need to stretch and her back to arch and she seemed inclined to purr as a cat will as it lies in the warmth from a fire, she didn't know why. Greatly daring she began to nuzzle with her mouth beneath his chin, just where a wisp of silky hair protruded from the neck of his open shirt. His hand moved to her throat, holding her as his mouth rose again to hers and it was then that she became aware of the changes in his body.

Hers was nailed against his and as, instinctively, she pressed it even closer, he began to breathe hoarsely and for a moment she felt fear. This was how Chris Andrews had been when . . . when . . . but this was not Chris Andrews, this was Jamie who must become, if not in name then in deed, her husband tonight.

She could sense him drawing away as though he were making a great effort to control himself, the fierceness of his need giving him what seemed to be a great deal of pain.

"Chloe," he almost snarled, kissing her, hurting her with it, he knew, savouring the satin smoothness of the skin at her throat with his open mouth. Her body was enclosed by the length of his, the trembling of his limbs mingling with hers.

He stood away for a brief second, his eyes glazed and helpless then swayed back again, his hands going to the buttons of her bodice, tearing them apart, pulling the soft cotton fabric away to reveal the creamy white smoothness of her shoulders.

"Oh God, Chloe, stop me," he whispered hoarsely. "I shouldn't be doing this . . . stop me . . . please . . . stop me."

But it was too late for anything which might be called restraint. Her breasts broke free of their covering, her small, almond-tinted nipples hard, like the ripe berries in the hedgerows in the valley and his mouth went to them eagerly, taking each one in turn between his lips, his tongue circling them, licking them with delight before allowing his hands their turn. They were big and brown, Jamie Hutchinson's hands, hard with the calloused palms of a seaman, or a farmer, but they were gentle with love and so were his eyes as he picked her up and carried her towards the stairs.

The one bedroom was in the sort of half gloom which heralds the coming of a thunderstorm but the bed and its plain, exquisitely sewn linen gleamed whitely beneath the two slopes of the roof. Its brass head and foot were bright with polish and Matty's elbow grease. Folded at its foot was the glowing bed quilt just as though in preparation for the lovers. There was a plain dresser and a wardrobe. Nothing of value but it was clean and immaculately tidy, everything stowed away as Jamie had been used to below decks.

She hung her head shyly when he began to undress her, hiding herself in her silken curtain of hair, uncertain, waiting hesitantly for him to tell her what to do and yet willing, not holding back or recoiling when his hands and mouth began softly but surely to explore her trembling body. She held his head to her naked breast, her own hands in his thick hair and then moving to smooth the long rippling muscles of his back since she meant to do this thing well, to give him no cause for complaint, to please him. She was not offended by him, by his weight and size and dark masculinity nor by his growing and strange male excitement. Her body found his not unwelcome and when, at last, his pierced and entered hers, though it was painful she did not cry out.

Later, when he was calm and she almost asleep in what she found to be his comforting arms, he turned her so that her back was pressed close to his chest. He cupped her breasts with marvelling hands and sighed, his breath moving in her tumbled hair.

"So, my dove," he murmured wryly, "this is to be our wedding night, is it?" pretending resignation but glorying in his mastery of her.

"So it seems, Jamie. Do you mind?"

"I'll not have to for it's done. You'll sleep in my bed tonight and every night of your life, my darling. You belong to me now and God help any man who tries to take you from me for I'll kill him."

They slept through the thunderstorm in one another's arms. He would find out who had beaten her tomorrow.

It was Ivy who discovered her bed had not been slept in and for an hour there was chaos since no one could imagine where she might have got to.

"It's not as if she's any friends, Mrs Tiplady," Ivy said plaintively, her heart going out to the poor young lady who had done her best to fit into this family, indeed to find some niche in their lives which she could call her own. " 'Appen she's gone back to 'er pa in Liverpool," for of course by now all the servants were aware of the circumstances of their mistress's young niece.

"Happen she has, Ivy, but that doesn't mean we shouldn't look for her here. Anyway, no doubt Mr Andrews has sent a telegram to Miss Chloe's pa by now so we'll soon know. Eeh, this is a bad do and no mistake. See, you, Tommy Jenkins . . ." turning on the coachman's lad who for some reason was hanging about the kitchen doorway. "You'd best be occupied looking for Miss Chloe instead of dithering on my doorstep. Go and find Angus and he'll tell you what to do. Him and Billy are to go up to Tintwistle Knarr since Saul Gibbon says he's seen her up there a time or two. Now then, Lottie, fetch me that saddle of lamb from the larder and you'd best start on the veg, Mabel. What? Who?"

She turned irritably to where Mabel, who was her kitchen maid, pointed her finger at Tommy Jenkins who still remained glued to the doorstep.

"I thought I told you to report to Angus, my lad, and I'd be obliged . . . what? A note. Who for? The master? Well, why didn't you say so? Come in, come in and mind them feet on my clean floor."

All about the kitchen work came to a complete standstill as eager young women, excited as those who have nothing in their lives but drab routine often are, crowded about young Tommy Jenkins, eyeing the piece of folded paper he held in his hand. But it was not just the paper which captured their attention but Tommy's air of positively bursting with something which threatened, if it was not let out soon, to explode.

"I'm ter put it in master's hands an' no one else's, Mrs Tiplady," he said politely, his own importance almost too much for his boyish composure, which was none too steady at the best of times. "That's what I were told ter do an' if Jamie were ter hear that— "

He stopped speaking abruptly and the maids exchanged bewildered glances for what had Jamie Hutchinson to do with all this? They were not awfully sure what they meant by all this, nor why this young lad's older brother . . . well, half-brother, should be involved but it was all very intriguing. Happen he'd found her wandering on the moor, poor little mite, and taken her in, but the note would reveal the truth and they could hardly wait to see what it might be. They nudged one another, whispering and lifting enquiring eyebrows, but even in the midst of this crisis Mrs Tiplady was not about to allow any slacking in the strict regime of her kitchen. Mrs Tiplady was not only cook here, but housekeeper and Mrs Andrews trusted her to keep these twittering housemaids and kitchenmaids employed as they should be and not wasting their time and Mr Andrews's good money in idleness.

She clapped her hands and at once, like a flock of starlings disturbed from a tree, they darted away to their respective tasks, leaving Tommy in the sole charge of Mrs Tiplady.

"Give me the note, lad," she said kindly. "I'll see the master gets it." But Tommy, just as though he expected her to snatch it from his hand, put it behind his back, his brother's words still echoing in his astonished head. He had taken it in, of course he had, for their Jamie's hard grip on his shoulders, which had made him wince, had forced him to, despite the incredible sight of Miss Chloe who was curled up wrapped in nothing but a quilt, from what Tommy could see, in his brother's fireside chair. And as for her face, well, if Jamie had done that to her he wanted a good thrashing and no doubt Mr Andrews would see to it when the time came. Not that Tommy could imagine his big, good-natured brother bashing a woman in the face, nor anybody's face for that matter, since he was the gentlest, most even-tempered man Tommy had ever known. Go out of his way to mend the broken wing of a bird, he would, or fetch home a lamb in need of shelter, but somebody had landed her one, which was another puzzle in the quite mystifying events which were taking place at Valley Bottom Farm.

"Nay, Mrs Tiplady, I can't," he protested. "I'm ter give it ter't master an' no one else." Tommy set his jaw at its most truculent angle, ready, it seemed to her, to dart away if she so much as put a hand out to him.

She tutted irritably. "Very well then. I'll take you through myself but make sure them boots are clean. Mrs Andrews is very particular about her carpets and Dilly doesn't want to have to brush them again, do you, Dilly?"

Dilly shook her head dumbly, her eyes popping, her mouth agape.

They were all in the breakfast room, Mrs Andrews and her daughter eating a late breakfast as was their custom, Mr Andrews stalking round and round the table in what looked to Mrs Tiplady to be a state of considerable annoyance, though there was an anxious frown dipping his eyebrows. Master Chris, who lounged against the window frame gazing out over the rolling lawns and crowded flowerbeds, had returned from the mill with his father when his mother's rather frantic note regarding her niece's disappearance had been delivered there by Dicken, mounted on Master Richard's chestnut bay.

Mrs Tiplady couldn't quite see why he was needed since he had made no effort to offer his services in the search for his cousin, but then any excuse was better than none to the master's son to get out of doing any work.

"Yes, Mrs Tiplady?" the master enquired, pausing for a moment in his pacing, eyeing Tommy Jenkins and his hob-nailed boots to which wisps of what looked like cow-dung still clung with some amazement.

"The lad has a note, sir, which he won't part with, only to you." She pushed Tommy forward unceremoniously, still somewhat incensed by his refusal to trust her in the delivery of the message.

"A note! Who from?"

"Nay, sir, he wouldn't let me see it, but happen . . ." She left the sentence unfinished, for all their thoughts were centred on the missing girl and what else could it be about despite what seemed to be some involvement on the part of Jamie Hutchinson?

You could have heard a feather drop, Mrs Tiplady thought, so quiet did they all go and from his favourite position before the small fire, Katy Andrews's dog, who had no business being there in Mrs Tiplady's opinion, raised an enquiring head.

He read it through twice, the master, without a word, without lifting his head, without looking at his wife, absorbed, or was it stunned, Mrs Tiplady was to wonder, by its contents.

"Jack?" Mrs Andrews quavered, her face as white as the napkin she held to her lips.

"Father, is it from Chloe?" his daughter asked, her young voice trembling with what seemed a genuine concern to Mrs Tiplady, while by the window young Master Chris said nothing at all.

"Jack?" Mrs Andrew repeated. "Please, Jack . . ."

Mr Andrews sighed heavily, his hand holding the crumpled sheet of paper falling to his side.

"Aye . . . oh aye, lass . . . she's safe enough."

"Oh, thank God, Jack."

"Hang on . . . hang on."

"What is it, Jack?"

"Well, I don't reckon tha'll like it over much when I tell thi'," reverting to the broad vowels of his youth in his distress. "It seems she's spent the night wi' Jamie Hutchinson. She's . . . she's his . . . his wife, he ses. Bloody hell, tha' knows what that means, don't tha', my lass? They mean to make it legal as soon as— "

Katherine Andrews stood up violently, so violently her chair flew backwards halfway across the room, and throwing back her head began to howl like a badly wounded animal.

10

It was a bad, bad time and how they managed to get through it was a wonder to them all, Mrs Tiplady was often to say sadly to Freda, the head parlourmaid. Well, she had to talk to someone, hadn't she, and Freda was a decent, sensible woman of more than thirty years, fifteen of them spent in the service of the Andrews family.

They'd known nothing like it before, even in this household where the children had been allowed a freedom no member of their generation and class was accustomed to. Miss Katy had been a law unto herself since she was a little thing, going where she pleased and when checked bellowing her outrage from the cellars to the rooftops. The boys not quite so bad, particularly the two older ones, though Master Chris caused almost as many ructions as Miss Katy, even if it was Mr Andrews who made the most noise about them.

But they had been . . . well, it sounded daft and she was sure Freda would understand, they had been wholesome disagreements with no badness in them. Hot and hasty but soon over. Tantrums really, the kind children have, if it was not out of place to call Mr Andrews childish. They all wanted their own way, every member of the family, that was the trouble, and with the exception of Mrs Andrews, fought one another to get it. It seemed Miss Katy had had plans for herself and that big lad of Matty Jenkins, from the way she carried on. In front of Tommy Jenkins, too, but they had turned to ashes on her tongue and she would never recover from it, she shrieked in her first dementia.

Mrs Tiplady, frozen for several long, appalled seconds, as they all were, by Miss Katy's heart-rending cries, by her absolute determination to hurt herself badly as she threw herself from wall to wall, had hurried Tommy from the room so fast the pair of them had almost fallen headlong over the damned dog which whined at the door to get out. To safety and sanity, she supposed, and who could blame the poor beast? Young Tommy was as white as the driven snow and she herself was shaking badly, but Mrs Tiplady had been in service for a good many years and had survived many crises and she was not about to allow this one to interrupt the smoothly running machinery of her kitchen.

The maidservants, having heard the commotion from the breakfast room, were milling about the room as she had fully expected them to be, except Freda who had more sense, and they turned as one as she hurried Tommy towards the kitchen door.

"Go home to your mother, lad, and say nothing. D'you understand? Not to anyone. Now I'm trusting you, Tommy Jenkins, to act like a man. They'll know soon enough, your ma and pa but it's up to the family to say when. Can I . . .?"

"I'll say nowt, Mrs Tiplady, 'onest ter God," but she could see the excitement in his eyes and the flush of anticipation in his face and, since he was only a boy of fourteen she was not awfully sure he would keep his promise. After all, it concerned his family just as much as the Andrews.

She sighed deeply. "Right then, off you go, and as for you lot," turning to her handmaidens as Tommy ran off across the back yard, "who gave you permission to stand about with your mouths hanging open? Mabel, have you done them veg? And what happened to the saddle of lamb I told you to fetch from the larder half an hour ago, Lottie Earnshaw?"

"But Mrs Tiplady, them screams . . . is someone 'urt? Miss Chloe?"

"Whether they are or whether they're not is none of your business, Ivy. As I told Tommy, when the master sees fit to let you in on his private affairs, then you'll know and until then you've a job to do so I suggest you go and do it. I'll say this," relenting a fraction for they had all been worried sick about Miss Chloe, "the mistress's niece is safe and sound. Now then, Dilly, I reckon you'll have to go over this floor again, don't you? That lad's boots look as if they've traipsed through a farmyard and he's left a trail from here to the breakfast room so you'd best get your bucket out again. Freda, you come with me and

Janet, make a fresh pot of tea and bring it to my room and then you can make a start on— "

It was not vouchsafed to Janet what she was to make a start on, for cutting off Mrs Tiplady in mid-sentence, the door, which led from the hallway to the kitchen and which she herself had just come through, was flung open with such violence Dilly dropped the bucket she had picked up. They all turned, Mrs Tiplady included, their faces filled with dread, the expression on them sharing the identical thought: What now?

When they saw the apparition in the doorway, every last one of them, even Mrs Tiplady, fell back from it in horrified silence.

Katherine Andrews's eyes recognised them for they were part of her everyday life and had been, some of them, since she was a child but they meant nothing to her now. She didn't acknowledge them just as she didn't acknowledge the table and chairs, the pots and pans or any part of the familiar room. She had been in and out of it since she had learned to walk, sitting on Mrs Tiplady's footstool before the fire, eating Mrs Tiplady's delicious biscuits, quite at home there since, as was her way, Katy Andrews could see no reason why she should not go where she wished to go.

Now she was to make her way to where she didn't wish to go at all but where she must. She had no coherent thought in her head, nothing that made sense or was reasonable, just a deep, primeval instinct which drove her on to what her breaking heart must know for itself. Her brain was numbed, empty really, and her body suspended in some merciful oblivion which, she knew quite definitely, would not last long. But while it did she was driven to this journey she must take.

She was dressed in her simple day dress, a separate skirt and bodice of jaconet, a fine cotton material in a colour somewhere between pale blue and green, with a sash of the same colour. The skirt had what was known as an apron front but as she was not yet seventeen her mother had forbidden her, and her dressmaker, the overskirt and bustle which were the fashion. Her shoes were high-heeled, dyed to match her gown, shaped like slippers with long uppers.

A very elegant and lovely young woman but somehow it was all tossed about, dishevelled, creased, even torn in places, the sash hanging loose, several buttons come undone. Her hair, though it was short by the day's standards, was hanging about her face in some curious way and from beneath it her eyes stared, blank and unfocused, the lovely, rich golden amber to which they were all accustomed turned to the colour of the brown mud which edged the reservoir when the water was low.

She stood for a moment or two in the doorway and from behind her her father's voice called out to her but she appeared not to hear him as she blundered across the kitchen towards the back door, banging her hip savagely against the solid table in its centre as she went.

"Miss . . . Miss Katy," Mrs Tiplady quavered, while all about her the maidservants stood rigidly in the position of whatever it was they had been doing before Miss Katherine crashed into their domain. Dilly held her scrubbing brush in a hand gone cold and numb and Lottie clutched the saddle of lamb to her bosom as though it were the only sane thing in a world gone mad, while in the chimney corner where she had been about to reach for the kettle for Mrs Tiplady's tea, Janet began to weep silently since she could not bear to witness the pain which was written on Miss Katy's face, she blubbered later.

Katherine moved through them with the speed and force of a charging bull, opening the yard door and flinging it back on its hinges against the wall. Through it they watched as she rushed headlong across the yard where she disappeared through the arch which led to the stables.

Jimmy was grooming Master Richard's horse, a bay mare called Jenny which he had just exercised in the big paddock at the back of the stables. When he had finished he would do the same for Hal who was Master David's chestnut. Neither animal was ridden as much as Jimmy would have liked but Mr Andrews wouldn't dream of getting rid of them, he had told the groom. When his sons came home they would need a decent mount and so the pair of them, groomed and glossy with good health and loving care, if a bit overweight, were quartered in the stables and paddock, eating their pampered heads off.

Dicken was mucking out, sweeping the malodorous contents of the loose boxes into the yard, and sitting on a bench against the stable wall, a pipe in his mouth and a tangle of harness in his hands, was the third groom, a wiry, bandy-legged little man called Noah. Jamie Hutchinson's father was nowhere to be seen.

They all three turned to stare at Katherine in much the same way the maids had, mouths open, eyes wide, for though they were used to Miss Katy's tendency to pop up, however inconvenient, at any old time of the day, demanding her mare, Storm, be saddled, she wasn't dressed for riding today. In fact she looked bloody queer, Dicken was to remark later to Janet, with whom he was "walking out" and it was perhaps the strangeness of her attire and manner, her complete oblivion to any of them, just as though the yard were empty, that allowed her to stride into the stable, release the sorrel from where she tossed her head in her stall and lead her out into the yard without a word from any of them. If it had not been for Noah's pipe which fell from his slack lips into his lap, scattering hot ashes on his "vitals" they might have been frozen to paralysis for the next hour, Dicken told Janet, they were all so bloody mazed, though of course Mr Andrews would have fetched them out of it soon enough!

There was a mounting block in the yard. She led the sorrel to it then, bunching her full skirts about her waist, unconscious of the men who stared in wonder at her frilly drawers, leaped astride the mare's back, thrust her hands deep in her mane, dug her dainty heels into her side and flew out of the yard like a bird on the wing just as her father staggered into it.

"Katherine . . ." he bellowed, his face like paper, his brown eyes flat and muddy, so great was his fear for his girl. "Katy. Oh, dear God, that bloody woman's come back from't grave to haunt us."

The bewildered men had not the slightest notion who he was talking about, continuing to stare, first at the open gate out on to the drive through which Miss Katy had disappeared, then at the frantic man who was her father.

"Jimmy, get up on that animal and follow her . . . bring her back. Be quick, man, for Christ's sake. No, don't bother with a bloody saddle, you fool. If my lass can ride bareback then so can thee. Hurry, man . . . hurry. You, Dicken, saddle me a horse an' one for thissen an' we'll follow."

She went by the most direct route through her father's wood and out on to the pasture beyond. There was a gate leading to a field in which cattle stood and which she usually stopped to open and close behind her, since her father objected to Jamie's small dairy herd, which for the past month had grazed there, wandering willy nilly on to his property. It was all his property, of course, including Valley Bottom Farm but it was leased to Jamie who was now her father's tenant.

Ignoring the gate, for she had not the time to be concerned with it, she set the sorrel at the stone wall which ran round the field, clinging with her strong hands and legs to the little mare's back. The animal took it bravely though her eyes rolled frantically as her hooves dislodged one of the top cam stones. The cattle scattered, flowing towards the edge of the field, ungainly in their alarm and Archie Bagshaw, the postman, who was riding placidly along the valley road, twisted about in his saddle so vigorously to see what all the commotion was about he damn near fell off his horse. He was on his second delivery of the day and with two more to go he couldn't afford an accident, could he?

It was a soft, late summer day. The thunderstorm of the night before had washed the skies and tossed away the clouds, leaving the sun to shine where it would, gentle and warm and benign. On any other day Katy would have idled along, drinking in the wine-like air, dreaming her dreams, admiring the wild spread of flowers in the long meadow grasses, and the heady lilt of the songs the skylarks poured out. It was not often the high peaks were favoured with such benevolence. The sound of water from above was a soft background to the loveliness of it all but Katherine Andrews neither saw nor heard any of it.

Jamie had not left Chloe's side since the moment he had carried her through the door the day before, like a bride, he had whispered to her later in the warm, comforting depths of what was now to be considered their marriage bed. She had awoken, dreadfully alarmed for the space of ten seconds, with his arms still about her, the weight of him tipping the bed so that her body had no choice but to lie directly against his. He was awake in the growing half light which the cock in the yard was declaring to be time to get up and when she opened her eyes his serious face was straining towards her.

"Have you any idea how much I love you?" was the first thing he said to her.

"I . . . think so," she murmured hesitantly.

"Are ... are you still of the same mind, lass, because if you're not you are bound by ..."

"What do you mean?"

"I mean that if you have ... are having second thoughts I'll not hold you to ... to anything. I'm glad what happened to us happened but I'm afraid I might have stampeded you into it."

She must have made some sound of distress for at once he turned her to him and, lifting himself on one elbow, looked down into her face.

"What have I said?" He smoothed her hair back from her brow, marvelling on how beautiful she was, even with half her face swollen and bruised.

"I'm ... I wasn't ... stampeded, Jamie. I wanted to." She ducked her head shyly and he was enchanted. "I was happy at what happened but if you ..."

"Dear sweet Christ, no," he almost shouted, and at once she relaxed and smiled, for only she knew what had really taken place. She regretted nothing and her smile said so and when, gently, tentatively, as though she were some breakable thing which should he damage it would be beyond repair, he kissed her moist, rosy lips and cupped her breasts with big, tender hands, she responded willingly, wanting nothing more than to please this man who loved her.

They made love again, easier this time since she knew what to expect, her heart flowing with gratitude towards him, for she sensed he was holding back what could be a stronger passion than she could cope with just yet. He shuddered and gasped at the end of it and she held him more confidently, glad that he seemed to get what she supposed men wanted from a woman. Her body accommodated his quite readily and painlessly despite the enormous difference in their weight and size, and when, later, he brought them tea on a dainty tray, his strong and beautiful male body completely naked, she allowed her eyes to study him for a matter of thirty seconds and, finding nothing in his masculinity to repel or frighten her, was glad when he slid back into bed beside her and, holding her close to him as though he could not bear to have her even an inch from his side, began to talk to her of his life at sea. He made her laugh and he made her gasp in wonder at some of the things he had done and seen and when, suddenly, he clapped his hand to his head and said, "Oh, my God, the bloody cows," she was sorry when he leaped out of bed and into his clothes.

"Get up when you're ready, lass," he said, leaning over to kiss her. When she did, wrapping herself daringly in the quilt she herself had made, and ventured down the narrow, crooked stairs, Tommy had been there, his face thunderstruck. A note was to be delivered to Cloudberry End and put into Mr Andrews's hand, Jamie had told him as Chloe curled herself in the big chair, and no one else's, and now, here was the result of it in the form of Katherine Andrews herself.

They heard her coming, her mare's hooves striking sparks off the newly restored cobbles on the track and though they had expected something they had not specifically imagined it would be Katy herself.

Jamie opened the door, placing himself in the frame of it, filling it, his body ready to protect Chloe from what promised to be a degree of violence. He was alarmed by Katy's appearance, which seemed to convey an ordeal through which she had gone and which she could barely manage. Her face was the colour of the ash in a dead fire and her eyes, for that moment, were blank and lifeless, just as though the flame of Katy Andrews which had burned so brilliantly, so jubilantly, so joyfully, had been snuffed out. Her gown was torn and she wore only one shoe which, like the hem of her skirt and her bare, stockinged foot, was filthy with cow muck, for Jamie's farmyard was not in the immaculate condition of her father's stable yard. The cows had been brought up and milked, then turned loose again and their excreta was thick and stinking in the churned-up ground. He should have cleared it himself, Jamie had time to think, but the truth was he was so enchanted with his new love he could not find the strength of mind to tear himself away from her.

Katy's hair was wild and tangled and from beneath it her eyes peered like an animal's from its den. When he glanced over her shoulder he was not surprised to see she had ridden bareback.

"Katy . . . ?" he said, keeping his hand on the latch, beginning to be afraid now, not just for Chloe who, he imagined, could possibly receive another black eye to match the one she already had if Katy reached her, but for this silent, empty young girl who stared at him so senselessly, on whose face was an expression of such crazed and terrible pain he was appalled. There would be more than black eyes exchanged this day, he told himself, for this was no temper tantrum thrown by a young girl who had been crossed in love, calf love, he had always thought it, but some deep and agonising emotion which might destroy the girl who suffered it, and anyone in her path who she thought had caused it. An explosive nature such as Katy's which she had never learned to control was a dangerous thing to encounter and he must keep it from inflicting damage to the woman he loved.

But Chloe Taylor, despite her fragile appearance, the wisp of swansdown look which implied she might blow away on any stray breeze, was deceptively strong and was no coward. All her life she had been protected from the outside world by her well-bred, devout, church-going mother, but the last year had taught her that it didn't matter whether you believed in God or not, followed the teachings of the Church, read and lived by your Bible, the blows came just the same and there was only one way to deal with them when they knocked you to your knees. Get up and get on! Face them and if you couldn't do that, then bend a little which prevented you from breaking. Courage, she had learned, came hard and though she had done wrong last night, and this morning, a wrong her mama would condemn her for, it had not felt wrong. Jamie had done what he had done to her in love and she had responded in the same way and if her cousin Katy had come to castigate her, Chloe could manage a bit of castigating herself.

When she opened the door wide and peered round the large frame of Jamie she was astounded by the sight of the swaying, what seemed the almost insensible figure of her cousin on the path. She would barely have recognised her had it not been for the colour of her tangled hair and the blown horse who stood, head hanging, beyond the mended gate. It was Storm all right, and it was Katy all right, but . . . Oh, dear merciful heaven, what had happened to her? How had she come to be in this pitiable condition, this state of near collapse, of suffering so great it was not to be borne? She was in pain so deep it was ready to destroy her, ready to drain her life's blood away, her eyes moving slowly, like that of a wounded and downed beast, from one tormentor to the other.

Herself and Jamie! Sweet Jesus!

"Jamie, bring her in," she murmured without hesitation, doing her best to dodge under his arm to get to the girl from whom, she realised fully now, Chloe had taken the only man Katy had ever wanted. Jamie Hutchinson. It was too late now, of course, for ignorant as she was she was fully aware that she could already carry Jamie's child in her womb. They could not go back, none of them, even had she and Jamie wanted to, despite what he had said this morning, but her compassion for her cousin, who had treated Chloe with nothing warmer than casual indifference, was immense. She must be brought inside, put in a cosy chair by the chimney corner, given tea, or perhaps brandy if Jamie had any, comforted, if such a thing could be managed, until her father came to get her. She could hardly be left to weave about in such a mindless fashion. So deep in shock her mind was gone.

But Jamie knew Katy Andrews better than did Chloe and when, with a shriek which lifted a flock of starlings from the trees at the back of the house and sent her mare skidding and flying back down the track, she launched herself at her cousin he was ready for her. She had nothing but her bare fists, her feet, her teeth, her fingernails to tear him to pieces with, then do the same to Chloe if she could reach her, but her despair gave her a strength which was not far short of his own.

"You bitch . . . you filthy whore . . . he was mine . . . mine . . . all my life, since I was a child I've loved him and . . . yes . . . left alone . . . waiting . . . he would have loved me. He would have seen me . . . Oh, God, I should have done what you did, taken my clothes off for him . . . anything . . . but I didn't know . . . you see, I thought you were nothing . . . I was blind . . . God damn you to hell, you bitch . . . your mother did something . . . to mine for which she never forgave her . . . and now . . . now you've done the same to me. Let me get at her . . . Jamie . . . please . . . I'll kill you both, I swear I'll kill you both . . . she's taken you from me, Jamie . . . Oh, Jesus, Jesus, what am I to do with the rest of my life? . . . let me go, dammit, let me go . . . let me hurt her, Jamie . . . I beg you . . . don't do this . . ." and all the while she shrieked and howled her pain and loss and devastation she struggled in the straining arms of the man she loved, not to claim his kisses as she had yearned to do, but to tear out his eyes, rake his cheeks with her nails, damage him, particularly his manhood, for if she couldn't have it then Chloe Taylor certainly wouldn't.

She drew blood as her teeth sank into the fleshy part of his hand between his thumb and forefinger and his left cheek had four bleeding tracks down it where she had run her nails. When she was free she would start on Chloe, her maddened eyes told her.

Chloe, appalled, her one good eye enormous and glittering in her bruised face, backed away from the scene of horror which was being played out on the doorstep. The young dog who had come to the door in welcome at the sound of the visitor was cowering on the blanket bed Chloe had made him and with a moan of anguish she sank down beside him, putting her head down to his.

"It will be all right, Captain, it really will," she kept repeating as though it was his fear she was calming and still, from beyond the door which Jamie had managed to close when she stepped back from it, the sounds of the struggle, the shrieks of demented rage and pain and desolation continued. She could hear Jamie's voice as he did his best to calm her cousin, soft, tender, even, for he was aware that it was because of him Katy was suffering. He had done nothing, ever, to encourage her belief that one day he would come to love her, as a man loves his woman, but all the same he felt guilty. She was a child, sixteen, a child who had suffered no pain, no unhappiness in her carefree life, not even the normal restrictions put on a girl of her class. She had got what she wanted, always, from the world she lived in and she had expected to get him and now, when she found she couldn't, she was ready to inflict any injury she could on those who had prevented it.

He couldn't calm her. Without physically hurting her he couldn't restrain her, so he did what he had to, which he had done before with recalcitrant, drunken seamen and when she fell, senseless as a stone, he caught her to him, ready to weep for her.

"Open the door, Chloe." His voice from outside was as cold as ice, just as though this was all her fault but Chloe rose to her feet and did as she was told.

"A blanket, if you please," he added and she ran to do his bidding as he laid the insensible figure of Katy Andrews on the settle, placing the quilt which was the first thing to come to hand across her cousin. There was a livid red mark on her chin, just to the right and below her jawline.

"You . . . you hit her?" She put her hand to her own bruised face and the eye which, this morning, would not open.

"I had to." His voice was stony.

"But surely there was no need?"

"There was every need. She would have injured you if I hadn't stopped her."

"Dear God, Jamie, was there not some other way to prevent her?"

"None. She was not herself." His voice was clipped and flat and Chloe was distraught, wondering where the loveliness, the sweetness, the promise of last night and this morning had gone. It could not be destroyed. Not so soon. It had been . . . lovely. He had been . . . she had liked his arms about her, his blue eyes shining into hers with the brilliance of his love. She had been ready to . . . what? Well, whatever it was she had been content with it, longing to see where it might lead. Was it now destroyed? Had her cousin killed it, as she had threatened to kill her?

"Jamie?" Her voice was soft and despairing and when he turned to her, his worry and distress plain on his strong face, she began to cry soundlessly.

At once everyone, including the unconscious girl on the settle, fled from his mind and he was across the kitchen in a stride, pulling her half-dressed figure into his arms. He cradled her against his chest, his cheek resting on her hair, his hands smoothing and stroking her bare shoulders, her back, her face.

"Don't, my dove, don't cry. I can't bear to see you cry. It breaks my heart . . . hush now . . . I love you and this doesn't change anything, you must know that. I was aware that she had . . . tender feelings for me but I thought, hoped, she would grow out of it."

"Oh, Jamie . . . poor Katy . . . poor little girl."

"I know, but you are my love, my heart, my very soul. Do you not know I would die for you? Your flower face is engraved in my mind so that if I were to go blind I would always see it." He was close to tears himself. "I love you . . . kiss me."

The girl on the settle opened her eyes and they were clear now, despite the blow to the chin she had suffered. It was as though Jamie's fist had jolted the mist of despair and fury from her head, leaving it steady and able to organise her thoughts for the first time since her father had read out the note from Jamie. She knew she would hurt savagely again, not physically of course, but in every other way and she must get away from here before it began, away from the man and woman who murmured in one another's arms on the other side of the room, away from this farm and from the family which was hers at Cloudberry End. She didn't know for how long. She didn't even know where she would go, but she must leave. She must leave at once. She didn't want to hurt anyone now. That was over and done with and the next step must be taken towards whatever was to happen to her.

Katherine Andrews, a child no longer, rose quietly and, with only the dog to watch her go, slipped from the kitchen. When she reached the gate she hesitated, bewildered that her sorrel was not there. She whistled softly, beginning to walk back down the track and with a whicker of greeting Storm appeared, nuzzling at her mistress's shoulder, recognising that the mad possession had gone.

Using the wall beside the track as a mounting block, Katherine climbed up on to the mare's back and, turning her round, steered her up the track towards Little Crowden Intake and the long climb towards the Black Hill.

11

Everything went in threes, they all knew that, Mrs Tiplady murmured to Freda, who had become her confidante, and as if the situation wasn't bad enough, what with Miss Chloe and her goings-on and then Miss Katy vanishing off the face of the earth, Mr Andrews's brother George had to go and have an apoplectic stroke right at the bar of the Old Swan, which was enough to put any man off his ale and no mistake, and all on the same day. Dead before he hit the sawdust on the floor, they said, and could the master, who was already out of his mind with worry over his girl, ever be the same again?

Three days now since Miss Katy was last seen at Valley Bottom Farm, or so Jamie Hutchinson reported, though how he dare show his face at Cloudberry End after what he and that hussy had got up to was beyond understanding. The mistress prostrate, shut up in her room with only the master and Matty Jenkins allowed to go near her, but then she and Matty had a lot in common, what with Matty's lad living in sin with that mim-faced niece of Mrs Andrews, who'd taken them all in, and the mistress's lass vanished as though the ground had swallowed her up.

Which, of course, was what they were all afraid of. Everyone in the district was aware of the vast areas of wet, boggy land which lay on the high wastes above the valley. The underlying stone cupped the water like a bowl and the peat held it, sponge-like, so that even in the driest summer there were still many places where the moor was a quaking morass, pitching and tilting and sucking the unwary into its depthless clutches. Whole waggons had been known to vanish without a trace so the ground would have no trouble absorbing a mere horse and rider, would it? The groom, Jimmy, muttered to Dicken, not in Mr Andrews's hearing, of course, that if Miss Katy's appearance that morning was anything to go by, the last thing she would have on her mind was where her mare might tread. Out of her bloody mind over something, though they were not privy to what it was. The events in the house were relayed to them third or fourth hand but it must have something to do with the other one, her cousin, who had gone missing the day before, apparently. What was up with them, he asked Dicken to tell him, as they set off on Hal and Zack to search the faint, stony tracks which criss-crossed Tintwistle Knarr. Couldn't the master keep his womenfolk in better order than this? If they were his girls they'd feel his belt on their bums, choose how. Not sit down for a bloody week, they wouldn't. Causing all this hullaballoo when he had work to see to in the stables, not to mention all the men whom Mr Andrews had mustered to search for his girl and must leave their jobs unattended.

And how would anyone know if she and the horse she rode had been sucked into a bog? the maids whispered to one another in the kitchen, their eyes wide and frightened at the very idea of it, the sheer horror of it. Without trace, without a footprint or hoofprint, with no one but the larks high above to hear her cries or see her . . . her . . . struggles. Dear Lord, it didn't bear thinking about, did it? Janet moaned and perhaps another cup of tea would be in order.

Every man in the district was drawn into the search, those who knew Butterley Moss, Sliddens Moss, Tooley Shaw Moss, all barren, shaking wastes which lay about the steep, sloping land up to the Black Hill. To the south on the far side of the reservoirs, Birchen Bank Moss and Featherbed Moss, for who knew which direction she had taken? Last seen at Valley Bottom Farm, they were told, but she could have crossed the railway track in her demented state, the one Jimmy and Dicken described to the searchers in shocked whispers.

They were forced to stop as darkness fell, for no man could search in the dark, Saul Gibbon said patiently to Mr Andrews who was nearly off his head. Saul was a shepherd and he knew what he was talking about, for he was as familiar with these hills and moors as he was with his own snug kitchen. If anyone could find Katy Andrews, he could, and so, with the sergeant from the local constabulary, who after all had the authority, Saul was more or less in charge, sending men

where he thought they should go, quartering the valley and
the hills which rose out of it with almost military precision.
It was no good thrashing about in the dark or there would
be more than Jack Andrews's lass missing, and as soon as
it was light they would begin again. Farmers and their sons,
labourers, those who worked the quarries, any man who could
be spared, and Saul would set his own two sheepdogs on the
trail, those which searched for sheep when the deep winter
snows fell. It was lucky it was mild out, and dry, he added
comfortingly to the distraught father, and the lass would take
no harm.

Chloe saw next to nothing of Jamie for three days, nor
indeed of anyone. She had been left with the problem not
only of how one made oneself a meal of any sort on the open
fire, but on how to light the thing if it should go out, which it
did. She knew how to boil an egg and make a pot of tea since
she had done it for Mama when she fell ill, but not on an open
fire. And then there was the question of a change of clothing,
especially her underclothing. She had nothing but the clothes
she had worn on the day Chris Andrews had accosted her and
she had no money to buy the materials to make others even
if she could get into Crossclough. Jack Andrews had been
more than generous with the allowance he had given her –
she suspected more to ease his own conscience than for any
other reason – but naturally she had not carried money about
with her when she went for a walk. Now, when she was really
in need she had nothing to ease it.

Not that that mattered when compared with the terrifying
strain of her missing cousin. Jamie was like a man possessed,
just as though he were to blame for Katy's disappearance.
Jack Andrews, when he had followed close on the heels of
his groom up to Valley Bottom Farm – for where else could
Katy have gone? – had made it plain that this tragedy could
only be laid at Jamie's door. Of course he was not himself and
when he was, being a fair man, would realise that it wasn't
so. If every man or woman who was rejected by the object of
their own desire acted as Katy had done the world would be
in a constant state of upheaval, her uncle would know that,
Chloe told herself, but he wasn't thinking straight and, she
supposed, the sight of herself lurking at Jamie's back half an
hour after Katy's disappearance had not helped his normally
reasonable mind.

"I'll bloody kill you for this, Jamie Hutchinson," he thundered in his demented fury. "If she's not found soon you're off this farm by the weekend, you and that trollop with you," before digging his heels into his mount's side and heading off back to Cloudberry End, the awkward groom behind him.

So Chloe could only remain in the farmhouse, her only company the dog, and wait forlornly for the moment, usually just after dark, when Jamie came stumbling home to fling himself in the chair and fall asleep. She knew she was no good to him. She could do nothing to ease his sense of guilt, to comfort his aching, weary body, not even cook him a warm meal to sustain him.

"It's all right, lass," he would mumble, his haggard face doing its best to smile reassuringly. "A bit of bread and cheese will do."

On that first day when she had been left so frighteningly alone she had moved slowly about the farmhouse, going from room to room, opening cupboards and drawers, the dog at her heels, familiarising herself, or trying to, with what was to be her home from now on. She had lived a comfortable life for eighteen years in the tall house in Liverpool, with a parlourmaid to answer the door, a cook and a skivvy in the kitchen and during the last four months in absolute luxury at Cloudberry End. She had never been in a kitchen except to convey an order from her mama to the cook, until the last weeks of Mama's life when she had learned how to boil an egg and make a pot of tea, but the rudiments of cooking, of cleaning, of how one went about the everyday tasks of washing and ironing one's own garments were a dark mystery to her. There was no running water in the kitchen and Jamie explained to her that every drop must be brought from the pump in the yard. These were the buckets to be used, he had explained, his eyes so dark and forbidding, she felt herself shrivel inside, wanting to weep for the loss of the loving warmth which he had shown her before Katy's disappearance. He was no longer the ardent, gentle lover who had taken her to his bed and then, after loving her, for she recognised that was what he had done, loved her, held her in strong, protective arms while she slept. He was no longer the smiling, good-humoured giant who had treated her as though she were a fragile stem of cut crystal who should not be allowed so much as to lift her own teacup to her lips and, in the soft depth of the bed they had shared for the first time only a night or two ago, he turned his back on her and slept the sleep of the exhausted, only to fling himself out of the farmhouse with hardly a word the minute it was daylight.

How Katy would have relished it, Chloe thought bitterly, her disappearance having separated the man she loved from the woman she loathed as effectively as death itself.

She found an old but clean white shirt presumably belonging to Jamie at the back of a drawer, one which had a frilled, tucked front, wondering in astonishment when he had ever worn it. She hoped it was not something he treasured as she cut into it with a pair of sharp shears she found in the kitchen drawer, not sure of their purpose but at least they suited hers. From the worn material and with a needle and some thread – black – she discovered in a small box on the mantelshelf she fashioned herself some rather skimpy undergarments, but at least it meant she could wash her own, though the ironing of them was beyond her. It had taken all her strength to pump the water into the bucket and carry it, half a bucketful at a time, into the house and then to ponder on the means to heat it. There were pans on the shelf and the fire, which Jamie had patiently relit with instructions not to let it go out, pointing to the plentiful supply of wood which was stacked in the yard, was crackling cheerfully in the barred grate. But in the end she had washed them as best she could in cold water, then draped them before the fire to dry.

The bread, which was all but gone, was as hard as rock, and the cheese box empty and she was wondering despairingly what she might give Jamie for a meal on this, the third and what was to be the last day of searching, when she heard the sound of horse's hooves on the track. For a second her heart leaped gladly for surely it was Katy come back from the . . . well, from the dead, but when she flung open the door it was not her cousin who stood there but Jamie's mother.

They looked at one another, the two women, for what seemed an eternity to Chloe, the expression on Mrs Jenkins's face quite inscrutable and yet in her eyes there was surely no mistaking the utter contempt and dislike. Chloe felt it slither inside her and wrap sinuously around her fast-beating heart. Mrs Jenkins was walking, leading a placid old horse which lowered its head and began to crop the rough grass just beyond the gate. On its back was strapped the faded, much worn carpetbag which had once belonged to Chloe's mama.

Chloe, with what seemed so much to do in this new life of hers, the bringing in of water and logs, the constant replenishing of the fire, the washing and sewing and even the sweeping out of the kitchen which she thought she should do, had not had the time to fasten up her hair in its customary neat chignon. It hung in a wild tangle of curls – since she had no brush and Jamie seemed uncertain of where one could be found – tied up with a bit of twine she had found with the needle and thread. Her dove grey gown was stained around the hem with the muck from the yard and though she had sluiced her hands and face at the pump and even stripped and washed her body in a bucket of cold water, there was about her the kind of dishevelment usually seen in those who care not a jot for their appearance. Her stout walking boots were weighted down with mud and muck and the scrap of towel she had tied about her waist in an effort to protect her one dress was torn and dirty.

Jamie's mother continued to study her, her blue eyes, so like his, running down the length of her, then up again to Chloe's face, her lip curled in what appeared to be almost a snarl.

Matty Jenkins had nothing against this girl as such and perhaps, if she'd proved strong enough to be the farmer's wife Jamie needed, could have taken to her. She was well bred, though that didn't matter, and good-hearted, they all agreed at the house. She'd kept her head up and her graceful back straight despite Sara's aversion to her, and Matty admired that, but Jesus God, she'd overturned the life of the Andrews family like a child with a stick stirring an ant-hill. She had created havoc and destruction, not just because of who she was, which Sara had found so hard to cope with, but because of what she had done to Katy and to Jamie. Jamie must be bewitched, his mother agonised, as she stared in growing horror at the slut in her son's doorway. And she'd no shame neither, standing with her tatterdemalion head up and her shoulders squared, just as though she were some elegantly gowned hostess welcoming a guest on the doorstep of her mansion.

"Mrs Jenkins," she enquired politely, "won't you come in and . . ." She was about to say "take tea" but she had used the last of the tea leaves an hour ago, having mastered the kettle and the trivet which held it, as she meant to master all the other strange gadgets in her new home. When Jamie was himself, of course, and could show her.

"I don't think so, lass. I'm doin' Sara, Mrs Andrews, a favour fetchin' yer things. She wants shut of 'em, yer see. Aye, I could've sent one o't lads but they're all out searchin' fer Miss Katy, poor lass, an' if she's not found tha'll not 'ave an easy life in these parts an' neither'll my lad."

Chloe's face spasmed in horror as the words struck her but she found her voice bravely though it was broken with her strong emotion.

"Why? Dear God . . . why? Why do you blame me and Jamie for all this? Even Mr Andrews has threatened Jamie with eviction but it is not his fault, nor mine that— "

Matty cut her short, her face contorted with rage. "So, yer've summat else to answer for, 'ave yer? For if my boy loses this farm an' everythin' he's purrin' to it he'll not forgive thi'. Miss Katy'd not've run off but fer thee an' what tha' tempted my lad ter do. Traipsin' up here an' doin' yer best ter get yer claws in 'im."

"No, no, it wasn't like that. Jamie has never loved Katy, not in that way. He was entirely honourable in his dealings with her but she refused to accept it. She wanted him for herself, you see and when she heard that we . . . that Jamie and I . . ."

Chloe stepped out from beneath the shadow of the porch, throwing out her hands in desperate appeal and for the first time Matty saw her face. She gasped and put her hand to her mouth.

"Dear sweet God in heaven, tell me my son didn't . . ."

Chloe tutted impatiently. "No, of course not. Surely you know Jamie better than that."

"I thought I did, lass." Matty's shoulders slumped. "But if it were'nt 'im, then who?"

Chloe hesitated. Should she tell Jamie's mother who had beaten her across the face in his frustrated temper? But if she did would it not cause more trouble for the Andrews family? So far only she and Chris Andrews knew who had given her the bruised and blackened eye, the swollen, red-wealed face but if Mrs Jenkins was told and it got out, Jamie would without a doubt go down to Cloudberry End and wreak havoc on . . . Well, he would have done a few nights ago, she told herself bleakly, but now . . . now, who knew what his reaction would be? From his attitude towards her since Katy had slipped out of the kitchen and vanished, probably that she had got what she deserved.

"It was . . . a man up on the . . . on the moor," she mumbled, hanging her head as though in shame, then looking up again sharply. "He wanted something I was not prepared to give him so . . . he struck me. Jamie found me and brought me here. Neither of us planned it, Mrs Jenkins, please believe me, but . . . well . . . Jamie has asked me to marry him and I have said I will. I cannot return to Cloudberry End, not now. Even if Katy had not run away, I could not return to the house where . . ."

Matty knew then who it was who had savaged Chloe Taylor's face, for had they not all noticed the way he waylaid this lovely girl, in the garden, according to Angus and Billy, and on the back staircase where Ivy had found them. He was the weak son of a strong father and though Matty did not like to believe that he would strike a defenceless girl, who else would have done it? Some rough fellow intent on rape? Hardly, for a refusal to allow it would have been ignored and Chloe would have got more than a smack in the face.

Matty sagged against the patient horse and pushed a hand through her windblown hair, her own head bending as though in pain. She believed her, that was the trouble. She believed every word this girl said, which made it hard to go on despising her. Sara was lying in a semi-drugged state in her bedroom at Cloudberry End, moaning for her girl to be returned to her, and if not her, then her husband on whom she leaned so heavily. Sometimes, when Matty looked back to the days when she and Sara had lived and worked in Liverpool, she could scarcely credit that this was the strong, resolute young woman Sara Andrews had then been. She had suffered sorrow and loss and the dreadful mischief her own sister had caused in her life but she had been unbowed by it. It was not until she married Jack, who insisted on treating her like a hot-house flower which would wither in the cold winds of everyday life, that she had become . . . weakened. He, with his strength on which he insisted she leaned, had weakened her imperceptibly day by day until she could barely function without him beside her, no more than an arm's length away. It had saddened Matty. It was not that Sara was melancholy.

Far from it. When all was well she was as merry as a child but it had to be within sight and sound of Jack Andrews, which was probably the reason he had retired from the business of building railways so as to be always near her.

"Tha's ter marry my Jamie?" she said at last, raising her head, surprised by the compassion she saw in Chloe's eyes, just as though the girl could sense Matty's pain. She didn't take after her mother, at any rate, which was something, for Alice Hamilton had been a cold-hearted bitch if ever there was one.

"Yes, I believe so."

"Don't tha' know?"

"Well . . . since Katy left he has been distraught. Like Mr Andrews, he blamed himself, you see."

"Nay, she were always hangin' about him when he were home. Puppy love, it were."

"Oh no!" Chloe looked shocked. "It was not that, Mrs Jenkins. She truly loves him."

"Loved him, lass."

"You can't mean . . . she's dead?" Chloe slumped against the door frame and the dog huddled up to her skirt, bewildered by the tides of emotion which flooded in and out of what he had begun to think of as his territory.

"Nay, she's not bin found. There's a hue an' cry out for 'er in every town within forty miles an' she'd hardly be missed, lookin' like she did, that's if she got that far. Them bogs up there . . ."

Matty shook her head dumbly and tears began to slide down her cheeks. She had not wept nor broken, as Sara had, for the three whole days of Katy's disappearance but now, in the presence of this quiet, dishevelled but dignified young woman, she felt it begin to break inside her and flow towards the surface of her skin.

"Oh, God, lass, where is she?" she wailed, then was amazed to find herself in the slender, but surprisingly strong arms of the girl she had been prepared to repudiate, even if she was Jamie's choice. She was led inside and placed gently in front of the lively fire, her hands chafed by the girl who knelt at her feet while she wept and wept and then, as women do, felt better for it.

"Put kettle on, lass," she said at last, sniffing her last sniffle, blowing her nose vigorously on the scrap of clean linen in her sleeve.

Chloe sighed disconsolately. "Mrs Jenkins, I would most willingly but . . . well, you see, there's no tea. I am so sorry. I feel quite mortified, but Jamie is . . . is so worried . . ."

"D'yer mean ter say he's gone off an' left yer, a gently reared girl ter fend for thissen? Is there nowt?"

"Well, milk by the churnful, for the cows have to be seen to," Chloe said brightly, just as though the routine of the farm was well known to her. "Tommy has been up."

"Aye, he would. A good lad is my Tommy."

"But he didn't stay to tell me where things were."

"What about potatoes in't barn? An' them carrots an' onions?"

"Carrots and onions?" Chloe said faintly.

"Aye, an' there was a rabbit in the ice house."

"Ice house?"

"Jesus God, girl, what 'ave tha' bin livin' on?"

"Cheese, and bread . . . and milk, of course."

"An' Jamie an' all?"

"He said he wasn't hungry, Mrs Jenkins and I didn't want to add to his . . . his burdens. He was so tired he slept like a log."

"Aye, well . . ." Matty wasn't sure she wanted to become acquainted with her son's sleeping arrangements but it was very plain that this lass needed a bit of help and who else was to give it to her but the woman who was to be her mother-in-law?

She began to feel more cheerful than she had for days. "Now then, let's get ourselves started. Tha's no tea, tha' say?"

"No." Chloe was devastatingly sorry.

"Well, we'll see about that. Put some water in't kettle."

"Oh, I can do that, Mrs Jenkins."

"Good, then go an' fetch some eggs an'— "

"Eggs?" Chloe looked bewildered.

"Don't tell me tha's not collected th'eggs?"

"From where?"

"Eeh lass, tha's a lot ter learn about bein' a farmer's wife."

"I know." Chloe's answer was humble, but Matty patted her hand comfortingly.

"Don't tha' fret. Now then, why don't tha' tekk that there basket an' go outside. Search about the yard an' round the places where tha've seen the 'ens scratch and look ter see if tha' can find any eggs. I'll be surprised if tha' don't. Mind you,

I don't suppose Jamie thought ter tell thi' ter feed 'em, did he? No, I thought not," as Chloe shook her head in bewilderment. "Now, I'll fetch in tha' bag. There's your 'air brush, which tha'll be glad of," eyeing the tangled mass which fell about Chloe's face and shoulders, "all tha' things, not much, lass, but enough ter tide thi' over till tha're wed. Oh, an' I found a little bag in't drawer with some money in it so tha'll be able ter mekk thissen a decent dress, fer I'll have no one in this valley say our Jamie wed a . . ."

She had been about to say "trollop" and she could see the awareness of it in Chloe's eyes and she was sorry. This girl was not the trollop they all called her. It was that lad down at Cloudberry End who had sent her running for cover with his greedy hands and lustful eyes. It was not the first time he'd gone after some girl, though usually it was a pretty maidservant or a dairymaid he'd taken a fancy to. Got a girl into trouble up Penistone way a year or two back and cost his pa a pretty penny to hush it up, the story went, and all this trouble could, in a way, be laid at his door. If he'd not done his best to seduce this lass would she have been as willing to wed Jamie who, though a decent, hardworking, attractive man, was not in the same class as she was and was illegitimate into the bargain? And happen, if there'd been no one else to take his fancy, who knows, Jamie might have settled with Katy who usually got her way. He'd have been in clover then, her Jamie, with the Andrews' endless supply of cash ready to flow into his pocket, and his infant farm. There were some bad seeds in the Andrews family, like that Paddy and now, it seemed, Chris Andrews was going the same nasty way. His brothers were as even-tempered and worthwhile as their father and young Davy was at this moment somewhere up on Ramsden Edge where Ramsden Clough plunged, cliff-like, into the turbulence of the rock-strewn water, searching frantically for his sister. Called home from the university in Edinburgh he had been, and there was young Master Richie, who was expected home in the next few weeks since the railway he was helping to build was all but finished, and how would he be affected by his sister's disappearance? Chris was galloping about here and there and every bloody where, they said, strangely excited by the drama, and glad, of course, Matty was convinced, of anything that got him out of the mill.

The horse beyond the gate was quite prepared, it seemed,

to browse on the sparse, almost colourless grass which grew there and when the sun came out the dog wandered into the bit of warmth beneath the kitchen window, happy with the feeling of calm which now flowed about his domain. Matty produced scrubbing brushes, polish and dusters from where they were kept in a tiny, hidden cupboard under the stairs and which Chloe had not even known was there.

"We'll give t'place a good bottomin', lass, then tha'll know how to go about it by thissen, then I'll show thi' where Jamie stores 'is veg an' the like an' how the ice house works. Made it 'isself, did Jamie. Oh aye, he's a clever lad is yon an' tha'll want fer nowt he can give thi'."

Having decided that she might as well accept this lass who could, for all Matty knew, already be carrying Jamie's bairn, she was bent on teaching her, in no more than a couple of hours, how to look after Matty's son in the way he deserved, and she demanded. She'd keep an eye on her, of course. Come up every day or so to make sure she was going on in the right way of things and, if there was a bairn, the lass'd need all the help Matty could give her. She was willing, give her that, setting to with the scrubbing brush as though her life depended on it and, when the place was as immaculate as Matty liked to see it, listening and watching intently as she was shown how to make a rabbit stew.

"It needs a bit of celery in it ter give it best flavour which we 'aven't got but these'll do fer now. No, don't fiddle wi' it, lass, give it a good chop across its legs," for Chloe had paled slightly, not only over the skinning and cleaning of the rabbit but the chopping of it into decent-sized pieces.

"Plenty o' carrots an' onions, that's right, an' a dash o' salt an' in the oven it goes."

She was quite flabbergasted to find that Chloe had no idea that those were ovens on either side of the fire, but then, could you blame the lass, for when had she ever had the need to know such things? She promised she'd come up tomorrow, and show her how to bake bread ... aye, that was flour in that crock, patient as patient, and then was ashamed when she realised that for the best part of two hours she hadn't given poor Katy Andrews a blessed thought and what was worse, for she loved her like a sister, Sara Andrews would be awake now and fretting for her.

It was completely dark when Jamie Hutchinson staggered

up the path towards the farmhouse door which stood half open. He had tramped thirty miles since daybreak and his mind was blank and empty of all thought but the need to lay himself down somewhere and sleep until the cock crowed. He knew she would be there, where she had been for the past three nights but somehow he couldn't seem to find the strength to care. He loved her, he knew that, deep in his bones and heart he loved her but just at this moment he had no time for her. She would be there when all this was over, he knew that, too, for she was not the kind of girl . . . woman . . . to run away, or have a paddy if she was neglected but just for now he wanted nothing but oblivion.

She was standing over a pot which she had just brought from the oven, a spoon in her hand, a delighted smile on her face. She turned as he entered. The room was lovely with firelight and candlelight and the aroma of cooking mixed with what smelled like lavender. It was clean and sparkling across every surface, even the snow white tablecloth which she had rooted out from somewhere. She was in her black gown but the top half a dozen buttons were undone to reveal the sweet cleft between her creamy breasts and their top curve almost to her nipples. She wore a snowy cloth about her waist to protect her gown and her hair had been brushed and brushed to a gleaming tawny gloss. It tumbled carelessly down her back in a curtain of living flame, caught casually with a knot of ribbons at the crown. She was flushed and bright-eyed and looked quite, quite enchanting.

"Rabbit stew," she said, smiling shyly in his direction before turning to put the dish back in the oven. "The potatoes will be ready in ten minutes if you want to have a wash."

"Bugger the wash and bugger the rabbit stew," he said.

"Your mama was here," she ventured breathlessly as he pulled her into his arms.

"Was she now?" His lips folded about hers in a way that drew the most delightful feeling to the pit of her belly. His arms held her tight against him so that even through her petticoats she could feel his need of her, knowing exactly what it was now, despite her lack of experience. He bent her back and his lips travelled down the column of her throat to her breasts and when his fingers pulled her bodice apart she made no objection.

They ate the rabbit stew later, much later, she on his knee, their naked bodies wrapped in the quilt while the dog dozed contentedly before the fire.

They were not to go out again since they had searched every square inch where she might be, quite fruitlessly, he told her quietly, holding her, guarding her, loving her while she wept for her cousin.

12

Katherine Andrews awoke from her deep and troubled sleep and for a moment or two could not recall what was troubling her, or even where she was. She felt calm. She had felt calm ever since she had slipped out of Jamie's house, climbed on to Storm's back and ridden away towards the summit of the Black Hill. As calm and frozen as an iceberg which floats imperturbably on an Arctic sea and which Jamie had once described to her. The sea is cold and the air is cold and so nothing melts it, just as nothing would ever melt Katy Andrews's heart again. She had the most curious feeling that she was not really present in her own body which had had things done to it in these last few days which she had never dreamed of. She existed in the tearless agony which had come upon her when she had seen Jamie and Chloe in one another's arms in Jamie's kitchen. Yes, agony, excruciating and yet at the same time numbing, and nothing, nothing of what was happening now touched her. She knew she must live for ever with these days, these hours, these minutes which ticked by so slowly, and yet flew backwards like birds tumbled in a windblown sky. They would be a part of her life, burned in her brain, sunk deep in her heart with the painful remains of her love for Jamie and whatever she did, whatever became of her, whatever else was forgotten as she grew old, this would be as clear in her memory as though it had just happened. Time would never dim or heal her pain. There was nothing she could do, nothing, except gather her strength to go back. She could not stay here, not in this cottage where no woman had dwelled for years and where the man who remained was content to live in the confusion her death had left.

She was naked under the sleazy sheet, the bedlinen which

a week ago would have made her shudder. Now, if she noticed it, which appeared unlikely, it made no ripple on the flat, smooth surface of her clouded mind.

She turned her head towards a window festooned with cobwebs, the small panes of glass smeared and dull. There was a jumble of objects on the windowsill, a pint pot from which he drank his ale, a sturdy boot with a sock hanging from it, a hammer, a picture of a dog and a cat in a basket, a relic from the days when Emily Andrews was alive, a small, rose-painted jug and a half-eaten sandwich on a plate. He had been munching on it as he came up the stairs last night, she remembered, but his eyes had become hot and narrowed when he saw she was awake and the bread and cheese had been unceremoniously put aside as he made himself as naked as she was.

She had not been out of this bed for . . . how long was it? . . . she didn't know, nor did she care at this precise moment. She was quiet, empty, without, for the moment, any need to make a decision. She needed this quietness, this emptiness, totally apart from those who, she supposed, loved her at Cloudberry End and who would, by now, imagine she was dead but it didn't seem to matter.

It was the dog who had found her. Strangely, she had not gone far, which was perhaps the reason none of the others had looked for her there, imagining that she would have galloped for miles before stopping. Just on the edge of Pikenose Moor which lay up beyond the back of her grandmother's cottage there was a circle of rocks, a curious outcropping of grey-pitted stones, some teetering on top of others to form an overhang. It made a shelter of sorts, a stockade in which she and Storm could hide. The beaten-down, springy peat created a soft bed on which to lie and for a long time, while Storm cropped the grass, in total silence and stillness, just as though she were dead, she lay and stared up unblinkingly into the clear sky. Grouse rose now and then, unafraid of her quiet presence, and invisible skylarks sang their hearts out as if to say though hers might be broken theirs certainly weren't.

He only found her by accident and had the dog not caught the scent of the mare and gone to investigate he would have tramped by on his way back from Crossclough to his cottage higher up the hill. He wasn't even looking for her, since he didn't know she was missing, he told her later, for when he picked her up in his strong arms and, leading her sorrel, carried her to his cottage, she was senseless and in a state which she would not have understood had he tried to explain. The mare was tied to a broken, hanging gate, then Paddy Andrews turned his attention to his cousin.

Carelessly he laid her on the littered table on which were the remains of not only his breakfast but his and his pa's supper last night. He had spent the morning seeing to the arrangements for the disposal of his pa's body, and had then gone rabbiting, and what the hell Katy Andrews was doing lolling about like a rag doll with half its stuffing missing was a bloody mystery, but as soon as he'd had a bite to eat he'd take her back to that mansion she lived in and perhaps his uncle, who, after all, was pa's brother, might be persuaded to chip in for the funeral.

She turned her head to look at him as he was shovelling a cold bacon sandwich into his mouth, and then sat up, making nothing of finding herself lying on the frowsy table, and Paddy was slightly unnerved by the fixed, unfocused depths of her transparent, golden eyes. Had she heard, he asked her, since he was a chap who liked a bit of a tongue wag while he ate, that his pa had died last night? He was not unduly concerned about it, though there was the question of this cottage which belonged to Jed Miller of High Shine Farm and was meant only for those Jed employed. George Andrews had laboured for most of his fifty-odd years for Jed Miller and Jed Miller's pa. Paddy had been born in this cottage and his ma had died here, a year or two back, did Katy know that? wondering what the bloody hell was wrong with her since she was obviously not what he would have called "right", not the Katy Andrews he knew and had fought with at his gran's cottage a month or two back. She'd not have allowed him to lay a finger on her then, let alone pick her up in his arms and cuddle her to his chest as he carried her to his house.

"D'yer want summat? A cup o' tea, 'appen?"

"That would be nice," she answered, her polite voice hoarse as though from misuse.

"Right, I'll put kettle on."

"Thank you."

"I were goin' ter clear up but then I got word me pa was dead ... well, you know 'ow it is." He shrugged his broad shoulders and smiled deprecatingly, his face not wearing its normal arrogant grin, nor his chin its usual truculent angle. He turned back to the kettle, the teapot, the tea caddy, the domesticity of his tasks seeming to soften him, though neither he nor the girl was aware of any change in him, or indeed why he should be changed at all. He had to rinse a couple of mugs out, for there was not a pot clean in the house and the milk was off but, Paddy decided, glancing at Katy, she'd not have noticed if he'd given her the contents of the chamberpot to drink.

What was up with her? he asked himself wonderingly for the umpteenth time, as he threw one long leg over the bench and sat down beside her. She was still perched on the table, her feet on the bench which he straddled. He pushed aside several plates, and the cat who had licked them clean, propping one elbow in the space he had cleared, studying the state of his visitor's dress and the windswept tumble of her hair. He knew she often roamed the moorland which surrounded her home, he'd seen her himself, even nodded to her as she passed him by when he had been tramping off with his dog to a fight in which either he, or the dog, was to take part. Dressed up to the nines she had been then, in her blue riding habit and polished boots. She'd returned his greeting in that haughty way she had, just as though Paddy Andrews was nowt a pound to her, a cowpat in which even her little mare would not be allowed to tread, but she'd lost it now, that hoity-toity "I'm better than you" look with which he was so familiar. Dragged about, she appeared to be, and for the first time he noticed she had only one shoe.

She sipped her tea in total silence, her great golden eyes staring somewhere over his shoulder to the greasy window, or sliding to the open door which led out into the cobbled yard. There were chickens strutting and pecking, several of them sidling into the kitchen and coming to roost on the top of the dresser but the constant sound of their cackling did not appear to trouble her. The dog lay on the step watching without interest, his little eyes half closed though he was alert to any danger which might threaten him or his master.

Paddy didn't know what to say and she didn't seem to care, or even notice the lack of conversation. When she had finished the tea she just sat there, incongruously, on the edge of the table, her feet together on the bench, waiting, it seemed to him, for someone to tell her what to do next. Had she had a fall from her horse, he wondered, perhaps a blow to the head which had stunned her? How could he tell without asking her and when he did she turned to stare at him as though he were talking a foreign language.

"Is summat up, Katy?" he asked her, bewildered by his own concern for her, for when had any of Jack Andrews's family ever given him the time of day, let alone their goodwill? But she was so unlike her usual self, almost like a bairn . . . well, no, not with a figure like hers, bits of which were showing through her torn, stained dress, but despite his curiosity and a strong need to know what had been done to her to get her in this state, he'd best get her home to her pa before a hue and cry was sparked off. It was already beginning to dim into the dusky, end of summer evening which fell at this time of the year and the track down to Woodhead was steep and tricky.

She had not answered his question, nor even turned to look at him when he spoke.

"Well," he said at last, his eyes moving across her face. He rubbed the stubble on his chin and gave her a sort of half smile as though to encourage her, to let her see he meant her no harm. That despite his reputation with women he had never yet damaged one, nor forced one against her will. He liked a joke. He liked to tease and frighten them a little, those he sometimes came across walking a quiet lane alone but Paddy Andrews had no need to force a lass. No need at all. There was a certain dairymaid on a farm near Woodhead who regularly and willingly dropped her drawers and spread her legs for him, so he didn't go short and he'd never paid for it in his life, never.

He sighed in some irritation, pushing a none too clean hand through the rough thatch of his short, curly hair. He wished to God the damned dog had not found her, and wondered why, when he did, he hadn't taken her straight down to her folks instead of fetching her all the way up here. Why had he even bothered to pick her up, for she'd no doubt have got up on her horse and gone home herself when she was ready? She was nowt to do with him. He'd enough to see to with his pa dying like that and the question of cash, or his lack of it. He'd been working as a labourer in the local quarry ever since Chris Andrews had got him the push from the paper mill, soft prick, and one day he'd get even with him, choose how, but in the meanwhile, with fights a bit few and far between, he was short of ready cash. Surely, if he took Katy home his uncle'd be so bloody relieved he'd not refuse his help with the laying to rest of his own brother? It was a worrying time, for this cottage would not be his for long, neither, for it would be given to the next labourer Jed Miller employed. Paddy thought he might sling his hook and find something for himself elsewhere. Perhaps America, if he could get together the fare, where their Lester and Walter and Arthur had gone years ago. He was strong, afraid of nothing and no one and the thought of carving out a new life for himself in the wilderness which he'd heard of out there appealed to the adventurer in him. He couldn't settle to anything here, and now seemed as good a time as any to leave.

He stood up. "Right then, we'd best get tha' home ter tha' pa, hadn't we?" he said, his voice almost soft, him, Paddy Andrews who had never in his life had the grace to see any woman home but then he was short of a bob or two and Uncle Jack would be very grateful to have his lass home safe and sound.

He was seriously alarmed, as was his dog which leaped to his feet when Katy began to rant and rave like a woman gone off her head.

"No . . . no . . . I won't go," she screamed, rocking backwards and forwards on the table, tearing at her own hair and face. Her mouth was wide and so were her eyes, as though she stared at some horror which was not vouchsafed to him. She swung about as though searching for some means to escape it, he thought, whatever it was, and as much to protect her from her own savagery as anything else, he sprang towards her and pulled her to him.

"Christ, Katy . . ." He was appalled, for the first time in his life totally at a loss as to how to handle a woman. He shoved the bench back and stood before her while her fists beat against him, but by now her cries were muffled in the open neck of his shirt though her words were still audible.

"I can't . . . I can't go home . . . not yet . . . oh please, don't make me . . . let me stay here."

"Bloody 'ell, lass, tha' can't stay 'ere."

"Why not? Why should you care? You've no time for us so why should it worry you what happens to me or my family?" Her voice was rough and gasping. Her arms went round his back and her hands clung to the thick fabric of his shirt as though she were resolutely determined not to be prised loose from him.

It was true. He'd despised them all, particularly that high, mucky-muck wife of his uncle's who, like her daughter, had looked at him as though he were no more than his own dog when they passed him in the lane. This girl's brothers with their grand horses and expensive boots and whose expressions of disdain, whose eagerness not to be associated with him were as plain as the nose on his face. Jack Andrews had made a lot of money and for reasons best known to himself had come back here to lord it over his own brothers, over his nieces and nephews and it had been a festering sore beneath the skin of Paddy Andrews ever since he had been old enough to understand. Stuck-up buggers, the lot of them and his greatest wish was that one of them would pick a fight with him so that he could knock the living daylights out of him. He'd almost had that bloody little sod, Chris Andrews, a month or two back but old Jack, who at least had guts, had come out and chased his son off in a funk.

Katy shook so much the table on which she was still perched trembled and all the crockery jumped and dithered. The dog growled warningly, not sure what at but ready to show his willingness to fight it, whatever it might be, and Paddy, in a state totally unlike his usual cocksure, defiant self, held her steady against him, his handsome face creased with an expression no one who knew him would have recognised.

"I won't go, Paddy." At least she knew who he was. "If you turn me out I'll simply run away again and they'll never find me."

"What were tha' runnin' away from?"

"Never mind that. Just let me stay with you."

"Lass, don't be daft . . ." but he was beginning to weaken since, from some deep, primeval part of him, some fundamental source which is buried in all men, it began to occur to him that here was a perfect way to assuage his desire for revenge on Jack Andrews and his family who had always been, in their eyes, so far above the rest of them. They'd done nothing to him, or his, he knew that, it was simply that their sneering attitude, which said that Paddy Andrews was not fit to lick their very boots, needed to be shown that he could do far more than that. And here, to hand, was the girl who would help him to it.

"Please, Paddy, let me . . . let me stay until . . ."

Until I feel better, she wanted to say, which was ridiculous for when would that ever be, but just a few days. No, she did not care that they would be out of their minds, her mother and her father. They shouldn't have tried to prevent her from . . . keep her from . . . from Jamie. Aah, God . . . God, she could not stand it. She must surely die from the wounds which had been inflicted on her . . . but a few days on her own . . . it would give her time to begin the building of the shell inside beyond which no one could reach, beyond which no one could touch, hear her cries of grief, see her suffering. They would be looking for her, even Jamie, she knew that, but let them hurt a little, or even a lot, for whatever it was they were suffering it would not be a fraction of her own.

She became aware of the change in the man who was standing between her legs. He had begun to breathe heavily and his hands had moved to her ankles. He removed her shoe and began to smooth the arch of her feet, then, his face closing in on hers but not yet touching it, his hands moved slowly up her legs beneath her petticoats. They reached her knees, stroking behind them, pushing her legs further apart, slipping beneath the ribbons at the bottom of her drawers, finding their way to the soft flesh between her thighs. With one enquiring finger he pushed his way through the thick mat of her pubic hair and moved very slowly into the warm, moist crevice at the junction of her thighs, stroking gently, experimentally, as though waiting to see if she had any objection. When she made none, he smiled.

"Good lass. Now, I'll just go an' 'ide the mare in the out-house," he murmured, his warm, heavy-lidded eyes running over her. "Don't move."

"No, I won't," she said obediently.

He returned quickly, moving to stand in the position he had left a moment ago. He put a hand to her cheek, cupping it without force, then letting it slide to her chin. She looked up at him, not afraid, for what would Katy Andrews ever fear again, her eyes deep and fathomless, great golden pools in which there was no life. She blinked as his mouth came down on hers. He was still holding her chin with one hand and as she sat in blank acceptance his other hand went to the back of her head beneath her hair as though to prevent her escaping.

She felt nothing, no surprise, no offence, even at his first intimacy, no warmth, no fear or distaste. She merely let him kiss her. Let his eager hands begin again their exploration of her body. What did it matter? If this was what he wanted and was the price for a few days of respite for Katy Andrews, could it concern her who, having offered her body to one man who had refused, must give it to another. Why not Paddy? One man was as good as another if his name was not Jamie Hutchinson and it was nothing to her. She was numb, cold, so perhaps Paddy's big warm body would help to bring her back to some sense of who she was. Not yet, of course, since she didn't want to be troubled with who she was. Not yet, but soon, when she was ready to leave. What did it matter?

He lifted her skirt and removed her drawers, bending her legs apart so that he could "have a good look at her" he said hoarsely. He seemed to find a great deal to interest him in that warm, secret part of her body which no one had ever seen, she supposed since she was a babe in arms. He parted it and even put his mouth to it, groaning in the most peculiar way while she sat obediently and stared out of the window at the moors where once she had been so happy.

He told her to remove her clothes then, one by one and slowly, and she complied obligingly, sitting on the littered table, her back straight, her breasts full and jutting. He was like a boy with a new toy, one which is his alone to play with, gloating, his hands and mouth roaming over her and into her before removing his own garments and coming to stand again between her legs. The rod which stood out from him was quite enormous but he tucked it up flat against his stomach between them, not yet ready, he gasped, to do what the stallion at Johnny Ashwell's place did to the mare. What did it matter?

He stood back from her for a moment, trembling as though he were ill, groaning deeply in his strong chest. He lifted her from the table, turning her about, bending her over it so that her breasts were flattened in a plate which had once held a joint of bacon. His hands were everywhere, smoothing the curve of her buttocks, lingering in the crease between, probing the centre of her. What did it matter?

"Jesus God, but tha're beautiful, Katy Andrews," he grunted huskily, "and tha're bloody mine. Tha're mine, dost tha' hear me? That bloody pa o' thine and the prick who's tha' brother . . . By God, if they could see thi' now, wi' me, Paddy Andrews who's scum of the earth ter them. But I'll tell thi' this, my lass, tha'll not forget what I'll do ter thi' in the next few days an' no man'll suit yer after that. Only me, I promise thi'. Now, I'm tekken thi' ter bed an' yer ter stay there, d'yer hear me? Wherever I go I'd like ter think of yer there, waitin' on me. On me, Paddy Andrews, waitin' in my bed whenever I want thi'. God Almighty, it'll 'ave ter be now cos I can't wait ter get yer up them stairs."

Sweeping the table clear with one mighty crash which made the dog leap towards the yard with a howl, and scattered the hens into a flapping frenzy, he laid her on it, her long and lovely back squashed against the litter of George and Paddy's last meal, opened wide her legs, put her heels on the edge of the table and tore through her virginity until her thighs were red with her own blood.

She did not cry out. What did it matter?

That had been several days ago, she supposed vaguely. How could she tell in this dream world, this nightmare world in which nothing existed but Paddy Andrews's powerful body and what it did several times a day to hers. He couldn't get enough of it, he said. He'd always had a fancy for one of them there slave girls he'd heard tell of, he said, and if she got out of his bed, even when he was forced to leave the cottage for an hour or two, he'd beat her until she was black and blue.

He fed her on something or other, mostly eggs and milk and cheese, introduced her to a chamberpot which she supposed he emptied. She slept like the dead in his arms at night, for which she was eternally grateful and when he wasn't making love to her, if what he did could be called that, or studying her in the poses he put her in, or instructing her in what she was to do to him, she dozed in the bed, the minutes and hours and days running in to one another in one long, timeless blur.

"How long has it been, Paddy?" she asked him that night. He had been to his pa's funeral, he had told her, which her pa and her brothers had attended but he did not divulge to her the quite dreadful appearance of all three. It was just a week since Katy Andrews had ridden off, never to be seen again, it seemed, and hope had long since gone that she might have survived, though there were still a few men paid by Jack Andrews who were to keep on tramping the hills and moors for some trace of his lost daughter.

They were all in black at Cloudberry End, it was reported and Sara Andrews had gone into such a decline it was only the constant presence of her husband prevented her from slipping completely away; but her eldest son was to be home in a day or two so that should perhaps take her mind off her loss, they were saying.

They'd not found her. They had been all about Paddy's own cottage only yesterday, wanting to poke into his outhouse and chicken house but he'd told them to bugger off, threatening them with murder if they didn't, doing his best not to smile at the thought of the girl they sought, naked and waiting in his bed only a few yards from where they argued.

She was sitting up in the bed, the sheets about her waist, her glorious breasts, on which there were several bites and bruises, flaunting, golden, rose-tipped in the candlelight. He had roasted a chicken which he had stolen from Jed Miller's chicken run on the way back from the funeral at Woodhead Chapel. He had chickens of his own, of course, but why use up your own provisions when you can "borrow" from someone else, he laughed. She had a drumstick in her hand and she bit into it with evident relish. Her white teeth sank into the flesh as they had at times sunk into his own and he felt the urgent, explosive desire for her flood the pit of his belly. Sweet Christ, but she was superb, his Katy, for she belonged to him now, the most superb woman he had ever had in his bed, or ever would, come to think of it. She was all he had ever wanted in a woman and now, she was his. He knew that, even if she didn't and though he wasn't sure how he would manage it, he intended that she would remain his until one of them died.

Tearing off his clothes, he threw back the tangled, greasy sheets, his eyes hot with passion on her long, stretching body but in them was also a strange expression which might have been tenderness, a soft look of something she did not see and he was not aware was there.

"Aah, lass . . . my lass," he whispered. His hands reached to smooth and fondle her, his fingers and mouth insistent, his tongue, his breath touching every full curve and exploring every cleft of her, fierce and possessive, and within her she felt something unfurl itself, like a bud in spring ready to burst into flower.

"Katy . . . Katy, tha're the most beautiful thing I've ever known," he murmured, out of his mind with some emotion he did not recognise, his body moving over hers. She arched her back, surprising them both, for though she had never resisted him her part in their coupling had always been passive. No matter what he did to her, sometimes rough and animal-like, she had made no demur, allowing him the most extreme and even painful familiarities.

Her hips rose eagerly to his and when he entered her he felt her muscles grip him fiercely, spasming about his thrusting manhood, gripping him in what seemed to be a reluctance against his withdrawal.

"No," she moaned, "no . . . I'm not . . . not ready . . ." then with an explosion which they both felt, the bud opened. It flowed and rippled and shimmered inside her, moving from the centre of her where she and Paddy were joined, to every tingling nerve and pulse in her body.

She cried out then in her first climax, clinging to him as though should she let go she might be flung into infinity for ever.

He smiled afterwards, holding her in his arms, well pleased with himself, for he knew what had happened to her and it would help to bind her to him more closely. A woman will follow anywhere a man who loves her well. Who gives her body what it needs. She was of the earth, as he was; the last few days had proved that, not like those high-nosed, gently reared ladies who, so he had heard, found their man's attentions distasteful and to be put up with only when they could not avoid it.

"Tha're truly mine now, lass," he murmured into her hair and for some reason she was sorry.

When he awoke she was gone.

Jimmy and Dicken and Noah froze into paralysed, slack-jawed silence, all three turning a sickly grey-white as she rode slowly into the yard and, throwing her leg over the mare's neck, slid to the ground. She wore only one shoe. Apart from that and the muck which coated her, she looked just the same, just as she had done when she high-tailed it out of here a week ago like a wild thing on its way to hell, except that she was quiet now, thinner in the face, her eyes cool where they had flashed with madness.

"Dear God . . . Dear God, Miss Katy," Jimmy stammered, the comb with which he was currying Master Davy's chestnut falling with a clatter to the cobbles. The horse shied, startled, and Jimmy was dragged a foot or so as he tried to calm it. Noah, who was an old man and who had been the first to put this lass up on a horse when she was no more than a tiddler, began to sniffle, bringing out a big white square of linen from his pocket into which he trumpeted, and Dicken could do nothing but stand and stare before a grin as wide as the stable door split his young face. A bugger she had always been but he was right glad to see her back just the same.

"Mrs Tiplady . . . Mrs Tiplady," he bellowed as he ran towards the back door of the kitchen, sent by Jimmy to warn them, for the mistress was very frail and a shock like this . . . well, who knew what a gently bred lady like herself might do?

"What, for heaven's sake?" Mrs Tiplady did a bit of bellowing herself as Dicken flung open the door, for she'd have none of the stable yard muck in her kitchen.

"'Tis 'er, Mrs Tiplady . . . 'tis herself tell the master. Look," turning to sweep his arm in a theatrical manner, somewhat like a magician producing a rabbit from a hat, towards the gate where Jimmy and Noah were slowly escorting Miss Katy, one on either side of her, longing to hold her up, to carry her if needs be, in her triumphal, heartfelt homecoming. She walked steadily enough without their help, not smiling nor showing much of anything in her face, though her eyes were glad to see them, they said.

The state of her was appalling, Mrs Tiplady had time to notice before the maids began to scream their joy, throwing their aprons over their heads and, from the corner of the chimney, a small brown bundle of rough fur flung herself rapturously against Miss Katy's skirt, leaping up in great bounds until Miss Katy caught her in her arms and held her, wriggling and licking her dirty face ecstatically. The blasted animal had never been out of the kitchen except on matters of duty since Miss Katy left, hanging about, first at one door, then the other as though, when Miss Katy returned she would be at the right one to greet her. Fretted she had, poor little thing, gone to skin and bone and now would you look at her. At least she brought a smile to Miss Katy's haggard face.

"Miss Katy," she breathed, sitting down hastily in her chair before the fire. "Lord save us and may we be truly thankful for His blessings. Oh child . . . child . . . Quick, Freda, run for the master."

"Oh, miss, we thought you was dead."

"We've bin asearchin' and asearchin' for yer." This from Dilly who gave the tearful impression she herself had been out with the men.

"See, sit thi' down, lass and . . ."

". . . a week an' we'd give up 'ope, 'adn't we, Ivy?"

"Where've tha' bin, child?"

And in the doorway the three grooms hung, elbowing one another aside for a better look, their weatherbeaten faces split into grins of huge delight.

"I must go through, Mrs Tiplady. My mother and father will . . ."

"Eeh, o' course, lass, get thi' gone. They're in't drawin' room."

Mrs Tiplady was so overcome with emotion she broke out into the thick, long-drawn-out vowels of her northern heritage, that which she had managed to eradicate from her speech for years now.

They all wept over her, her father, her mother, even her two brothers, though she herself shed not a tear. Dry-eyed, she stood first in one embrace and then another, saying nothing except, yes, she would like a bath and a change of clothing, and no, she was not harmed and they had no need to worry over her.

"Worry over you, lass. Worry over you! We thought you were dead . . . in the bog . . ." Weary tears slid down her father's face, her strong, unbowed father who, as far as she knew, had never wept in his life.

"Darling . . . darling, we thought we had lost you," her mother cried, her frail body shaking in her daughter's arms which were so much stronger than hers.

"God, you're a bloody nuisance, Katy Andrews, but bloody hell, it's good to have you home," Chris whispered, his keen male eye wondering what it was that had changed his spoilt brat of a sister into this quiet-eyed but strangely exotic young woman. He recognised it, that look of maturity, that look of . . . Jesus, what was it? He had seen it on many women's faces, young as he was, but it made no sense in connection with his sixteen-year-old sister.

"Where have you been? Christ, we've been out of our

minds," Davy said, hugging her swiftly and thanking God, she was well aware, that he could now get back to his studies.

She wouldn't tell them. Her father thundered, her mother wept quite frantically, her brothers threatened, since they were well aware that she had been sheltered somewhere. She could not have survived out in the open, dressed as she was, with nothing to eat but bilberries so where and with whom had she been?

She wouldn't tell them.

It was no concern of theirs.

13

Chloe Eleanor Taylor and James Paul Hutchinson were married in a quiet ceremony at Woodhead Chapel on Chloe's nineteenth birthday, the only persons present beyond the parson and his wife, Jamie's mother, his stepfather, his half-brother Tommy and his half-sister Dulcie, who would not have missed the occasion for the world, she told her mother.

The Andrews family, even if they had been invited which they were not, would have declined, since Katy's disappearance for a whole week was still far too fresh in their minds. Of course Jack Andrews had not made good his promise to evict Matty's son from the farm he rented, but there was still that feeling that none of what had happened would have happened but for him and Sara Andrews's flighty niece.

The quiet service, the unhurried and peaceful tranquillity of the old church which had stood since it was founded in 1487 as a "Chapel of Ease" for outlying parishioners, the absence of prurient spectators gave their wedding day a dignified joy which pleased both the bride and groom. They had told no one of the date they were to be married except Jamie's small family, and as they came out from the plain, foursquare little chapel the autumn sunshine laid its golden rays about them in what seemed a blessing, a delightful omen which augured well for the days and years ahead.

Chloe wore a gown of rich cream muslin over silk. A collar of frothy ruffles stood up at the back of her neck under the fall of her loosely fastened gold and copper curls. The neckline was square cut just above the tops of her creamy white breasts. The bodice fitted her like a second skin, the ruffled sleeves ending just above her elbows and the skirt was a full waterfall of gathered flounces, each one edged with cream satin and scattered with cream rosebuds, gathered up at the back in a small bustle. She wore a "Dolly Varden" hat tipped slightly over her forehead, the front of the brim turned down, the back turned up. It was decorated with cream satin ribbons and roses to match her gown. She held a single cream rosebud in her hand, begged by Thomas, who had been told of the colours she was to wear, from Angus the gardener.

Her delicate beauty – thank the dear Lord her face was healed – was startling, not quite of this world, her mother-in-law decided. Totally unsuited for a farmer's wife with her dashing hat, her lovely dress which she had made herself, the pale cream of her kid boots which peeped from beneath her skirt. Jamie had had to carry her across the yard to the gig Thomas had borrowed from the Andrews' stable, so as not to spoil the hem of her dress and her dainty boots, but could you help but be struck dumb with awed admiration for her? Matty couldn't. She'd grown fond of her during the past month, for no matter what Chloe was asked to do, no matter how hard the task, by God she had a go at it and every surface of the little farmhouse shone like the newly burnished copper pans which winked on the mantelshelf. You couldn't help but take to her. A little bit of a thing doing her best to hump great buckets of water from the pump in the yard, the skirt of her black dress which she wore to work in tucked up in her waistband. Her hair tied up in a bright froth of coloured ribbons, her boots caked with cow muck, she'd even had a go at milking the cows, squealing with delight when she had squirted her first milky stream into the bucket.

Jamie worshipped her. His eyes were a narrowed, vivid blue, blazing with a love for his wife you'd have to be blind to miss. A bit embarrassing really, his mother was tempted to think, for it was very evident what he had planned for her when he'd got rid of his guests. And it was not as though he was the usual bridegroom who, having been held at straining point for months, years sometimes, was at last to get his hands on what he'd ached for. That big bed of theirs, which Matty had helped to change only this morning before the gig had brought them down here, had been most thoroughly used ever since Chloe had been brought to Valley Bottom Farm, for it seemed they cared nought for Crossclough's opinion on the sinfulness of their situation.

Of course, Katy Andrews had diverted a lot of the talk away from Matty's son and his intended bride, and they *were* to be married, Matty made sure everyone knew, those in the kitchen included, for she'd have no talk in front of her about loose morals and such like. It had been hard not to disclose the date of the wedding, which would have made her feel better, but Jamie and Chloe had been adamant that they wanted no curious spectators.

Now her joy was unbounded as she watched her son and her new daughter-in-law move in what might have been described as a "languorous" fashion – had she known the word, which she didn't – down the short, steep path to the chapel gate. They held hands and looked fondly into one another's eyes and Matty took her Thomas's arm, turning to smile at Tommy who looked most uncomfortable and not at all himself in his new black suit. A big lad was Tommy, like Jamie, and she hoped to God he didn't grow any bigger, for the suit had cost a pretty penny and would be hard to replace. He was like Jamie in looks, was Tommy, both of them taking after her, she thought complacently, dark-haired and blue-eyed and with any luck, though she was narrow-hipped and as insubstantial as the daisies growing in the grass between the graves, James's Chloe might put a blue-eyed baby in Matty's arms by this time next year, or even sooner!

They hadn't a lot to say but they were all smiling broadly except for Tommy who couldn't wait to get his bloody collar off. Thomas was smart in his one good suit, Matty quietly elegant in a blue silk gown she had made herself, for Matty had been a seamstress in her younger days, and a good one, like Sara Andrews. Her blue hat, decorated with a racy-looking stuffed bird, was stylish and she was proud of her family, of her new daughter-in-law who was "respectable" now and of her eldest son who, for the first time in his twenty-five years, wore a dark grey suit with a light grey waistcoat and could be mistaken for gentry any day of the week.

"Right, lad," she said cheerfully to her husband. "Let's be off ter cut t'wedding cake, an' give over kissin' tha' wife, Jamie Hutchinson. Tha'll have plenty o' time fer that later," glorying in the fact that she could make a joke of it now since Jamie and Chloe were decently wed.

*   *   *

The girl who crouched behind the stone wall at the side of the chapel waited until the gig was out of sight then straightened up stiffly, just as though she were as old as her own grandmother. Her face was bleak. Her eyes were brown and dull like the soil on a newly dug grave in the cemetery about the chapel, staring at nothing in particular, empty of any expression. Her wide, full-lipped mouth, the colour of the red berries in the hedge, was compressed into a thin white line but she made no sound as she made her way slowly up to the back of the chapel where her mare, her reins fastened to a cam stone at the top of the drystone wall, cropped peacefully.

By the simple expedient of keeping her eye, not on Jamie or the girl he was to marry, but Matty; on Thomas and his comings and goings and the sudden use of the gig this morning, she had ascertained when the wedding ceremony was to be. She was the only one who knew.

Katy Andrews wore breeches of doeskin, well cut, in a shade of creamy beige, made for her by her mother's dressmaker who had at first refused flatly to be associated with such a disgraceful, indecent item of clothing.

"Very well, I shall take my custom elsewhere," Miss Andrews said coldly, picking up her reticule and turning towards the shop door. "There are other dressmakers besides yourself, Miss Mason," which was true and, seeing a great deal of business leaving her establishment, for Mrs Andrews, who no longer made her own clothes, was a wealthy client, Miss Mason hesitated.

"Can you not make such a garment?" Miss Andrews wanted to know. She was alone. She had come in her father's carriage, driven by her father's coachman. She was beautifully dressed in a gown of white muslin, her sash a lavender blue to match the ribbons on her small hat. Just as a girl of her age should be.

"Naturally I can, Miss Andrews, for have I not made the breeches you wear with your riding habit? I can make any garment I set my mind to but I'm sure your mama . . ."

"My mother is not well, Miss Mason, otherwise she would be here beside me."

"I'm sorry to hear that, my dear, but really, would it not be . . .?"

"Can you do this, Miss Mason?" Katy Andrews continued doggedly. "And will you do it?"

Miss Andrews was perfectly polite, calm and more dignified than Miss Mason had ever seen her, but there was a certain look about her, in her brooding eyes, in her unruffled belief that she would get what she wanted which made Miss Mason uneasy.

Resigned, Miss Mason gave in. She had heard, as who had not in Crossclough, of the worrying state of Mrs Andrews's health and if Miss Andrews were to be allowed to wear such a garment, as it seemed she was, who was Miss Mason to argue? She measured her customer, not only for one pair of breeches but two, several jackets of various materials and colours, an enveloping waterproof cloak lined with a sturdy woollen material which Miss Andrews explained must be full enough to be spread back over her mare's rump, and half a dozen pairs of riding gloves.

Miss Mason watched from her window as her client walked calmly across the road to Mr Wilson's, the hatter, where, she heard later, she ordered a man's tall riding hat, and from there to Mr Potter who made riding boots for gentlemen.

Miss Mason shook her head. What was the world coming to, she asked her young apprentice to tell her, but the girl had no answer.

Katy sprang lightly on to Storm's back, unhindered by the full length of the riding habit she had once worn. They made no attempt to force her now, her mother and her father; to stop her going where she pleased since she went anyway. Her father might have made more fuss, created the dreadful arguments which upset her mother so, but the very fact that they did kept him tight-lipped and grey-faced with the growing realisation that his daughter, his Katy, was gone for ever. Ever since she had returned from the dead, so to speak, she had, without fuss, or any of the shenanigans she had once got up to, gone wherever she pleased and there was a rumour rippling about the valley which made her smile, since it said she had been seen with a man up on the high moorland of the Dark Peak.

It was hard going up through the stand of trees which lay at the back of Woodhead Chapel, oak and birch and rowan, acorns lying thickly on the spongy ground, last year's growth of leaves forming a carpet which deadened the sound of her mare's hooves. The downy birch trees, which were the only species to survive in the cold uplands of the north, their leaves turning a bright yellow and ready to fall, showed their gleaming trunks, a pale white in the soft shafts of sunshine and russet bracken crowded about their roots. Rowan, its handsome trunk covered with smooth, slate grey bark, its foliage providing a glorious display of bright, shiny fruits ranging in colour from orange to vivid scarlet. It would be short-lived, this splendour, for already the woodland birds were stripping the trees bare.

She came out from beneath the trees on to the tussocky moorland, allowing Storm her head, galloping flat out, her hair, which she no longer bothered to cut or fasten back and which had grown quickly, streaming out in a molten copper flag behind her. The wind plastered her silk shirt to her full, round breasts and it was very evident that she wore nothing under it. Her face, despite the force and drive of her gallop, was white and strained, her eyes glazed, anguished.

The sky was shining and translucent, like silvered mother-of-pearl with barely a hint of blue in it but she did not see the beauty around her, nor above her. Her expression was haunted and she gave the appearance of being in a kind of dreadful limbo in which nothing was real or relevant. She was sunk in her own agonising, dry-eyed grief, washed up alone on some deserted shore where her inner self had nothing to do with her body which continued to function as those about her expected her to function. The armour of numbness, which had formed about her in Jamie Hutchinson's kitchen and which had shielded her to a degree, had begun to develop chinks in it which would soon become great gaps and eventually fall away altogether and Katy knew she would be raw and vulnerable. Her face felt cold, clamped tight with the pain which devoured her, a pain so deep it seemed to come from somewhere inside her she had not known existed.

Despair, that worst of all emotions, tore at her, for at last she truly knew she had lost him. He was married, husband to Chloe, lost to her for ever and somehow she must find a way to go, something to fill her days, and nights, a purpose in life which would exhaust her so that she might sleep.

Jamie. His name slashed across her heart like a saw-edged blade and she doubled up in agony, her face pressed to Storm's wind-tossed mane. The piercing sorrow hollowed out a space inside her that only Jamie could fill and at last, with her hair falling to mingle with the mare's mane, she wept. Not a cascade of tormented weeping but silent tears which slipped from beneath her closed eyelids and fell in slow desolation to Storm's neck.

The wind whined over the moors but she dawdled about the tops for several hours, stopping now and then to alight and lean against her mare's strong back and stare down across the rolling uplands of the valley far below. The hills went on and on into the distance, rising up in dark-shaded, gold-shaded, blue-shaded grandeur. There were deep grey cloughs littered with stones and, winding like a thread of silver ribbon, Great Crowden Brook which emptied just by her grandmother's cottage into Woodhead Reservoir.

She rode again, stopped to rest again, her back against a sun-warmed rock as big and as square as the stable block at Cloudberry End and all about her great chunks of stone rambled down the slope, cracked and broken as though a giant hammer had shattered them and a giant hand flung them away.

She was just inside the encircling woodland which surrounded her father's property when he sprang out at her from behind the broad, gnarled trunk of a vast oak tree. His arms went round her waist, dragging her from the saddle but her feet were still in the stirrups and for a moment, as her legs twisted agonisingly, they were both carried along by the terrified mare.

"You bloody fool," she snarled in his ear. "You'll injure her," but already her teeth were beginning to nip at his flesh and her tongue to lap about his chin like a kitten at a bowl of cream.

He brought them to a halt just before the wood ended and the smooth lawns and ornamental gardens of Cloudberry End began. The mare tried to escape him, rolling her eyes, ready to snap at his hand for she was afraid of him, as most animals were, but he hauled her back deeper into the wood and tied her to a sapling.

Paddy Andrews turned to Katy, his eyes burning pits of brown coal in his strong, sunburned face. He had not shaved for days nor had he bathed and the smell of his male sweat was acrid in the leaf-scented, fern-scented fragrance beneath the trees, the familar scent of him already uncoiling that sensitive bud deep in her belly which she had come to know so well in the past weeks.

He swayed towards her and she began to smile, for by God this was what she needed to block out the sight of her cousin Chloe in her wedding dress and the look in Jamie's eyes as he brought his bride out of the chapel on his arm.

They came together with an impact which jarred the breath from their lungs, tearing at one another, their mouths opened wide as they bit and snapped and sucked and licked, their snarling breath growing hoarse with desire. Frantically they threw off their clothing though her bloody breeches were not as easy to remove as her skirt and drawers had been, he growled at her.

They smiled as they circled one another like two prize fighters, both totally naked, both strangely beautiful in their fierce lust. They had shared many hours together since the days he had turned her into a woman, up on the moorland, lying on the springing turf among the rocks, their bodies turning to lustrous shades of burned honey and polished amber in the hot sunshine which had bathed the Dark Peak throughout the month of September. He had loved her until she purred like a cat, hurt her until she screamed for mercy, then loved her again until she slept in his arms. On waking, bruised and sore, he would take her again and it was as he had said it would be. She could not get enough of him, nor he of her. He put his mark on her, though she would have denied it, as though he branded her with a hot iron and the clamour they made silenced the small moorland animals and flushed out the larks which rose crazily into the sun. He caressed her body until, her hips and buttocks rolling boisterously, she laid herself along his hard body and impaled herself on his jutting manhood. When it was done, not satisfied, she explored him from the curling, tumbled hair on his head to the soles of his none-too-clean feet with her fingers and her mouth until he groaned in agony, her breasts, golden and tipped with rose, big and full and exuberant, poised above his face until her nipples slid into his mouth and this time it was his turn to dominate her, flipping her over on to her back, the full weight of his muscular body pressing hers down into the soft grass. He took her every day and longed for her every night, careless who knew it, for she was his.

They were quiet at last. It was the first time they had lain together so close to her home and it was in his heart to wish that her father or her poor sap of a brother would come across them, sprawled naked together on the sorrel-carpeted woodland of Cloudberry End. They'd have to accept him then. Accept him as a husband for Katy Andrews, for what man would want damaged goods when it came out she'd been had by Paddy Andrews? He'd like that. It'd suit him down to the ground to have not only Katy Andrews in his bed but Jack Andrews's cash in his pocket. A decent job at the paper mill, not too exacting, for he fancied the life of a bloody gentleman and by Jesus, he'd put that little pipsqueak's nose out of joint, see if he didn't.

He had hoped, in the last few weeks, that she'd tell him she was pregnant, for with what joy would he have greeted such news. He had to smile when he thought about it, for in the five years or so since he had taken his first woman he'd done his best to avoid the very situation he now hoped for. It was what all men dreaded, the accusation that they were the father of what was in a woman's womb, but by Christ he wished he could claim that predicament with Katy Andrews.

"I'll have to go." Her eyes were a deep, glowing golden brown surrounded by the faint smudges he recognised were the result of her utter satiation. Her face was flushed and there was still a patina of sweat between her breasts and on the inside of her thighs. He began to lick it with a greedy tongue but she pushed him away and he knew it was all over. She had had what she wanted from him and the familiar feeling of frustrated fury ran through his veins. He did his best to be patient. He had never been patient in his life but then he had never loved a woman in his life and if he was to have this one, who had become his life, then he must show restraint. At the moment she was mad for him, as he had told her she would be on that first night, but she still did not consider him as anything but a lover. A plaything, an interlude to relieve her boredom and fulfil her newly awakened needs in much the same way men looked on a mistress. Until he had her in the palm of his hand, eating out of the palm of his hand, pregnant, then he must not try to rope her or she would simply turn her back on him.

It was hard but he managed a grin, a grin of great wickedness and she began to smile as she pulled her breeches over her hips. She wore nothing beneath them. She sort of wriggled and twisted and slithered into them, her breasts bouncing, her waist and belly sinuous and fluid and for a moment he was diverted.

Hurriedly he reached for his own trousers, holding them in front of him before she noticed his renewed interest.

"What?" she asked him. "What mischief have you got planned? You're up to something I can tell, so you'd better spit it out."

"I'm fightin' ternight."

She stopped fiddling with the buttons of her breeches and her eyes widened. He was fascinated to see that, for some reason, her nipples had hardened, standing out from the dark circles which surrounded them. She was excited, he suddenly realised and at once his hands reached out to hold them. She did not stop him.

"Fighting?" she murmured, her breath beginning to quicken again.

"Aye, would tha' like ter come an' see me fight, Katy Andrews?"

"Yes . . . oh yes," making no resistance when he began to pull her breeches down about her thighs.

She slammed through the back door and, about the kitchen as it always did, everything came to a halt, just as it had done in the stable yard where the men's eyes didn't know where to look. Dilly's hands froze in the water in which she was peeling carrots and her eyes swivelled wildly in her head. Her mouth dropped open and she almost fell off the box which elevated her to the right height for the scullery sink. They'd seen her before, naturally, in this "get-up" but it took some getting used to. No wonder her poor ma was not in good health.

Ivy carefully replaced the fine bone china milk jug on the tray which she had been about to take through to Mrs Andrews, afraid she might drop it in her spellbound contemplation of Miss Katy's rolling behind and Janet, who was diligently following Mrs Tiplady's instructions on the making of light, fruity scones, dropped the baking spoon on to the clean floor where Muffy leaped upon it in great glee.

It had been noticed and remarked upon that Miss Katy no longer took her little dog with her on her daily outings to only God alone knew where. They didn't know why, for the animal had gone everywhere with her at one time. Another mystery to add to the one which none of them could solve and all, probably, to do with the week she had spent, again they didn't know where, when she had gone missing.

"No, naughty girl," Katy told the dog, scooping her up into her arms and kissing her. She handed the spoon to Janet with an apologetic shrug, then, "I think I might have something to eat, Mrs Tiplady. I'm famished." She threw herself down in the chair Mrs Tiplady had just vacated, the dog in her lap and waited with absolute certainty that she would be fed.

"Will you not go through to the drawing room, Miss Katy?" Mrs Tiplady wheedled. "The mistress is about to take afternoon tea and I could bring some extra . . ."

"No thanks, here will do, Tippy," calling the cook by the name she and her brothers had used as children. "I can't be bothered to change and Mother will only go on about my breeches."

And could you wonder, Mrs Tiplady's expression suggested as Miss Katy placed her right ankle across her left knee, as her brothers did, and waited.

"Those scones smell good, Janet. I love them hot," she went on. "Lots of butter, please and a cup of tea. I've no idea what's made me so hungry," and neither had they and they had never seen her look so well. She was flushed and shining, like a rosy apple, her skin right down to the opening of her shirt a soft, honey brown, as were her bare forearms, her neck and where else they shuddered to think for not a bit of white flesh could be seen anywhere. The Lord alone knew where she went all day long, what she got up to and with whom, for nobody reported seeing her in Crossclough or Woodhead so what were they to make of that? Her eyes were sort of unfocused, deep and somehow dreaming, her lashes lifting and drooping slowly, her long body lying boneless and graceful in the depths of the chair. The dog draped herself across her stomach while her mistress ate half a dozen scones, watching each mouthful unblinkingly, rewarded now and again with a morsel which went straight down without touching her teeth.

Katy stood up and placed the little mongrel on her cushion by the fire, dusted down her indecent breeches beneath which they could all see, as plain as plain, the crack in her behind and in . . . in another unmentionable place, smiled her thanks and strode out of the kitchen.

"Well, I don't know what ter say, really I don't," sighed Freda. "She were a handful before, we all know that but since she come back from . . . wherever it were she got to that week, she's like some . . . well, I dunno . . . Her poor ma and pa must be outa their minds with worry. She's lost that wildness, wouldn't you say, Mrs Tiplady, but what's come ter take its place, tell me that? A madam she might have been, and was, but she was always warm with it, you know what I mean? Now she's so damned cool, composed like, it's frightening. Ride roughshod over everyone, she will, to have what she wants, whatever that might be, an' I for one wonder where it will all end, honest to God."

Chris Andrews yelled with the rest of the howling mob as the bare fist of the smaller fighter glided off his opponent's cheek and whistled past his ear. They fell against one another, the blood which slicked both their bodies glueing them together for a moment before one pushed the other off and danced away on light feet. He was graceful, the big one, lean and dangerously cool-headed, his powerful shoulders shining with sweat in the torchlight.

The contenders were not restricted by the 1867 Marquis of Queensberry rules here, fighting bare-knuckled, throwing, gouging, tripping, hair-pulling and scratching being the order of the day. There were no weight divisions, though the two who fought each other tonight were evenly matched, one being slightly taller than the other. There were no timed rounds, for they lasted as long as it took one man to knock down the other which was followed by a thirty-second rest period when both challengers were then required to "come up to scratch". This was a line drawn in the centre of the rough ring and the loser of the fight was the man who was unable to crawl or stagger to the "scratch" line. A test of endurance then, with no real skills required. This fight had already lasted two hours.

The purse was for twenty guineas and the bets were flying, tempers rising, other scraps threatening to break out as men extolled or belittled the skills of the men in the ring. There was an enormous crowd, working men mingling with the gentry who were diverted by the sight of one labouring man beating the living daylights out of another. They yelled hoarsely, then guffawed mindlessly as one almost slipped in the blood. There was an avid hush, a dreadful silence followed by an explosion of maniacal noise as one of the fighters went down.

"Get up, man, get up."

"Yer bloody nancy, it were nowt burra tap."

"'Ang on theer, lad."

"Come up to scratch, for God's sake, I've a guinea . . ."

"What's up wi' yer?"

"Gerrup . . . gerrup an' kill 'im."

The crowd howled and swayed, mindless in its bloodlust, wanting murder, or at least mutilation and Chris Andrews, who was already deep in debt and would be deeper still if his "man" did not win, clapped his hands to his head in a ferment of excitement.

It ended suddenly when the taller man drove one of his hard fists into the centre of his opponent's face, smashing what was left of his nose to bloody pulp and with the other almost lifted him from his feet with an upper cut to the jaw. He went down with a thud which seemed to make the ground judder.

"Come up to scratch . . . come up to scratch," the timekeeper roared after the required thirty seconds had gone by, but the man was coming nowhere, not even round, and the arm of the winner was lifted high above his head as the crowd howled its approval, or not, depending on where the wagers had been laid.

They were spellbound, the hundred or so men who surrounded the ring, falling silent at the spectacle of the tall, blood-streaked winner striding from the ring and taking in his arms a tall, slender, cloaked, top-hatted young gentleman who, to their astonishment, kissed him again and again on his bloody mouth, so vigorously his hat fell off, his cloak fell open and he was revealed to be, not a young man but a young woman!

And not any young woman, either, but Jack Andrews's lass, who had vanished a month or two back and then returned in the most mysterious fashion. Now she was hanging about Paddy Andrews's neck, Paddy Andrews who was her own cousin, and in a way which could only be called disgusting. Not only disgusting but surely criminal for her even to be here. Impropriety apart, she was in real danger amongst such rough company, though the way she and Paddy were carrying on it was obvious what was between them and there was not one man ready to insult her, not with the winner of the fight to protect her.

But Chris Andrews had no such compunction. With a roar which could be heard a mile away in these silent hills and in this silent company, he launched himself across the slippery ring, his arms going round Paddy's waist, his face twisted, contorted into a rage and disgust so powerful he actually pulled the bigger, more powerful man from his feet. Katy Andrews staggered, losing her balance but was saved by the hand of an excited onlooker who leered at her brazen, what seemed to him almost naked body beneath her cloak as though he would dearly love to lay more than his hand on her.

"Chris," she was shrieking, shaking herself free. "Get off him. Paddy, for God's sake, it's Chris, damn you. Chris . . . Oh, dear sweet Christ, he'll kill him," for Paddy, not recognising his attacker in the flickering light of the torch and who would not have cared if he had, was raining blows on her lightweight brother's face and head, doing him damage from which he might never recover.

Paddy still had the killing force in him and did not understand or care for the troublesome fly which buzzed about him.

"Paddy, stop it . . . stop it," the fly shrieked and when he at last recognised her and who it was he was murdering, he stepped back in disdain from the bleeding, crumpled heap at his feet. He wouldn't soil his hands, nor his reputation on a bit of shite like Chris Andrews, his expression said.

"Leave 'im," he snarled as Katy would have gone to him.

"He's my brother."

"An' what am I?" His eyes were menacing, not allowing her to see his fear. She must choose between them, his slitted eyes told her, here before this assembly who were watching, hypnotised and soundless, but this was Katy Andrews who feared no man and was beholden to no man. Katy Andrews whose warm, loving heart had been broken then effectively hardened until it ached for no one.

Still, she did not ignore him.

"I'll come back, Paddy, but I must see he gets home. Johnny, is that you? Is his horse here? Oh Tim, thank God . . . get him into the saddle and make sure he gets home, will you? Thanks."

She turned when her brother was draped across his saddle and led away and with a shameless, graceful stride which silenced even those who whispered at the back of the crowd, moved across to Paddy Andrews and kissed him again on his torn mouth.

He grinned triumphantly, turning to the men who watched,

his arm possessively about her waist, his grin confirming that, yes, this woman was his and if there was any other man who wished to dispute it then now was the time to do it.

They shuffled their feet and lowered their eyes, not in shame for themselves but for Katy Andrews who was breaking her family's heart.

14

The full and shameful horror of it rocked not only the house of Cloudberry End but the small town of Crossclough and the length and breadth of the Longdendale Valley as well. They talked of nothing else and it was then that Madge Andrews, who had scarcely had a day's illness in her life, suddenly seemed to falter, to look frail, to look her age, saying she did not feel up to fettling and would have a day or two in bed. Her son's lass, Dorcas, a sensible young woman, plain to be sure but trustworthy, was sent over to stay with her until she was up to her old fettling ways but Madge was beyond that now. Paddy was her grandson. A young devil, if ever there was one, and Katy, her granddaughter, the joy of her heart and she just could not reconcile the two, nor the talk about them.

Katy Andrews, during the week she had spent in Paddy's cottage, her mind numbed with grief and despair, had given no thought to those who loved her, who searched desperately for her, since their feelings had not mattered. In a curious way she had been half ready to believe that her father and mother were to blame, for if they had encouraged Jamie to think of their daughter as, perhaps, a prospective bride, had him up to the house to dine, allowed him to become a welcome guest and not treated him as merely the son of a servant, could not the result have been vastly different? After all, her father was of humble stock and so could he not have been less rigid in his refusal to accept Katy's obvious feelings, for she had never kept them hidden, for Jamie Hutchinson? Calf love, puppy love, those were the words which had been bandied about, no one ready to believe that her young love was given whole-heartedly, irrevocably to Jamie.

So, let them suffer, let them weep, let them spend sleepless nights and heartbreaking days; the only person whom she regretted hurting during that week was her grandmother who had never, in all the years Katy had been galloping over to Woodhead, reproached, or criticised her arbitrary defiance of the rules of society. Nor had she treated her granddaughter as other than a human being who must decide her own course through life. As Madge Andrews had. Even if it proved to be the wrong course, then that was all right as long as one had the guts and resolution to recognise it and get back on the appropriate track, then no harm was done. Katy had respect and love for her grandmother and it filled her with guilty shame in the weeks following her homecoming to see the way her grandmother, worn out by that dreadful week, was fading. Of course she was very old, well past the time when women could expect to live, but Katy could not forget how spry her grandmother had been only a few days before Chloe Taylor ran away to Valley Bottom Farm.

"What were tha' thinkin' of, my lass?" she asked Katy sorrowfully when her granddaughter rode over to visit her a few days after the fight. Chris was still lying in his bed, no bones broken, no more than two black eyes, a bloody nose and a livid bruise below his breastbone, but the damage to his self-esteem, to his pride and sense of who he was in this community, not only in the valley but in the eyes of Johnny Ashwell and Tim Warren, was vast, brooding and hidden, ready, though no one knew of it, to do murder to Paddy Andrews when the time was ripe. His mother had risen from her own couch where she was fast becoming a semi-invalid, exclaiming in horror, clinging to her husband but refusing to leave her son's bedside until the doctor had assured her that he was in no mortal danger.

Later that night, when she had drifted home on the back of her mare, Paddy's kisses still hot on her mouth, the bruises he had given her chafing her thighs, Katy had not been astonished when her mother had turned on her.

"This is your fault," she had hissed, ready to clench her own fist and drive it into the face of this girl child of hers, but Katy had merely shrugged, her own eyes untroubled, for whatever had caused her brother to be as he was could not be laid at her door.

"Why, lass?" her grandmother repeated, putting out her hand

to her, beckoning her to sit beside her on the bed where she lay. "Dost tha' enjoy hurting them as loves thi'? And what did tha' think to achieve by going to watch a prize fight?"

Katy, in deference to her grandmother, wore her blue riding habit, though naturally Madge Andrews had been told of her granddaughter's indecent outfit which she ostentatiously sported up hill and down dale and even in the centre of Crossclough where the sight of her lounging on her mare's back in a man's silk shirt and riding jacket, doeskin breeches and a dashing top hat had brought the traffic to a standstill.

"Nothing, Grandmother. I just wanted to see how men spent their time. To find out what pleasure they get from such a spectacle."

"An' did tha'?"

"No, not really. But I did find out something and that is that I need the choice to see such things, if I wish to. I may not go again but I shall decide one way or the other. I have been persuaded, all my life, to follow other people's inclinations and not my own. I have not, as you know, been easily persuaded." She grinned. "Now I have decided to consider no one's preferences, only my own. The other night my . . . my cousin was to fight and when he invited me to watch him I accepted."

"No matter who tha' hurt?"

Her grandmother's eyes were misted with what looked like tears and in a fit of remorse Katy lifted her blue-veined, liver-spotted hand to her face, brushing the back of it with her lips.

"I'm sorry, I know it hurts you but sometimes . . . I hurt so much myself I seem unable to feel for others, even you, Grandmother. I love you."

"I know that, lamb, an' I know what ails thi' but tha' must get on wi' tha' life an' not try to destroy others."

"I don't, Grandmother. I'm not trying to destroy others but I feel the need to live as I want to live. Is that wrong?"

"An' how's that then, Katy Andrews? Tha' can't go through life treatin' other folk as though they meant nowt. Tha's chosen a hard road to walk, lass, if tha're to be at odds wi' everyone tha' meets on it."

She put her gnarled old hand against Katy's cheek and in her face was a mixture of sadness and yet a pride in this headstrong granddaughter of hers.

"Paddy Andrews, though he's me grandson an' I'm fond of 'im fer all his wild ways, will bring tha' nowt but trouble, Katy. Don't play wi' fire, lamb, fer that's what tha're doin'. He's a man not a boy an' won't be put down an' picked up again when tha've a fancy for . . . for whatever it is he is ter thi'."

Though Katy still obstinately refused to reveal where she had spent the week of her disappearance, the farrago at the prize fight surely pointed to only one conclusion and that was Paddy Andrews's place, and what had gone on there? Madge Andrews asked herself despairingly. And had the same thought occurred to Jack, this girl's stricken father who, short of tying her to the bedpost to keep her at home, since the law was on his side, had no control whatsoever over her movements?

"Grandmother!" Katy was ready to be appalled.

"I'm old an' me time's nearly up but I'm not blind, lass, nor soft in th'ead. I've heard the rumours, aye, even lyin' here in this bed for Annie Lennox an' Jinty Pickles are only too glad ter tell me tha's bin seen wi' him up on Tintwistle Knarr. Saul Gibbon tells his Agnes who passes it on ter Percy Clarke's missus whose maid tells Jinty when she goes up theer to do't laundry. Leave well alone, lass. Paddy's not the sort ter tekk up wi' any lass unless theer's summat in it for 'im, one way or t'other. Theer's nowt round 'ere fer a lad such as 'im an' I'd not be surprised ter see 'im tekk 'imself off across the world ter join his brothers, that is unless he found summat here more to 'is likin'. And tha' pa's got a bob or two in his pocket."

"I'm not sure I know what you mean, Grandmother."

Madge Andrews's face was filled with compassion and understanding. She should be worried about this girl of Jack's and she would if she had the strength for it but somehow these days she found her mind turned more and more to Chris, her Chris who had died so long ago but who had lived on in her heart ever since. She'd not mind seeing him again and as soon as the good Lord liked. And then there was George, her eldest, dead only a few weeks ago which did not seem right, for surely a mother should go before her child. She'd not attended his funeral, letting the men of the family see to the putting away of one of their own, but sorrow had burdened her and helped to bring her to this bed of hers.

Aye, she could understand her granddaughter's misery, her sense of loss for she'd known it herself. Katy was young, seventeen next month and though it sounded heartless, she'd get over this pain she felt over Jamie Hutchinson. You got over everything in the end. You had to, or go under.

"I'm tired now, my lass," she murmured, her interest in and concern for the events of this world slipping gradually away from her as she edged towards the next. "Off yer go an' mind what I say. Listen to tha' pa an' ma for they only want what's best for thi', as we all do."

It was the last time Katy saw her grandmother alive. Her heart had simply stopped beating as she slept, the doctor informed them, but it made no difference to Katy Andrews, for she knew beyond question that she had killed Madge Andrews as surely as if she had held a pillow over her face and she knew also that she would never forgive herself for it as long as she lived. She sat on the edge of her chair in her mother's drawing room, her hands in her lap, her face carved from grey granite, her eyes wide and tearless in shock as her father discussed the funeral arrangements with her mother as casually, it appeared to her, as though his mother were no more than a slight acquaintance. It would be a splendid affair, of course, and so it was, for, contrary to Katy's belief, Jack Andrews had been very fond of his mother. But she had been ready to go. It was the natural order of things for the generation ahead to "pass on" and Jack accepted it and what he had to do.

There was a vast crowd all but swamping the small cemetery at Woodhead Chapel and standing in silent rows beyond the wall and down to the road which meandered alongside the reservoirs. Katy had been unable to contemplate the funeral, saying she was off to the tops to do her own mourning, but her father, speaking quietly and in a voice which brooked no argument, of his mother, and his mother's love for Katy herself, her hurt at not having her granddaughter to stand at her graveside in a last respectful farewell, persuaded her, and she stood on that cold autumn day, staring out over the heads of her cousins, one of them Paddy Andrews. She did not look at the coffin, just as she had not looked at her grandmother's dead face as it reposed in it, not caring how beautiful she looked, not believing them when they told her she was only sleeping. She was dead, the only person she had ever truly loved besides Jamie, which was quite a different sort of love. She felt irritated by the tears about her, for what did they know of true desolation? She and her mother wore black silk gowns beaded with jet, hats with black, silk bows and feathers and knee-length mourning veils. She did not see, or care what the rest of the family had on, the shuffling rows of them, men and women. There was a black-draped hearse and several carriages, black horses and a blackness about her which did its best to drag her into the grave with Grandmother. How blissful that would be.

It was then she saw them standing on the far side of the drystone wall which surrounded the cemetery, their heads bowed, his arm solicitously about her as though she were as fragile as a newly flowered snowdrop. She was in black, the black she had worn on the day she had climbed down from the Manchester to Sheffield train, pressed and sponged for the occasion. She lifted her clouded, blue-green eyes from her sombre contemplation of the freshly dug earth about the grave and her glance was nailed to Katy's, neither of them able to look away. They were trapped, as the parson droned on of everlasting life and women wept as women do, in a timeless moment of what could only be called remembrance. But remembrance of what, since neither of them could recall memories, shared memories that were pleasing to them both. It was then, as blue eyes searched brown, that they realised it was not what had been but what might have been that they shared. What, in time, might have grown between them if a man had not forced them apart.

Chloe had not known Madge Andrews and could not honestly mourn her as Katy did but her warm gaze said that she understood Katy's desolation, for had she not lost her own mama not so long ago? It was all there, the sympathy, the sadness that she could not give to Katy what she needed. She seemed inclined to smile a little, no more than the compassionate lifting of the corners of her soft mouth. They had never been friends, as they might have been and now, with Jamie Hutchinson standing irrevocably between them, they never would. But for that moment Katy allowed the gentle giving of something which might be of value, perhaps comfort, from her cousin, a willingness, if Katy could bring herself to . . . what? What could there ever be for Katy Andrews and Chloe Hutchinson now?

Nothing but bitterness and knife-edged pain, Katy's eyes told her, hardening to brown pebbles in the absolute stillness of her white face. Then the moment, the strange moment was over almost before it was acknowledged and it was Chloe who looked away first. She turned her face into Jamie's shoulder and at once he bent his head tenderly, murmuring something to her. They had come as a mark of respect to the family who had been closely involved with Jamie and Jamie's mother for nearly thirty years and for no other reason. Certainly not to be stared at, though there were those who were staring since not many had actually seen a couple who had lived in sin.

Now, as the coffin was lowered into the ground, as Sara Andrews, pale and frail as a drift of lily of the valley, swayed in her husband's strong arms, Chloe and Jamie moved away, Jamie's arm still comfortingly about his wife's shoulders.

Across the gaping hole in which their grandmother was laid to rest, Chris Andrews stared grimly at his cousin Paddy, his livid face quite without expression. There were still deep plum circles about his eyes, turning mauve and yellow at the edges and he was seen to take his brother Davy's arm as he moved slowly away towards the carriage.

Richard Andrews, recently arrived from some God-forsaken place none of those hereabouts had ever heard of, put his arm about his sister's stiff shoulders, attempting to lead her away, and those who watched were diverted to see her shake it off, indicating that she would join the others in a minute.

There were only herself and Paddy then and those who had gone would have been astonished to see the expression on his somewhat battered face and hear the soft words he spoke.

"Are thi' managin', Coppertop?" A name he had given her at his cottage when she had flamed into life for him. His usually rough voice was warm, soft-toned.

"Not really," she sighed, showing only to him the true depth of her sorrow.

"Can I . . .?"

"No . . . no, Paddy. It will get better. I loved her."

"Aye, I know that, lass. Listen, I'll not come round ter't house wi' rest."

"It would be . . . for the best."

"I'll see thi' soon, Coppertop?" The longing in his voice was very evident and she smiled a little. The men were shuffling about them, their spades ready to fill in the grave but Paddy moved round to stand beside her.

"Katy?" he insisted.

Audrey Howard

"Yes . . . soon, Paddy, I promise," and for a second or two the gravediggers were confounded to see Jack Andrews's lass lower her head to Paddy Andrews's broad shoulder.

They trudged or rode back to Cloudberry End where Mrs Tiplady had prepared some sort of repast. How would these plain working folk, Jack Andrews's brothers and sisters-in-law, his nephews and nieces and their offspring, fit in there? But they were Madge Andrews's family when all was said and done and must be sustained. Madge had left a will, at Jack's insistence, since he meant to have no haggling over her bits and pieces, he told her. There was her china tea-service, her mother's chiffonier standing in the parlour, some trifling pieces of jewellery, but best to say who got what, he said firmly, and now they were to find out.

They ambled about the house in their Sunday clothes, Will and his wife, Anna, Harry and his wife, Jane, their children and grandchildren, those who had not died or emigrated. Dozens of them, it seemed to Freda and Lottie and Ivy who were seriously offended to find the women gawping about the first floor of the house, peering open-mouthed into bedrooms, one even trying out Mrs Andrews's pretty summer parasol of cream lace and silk which she had discovered on a chair in the master and mistress's own room.

Will Andrews's two youngest, Josh and Jake, had frightened Dilly to death when they loafed into the kitchen demanding a "proper" drink of ale and not this sweet stuff which tasted like bloody medicine, referring to Mr Andrews's best sherry. Their big, dark, powerful bodies had seemed to fill the kitchen with some dreadful male menace, since it seemed they were ready for a bit of "fun" with the younger housemaids. Mrs Tiplady soon put them in their place, of course, sending them off with a flea in their ear, the pair of them, and she didn't care if they were related to the master. The housekeeper was heard to remark that it could have been worse. Their cousin Paddy Andrews might have accompanied them.

None of them was quite sure why they had been assembled in Sara Andrews's elegant drawing room. They jostled one another, the young ones inclined to giggle and stare at this uncle of theirs and his frozen-faced, gimlet-eyed sons, his stiff-necked daughter whose curling lip said she despised them all, and his wisp of a wife whom none of them had cared for, and most, truth to tell, had never met. A will!

668

What would old Grandma Andrews want with a will, the men muttered amongst themselves, twisting their Sunday bowlers in work-roughened fingers while their womenfolk looked about them wondering what half the objects in the room were meant to be.

"This is a short, simple will," the solicitor from Crossclough began, deciding from the first to use short and simple words in order to be understood. "Bequeath" would be beyond most of them so, to save time he went right at it.

"Mrs Andrews has left everything she owned to her granddaughter . . ."

There was a stir. Which granddaughter?

". . . from whom, she says, she received more affection than she could ever repay."

What in hell's name did *that* mean? they asked one another, turning to stare about them.

"There is only the property in Woodhead . . ."

Property? In Woodhead?

". . . a cottage, but it, and everything in it is . . ." Should he say *bequeathed*? No, best not, ". . . given to my granddaughter Katherine Andrews."

He could see that even Jack Andrews was pole-axed. It was he who had insisted on his mother making a will but he had no idea what its contents might be and if he had known that Madge Andrews had actually owned her sturdy little cottage he might have discussed with her the disposal of it and would certainly have done his best to dissuade her from putting it in his daughter's careless hands.

Ever since he had begun to make money in what he called "a fair way of things", he had arranged for a generous weekly sum to be sent to his mother and, he supposed, over the years, more than twenty of them, she had been able to put some by. And why not, since there was quite a lot of it, at least by her standards, his twisted, feverish thoughts whispered and she had spent it on nothing for herself. He had been aware, but had said nothing, that she often put her hand in her purse to help out one of her family but the rest, it seemed, had gone towards the purchase of her little cottage on the shores of the Woodhead Reservoir. The cottage which she had just passed on to her wilful, headstrong, uncontrollable granddaughter, giving her a bolt-hole to which she might escape whenever the fancy took her. Which would be frequently.

"Jack ..." his wife faltered, reaching out for him though the expression on her face was bewildered.

"Christ!" Chris Andrews pronounced, turning to look at his two brothers who, being away from home so much, were not aware of the implications, while the silence continued as those not quite as quick-witted as their educated cousins did their best to grapple with what they had just heard.

"D'yer mean ter say the ... that it belonged to th'old woman?"

"I allus thought it were rented."

"Wheer'd she get brass?"

And then, when the explosion settled slightly another began.

"She's give it to ... to 'is lass?"

"Talk about much gets bloody more."

"That'd 've medd a right nice little 'ome fer our Patty," who was to be married at Christmas, as they all knew.

"T'aint fair."

"What's she ever done that we didn't, tell me that?"

"Bloody nowt that I can see."

"I allus liked them cups an' saucers."

"Aye, an' I 'ad me eye on them copper pans."

" 'Tis wicked ... wicked."

In her straightbacked chair Katy stared at the solicitor, her eyes ready to shed tears at last, bright and hot, though her face was perfectly still and as blank as an empty page. There was no expression there. Not gratitude, not remorse that she should benefit from her grandmother's death where others, perhaps more deserving, hadn't. Not relief, nor speculation of what she might get from such relief. She simply sat, a study in black and white, even her glowing hair completely hidden beneath the black hat and ruched black veiling which swathed the brim.

They had stopped muttering when they finally left. By then they were in a full-throated roar of resentment, swearing they'd not let it lie even though the solicitor told them firmly again and again that Mrs Andrews had been in full control of all her faculties when she made the will and there was nothing to be done about it. It could not be overturned, though they were not awfully sure what he meant by that, harbouring the thought that somehow they were being diddled. She had been their mother and grandmother and so surely, just as much as

Katy Andrews, who was no better than she should be, they must be entitled to something, even if it was only a copper pan or two, Harry's wife Jane said aggrievedly.

Katy sat where they had left her, the solicitor's card in her hand for, he said, he would be obliged if she would call, at her convenience, of course, at his offices in Crossclough since there were some legal papers to be signed. He had tried to settle the appointment with Jack Andrews, who, as her father and legal guardian was surely the one to deal with, but she had coolly told him, with a polite smile of apology at her father, that she was quite capable of settling her own affairs. The days had gone when a woman's inheritance went at once to her nearest living male relative, her cool smile reminded him, and she would be down the following day to see it all neatly tied up. She was just seventeen years old.

They had all gone their separate ways, her mother and father to the room they shared where, presumably, they would console one another with the thought there was simply nothing more to be done with her. Her father, doing his best not to upset her mother, had done everything in his power to persuade Katy to put it all in his hands. He would sell it and put the proceeds into something which would bring her in a small income. She had no need of it, he begged her to admit, since it was not the sort of home she would ever live in when she married. Or she could rent it if she didn't want to part with it, he pleaded, while her mother wrung her hands and her two older brothers looked bewildered, wishing to God they could get away to their own worlds, she could see.

While her father argued, Chris sat and stared into the fire, his face brooding and unreadable, his eyes hooded, a brandy in his hand, a cigar between his lips and it was a measure of his father's distress that he noticed neither. He said nothing. He didn't look at her and it seemed to her it was then, at that moment, that the frail but up to now determined thread which had tied her to her mother and brothers, to her father and to his ruling of her, frayed and snapped, leaving her suspended in a light bubble of time, which, when it burst, would drop her into a completely new and undeniably shiny world which might be to her liking. She had never been tied to the conventional mores of her mother's world, and her father, though he had done his best to tame her when he was at home, had been too engrossed with her mother to concern himself unduly with his growing daughter who had, after all, a nanny, then a governess to take charge of her.

So what, her calculating mind asked, was she to do with this gift her beloved grandmother had put in her hands? Was she to waste it as her father wished, or was she to use it to her own advantage, as Grandmother, in giving it to her, seemed to be telling her to do?

She lifted her head, turning it as though to listen for something which sounded on the edge of somewhere far off, then let out her breath on a long, exhausted sigh. She had seen put in the ground today the only person who had truly loved her and how was she to replace that? She sensed that there was a depth to Paddy Andrews's feelings for her which had not been truly revealed but he meant very little to her except as someone to warm her cold body against. His flesh set hers alight, while in the midst of the consuming flames her cold heart beat, perhaps faster but certainly not warmer. Her heart! Dear sweet God, her heart, that bothersome organ which nothing and nobody could cure of the dreadful injury inflicted on it by Chloe and Jamie Hutchinson.

Pain knifed her as her closed eyes saw them as they had been today. Jamie's tender care of the slim, flower-like woman who shared his bed, who had stolen his heart and love, who lived his life with him, the life which should have been Katy Andrews's.

She could go away, she supposed. Pack a bag and take the train to . . . to somewhere and make a life for herself, but she was trained for nothing and certainly not for earning a wage on which to live and anyway, that would be running away and Katy Andrews had never been known to back off from a challenge in her life.

Her mind shifted in subtle shades of warmth and light and then to the cold greyness of despair. For the life of her she hadn't the faintest notion of what she wanted to do. What looked exciting to her, thought-provoking, a gamble, a risk in this safe world which her mother and father had built around themselves and which included her? What was there? What could there be? And all she could see was Paddy Andrews's wicked grin, his narrow-eyed desire, his strong demanding body which was as familar to her now as her own. At least when she was with him she felt alive, recklessly alive, which was what she needed to soothe the wounds a girl of just seventeen should not have been asked to suffer. Why did she feel as she did? Why was all her life, her love, her heart and mind and soul focused on one man, a man who was husband to another woman? Five short months since Chloe had come to Crossclough, stepping – ominously, why hadn't she seen it? – from the same carriage as Jamie and in that time had successfully taken the meaning of life from Katy Andrews.

Her eyes narrowed then. She leaned forward in her chair, focusing on the chuckling flames in the fire, yellow, orange, gold, a touch of blue here and there as the coals hissed.

Meaning, that was what life must have. A purpose, and surely the cottage her grandmother had given her must have some purpose otherwise her death would have been for nothing. Love had gone, not only with Jamie but with Grandmother, but perhaps in Grandmother's own house Katy might find what she sought. God knows what it was but even if it were only a space in time to be alone, a space to think and plan and hope, then she must take advantage of it.

Slowly she rose from her chair, left the empty firelit drawing room and went upstairs to pack.

15

The five men were no more than shadows, the outline of them revealed only as slightly darker than the black night itself.

It was Christmas Eve and the inn on the far side of the moorland road near Saltersbrook was raucous with men's voices, men who were merry with ale, with mulled wine and spiced rum and Christmas spirit, men who had just been paid and, with a week's wages in their pockets, were eager to pour it down their throats as fast as the innkeeper and his barmaid could refill their glasses. Through the small leaded windows, the low, smoke-blackened, age-blackened bar-room could be seen to be jammed with working men and not a few of the gentry who had a fancy to drink in what they considered to be the "quaintness" of a working-man's bar. There was the sound of drunken singing, appropriately, "The Holly and the Ivy", and each time the door opened a beam of golden light spilled out in a long rectangle across the track.

It was bitterly cold, the ground beneath the waiting men's feet crunchy with frost. A dark night with no moon as yet, though there was a wind getting up which would shift the clouds to reveal it soon enough. The weight of the darkness pressed down on them and they shifted uneasily, but what they had come to do needed doing, they all knew that, distasteful as it was. Distasteful, yes, but at the same time each one felt that small, completely male frisson of excited anticipation which comes to soldiers as they wait to go into battle.

The door to the inn began to open and close with more frequency, letting out the merrymakers, most of them in amiable groups, their arms about one another's shoulders, their feet inclined to stumble. There were shouts, appropriate to the season, shouts of farewell, shouts of derision as one of the group lost his footing, and of warm friendship, that of men who had the drink in them.

"Is this him?" one of the five waiting men whispered, his voice rising in excitement.

"Be quiet, you bloody fool," the soft answer came and for another half-hour they shivered in the biting wind which searched among their warm clothing.

Moonlight suddenly flooded the land, carving areas of grey shadow in the dips and hollows about them and the silver-white glitter of the hoar frost created a mysterious beauty which the waiting men were too preoccupied and nervous to notice. They bobbed down hastily, looking about them as though expecting shouts of discovery, then, just as suddenly, the moon disappeared behind a cloud again, leaving them in the welcome pitchy darkness.

The inn door opened once more and one man came out, a tall, broad-shouldered man who called back something to those still inside, his laughter carrying across the cold air to the men who crouched in the dark.

"It's him," one of them whispered. "Let's hope to Christ he hasn't got his bloody dog with him." There was a tense pause then, when it was apparent the man was alone, a collective sigh of relief. "He'll have to come this way to get to his place," the man continued, "or to Woodhead." There was a bitter note in his voice. "Wait until he's got past us and don't move until I tell you."

"What if he . . .?"

"Be quiet and wait until I give you the signal."

The man who had come out of the inn crossed the track and, unbuttoning his trousers, casually urinated in a long arc on to a clump of gorse, the steam from its warmth clearly seen in the light from the inn's window. He was about to take the rough path which led off the track where the inn at Saltersbrook stood when he paused as though some deeply buried, primeval instinct in him sensed danger. He stood, as silent and indistinct as one of the trees which were grouped in a small acre of woodland to his left, his head turning this way and that, like an animal which scents the air, but he had drunk a great deal of ale that night and his normally keen awareness of all that went on about him, wherever he was, had been lost in his glass.

Grunting as though at his own foolishness, he moved on

up the path which led from Saltersbrook, across Longside Edge and on to the village of Woodhead which was his destination.

They let him go half a mile. He was blundering and cursing as the moon slid in and out behind scudding, silver-edged clouds. He sang "The Holly and the Ivy" with great gusto and the night creatures cowered down as he went by, creeping out as the sound died away only to scuttle back to safety as another group of intruders disturbed them.

The clouds had fled away, leaving a blue-white radiance, when the man they followed finally sensed them at his back, whirling in crouched alarm, wary in that moment but relaxing contemptuously when he saw who it was. He picked out the face of the man who was his enemy and began to laugh, despite the four shadowy figures who were grouped about him. Five against one, his mocking gaze said, not at all alarmed and it was obvious he felt he still had the advantage in view of who the five were.

"Well, well, well, if it's not the Andrews boys, an' who's these two mannikens wi' thi', lads?"

Paddy Andrews's laughter became more merry and he slapped his thigh in huge delight but Chris Andrews did not share his humour, it seemed. His voice was cold, cutting, belying the white-hot, dangerous anger which burned inside him.

"Yes, the Andrews boys, Paddy. My brothers Richard and David who are home for Christmas as you see." His voice was as smooth as silk but heavy with menace. Paddy appeared not to care. "And allow me to introduce my friends, Johnny Ashwell and Tim Warren, who are of the same opinion as myself and my brothers since they have sisters too."

"Aah, so that's it, is it? Tha've come ter tell me tha' don't like the idea of a common chap like me makin' free wi' a lady like Katy. Is that it?" He laughed derisively. "Well, Mr Andrews, sir, your sister needs no persuadin', believe me. Drops her drawers, or should I say 'er breeches, whenever I 'ave a fancy fer it, which is most days, let me tell thi'. That cottage o' Gran's 'as come in right 'andy an' when me an' Katy's ready fer it 'er an' me'll be married an' settle down in it."

"You bastard, you filthy rotten bastard," Richard Andrews screamed and before his cooler-headed younger brother, who knew exactly what Paddy Andrews was capable of, could warn him he leaped at his cousin and swung at his face with the cudgel he carried.

Paddy Andrews's reputation was as a hard and vicious fighter who would use any means at his disposal to injure his opponent. A champion he was, for three of them had seen him fight and had even won a few guineas on him. But only in numbers could he be bested, Chris Andrews had emphasised and his older brother, in his rage, had forgotten. Only if they moved in on Paddy as one man could they hope to defeat him. They were all aware that they could not tackle a man who fought in a bare-knuckle boxing ring, not unless they had something to knock him down with and even though Richie had such a weapon Chris distinctly heard his brother's arm snap as Paddy caught him and threw his lighter frame towards the other four.

"Stay together, dammit," he yelled, brandishing his own club. "Move in together. At his back, Davy . . . Johnny, over to his right . . . here, Tim, beside me. Together, damn you, together."

Stepping over the prostrate form of his groaning brother who was doing his best to get out of the way, Chris Andrews, whose mean temper and boiling rage, whose frenzied need for revenge, not only on his sister's account but his own, made him strong, moved in and the rest followed, and though he put up a long and deadly fight, damaging each one of the young gentlemen in some way, they steadily beat him down, striking in unison, using their boots as well as their weapons when he was on the ground, five dark, intent, mindless figures, since Richie found he could still utilise his feet, mangling and mauling Paddy Andrews until he was compelled to curl himself up in an attempt to protect the most vital parts of himself.

There came from the brow of the small rise behind them the sound of someone singing. A Christmas carol, probably one of the last revellers from the inn making his cheerful way home, since there were a few men from the direction of Woodhead who liked to drink at the Feathered Cock in Saltersbrook where the ale was cheap and the barmaid saucy

"Someone's coming," Johnny Ashwell hissed, launching a final kick at the foetus-like form on the ground.

"Dammit, dammit . . ." Chris Andrews's voice was almost a moan, a thwarting of his violence which was not yet spent.

"Help Richie."

"For Christ's sake, come on, Chris."

"I hadn't finished."

"An' neither 'ave I," the man on the ground mumbled.

Shambling and stumbling with Richie Andrews between them, the five young men made their way on the moonlit path while their victim fell into a merciful state of insensibility.

Katy Andrews, surprised that she had not seen Paddy since early the night before, had ridden over to Cloudberry End. It was Christmas morning, which meant nothing to her since she would spend it as she spent every morning. A ride up to the peat moor to drink in the peace and grandeur of the undulating hills and valleys and cloughs about her. A good gallop across Arnfield Moor, leaping Arnfield clough and then back down through Spring Intake and eastwards beyond Spond Moor and Crowden Brook to the cottage at Woodhead. She meant to have a word with Annie Lennox about the state of Grandmother's cottage since she had moved into it. Annie was a decent woman, of course, and probably would refuse to have anything to do with her and the cottage her grandmother had once kept in such an immaculate condition but Annie was recently widowed with three children to feed and clothe and perhaps the inducement of a few shillings a week might overcome her aversion. Katy felt her grandmother's reproving presence there whenever she herself noticed the muddle in which she lived, for she knew Madge Andrews would not have approved. The place had not been cleaned properly nor the bed in which Katy herself uncaringly slept changed for weeks and, if only for her own sake, after all she was used to better, she must see that it was cleaned up a bit.

She didn't really know why she had felt the compulsion to ride over to Cloudberry End just because it was Christmas Day. Perhaps because her father and mother had, at last, begun to treat her as an adult and not some silly girl who could not be trusted to cross the lane on her own. It had taken a great deal of tight-lipped resolution on her part. Indeed, on that first day when her father had driven over to Woodhead accompanied by Jimmy and Dicken with the express intention of bringing her home by force, she had been ready to defend herself, and her intentions, with anything which came to hand.

"Fetch her to the carriage," he had thundered, ordering

the grooms to lay hands on her, but when they hesitated, looking apprehensively from their master to their master's narrow-eyed, spitting daughter, it had been Mr Andrews who had slowly bowed his head in despairing compliance. His shoulders had slumped. He had ordered them out of the cottage, telling them to go home and only that dog of hers and the four walls of the cottage had heard what was said between them. She had defeated him and he had driven home to tell his wife so. If they wanted to keep her they must let her go and that meant allowing her a weekly sum to feed and clothe herself. She was their child and they could not see her starve or go about in rags.

She was shunned wherever she went, not only by those who were her parents' friends and acquaintances, but by men and women from the lower classes who treated her with the insolence she deserved. She became invisible to the tradespeople of Crossclough, Miss Mason the dressmaker and others averting their faces and pinching their lips, for if they should be seen to serve her who was a harlot then they would be bound to lose customers who were not. She flaunted her looseness, for it was widely known that Paddy Andrews often spent the night at that cottage her grandmother had left her. She was cut dead by everyone who knew her but somehow it didn't seem to matter. When it was ready, the shape her future was to take would come to her and in the meanwhile she had Paddy to make her laugh, to set her flesh on fire, to exasperate and irritate her and it was enough for now.

She was surprised when her three brothers came into the breakfast room, where she was tucking into one of Mrs Tiplady's excellent breakfasts. They were inclined to strut, she thought, their faces, or at least those of Davy and Chris, somewhat knocked about and Richie with his arm in a sling which he held to his side as though in some pain.

"Are you sure this splint and sling is enough, Davy?" he was asking his brother. "Should the arm not be strapped up more firmly and do you think you could make up some more of that stuff you gave me last night? It eased the pain considerably and it hurts like the very devil now."

"It's as good as old Dr Highcroft could do, lad. Probably a lot better since his methods will no doubt be completely out of date by now. No, don't fiddle with it, it's perfectly all right as it is. You will be somewhat handicapped for a week or two but a fine, healthy specimen like yourself should soon heal. I'll get down to the chemist after breakfast and knock him up. See what he's got in stock. I don't carry vast stores of medicine about with me, you know."

They were all three grinning in what seemed to be high good humour and a vast degree of self-approval and Katy sighed in resignation. They had evidently been involved in some boyish prank, the kind of brawl to which young men seemed prone, but she'd be damned if she would ask them to tell her about it as it appeared they would like to do. Chris, glancing in her direction, smirked and whispered something in Richie's ear which made him laugh out loud, then wince as whatever it was he had done to his arm pained him.

She stood up abruptly. She was well aware that her brothers would have liked to cut her dead like the rest of the community and were quite appalled at their parents' willingness to have her at Cloudberry End. It made their own position, with people like the Ashwells and the Warrens, extremely delicate and it took all their tact and charm and exquisite manners, their crushed and sorrowful oppression of spirit which would obviously strike a man whose sister was no better than she should be, to remain on good terms with the circle in which they had always been welcome.

Katy was as unwilling to be involved in the usual family Christmas Day as her brothers were to have her here. The giving and receiving of gifts, the drinking of sherry in the drawing room, the enormous Christmas dinner, and meant to leave as soon as she had greeted her parents. For some reason, perhaps a residue of feeling which she did not care to call compassion for her mother, she had resisted the temptation to put on her breeches and instead wore her riding habit of blue boxcloth. Her hair was long enough now to sweep up and tie in a tumbled knot of ribbons at the crown of her head and the curls bobbed merrily as she moved towards the door.

"Well, I'm off," she declared. "Tell Mother and Father I'll see them later, perhaps for dinner. I've . . . well, I've left a gift or two under the tree so . . ."

"And may one ask where you're off *to*, little sister?" Chris drawled, his cat's eyes narrowing in a way which puzzled her, for everyone knew where she went to these days and nobody tried to stop her. Not now.

He was helping his brother to bacon and eggs and kidneys

while Freda and Ivy stood awkwardly to one side, sensing something unpleasant was about to take place and unwilling to be caught in the midst of it.

"No, you may not," Katy answered coolly, sweeping the wide hem of her skirt to one side as she manoeuvred her way towards the door, "and quite honestly I wonder why you ask me. I no longer live in this house and am not bound by its rules. What I do is my own concern and I'd be obliged if you would keep out of it."

"I wouldn't dream of interfering with anything *you* might do, my pet." Her brother sat down, exchanging smiles with Richie and Davy who had arranged themselves on either side of the table, setting to with gusto as though whatever it was they had been up to had given them an appetite. Davy leaned over and helped his older brother to cut up his food and their smiles became deeper, almost, Katy was inclined to think, if they had been females, turning to giggles.

She hesitated at the door. The you, the emphasis on the word, suddenly caught her attention. Not *you*, Chris had said, as though . . . as though . . .

"Are you trying to say something, Chris, or is this just you being your usual fatuous self? I've no time for games and you should know that by now."

"Oh we do, little sister, but then neither have we, have we, brothers? We are very serious when we have a mind to be, is that not so, lads?"

Davy shrugged and speared a morsel of bacon, a small smile still playing about his mouth. Richie nodded at Freda who sprang forward to refill his coffee cup and, in the tense atmosphere, for there was no doubt it was tense, Ivy looked calculatingly towards the door as though measuring the distance and how long it would take her to cover it.

Katy took a step back into the room and despite her own determination not to, said in a cool voice, "What have you done?"

"Done?" Chris took a bite out of a piece of toast. "Done about what?"

"Don't play the fool with me, Chris Andrews. The three of you have been up to something. A fight of some sort, I'd say, by the bruises you carry."

Her brother raised his reddish brown eyebrows, still

smirking, and Richie and Davy exchanged further meaningful glances.

"Yes, you might say that, my dear," he drawled, "though I think a beating would be a more apt word, would it not, brothers? A well-deserved beating. Sometimes a man needs teaching a lesson when he interferes with something which is not his to interfere with. When he gets above himself and so must be shown the error of his ways."

Katy took another step in the direction of the breakfast table, her eyes slitted, her fine eyebrows dipping, her mouth thinned to a narrow line of annoyance with this exasperating brother of hers. She was seventeen and for the past ten years or more her two older brothers had been first at school, then at university and in Richard's case abroad and she was close to neither of them. And it was at neither of them that she flung her concentrated gaze.

"Who are you talking about, Chris Andrews?" she snarled, though of course it was becoming clearer with every moment and every exchanged smile who he was talking about. "What have you done to . . .?"

"To Paddy Andrews, is that the name which comes to mind? Why, only what he deserves, little sister," and Chris's gleaming eyes told her he would like nothing better than to do the same to her. She had shamed them, made a laughing stock of them with her blatant and persistent preference for the coarse, uncouth labourer who was their cousin and though Chris Andrews was just as wild, just as rebellious, just as disobedient, he had always stuck to the codes of the society in which he had been brought up; besides which, he was male and she was not. She had been seen as far afield as Tintwistle, Mottram, Holmfirth and Penistone, following the prize fights in which Paddy took part; at the illegal cock fights and dog fights which took place at the back of isolated inns on the moors and was known to smoke cigars and drink a glass of claret, or brandy. She did, in fact, what young gentlemen did, what her own brother did and her own brother was incensed by it. Paddy Andrews was his cousin. His father and Paddy Andrews's father were brothers and in some way Katy's behaviour had been, if not accepted, then overlooked when she lived at home.

But she no longer lived at home. She treated her mother and father with politeness, only turning into a spitting, clawing she-cat when her father tried to remonstrate with her which he did less and less.

In short, she was beyond anyone's control but perhaps with Paddy Andrews out of the picture, which he undoubtedly would be after the thrashing they had given him last night, then she might, for lack of a companion if nothing else, be forced to return to her parents' home where she belonged. The chances of getting her decently married were long gone but they might be able to unearth some member of the lesser gentry who would be willing to take her on with the right amount of inducement. Hard cash, of course.

"You bastard," she spat at him, then turned to glare savagely at Richie and Davy. "You bastards, all of you. D'you mean to tell me the three of you took on Paddy?"

Suddenly she smiled and the colour which had fled from her face flooded back beneath her skin.

"D'you honestly expect me to believe that you three gave Paddy a beating?" And as it had on Paddy's face the night before, an expression of sneering mockery lit hers. "I don't believe you. He could whip the three of you with one hand. In fact it seems he did for Richie's arm, which I presume is broken, and those cuts and bruises you are all three wearing . . ."

"Not three of us, my pet." Chris interrupted.

"Not . . .?"

"Oh, we are well aware of Paddy Andrews's prowess with his fists and not being fools, and not needing to fight him but merely to thrash him, as one would a disobedient dog, we took along— "

"You bastard," she shrieked again. "You cowardly bastards. How many of you? Jesus, you're quite unspeakable, all of you. Where is he? If you've hurt him . . ."

"Hurt him! He'll be lucky to walk again . . ."

But his sister waited to hear no more. Whirling frantically, her skirt tipped to reveal her tight breeches, she tore open the door and, leaving it standing wide open, made for the back kitchen and the stables.

The two parlourmaids listened to her feet pound up the hallway, their eyes wide and appalled, both of them wondering what on earth was to happen to this family, and therefore them, if this tearing one another to pieces was not stopped. First Master Chris and his father, then Miss Katy and her father, and now Master Chris and Miss Katy.

"Should we not try to stop her, Chris?" Richie asked anxiously, nursing the arm which was broken and which his brother, who was almost a doctor, had set for him. "Or perhaps fetch Father, surely."

"Listen, Richie, my lad. You've been away a long time so you don't really know the state of affairs in this family. But let me say this, there is nothing you, nor Father, nor anyone . . . well, perhaps there is one man but he is . . . not available, could retrieve our sister from the path she is on so let her go and look for our cousin, which she will do if only to defy us. When she sees the state of him she'll be back within the hour, for our sister is not known for her mercy, or compassion."

He was wrong. They brought Paddy Andrews to Katy's cottage, for where else could they take him, his cousins Jake and Josh Andrews, sent for by the man who had found him on the moor. When Katy flung herself up the stairs and into her bedroom they were standing beside her bed, awkwardly sorry since they had never seen Paddy Andrews take a beating. In all his years as a prize fighter he had managed to avoid having his body broken or even his face seriously marked but now it lay on the none-too-clean pillow, hideous with torn skin, one cheek gashed to the bone, both eyes blackened and almost closed, and his nose peculiarly askew. He was a big, solid, well-nourished man, strong in body and mind, refusing ever to lie down, but now his flesh all over his fine body was black with bruises, scraped raw and clotted with dried blood.

"Tha' . . . can . . . clear . . . off now, lads, thanks," he gasped to his cousins who were glad to go, his tongue in the hole where a back tooth had been torn out, his breath rasping in a way which obviously hurt him. "Me . . . nurse is . . . 'ere ter . . . 'old me . . . 'and. Tha' 'ave . . . come ter . . . 'old me . . . 'and, . . . 'aven't thi', Coppertop?"

He did his best to give her his usual wicked grin which she knew quite certainly was causing him a great deal of pain and effort. Between the blood-caked slits of his lids his eyes were asking her something. The muscles in his throat were taut with unspoken words and his hard, fighting jaw was inclined to tremble, she thought.

"Do you need your hand holding, Paddy Andrews?" she asked him, her own voice wobbling a bit.

"Just . . . fer a day . . . or two, I reckon. But tha'd . . . best

ride . . . fer't doctor, lass, fer I've . . . an idea . . . me leg might
. . . be broke."

With great difficulty he pushed aside the bedclothes which
the twins had piled on him, since that was what one did with
an invalid. They had removed his trousers and though Katy
was not aware of it, while they did so, and on numerous
other occasions on the long drag home, he had mercifully
lost consciousness.

When Katy saw his leg she felt inclined to do the same.
Pushing through the oozing skin of his shin was a shaft of
white, jagged bone.

"God above, Paddy," she gasped, fighting off nausea as
she backed away, her shaking hand to her mouth, then she
turned, threw herself down the stairs and on to her mare's
back, clattering off as though "owd scrat" was after her, Jinty
Pickles remarked.

It was several hours later, the doctor gone, the light going,
when Paddy mumbled from the laudanum-induced sleep the
doctor had put him in in order to set his leg.

"I'm . . . a bit bashed . . . about, lass, as tha' . . . can . . . see.
It were tha' brothers . . . what did . . . it. I'll not let . . . it pass,
Coppertop, tha' knows that. When . . . I'm on . . . me feet . . .
again, an' it'll . . . not be long . . . I promise thi' . . . I'll teach
'em . . . a bloody . . . lesson they'll not . . . forget."

The effort of talking had opened the deep gash at the
corner of his mouth and the blood ran freely on to the grimy
pillow. It was this, this added stain which seemed to draw
her attention to the state, not only of the pillowcase, the rest
of the bedlinen, the room itself, but the whole disreputable
cottage, and it stiffened her resolve to put it all back to what it
had been before her grandmother's death. Besides, she would
need help to nurse Paddy.

She smiled and knelt down beside the bed. "Well, we'll
talk about that, later. They had no right to do this to
you but I suppose they thought they were defending my
honour but it's too late for that, isn't it, Paddy-me-lad? Far
too late."

She bent forward and placed her strangely tremulous mouth
on his, soft as a butterfly but still he winced. "You're not
ready to have me climb into bed with you, then?" She grinned
impishly.

"Sweet Jesus, girl . . . don't . . . make . . . me laugh."

"Who's laughing?" and she winked broadly. "Righto, then, I'll just go and . . ."

"Tha'll . . . not . . . leave . . . me?" he asked her anxiously, his expression telling her he was furious that he, of all strong, fighting men, should be brought to this and she knew it would be difficult. Begging for help from a woman, for a woman's comfort, but most of all from her over whom he had always held dominance.

"No, I'll not leave you but it's time I stopped living like a pig in shit, Paddy Andrews. You must surely remember what this place was like when Grandmother was alive?"

"Aye." His eyes wandered as best they could round the room. There were garments strewn about the floor, his own, bloodstained and torn, hers just tossed anywhere they fell. There were riding boots and a plate on which the last meal they had shared reposed, a half-drunk glass of wine. On almost every surface there was some littered object, even a trap with which he snared rabbits and which he had dropped carelessly as he flung off his clothes to get into her bed with her. Paddy had not worked for months now, ever since the week of Katy's disappearance in September. Not even at the casual work which had allowed him to wander the moorland to trap rabbits, to shoot whatever came into his gun sights to supplement his table. He still went out on most days from the cottage belonging to Jed Miller from where, as yet, they had not managed to evict him, trapping and shooting, and a week barely went by when he did not win a decent purse in the boxing ring. A fighter, a hunter was Paddy, skilful and cunning, a man who called no other man master but who, though he had not yet fully admitted it to himself, had bowed his head and his knee to this girl who knelt at the bedside.

"What . . . tha' gonna do . . . then? I can't . . . see thi' . . . in a . . . pinny, my lass," he mumbled through his broken mouth.

"No, neither can I but I can pay someone to put one on and give this place a thorough clean."

"Eeh, Coppertop . . . must tha? I've a . . . mind . . . fer a bit . . . o' . . . peace," closing his eyes fully and turning his head away from her.

"You shall have it, Paddy, never fear."

Annie Lennox took a bit of persuading. Well, Katy Andrews was considered a loose woman by decent folk like her and

Jinty, and that ox of a man who frequented Madge Andrews's trim little cottage was no better than he should be, neither. But how could she refuse the money Madge's granddaughter slapped briskly on Annie's well-scrubbed table top, not with her Frank gone and three young 'uns to rear. She did a bit of scrubbing at the Queen's Head in Crossclough and for the parson's wife and anyone else who would employ her and the offer of regular work, and only next door, was surely something she couldn't afford to turn down.

"I'll not come in when the pair o' tha's theer," she said doggedly.

"I'm sure a time convenient to yourself can be arranged, Annie."

"Mrs Lennox ter thi'."

Katy felt a spurt of irritation rise in her, quickly suppressed, for how could Annie Lennox's opinion, or anyone else's for that matter, concern her? Beggars can't be choosers, she told herself and she really couldn't quite see herself tackling the clutter which had accumulated in Grandmother's cottage since last October. Besides which, Paddy would need some looking after until his leg healed. Bedpans and such and the invalid food the doctor had advised and which she herself hadn't the faintest notion how to contrive.

"Very well, Mrs Lennox," she answered crisply, "but I would like you to make a start right now."

"Nay, I saw 'im bein' brought 'ome a while back. Drunk as a lord, 'e were an' I'm goin' nowhere ..."

"Then the arrangement is cancelled, I'm afraid. Either you start now or I shall find someone else to ... to help me."

It was perhaps those last few words that did it, for beneath her grim exterior Annie Lennox had a kind heart. She didn't bow her head, though, not to this baggage, but she nodded it stiffly in compliance.

And so it was Annie Lennox, having committed herself punctiliously, as was her way, to the job in hand, which was the scrubbing and deep scouring of Madge Andrews's cottage, as she still thought of it, who told Katy she'd best send for the doctor again.

"Why? The leg is set and surely that's all that's needed. Paddy is a strong man and will soon heal."

"I don't like look of it."

Katy's voice was sharp. "What do you mean, you don't like the look of it?"

"Just what I said. I've not seen it fer a few days an' . . ." since Katy had taken over the dressing of the wound.

"What, for God's sake?"

"'Ave thi' not noticed smell?"

"Well, yes, but . . ."

"An't colour's not right."

"The colour? What's the colour got to do with it? Really, Mrs Lennox, don't you think you are . . ."

"Never mind that, lady. You get Jinty Pickles's lad ter run fer't doctor an' tell 'im ter be quick about it before it's too late."

But it was already too late, the doctor said, none too pleased to be brought back to the foul-mouthed brute who seemed intent on doing them all a serious injury if they so much as came near him with a knife.

"It's no good cursing me, my good man. The flesh is already dead due to the lack of a healthy blood supply to the affected part and if something is not done soon you will— "

"Don't talk so bloody daft. It don't even 'urt."

"That is why. Because it is already dead."

Seeing where the doctor was leading, Paddy began to scream.

"No . . . Oh no . . . yer not cuttin' my bloody leg off . . . oh no . . . I'll not 'ave it . . . no . . . no . . . please, Coppertop, don't let 'im cut me leg off, please . . . please." His voice took on the high-pitched hysteria of a man in mortal terror, his mouth a cavern of horror in his bleached and sweating face.

"Oh, dear God in heaven," Katy moaned, "please, Doctor, can you not . . .?"

"There is nothing else to be done, young lady, nothing."

It was like a nightmare. The stink of it in Madge Andrews's once sweet-smelling cottage made them all gag, though the doctor and his nurse, and Annie herself, were accustomed to the nastiness which illness brings. Annie's own Frank, who had died in the grip of some fever, had suffered a violent emptying of his bowels which Annie had patiently dealt with but this was even more punishing to the nerves and stomach.

But worse, far worse than the abomination of the stench of his flesh was the sight of Paddy's body tissue which had degenerated in two weeks from the well-muscled firmness of a young and healthy man to the blackened, oozing, wet mass which had simply rotted away below the knee and was visibly spreading upwards.

It took five of them, one the hastily summoned and reluctant Barty Pickles, to hold down the writhing, screaming, demoniacally strong figure of Paddy Andrews while Doctor Highcross administered the merciful chloroform.

"Well above the knee, I think, Nurse," the doctor stated matter-of-factly when Paddy was at last still, "if we are to part it from the healthy flesh. And perhaps it might be as well if you were to leave the room now, Miss Andrews," he told Katy, turning from the kitchen table where, with the help of Barty Pickles, they had laid out the unconscious man. "Now I am aware that it is not a pretty sight," referring to the repulsiveness of Paddy's leg which seemed to have in it every colour from the deepest purple and black of the dead flesh to the green and yellow of the pus which exuded from it, "but it will soon be put right." It was as though he had suddenly become aware that though this girl no longer lived in the bosom of her family, indeed had been cast from it by her behaviour with this man, she was still the daughter of one of the most influential men in the neighbourhood. He himself would not be here if that had not been so, since he did not give his services to any Tom, Dick or Harry who had an accident.

The last thing Katy saw was the lethal-looking surgeon's saw which the doctor took from his bag before she fell into the compassionate arms of Annie Lennox.

It was two weeks later that Katy Andrews's brother Chris was found at the bottom of Deep End Clough. Drunk as usual and fallen off his horse, the rumour was and had it not been for Saul Gibbon, who was up that way searching for some of Farmer Clarke's flock which had wandered up beyond the snowline, and who had heard his weakening cries, he would certainly have perished. The clough was deep, filled with jagged rocks, almost impossible to climb out of, especially in the dark, but the puzzle was, what on earth was he doing riding up there at that time of night? Crossclough asked, shaking its collective head. And if he had fallen why was he not injured? Apart from the effects of a night spent out in the icy depths of January and which, as he was young and healthy were no more than a chill and a "wheezy" chest, he had suffered no injuries.

A lucky lad was Chris Andrews who, strangely, had nothing to say on the matter.

16

The following July Chloe Hutchinson had reason to believe that she was pregnant but she told no one, not even her husband who she knew waited and watched her every month for the sign that they were to have a child. It was nine months since they married and really, she often smiled to herself as she did her best to make her butter "come", something which was often beyond her for it required strength, it was not for want of trying on Jamie's part.

Not that she was an unwilling partner, far from it. She had known no man's body before Jamie's but despite her previous ignorance she was aware that Jamie was a considerate lover. How did she know? she often wondered, lying in his arms, her breath beginning to slow and her heartbeat to calm, her body slumbrous and stretching after the touch of his hands and mouth and the enchantment they brought to her.

He seemed to delight in studying her naked body for hours on end, turning her this way and that, placing the candle a little closer in order to alter the shading of gold and honey and tawny rose which played over her skin in the candle's flame, arranging her hair to please some need in himself, the very manner in which he did it, even before his touch began to delight her, putting a taper to the excitement which was lit in the pit of her belly. Every night this happened, and sometimes when his waking body turned to hers in the early morning.

Once they had been in their bed on a sunny, wintry Sunday afternoon when her mother- and father-in-law had taken it into their heads to walk up from Cloudberry End. The silent laughter had been quite hysterical as she and Jamie had fumbled their way back into their discarded clothing, Matty shouting up the stairs – since they had neglected to lock the door – demanding to know what they were up to. Flushed they had been, and dishevelled, Jamie's shirt on inside out and his hair, which her hands had been clutching as he explored with his tongue the exquisite tenderness between her thighs, standing up like that of a porcupine.

She had caught the blue twinkle in Matty's eye and though Thomas had been so embarrassed he had stamped off with the excuse he wanted to check on Jamie's plough horse, she and Matty had shared a conspiratorial smile which they had not allowed Jamie to see.

She was happy. She was well aware of her own short-comings as far as being a farmer's wife was concerned. There were some jobs about the farm which were beyond her strength which was where Adah-May came in and glad of her, Chloe was. A big, strong girl of fourteen whose mother had despaired of ever getting her in work, for Adah-May was simple and could do nothing without constant supervision. Sweet-natured and hardworking with a smile on her that lit the darkest day, she was a willing workhorse which no amount of work could tire. Show her, tell her, stand over her for five minutes to make sure she'd got the hang of it and whatever it was she'd go on doing it until she was told to stop. She'd scrub the colour off the kitchen flags if left alone but couldn't be trusted, even when watched, to handle the pretty, bone-china tea-service which had been a wedding present from Mr and Mrs Jack Andrews.

And put her to the butter churn, watching her, of course, as she dashed the long plunger up and down, and she would go on long after the thump which said the butter had come.

Jamie had promised to look out for one of the new "end over end" churns without paddles which would make the job simpler and easier for Chloe, but in the meanwhile Adah-May went at the old one as though it were a mortal enemy she was determined to best.

Chloe was very proud of her dairy and of the butter and cheese Jamie took to market each week, along with "her" eggs. The dairy was sited next to the farmhouse on the cool, north side, though as Jamie said, there was seldom a warm side up here on the edge of the moorland. There were two rooms to the dairy, one for butter-making and one for the making and storing of cheeses. Jamie made sure there was a good water supply from the pump. There was a boiler, a stone floor with a slight slope to allow for drainage, and walls lined with plenty of stone shelves. Adah-May kept it spotlessly clean, pails and crocks scrupulously scrubbed out along with the floor, the shelves and indeed every blessed thing Adah-May could lay her hands on. She idolised Mrs Hutchinson, who was everything Adah-May was not and if Mrs Hutchinson needed carrying about the farm on Adah-May's back then Adah-May would get down on her knees and gladly do it. She went home to her ma every night, her round, dough-like face as lugubrious as a hound-dog's and presented herself each morning, sometimes before she was required, as Jamie made love to Chloe in their deep, warm bed, her face lit up with a smile of pure heaven.

They lived a solitary life at Valley Bottom Farm with only Adah-May and Tommy, who helped Jamie in the fields with his small dairy herd, in the planting of his crops and up on the intake where his sheep were grazing, but when the two of them went home it had become a matter of deep pleasure to Chloe to share the warm, firelit, candlelit evenings with the man she considered to be not only her husband, her lover, but her true friend. She could still not bring herself to say that she loved him, she only knew that when he was away from the farmhouse she felt a small prick of loneliness, of unease as though the drawbridge had been left down, allowing in perhaps a presence she would not care for. His weatherwise, earthbound calm was a joy to her and she lowered herself into it each night as into a warm and easeful bath. He was a constant source of comfort, of quiet protection against a world which, though it had held no particular terrors for her, had held no particular joys either. When she heard his step in the yard or his cheerful whistle to Captain as he came down the track at the end of the day, her head lifted thankfully and she could not help nor deny her inclination to run out into the dusk to embrace him which she knew pleased him inordinately. He loved her. He said so at least twice a day and she sensed his own happiness with her, in what she gave him.

She had not failed nor disappointed him, she knew that, but did she love him as a woman loves her man? she asked herself. In that unique way which exists between a woman and the man who is all the world to her. In that blissful committed state shared by two people who cannot live apart and the answer was she didn't know.

She was a farmer's wife now and though she sewed in the evening by the fire it was no longer the intricately embroidered pretty things her fingers were accustomed to but warm winter shirts for her husband, skirts and blouses for herself in practical colours of chestnut brown, burgundy and charcoal grey, but all well fitting and beautifully made, simple but at the same time elegant since her mama's training and her own sense of good taste were deeply ingrained in her. She made pretty underwear of sturdy white cotton, smothered in lace and frills, for she knew her husband liked it, the fabric all bought from the accumulated allowance her uncle had made her. She replenished Jamie's slender stock of bedlinen and soon it would be tiny garments by the score.

When spring came they spent long Sunday afternoons together, climbing the tortuous, stony paths and the winding tracks between walls of heather in the direction of Bare Moss at the back of the farm. They found a sheltered spot in a grassy hollow, tall rocks at their back and admired in companionable silence the splendid panorama of the valley set out below, threaded with the shining expanses of the reservoirs. Jamie would stretch out beside her, his hand holding hers, telling her the names of the grasses and wild flowers, of the trees below and the birds above, many of which he could identify by their song.

"However did you come to know such clever things, Jamie? You were away at sea so long."

"I was a boy round here, my little dove, and grew up knowing country ways from the grooms and stable lads at Cloudberry End, the shepherds on the hills and all those who came from these parts. It was this which encouraged me to think I might make a farmer." He smiled from under the shade of his hand, his eyes soft and dreaming.

"You're an amazing man, Jamie."

"A lucky man, my dove."

When Jamie went into Crossclough she accompanied him on occasions, bringing back farming manuals from the second-hand bookshop which they both studied in the evenings, for was she not a farmer's wife and would it not be beneficial to Jamie to share his work with a woman who knew what he was talking about? She could milk a cow, care for the hens, the sow and her piglets, and even, when Jamie got up in the night to attend a sick cow or deliver a calf, get up to help him

– aided by the good advice in the manual – and had managed to quell the churning of her stomach at the sight of the blood and detritus of birth.

Matty came over to see her perhaps once a week, a fount of sensible, practical advice, glad to be of help to the slight but stubbornly determined girl her son had married and it was these visits more than anything which helped Chloe to decide to keep her suspicions about her own condition to herself for the moment. She knew that once Matty was told that she was to be a grandmother nothing short of an earthquake, a tidal wave or a blizzard would stop her from making her way up to Valley Bottom Farm as many times in the week as there were days.

And there had been a few of those in the winter. Blizzards! Jamie had been tied to the farmhouse for two whole days just after Christmas, going no further than the manure-scented, steaming barn where his beasts were quartered, to the hen house and the pig sty, Captain floundering comically at his heels. The world had become a magical place – at least to the eye – when the storm was over, its coming announced by bottom-heavy, fat clouds bouncing over the hills. A world of vast white spaces in which only the hazed shapes of snow-laden trees were visible and the solitary white-topped greyness of a farmhouse down in the valley. Chloe had stoked the fires and drawn the warm woollen curtains she had made for every window and they had not wasted the hours they had been shut in together.

It was in April that she conceived. One of the days on which she and Jamie had climbed up the track as far as Crowden Meadow. There had been no sign of life beyond a skylark high above and a few cropping sheep and when he had drawn her to him in love, cradling her, caressing her until she moaned her delight, he had eased himself into her and planted the seed which grew in her now. She had conceived. That was the word for it, the proper word which she knew her mother would have shuddered over, just as she would have shuddered over the very idea of making love, not just in broad daylight, but out of doors. But as a farm wife Chloe had no time for shuddering or being ladylike. She knew exactly what lay ahead of her when her time came, for the farm manual on breeding described it to her in detail and she supposed it was pretty much the same for humans as it was for animals.

Lambing time had come and gone by then and she had helped her husband with several weak lambs, feeding them by hand and nursing them in the warmth of her own hearth.

She was content.

She saw nothing of Katy Andrews but her mother-in-law brought her the news from Cloudberry End, none of it good.

"They say he sits in that special chair what she had made fer 'im, the one wi' wheels, though he never turns 'em, an' does nowt but shout at her as if it were all her fault. She has ter keep out of 'is way, Annie Lennox told me t'other day in Crossclough, when the black mood's on 'im or he'd knock her teeth down her throat. Them cousins of his, Jake an' Josh, fetched him downstairs an' he sleeps in a bed in the parlour, Annie said. God only knows how Katy'd manage if it weren't fer Annie." Matty shook her head sadly. "That girl waits on 'im hand an' foot. Lord, will yer listen ter me, poor bugger only has one foot ter wait on. Mind you, I reckon it's a good job he can't gerrup them stairs or the poor lass's life would be a hundred times worse than it is."

The mental picture of the one-legged hulk it was said Paddy Andrews had become doing to Katy what Jamie did so lovingly, so joyfully to Chloe was too much for her and she turned away in distress, the slight nausea which had troubled her recently turning her stomach over.

"Dear heavens, Matty," she whispered, "what is to become of her?"

"Nay, lass, she made her bed an' now she must lie in it." Matty's face was grim.

"But don't you think . . . circumstances . . . have helped to shape what has happened to her?"

"Aye, happen, but you should see her. You'd think she were Queen of England the way she carries herself. There's just summat about her . . ." Matty's eyes became unfocused as they dwelled on what it was about Katy Andrews that was so fascinating. "She's . . . matured. No, that's not the right word . . . she's become a woman, gloriously beautiful. Eeh, will yer listen at me?" Matty sighed. "But it's her poor mother I'm sorry for," she continued dolefully. "She's not strong, what with all them miscarriages. Oh aye, in between Master Richie an' Master Davy an' them with only eighteen months between them. One she had then. Only a couple o' months gone, she were, but she'd a bad do. Then after Master Davy she'd another two before Master Chris come along and then if she didn't have another after him. Four in all an' her like a bit o' swansdown with no substance on her to speak of. That's why Jack, Mr Andrews, is so clucky wi' her. Fusses like a mother hen, he does but then, after what happened years ago is it any wonder? It seemed for a while, afterwards like, he just couldn't bear her out of his sight. An' then them years she spent in Canada did her no good. Great cold place it were, not fit fer humans, I shouldn't wonder. Well, I'll say no more but when she come back I was shocked at the change in her, I can tell thi'."

"What *did* happen, Matty?" Chloe tried to keep her voice light as though to reveal her true interest might bring her mother-in-law back from the past just when it seemed the mystery about Sara and Alice Hamilton might be about to be revealed.

"She were only fifteen when they met, Sara, I mean. Jack were a navvy buildin' the railroad near where the Hamiltons lived and . . . well, they fell fer each other like a ton o' bricks. But Sara's pa were a doctor, her ma related to a lord or summat, an' Jack were nowt burra rough workman. Miss Hoity-Toity didn't like it one bit from what Sara told me— "

"Miss Hoity-Toity?" Chloe was enthralled. That day she had made her first successful batch of fruit scones in the hard-to-manage ovens beside the fire and she had been so pleased with them she couldn't wait for Matty to try one with the cup of tea she was sipping, but the scones stood neglected as did her newly churned butter while Matty wandered back into the past and Chloe encouraged her. Adah-May was warbling on about, ". . . going to Scarborough Fair . . ." in the dairy and in the cosy kitchen Alice Hamilton's daughter leaned forward expectantly towards her mother-in-law. At last she was going to find out what it was that made her mother's sister, her Aunt Sara, unable to bear the sight of her. In all the months Chloe had lived at Cloudberry End she had received no more than a cool "Good morning" or "Good evening", her aunt's eyes unable to find the courage even to meet Chloe's gaze. Since then, apart from the tea-service which Thomas had delivered with not even a note to accompany it, there had been no word from the Andrews family.

"That were what they called 'er. Miss Hoity-Toity. We all

did 'cos that's what she damn well was." Matty's face became flushed with the memory of some offence she still obviously felt and she folded her arms grimly over her matronly bosom.

"Who?"

"Alice bloody Hamilton, that's who . . ." Then, suddenly appalled as she realised what she was saying to this girl of whom Matty had grown enormously fond, and about her own mother, too, she clapped her hand to her mouth.

"Eeh, lass, will yer listen ter me babblin' on about summat what's got nowt ter do wi' me. An' about yer ma an' all. No matter what she did, she were yer ma an' yer must 'ave bin fond of her."

"What *did* she do, Matty?" Chloe clutched at her mother-in-law's arm, her eyes quite frantic in her face from which all colour had fled. First of all there had been the revelation of Sara Andrews's frequent miscarriages, which, to a woman who was possibly three months pregnant was not exactly the kind of conversation which should be embarked upon. Of course, Matty didn't know about Chloe's condition and would be stricken with remorse if she did but it was Matty's evident loathing, her bitter contempt, even after all these years, of Chloe's mama, which demoralised her.

"Please tell me, Matty," she pleaded desperately. "I know I am hated by all of them at Cloudberry but none of it can be blamed on me. I had nothing to do with Aunt Sara and Mama and what happened between them. Uncle Jack and Aunt Sara . . . well, you know how they are and now there's Katy. I feel to blame about that. She has run wild and now look at the consequences. If I hadn't married Jamie, well, who knows, perhaps he and Katy might . . . but that was forced on me by Chris. Oh God, Matty, I don't mean I was forced into marriage with Jamie," for Matty's face was becoming more and more horror-stricken. "It was Chris's . . . attentions . . . he hit me, Matty. That's where I got that . . . that . . . last year. Jamie found me and brought me home . . . Oh, dear Lord . . ."

She began to weep, all her pent-up emotions, which she had not really been aware she was clenching inside her, those that she had pushed to the furthest corner of her mind, flooded in a torrent from her wide, distressed mouth.

"I haven't told Jamie though he's asked and asked . . . Matty, he'd kill him . . . you know how he is about me."

"Aye, chuck, aye, now give over greetin'." Matty had her in her arms, pulling her along the settle on which they were both sitting until Chloe's face was buried in Matty's capacious, comforting bosom, patting her back and shoulder consolingly, sniffing a bit herself, for she was the sort of warm-hearted, emotional woman who would always weep in sympathy for another's tears.

"Promise me, Matty," Chloe begged her frantically. "I want no more trouble which can be laid at my door."

"Nay, lass, none of it can be laid at thy door." Though Matty was Liverpool born and bred she had lived in this land which was somewhere between Lancashire and Yorkshire for so long, it showed in her speech. Now and again she lapsed into the "thee"s and "thou"s and other dialect of her neighbours. "I had me suspicions about Master Chris fer he's allus bin a birrov a lad. For ever sniffin' round every maidservant with a claim ter looks but I'd not've believed he could hit a lass."

"I wouldn't allow him to . . ."

"So he hit yer?"

"Yes."

"A bad bugger he is an' he deserves a good thrashin' but I don't want our Jamie givin' it 'im. I'm frightened he'd not stop there."

Matty hugged Chloe closer to her, hesitating before she spoke again.

"Did yer know there's rumour goin' round it were Chris what did fer Paddy Andrews?"

Chloe lifted her head in amazement. "Chris couldn't do that, Matty. He's half Paddy's weight and size. Paddy would kill him."

"Aye, I know that but with his brothers and them pals of 'is from't gentry he could manage it. Chris an' Davy were a bit knocked about at Christmas an' Richie had a broken arm which he said he got fallin' off his 'orse."

"Oh Matty, Matty, ever since I came to Cloudberry End there's been trouble."

"An' none of it your fault, so yer not ter dwell on it, d'yer hear?"

There was no more said on the subject of Sara and Alice. Chloe calmed herself enough to butter a scone for her mother-in-law which Matty thought was a "fair treat" and later, when she had gone and Chloe lay drowsing on her husband's lap before their fire she told him she was to have his child.

It was another week before Matty heard the news, whispered with great delight in her ear by her son, who had called to bring her some eggs, but within the hour it was all over Cloudberry End.

Katy had taken to galloping up to the top of the rough hill at the back of Jamie's farm, though it was becoming increasingly difficult as the months passed, dismounting from Storm's back and standing, sometimes for more than an hour, amongst a huddle of tall concealing stones. Wrapped about in her capacious cloak she would watch as Chloe moved about the yard from the farmhouse to the hen run or the barn, or, if the day was fine, merely standing and gazing about her in evident pleasure. That was what stabbed Katy to the heart, Chloe's pleasure, her great content, her settling like a cat which has finally found a place by a welcoming hearth, the hearth which should have been Katy Andrews's, and the contrast with her own devastated life was horrific. She didn't know why she rode up here for it did no good. It was as though the clean, sweet, undisturbed direction of Chloe's life with Jamie might somehow deaden the hideous distortion of her own with Paddy. As though, if she came within a certain radius of its goodness it might warm the frozen stillness in herself, though the thought often amazed her, for it was Chloe's fault, wasn't it, that this had happened at all.

Her face expressionless, her eyes dead, she remounted Storm and made her way back to Cloudberry End where the mare was still stabled since there was nowhere to house her at the cottage in Woodhead. She would walk back from there as she always did. But today, with the peace and goodness of Valley Bottom Farm still laid about her she found she could not face it, not yet. Paddy, and possibly the twins, would be there, swilling down the whisky they bought him with the money, her money, he gave them and she needed an hour or so to regain her strength for the never-ending war which was waged in Grandmother's cottage. She would go and sit in the kitchen of her old home and drink a cup of Mrs Tiplady's hot chocolate, eat a mouth-watering biscuit, just as she had done as a child. She would be a child again if only for a short time.

"What's all the excitement about, Tippy?" Katy smiled up at the housekeeper as, seated by the fire and still wrapped in her figure-disguising cloak, she accepted the cup of chocolate and the plate of biscuits which were pressed into her hand.

The housekeeper beamed. It was not that the coming event would in any way affect her, or indeed any member of the Andrews household, but Matty Jenkins had been so enraptured, so overwhelmed with joy, flinging open the kitchen door to announce the news as though it were world-shattering, her delight had infected them all, even Mrs Tiplady. Well, Matty would be excited. Her Dulcie already had little ones but they all knew Jamie Hutchinson held a special place in his mother's heart, him being her first, perhaps, and this coming child would bring her a special joy. Matty had grabbed the squealing Dilly and whirled her about the kitchen table, the scullery maid ready to have hysterics about it and it was all Mrs Tiplady could do to disentangle her from Matty's ecstatic embrace and restore order.

"Now sit down, Matty, and calm yourself," she had told her. "See, Janet, pour Matty a cup of tea and I'll have one myself. Now then, when's it to be?"

Matty had gone but the happiness such events bring had remained in the warm, bread-scented kitchen and before she had time to consider the advisability of revealing to Miss Katy the fact that Miss Chloe was with child, since they were all aware of Miss Katy's feelings for Miss Chloe's husband, it was out of Mrs Tiplady's mouth with a smile of pure delight. For a moment she had forgotten the connection Matty Jenkins's grandchild would have with this family. Babies were a delight, Mrs Tiplady believed, though she'd had none herself and Matty was so overjoyed, so proud you'd have thought it was all her doing.

"It's Matty, Miss Katy. Mrs Jenkins. She's just heard she's to be a grandmother and she's that tickled she's got us all in a . . ."

Mrs Tiplady had been about to use the word turmoil but that didn't say much for her own control of her staff, did it, besides which Miss Katy was looking at her as though she had said something offensively rude.

"I mean . . . well, I know it's not her first but with it being . . . well . . ." Mrs Tiplady's voice ran down to a whispered entreaty for forgiveness as she realised what she was saying.

"Indeed," was all Miss Katy said, but she stood up so violently Lottie, who had been about to pass her another plate of biscuits was almost knocked from her feet.

"I beg yer pardon, Miss Katy," she babbled, though it was not her fault that the biscuits were all over the floor and the plate smashed to smithereens.

They all stood in paralysed silence, the servants, each one waiting for another to speak, or move, or for Miss Katy herself to explode which she seemed in imminent danger of doing.

"Miss Katy, won't you sit down and let Lottie get you another plate of biscuits?" Mrs Tiplady begged nervously. They didn't see her all that much but when they did they were all like that with her. Nervous, for she was as unpredictable as one of the storms which blew up over Black Hill and just as dangerous, and could you blame the poor child though what had happened had been brought on by her own wilfulness. Even so, Mrs Tiplady wouldn't wish on her worst enemy the life Miss Katy lived with that . . . that brute up at her grandmother's cottage.

Katy Andrews didn't answer. From the secret part of herself to where she withdrew when she could stand no more, she peered out at them, quiet as death, pale as marble, and Freda and Mrs Tiplady exchanged glances, for they were of the private opinion that their master's daughter was not far from the edge of . . . well, they hated to call it "madness", but surely, "out of her mind" might describe the state into which she seemed about to topple and it frightened them all to death.

As though to confirm Mrs Tiplady's thoughts Miss Katy began to laugh. Her hand made some gesture which might have been denial of the news just disclosed or simply a matter of steadying herself against something which threatened to consume her, then, still laughing merrily, she turned on her heel and left the kitchen. They heard her footsteps clatter across the cobbled yard and when Janet ventured to peep through the open door she could be seen striding towards the drive which led to the gates, and from there to Woodhead and what awaited her there.

17

It was a day of warm summer sunshine. Jamie and Tommy had
gone up to the high intake to check on the almost full-grown
lambs, ready to select which to keep and which to send to
market and Chloe knew, as she slipped her light cloak over
her shoulders, that they would not be back for hours. She sat
down to pull on her sturdy boots since she had a fair walk
ahead of her, then, after one last glance round the peaceful,
sweet-smelling tranquillity of her kitchen, she stepped out
into the yard.

"I'm off, Adah-May," she called, turning in the direction of
the dairy where a tuneless rendition of "O God our Help in
Ages Past" was being performed. It was Monday and yesterday
Adah-May would have gone to church with her family which
explained the hymn, the words and music which would
have been the last Adah-May had heard and so retained in her
memory. A bucket clattered against the rim of the old stone
sink and there was the sound of one of the wide, shallow
slipware bowls in which the milk cooled being placed on a
shelf. Adah-May was to scrub the dairy from floor to ceiling
which included the shelves and the sink. She was to remove
the gauze which was placed over the windows to keep out
the flies and when she got back "the missis" was to help her
to put up fresh. All Adah-May had to do for the moment was
scrub, since it was the only job she could be trusted to do
on her own and having no idea how long she would be,
Chloe had given her the most time-consuming task she could
think of. When she was finished she was to go home, Chloe
had impressed on her, though she could see Adah-May was
bewildered. She didn't actually ask her mistress where she
was going, or why Adah-May was to go home so early, for

her thought processes could not cope with more than one order at a time.

Her alarm at the idea of being here without Mrs Hutchinson to run to should something go wrong showed clearly in the biting of her lip and the screwing up of her homely face, but when Chloe popped her head round the dairy door Adah-May turned to beam at her and Chloe knew she had forgotten all that she had been told no more than fifteen minutes ago.

She sighed. "Good girl, just keep on in the dairy and then . . . well . . ." Perhaps she would be home before Adah-May had finished the scrubbing and if she wasn't then the girl would just have to manage as best she could. She would come to no harm, surely, in the farmyard where there was nothing more dangerous than the strutting, pecking hens.

"Goodbye, Adah-May," she murmured, working on the assumption that if she were quiet and calm and matter-of-fact Adah-May would be the same and accept her leavetaking without noticing that she had actually gone.

"'Bye, missis," Adah-May answered shyly, returning at once to her deep scouring, for was that not what the missis had told her to do?

There was still a hint of mist on the tops, breaking up into floating wisps and wavering curtains as larks rose to greet the sun. Heather flowed away like a purple sea, lapping in wavelets against the outcropping of grey spotted rocks, golden with lichen. The cotton grass rippled in the gentle breeze and Chloe sighed in contented pleasure as she stepped out on the path. She had come to love what she had once called "this God-forsaken spot". The great empty spaces in which the serenity of it all wrapped about her, with no sound but the chuckling of the water, the lyrical song of the birds, perhaps the faint barking of a distant dog. Blue shadows filled the valley below, moving steadily to climb the opposite hill in unison with the clouds.

Growing in shy clumps in the rough grass and sprouting from fissures in the rocks were the white, mauve-tinged delicacy of eyebright and the yellow and purple of mountain pansy. To her right and just below her, where the track led up, was an acre or two of woodland: sessile oak, birch and mountain rowan which were native to this part of the high peakland.

She sighed again in pure happiness. It was just over a year

since she had left Liverpool, sent with scant regard for her own wishes to her mama's sister, an aunt Chloe had never met, nor indeed scarcely knew the existence of. Forwarded like a parcel to get her out of the sight of her new stepmama who was to have her papa's child and now, fourteen months later, she was to have a child of her own.

Had her papa another daughter now, or perhaps a son to carry on his name? Why had he not written, at least once, to tell his first child of the birth of her new brother or sister, or even to enquire of her if she was managing in the strange and unfamiliar life to which he had abandoned her? But the triumphantly smiling face of her stepmama came between her and her thoughts and her question was answered.

She stopped for a moment on the track which led to the road, basking in the warm sun of midsummer, chasing the thoughts away since she did not wish to cloud her new happiness with bleak memories of the past. She was happy with Jamie. Happy and loved as she had never, she realised it now, been loved before. Even her mother-in-law showed her a deep affection, inclined to hug her and give her a smacking kiss on the cheek to show her approval, and though Chloe had not been accustomed to it with Mama and Papa, she did not find it unwelcome. Her world was small, isolated but she was happy in it. She was not to be afraid of the coming birth, Matty had told her stoutly for she would be there and Chloe was given the distinct impression that if Matty could manage it she would labour alongside Chloe.

The faint, morning breeze moved in her hair which she wore loose, since it seemed Jamie liked it that way and it was always her pleasure to please him. Only when she was busy at her household chores, or working about the farm did she tie up her hair in a three-cornered kerchief. The moor above her was loud with birdsong, lulling her to a state which was almost like sleep-walking but she knew she could not afford to dawdle. Not only might she lose her nerve, so bravely scraped together over the last few days, but she had a long walk there and back and if Jamie were to come home and find her not there he would be frantic.

There was a short cut from the farm in a direct line across Great Crowden Brook, through Springfield Wood and on behind Woodhead Chapel. From there it would take her across ploughed and planted farmland and meadowland, over the steep-sided Enter Clough which was tricky and then on to the road which led to her destination.

The trouble was she was not really familiar with the route although she had been on it with Jamie, and if she lost her way, or her footing, she could be in real trouble. Jamie had taught her a very real respect for these parts which could be treacherous, even on a sunny day. She placed a protective hand on her still flat belly – though Jamie swore it was fuller – and turned towards the safety of the muddy road. It might take her longer but at least she was on a well-used thoroughfare.

The sun was bright on the water which lapped peacefully on her right. Torside Reservoir, as placid and unruffled as a duck pond, the blue of the sky, the mottled brown and green and gold of the land and the brilliance of emerald-leaved trees reflected in its mirror-like surface. It stunned her heart into silence with its beauty, the silence and stillness which only the land in its glory can command. There was nothing to intrude in the peace as she passed Woodhead Chapel, her face smiling in remembrance of the joy of her wedding day and all the joyful days which had followed.

There was a cottage at the foot of Enter Clough, its garden vivid with the blue of Michaelmas daises, the spikes of yellow hollyhock and the scarlet of dahlias. The hedges which bordered the road flamed with ripening berries and beyond them the corn was turning a rich gold. Cattle dozed in the shade of the trees and the small golden domes of beehives hummed with thronging bees in the frantic activity of making honey. Had it not been for the hazard ahead Chloe would have enjoyed every lovely mile.

The track turned off about halfway along Woodhead Reservoir, moving upwards steeply then turning to the right, and as she clambered up it, her heart pounding in her breast, there they were, perched like a row of birds on a washing line. The half a dozen or so cottages which made up the hamlet of Woodhead.

Her mouth became instantly dry and she would have given a great deal for a long drink of the cold, clear water Jamie drew from the pump in the yard. Oh, Lord . . . Oh, Lord . . . it was not just what she was about to attempt that frightened her, though that was bad enough, but what Jamie would say, and do, when he found out. Of course it would be done by then and too late for anything but the inevitable recriminations but if he should be aware that she was hazarding not only herself but their unborn child in this foolhardy venture, his rage would be unimaginable.

The end cottage which was her goal was quite, quite enchanting. There were roses scrambling up its walls in their full summer glory and even sprawling over the well-kept tiled roof. In comparison with the other cottages, some of which were in a sad state of repair, it was freshly painted. The windows winked cheerfully in the sunshine, the step was freshly scrubbed and even the bright daisies and lobelia in the window boxes stood up proudly to attention.

Hesitantly she approached the front door, clutching her cloak about her as though for protection. She could feel pulses she had not known she possessed beating frantically in various parts of her body. Her last thought as she lifted her hand to the bright, freshly buffed brass door-knocker, which was in the shape of a lion's head with a ring in its mouth, was that this surely could not be good for a woman in her third month of pregnancy?

She had lifted the ring in the lion's mouth and was about to let it fall when, from the other side of the door, there came a roar which nearly stopped her heart beating. She felt it falter, then race in an even more rapid tattoo and despite her courageous determination to do this thing she took half a dozen steps backwards. There was a window open upstairs which allowed the sound, the bellowing, free escape. A dog howled ferociously from somewhere in the cottage, a great angry tidal wave which washed out and over her and beyond to join the waters below, a sound so terrifying she had turned to run, to scurry home to the peace and security of where Jamie was, when a woman screamed.

The scream was even more terrifying than the roar and the howling dog and it seemed to Chloe that every living thing within hearing distance had curled up and put its hands over its ears to shut out the horror of it. A high scream of pain and yet even worse was the whimpering which followed, a whimpering which said that the woman who was doing it was in a state of total terror.

Dear sweet God above, what shall I do? Chloe distinctly heard someone say out loud, unaware that it was herself. She was conscious that she was shuffling about indecisively, moving from foot to foot and she could hear someone moaning in the back of her throat and realised that it was her own throat and her own voice which was making the sound.

"Don't, Paddy . . . I'm warning you . . . don't," she heard the woman say in a high, pain-filled voice and she knew as she had known from the first that the woman was her cousin and that something dreadful was happening to her on the other side of the beautifully painted door.

She didn't give herself time to think, since she knew if she did she would pick up the skirt of her second-best gown and run like a hare down the track for the safety of her home. Paddy Andrews might be murdering Katy Andrews in the cottage which had once belonged to her grandmother but it was nothing to do with Chloe Hutchinson, was it? Chloe Hutchinson was to have a child and she must protect it, her female, breeding body was screaming, but the screams from inside the cottage were just as insistent for they were female too.

Flinging herself at the door, ready to shout and bang and create as much noise as she could in the hope of distracting the man from what he was doing to Katy, Chloe found it opened before her onslaught and she was flung into the room almost at the feet of the seated man and the woman who knelt in front of him.

He had her by the arm, which he had twisted up behind her back at what seemed to be an impossible angle, her hand almost hidden under the tangle of her own hair. Her head was thrown back and her mouth was wide and straining in a rictus of agony. Tears poured from her eyes and as Chloe scrambled to her feet and began to back away, the man in the wheelchair grabbed Katy's hair with his other hand and forced her into an even more awkward position, one that had her almost on her back but with her legs twisted under her.

"You whore . . . you filthy whore," he was spitting, the saliva from his mouth spraying her face. "I'll bloody kill thi', I swear it. I'll 'ang fer thi' gladly since there's nowt much else ter be done wi' me, an' when I find out who it is tha've bin with . . ."

"Paddy . . . Jesus, Paddy . . . would I be likely to go out and lie with another man like this? Let me go, you bastard, or I warn you I shall abandon you to fend for yourself. Take your bloody hands off me."

"I've not done wi' thi', bitch, not yet. It's not often I get me 'ands on thi' now but I reckon . . ."

It was at that moment that Paddy suddenly became aware that they were no longer alone. The sunlight from the open door fell in a golden stream across the kitchen, touching the hem of Katy's dishevelled gown which was somewhere up about her thighs and Chloe remembered wondering when it was that her cousin had discarded the breeches which she had flaunted about the valley for so long. She wore no stockings or shoes and the skin of her shapely legs was white, smooth as porcelain but mottled with unsightly bruises, some of them deep and fresh, others fading to green and yellow.

Paddy Andrews, an expression of surprise taking the place of uncontainable rage on his red and sweating face, stared over the sprawled body of the woman he was abusing, and so great was his amazement to find the dainty wife of Jamie Hutchinson in what he had come to consider as *his* cottage, since he now lived here with Katy, he allowed his grip to slacken and at once Katy scrambled awkwardly away. Not far but far enough to be out of his reach. She remained on the floor, her skirts still bunched up about her, hugging the arm Paddy had nearly torn from her shoulder, rocking slowly in pain as she nursed it to her. Her hair hung about her face like a curtain, hiding all but her bitten mouth, but from the tangled mass of red-gold curls her tawny eyes, narrowed and venomous, glared at Paddy.

"You do that again, Paddy Andrews, and it won't be you who'll swing but me." Her voice was low, husky. It was as though her throat hurt her and Chloe had time to notice that the bruises on her legs and thighs were repeated on her neck. "I'll kill you, I promise. I'm sure I could persuade my brother who is now a qualified doctor and who hates your guts to give me some potion which would do for you. Slip it in your whisky, I would, and no one the wiser and, what's more, no one to care, not even those two idiots who— "

"Now then, Coppertop, that's enough of that. Can thi' not see we 'ave a visitor an' that's no way ter talk afore a visitor. Good day ter thi', Mrs Hutchinson, an' what can we do fer thi' on this fine, bright an' lovely mornin'?"

He grinned and for a moment, from inside the ruined, sweat-streaked face, the bloated flesh, the bloodshot eyes and twisted, bitter features of the man in the chair, the old handsome, winsome charm of Paddy Andrews shone through. Chloe could remember him clearly, striding athletically down the track from his father's old cottage, jumping lightly across rocks and crevices, his powerful, muscular body quite magnificent in its flagrant masculinity. Tall, strong, invincible, winking devilishly at her as she gathered bilberries for a pie.

"Good mornin' to yer, Mrs Hutchinson," he had cried out then, for it was just after she and Jamie had married, bowing and doffing his cap with a sweeping gesture, his dark curls alive and springing about his head. "A lovely mornin', is it not?" he had gone on, before disappearing jauntily in the direction of Woodhead and, presumably, this cottage.

Chloe simply stood there, her slight figure outlined by the shaft of sunlight, slender enough as to be almost transparent, her body as fragile and breakable as the lark which soared in the sky and yet prepared, or so it appeared to the grinning Paddy Andrews, to defend to the death her cousin who hated the very air Chloe Hutchinson breathed.

"Look 'oo's come ter visit us, Coppertop. It's Mrs Jamie Hutchinson as I live an' breathe. Tha'd best gerrout that fine tea-service Grandma left us, fer I'm sure a cuppa tea'd be most welcome, wouldn't it, Mrs Hutchinson?"

She turned her head then, Katy Andrews. Her face, still hidden in the curtain of her hair, showed no surprise, for Katy Andrews had learned in the last, bitter seven months to hide all emotion, all thought, all feeling, to keep to herself what once had exploded from her in a great fiery conflagration, since then she had seen no need to suppress it.

Slowly she hauled herself to her feet, hampered, Chloe thought, by her injured arm, clinging to the corner of the highly polished dresser but as the hem of her gown fell down about her bare feet, the reason for her discarding of her breeches became clear. Chloe felt the blood drain from her face and almost succumbed to her own need to fall down if she could not, and as soon as possible, find something of her own to hold on to.

Katy Andrews was in what looked to be the last month of pregnancy. Not that Chloe knew much about pregnancy. She was in her third month and barely showed. Her stepmama had been in her sixth month when Chloe last saw her and had appeared quite enormous but not nearly so enormous as Katy, whose belly jutted out from her straight and slender frame as though it could not possibly be a part of it. It was like some monstrous appendage which had attached itself to her, dragging her forward, altering the way she stood, forcing her back to a concavity which made her look deformed.

She stood as straight as she could though, her head held high, her jaw thrust forward. She pushed her hair back from her face with both hands, fastening it with a scrap of ribbon she retrieved awkwardly from the floor before she spoke.

"Get out of my house."

That was all, just those five words, but in them was a venom which plainly revealed all her loathing, all her revulsion, all her bitter, pent-up enmity for her cousin who had caused, knowingly or not, the nightmare world in which Katy now lived. Her face was cut like a cameo as she turned icily away, clear, unblurred by her pregnancy, white as marble, and as cold, but she had not bargained for Chloe's frail but resolute courage which had brought her here. Chloe had not known of Katy's condition. She had come, persuaded by the conversation she and Matty had had a few days ago, to see if . . . well, to find out if perhaps . . . perhaps . . . If Katy would allow it, she might give her cousin . . . dear God, it was so hard to put into words since she wasn't even sure what she meant herself, what she meant to offer, but what it boiled down to was . . . was a helping hand! A sympathetic . . . no, oh no, that was the last thing her hot-headed, stiff-necked, brave-hearted cousin would want, sympathy, so really it was anything that Katy might have a need for which Chloe could give.

She spoke for the first time since she had erupted into the pleasant kitchen – and it was pleasant, as clean and fragrant as her own – but it was not to Katy she spoke but to the man in the chair.

"You must not treat her so, Mr Andrews, not in her condition. You could harm the child." Her voice was severe, scolding, ludicrous really, she knew it herself, in the bitter, menacing atmosphere which charged the cottage, but it was all she could think of. The man might have broken Katy's arm, or her neck and here was Chloe Hutchinson lecturing him as though he were a big, naughty boy, one who had been caught bullying a smaller. He needed horsewhipping for the way he had handled her cousin, and her so close to her time, she thought, idiotically, she realised later. Taken outside and bent over a rail like one did with naughty boys, or so she had heard, and . . .

It was then that her eyes dropped to his hands which were clenched furiously in his lap as though in the deepest frustration, and from there moved down to his legs . . . to his one . . . one leg which ended in a bare and dirty foot, and to the other which didn't. A half a leg then, not even that, for the stump of it finished obscenely about six inches above his knee. It was wrapped about in what looked to be a bit of soiled cloth. His trousers were filthy, crumpled rags which looked as though they were never removed and his torn shirt was the same. It was evident that he had shaved, or someone had shaved him, but not for the last week.

He was still smiling as she lifted her appalled gaze to his face, his mouth cruel over his even white teeth which were the only thing about him which still remained attractive.

"Norra pretty sight, is it, Mrs Hutchinson, but my Coppertop still loves me, don't tha', Coppertop? Well, she did once since she's to 'ave me bairn, or so she ses. That it's mine, I mean. But she likes it, if tha' know what I mean, Mrs Hutchinson, an' wi' me like I am it occurs ter me she's gerrin' it elsewhere. Dost tha' tekk me meanin'?" He winked roguishly as though he and Chloe were kindred spirits in matters of the flesh.

"Be quiet, Paddy, you're making a fool of yourself." Katy began to move ponderously towards Chloe, her enormous belly swaying before her, her eyes glittering in her bone white face and, despite her determination to be heard, Chloe found herself moving back before her, almost tripping on the step, though she kept both hands resolutely on the frame of the door in order to prevent Katy from slamming it to.

"Katy . . ." she ventured tentatively. "Won't you . . .?"

"I thought I told you to get out of my house. You and I were never friends and why in hell's name you've come here I don't know, nor do I want to know, so get off my doorstep now before . . ."

"Katy, let me help you . . . please." She released her frantic grip of the door frame for a moment, using it to indicate the grinning man who would plainly be of no help to a labouring woman, the dog which could be heard throwing itself against a door upstairs, still clamouring to be let out and the awful, awful sense of hatred and fear which permeated the place.

"I don't want, nor need your help and why you should imagine I do is beyond me."

"But you are to have a child . . . I didn't know."

"Well, I did," Katy sneered, "and so does everyone else in this valley except you."

"Jamie didn't or he would have told me."

Chloe knew she had made a grave mistake as soon as the words were out of her mouth.

Katy's face twisted and the clamped-down, tightly held emotions within her, despair, hopelessness, fear, were beginning to surface despite her bitter struggle not to let this hated woman see them. No one was allowed to see what festered inside Katy Andrews. The deep, yearning, living love for this woman's husband which just would not die, the misery, the grief which had altered her until she was just not the same person any more as she struggled to come to terms with her appalling sense of loss. And then there was the remorse, yes, she who had not known the meaning of the word, when she heard from Annie Lennox of the slow deterioration of her mother's health and her father's devastation over it. The compassion she did not want to feel for the big, once handsome man in the chair who had been crippled by Katy's brothers for what she had done. Not shame, no, never shame, though she didn't know why, for surely she should feel some and now detestation for this . . . this thing which grew and jostled for space inside her. Paddy's child. The child which the gross man in the wheelchair had given her before he was crippled. Dear God, with what hot joy her body had welcomed his then and with what disgust it contemplated it now.

She could actually feel the tears welling up within her like some pool which slowly fills up with rainwater in a storm and, when it is full, overflows, but she would not weep in front of Jamie's wife, who was looking at her with such sorrow, such gentle compassionate sorrow Katy wanted – to her own amazement and horror – nothing more than to be gathered into the arms which were stretched across her doorway.

Dear God . . . dear sweet God! She opened her eyes wide, then blinked rapidly but Chloe had seen the moisture which was forming. It encouraged her and her face softened into a smile.

"Please, Katy, can we not . . .?" She could not quite bring herself to say "be friends", not yet, but surely, surely now they were both facing motherhood . . .?

As though reading her thoughts Katy stiffened in what appeared to be deep offence and her face, which had been wavering into tears, hardened. Her lip lifted in contempt and she bared her teeth for a savage moment.

"Don't start prattling on to me about babies or as God is my witness I'll knock you to the ground. I heard about you when I was at . . . at Cloudberry End but let me tell you I have no interest in, nor concern for this," placing a hand on the mound of her belly, "and I would be obliged if you would give me the same consideration. It is nothing to do with you and I don't need . . ."

"But you do, Katy, you do. You'll need a woman's help." Her eyes went over Katy's shoulder to the bloated carcase of the man behind her. "You can't manage . . ."

"I can certainly manage without you, madame."

"No . . . no, Matty says— "

"What Matty says is again nothing to me. And how dare she gossip?"

"She didn't. I was only going to say she has told me what will happen . . . explained it to me so that I would not be afraid and I believe you should have someone . . ."

"You? D'you mean you? Are you saying that I should have you in my home to help me with the birth of this . . . this child?" Her eyes blazed with incandescent fury and her lips curled. She placed her hands on her hips in a stance which would have been glorious but for the shape and size of her. Instead she looked pathetic and Chloe felt the tears flood to her eyes.

"Please, can we not put what has gone . . . behind us? I have come to ask you . . . to see if I can . . . well, in the circumstances . . ."

Again her eyes went beyond Katy to the man at her back but it was no use. She was no use to Katy Andrews who reviled the very ground on which Chloe Hutchinson walked.

Katy laughed. "Oh, you mean Paddy? Now don't you worry about me and Paddy." Her voice was mocking. "We're just like a couple of love-birds, aren't we, Paddy?" turning to smile brilliantly, heartbreakingly in his direction. "Him and me will manage just fine, won't we, lad? He'll act as midwife and then there's always Josh and Jake."

"Please, oh please, don't joke."

Katy's face hardened. "Who's joking? Now get out of my sight, you unspeakable trash. Get out of my house and don't come back here, ever. I detest the very thought of you and your . . . your . . . what you are carrying almost as much as what is inside me. If you don't take your hands from my door frame I shall trap them without the slightest compunction."

To prove she meant it Katy crashed the door to and Chloe had time only to leap backwards, sitting down in a graceless heap on the track.

Inside the house the man began to laugh.

It had never once occurred to her to turn him out. She lay in the dark that night listening to him as he and his cousins sloshed down their throats the whisky the twins had brought over to "cheer him up" and for which she would be expected to pay. There was laughter and something crashed to the ground. The dog barked furiously and through her open bedroom window she heard Jinty Pickles's husband, who must have come to his door, complain bitterly that it wasn't fitting and they had no right to be disturbing decent folk who were trying to sleep. It was a bad day indeed when Madge Andrews had passed on and left her pleasant, peaceful little home to the bad lot who occupied it now. He wouldn't say it to Paddy's face, of course, for though Paddy was no longer capable of felling a chap, not unless he came and knelt in front of him, Josh and Jake were and Barty Pickles valued his hide too much to chance it.

Though she did her best to fight it, the face of the woman who had knocked on her door this morning imprinted itself on the inside of her closed eyelids. At once she opened them, staring at the silent shapes of the things which had once known the calm presence of her beloved grandmother, praying – though not in the true sense of the word – that her grandmother's memory would disperse that of Chloe Hutchinson but she could still see her, distressed, afraid even, but determined, nevertheless, to have her say.

Help her . . . Help her . . . Help Katy Andrews! That's what she had offered to do and dear God, the temptation to accept had been so great it had almost had her over. But what action could Chloe Hutchinson possibly take, had Katy herself wanted her to, that would rescue her from this impenetrable greyness, this perilous dread she was slowly sinking under? The naïvety of the woman was laughable had it not been so infuriating, but at the same time, though she hated the thought, she could not help but admire the bloody nerve of the woman. Of course, everyone knew there was nothing to be done with, or for Katy Andrews now. Her own family never came near her, though she knew in her heart where truth lay that if she asked for help it would be given. Every week Jimmy or Dicken rode up, their faces averted, to deliver the envelope which contained enough money for her to live comfortably and even feed Paddy's increasing appetite for alcohol. As long as she kept out of his reach and those cruel hands of his which, now that he was incapable of giving her pleasure, loved to pinch and bruise, not as once they had but simply for cruelty's sake, she could go on.

Annie – Mrs Lennox – came in every day while Paddy lay insensible in his bed to clean up after him and put the small cottage to rights, but she was another one who kept her face averted and had it not been for the generous wage Katy paid her would not have set foot inside the place. They were polite with one another, that was all and it would have been . . . pleasant to have another woman, a young woman . . .

God Almighty, what was she thinking of? What had put that preposterous thought in her head? What preposterous thought? her bewildered mind asked, for it had never been completed, and never would, for there was nothing more certain in her life than the truth that she would consider Chloe Hutchinson with loathing until the day she died. Chloe Hutchinson, the woman who had stolen Katy Andrews's life.

18

She was up on Great Crowden Intake when the first pang struck her. Low down in her back it was, more like the start of the dull cramps which came to plague her each month, moving dully to the pit of her belly. Well, if that was all it was going to be she'd manage it fine, she told herself. Up here with no one to see but a hawk which floated on the flickering wind, a skylark or two doing acrobats against the grey sky and some sheep who called fretfully to one another across the dense carpet of purple heather above the intake.

Though the day was dull it had not been cold when she lumbered down the stairs. Paddy had been snoring on his bed where his drinking partners had flung him the night before, his face slack and puffy, his mouth open, his lips coated with some nasty white substance which made her stomach heave. The dog lay next to him. He raised his head and watched her as she began to move things about haphazardly, an empty whisky bottle, a plate on which a half-eaten meat pie congealed, Paddy's shirt which, unusually, he had removed. After a moment or two, knowing she was no threat either to him or his master, the animal lowered his muzzle, resting it on the stump of Paddy's leg, not at all revolted by it as she was.

Moving back into the kitchen she began to fidget with dirty cups and plates and cutlery, finding, to her surprise, she felt a great need to have them washed and set to rights, to tidy the place up. Even, God forbid, to fetch a pail of water and scrub the table top which was stained with whatever the men had eaten and drunk the night before. What in blazes was the matter with her? Katy Andrews who had never willingly washed a plate in her life and certainly had barely noticed the state of the table top, let alone felt the need to scrub it.

The fire had still been in, for despite their negligent attention towards anything which smacked of cleanliness, and their drunken state of the night before, all three men had been brought up with the ingrained principle that a kitchen fire, once lit, must never be allowed to go out. It was the centre of cottage life, the focal point, its heart. It kept them warm and it fed them, for all the cooking was done in the ovens on either side of it and in its slumbering coals which one of the twins had replenished. The kettle whispered softly above it and her grandmother's chair rocked before it. Peace was total and Katy savoured it while she drank a cup of tea and ate an enormous dish of porridge Mrs Lennox had made and left in a pan to the side of the fire. With syrup trickled into it it made a satisfying breakfast. Mrs Lennox, though she had nothing to say on the matter, or indeed on any matter, often left some culinary offering. A dumpling stew, a steak and kidney pudding, a slab of boiled bacon with pickles, bread on most days, the extra few shillings Katy put in her hand for payment going completely unremarked. It was as though Annie Lennox could only manage the dreadful state of affairs in Madge Andrews's cottage and her own financial need to be involved in it if she did not speak of it, or to its present occupants. A nod, sometimes a muttered reminder that his bed needed changing, which meant Katy was to have him out of it while Annie tackled the slovenly mess it was in.

Katy was aware that without Annie Lennox's reluctant help she would have gone under.

She was restless, wandering from the scullery where, again to her astonishment, she found herself with a passionate desire to clean the windows, for heaven's sake, which naturally she resisted. Back to the glowing hearth, then over to the front door, flinging it open to stare down the track towards the reservoir, where the water rippled in a gentle, aimless way, eddying this way and that as the wind caught it. Grey clouds, their undersides lined with dark blue, sat almost motionless above distant Bleaklow Hill and from the railway track which ran on the far side of the water came the shriek of an engine's whistle.

It had rained in the night and the hedgerows were spattered with moisture. Wild flowers bloomed, bright and unruly. The trees, product of the abundant rainfall which predominated in this high peak land, were garbed in lush green foliage, dripping somewhat disconsolately to soak into the already sodden ground. Barty Pickles's gnarled, mossy trees were laden with apples and plums and Katy smiled, for at this very moment a plum pie resided in her cupboard, baked by Annie, the plums, though he was not aware of it and would have been highly indignant if he had known, from Barty's trees.

She sighed, leaning her shoulder against the door frame, her hands linked beneath the awkward, hated burden of her distended stomach, then, turning clumsily, she reached for her warm, lined cloak. She threw it round her shoulders and, closing the door quietly behind her, she left the cottage, going not down the track but crossing it behind Enter Clough. The clough itself was not deep and neither was the water which chuckled down it and she was able to reach the other side without getting her feet wet.

Working her way steadily across the horizontal waves of gritstone which lay above the farmland she felt her spirits lift. She breathed deeply, filling her lungs with the pure, heady air which had in it the scent of heather and gorse, of rich soil and rough grass, of all the things she had known and taken for granted all her pampered childhood.

A lark, despite the cut-throat and buffeting wind which had sprung up as Katy climbed higher, rose straight up in front of her into the whirling air and poured out its bubbling song. She stopped to watch it and to catch her breath, bending over a little to ease the stitch which pierced her side.

She stood for several minutes, wishing she was on Storm's back with Muffy racing along at the mare's heels. What with one thing and another, she thought grimly, Paddy Andrews had a lot to answer for, though she supposed she could not blame him entirely. First there was this blasted infant which surely must come soon and when it did a home had to be found for it since she knew nothing about babies and had no intention of learning. Second, because of her condition she had been unable to ride Storm for weeks and third there was the loss of her constant, devoted companion, her scruffy little dog whom she had been forced to leave at Cloudberry End. How she missed her and she knew Muffy fretted but there was nothing to be done about it, not with that ugly brute which never left Paddy's side taking up residence in what he evidently believed to be his rightful place on Katy's hearth. Now and again, when his furious barking at every damn thing which annoyed it, annoyed *him*, Paddy begged her to lure him up into the spare bedroom so that he could have a bit of peace, but even there he was forever whining and howling and throwing himself against the closed door. Damned dog! She hated the thing.

The deep gully down which Little Crowden stream ran had her panting badly by the time she had traversed it. It was more of a climb than she had bargained for, since she had never done it on foot. Still, she managed it, her breath heaving triumphantly as she rested for a moment, looking down the steep slope towards Woodhead Chapel. The trees surrounding it hid it from her view and it seemed to her the bunched clouds which had begun to tumble across the sky were lower than when she had left home.

Great Crowden Breck, the largest of the waters which ran down to the reservoirs, was easier to get across. There were numerous scattered rocks in the smoothly flowing, white-dashed water and holding the awkward weight of her unborn child with both hands as though for balance, she managed to flounder from stone to stone, clambering up the bank through the vivid yellow gorse bushes which lined it to flop on her back with relief.

It was then that the first pain nudged her. The rough grass of the intake was damp but soft. Her cloak was thick, warmly lined and would provide her with a comfortable bed, especially if she could reach an outcrop of dizzily balanced rocks higher up the intake which would give her some shelter from the wind and what appeared to be a coming rainstorm.

She had almost reached them when another pain rippled through the small of her back, down her loins and up to the pit of her belly, this time stronger than the twinge she had first suffered and she had to pause, panting a little, waiting until it had passed but it didn't. Instead it lingered, a persistent nagging backache which, no matter how she stood, would not ease.

She was not frightened. "Oh damn and blast," she muttered, vaguely annoyed somehow for she had never been ill or known pain of any sort beyond a skinned knee in childhood since her birth seventeen years ago.

The rain was falling more steadily now, droplets catching in her hair and beginning to run uncomfortably down her face. They clung to her eyelashes, making her blink and she knew that if she didn't get into the shelter of the rocks, even with her sturdy cloak about her, she would soon be wet through.

She was still not frightened. "Damn you to hell, Paddy Andrews," she snarled savagely as she struggled up the incline, slipping on the wet grass, until she reached the grateful, if not entirely waterproof shelter of the rocks. She knew nothing of childbirth, only that it could take a while and that there was not much to be done about it until the end when, presumably, you wrapped the result up in a shawl and handed it to someone who would know what to do with it. In the meanwhile she'd lie here and wait.

Wrapping her cloak about her, glad of the warmth, she huddled against the biggest stone, doing her best to keep out of the drizzle which the wind would persist on flinging against her. No matter which side of the stone she crawled to, it still found her and she began to shiver.

She was alarmed several minutes later when she suddenly found her lower body, her thighs and legs, her drawers and petticoats, soaked with something which gushed from between her legs in the most undignified manner. It was warm and for a dreadful moment she thought it might be blood but as the pain began to attack her with a vengeance she found it no longer mattered. Blood, or perhaps she had wet herself in this disgusting thing which was happening to her, but did she care? Not at all! She only cared about the increasingly agonising crescendo of pain which knifed into her body at shorter and shorter intervals and her need to get it over and done with so that she might be returned to the person she had been before Paddy Andrews had got her with child. She'd known him and his body and this was the outcome and as God was her witness it would never, *never* happen again. Not any of it.

Jamie heard the scream, well, a succession of what sounded like screams, from where he was just starting the descent between Rakes Rock and Black Tor. He had gone to search for one of his flock. All sheep were stupid in his opinion, following one another blindly, even over the gritstone edge of Oakin Clough, which he knew to his cost, for three of his had done just that. But this particular beast did not seem to have the flock instinct, wandering off by itself as though in search of something, though God alone knew what. What would a ewe look for? he asked his wife, shaking his head in wonderment but there seemed to be no answer and every now and again he was forced to search for the bloody thing. He had not found it today.

The driving rain slanted almost horizontally into his face and the wind lashed the bracken to frenzy. Already, though it had been raining for no more than two hours, a fast-moving swathe of water was flowing across the sodden grass and over his stout boots and the track was almost invisible. It was slippery and he had gone down more than once on to his behind. The rain was coming down faster, or rather across faster, hurtling directly into his face, almost with the ferocity of hailstones, it was so hard and cutting.

He hesitated as the sound was repeated. At first he had been inclined to put it down to the keening of the driving wind, cursing the bloody weather which could turn from the warmth of summer to the raw chill of winter in a couple of hours. Jesus, it was July but it might have been January it was so bitter and he wouldn't have been surprised to see the rain turn to snow.

There it was again. He saw Captain prick his ears and turn his head in the direction of Great Crowden Intake which was away to his left, then look up at him as though seeking a command. The animal was becoming a well-behaved and competent sheepdog, alert and obedient, mindful of his job as the keeper of his master's flock and though his sharp ears were well aware the sound was not that of a sheep it was one which needed investigating, surely?

"What is it, Captain? You can hear it too, can't you?"

The dog almost nodded his head. He was poised, one foot raised, ready to dart off when his master said he might and when Jamie's hand waved him on he was off like a greyhound from the slips, a fast-moving blur blending into the soaked, mud-coloured ground and the slanting rain before vanishing from Jamie's sight.

"Captain?" Jamie called, his hands cupped round his mouth and when the dog answered with a short, yipping bark which meant "over here", he moved as fast as he could go across the sloping, greasy grass in his direction.

* * *

She had fallen into a light doze between the tail end of one slash of the knife and the beginning of the next. She had been writhing and screaming for hours, days, weeks, up here with no one to see her, or hear her, which is what she had wanted, she remembered thinking dazedly. To get this over by herself without any other woman fussing about her and by God, she'd got her wish and now look what a bloody mess she was in. As far as she could tell, and how was she to know, the child showed no sign of making an appearance and not only was there a claw scrabbling at her back and her belly, and every other part of her racked body, her throat was on fire with her own screams. Several times she had turned her face up to the pelting rain, opening her bitten mouth wide and allowing the icy water to fill it up and then slide down her throat but she was so tired now, so battered, so dazed and uncaring, she no longer had the strength. At the beginning she had stood up and walked about, holding on to the rough stones among which she sheltered and she had found some benefit, but that was a long time ago and so now she would lie here and let this thing continue to tear her to pieces, when, presumably, she would die. And the child, which would concern no one. In fact there most certainly would be more than one who would be glad to see the back of her, and Paddy Andrews's bastard. Chris, for one, and who could blame him, although it had been his initial attack on Paddy which had brought about this maelstrom of events.

Oh God . . . Oh sweet Jesus . . . it was here again, that agony which was slowly tearing her apart.

Her head was jerked back and her throat became taut, the tendons in it straining and rigid, her voice no more than a thin wail, when something wet and warm and rough moved across her face. Her eyes were tight closed, her mouth opened wide but the tongue, for that was what it was, continued to lap at her with the cheerful abandonment of a young dog.

Muffy? Was it Muffy? Was she at home then in the kitchen at Cloudberry End, her own little dog in her lap, her ecstatic tongue licking at every bit of bare flesh it could reach? Her face and neck and now her hand which she lifted weakly to ward it off. But she was so cold, so cold and tired and hurting and someone was sawing at her with a blunt knife and she really ought to raise her voice in protest but the thing was she was just too exhausted to care any more.

"Muffy . . . good girl," she said hoarsely, glad to have her, for if she were to be alone up here . . . up here . . . aah, she wasn't in the kitchen at Cloudberry End then . . . of course . . . too cold . . . then in what better company to die than Muffy's who loved her?

But she must be dead already . . . and gone to some heavenly place, for here was Jamie, her love, her joy . . . the reason she lived . . . for Jamie . . . for the only man she had ever wanted . . . needed . . . Jamie . . .

"Katy!" His voice sounded strange, hoarse, and in it was something odd which she could not recognise. His eyes, blue as the sky on a midsummer day, blue as turquoise in candlelight, were glittering, wide.

"Jamie . . . Jamie . . . have you . . . come to . . .?"

"Dear sweet Christ, Katy . . . what in heaven's name . . .?"

She smiled and her hand gripped his sleeve with a strength which surprised her, for she had been fighting this thing for so long and she was burned out, finished, but there was something she must say before the end.

"I love you, Jamie. This . . . with Paddy . . . is nothing. I love you . . . and I always will." She wanted to tell him that. She wanted him to understand about her and Paddy . . . it was most important before she died. She could feel the claw beginning to rip at her again but when he put his arms about her and lifted her contorted, contorting body against his strong one she didn't mind so much.

"Put your arms round my neck, sweetheart."

Sweetheart! He had called her sweetheart, so what else mattered in this bad, mad world, this agony, this bitter, joyless day on which . . . she couldn't quite remember what it was . . . on which something awful was happening to her.

Her arms felt so heavy though, so lifeless, boneless, useless.

"I don't think . . . I can, Jamie."

"Never mind . . . never mind, my love. Just rest . . . I've got you. Just rest until I get you home."

"Are we to . . . go home then, Jamie?"

"Yes, sweetheart."

It took him over two hours to negotiate the steep track which led down from Great Crowden Intake to Valley Bottom Farm.

Again and again he was forced to kneel and put her on the ground, her labouring body too much for him to hold and with each contraction she threw herself about, screaming and begging him not to let her go. She was off her head, her eyes deep pools of dull brown amber in her putty-coloured face. She was as wet as if she had dragged herself through the rapidly filling breck which he followed, and so was he, doing his best to stay on his feet in the headlong race of rainwater which was on its way to the storm-tossed fury of the reservoir in the valley. It was growing dark and several times he was convinced that he and Katy, her unborn child and the brave dog who never left his side, were to go too.

Chloe had a dozen candles lit in the kitchen, making sure he would not miss the farmhouse in the black fury of the storm which had come upon them so suddenly and as he staggered through the gate and round the corner of the building into the yard, sheltered from the shrieking wind at last, she was there, the door standing wide, a shawl about her head, for she had been up to the drystone wall at the back of the farm a dozen times to peer up the track from which he would come.

For a moment she thought he had a sheep across his arms, grey, sodden, senseless, perhaps injured in some way and was alarmed when he moved towards the kitchen door with, it seemed, every intention of bringing the animal inside.

"Jamie . . .?" she questioned.

"Quick, for Christ's sake get out of the way."

"Jamie!" He had never, as long as she had known him, spoken to her in other than the gentle tones of a lover and her mouth dropped open in astonishment.

Then she recognised what it was he carried.

"Blessed Lord," she gasped, rearing back from him and his burden, her eyes wide and frightened, her hand going to her mouth. "What . . . who . . .?"

"Quickly, it's Katy and she's in labour, and in trouble by the look of her. God knows how long she's been up there. We've got to strip her off, Chloe, and get her warm or she'll die."

Yes, Chloe could see who it was now, the woman who had put that anguished look on Jamie's face and made his voice so hoarse and afraid. She already looked dead to her, her arms and head lolling back across Jamie's arms, her hair streaming like tangled seaweed towards the floor, dripping and limp, its vital colour completely gone. Her eyes were closed and her wet face was carved as though from stone and Chloe was about to put out a tentative hand to her cheek, for surely it would be cold and lifeless, when Katy suddenly stiffened, then arched her body in some dreadful spasm and began to scream, a high-pitched scream of pure, undiluted agony.

"Oh sweet God," Chloe whispered. She could feel the blood freeze in her veins but Jamie would have none of it.

"Chloe, pull yourself together or they'll both die."

"Both?"

His voice was harsh as though he was angry with her and she wanted him to put down Katy Andrews and take her in his arms. To put to one side the woman he held who was nothing to do with Chloe and Jamie Hutchinson and their life. To take hold of his wife who was – dear God, forgive her – jealous of his attention to the woman who was her cousin.

She had no time to examine this astonishing thought, for Jamie was becoming increasingly impatient.

"Chloe, she's in labour, for God's sake. You know what that means. Now move. Clear a space in front of the fire and spread that rug. Yes . . . yes, that will do. Then we must take off these wet clothes," and all the time he spoke Katy's voice rose higher and higher in a wail of white-hot agony.

"I'm not sure I can manage her on my own, Jamie," Chloe heard herself whisper, clutching at her own belly where her child slept.

"I'm not proposing that you should, my dove. Now run upstairs and bring down the blankets from our bed and some clean sheets . . . quickly . . . quickly."

For perhaps the last time in her life Chloe's early training at her mama's knee rose to the fore.

"But surely you cannot mean that *you* are to help?"

"For Christ's sake, woman, stop dithering about and do as I say."

She became calm then. His concern for Katy was only natural and this was not the time to be studying her own sudden and strange feeling for this man who loved her and who had been her husband for nine contented months. She became the woman she really was beneath the veneer her mama had painted over her. The woman who was now a wife, a true wife. A farmer's wife who would shortly go through herself what her cousin suffered and she did not intend to flinch from it.

They stripped her while she mumbled and screamed and writhed and bucked beneath their hands. Chloe was strong now, soothing her, stroking her face and her sweat-streaked hair, unembarrassed to have this naked woman straining on her kitchen rug beneath the pitying gaze of her own husband, for that was what was in his face for Katy Andrews, his wife saw it plainly.

Even like this Katy was beautiful, earthy, a female labouring to bring forth life. Her fine white skin stretched dangerously tight over the distended mound of her belly. Already her swollen breasts leaked some milky fluid, Chloe noticed, as she eased Katy gently into one of the capacious nightgowns she had already made in preparation for her own pregnancy.

"Oh God . . . God help me . . ." Katy Andrews, as though her body knew that it must take an active part in this last stage of her labour, came to her senses to find the compassionate face of the woman she hated more than any other bending over her. Her heart, which was already banging away inside her chest as her body strained to rid itself of its burden, gave a sickening lurch and though she scarce had breath to breathe let alone speak, she heard her own voice rasp in her inflamed throat.

"What in hell's name d'you think you're doing?" she snarled. "Take your filthy hands off me and bugger off before . . ."

"I have no intention of buggering off, as you so engagingly put it, Katy Andrews," Chloe answered serenely. "This is my house we are in. That is my nightgown you are wearing and my rug you are staining with your blood, so kindly lie back and allow Jamie and me to deliver your child."

Katy's mouth popped open even wider, then stayed that way as she began to bellow.

"Oh Jesus . . ." She was up on her elbows. Her head fell back and her heels dug into the bright rug as her splayed legs moved instinctively wider to allow passage for the child she was pushing out of her.

"Where the bloody hell is Jamie?" she screeched, panting like a dog on a hot day.

"Here, at the working end" – his voice smiled – "and you're not to worry. Chloe and I have done this before, you know, so we're quite experienced."

"Who . . . who with?" she managed to ask as she bore down relentlessly, unable to do anything else.

"Oh, several calves and at least half a dozen sheep."

"Calves . . . sheep! God help me . . ."

"No, lass, just me and Chloe."

It took no more than fifteen minutes, minutes through which Katy roared and raged, for Jamie kept telling her to stop, to rest a moment, to slow down then to bear down, to stop . . . stop, until she said she had had enough and was off to old Dr Highcroft who wouldn't keep her hanging about like this.

A final heave, a sort of plopping noise like a landed fish coming to rest on a river bank and then, with a bellow which had Captain leaping to his feet and barking furiously, Katy Andrews's son was born into the hands of the man she loved.

The woman she loathed held her hands and cried and Katy allowed her to kiss her brow and cheek before being taken into her strong and slender arms, glad to be there at the last.

19

She walked up the gravelled driveway, her skirts swinging, her ankles bare, her son tied to her breast in a shawl, just like a gypsy woman selling pegs at the back door, Mrs Tiplady moaned to Freda, though of course, Miss Katy didn't use the back door but marched boldly in at the front.

"Is my father at home, Freda?" she asked the flustered parlourmaid. "I've come to introduce him to his grandson."

And there he was, Freda reported later to the open-mouthed servants who clustered round her, undeterred by the presence of Mrs Tiplady, who was not as commanding as usual in her astonishment. Paddy Andrews's son, lying sweetly in his mother's arms, plump and brown and with eyes and hair exactly the colour of hers. They said she took him up on the moors, striding out like a man, though she no longer wore her breeches, nor did she ride her sorrel mare. Saul Gibbon said he had seen her as high as the Black Hill itself, sitting on a rock, the wind in her hair, the child suckling at her breast.

"Good day to you, Saul," she had called out, bold as brass. "A lovely day, is it not?" and Saul had no choice but to answer that it was. Well, he was that taken aback he'd had no time to remember that she was the scarlet woman of Crossclough, with her crippled lover and her bastard child and that no one had a good word to say for her except that cousin of hers who was herself suspect. She looked so . . . well, Saul was not familiar with words such as "tranquil" or "serene" but that was what Katy Andrews was now, despite what had happened to Paddy Andrews and Chris Andrews, for which she was surely to blame, the wildness gone from her with the birth of her boy.

Jack, she'd called him, though naturally he'd not been

731

baptised, not with him being illegitimate, but perhaps if Jack Andrews, his grandfather, were to get a look at him, things might be different.

He was sitting in a leather chair drawn up to the fire in his study and he did not get up when she entered. Neither did he turn round. He was smoking a cigar, his head wreathed in the fragrant smoke from it and Katy breathed it in deeply, realising how she had missed it. It brought back memories of her childhood, of her father coming home from his travels laden with presents, big, strong, handsome, his smile wide as he swept her up into his arms. Not for long, of course, for her mother would detach him from his children and carry him off to the private world she and he lived in and it would perhaps be twenty-four hours before they saw him again.

"Father," she said quietly, for Katy Andrews had learned to be quiet now she had a child. "Father."

He turned then, sighing deeply as his eyes lifted to hers and she was shocked to see the change in him. She had not seen him since he had come to the cottage to try and take her home, and she had thought him to be ageing then but he looked ten years older now. He was no longer big and strong, though she supposed he could still be called handsome in a lean and furrowed way. Where his face had been smooth, well shaven, amber-tinted, it was now lined and sallow, the flesh dwindled somehow, his dark brown eyes, so like hers, so like Paddy's, sunk deep in dusty shadows. He had grown so thin, his well-cut jacket standing away from his neck where once it had fitted snugly and when he stood at last she could see his waistcoat hang away from his stomach.

"Katherine," he answered courteously, as though she were no more than an unexpected guest. His eyes strayed briefly to the child but he showed no particular interest, not even when her son awoke, blinking his eyes slowly like a baby owl. After a lingering contemplation of her own face, which the baby always seemed to find of immense interest, especially when she talked to him, he looked about him, turning his well-shaped head on which russet curls had begun to spring until his gaze came to rest on his grandfather. He smiled briefly, a sort of bobbing half smile which seemed to take him by surprise, then he turned his face to her breast in search of nourishment. His mouth nuzzled against the cotton of her bodice, open and demanding and Katy knew she would either have to feed him or be quick in what she had to say to her father.

She smiled hesitantly. He was so distant, so unconcerned, not only with her but with her son whom he surely could not resist. This was his grandchild, his first grandchild and though circumstances were . . . well, she could only call them disastrous, surely her parents would recognise that things were different now. She was different since Jack's birth. This was her family home and in it was her family and she wanted Jack to be welcome in it, to have a family, a grandmother and grandfather, uncles and . . . well, a proper place in the way of things. Paddy treated him like a plaything, something to divert him when he was bored, wanting to dandle him on his good knee, tossing him about roughly, making a man of him, as he put it, boasting to his cousins on how brave and handsome his son was. His son who was the dead spit of him except for his hair, he said, and that, of course, came from his Coppertop, leering in her direction, giving the impression to the grinning twins that he and Katy still shared a physical relationship. Not that she ever left Jack alone with him, not for a second and when Paddy had him in his rough embrace she hung about no more than an arm's length away in case Paddy got too boisterous. Truth to tell she didn't like him to touch her son at all, even though Jack was his as well. Paddy was so gross now, eating and drinking from daybreak until he fell into his bed at night, the fat hanging in folds down his once arrow-straight, fighter's body. What had once been hard muscle was now creeping obesity, flabby and disgusting and to see her sweet baby on his knee, her son whom she loved with all the passion she had once lavished only on Jamie Hutchinson, was something she could not bear.

She was not sure, even as she stood before her father, what she expected of him, what could be done to put right the wrongs she had committed but she had to start somewhere. This child was the catalyst. Already he had shown her that love was never-ending, ever-growing; that it took many forms. That it could not be divided, or subtracted from. That no matter how many there were to share it it was always the same size. She loved Jamie. That was a fact and was unalterable. That love would never wither but now her son took her love for himself, for did she not have an everlasting abundance of it, stealing nothing from Jamie since love was indivisible.

Her father waited patiently for her to begin. She felt a tremor of apprehension for she had not expected this indifference, this complete lack of concern for anything she might have to say. She was his daughter and so he had agreed to see her but it was no more than a gesture, his attitude said, as if he were waiting civilly for her to get on with it and then leave him in peace.

"Is Mother well?" she asked for want of something to fill the dreadful emptiness while the baby, whom she had hoisted to her shoulder in order to divert him from the smell of her milk, did his best to turn his head. He was almost three months old now and beginning to take a great deal of interest in what went on around him and she patted his back pacifyingly.

Her father looked at her for a long time before breaking the silence. His face could not be said to have come alive but there was an expression on it which she did not recognise.

"I was going to write to you," he said at last, his voice quiet, "since you have a right to know but as you are here now I may as well tell you."

The apprehension began to grow in her, to become something more than apprehension and she felt her heartbeat quicken. The clock at the back of the room sounded the quarter hour with a solid clunk and it made her jump. She held the baby more tightly to her and he began to struggle strongly. She patted his back feverishly and began to sway to and fro, doing her best to avert the full-throated roar of his demand for the breast.

"Father, you're beginning to frighten me. I came to— "

"Really, lass, d'you think it matters to me now? What you came here for? I'm sure whatever it is will be to your advantage as has every action you have ever taken since you were a child. At least what you imagined to be to your advantage— "

"No, Father . . . no," she interrupted him. "I came not for myself but to show you your grandson." She turned the baby to face Jack Andrews, holding his back against her breast, but her father, after a casual glance into the child's appealing face, looked back to his daughter.

"See, Father, is he not a lovely boy? Please, don't look away. I named him Jack . . ." After you, of course, though without the conscious intention of pleasing you. "Father, he is your flesh and blood . . . please . . ."

"Aye, an' Paddy Andrews's." Her father's face became

animated for a moment and his voice was harsh. A flush of blood ran under his skin making him look more like his old self, then it died away and so did his show of animosity.

"Father, I know it has not been . . . pleasant," she mumbled, "but Jack is your grandson, and Mother's, so may I not go up and show him to her?" Her voice had became pleading, desolate but her father cut it off, his own sharp and positive.

"No, you may not. That is what I must talk to you about. Your mother . . . is not well." His voice broke and he passed a trembling hand over his face. "She has not been strong, not for years, but I dare say with a peaceful, trouble-free life she might have remained in good health. But of course that is just what she has not had. None should know better than you. It has broken her heart, Katherine. You have been a trial to me and to your mother, lass, you must know that?"

"Father, I did not mean to— "

He cut off her wail of protest with a dismissive movement of his hand.

"Maybe you did not mean to, Katherine. Nevertheless you did, so I am taking your mother away. I have bought a house in Scarborough. It stands on a cliff overlooking the sea. The air and a life of tranquillity free from the pressures her family have forced on her in the past will, Dr Highcroft assures me, be beneficial to her and she may, to some extent, recover. She is to lead a quiet life with only those people about her who care for her."

"Father, I love her," and it was true though she had not been consciously aware of it.

"You have a strange way of showing it, lass. You have broken her health and her heart. Your wildness, your flouting of every rule her society believes in has become more than she can bear. She has been forced to listen to tales of your . . . your depravity. Yes, that is the word I would use, and I mean to see she is protected from it from now on. We leave at the end of the week and— "

"But, Father, please . . . please don't shut me out."

"Shut you out! Girl, you did that to yourself when you took up with Paddy Andrews."

"I know, I know I was to blame, for Paddy and his feud with Chris which is . . . Oh, please, Father, now that I have a son, won't you . . .?"

Her father looked at her sadly, then, putting out a

trembling hand, laid it for a moment on his grandson's head.

"Now you know, Katy. Now you are a mother yourself you will realise what you have done to yours."

She scarcely heard the rest of his words which explained to her the arrangements he had made for his children, which, presumably, included her, and for his property. Mrs Tiplady, Ivy and Freda were to go to Scarborough with their mistress since they were used to her ways and she to theirs. Lottie and Janet would remain at Cloudberry End with the remainder of the kitchen staff to take care of the house and of Christopher who was to be in charge of the paper mill.

He would need a home and there were his brothers, Richard and David, who would require some place to come back to from their travels.

The outside staff would remain, since Jack Andrews did not wish to see his property go to rack and ruin. Jimmy and Dicken would continue to see to the stables and the horses, Storm included, if she so wished and he himself would travel back now and then from Scarborough to check on things. Cloudberry End was to remain as it was and, if she needed it, he added distantly, doing his duty, no more, and, not wishing either himself or his beloved wife to be concerned with it, there would always be a home for her here.

"A home?" she repeated dully.

"Yes, I really cannot see you living your life out with that . . . that . . ."

"Cripple? Is that the word you're searching for, Father?"

"If you wish."

"Have you never wondered why I stay with him?"

"No, I can't say I have, Katherine. Not lately, at any rate."

"He is a cripple because of me, Father. Chris and the others gave him a beating."

"Richly deserved, my lass. Had I been young enough I would have helped them. For a man to . . . to violate an innocent girl— " He stopped abruptly and the glow of madness which coloured his face faded. "Well, what's done is done, Katy, and we are left with the results. We must make of them what we can. My concern is for your mother now. No one else. Now I must go, if you'll excuse me. I have things to do."

"Yes . . ." She stood up, the child in her arms, not thrown out, oh no, far from that, but abandoned just the same, by the man and woman she herself had abandoned so carelessly.

They watched her go, Janet and Lottie, from the upstairs window where they were packing their mistress's clothes. They had no idea why she had come, apart from what she had said to Freda about showing her boy to her father, but even now, when she surely must have been told of her parents' departure for Scarborough, she did not droop nor falter. Her head was up, brilliant and glowing in the "back-end" sunshine, her back straight, her skirt swinging, her stride long and graceful as she turned into the woodland just before she reached the gate. Now where was she going? they asked one another. Taking a short cut beneath the brown and copper and tawny orange of the autumn trees and then on through the fields where the crops were being harvested, perhaps.

Well, wherever she was off to it was none of their business, though they did admit to one another they would have liked to get a look at Miss Katy's little lad.

It was a mellow, sunny day and Katy could hear through the misted jumble of her thoughts the voices of children blackberrying on the other side of the hedge and the sweet, solitary singing of a robin. A mist was gathering in the hollows and the sky was turning to the pearly blue of the coming evening. Her child was beginning to clamour with more persistence for her breast which was full and doing some clamouring of its own. She felt dazed, a sense of disorientation which was foreign to her, she who had always known her own mind, her own needs and her own ruthless determination to follow them.

The sun was sinking in a blaze of crimson glory at the back of the peaks towards Black Hill but there was still a patch of warm sunlight on a bit of drystone walling facing the west. Just below her lay Valley Bottom Farm. She could hear the constant cackle of the hens in the yard, quietening slowly as the day drew towards its ending and the voice of young Tommy shouting goodbye to Chloe. Soon Jamie would be home, his eyes darkening with love for his wife. Katy had seen them do so, his arms reaching out for her with a hunger which spoke, as words could not, of his need. She had seen that, too, in those few days she lay in their house after Jack was born and she had also seen Chloe's answering ardour, her eagerness to be in the arms he held out to her. She had lain on the truckle bed in the warm kitchen, her new son snuffling beside her, for three long and endless days and nights until she could stand it no longer and Thomas had come to take her back to Woodhead in the gig.

The baby nuzzled contentedly at her breast, his eyes beginning to glaze with sleep and the fullness of his small, distended stomach. His mouth relaxed and released her nipple which was moist and shining with milk and she rested him across her lap, studying the perfection of his face. The fluff of red curls just over the pulsing fontanelle, the honey tint of his silken flesh where the sun had touched it, the length of his curling auburn lashes, his rosy, pouting mouth which still sucked even in sleep. His hand rested peacefully against his own cheek and she bent her head to it, lifting it gently, kissing the plump palm.

She did not hear his boots on the tufted grass and her breasts were still exposed, rich and ripe with motherhood, heavy and yet not drooping, for Katy Andrews was not yet eighteen. Young, proud breasts with peaked, almond-tinted nipples in the perfect circle of the areola. Her head was bent to her child, her glossy, burnished hair pulled back and tied on the crown with a knot of bright green ribbons and her face was so unutterably sad Jamie Hutchinson felt his heart move for her. She looked quite startlingly beautiful, her skin honey smooth with a rose flush on her cheekbones. Her wide, passionate mouth, a vivid poppy red, began to curve in a smile as she studied her son and he found himself unable to move. She was the perfect woman, the personification of motherhood, everything female which a man dreams of and yet there was a sensuality about her, an earthiness which awoke a stirring in the pit of his belly. He was scarcely aware of who he was, or who she was as he allowed his eyes to roam dreamily over her shadowed face, the strong column of her throat, her half-bared shoulders, the glory of her breasts and thrusting nipples on which milk still glistened.

She looked up then, suddenly aware of his presence. For a split second she recognised what was in him, the shock he was experiencing, the flare of awareness of her as a woman. Not Katy Andrews who had tagged along at his heels as a child and young girl. Not Katy Andrews the wild, defiant creature who had become embroiled with her own cousin, nor Katy Andrews the mother, but herself, a beautiful sensuous woman in whose eyes glowed her deep love for Jamie Hutchinson.

Neither of them moved or spoke. She made no attempt to cover her nakedness and the moment stretched on endlessly as the blood ran hot and rich in her veins. He was seeing her, really seeing her, she knew, for the very first time and she gloried in it, wanting the moment never to end.

A cloud shifted across his face and his mouth moved and lifted as he tried to smile, to be casual, for had he not seen her suckle her child in his own kitchen. But this was not the same and they both knew it. Her breasts were uncovered but she was no longer suckling her baby. They were alone up here but for her son who was peacefully sleeping and for several long, throat-catching moments she allowed Jamie's gaze to flicker about her then, with deliberate slowness, she pulled her bodice together.

At once he became brisk, clearing his throat, doing his best to pretend that nothing unusual had happened between them, that her exotic beauty had not disturbed him. She was Katy, for God's sake, his wife's cousin, his wife whom he loved so tenderly, so deeply, so endlessly he would die for her.

"You're a long way from home, Katy," he managed to say.

"Yes, I walked over to Cloudberry End. I had something I wished to discuss with my father. I left in rather a hurry and . . . well, Jack was hungry so I sat down here in the sunshine to feed him but I suppose I had best be off."

She made no attempt to stand though, continuing to smile up at him, her eyes narrowed with a message he had no wish to read. There was a silence between them overlaid with the call of sheep up on the intake, the song of a thrush nearby and the panting of Jamie's dog which had flopped down in the shade of the wall.

Jamie did his best to avoid Katy's eyes for there was nothing more certain in this world than the love he had for his wife, but some invisible cord, some signal from Katy to himself, from her deep brown eyes to his, was drawing him to her as though she had him on the end of a rope and he knew he must put an end to this madness before it was too late. Before this sudden fascination with Katy Andrews's ripe and lovely body, which she seemed to be telling him was his for the taking, overcame him and ruined not only his life but hers and Chloe's.

"Your father?" he managed to croak and was relieved when the expression in her eyes altered, becoming vague as though she were looking inwards, or backwards to something which gave her no pleasure. Her gaze left his to wander up towards the peat moorland at his back and he felt as though he had been released from some possession which had him in its tenacious grip.

He edged backwards, wary, ready, should she scorch him with those hot, burning eyes again, to have plenty of space between them but it was as though she had moved from one dimension to another, from this time to another. Her voice was soft and weary, pain-filled, her expression one which asked was Katy Andrews never to know the simple, day-to-day content other women had? Like Chloe, for instance.

"Yes, I . . . well, I suppose I wanted to mend the rift between us. Between my family and me. Because of Jack, you see."

"Not while you live openly with Paddy, sweetheart." The endearment seemed to come naturally. As her sadness had grown so had his compassion and he momentarily forgot the bizarre emotions he had felt only seconds ago.

"Yes, I realise that but as it happens, it doesn't matter."

"No?" Despite himself he moved closer to her, leaning over her seated form.

"No. He and my mother are to go and live in Scarborough. She says she can take no more of my . . . the word he used was . . . depravity."

"Aah, no."

"And so he is to take her where it will no longer weaken her. He is to leave the house and some of the servants to look after Chris."

"My mother has not spoken of it."

"Perhaps she is not to go. She is very . . . attached to Chloe and with the child coming she will not want to leave. Her family, her life is here and she has already given so much to Mother."

"Yes." Jamie sighed and lowered himself into the patch of sunshine where Katy sat, leaning his back against the wall, his shoulder no more than six inches from hers. The sun was almost gone. Shadow crept down the slope of Round Hill towards them. Soon they would be in it and the warmth and light would be gone and she had several miles still to trudge to Woodhead but neither seemed to care about it.

"And then there is Tommy."

"Yes," he said again.

"But I am, if I wish it, to move back to Cloudberry End." Her hold on her baby tightened. She lifted him up to her face, resting her cheek on his downy curls, then kissed him in a passion of love. "I want what's best for him, Jamie. I didn't know I would . . . love him so, you see, and what kind of a life will he have with me and Paddy in Grandmother's cottage? Even if we married . . ."

"Aah, no . . . no, you cannot be thinking of that, Katy?"

She turned to look at him in surprise, clearly startled.

"Why not, Jamie? It would be the proper thing to do. For Jack, I mean."

"But not right, Katy. Not you and that . . . that . . ." Though he had not seen Paddy Andrews, indeed no one had bar Josh and Jake and Annie Lennox since his leg was removed, Jamie could imagine what he had become and the idea of this fine and lovely young woman who seemed bent on making reparation for what she had damaged in her wildness, tied for ever to what was left of Paddy Andrews revolted him beyond measure.

"Move back home, Katy. Now that you have the chance bring up your child among your own people. In the way he should be brought up. As your brothers were. A decent education, all the things he should have."

"And what about Paddy? Who is to look after him?"

"Surely Mrs Lennox . . .?"

"Annie? She loathes the sight of both of us."

"Not from what I heard."

She turned to look sharply at him. "What have you heard?"

"She talks to my mother . . . not gossip, you understand," he added hastily, "but my mother is concerned for you and Annie knows it. She admires you enormously for what . . ."

Katy snorted disbelievingly and the baby stirred. At once her hand cupped his rosy, rounded cheek and, comforted, he settled again.

"She can barely bring herself to take my money, Jamie. Had she not been so desperate . . ."

"Oh no, you're wrong. Annie Lennox would scrub floors until her knees bled rather than work for someone she despised. She disapproves of you, lass, but at the same time she respects what you have done since Jack was born. And though she has no time for Paddy she recognises the way you have stuck to him, cared for him since his . . . his . . ."

"Since the beating my brothers gave him. *That* is why I stayed, Jamie. Not for some high-falutin' sense of honour but because it was my bloody fault."

"Katy, Katy, don't blame yourself for everything that has happened."

"Oh please, Jamie, don't be nice to me or I shall cry. All that has happened in the last year is because . . . because . . ."

She turned her head to look at him. Everything except their faces was in shadow now but the last of the sun's rays lit her eyes to deep molten copper and his to the brilliance of sapphire. Brown looked into blue, the message again shining brilliantly for him to see. The message which said, "Because I loved you, Jamie, because I love you still and you don't love me."

Jamie was often to wonder what might have happened had his wife, now in her fifth month of pregnancy, not taken it into her head to wander up the gentle slope at the back of the house to meet him.

The dog heard her first, springing up rapturously, leaping the drystone wall and charging down the field to greet her. The sun was in her eyes, the dog bouncing joyously about her skirt and when her husband and her cousin rose she saw nothing confused or furtive or guilty in either of them.

"Katy . . . oh, Katy," she cried out, her pleasure genuine at the sight of her cousin who, despite Chloe's pressing invitations, had not been back since the birth of her son in Chloe's kitchen ten weeks ago.

"Jamie, darling, bring her down, and the baby. Oh, will you look at him . . . so big now. Let me hold him. May I, Katy? I promise to be careful. Oh Lord, oh dear Lord, is he not perfect, Jamie? Katy, he's beautiful. Look at him, Jamie. Oh please, come down to the farm, Katy."

A mother will love anyone who loves her baby, it is said and Katy Andrews was no exception. Chloe's genuine admiration for Katy's son eased another fraction the animosity she still could not help but feel towards the woman who had married Jamie.

"Well . . ." she answered awkwardly, watching anxiously as Chloe held her sleeping child in careful arms.

"Please, Katy, say you will, please. I have a steak and kidney pudding big enough for six. Stay, we would love to have you and then Jamie will take you home."

And all the way down the field and for the two hours Katy remained in his wife's kitchen Jamie's eyes did not once meet hers. If Chloe was aware of the constraint, the tension, the attempt on Katy's part to be polite since, after all, but for Chloe and Jamie, Jack might not have survived, and neither might she, she showed no sign of it. She made the teatime small talk her mother had taught her, effortlessly filling in awkward gaps with details of her own, often laughable attempts to be a farmer's wife, bringing a grudging smile to Katy's face. This was a different Katy to the one she had known a year ago. Quieter, calmer but still not inclined to be a friend to Chloe Hutchinson with whose husband she was in love.

Only when the child woke and began to display his cleverness, which at ten weeks consisted of a wide, lopsided smile, a deep, infectious chuckle, a vigorous kicking of his sun-tinted, sturdy legs and a sudden intense interest in his own hands, did the two women form that link, that smiling delight which is part of the female nature when an infant is present.

They bade one another goodnight, Katy polite but non-committal as Chloe begged her to come again and when Jamie walked her home in the dark, endeavouring to make obliging conversation, his manner told her irrefutably that Jamie Hutchinson loved his wife and no one else.

Only as he stood at the bottom of the track which led up to her grandmother's cottage did he allow himself to escape the restraints he had put on himself, admitting only to himself that they were needed.

"Go home, Katy. Go home to Cloudberry End. My mother will help you, and so will Chloe, if you would let her. She has become . . . fond of you."

"I know." Her voice was low and sad.

"And you have a friend in me, Katy," but only a friend his voice and manner seemed to add.

"I know that, too, Jamie."

She bowed her head over her baby then lifted it resolutely as she started the climb to the cottage.

20

Paddy Andrews was still in his bed when the crash woke him. It sounded as though someone had dropped a heavy object from a great height and he winced as the noise collided painfully about like cannonballs inside his head. The dog who lay stretched out beside him leapt frantically to his feet and jumped from the bed, making for the closed door which led from the parlour, where Paddy slept, to the kitchen, growling ominously. Something was happening on the other side of it and the dog didn't like it. To prove it he began to bark, a deep-throated, gasping bark which showed, like his master, he was not in the condition he once had been.

"Shurrup, yer daft sod," Paddy snarled, putting his hands to his splitting head. Last night he and the lads had put away . . . well, he'd lost count of how many bottles they'd seen off, but however many it was it had done neither his constitution nor his temper any good. And who could blame him for drinking himself into an unconscious state? he asked himself peevishly, after what that bitch had told him she meant to do. Not that he had any intention of letting her get away with it, naturally, and he'd said so to the lads when they arrived and they'd promised to back him to the hilt. Good lads they were, vowing that no man should be treated as she was threatening to treat Paddy, since he was an Andrews and Andrews men were used to ruling their womenfolk with a rod of iron. Who the hell did she think she was? And after all Paddy had done for her, an' all. What that was specifically none of them could have said by then, being far gone in their cups, maudlin and sorry for themselves, as men are at such times, though why Josh and Jake, who both had two good legs, should include themselves in Paddy's ill-fortune, again none of them could have said.

"What the bloody 'ell's goin' on?" he roared now, then clutched his head in agony. God, he could do with a drink and where was that bloody woman, either of them bloody women, meaning Annie and Katy who were supposed to have the looking after of Paddy's needs. His mouth felt as though the cat had shat in it and he could barely see through the slits of his eyes. His stomach rolled and churned and heaved and with a muttered oath he leaned over the bed and vomited in great waves all over his gran's colourful rug. The stink was appalling but what did he care? He hadn't the cleaning up of it, had he? It'd give that bitch something to do and serve her right for upsetting him so.

"Katy, will yer get yersen in 'ere an' on't double," he bellowed, beyond caring about his head but there was no answer except for more strange noises, bumps and footsteps across the flags, a soft voice instantly hushed and what could have been the whinny of a horse from somewhere beyond the closed window.

The baby began to wail for no more than a second or two, then became silent as if something had been shoved hastily in its mouth. That'd be Katy's titty no doubt, and by God, he wished he could get it in his mouth now and again.

At first, after his leg had gone he had felt a great reluctance to expose what was left of him to Katy. Afraid of what she'd do, or say. Afraid to see her recoil in horror which, while the rest of him was still in a reasonable condition, attractive to women, he'd say, he'd been terrified to attempt. Now he didn't give a fart. He was in a bit of a mess, he knew that. He'd seen himself in that mirror over the mantelshelf which Annie Lennox had lifted down to clean. Gave him a shock, it did, and for several weeks he'd felt like getting shut of himself but that'd worn off, especially with the help of the whisky or the brandy, and so had his consideration for how Katy might act if he tried to lay a hand on her. Give him half a chance and he'd have her skirts up over her head, her bum on his knee, his cock inside her and bugger her feelings.

The door opened and there she was, the subject of his lustful thoughts, his son in her arms, her flaming copper hair brushed smoothly back into an enormous bun at the crown of her head. She was dressed in a plain, pearl grey gown of soft wool with white at the collar and cuffs and a knot of ribbons in her hair to match. On her face was an expression of steely determination which quickly changed to one of revulsion when she saw the mess he had made on the floor. She drew her skirt to one side as the dog lumbered past her on his way outside to relieve himself and Paddy began to smile in satisfaction. She looked bloody marvellous, there was no doubt about it. A real lady in her elegant gown. He wondered where it had come from, since he had never seen her in anything like it in all the time he had known her. Mind you, you'd have to go a long way to beat the sight of her in those tight breeches she had worn and the sheer silk shirt which had showed off every peak and curve, including those tasty nipples of hers.

Never mind, he'd take a great deal of satisfaction in seeing her clean up after him in what she had on, since the nasty task would soon spoil its immaculate stylishness.

"Where in 'ell 'ave you bin?" he snarled, prey once more to the cannonballs in his head. "I've bin yellin' me bloody 'ead off fer 'alf an 'our but could you or that old 'arridan come an' see what I wanted? Oh no, too busy bangin' about the place ter bother wi' the likes o' me. Can't a man gerra bit 'o peace of a mornin' in 'is own 'ouse?"

"It's afternoon, Paddy. Half past one to be precise."

"Oh, be precise, do, my lady, but not fer my benefit. Time means nowt ter me." His snarl had turned to a whine of self-pity but Katy ignored it, wrinkling her nose and making some movement with her hand to indicate her distaste and indifference.

"I came to remind you that I'm leaving, Paddy, as I said I would. I am going now so I . . ."

His head, which he had been about to lay wearily back on his pillow, shot up and he reared into a sitting position. The sheets fell away to reveal the fleshy folds of his naked, sagging body, the pendulous breasts which were as big as a woman's, the enormous paunch of his belly, the sagging, dough-like remains of what had once been the well-proportioned and masculine beauty of Paddy Andrews. For a moment he saw the pity in her eyes and his face became engorged with the blood of his fury.

"Oh no, madame . . . oh no. I told yer last night tha' were goin' nowhere, an' neither is my lad. This is 'is 'ome, an' thine, an' this is where tha' stays. I'm master in this 'ouse an'— "

"Oh, Paddy, don't. There is nothing you can do to stop me leaving you, nothing. We are tied together by no more than . . . what we once were and those two people are gone."

"What yer talkin' about, yer daft cow? I'm still 'ere an' so are thi' an' that's our lad tha're 'oldin' an' tha's tekkin 'im nowhere."

Her voice was low and sad. The baby's eyes were round and alarmed in his rosy face and his lip was ready to tremble, but she held him close, pressing his face into the curve of her neck as though to prevent him from seeing the hateful state, not only of the room, but of the man who was his father.

"You can't stop me, Paddy, and it's my fault that you can't. But then if you'd not lost your leg we would none of us . . . I know he – Chris, I mean – was at fault as much as me but I cannot . . . I have tried for the past . . . since it happened to forgive both of you, and myself, but . . . well, there's no good dwelling on what might have been." She shook herself, like a dog coming from water and her voice became steely. "I'm going home to Cloudberry End as I told you. I can't bring my son up in this . . ."

"*My son*," he howled.

"No, not any more. If you had . . . well, accepted what had happened and tried to make something of yourself I would have helped you, Paddy, but you didn't. You have drunk yourself— "

"Because of you . . . *because of you*."

"I know and I will look after you, financially. My father is not without means and has been generous. This cottage will be yours. Annie, and anyone you want to employ to help you, I'll pay for but I must get my son— "

"Never . . . never, d'yer 'ear? Tha'll not gerr away wi' it. Josh an' Jake'll 'elp me. Good lads they be an'll do 'owt I tell 'em. So you just watch out, my lass. They'll do fer thi' if I say so an' that brother o' thine, fer I've not forgot it were 'im what took me leg. 'E gor away wi' it last time but I've not forgot, Katy Andrews. Tell 'im when tha' sees 'im. 'Im an' thee'll live ter regret what tha've done ter me, lady. An' watch out fer't bairn an' all. Don't tekk yer eyes off 'im fer I'll 'ave 'im back. As God is me witness I'll 'ave 'im back."

The excitement was intense. Janet who, now that Freda and Ivy were gone, had stepped into the role of head parlourmaid, kept saying she was sure she could hear the doorbell, running up the hall a dozen times to check. Lottie and Mabel, though Mabel was, strictly speaking, only the kitchenmaid and therefore did not go beyond the green baize door into the house, had cleaned and polished every room from the top of the house to the bottom, as Mrs Tiplady had trained them, and though she had been gone a fortnight and standards had slipped slightly, since a servant needs a firm hand and a firm voice of command, they had felt a compulsion to prove their reliability. The place looked grand, all clean and shining and smelling of the polish Lottie had made from a mixture of common beeswax, white wax, curd soap, turpentine and water. She and Mabel had applied it to every piece of furniture in the house, using a piece of flannel, then polished the surfaces up with a duster and finished off with a buffing with an old silk rubber. It had brought everything up a treat, Lottie informed the others in the kitchen, Janet and Dilly and Chuckie who had recently been taken on as odd-job boy and was busy polishing the cutlery.

They had cleaned the marble of the drawing room fireplace with a blend of soap, turpentine, pipe clay and bullock's gall, applied with a soft brush, leaving it to dry before polishing it with a duster. The gilt frames round Mrs Andrews's lovely pictures had been brightened with sulphur, water and garlic and honestly, Lottie said to Mabel, Mrs Tiplady would have been proud of them. They had neglected nothing, dusting the books in Mr Andrews's library, polishing the deep leather chairs, cleaning the long windows with vinegar, brushing as best they could the green baize top of the table in the billiard room which Master Chris and his wild friends had damaged, beyond repair in Lottie's disapproving opinion.

They made up Miss Katy's bed with snowy linen, the high, old-fashioned bed smelling of honeysuckle and lavender from the sachets of pot-pourri beneath the mattress and tucked into the pillows, and for half an hour argued on the best place to put the cradle which had been brought down from the attic.

They did not stop to question why they should be taking so much trouble to please Miss Katy, for knowing her as they did, and her complete disregard for anything of a domestic nature, would she even notice? It was just that it was all so dramatic, the return, not of the prodigal son, but the prodigal daughter and what would their lives, which had been turned upside down by the events of the past month, be like from now on? No Mrs Tiplady to tell them the way of things. No Mrs Andrews who was, after all, their mistress. No Freda or Ivy who were trained up to be efficient servants, to give a hand or a direction. Just Miss Katy who had set the valley aflame with her doings and Master Chris who was scarcely ever in evidence before two o'clock in the afternoon.

And Miss Katy's illegitimate child, son of Paddy Andrews who, it was said, was drinking himself to death since they cut off his leg. How were they to manage, they asked one another, since they really did need a hand to guide them, to steady them and was Miss Katy's hand, once so unsteady, the one to do it?

"Will she be tekkin' on another cook, d'yer think, Janet?" Lóttie asked anxiously. They had been making do, all of them, trying their best to produce something for Master Chris to eat of a night when he came home from the mill, which was not often but none of them, except Janet, knew anything about the culinary arts and Janet's talents lay more in the baking of scones and biscuits and perhaps a custard tart. She was a housemaid and Mrs Tiplady had only been letting her try her hand because Janet was walking out with Dicken and was eager to learn a bit of baking for when she and the groom were wed. She could make a decent vegetable stew, of course, and a suet pudding but that was not the sort of thing one served a gentleman amongst his crystal and silver. They had mackled up a slice or two of bacon, some mushrooms and such for Master Chris's breakfast, which had proved to be a complete waste of time since, with his pa gone, he was hardly ever out of his bed before noon.

"Nay, don't ask me, Lottie. I'm as much in the dark as you. We'll need someone ter take the place of Mrs Tiplady, if such a person exists," Janet added sadly, for they all missed the cook's firm but kindly hand, "an' we'll need a kitchenmaid if Mabel's to be housemaid with you. Anyroad, let's wait an' see, shall we? I suppose there'll be a nursery maid needed an' all. Eeh, it'll be grand ter see that there nursery bein' used again. You made a right good job of it, both of you. Dear God, there's the bell. Now, is me cap on straight?"

They were all there except Chuckie who said if you'd seen one baby you'd seen 'em all, even Dilly peeping round the green baize door for a sight of the young woman and her child, who, Dilly was aware, had committed a dreadful sin, or so Dilly's mam had told her. In fact her mam had been in two minds whether to fetch her away from Cloudberry End for she did not want her girl associating with such a person, she said. But then Dilly was not likely to have much, if anything, to do with the infamous Katy Andrews, was she? Not in her humble capacity of scullery maid and good jobs were not easy to find, especially if you were a bit undersized and childlike as Dilly was.

Muffy was barking frantically with joy, doing her best to climb up Katy's skirt, the one the new dressmaker in Crossclough, not knowing Katy's past at that time, had made for her, and for several minutes pandemonium reigned.

"Good morning, Janet. What a simply lovely day," Miss Katy remarked as the maidservant held open the front door and bobbed a curtsey. Behind her mistress on the drive, Thomas and Dicken were busy with the unloading of her boxes. It was October and pale amber sunlight fell through the reddening trees. Leaves were beginning to fall, yellow and gold and tawny brown and rooks were clamouring about the empty nests which had been their homes in the spring. Smoke rose on the still air, drifting lazily from the side of the house where Angus and Billy were burning leaves. The aromatic fragrance mingled with the smell of the withering leaves and dying flowers and suddenly a great burst of joyousness rose in Katy and she smiled at Lottie and Mabel who had come to help with the luggage.

It was good to be home. She said so.

"Eeh, 'tis grand to have thi', miss," Lottie cried, so carried away with the singularity of it all she was ready to gallop about and shout it to the four winds. And her a maidservant in this house for six years and should know better! Anyone'd think she was as young and daft as Dilly. She quite forgot what Miss Katy had been up to this past year, which by rights she should deplore, and of course, being a decent girl, she did, but could you resist the results of it who peeped boldly from his mam's arms, his toothless smile and bobbing head which he could now hold up unaided enchanting her until she longed to hold out her arms for him.

It must have shown in her rosy-cheeked, freckled face and her smiling, shining eyes. Katy recognised it at once.

"Here, hold him for me, will you, Lottie, while I sort out what is to go where. Aah, Dilly, isn't it?" dashing Dilly's mam's hopes that her innocent daughter would not be contaminated by her mistress whose own innocence was long gone. "Come and help Janet, will you?" for Katy Andrews cared naught for the nuances in the ranks of the servants. Janet was supposed to be head parlourmaid now and Dilly was only a scullery maid and that they should be asked to share the carrying, one to each end, of one of Miss Katy's boxes was quite irregular. It was very evident that Mrs Tiplady was no longer there to guide them all, including the young mistress, in the way a house should be run.

Thomas and Dicken were shouldering a box between them, both of them directing orders at the other when a voice from the path leading to Thomas and Matty's cottage hailed them cheerfully. Thomas recognised it and breathed out thankfully, for with his wife in charge all would soon be in good order.

"Mornin', Katy," Matty called, the only one of the servants, if you could call her that, who did not preface the young mistress's name with the title of Miss. Matty held a special position here at Cloudberry End, due, no doubt, to her long friendship with Mrs Andrews. "I've come ter see if yer need a hand, lass. P'raps wi't baby, seein' as how this lot's had nowt ter do wi' one."

"Well, Lottie seems to be managing nicely, Matty," Katy remarked smoothly, earning a gratified and triumphant smile from the parlourmaid, "but if you could direct where these boxes are to go I would be grateful."

"Rightio, lass, glad to 'elp. Now then, what's in that there box them lads is chucking about?"

"Grandmother's china."

"Dear God above, will yer tekk more care, Thomas Jenkins or yer'll 'ave it all smashed ter smithereens, and don't go jerkin' it about like that, Dicken. Them's valuable ornaments in there."

Katy had been determined not to leave any of her grandmother's precious things, precious to her at least, if not in value, and each piece had been reverently wrapped and carefully packed by her and Annie. She had been desolate that she could not fetch the chiffonier from the parlour, the one which had belonged to her great-grandmother, but during the night as she and Annie tiptoed about, quietly putting all they could manage into boxes, she had been reluctant to enter Paddy's room and manhandle the lovely piece of furniture from directly under his snoring nose.

It was like bedlam with everyone running hither and thither, all giving orders and none taking them – Mrs Tiplady would have been appalled – as the last box was heaved up the steps and into the hall. Janet and Dilly were falling over their own feet as they dithered over who should take the lead up the stairs. Dilly was so excited she could barely restrain herself from bursting into hysterical laughter and she swayed to and fro as she waited for Janet to tell her which end to get hold of. Mabel was already struggling up the stairs with a box containing Jack's baby clothes, while at the bottom Lottie was performing a little jig to amuse the child in her arms. Matty was still berating her long-suffering husband on the correct way to handle a box of china and Dicken had his arms full of what looked like old Mrs Andrews's exquisite patchwork quilt, the last one she had made before she died.

"Where d'you want this put, Miss Katy?" he asked fretfully, for he was a groom and this was really not his job. "Where'd she want this?" he demanded of Matty but Matty had turned her attentions to what she considered she was best at and that was getting her hands on Sara Andrews's little grandson. She and Lottie were both becoming red in the face, ready, or so it seemed, to tear the lad apart and Jack looked as though he were about to howl for his mother.

"Well, I might have known that when Katy Andrews walked through that door she'd bring nothing but chaos with her," a male voice drawled from the study doorway.

It brought them all to a faltering standstill. Even the baby turned his head to stare at the man who had spoken.

Katy, who was a third of the way up the stairs, following close on Mabel's heels with the intention of supervising the unpacking of her son's tiny clothes, many of them made and sent over with Tommy by Chloe, paused, causing serious confusion to Janet and Dilly who were directly behind her. She turned slowly, then, doing her best to avoid the unsteady servants, moved slowly down the stairs.

Standing at the foot, she faced her brother who was leaning indolently, hands in pockets, a cigar between his teeth, one of his father's best she was sure, in the study doorway.

"Chris, good afternoon. I had not thought to see you here."

She lifted her neatly coiffed head and smiled, a tight smile which had no warmth in it. She had known he would be here, of course. Well, not at this precise moment which was half past three in the afternoon when a man of business might be expected to be performing it, but here at Cloudberry End where at some point they would be forced to face one another.

She had not seen him since Christmas Day and though there was no visible change in him she sensed a restlessness, a rawness, a snapping tension which made the very air about him uncomfortable.

"I live here, Katy, or were you not aware of that when you made your arrangements with Father?" His own smile was no more than a rearrangement of his mouth and facial muscles and did not reach his eyes. It was very evident she was not welcome.

"I meant at this time of the day, brother." Her voice was soft but with a slight touch of menace in it which said, "Do nothing to endanger me or mine. Stay out of my way and I'll stay out of yours." "I imagined, for some reason," she went on, "that since Father left you in charge at the mill that was where you would be."

"To what purpose when I have a perfectly capable manager to see to it all for me? What is the saying? Don't keep a dog and bark yourself."

"I believe it is, but surely a dog needs a master to keep it in check. To give it orders and— "

"Really, sister, you have, through your own choice, lived apart from this family for a year and yet you have the gall to come back the moment Mother and Father are gone and presume to tell me— "

"I am here because Father told me I might. This house belongs to him and it is up to him who lives in it. I and my son . . ."

"Your son!" Chris's mouth curled in an ugly sneer and his moss green eyes grew diamond-bright with venom. "Paddy Andrews's get! A bastard who has my name and you expect me calmly to accept him, and you, into this house where decent members of society— "

"You mean Johnny Ashwell, I suppose, by decent society, and Tim Warren and all the other wild-riding, wild-gambling rakes you associate with?"

"Of which you yourself were a part not so long ago, remember?"

"Oh for God's sake, Chris, stop it." Katy put a weary hand to her head, conscious suddenly of the paralysed figures of the servants hovering, for want of a word of command, about the hall and staircase. "We are to live in this house together but if, as it seems, we cannot do it in some sort of peace then I suggest we avoid one another as much as we can. I should perhaps warn you that I mean to run this place as it should be run. I have nothing else to occupy me but my son so I shall make a career of . . . of being a competent mistress."

"I thought you had been that for some time."

"If I have I did it well."

"Is that so?" There was a sneer in his voice but she lifted her head and squared her shoulders.

"Yes, but that is over and as I must fill my life with something then I shall embark on this . . . this new vocation. I am fully aware that I shall never be a hostess, as Mother was, for there are none in this valley who will call on Katy Andrews but I am a mother and intend to make a decent home for my son."

"Oh, spare me," he groaned, putting a hand to his brow with a theatrical gesture.

"There will be proper meals at the proper time and you are welcome to join me."

"Jesus Christ, what bloody game is this you're playing, Katy? Surely you don't imagine that you and I can . . .? He tried to kill me, your lover, you know that, don't you?"

Ignoring the horrified gasps which whispered about the hall and up the stairs, Katy took a step closer to her brother.

"You were not without blame, Chris."

"And neither were you."

"True. And I cannot tell you, except for my son, how much I regret it. Because of him I intend to put it behind me and try to make a respectable life in a respectable home for both of us."

"Is it not too late for that?"

"Whether it is or whether it isn't, I mean to try. He is all I have. Now, if you'll excuse me, I have things to do."

As though she had given a signal the servants snapped to attention and began to move about in a somewhat aimless way, for the encounter between Miss Katy and Master Chris had unnerved them. They none of them, for a moment, could quite remember what it was they had been doing, or where they were going and it seemed Dilly might break out into hysterical tears this time since, for the life of her she couldn't recall whether Janet had told her to go first or last up the stairs.

Katy pulled them all together. It was as though the confrontation with her brother had put a heartener in her. Stiffened her backbone which was already perfectly stiff and straight and strong.

Before the day was out she and Jack were comfortably settled in her old room, her boxes unpacked, her things put away for now in the empty drawers, since she did not intend to remain in this room which was smaller than she required now she had Jack. She and Lottie and Janet had gone through all the gowns in her wardrobe, those she had left behind when she went to live in Woodhead last year, searching for something she might wear in this new life of hers, at least until she had a chance to see her dressmaker and order some more.

They had all three been disconcerted to find they were too small for her, especially in the bodice.

"Tha've put weight on wi't baby," Lottie told her sagely. "It allus happens."

"Mrs Jenkins can alter them for thi', miss," Janet added. "Yer know how clever she is with a needle."

"Yes, there's no hurry. It's not as if I am to be overwhelmed with callers, is it?"

It was said without bitterness, just a simple statement of fact and the maids exchanged glances, for what she said was true. How was she to manage, this young girl, only just eighteen last week, this wicked girl, as everyone knew she was and yet somehow, as they watched her quietly going about the business of settling herself and her son back in her old home, they could not quite bring themselves to believe it. She had her boy, a lovely little chap, to prove how wicked she had been, a boy of whom they would all grow fond, they were sure, but what was she to do with the rest of her life? What she had said in the hall about running the house would have to be seen to be believed, for if there was one young woman who was totally and irrevocably undomesticated it was their new mistress. They all knew her and were used to her wild ways which surely could not vanish overnight even if she were a mother now. She'd be off on that there animal of hers in those breeches she had once worn as soon as someone could be found to care for Master Jack, for leopards don't change their spots overnight, now do they, Lottie told Janet. They were all prepared to overlook what she had done in the past since this was a good place to work in and fond as they had been of Mrs Tiplady, without her eagle eye about them they could relax a bit and you couldn't say the wages weren't fair, could you?

So, they'd all see how things went, they told one another complacently. With a young woman who in the past had cared not a tinker's toss for things of a "housewifely" nature and a man who was scarcely ever at home, life could be very pleasant at Cloudberry End.

21

Katy Andrews was wrong. There was one woman in the Longdendale Valley who was only too happy to call on her as she had been taught by her mama.

Katy was in the drawing room. She was down on her knees playing with her son on the rug before the brightly glowing fire. She had removed his nappy and flannel pilch and pushed up the skirt of his long petticoat, allowing his rounded, sun-tinted legs freedom to kick vigorously. His tiny penis bobbed merrily, his heels rose and fell, his legs stretched and bent and his hands clutched at one another, then reached for her as she leaned over him. She blew a raspberry, her mouth warm on his bare stomach and he chortled with laughter.

"Do you like that, my darling?" She smiled. "You do, don't you?" repeating the action several times then, sighing with pleasure, bent closer to study the handsome, irresistible face of the child while he gave her the same careful scrutiny.

The dog, who was sprawled as close to the fire as she could get, lifted one eyelid and lazily moved her short, stubby tail, then resumed her doze, for she knew the words were directed, not at her but at the strange creature on the rug who had come to intrude on her space. She sighed heavily, hitching closer to the fire.

The warmth and glow of it fell about mother and child and painted the delicate furniture which Sara Andrews had chosen, glinting on silver and crystal and delicate porcelain. On Sèvres and Meissen and Wedgwood and Coalport. On the chandeliers, two of them, each with eighty gently shimmering candles apiece. On the French ormulu clock which sat above the mantelshelf. On wide peach-coloured velvet sofas and matching balloon-backed cabriole-legged chairs. It warmed the ivory carpet to a rich cream and turned Katy Andrews's coppery hair to a fiery red. It flushed her cheeks and put dancing reflections of flame in her warm brown eyes. She was in a gown of tawny silk, the one she had worn long ago in another time when she and her mother and brother had gone to the railway station to meet her cousin, unaware that the day was to alter her life. It had fitted her then, as it did now, but not until Matty had let out the seams in the bodice. The gown suited her, its colour catching the fire's glow in its folds, shading the richness of the silk from palest amber to the deepest burgundy.

There was a light tap on the door and the astonished face of Janet appeared, her eyes wide, her cap somewhat askew as though she had come in a great hurry from whatever it was had caused such consternation.

She had been in the kitchen, sprawled in Mrs Tiplady's chair, her feet up on Mrs Tiplady's stool when the doorbell rang, discussing with an equally lethargic Lottie what they might put together for Miss Katy's and, if he should put in an appearance, Master Chris's dinner that evening. Mabel was peeling the spuds and Dilly, who had dropped a jar of Mrs Tiplady's raspberry preserve which they had fancied with the sponge cake Janet had made, and a bit of custard, of course, shattering it all over the flags, was on her knees scrubbing half-heartedly at the stains it had left. Chuckie had been given some vague instructions to sharpen the knives an hour ago and had gone to fetch the knife sharpener but as yet he had not returned.

It was two weeks since Miss Katy had come home and in that time the two maidservants had sent in a menu of endless chicken broth, dubious soggy vegetables and tough meat with bread and butter pudding to follow, which was not exactly up to the standard of Mrs Tiplady, was it, but Miss Katy had not complained. And neither had Master Chris for the simple reason he was never there to eat them. Should they try a bit of haddock tonight for a change? The fish man had been that morning, telling them it was straight off the boats but how were they to know? Perhaps a custard tart might be a welcome change, which Janet could manage but as Miss Katy seemed quite content with what they had served, so far, despite what she had said to Master Chris, should they let well alone and stick to what they knew?

"What is it, Janet?" Katy looked up from her absolute contemplation of her son, something she did a lot of, Janet thought, wondering if it was right. Of course the women in her class had no time for such nonsense and those who were not of her class, like Mrs Andrews for instance, had not the inclination, but then Miss Katy was like no mother Janet had ever known, falling into neither category.

"A visitor, miss, an' are you at home?"

"A visitor? For me? Are you sure they don't want Mother, or perhaps my father?"

"Oh no, miss. Asked fer you particular."

"Who is it, Janet?" beginning to look a shade apprehensive, for though she had talked of living the life her mother had led, which included, if they came, the receiving of calls, she had not really expected them.

"Well, she give me this, Miss Katy. In the absence of a card, she says, an' would you forgive 'er."

Janet held out the silver tray on which Sara Andrews had been used to receiving the calling cards of Mrs Ashwell and Mrs Warren and other ladies of a similar background. On it lay a neat square of paper, perfectly clean but plain with nothing on it except a name inscribed in exquisite copperplate. It said, "Mrs James Hutchinson".

Katy studied it carefully, reading and rereading the beautiful writing, aware that Janet was watching her with intense interest. She was also aware, wondering why she had not noticed it before, perhaps seeing her head parlourmaid with the eyes of the caller, that there was a dirty mark on the maid's apron and that her normally immaculately ironed, frilled cap with its long streamers down her back to her waist was crumpled. She was in the correct black which was usual for afternoon wear but somehow she did not appear to be in the proper state of immaculacy Mrs Tiplady had insisted upon.

Janet waited. None knew better than the servants in this house how Miss Katy felt about Mrs James Hutchinson, her own cousin, Chloe, and Janet held her breath, wondering what her young mistress would do. Mrs Hutchinson sat where Janet had put her on a hall chair, in view of her condition, the gig in which presumably her father-in-law, the Andrews' own coachman, had brought her, waiting on the gravelled driveway to see if she were to be received. Talk about cheek, her coming here after all this time. The master and mistress scarcely over the doorstep and in their carriage on the way to the railway station and the young woman neither of them had seemed able to stand handing in her card as if she had every right to be calling on her cousin, their daughter. Perhaps she had. Miss Katy had given birth to her baby on her cousin's kitchen floor, rumour had it, and happen she and Miss Katy had become friends over it but if they had the servants at Cloudberry End hadn't heard about it and Matty Jenkins would have been the first to tell them of it, wouldn't she?

"Shall I send her in, Miss Katy?" she asked somewhat impatiently for she was dying to get back to the kitchen and spread the news.

Katy sighed deeply. Her son crowed on the rug before the fire and as she watched him he urinated in a delicate filmy arc almost into the fireplace. Janet gasped then laughed and at once Katy relaxed, beginning to smile. It was as though the child had intentionally performed his little trick to remind her that nothing really mattered but him. He held in contempt her mother's expensive rug, the maidservant's avid curiosity, even the visitor who would have to take him just as he was.

"Show her in, Janet," Katy said coolly, just as though she were quite accustomed to "morning callers", who came, as was socially correct, directly after lunch, and indeed would not be surprised if another dozen arrived in the next hour. She reached for the baby, lifting him to her shoulder, her forearm under his plump, bare behind, her left hand holding his right to her mouth.

Chloe Hutchinson was in her sixth month of pregnancy, her figure thickening about the waist but with a carriage so straight and graceful it was barely noticeable. She looked quite glorious with that peach bloom some women acquire when bearing a child. A sort of sheen, a polish, a tawny look of good health which glowed through her fine creamy skin like a candle behind gauze. Her eyes were a clear blue-green, steady and unafraid, looking first at Katy then going, with obvious pleasure, to the half-clothed boy.

She began to smile, the hesitancy with which she had come into the room slipping away and again her very evident approval of her son had its effect on Katy, who felt her heart move gently then relax. The dog rose to her feet, stretched, first one back leg then the other, yawned and padded over to Chloe while the baby watched with great interest.

"Katy . . . and Jack! I had not expected to see him so this is a lovely surprise. Oh my dear, what a handsome boy and so sturdy. And Muffy," bending to pat the dog. "She must be pleased you are home. I know how she missed you."

"Yes." Katy's voice was gruff. She still knelt on the rug, holding her son somewhat in the manner of a shield but her eyes had lost that guarded look of wariness.

"May I hold him?" Chloe asked softly.

"He has nothing . . . no pilch."

"I don't mind. I see he has already relieved himself," nodding at the small puddle in the hearth.

"Yes." Both women began to smile at the rudeness of the young male who is able to perform his bodily functions wherever and whenever he pleased. The boy was passed to Chloe and he didn't seem to mind. He settled himself in a companionable way in her arms, watching her face and when she smiled so did he.

"May I sit down?"

"Oh, sorry." Katy indicated the sofa beside the fire, waiting until Chloe was seated, the boy held gently on her lap before she sat down on the matching sofa opposite. They were very conscious of one another, the two cousins, wary even, though there seemed to be no actual antagonism, both wondering what they were to talk about, since not only did they have nothing in common, not in their nature nor their outlook on life, they were both sharply aware that they loved the same man. It was past, that savage time when their lives had been devastated by a love so passionate and destructive it had mangled many lives. That devastation had been forced by Chloe's marriage to Jamie and the irrefutable fact that it must be accepted, unacceptable as it was to Katy. So much had happened in the past year. Doors had been opened, passed through and closed again, leaving behind them pain and sorrow, hatred and bitterness, but it was over with. They were both to make new lives with their children, one of whom, as he gurgled unknowingly on Chloe's lap, seemed to be destined to draw them slowly closer together. He had been born to Katy on Chloe's kitchen floor and even now his mother could still feel that strange and unbelievable feeling of comfort which had sighed thankfully through her after her labour in Chloe's arms.

"I never thanked you properly," she said abruptly, surprising not only Chloe but herself. Chloe's eyebrows lifted questioningly, though she still allowed her fingers to be firmly gripped by the baby who seemed intent on getting them into his mouth.

"Thank me? For what?"

"For what you and Jamie did last July. If Jamie had not found me and brought me down I don't suppose either of us would have survived. I thought, in my naïvety and stubbornness, I could manage the whole damn thing on my own. Have the child then tramp down to Woodhead where I meant to ... well" – she shook her head dismissively – "never mind. Anyway, thanks to you both ..." Her voice trailed off. Her eyes strayed to her child and a rosy flush of embarrassment stained her cheeks.

"Don't be silly," Chloe protested. "We only did what anyone would have done, Katy, you must surely know that."

"Not for me, they wouldn't. The people of the valley would have stepped over me sooner than be associated with the hussy Katy Andrews."

"I can't believe that, Katy."

"Oh, come on, Chloe, just because you're a bloody saint doesn't mean everyone is."

For a moment there was a breathless silence then Katy grinned. "Go on, you know it's true."

"I am not a bloody saint, Katy Andrews," Chloe said indignantly, "and don't you dare call me one. Dear God, not only do you insult me, you provoke me to swear in the most unladylike way. You are a bad influence," but she was smiling as she spoke. "As for Jack, I only did my duty."

"Rubbish, you're too good by half and it'll get you into trouble one day."

"Katy!"

Katy began to laugh then, throwing her head back and opening her mouth wide to reveal her perfect white teeth while her son watched her with startled bewilderment, for though his mother smiled and talked to him for hours on end he had never once seen her shout out loud in joyful laughter.

"Katy, you are startling your son. And can I take it you are poking fun at me?" Chloe smiled ruefully.

"Yes, cousin, I'm poking fun at you but only because I'm not used to being polite."

"I can see that. I have been here for fifteen minutes and have not yet been offered tea."

"Dear God." Katy clapped her hand to her brow. "Is that what I'm supposed to do?"

"Of course. Did your mama not teach you?"

"Don't be daft. When was I ever at home to serve tea to Mama's callers? I suppose I'd best do something about it." She rose to her feet with the evident intention of going to the door and shouting down the hall for a servant.

"Katy, what are you doing?"

"You wanted tea, didn't you?"

"Yes, but there's a bell beside the fireplace. Don't tell me you did not know of its existence. If you ring it one of the housemaids will come. You tell her what you want and she will fetch it."

"Aah, now I remember seeing Mother doing that." She grinned to let Chloe see she had known all along. "Of course, it's just that in the past year I have forgotten everything I was ever taught. Not that that was much, I can tell you, but she did try, poor Mother, to make me into a lady."

Katy pulled the bell and when a flushed and excited Janet had gone off full-tilt to tell the others that the visitor was to take tea, sat down to face her cousin, inclined to smile as though at some foolish memory.

"How is your mother?" Chloe asked courteously, remembering the cool woman who had barely allowed her niece a brief "Good morning", never mind a friendly smile.

Katy's face became shadowed. "Not well," she answered abruptly, "though I did not see her. Father wouldn't allow it."

"Not allow it?"

"No. He said I had broken her heart."

"Oh no, Katy . . . no, surely he did not mean it."

"He did, cousin, and I suppose it was true. I was a . . . well . . ." She sighed deeply, her face pensive, her eyes deep brown pools of sadness. "I was a bad girl. I haven't changed, you know. Not really. It's just that I'm afraid I have damaged irretrievably Jack's chances of a decent life. I didn't want it particularly for myself but I do for him. I was going to give him away, you know."

"Give who away?"

"Jack. Of course, he wasn't Jack then, he was . . ."

"Katy! Katy Andrews, how can you sit there and tell me . . . how could you even contemplate such a wicked, wicked . . ."

"Oh, for goodness sake, cousin." Katy's voice was irritable. "That was then. Before I met him and by the way he has fallen asleep so I'd best put him on his sheet. He's inclined to widdle in his sleep."

"Widdle?"

"Yes, relieve himself as you so politely put it."

The sleeping baby was placed beside the dozing dog. The tea was brought and sipped, though when Katy asked for biscuits or cakes, those which Mrs Tiplady had once made for her, she was astonished when Janet said there were none, besides which it was not the correct thing to do to serve cake and biscuits to a caller, morning or afternoon, though naturally Janet did not say so.

"No, miss, I'm sorry but neither me nor Lottie is really a cook, yer see."

"Yes, I had noticed."

"We was wonderin' like . . ."

"Yes?"

"Whether yer meant to employ one, miss. A cook, I mean." Janet twisted her hands in her apron while her young mistress stared at her in bewilderment as though the idea had never once occurred to her. Chloe watched her with breathless fascination, for this was a side of her wilful cousin she had never seen before. Indeed, had never expected to see. It was hard to visualise Katy managing this household, in fact it was downright impossible and yet from what she had just said it seemed she was to make a stab at it if only for the sake of her baby son. He would have no chance at all of mixing with the children of decent society if he were to be brought up in a cottage in Woodhead with Paddy Andrews to influence him, to fill his childhood days with the brutality she herself had seen Paddy employ against Katy. Katy's child would be coarsened, knowing nothing but the boorish manners and attitudes of his uneducated Andrews cousins. A child of working-class parentage with an education to match and though it was how his grandfather had started it was just not appropriate for a generation to revert back to the humble origins of its predecessors.

But what of young Jack Andrews? Even living and being

reared at Cloudberry End, which was a gentleman's residence, as the grandson of Jack and Sara Andrews, as a child born out of wedlock he would have a hard enough time of it for how many of the Ashwells and the Warrens and others of the local gentry would allow their offspring to be tainted by the slur of illegitimacy? Katy was being very optimistic if she thought she had only to return with her son to her old home and they would both be accepted again.

Chloe herself was married to a farmer, the son of a servant and, like Jack, illegitimate but Jamie had pulled himself up by his bootstraps, taking advantage of the education Jack Andrews had given him, travelled the world, even if it was only as a common sailor, saved his money, learned things, bettered himself and through sheer hard work and a resolute determination was making a success of his life. Their child would have the best they could give him. She was what was known as a lady, or so her mama had told her, with a great-uncle, or was it a great-great-uncle? who was titled and she meant to claw every advantage she could from her birthright for her child. She was well educated, for Mama had believed in it and she would bring up her and Jamie's child in the ways of a gentleman. He would be a farmer, but he would be a gentleman as well. Katy wanted, no, *demanded* the same for her son. Not to be a farmer, of course, but to be accepted into the class of society of which her mama and papa, her brothers and herself were a part. It would be a hard, grinding task, the sheer immensity taking Chloe's breath away. Katy had offended Crossclough and Crossclough would not forget it. She had laughed in their faces, snapped her fingers at their horrified disapproval, swaggered about the valley in her silk shirts, her tall top hat and her mocking smile and they would not take kindly to her expectations that now she was repentant they must forgive her and take her, or at least her son, to their hearts.

"What d'you think, cousin?" she heard Katy say, her voice impatient since, though she was determined to do it, it was hard to be serious about playing the role of mistress of Cloudberry End.

"I'm sorry?"

"Really, cousin. I am trying my best to take up the reins of running this house and what are you doing? Daydreaming! I am asking your opinion since I suppose you will know more about such things than me, on whether I should employ a cook and perhaps a housekeeper, and if so where on earth might such a person be found? What d'you think?"

Chloe lifted her head decisively, squaring her shoulders and straightening her back which, despite the dull ache in it, she did not allow to touch the cushions on the sofa. Her memory took her back to the tall house in Liverpool and her mama's cool and ladylike control of the few servants they had. She could recall the way Mama had spoken when she was interviewing their last cook, one of many, unfortunately, for Mama had a way of getting the back up of every servant she employed and none stayed longer than six months. Still, it had given Chloe an insight into what was required in a servant and how not to treat one.

"Neither Janet nor Lottie can cook a meal, Katy, so it seems only sensible to get someone who can. If you are to do any entertaining you will need a good cook."

"Entertaining! You are joking."

"No, I am not. The time will come" – determined to be positive for Katy's sake – "when you will invite perhaps not friends of your mama but friends you yourself will make."

"Where, for heaven's sake?" Katy hooted.

"I don't know." Chloe's expression became stubborn. "If you make up your mind to it you will do it, I know you will, but you'll need a decent woman in your kitchen. Someone who can cook well and also manage the household as Mrs Tiplady did. You must interview."

"Interview! Oh, God, I wouldn't know where the devil to start. How does one go about such a thing? Do you know? Would you help me?"

"Well, I suppose one would advertise, or perhaps Matty might know of . . ."

"Perhaps Matty might even be persuaded to do it, cousin. What d'you think? She knows the house and . . ."

"She is not a cook, Katy, but perhaps, if she were willing, she might agree to be housekeeper."

"D'you think so?"

"You could ask her, I suppose, and then, of course, a lady in your position will need a nursemaid to look after— "

"Oh no, no one will have the caring of Jack but myself. I have done so for the past three months and can see no reason to stop now."

"Katy, are you to bring him up as the son of a lady as your mama would have done?"

"No, not as Mama did." Katy's voice was brusque.

"I know what you mean and I can understand your reluctance to put him in another woman's care but there is surely a way to . . . to rear and nurture a child so that even if he has a nursemaid, you are involved in it and the centre of his universe. You will have . . . well, I don't know, things to do that will require attention and you cannot walk about with a child on your hip as women do in certain classes."

"Jesus, oh Jesus, this is going to be harder than I thought," Katy moaned while Janet's eyes moved in a mesmerised fashion from one face to another, wondering on the strangeness of seeing these two young women so involved with one another, and, even more amazing, Miss Katy's evident intention of whipping this household into some sort of shape. Not that it had slid far since Mrs Tiplady had gone but even she was aware that things weren't quite what they should be. Wait until she told them in the kitchen that Matty Jenkins was being considered for housekeeper!

Matty refused. She was too old, she said, and besides, would the maidservants take kindly to being ordered about by a woman with whom they had all been on familiar terms? And then there was the expected birth of Chloe's child, looking fondly at her daughter-in-law, so all in all she'd have no time for it, she said apologetically to Katy. She'd help out in any way she could. She might even know of a good woman who had once worked for Mrs Ashwell until the Ashwells had gone in for fancy chefs and such like. Though she didn't say anything to Katy Jess Kelsall was getting on a bit which was another reason why Mrs Ashwell had got shut of her, but Jess, having found no other work, might be persuaded to work for the "scarlet woman of Crossclough" as Matty had heard Katy described. She wondered as she spoke what on earth this girl, the daughter of the woman Matty had loved dearly for thirty years and missed more than she could say, imagined she was up to! Did she honestly think she could move back to this house and live the life she had known before she left? The daughter of Jack and Sara Andrews and, therefore, despite her wild ways and shocking behaviour, recognised as a young lady of class. She'd taken on a heavy load, poor lass, but then most mothers fought tooth and nail for what they thought best for their child and that was just what Katy Andrews was doing.

She sipped her tea and, like Janet, marvelled at the tentative show of cordiality which seemed to be budding between her daughter-in-law and Sara's lass. Katy kept addressing Chloe as "cousin" but it was a vast improvement to some of the names she had laid about her last year when Chloe had moved in with Jamie. Matty sympathised no end with Katy since she herself had borne a child out of wedlock and but for Katy's mother would have finished up in the gutter, or a brothel. Aye, she'd not forgotten that and she'd like to see Katy Andrews claw her way back to respectability as Matty had done.

The gig jolted sickeningly on the rutted road back to the farm and though it was only a few miles it seemed interminable to Chloe. It was a glorious day, a vivid blue sky streaked with hurrying clouds above the deep reds and gold of October but Chloe didn't notice as she concentrated on keeping down the tea she had drunk at Katy's and the infuriating pain in her back.

Jamie was up at the back of the farm, he and Tommy busy with the last of the harvesting as Chloe, after saying goodbye to her father-in-law and thanking him for driving her up to Cloudberry End, moved slowly into her kitchen. Adah-May had been put to scouring the setting dishes and butter churns in the dairy, a task she was capable of performing without supervision and Chloe could hear her intoning the words of one of her favourite songs as she clattered the churns in the sink.

"Early one morning,
Just as the sun was rising,
I heard a maiden sing in the valley below,
Oh, don't deceive me . . ."

The tune bore no relation to the words but Adah-May did not seem to notice as she warbled on.

It was warm. The fire glowed in the grate, its embers spitting a little in flames of orange and yellow and fierce crimson. Everywhere sparkled and gleamed, for only yesterday Adah-May had declared her intention of giving the place a bit of a spring clean, despite the autumnal nip in the air. The dark lustre of the polished furniture reflected the glow from the fire. The little chair which Chloe knew her child would not be able to use until it was at least a year old had been furnished with a new, brightly embroidered cushion and set before the fire and she smiled at her own insistence that it should be ready. Jamie humoured her, his eyes gentle, his hands gentle as they curved about her belly, since he was as eager as she to see their first child seated in it. There was a lovely aroma, for she and Adah-May had baked a fresh batch of bread this morning before Chloe left for Katy's.

Not wanting to call Adah-May, moving slowly, she made herself a pot of tea, more for something to do than for any need or desire for it, drank a sip or two then moved outside again into the crisp amber day, shivering a little as the wind, coming straight from the moor, struck a blow at her.

The dairy was on the far side of the farmhouse and Adah-May had not seen her return. Breathing deeply, her hand protectively about her unborn child, she strolled up to the wall at the back of the house, shading her eyes for a sight of Jamie, wondering why it was such an enormous effort to move one leg after the other, of keeping her aching back erect and forcing her uneasy stomach to remain calm.

She clenched her teeth as a brief pain bit into her and suddenly she was afraid, deathly afraid, for it seemed to her that something inside her body appeared to be breaking. She must get into the house, find a corner in which to crouch and mend the damage which her woman's mind knew was happening to her woman's body. She must find safety, shelter. Oh, sweet God, where was Jamie? She needed Jamie . . . where . . .?

Slowly, like an old, old woman she moved in a half crouch down the gentle field, her hands to her belly as though, in this strange position she might protect the treasured burden inside her. She must not miss her footing, nor must she jar herself. It was as though she were a vessel carrying a precious liquid which if it tipped would run away. The more carefully she walked that endless distance from the wall to the house the less likelihood there would be of spilling it, and it must not be spilled.

She reached the kitchen doorway and stumbled inside. Everything seemed to have come to a stop, the clucking of the hens, the tuneless singing of Adah-May, the hissing of the fire, the ticking of the clock and the absolute silence enveloped her in a frightening cocoon. She put out a hand to the table, first to steady herself but more importantly to convince herself that it was still there, but as she reached for it her hand found nothing but empty space which she went headlong into.

She felt it then, the bleeding, and understood she had started to lose her child.

22

She couldn't summon the strength or inclination to be concerned about anything in those next few months and certainly could find nothing to interest her in her cousin Katy's efforts to take over the running of Cloudberry End. It had been weeks before she had allowed Matty to coax her from her bed where she had lain, hour after hour, her head turned to the window, watching the seasons slowly move from autumn to winter. The skies had changed from the sun-warmed, sun-tinted blues and golds of the fading year to the hazy, opalescent hue of the coming winter, matching the feelings in her heart. She could hear the sheep cough in the meadow where Jamie had brought them down for wintering. A bright fire sang cheerfully in the bedroom grate and mixed with the fragrance of the burning wood she could smell the frost which had begun to crisp about the window frame and coat the rough grass of the slope where her child had begun to die.

She vaguely expected, for so it was said, that time would diminish the pain of her loss. Matty had repeated it gently again and again. Time soothes the raw pain of wounds, she said, and perhaps she was right. If it was so Chloe longed to go to sleep and wake a year from now, or even two, when, presumably, she would have recovered. She had carried her child for six short months. Their time together had been brief but she had loved her and now she mourned her, though her daughter had never breathed. She allowed herself to imagine now and again, as she lay in her bed, how it might have been, dreamed of it until reality returned and her child was dead.

She had felt nothing at first, huddling in the grey wrappings of her grief through which no pain could reach. Her mind drifted but she allowed no thought or memory to assault her by the simple process of falling asleep whenever her mind's eye recaptured the happiness she had known. Her body had been bruised and tender, as though she had been severely beaten, but Matty, who had suffered a miscarriage herself, told her this would wear off.

For five days she had been troubled with a fever, neither knowing nor caring whether she lived or died and at the fringes of her semi-conscious mind she had been aware of Jamie. Jamie weeping and begging her not to leave him and, knowing how he loved her, and how, at last, she had come to love him, she made a great effort not to follow the tiny girl who had been born dead into Matty's hands. She had seen her, held her, a perfect child whose head had fitted in the palm of her hand and whose skin had the glow of the pearls her own mama had once worn. She had no eyelashes, no finger- or toenails but her beauty was so fragile, so delicate Matty had wept bitterly and so had Jamie as they put her in her tiny, satin-lined coffin.

But Chloe couldn't. She hadn't shed a tear, not even when Katy, quite distraught since she could imagine exactly how she would feel if her own precious child were lost to her, flung herself on Chloe's bed, weeping in that dramatic way she still retained. With the compassionate, headlong warmth that, despite her wildness, had always bloomed in her, she let her emotions flow from her like a bursting stream. Poor Adah-May had given way to hysterics before collapsing in such a storm of grief they had been forced to send for her mother to fetch her home, though she had returned the next day and been a tower of strength in her own simple way to Matty and Jamie. They had all wept, even Thomas and Tommy, her mother-in-law told her, but somehow it didn't seem to matter to her inside the bubble she was trapped in. Nothing did.

She watched snow fall in early December, sitting in her chair by her kitchen fire, just a few scattered flakes at first which grew in size and ferocity until it was a dancing white wall beyond the kitchen window, a few flakes finding their way down the chimney to hiss on the coals.

"I'd best gerr 'ome, chuck," Matty said uneasily, "or I'm likely to get snowed in. Thomas'll be worried."

"Of course," she answered politely, since she was unfailingly polite with them all, not turning her eyes away from the window.

"Will yer be all right till our Jamie comes 'ome?"

"Oh, yes."

"I don't reckon 'e'll be long. Not with this lot," nodding her head towards the window. "It'll be dark soon, anyroad."

"I'll be fine, Matty. You go. I'll just sit here and wait for Jamie."

And that is just what she would do, Matty brooded, biting her lip and sighing. Her son would come home to a warm house and a steak and kidney pudding in the oven because Matty herself had provided them. But for her, God only knew what poor Jamie would have to put up with and if Chloe didn't snap out of it soon she'd tell her so an' all. Every woman who lost a child must grieve, must suffer the bereavement, the loss, the pain, but she must also share her sorrow with, and comfort the man who had given her that child. It would be Christmas soon and dearly as she loved her son's wife Matty couldn't keep running up here every day to see to her. Chloe had her physical health back. It was just her mind which seemed to have withdrawn itself to some despairing corner where it hid and suffered and would let no one, not even Jamie who suffered too, get close enough to comfort her. Oh, she allowed him to put his arms out and draw her slender body against his but she could not be said to be responding in any way. She merely allowed it.

"I'll be off then," she murmured, placing a gentle hand on her daughter-in-law's soft cloud of curls.

"Righto, Matty, and thank you."

"Can I get you a cup of tea before I go, lass?"

"No, thank you, Matty. I'll just . . ." Her voice trailed away and Matty sighed as she turned towards the door.

It could have been no more than ten minutes later, both Katy and Matty agreed, laughing and marvelling on how they could have missed one another, that the kitchen door was flung open and the room came alive with the exuberance of Katy Andrews, wrapped around in a mantle of snow, her son in her arms, peeping and blinking from his multiple wrappings, both of them glowing with the simple, joyful excitement of arriving through the snowstorm.

"For goodness sake, cousin, do come and take this heavy

boy from me and let's get the door closed before we have a snowdrift halfway across your kitchen floor. Now I can see it in your face," as Chloe remained where she was, staring in open-mouthed astonishment, "that you are about to say I shouldn't have come but I couldn't resist it. You know me. A challenge cannot be ignored, besides which, I'd promised Jack I'd bring him up to see you today and one can't let a child down, don't you agree? He would have been so disappointed."

Katy pushed the door to with her behind, leaning on it as she caught her breath, fully believing what she had just told Chloe. She credited Jack with an understanding well beyond his five months, talking to him endlessly on any subject which at that moment concerned her, from what Mrs Kelsall should serve for dinner that evening to the undeniable fact that Jack Andrews was the centre of Katy Andrews's world. She never tired of telling him so and he seemed to find what she said to him fascinating, smiling and reaching for her as though he knew he and his mother were special to one another, for were they not two against the world?

Despite Chloe's advice she had not yet employed a nursemaid for him and had totally rejected the idea that her son should sleep in the nursery on the top floor, declaring that the room was too far away for her to hear him should he wake in the night.

"That's what a nursemaid's for, Katy," Matty had admonished her. "She an't little lad'd sleep up there an' . . ."

"But I feed him in the night, Matty, and so it seems to me that it is much more convenient to have him close to me. He's not yet old enough to be weaned. I have plenty of milk and he is thriving," which was true. You had only to look at him, Matty agreed, to see what a bonny lad he was and what a bonny man he'd make. The dead spit of the Andrews lads with none of Sara's side in him except the colour of his hair which was turning to a rich, fiery copper.

And he was sunny-natured too, so God only knew where that came from, though Sara had been merry as a girl. He got it from neither of his parents, that was for sure. Jack, the lad's grandfather, had once been an even-tempered, good-humoured sort of a man so perhaps young Jack had inherited his disposition from his grandparents. Anyroad, he was the apple of his ma's eye, any fool could see that and who'd have believed that undisciplined, untamed

Katy Andrews would turn out to be such a gentle, loving mother?

Katy, with an air of making a great concession to the woman whom she was finding more and more of a friend, a support and an adviser, had moved into the bedroom which had once been shared by her mother and father. It was the biggest room in the house with two large bow windows and an area about the fireplace where a sofa and deep velvet chairs stood, with several small, pie-crust tables scattered between them. The room was quite exquisite, as Sara herself was, decorated in a shade of dove grey, duck egg blue and white. There was a vast double bed with a pleated silk canopy drawn up to the ceiling like an Arabian tent. A great deal of white in cushions and floor rugs. A white lace counterpane over duck egg blue silk, white muslin curtains, a muted shade of dove grey for the plain, rich carpet. A serene room which had the effect of soothing Katy's often troubled thoughts into a state of such tranquillity she was often reluctant to leave it to struggle with her self-imposed problems.

But its main advantage apart from its size was the modern bathroom her father had had installed which led off it and a room, once her father's dressing room, which Katy had converted into a nursery for Jack. There was a fireplace tiled in cheerful shades of yellow in which a fire burned behind a burnished brass fireguard, a deep bow window with a wide window seat. Once her father's things had been removed there was plenty of space for a crib with polished, turned rails, since young Master Jack had already outgrown his bassinet. There was a chest of drawers in which his baby garments were stored and a great many soft toys and books. Mechanical clockwork clowns and mice were scattered about the deep-piled carpet which was the same shade of pale grey as that in his mother's bedroom. The walls were painted yellow, the curtains were a bright shade to match and though the servants all deplored her carelessness in allowing an infant who would soon be crawling to lie on the dove grey elegance of Mrs Andrews's carpet, Katy Andrews took no notice.

When had she ever?

As the door clicked to behind her the snow was beginning to melt and drip from the rich, russet curls which tumbled over Katy's forehead. The drops of moisture made her blink and her smile deepened.

"I know you will be angry with me for coming through the blizzard, cousin, but I swear it wasn't a blizzard when I set off. Here, take Jack, will you?" since her cousin had still made no move towards her or her son, and without waiting for her approval she placed him on Chloe's lap where the snow on his wrappings immediately began to slide on to Chloe's pale grey gown.

"Take his things off, will you, there's a dear, while I get out of this cloak. I should have put up my hood but with Jack to carry and this," indicating the basket she had flung carelessly on to the table, "I hadn't a hand to spare."

She shook her head energetically and her hair swirled about her in a burnished mantle, the pins in it scattering everywhere. Her baby watched her in great admiration as if he could scarcely believe his luck in having such a splendid mother, then turned to Chloe, his wondering smile asking didn't she agree as he displayed the pearls of his new teeth which were also much to be admired.

Chloe seemed unable to move. Her hands had automatically gone to steady the child as Katy arranged him on her lap, but the depression which clouded her mind by day and by night appeared to have stolen her ability to think coherently. She had dwelled in near-oblivion for so long, transformed by her loss into an empty chalice which nothing could fill, she could not quite understand what it was she was being asked to do. This was Katy's child on her lap, she knew that. He was warm, solid, heavy as he turned again to look trustingly into her face and she supposed . . . what was it she was supposed to do?

"Do get his things off, Chloe, or he will take a chill."

There was a sharp, anxious note in Katy's voice which she did her best to hide. Her child was hanging about in wet clothes which must be got off him as soon as possible but she wanted Chloe to be the one to do it. It was an experiment and one she was sure was as cock-eyed as many of the other ideas she had had in her life, but something must be done to drag her cousin from the treacle-like morass of despair which the loss of her child had tumbled her in. She had thought of it this morning and with her usual impetuosity had dashed up here to try it out, but as she watched Chloe's look of blind panic and the way her hands trembled, letting Katy know that she was longing to be free of the baby on her knee, Katy could see she had made another error of judgment.

It did not once occur to her that not many months ago she would have been gratified to see her cousin, her enemy, adrift in this sea of senselessness. Before Jack was born she would have looked for some advantage to Katy Andrews in this tragedy of Chloe's, some edge which might have driven Jamie into her own arms but Jack was her guiding star, her conscience now and she found she could not contemplate any action which might shame her in his eyes. She had done enough of that in the past and to entangle herself with Chloe's husband, with Jamie whom she loved still, would certainly do Jack no good in the community. She must be circumspect now, for her son's sake and besides, there was something . . . something vulnerable, something defenceless about Chloe, something which awoke a strong feeling of protectiveness in Katy. Chloe who was so frail. Katy who was so strong. She had come to . . . she found her . . . Goddammit, she seemed to . . . to *like* her! This young woman had always done her best to support Katy, even if Katy hadn't wanted that support. Like the time she had come down to the cottage and stood up to Paddy, a fragile kitten squaring up to a battered, evil-tempered bulldog which if it could have got its jaws about her would have snapped off her dainty head. When Jack was born she had been magnificent in her strength and then, the moment Katy moved back to Cloudberry End she had come to call in the formal manner which was meant to say this was how Katy Andrews should be treated.

She had removed her own cloak, hanging it to dry over a chair, pretending an air of unconcern with what Chloe was doing to her child. She crashed cups and saucers about on the table and made a great display of interest in the kettle and teapot and when timidly and with great care Chloe began to unbutton Jack's little jacket Katy let out a slow and triumphant sigh of relief.

"I've brought an enormous batch of biscuits and cakes and scones and God knows what else for you to try, cousin. Mrs Kelsall seems bent on showing me she's a better cook than old Tippy and I must admit she's not bad. We had a splendid leg of lamb last night, the best I have ever tasted, with mint sauce and roast potatoes. Very simple but cooked superbly. Mind, when I say 'we', of course you will know I mean just myself. That brother of mine might just as well have gone to Scarborough with Mother and Father for all I see of him. Not that I mind, you understand, for we only argue and upset the servants. Lord knows where he spends his time for Chris doesn't tell me, but there have been nights when the place is alive with drunken young men and – now don't be shocked, cousin, though I swear I was – I have heard women's voices too. I am in bed, naturally, with my door bolted, I don't mind admitting it, and in the morning when I see the havoc they have caused in Mother's drawing room I could cheerfully wring his neck."

She turned abruptly, her exercise with the tea caddy and sugar swept to one side, her heart beating faster, then slowing again, dreading that she might find Chloe sitting like a frozen mannikin with Jack awkwardly on her lap, but she was easing his arms out of his coat, bending to smile into his face, chafing his little pink hands to warmth. Jack was watching her in that intent way young children display, vastly interested in her, ready, should she seem inclined, to be friends.

Katy felt her body relax into boneless relief. She took a quiet step or two across the kitchen, reluctant to intrude on this special moment, this healing moment between her son and her cousin, but drawn by something unique which had begun to flower.

"There," Chloe was murmuring softly, "there, that's better. Were your hands cold, darling? There, let Chloe warm them for you," and Jack watched her with big, unquestioning eyes, giggling as she pretended to nibble his fingers.

Katy quietly took his coat and the shawls she had closely wrapped about him before she left home, spreading them out to dry before the fire, then, sighing, sank down to kneel beside the woman and child in the rocker.

They were all considerably startled by the sudden appearance of Adah-May who had been bottoming the bedrooms, a task she had been set by Matty and, since no one had told her otherwise, she had continued until the light failed. She was like that, was Adah-May. Although she was certainly not quiet about it you often found you had completely forgotten her presence, Matty often said, and for the next few minutes it was pandemonium as Katy got her into her coat and boots and scarf for her journey home to her mam's.

When she had gone with Katy's exhortations to "Go straight home and keep to the path" ringing in her ears, Katy resumed her position at the feet of her cousin.

There was silence for several minutes, then, "I want to take him to Scarborough, cousin," she said abruptly. "What d'you think?"

It was the first time anyone had asked Chloe Hutchinson what she thought for a long time. She turned her gaze, which had become soft and tremulous for the boy, to Katy and in her eyes was a cloud, an indecision, or was it a reluctance to return to the world where decisions must be made, to the reality of everyday living? Let me, for just this moment, stay in my corner, it pleaded, where, if I know not content, at least it is not pain. It did not last long.

Almost without knowing she did it she drew Katy's child to her breast, resting her chin on his bright fluff of curls. She gazed into the fire, her eyes still clouded and pensive, her teeth unconsciously nibbling at her bottom lip.

"I think . . ." she said hesitantly, not quite sure of herself in this devastation which had shattered her. She would not have vacillated before. Before the death of her daughter she would have known exactly what to say, for there was no one more loving, more dedicated to the concept of family than she was. She had been unloved for most of her life. Now she knew she was the soul, the heart of her husband. She knew that Matty loved her and, she suspected, deep in her heart, so did Katy Andrews, her awkward, forthright, unconformable cousin. Surely, where love was there should be no doubt, no reluctance, absolutely no prevarication.

"Go," she said huskily. "Take their grandson to them, Katy, or you will never forgive yourself."

"They might not accept me."

"You must try." Chloe's voice was throaty with something which seemed to stick there, clogging it so that she could barely speak. "Don't ever miss the chance to make amends, Katy."

"No, you're right. It's been so long since I saw Mother. I didn't care much once. I'm sure you're aware of the . . . the great passion between my parents?"

"Yes."

"We, my brothers and I, were shut out, but now I have Jack I realise how much I must have hurt her."

"Go, Katy, and take Jack to meet them." Her voice became even lower. "I would have taken my . . ."

"Chloe . . . oh, darling . . ." Katy put her arms about her cousin, hugging her to her, knowing exactly what she suffered since she had a child too and could imagine the agony of his loss. The baby, owl-like, blinked between them, then decided he did not care for this close confinement, struggled and let out a howl of protest.

Instantly Katy let them go, reaching for the baby with hungry, suddenly empty arms, but Chloe looked up at her, on her face written her appeal though she said nothing. Her eyes were wide and bright with the tears she had never shed but which, Katy suspected, would come soon.

"Hold him for me, will you, cousin," she said, doing her best to be casual, "while I make this pot of tea I promised us. And we must sample some of Mrs Kelsall's fancies. She will be most offended if I don't report back the moment I get home on your opinion."

"Why should my opinion matter, Katy?" There might have been a glint of a smile on Chloe's face.

"Don't ask me, cousin, but it does. Now me, I count for nothing. Oh yes, she made it very plain when Matty brought her over that it was she who was conducting the interview, not me and that she was doing me a great favour in even considering gracing my kitchen with her presence. You must come over soon. When this damn snow has gone and Thomas can get the gig through I shall beg Mrs Kelsall to make us lunch. I want you to see Jack's nursery . . . Aah, I'm sorry."

"Katy, please, Matty and Jamie walk round me as though they were treading on eggshells and I know they mean to be kind. They love me and don't wish to hurt me but this . . . with Jack . . . though it grieves me that it is not my child I am holding . . . God, you cannot realise . . . but this is real. I long to nurse my own child, Katy, but until I do I should be glad to borrow yours now and again."

She had fallen asleep and so had Jack when Jamie came home. Katy stood up, the chair in which she had been sitting opposite Chloe rocking gently. She had been watching over them, her son and her cousin, while they slept but her eyes could not help themselves as they hungered across Jamie Hutchinson's face. He seemed thinner, older, his lean cheeks gaunt with worry, but when his gaze fell on his wife and the child in her arms Katy saw quite distinctly the relief sag through him.

He smiled briefly in her direction, going at once to kneel at Chloe's feet. He placed a big, gentle hand about her cheek, his eyes dreaming, then moving to Jack who had his rosy face pressed against the swell of her breast. His hand moved to push back a tendril of hair from Chloe's forehead, lingering in an agony of possessive and compassionate love and Katy watched, the knife in her heart twisting cruelly though she was aware he did not mean to cause her pain. He was simply demonstrating his love for his wife who had lost her child, his child, but was now sleeping peacefully with Katy's son in her loving arms.

Katy loved him. She loved his quietness, his strength, his air of knowing exactly who he was and, though it was ready to destroy her, who it was he loved. She loved the set of his chin, the way his dark hair curled into the nape of his smooth, amber neck, the quizzical tilt to his eyebrows, even in seriousness, the way his mouth turned up at the corners. She was aware that her love for him had changed. It had grown steadier, deeper, coming as naturally to her as her milk flowed for her son. Whatever she might have told herself earlier he had only to turn, hold out his hand and she would go with him in an act of complete surrender.

Had he not loved his wife.

At last he rose, turning thankful eyes to her, inclined to be embarrassed, for this thing, this strange unwanted feeling begun when he had found her suckling her child behind the wall, or perhaps, if he were truthful, even before that, would always be between them.

"Thank you, Katy," he said simply, putting out a hand to her then dropping it hastily before she could respond.

"She didn't want to hold him. I made her."

"Your instincts are sure and you have a good heart, Katy Andrews."

"Jamie . . ." Her eyes were as clear and golden as amber. Her love for him shone from them like a beacon. She could not hide it and it lit up the dim room, illuminating every corner, but he turned away from it lest he be burned, or blinded, or both.

"It's stopped snowing," he said, addressing the clock. "There was only a thin fall though it seemed a lot and it's frozen hard so we should be able to walk on it. Stay and have some of Ma's steak and kidney pudding which I can smell in the oven and then I'll walk you and Jack home."

"Thank you, Jamie," she answered gravely, knowing how it was between them. "Let Chloe sleep a while though. She seems to find comfort in Jack. He'll wake up as soon as his belly commands him."

She smiled, wanting to talk of anything but her child, Paddy Andrews's child, but conscious of the relief on Jamie's face. He was afraid of her, she knew that, wondering why since his love for Chloe was incontestable. Perhaps it was because he knew she loved him. That even after all that had happened, Paddy, and then Jack, her love for Jamie had never wavered. It glowed like a candle in a dark room, lighting her heart, warming her. Perhaps, when she turned her gaze on him he could see it, that candle which would never go out, never flicker and die until the day she did. He was uneasy with it. Whenever she called he was courteous, hospitable, begging her to make herself at home, inviting her friendship with his wife but she had noticed that he had always found some excuse never to be alone with her.

She sat down again while behind her Jamie moved about the kitchen, setting the table for their meal. It would be Christmas in a week or two and she intended, if Chloe was recovered, to invite them to dine with her at Cloudberry End. Now that she had a decent cook. A proper affair with herself and Chloe in evening gowns though she doubted if Jamie had an evening suit. It didn't matter. She would have candles and a Christmas tree with presents under it and it would be her first attempt at entertaining.

The dog, Captain, who had come in with Jamie, nudged her hand with his muzzle and she fondled him, smoothing his rough coat. She felt strangely at peace. She was not a part of this household, merely, she was aware, a welcomed guest, at least by Chloe, but she was also aware that there was something here that – what was the word? – gentled her. Moved her imperceptibly away from the wildness which had caused so much pain and desolation to so many people in the past. It was all her fault, the whole dreadful débâcle. Paddy, Chris, her parents' escape from her to Scarborough. Yes, her fault and yet, could she choose where she loved? Could anybody? It was her love for Jamie and his inability to return it, and then, to exacerbate the situation further, his love for Chloe which had set them all on the devastating path which, strangely, had led to this peaceful room.

She turned her head to look about her, sighing for what might have been and gazed directly into Jamie's troubled eyes.

He looked away at once, his eyes dragging from hers, his hands going to the cutlery he was placing on the table and as it rattled Chloe awoke. Her sudden movement disturbed Jack and he turned, still half asleep, his mouth seeking sustenance from her breast.

It did not seem to trouble her. She smiled, then looked at Katy and in her smile was a lessening of her pain.

"Thank you," she said simply and they knew she would be all right now.

Katy and Jamie studiously avoided one another's eyes.

23

She took the train to Scarborough, accompanied by Matty, determined to do this thing properly since she knew it would mean a lot to her mother. Ladies did not travel alone, especially with an infant. Katy, who had never listened to Sara Andrews's remonstrances, knew that. Remembered it from somewhere or some other time when her mother had still hoped to make a lady out of her.

She had not told them she was coming, she confided to Chloe, who had looked at her with some misgivings, dwelling perhaps on the possibility of the front door being slammed in her face. No, they would not do that, she was certain, but Katy might find that her parents might see her impetuous journey as just another example of her heedless irresponsibility and close ranks on her. They were not to know of their daughter's new, gentler approach to others now that she had a child to consider, a part of herself, another human being who depended on her, not only for his life but for what his life would be as he grew.

It was a long journey necessitating a change at Sheffield and Leeds. Jack was fretful, for with her usual hasty need to be at whatever it was that challenged her and her disregard for what might be described as setbacks, she had made no provision to feed him, blithely assuming, if she assumed anything at all, that she would find some secluded corner in the ladies waiting room in which to do it. The ladies who waited there, of the same social class as her mother, looked quite scandalised as she sat down, Jack squalling on her knee, with what seemed to them the obvious intention of baring her bosom like any low and common woman and nursing her child, and she had fled in confusion, hoping the journey to Scarborough would not take too long. Her breasts were dangerously full and tender when the hansom cab they had hired at the railway station finally delivered them, the baby wailing miserably, on to the front step of the house in Scarborough, the address of which had been given her by her father in case of an emergency.

The town itself was situated in the recess of a bay, rising to the summit of a cliff or "scar" from which it had got its name. It combined the advantage of sea bathing with mineral baths and had a beach of the finest sand, or so Katy had heard, though she had no great hopes of ever sampling any of it.

But she was concerned with none of these things as she and Matty climbed stiffly from the cab, the grizzling baby protesting so loudly the horse which pulled the cab almost dragged the driver off his seat in its alarm.

Katy was elegantly dressed in a travelling outfit made for her by the new Miss Johnson who, having set up in competition with Miss Mason in Crossclough, saw no reason to cease sewing for Miss Andrews, even though she now knew her story. She could not afford to turn customers away, even one as infamous as Miss Andrews, in fact, she was of the opinion that her other clients found the possibility that they might come across the "scarlet woman of Crossclough" in her smart little salon and whom of course they would cut dead, quite exhilarating. The pale sand-coloured pleated skirt and Norfolk jacket, the very latest fashion imitating the male garment, the dashing hat, so-called because its ribbons tied beneath the chignon and not the chin as did the bonnet, were a testament to Miss Johnson's considerable talent.

"Ring the bell, Matty," Katy said autocratically, her nervousness so great it made her sound rude. The house, set high on the clifftop if the climb up to it was anything to go by, was surrounded by trees, dark, moaning winter trees, for dusk had already fallen and she was vastly relieved when the door opened and an oblong of bright golden light fell across them.

"Mr Andrews, if you please," she told the astonished housemaid who opened the door. "We will come inside and wait in the hall since the child is cold. Oh, and would you send someone to fetch our luggage?"

"Beg pardon," the housemaid piped, quite overwhelmed by this patronising young woman, by the protesting child who stank of something unpleasant, though the second woman, older, sensible and unruffled, seemed well enough.

"I would like to see my father as soon as possible," Katy went on, her voice imperious and it was only when Matty dug her in the back, shaking her head warningly when Katy turned towards her, that she was made aware that she must not take the high-handed attitude that had been hers in the past. She was doing this for Jack and, she admitted, if only to herself, because of a strangely uncomfortable need to see her mother. It was over a year, a year last October on the day of her grandmother's funeral when they had last met so how would they greet one another? Would they greet one another or would Jack Andrews, his face turned against her, simply ask her to be on her way?

He walked down the wide, shallow staircase, his usual cigar held between his fingers and her heart leaped with gladness for he looked so much better. In the four months he had been at Scarborough he had regained some weight and his usual sun-tinted colour had come back, no doubt due to walks along the beautiful sandy beach Katy had heard about.

"Father?" She could say no more. The yearning in her voice was very evident and Matty could see Jack Andrews was affected by it.

"Katherine. You're a long way from home, lass. I hope there's nowt wrong. Is Chris all right?"

Katy felt a great need to tell the truth. To say, "As far as I am aware for I never see him and only hear the sound of his wild parties from behind my locked bedroom door," but she smiled instead.

"Yes, but I have come to ask about you and Mother, not to talk of Chris. How is she?"

"Better. We both are. The sea air is very bracing and we are comfortable here." He turned to smile at Matty. "Go on up, lass. She's waiting for you. When the maid said it was my daughter and an older woman we thought it would be you."

"Which way, Jack?"

"Up the stairs and the first door on your right."

The sound of Matty's pounding feet followed by the banging of a door died away. There was a small but very tense silence as Katy studied this deliberate – or so it appeared – slap in the face aimed at her. Her father was at ease, waiting for her to declare her purpose in coming here, unbending, not unfriendly, cool, but despite himself his eyes strayed to the grizzling, somewhat unsavoury child in her arms.

"Perhaps I might beg the use of a room, Father?" she ventured. "The boy is hungry and . . . and needs changing." She grinned suddenly, her old challenging grin that said that though she was no longer the hellion he had once known she still had spirit in her. "Your nose has probably noticed it."

"Er . . . yes." He smiled somewhat uncertainly.

"Perhaps . . . afterwards we might talk?"

"Well . . ."

"Please, Father. I have travelled a long way to see you."

They put her in a small parlour at the back of the house. There was a good fire, a comfortable chair, tea on a dainty tray which she drank as she nursed Jack. He had been changed and washed and now, warm and dry, with a full belly, he lay heavily in her arms, his head lolling back in a deep sleep.

She rang the bell and when the housemaid, who must have been hanging about outside she came so quickly, bobbed her smiling, eager face round the door, asked if she might beg a blanket or two and perhaps someone could be spared to watch her son.

"Eeh, raight gladly, miss," the housemaid said in her broad Yorkshire accent, obviously claiming the privilege for herself, though when Katy left the room there were two or three of them, Freda and Mrs Tiplady among them exclaiming how he had grown, hanging over the sleeping child. It was always the same. Put a woman, or several women in the vicinity of a young child and they would become as clucking as the hens in Chloe's yard. They took no notice of her, even Mrs Tiplady and Freda, considering as the daughter of their master she could go anywhere she pleased.

"Up the stairs and first door on the right."

She knocked hesitantly and when her mother's voice bade her to enter she did so. She closed the door behind her, standing with her back to it, noticing the way her father stood up at once, placing himself between her and her mother and it was perhaps at that moment that she recognised precisely what she had done to her parents and the reason for her father's subsequent removal of his wife from her daughter's excesses. Roughshod she had ridden over their hopes for her, their ideals and belief in what they considered proper, what everyone in their social circle considered proper. She had cared naught if they were damaged, concerned only with her own pain, her own needs.

Now they no longer trusted her and could you blame them and certainly her father was about to make sure that his wife, her mother, would not suffer again.

"Katy . . ." he said warningly.

She held up her hands placatingly. "I know, Father, and I understand. I promise, on the life of my child who, everyone knows, is the most precious thing in the world to me, that I have not come here to upset Mother. Matty here will tell you I have . . . changed . . . since Jack was born."

"'Tis true, Jack," Matty murmured.

"I am living an exemplary life at Cloudberry End and though I am aware that nothing will ever change what I did, that Jack will always be . . . illegitimate, I have come to try and make peace. To become . . . friends, if you will let me. I don't intend to make a nuisance of myself, to pester you and Mother but now and again, if you will allow it, I should like to bring him to visit his grandparents. He is a lovely boy— " her voice was thick with tears— "and does not deserve what I have done to him but . . ."

"Sit down, darling," her mother said to her father. "I think we may safely assume that our daughter would not plead her case so eloquently if she did not mean it. That was one thing you could always rely on, you know. Her total honesty. Her passion for the truth no matter who it hurt."

"Mother . . ."

Her mother sighed as Jack Andrews moved slowly towards her. She and Matty were seated hand in hand on an elegant little sofa in front of an enormous fire. The curtain had not yet been drawn and through the bay window the lights of the little grey town climbing down to the bay twinkled in the darkness. Katy could hear the pounding of the sea on the beach below and smell the tang of sea spray and sensed suddenly the lovely peace which her parents had found here away from their troublesome children.

"Bring him up, Katy. How can a woman refuse the sight of her first grandchild?"

"Sara . . ." her husband said warningly.

"She is a mother now, Jack, and knows how I feel."

It had been surprisingly easy, helped by the engaging charm and copper-haired good looks of her son, and by Matty who eased them all through three days of careful attention to one another's needs and fears and hopes.

How strange it was, Katy was to think later, that this child about whom Crossclough had thrown up its hands in horror, a child born of sin, they said, in his short, sweet life had, unknowingly, begun the healing process in Chloe and now was perhaps to do the same with the raw wound between her parents and herself.

"Yer ma an' pa do care about thi', Katy," Matty adjured her, "yer know they do, but, well, yer know 'ow they are about one another. Yer ma 'ad a poor sort of a life until she married yer pa. Get 'er ter tell you about it sometime, an' then you an' Chris were never easy. With yer pa away so much when you were little, an' now with this last – you an' Paddy Andrews – it were more than she could take, burrif yer mean what yer say about bein' different, towards 'er an' yer pa, I mean, actin' proper an' such, they'll stand by yer. They've tekken a shine ter't little lad an' can yer blame 'em but . . . well, my lass, I've this ter say. If yer let 'em down again yer'll 'ave Matty Jenkins to answer to."

Though the farewell they gave her was not exactly fulsome, for they could not quite hide their satisfaction at being alone together again, it was at least affectionate. Their manner seemed to say they were glad the rift between them was on the way to being healed but they could not at once put behind them all the years and all the anguish she had inflicted on them in those years. Not on the basis of one visit. But they were willing to give her a chance, for was that not what parents always did? Give a child a second chance. She would know now what that meant. They stood together on the wide steps, her mother leaning slightly on her father's shoulder, a handsome, well-dressed couple of middle years, smiling, waving, her mother's eyes turning more to her grandson than to her daughter.

A start had been made and Katy leaned back in the cab well satisfied.

It had been the practice of Annie Lennox to walk up to Cloudberry End from Woodhead once a week to collect her wages. She would have a cup of tea in the kitchen of Matty Jenkins with whom she had grown increasingly friendly in the past few months, before being shown into the drawing room of the big house where Miss Katy waited for her. Ever since those days when Annie and Matty had bumped into one another in

Crossclough and had sadly discussed the awful predicament Miss Katy Andrews had got herself into they had recognised one another in each other. They were both decently wed women, Annie, sadly, a widow now, with an interest in Katy Andrews which was not one of ghoulish curiosity, which could not be said of most folk in Crossclough. They were genuinely concerned for her, pitying the wild streak in her which had brought her to her present deplorable position. Approve of her? No! Admire her spirit? Yes, for had she not dragged herself from a situation which, had it happened to almost any other woman, would have extinguished the life from her.

They enjoyed the transference of these amicable chats in Crossclough to Matty's cosy kitchen at the lodge of Cloudberry End, spending an hour or so exchanging recipes for almond macaroons and Aunt Nelly's pudding which Matty had brought with her from Liverpool; the best way to make old crape look new again and the worry of growing sons since they were both blessed – or tormented – with one. Thanks to Katy Andrews, Annie Lennox had no need to worry where her next shilling was to come from and all through the winter she had fed her well-clothed, well-shod children on nourishing broths with the best cut of stewing steak in them, custards with milk and eggs, thick soups brimming with vegetables and the improvement in them had been remarkable. Poor old Frank, she often thought. He had done his best, working himself literally to death, but he had never had the joy of seeing his children thrive as they did now.

Of course there was a price to pay as there was for anything in this life. A cross to bear, a fly in the ointment and Annie's was Paddy Andrews. It had taken her nearly ten days after Katy left him last back end even to get inside the front door of what had once been Madge Andrews's spotless little cottage to do the job she was paid to do and Annie Lennox was not one to take money she had not earned. When she did finally gain access it was only on account of them Andrews twins who had no desire to clean up the foul mess Paddy had got himself into. Knocked on her door, they had, muttering that he was dead to the world, drunk as a stoat, lying unconscious in his own body wastes – though they had used a coarser expression – and if she would come in and give the place a bit of a clean they'd guarantee he'd not bother her, should he come to. Even their strong stomachs could stand it no longer, they had implied, hanging their unkempt heads and shuffling their enormous feet like two overgrown lads who have been up to no good.

It must have been a bit of a shock to his system, she often smiled to herself, to fall into a stupor one evening in a state of such filth even a pig would have been ashamed, and wake up the next morning with the place like a new pin about him. She'd not touch him, she vowed to his ham-fisted, red-faced cousins, but if they would attend to that part she thought she might see her way to buying them a pint or two in the Queen's Head in Crossclough.

It all worked out a treat. Between the three of them they kept Paddy Andrews in some sort of state halfway between cleanliness and beastliness, the lads glad of a bob or two, which, of course, Miss Katy supplied and Annie was made up with her family's new standard of living. With that and several other little jobs Annie managed, her life was free from the dreadful ogre of poverty which had always hung over her and Frank.

It was no fun living next door to him, mind, she told Matty, with his drunken shouts in the dead of night, his obscenities flung at her when she ventured into the cottage, his threats and abuse directed at his cousins who only grinned and leaped out of the way of his lethal fists. He was a devil and so was that dreadful dog of his which regularly butchered Barty Pickles's chickens. Again it was Miss Katy who patiently replaced them and any other damage or loss that was reported to her and which could be laid at Paddy Andrews's door.

But all that had ended four weeks ago and Annie was not sure which was worse, the squalid drunken chaos in which Paddy had lived or his sudden transformation into what she could only call "a new man".

It was quite nerve-racking. He had stopped drinking. Just like that he had stopped drinking and how could a man who had put away at least two bottles of brandy a day – she knew, for didn't she have the clearing away of them – stop drinking overnight? she asked Matty wonderingly. His temper, of course, was absolutely foul, terrifying in fact, and she had refused quite positively even to take his food in unless the twins were there with him. They were not very bright, she confided to Matty, but they were both like young bulls and between them they held him down until he had roared himself out.

And then there was this chap. What chap? Matty wanted to know, for the shenanigans that went on in the cottage of Katy Andrews's erstwhile lover sickened and fascinated her at the same time.

Well, Annie didn't rightly know. He came up on a horse, an old mangy thing with a basket over its rump and left half an hour later, in which time there had been absolute silence in the cottage. Four times he'd been now and when Annie had found out why she had raced up to tell Matty and now if Matty would excuse her she'd best go and warn Miss Katy.

But Matty could no more contain her curiosity than she could her own good nature. "What? What is it, for goodness sake?"

Annie paused in the doorway, her hand dramatically to her bosom. She was not a woman taken to dramatics but this was enough to alarm the most imperturbable of women.

"I went in not an hour since, Mrs Jenkins," for she and Matty recognised the proprieties and still addressed one another by their surnames, "an' I nearly fainted. Honest to God, I thought me heart'd stop beatin'. There he was as large as life an' twice as ugly . . . standin' up."

"Standin' up!" Matty put her hands to her mouth in much the same dramatic fashion as Annie.

"Aye, as God is my witness he was standin' on his own two legs."

"Never!"

"It's the truth, Mrs Jenkins. At least it were one real leg an' one wooden leg which stuck out of the end of his trousers like . . . eeh, like I don't know what. He was wobblin' all over't place but he laughed when he saw me, laughed an' laughed an' I tell thi' this, it scared the livin' daylights outer me."

Which was saying something since it took a lot to frighten Annie Lennox. During his long sojourn in his wheelchair in the cottage next to hers, though he swore and bellowed and flung himself about in order to get at her, he had never scared her, not once, but now he did and Miss Katy must be warned.

"'Aye,' he says, 'I'm up on me pins, Annie. Not walkin' yet but I will be. By God, I will. I've 'ad enough sittin' on me bum, lass, so I decided ter get messen a new leg. So yer can tell them what might be interested that Paddy Andrews is back in business.'"

It was the talk not only of the small hamlet of Woodhead which he and his cousins had terrorised as he floundered up and down the narrow, sloping track which ran through it, but of Crossclough where the news reached by the end of the week. Paddy Andrews was up on his legs again, even if one was made of wood. Josh and Jake supported him at first, one on either side until he had regained his balance and then, when they were elsewhere, he wobbled about on the crutches, presumably fashioned by the same man who had made his "peg-leg". They watched him from their cottage windows, not even the children daring to laugh at his comical hop-step-jump. "Peg-leg" they would have chanted after him, or "Hoppy" if he had been anyone but Paddy Andrews. "Fatty" or "Lumpy", "Dumpling" or "Tub o' Lard", from a safe distance, of course, for his girth was enormous with folds of flesh hanging about him and his wicked eyes sunk in the unhealthy pallor of his bloated face.

After a while they got used to him stumping up and down, keeping out of his way, naturally. Hop-step-jump he would go, his bull-like neck folded down, his chin on his chest, his eyes on the cobbles which threatened to catch the end of his crutches. Soon he no longer needed Josh and Jake and neither did he need Annie Lennox, he told her two months later, since he would get about the cottage on his own now. In one way it was a relief to Annie who had not felt safe with him on the move, though she had to admit he made no attempt to threaten her as he once had, but how was she to manage without the wage Miss Katy had paid her all this time?

"You're not to worry, Annie." For by this time the animosity shown by Annie Lennox towards Katy Andrews had vanished. "I am in need of a daily . . . what d'you call them?"

Annie bridled, on her high horse at once. "Nay, there's no call ter mekk a job fer me, Miss Katy. I'll manage well enough," though the prospect of being returned to "managing" after all this time was daunting.

"Rubbish," Miss Katy said in that high-handed way she had. "A good woman, in any capacity, is hard to find and if you think I am going to dispense with you over this then you are very much mistaken. Besides, I need to see you every day so that you can let me know what . . . what he's up to. You do see that, don't you? I know you're not afraid of hard work and not too proud to earn an honest shilling doing it. There is the washing and the ironing which, I'll be honest with you, Mabel cannot make a decent fist of. She is heavy-handed with the goffering iron and . . . well, you will know what I mean. Will you not come up to Cloudberry End each day as . . . as . . . general cleaner and factotum. I will pay you the same wage and it will be a great relief to me to know exactly how much progress that devil makes."

Katy was glad, of course she was, that Paddy was taking his life and putting it back together again. In a way it took away some of the heavy sense of guilt she had known ever since the doctor had cut off his leg, and also reduced the responsibility which she had expected to carry until the day of his death. Perhaps, if he could get about he might find life worthwhile again although, a small voice whispered inside her where she had cherished a certain peace of mind knowing he was tied to the cottage at Woodhead, if he can get about what mischief might he get up to?

Annie hadn't the faintest idea what a factotum might be but she was so thankful she didn't care. If it involved the heaviest cleaning or the mucking out of the damned horses in the stable, she would do it.

She wouldn't show it though. She was a decent woman who had earned her own living and paid her own way since she was a little lass. She bleached and scoured her kitchen table every day no matter how tired she was. Her stone floor was as meticulously scrubbed and her washing, hung out in the stiff wind which cut down from the moors, smelled of strong soap and lye. She was used to carrying heavy burdens, and she'd had plenty to carry in her time so she'd not bend her head to this slip of a girl, no matter how . . . fond . . . yes, fond she had become of her, nor how grateful she felt towards her.

"Right," she said, as though she was doing Katy a favour. "I'll start termorrer. Six o'clock do thi'?"

"Well." Katy was not at all sure what time her kitchen staff began work. "Perhaps we'd best go and see Mrs Kelsall," who, by now, ran the kitchen, the servants, the house and even the grooms in the stable like a general in charge of an army.

When she had anything to report, anything unusual that is, Annie would knock on Katy's drawing room door, stepping inside with no sign of the overwhelming awe she always felt at the sight of so many beautiful things. Shining, glittering, polished things that winked and shimmered at her from every corner of the room. Lovely colours and lovely pictures, flowers and even, in an enormous glass room she had heard Janet call the conservatory, birds singing in cages. If for nothing else it was worth the tramp twice a day to see this lovely room.

"He 'asn't half lost weight, Miss Katy," she reported several weeks later. "'Appen it's all them exercises he's doin'."

"Exercises? What sort of exercises?"

"Nay, I don't see 'im do them but I 'ear him sometimes, thump, thump, thump, an' Jinty Pickles ses he can get up that track as fast as you an' me. Sticks, he 'as now but he don't hop no more. He walks proper, one foot in front of t'other, like. It give 'er quite a turn, she said. It were like Lazarus come back from't dead, seein' him up an' about an' chirpy as a bird in a tree. 'Mornin', Jinty,' he ses to 'er. 'Fine mornin' fer a walk,' grinnin' like he used to," for there was no denying Paddy Andrews had been a fine, handsome, laughing man before he lost his leg.

"What . . . what d'you think he means to do, Annie?" Katy's voice trembled for though she had not taken his threat seriously at the time, for what harm could wheelchair-bound Paddy Andrews do to her and her son, Paddy Andrews up on two legs, even if one was made of wood, was a different matter altogether.

"Lass, I don't know, but I'd tekk care if I were thi'."

24

The man was admitted to Cloudberry End just as Katy and Chloe were about to sit down to lunch. Katy wanted Chloe to judge her once again on her skills as a hostess, though God only knew when she would have a chance to show them off, she laughed, not, Chloe understood, particularly concerned. No one had called on her since her return to Cloudberry End, which was only to be expected and had it not been for Chloe and Jamie she would have had no visitors at all. Truth to tell she was becoming slightly bored with being mistress of Cloudberry End, since Mrs Kelsall was excellent at her job and though she consulted Katy – tongue in cheek, Katy was inclined to think – on every household matter, there was no need for Katy to be involved apart from the accounts which Mrs Kelsall kept meticulously.

Katy saw Chris every now and then, sometimes at dinner, sometimes passing one another in a hallway like guests in a hotel but they had little to say to one another, speaking only to argue.

"Do your . . . er . . . friends have to make such an infernal row at two o'clock in the morning, Chris? Half the servants were out of their beds and Angus is quite incensed by the state of his lawn after someone galloped a horse across it."

"Really, and what is it to do with you, or Angus what I do in my own home? Besides, that brat of yours is for ever caterwauling. Sounds like a bloody cat on the tiles. I was quite mortified when I had to explain to my . . . well, a lady guest I was entertaining that it was not a cat but your— "

"That's enough, Chris. And I'd be obliged if you would not bring your loose women into Mother's house."

"You mean besides yourself."

"You bastard . . ."

"No, it is your son who is the bastard, Katy, and the sooner you remove him from a decent household the happier I will be. Why do you not return to your lover now that he is back on his feet? I'm sure a man with two legs must be infinitely more appetising than the wreck he was purported to be."

"Chris, I'm warning you . . ."

"Oh go to hell, Katy, and take your bastard with you."

On the whole they made a point of avoiding one another. The dinner at Christmas to which she had invited Chloe and Jamie had been somewhat strained and also on the several occasions in the past few months when they had driven over to Cloudberry End, borrowing the gig which spent most of its time in the barn at Valley Bottom Farm. Chloe must have some sort of transport, Katy declared, since she did not ride and Katy had no need of it since she did ride and besides, she had the use of her mother's carriage so it seemed only sensible to have the gig and the horse that pulled it stabled at the farm. Call it a Christmas present, she had pronounced carelessly. Yes, she knew she had given them both some trifling thing or two from under her Christmas tree but it was a waste to have it and the animal where no one used them. The horse could pasture in Jamie's meadow and would cost nothing much to feed and as it appeared she was to entertain no one but her cousin and her cousin's husband in her home, she said cheerfully, and was invited nowhere, what would she need with a gig?

She had taken up riding again now that Jack was old enough, or so she said, to be taken up before her on Storm's back. It did no harm to start them young, she argued when Matty protested, and Jack was nine months old now. He loved it, sitting up before her on the gentle slopes she took him on, wrapped in a warm shawl, the ends of which were tied firmly about his mother's waist so that there was no danger of his falling off. His face glowed as the wind touched it and his bright eyes roamed across the burgeoning moors just beyond Cloudberry End. Not far, since he was still young but he seemed to have the same empathy with its broad and sculpted emptiness as his mother. Bracken, its tall fronds rising to greet the spring, green and restless above the heather moor. The broken ground exploding with cotton grass, with bilberry which formed a continuous fringe above the gritstone, a wildness, a lonely wilderness to which the heart and soul of Katy Andrews responded. She loved it. The vastness which stretched on into infinity. The rolling moorlands, the steep-sided cliff faces, the sighing trees, the whisper of the wind through the undergrowth. It had never frightened her because it was her land and she loved it. There was nothing up here but sheep sheltering behind the cobweb of drystone walls which criss-crossed the peaks, a solitary shepherd who raised a hand in surprised greeting, a hawk hanging on the wind, rabbits showing off their little white scuts as they darted out of her way. She was never lonely. Just she and Jack, Storm and Muffy and if, sometimes, when her son slept in her arms after his feed she wept for her lost love there was no one to see or hear it.

"Now let us see what miracle Mrs Kelsall has prepared for us today," she was saying laughingly as she and Chloe entered the dining room followed by Janet who was to serve. They were all three considerably startled when the doorbell rang. In fact they looked at one another as though to ask who on earth this could be at Miss Katy Andrews's door. Janet, who had been heard to remark, not by Miss Katy, of course, that she was sick of sitting on her bum all day since it was her job as housemaid to answer the door, ventured a step in its direction.

"See who it is, Janet," Katy said firmly, noting that her heart was missing every other beat at the prospect of seeing Paddy Andrews on her front doorstep. Surely he could not have walked all this way from Woodhead, despite the progress Annie reported he was making on his new leg. She found she was hovering at Janet's back and behind her, Chloe, who seemed to be beset with the same fear, did a bit of hovering herself.

Jack was in his nursery having an after-lunch nap with Lottie sitting beside him, for Katy had still not got around to hiring a nursemaid for her son and the housemaid appeared to find the occasional hour she spent watching over him something to enjoy. Indeed the maidservants argued over whose turn it was to do it.

The gentleman at the door seemed vaguely familiar, though Katy could not quite place him. He was, she supposed, in his late forties or early fifties, a stocky, well-dressed gentleman who, at the sight of her behind her maid, whipped off his low bowler hat and held it politely against his plain waistcoat. He wore a sombre grey frock-coat which was not buttoned and trousers to match. He was decently dressed, neat and immaculate but he was not a "gentleman" and both young women, and indeed Janet who had been housemaid for enough years to recognise one, instinctively knew it.

"Aah, Miss Andrews," he said at once and somewhat breathlessly as though he had been running. Though he inclined his head at Chloe, his manner was brusque, businesslike, with no time to spare for polite conversation.

"I am Miss Andrews," Katy said, stepping forward and, though as usual she did not mean it to be, her attitude was imperious.

"Aye, I know, but it's actually Mr Andrews I'm after, Miss Andrews. Is he at home?"

"Mr Andrews?" Her voice rose on a questioning note and she arched her delicate copper eyebrows. She was looking quite magnificent. If she had been a lovely girl before the birth of her son, motherhood had matured her to a womanly beauty, a shining, glossy beauty which most men, had she met any, would have found hard to ignore. She was tall, her back straight but graceful, her posture and bearing that of a young queen. Her breasts were full, high and rounded and though she had almost weaned Jack there was no droop or sag to them. Her waist was slender, her hips curving, her legs long and in perfect proportion to her body. She wore her hair in an enchanting tumble of long, floating curls, thick and springing, fastened carelessly to the crown of her head with a knot of silver and cream ribbons to match her gown, which today was of a rich, creamy silk. Her skin was lustrous, smooth as honey, her cheekbone touched with rose as was her mouth, and her warm, golden eyes snapped and gleamed with good health and at that moment with keen interest, for she had just recognised the gentleman on her doorstep.

"It's Mr Harrop, isn't it?" she exclaimed, smiling at him with such brilliance he blinked. He had heard of her comeliness, as who had not in Crossclough; of her association with her cousin and the illegitimate boy who had been the result of it and like them all he had been shocked, appalled even at her behaviour, sorry for Mr Andrews and his wife who had so much to bear with their two youngest children. He had seen her about Crossclough in that shameless get-up of hers, averting his eyes, which was hard to do for how was a hot-blooded male to resist those bobbing breasts and hard-peaked nipples, those spread thighs which opened across her horse's back. Even a respectable man such as himself was not immune and he was glad to see she was modestly dressed today.

"Yes, miss, but I'm somewhat pushed for time, if you'll forgive me. I'm after Mr Andrews . . ."

"Do you mean my father, Mr Harrop?"

"Eeh no, Miss Andrews. He's away to Scarborough or so he told me last back end and a sorry day it was when . . . well . . ." He interrupted himself hastily, the expression on his face telling her quite plainly he really had no time to be chitter-chattering with a woman and certainly not a woman such as her, pretty as she was.

"Well, do come in, Mr Harrop," she entreated, opening the door wider, smiling again in a way which did nothing for Mr Harrop's pulse.

"Nay, lass . . ." getting irritated, with himself and her but trying not to show it.

"I insist, but first let me introduce my cousin, Mrs James Hutchinson."

"Ma'am."

"And this is Mr Harrop, Chloe, who is, I believe, manager at my father's paper mill. Have I got that right, Mr Harrop? You are manager, are you not?"

"Aye, I am that, Miss Andrews, but I'd take it very kindly if . . ."

"Oh, do come in, Mr Harrop. We can hardly continue to chat on the doorstep like this. My cousin and I were about to sit down to lunch. Will you not join us?"

"Nay!" Mr Harrop was deeply shocked. In his social group you just did not associate with a woman, no matter how well bred, who had done what Katherine Andrews had done, and besides, he had come here on urgent business and certainly had no time for socialising.

He stood firmly on the doorstep, refusing stolidly to put one foot over the threshold, just as though the three women who stood in the hall were sirens who might lure him to some dreadful bacchanalian orgy he might possibly regret.

"It's Master Chris I'm after, Miss Andrews," he declared firmly. "There's a problem at the mill which needs his attention so I'd be obliged if you wouldn't mind asking him . . ."

"My brother isn't here, Mr Harrop, and . . ."

"Perhaps you could tell me where I might find him then, Miss Andrews. I really must— "

"But I thought he was at the mill, Mr Harrop. I must admit our paths don't cross much. He lives his life and I live mine."

So Mr Harrop had heard, his grim expression said, but that was nothing to do with him, he just wanted to get his hands on the young wretch whom Mr Andrews had, much against Mr Harrop's advice, put in charge of the bloody mill when he took flight to Scarborough. He'd begged him and begged him, if he didn't want John Harrop to do it for him, to get in a decent engineering manager to help run the paperworks but Mr Andrews had seemed unwilling or unable to make a decision about anything at the time, for ever dashing off, so Mr Harrop had heard, to see that wife of his as though all those servants up at Cloudberry End couldn't manage without him. Daft he was about her, any fool would agree, and to go gallivanting off to Scarborough and leave a good business in the hands of a bone-idle young pup who cared for nothing but drinking and wenching and gambling was, in his opinion, nothing short of criminal.

"So he's not at home, Miss Andrews?"

"I have just said so, Mr Harrop."

"I must find him, Miss Andrews. I will be frank with you," though she could tell he didn't want to. "Perhaps a moment of your time?"

"Of course. Come into the small parlour. Chloe, do you mind? Janet, tell Mrs Kelsall lunch will be a little late, oh, and bring the brandy. I'm sure Mr Harrop would not refuse."

The tale was short, simple and so characteristic of her brother she wondered why Mr Harrop should be surprised not to find him here.

"It's over three months, Miss Andrews, since he was last down at Waterway which, pardon me if I speak bluntly . . ."

"Please do, Mr Harrop."

"Well, it was no loss, for I am quite well able to run it without him. Your father left ample funds, for the men's wages and any other need which might arise and, of course, any profit made has been paid into the account. Your father gave me and Master Chris power to draw on that account. Today, when I went to the bank to withdraw cash for the wages, tomorrow being pay day, the bank manager tells me the account is empty. That Mr Andrews, meaning Master Chris, had taken every last farthing from it a week ago. Unless I can lay my hands on a considerable sum, Miss Andrews, the men will not be paid and no man is willing to give his labour free. In other words there will be trouble, Miss Andrews, and your father would not like that."

"Of course not, Mr Harrop, I quite see that, but surely you could telegraph my father."

"Where, Miss Andrews? He was so adamant about keeping his whereabouts secret he gave his address to no one. For some inexplicable reason he decided that Master Chris was capable, and willing, to run the paper mill. He put his trust in him and now see where that trust has landed him."

"I don't think that was in his mind when he went, Mr Harrop? He and my mother were . . . well, let us say they were not themselves; family problems, if you take my meaning, and my father was concerned only with my mother's health. Truthfully, I do believe he did not really care what happened to his mill, but that is not the problem now. I know where he is, Mr Harrop, and I'm sure if I telegraphed him he could do the same to the bank manager, transferring funds from . . . I know he has a private account since I draw on it for the household— "

She stopped speaking abruptly, biting off her words, her narrowed eyes so vivid and startling a colour, so excited, so lit up with energy and force, Mr Harrop nearly choked on his welcome brandy.

"I could get the money for you, Mr Harrop," she said softly, "providing there is enough in the account. I dare say Mr What's-his-name at the bank will kick up a fuss but he cannot stop me. My father signed a legal document and so did I, giving me – what's the word? – power of something or other and I know he could only agree that, in this emergency, I might use this power."

She sat back in triumph and Mr Harrop could see quite clearly what it was Miss Katherine Andrews had which allowed her to get her own way as, it was said, she had done all her life.

"Happen you'd best telegraph your father, Miss Andrews," he said a little uncertainly. "Mr Wainwright's a bit of a . . . well, he likes things done the right way."

And so do you, Katy thought. They were all the same, of course, men! They thought they were the only ones with a brain in their head and that a woman was incapable of making any decision except what colour her drawing room curtains were to be and now look where that opinion had landed them. Now that she recalled, she had neither seen nor heard her brother about the house for over a week which was unusual, for though they rarely met he never failed to make his presence felt in some explosive way or other. She must ask the maids if his bed had been slept in and the grooms should be questioned on the whereabouts and movements of Chris's grey, Zack. In fact there were several questions which must be asked before she contacted her father but in the meanwhile she must put into some sort of order this dilemma into which it seemed her brother had tipped poor Mr Harrop.

She stood up so joyfully, so suddenly, Mr Harrop jumped and sloshed his brandy over his plain grey waistcoat but she did not appear to notice. He was struggling to his feet but she shook her head, her red-gold curls bobbing vigorously, indicating that he was to remain seated.

"No, no, Mr Harrop. Finish your brandy. Indeed help yourself to another. I won't be long. I must see to the care of my son and tell my cousin what I am about and then I will be with you directly."

"But Miss Andrews, what are you to do?"

"Now you are not to worry, Mr Harrop. We'll have this situation sorted out in no time. I will just go and speak to my cousin and the servants, then I shall put on my hat and return at once. I think we had best go in my carriage so I must ask Janet to tell my coachman to fetch it to the front door."

She smiled brilliantly. "Is it not a splendid day, Mr Harrop? I always think April is one of the loveliest months of the year, don't you?" Then she was gone with a graceful dipping of her cream silk skirt to reveal the inch or two of scarlet ruffles on her petticoat which made Mr Harrop gasp. Wait until he told Mrs Harrop that Miss Katherine Andrews wore a scarlet petticoat! No, on second thoughts, best not. Women were funny creatures and his wife might put some connotation on it that could cause no end of trouble and he was in enough of that already.

Though he protested volubly that all it needed was a note from herself, in the absence of her father, to Mr Wainwright, instructing him to transfer enough funds from the private account to the business account, she wouldn't hear of it, telling him it was no trouble, none at all, as she sat beside him on the journey to Crossclough. He could distinctly see, wherever he looked, the slack-jawed amazement of passers-by, many, of course, with whom he was acquainted, for Crossclough was a small town. Jesus Christ, what had that bloody little whippersnapper Andrews brought him to when he, John Harrop, a respected member of the community and a sidesman at the local church in Pilkington Way, should be seen riding in the same carriage as a woman who had not only lived with a man without benefit of marriage but had borne him a child.

Mr Wainwright was considerably taken aback by the unprecedented sight of Jack Andrews's harlot daughter sweeping into his office, her wide skirt held up to reveal the scarlet frills on her petticoat which matched exactly the scarlet feather on her jaunty hat. His clerks, like the good folk John Harrop had passed in the street, were open-mouthed with wonder. Strangely, it was then that John Harrop began quite to enjoy the situation, for after all there was nothing he could do but sit back and, hopefully, at the end of the day have the necessary cash put into his hands. She was a beautiful young woman and on the drive from Cloudberry End to Crossclough had chatted to him pleasantly in a way he would not have thought possible from what he had heard of her. She was bright, intelligent, even witty, and he found himself regretting the circumstances which had driven her to a point where no decent folk would so much as speak to her, let alone receive her in their homes. Her own fault, of course, but still, she would have made a fine wife for some man of business, charming them in that way a man in business needs in a wife.

"Now then, Mr Wainwright," she said briskly after they had been introduced, though naturally Mr Wainwright knew exactly who she was. He had not dealt with her himself when she came into his bank to withdraw funds for her household, leaving that to his head clerk, but he certainly knew her, as who didn't in Crossclough. "I have come here today," she went on, "to transfer enough funds from my father's private account into his business account which, Mr Harrop informs me, has been emptied. May I sit down?" For Mr Wainwright in his consternation had omitted to ask her, or Mr Harrop, to be seated.

"Oh, please do, Miss Andrews, but I'm afraid— "

"There is nothing to be afraid of, Mr Wainwright." She smiled, showing him her strong white teeth and sitting down with a flourish which allowed him another peep at her scarlet frills. "I'm sure it is a simple enough procedure which needs only my signature on a bit of paper and then Mr Harrop here" – smiling vividly in Mr Harrop's direction, a smile he found he was returning with a beaming nod of his own – "can pay my father's workers."

"Miss Andrews, you surely cannot expect me to transfer . . . how much?" – turning to Mr Harrop who mentioned a sum – "from one of your father's accounts to another without his permission?"

"Why not, Mr Wainwright? He gave me the legal power to withdraw cash."

"For household expenses and your own allowance, Miss . . . er . . . Andrews," clearly finding it distasteful discussing with a woman, and a woman such as this one, the affairs of a client, even if the client was her father. True, she came in every week and signed her name to the papers her father had had drawn up but that was for funds which a woman, a mistress of a household, would ordinarily deal with. Not this! Not this large amount which, to his amazed disapproval, Mr Harrop seemed to connive at.

"Mr Wainwright, tell me this. Does it specify on those documents how much cash I may withdraw at one time?"

"No, but— "

"And would you agree, as a man of business, that those who are in your employ must be paid the wage they have earned?"

"Of course, but— "

"And that my father, who is a wealthy man, has put his trust in you to manage his financial affairs in his absence in a manner which is beneficial to him?"

"That is precisely why— "

"And do you think that, having given the same trust to myself as he has to my brother who, it appears, has run off with a considerable sum of money belonging to my father, which you allowed, my father will be pleased to hear that his men have refused to work until they are paid and his mill has come to a standstill because of it? Surely you, who have done business with him for so long, must know that my father would beggar himself rather than withhold the wages they have earned from his men?"

She sat upright in her chair in a way which would have gratified her mother and waited, exuding authority in a way which astonished both men.

"Miss Andrews, what you say is true. There was nothing I could do to prevent your brother from emptying the account though I protested vigorously. But your father had given him authority to do so and I had to allow it." Mr Wainwright sat back in his chair and caressed his side whiskers in a way which told this young madam there was nothing more to say on the matter.

The young madam did not agree.

"Because he is a man."

"I beg your pardon?"

"We share exactly the same right where withdrawals of cash are concerned, my brother and I, albeit from different accounts, and yet what you allowed him you will not allow me. I can only presume it is because I am a woman."

"Miss Andrews, you go too far."

"Do I indeed, but it is the truth, is it not? So all I ask of you is to show me where in my father's document it says that his daughter does not have the same entitlement to draw out cash as his son."

She lifted her head regally and Mr Harrop felt like applauding. She was a rarity indeed, was Miss Katherine Andrews, with a square set to her chin and a firmness about her full mouth which spoke of a resolve so obstinate, so bright and positive, Mr Harrop had a great deal of difficulty in restraining himself from showing the same enthusiasm. He felt himself to be magnetised by her absolute certainty that she was right and of course, she *was* right, a fact Mr Wainwright finally conceded.

"Very well, but I shall expect to have your father's written authority in my hand by the week's end, Miss Andrews, and I shall impress it upon him when I write to him," he pontificated, as he watched his clerk count out the required money into Mr Harrop's bag.

"Tell me, Mr Wainwright, when my brother emptied the business account did you not think it worth writing to my father at the time?"

She smiled in triumph, then, giving the bank manager no

time to answer, swept from the bank, bestowing on each clerk at his tall desk a smile of such shimmering brightness they fell back from it, blinded by it and by something in her which looked surprisingly like intoxication.

"Well done, Miss Andrews," Mr Harrop murmured as he handed her into her carriage, smiling broadly as Mr Wilson, the hatter, walked smack into Mr Garfield, the chemist, both of them so intent on staring at himself and Miss Andrews they neither of them saw the other until it was too late.

"I am most grateful for your help," he continued, "but I think I will take a cab back to the mill. There is no need to trouble you any further."

"It is no trouble, Mr Harrop, none at all, and I insist I drive you there. I find I have a curiosity to see what goes on in that paper mill of my father's and so if you will hop up we will be on our way."

Hop up! "Miss Andrews, I cannot allow it, really I cannot. Your father would never forgive me if I were to expose you to the rough atmosphere of a working mill. There are sights to which you are not accustomed."

"Mr Harrop, you have no idea what sights I am accustomed to, really you haven't." She positively twinkled in his direction as she said it and Mr Harrop could feel the hot blood rush beneath his skin in the most appalling way as his imagination ran riot with pictures of her and Paddy Andrews. Dear God . . .

He argued with her all the way back along the road from Crossclough. When they reached the gate which led up to Cloudberry End he begged her to allow him to get down and walk the rest of the way but she merely ordered her coachman to "Drive on, Thomas", adding that, now that she had retrieved the men's wages for him she had a fancy to see, not only the men who were to be paid, but the place in which they worked.

"Have you women working there, Mr Harrop?" she asked him civilly.

"Yes, we have, but— "

"What do they do?"

"Miss Andrews . . ."

"Never mind, Mr Harrop, I shall see for myself."

When she got home Chloe was still there, sitting with Jack

on her lap while she played some clapping game she was trying to teach him.

"Pat a cake, pat a cake, baker's man," she was chanting, "bake me a cake as fast as you can," holding his small, plump hands between hers, then bending her head to drop a kiss in each palm. She had recovered from the loss of her child, outwardly at least, regaining that tranquil look of composure which her husband loved and which her cousin unknowingly leaned on more and more. She was often quiet, dreaming off into some distance, but inclined now and again, particularly with Jack, into bubbling laughter. Katy knew she wanted another child. Chloe had confided as much but she had intimated that Jamie was not yet prepared to chance it.

And could she help but be glad, Katy brooded in the tossing restlessness of the dark night, that it appeared that Jamie Hutchinson was not yet making love to his wife.

But these thoughts were far from her mind as she tossed her red feathered hat on to the nursery table and began to dance round it in a lively polka, her arms about an imaginary partner. They were both laughing, Jack and Chloe, their smooth cheeks pressed together as she spoke.

"Chloe, you are not going to believe this but I have just spent the most exhilarating afternoon I can remember. It was quite wonderful and I do believe I have found exactly what I want to do with the rest of my days."

25

It appeared that young Chris Andrews was in Baden-Baden, where, it was reported in Crossclough, though they could not swear to the authenticity of it for what did they know of such things, the nobility and even royalty did their gambling.

"He's in debt, Katy. He's lost the money he withdrew from the business fund and has telegraphed begging me to let him have a draft to cover the debt. He'll never gamble again, he swears to me, if I will only help him out of this mess and I suppose, for your mother's sake, I cannot refuse but I know what I'd like to do to the young bugger."

Jack Andrews sighed heavily, doing his best to restrain his grandson from clambering up on to the table in his study and playing havoc with his inkstand and pens. The boy was sitting on Jack's lap, diverted for the past five minutes, which was the span of his baby attention, by his grandfather's solid gold watch and chain, listening with awed delight to its repeating chime and solemn tick. It was a calendar railway watch with three dials showing the date, the day and the seconds and had been bought for Jack by his wife on the occasion of their twenty-fifth wedding anniversary. It was very precious to him and his reluctance to allow young Jack to grind at it with his sharp new teeth had frustrated the baby who was now intent on targeting his lively curiosity in another direction.

"Put him on the floor, Father," Katy told him.

"And have him remove the coal from the scuttle as he did yesterday?"

"I know, he's very lively," his mother said fondly. "Never mind, I'll ring for one of your maids. Perhaps Ivy will amuse him for half an hour."

The child, who was already pulling himself up on to his

brown and sturdy legs, objected at first when Ivy swooped down on him but his baby mind remembered where this smiling person came from and he was carried off to the kitchen where he would, his mother knew quite well, be completely spoiled, played with and sung to and fed Mrs Tiplady's biscuits until he was sick.

"You have heard from Mr Wainwright then?" she went on mildly, though her eyes gleamed the colour of pure malt whisky between her long, coppery eyelashes.

Jack smiled, a smile which lit up his face and made him look like the dashing young navvieman Sara Andrews had fallen in love with over thirty years ago. His grin was wide and his teeth, which were still white and sound, gleamed in the dim, wood-lined shadows of the room. His eyes narrowed and Katy felt her heart lift to see her father, on whom she had inflicted so much distress, evidently enjoying a moment of humour.

"By God, lass, you must have made an impression on the old buffer, and no mistake. Anyone'd think you'd stolen the money from him, or got it under false pretences and not only that but it was his money you'd wheedled out of him! Hell's teeth, I'd've liked to have been there, Katy." He grew serious. "You did well though and I'm grateful to you. Harrop wrote and said he couldn't have managed if you'd not stepped in like you did. And of course, you did the only thing you could in the circumstances. The men had to be paid from somewhere, surely the old fool could see that. I'm . . . grateful, Katy."

"And surprised, Father?"

"Aye, I'll not argue with that. You've not shown a great deal of sense in the past, my lass, but . . ."

"But?"

"You've . . . you seem to have made some effort to control that wild streak. Well, you'll know what I mean." His voice was gruff and he fiddled with the watch he had allowed his grandson to play with, not meeting her eyes, not wanting, she was well aware, to allow her to get under the guard he had erected around himself and her mother lest she inflict further damage on their hard-won peace of mind.

She had arrived in Scarborough earlier in the day to find her parents were out, Freda told her, and when they came home hand in hand from a walk on the long, sandy beach, her mother's uncovered hair tangled with sea-wind and sea-mist, her cheeks poppy flushed, she was glad when they showed a degree of pleasure at her arrival. Jack was kissed and admired and taken on to her mother's lap for a moment and they both agreed he was a handsome, taking little chap, though Paddy Andrews, whom he definitely favoured, was not mentioned.

It was four months since she had first come to Scarborough. She had not been back and she knew they were grateful that she had not become troublesome to them in their hard-won struggle for the peace and harmony they sought in their declining years. Knowing her impetuous, demanding nature, she was aware they were afraid she might intrude on them, constantly harangue them to forgive her, as she might once have done. Overwhelmed them with her guilt and shame, but she had gone away quietly and got on with whatever she did at Cloudberry End, causing no trouble, nor gossip, making no ripples and, surprisingly, being a big help to her father over the worrying matter of Chris and the missing money.

Now she had come again, giving Mr Wainwright time to put his "two pennorth" in, as her father said wryly, travelling with Matty as a decent woman should, to discuss it with him, though what was there to discuss now it was all over? Jack wondered.

"Have you heard from Mr Harrop again?" she went on diffidently, beginning to fiddle with the sash at her waist. She had changed into a gown of the palest yellow, soft and elegant and very feminine. She wore kid slippers dyed to match and ribbons in her hair of the same colour. She knew she looked as her mother and father had always wanted her to look, as she herself needed to look now that she was the mother of a son whom she was determined not to let suffer because of her wickedness.

She glanced up to find her father watching her with a slight air of apprehension, as though he had caught some whisper of why she was here and she was suddenly aware of how difficult this was going to be.

"No. I wrote to him and gave him this address, since I realised, after what had happened with Chris, it was foolish to allow him no contact except through you or the bank, but it seems, now that the emergency has been resolved, he has nothing further to say on the matter. Why do you ask?"

She took a deep breath.

"I . . . well, I know you will not like it, Father, but I went to the mill with him," she answered in a rush as though she must get it out before she took fright. "I wanted to see what went on there and I'm afraid I rode roughshod over his wishes so please don't blame him, but . . . well . . ." Her smile broke free, a smile like a sunburst, an explosion of light, of fireworks against a dark sky, stars glittering and flashing and her father's heart sank like a rock in deep water. Dear, dear God . . .

"I was interested, Father, and so, though I know you will not care for it, I go there for an hour or two on most days. I sit with Mr Harrop in his office and study the accounts and, well, I find it absolutely fascinating. I realise I have a lot to learn but as Chris is not in the least bit interested I thought . . . Oh, Father, unless you give your permission Mr Harrop says he cannot countenance, that is the word he used, having a woman intruding in a man's world. I took him by surprise, I think, with my curiosity and so he did not try to stop me at first, thinking, I suppose, that I would quickly lose interest but now he can see I am serious he has dug his heels in and insists that you . . . advise him on your wishes."

She was doing her best not to break out into the turmoil of excitement her visits to the Waterway Paper Mill had induced in her. The excitement the Katy Andrews she had been before the birth of her son would have engaged in but it was very hard. Her stomach was lurching in the most violent way and she could feel every breath catch like a barbed fish-hook in her chest but she did her best to remain composed. Her father was staring at her with growing horror as though he could not believe what she was asking of him and even as she watched, his head began to shake in violent denial.

"There is no one else but me, Father," she added desperately. "The boys don't care and it is hopeless with Chris, surely you know that after what has just happened. Mr Harrop says it is three months since he even showed his face at the mill."

"Are you daring to ask me if you can take. his place?" her father thundered. He hit the flat of his hand violently on the desk and the inkstand jumped several inches into the air, spilling the ink.

"Yes. Yes, I am." Her voice was defiant. "It is a sound business and it would be a shame to let it run down, for it cannot be left under the leadership of a manager for ever, Father, diligent as Mr Harrop is. I would go there perhaps no morem than two or three times a week, since there is

Jack whom I would not like to neglect. Besides, I think it is time to face the truth which is that no matter what I do, no matter how respectable I have become, it is too late. When I go into Crossclough faces are still averted. I am a leper in their eyes, not worth a moment of their time. As for calling on me or inviting me to their homes I must face the fact it will never happen. So, I must make a life in another direction. As I said, none of the boys are concerned with 'trade' as Chris so scathingly calls it, but I mean to be. If I can find something worthwhile to do with my life and Jack's life, for it will be there for him when he is a man, then that is all I ask. I shall never marry, we both know that so I will devote myself to creating a life, a purpose for my son. I want to do it, Father. I can do it. Mr Harrop said he had never met anyone who had grasped— "

"Bugger Harrop! He had no right to take a woman into— "

"He didn't, he didn't! I forced my way in."

"Just like you have always done, Katherine. Force! You know of no other way. And just when your mother and I were beginning to think you might . . ."

"Might what? Become respectable?" Her voice was filled with painful self-mockery. "I've tried. For over six months I've tried to be what a daughter of yours should be but I find I cannot fill my days with nothing but counting the linen and discussing menus."

"You have a son. Is he not enough? Don't you realise that if you do this thing you will further jeopardise any chance he may have of a decent life among decent people?"

"Why, for God's sake, why?" she demanded passionately. "What is wrong in honest, honourable work? And don't tell me it's not for women. There are women in business. Only the other day I read of two, years ago now, who ran the North Wick Mill in Somerset, a paper mill like yours."

Suddenly, with a savage movement of his hand he capitulated, turning away from her with great bitterness.

"Very well, then, further humiliate and degrade yourself by mixing with men who are the roughest, most uncouth you will ever meet, who use language you have never before heard. But I tell you this, expect no quarter from Harrop because he will be humiliated himself when he finds he is forced to work alongside my daughter. He will take it as an insult and so will the men. They won't like it and they won't hesitate to let you know. They will make your life such a bloody misery you'll be glad to get back to your menus, believe me."

"No . . . oh, no, all I want is a chance to prove I can— "

"As you always have done, you mean? You haven't really changed, have you, Katherine? You still have that stubbornness which demands what you think you should have, no matter how it might affect those who care about you. Well, do as you like, lass. Just leave your mother in peace, that's all I ask. If Harrop will put up with it then I shan't argue. I find I care less and less about business matters. I'm a wealthy man and I have no need to work. I have a fancy to spend the years I have left in peace with your mother. We are going to travel. Through France and Germany, Switzerland and on to Italy. Did she not tell you?"

He was informing her that they were escaping again. Distancing themselves even further from the turbulence their youngest son, and now their daughter, it appeared, was again to fling them into. They had allowed themselves to believe that everything was going to be all right. That Chris was knuckling down to his position, as the owner's son, of running the small family firm of Waterway Paper Mill and that their daughter, though she would never be the proper young lady they had hoped for as she grew, and whose past would always haunt them, was at least giving the community of Crossclough no further chance to point the finger, nor to gossip about her. The dust was settling, not as neatly as they had hoped it would, but enough to be able to breathe deeply without choking on it and now, within the space of a week or two, it had all blown up again into a gigantic storm which it seemed would never be stable.

"Father . . ." Katy's voice trembled but she held herself stiffly erect. "What are you to do about Chris?"

"Fetch him back, of course. For some reason he has run off to Baden-Baden, taking a considerable sum of money with him, money which did not belong to him and which he has lost in the gambling casino . . ."

Her father's voice began to grow fainter, fading away until she could hear no more than a murmur, a murmur which needed no concentration on her part but allowed her mind to travel back to the day she had left the cottage in Woodhead and moved back to Cloudberry End. She could hear another voice, not soft and filled with resignation as her father's was, but coarse, harsh with fury and frustration.

"I'll get thi', my lass, an' that brother o' thine. I'll not forget . . ."

And they had tried, hadn't they, she was convinced of that, Josh and Jake, under Paddy's direction. They had waylaid Chris, knocking him from his mount, abandoning him at the bottom of Deep End Clough where he had almost perished in the freezing January night. He had been drunk and had fallen from his grey, or so it was said. His animal had found its way home and Saul Gibbon had discovered Chris who, though Deep End Clough was faced with jagged, bone-breaking, flesh-tearing rocks, had been found without a mark on him. The mystery of it had kept the gossips at it for weeks but no one was ever to hear the true story.

Which was what? Katy had her own opinion but Chris had had nothing to say about it, probably because he had been too drunk to know what had been done to him, or by whom, but Katy had been troubled with thoughts of the revenge Paddy had sworn he would exact, against Chris who had beaten him, against her who had caused the beating and then stolen his son.

And was it just coincidence that Paddy, who had suddenly risen from the dead, or from what must have seemed like a living death to a man such as he, could now walk upright again, could even clamber up the rough sheep tracks and trails of the moorland, and that, at the very moment Paddy was mobile again, Chris Andrews should take it into his head to steal his own father's cash and slip quietly abroad?

Was she being unbalanced? she asked herself, as her father's voice continued to rise and fall in the far reaches of her mind, or had some threat been made against her brother, one that had caused him to bolt in panic? Dear God in heaven, where was it to end? Where was the sweet and enduring strength of her love for Jamie Hutchinson, which had set off this explosive chain of events, to bring them, all of them, since it affected so many people? One event had led to another and now there was this last. Of course, Chris was a weak, wilful man, much given to self-indulgence, with an ability to avoid anything which smacked of hard work, of trade, which he despised. Even without the threat of Paddy Andrews, which had been no real threat at all to him, he had believed, until Paddy had risen to his feet again, he would never have settled to this function, this role, this job to which she herself was so eminently suited and which had suddenly become such a fascination to her. Which she must have, even if it meant defying not only her father, but Mr Harrop, Mr Wainwright and every other damned fool man of business who got in her way.

". . . is not very far from Strasbourg," her father was saying, "and the Rhine where we mean to spend a week or two, so when I have got your mother settled I'll go and see him. Inform the young limb of Satan that unless he returns home and settles down to his work I'll not put my hand in my pocket for him again. I made an error in trusting him with the business, thinking a bit of responsibility might do him good, but I'll not do it again. Perhaps if he can't lay his hand on some cash he'll buckle down and face up to where his duty lies."

Aye, if he promises to be good and turn over a new leaf you'll give him another chance, but what about me? she thought bitterly. And it was this that hardened her resolve perhaps, or was it the thought that her father was willing to do almost anything to oblige his son, even if that son had proved a bitter disappointment, but was unwilling to give her, his daughter, a chance to do what should have been done by Chris?

"So Chris is to come home and take over again, is that it?" she asked sharply.

"I can see no other option. He'll be under Harrop's control, of course."

"I see, but what would be the point of that, Father? He will only do the same again. Go galloping off here and there with his wild, hell-raising, pedigreed friends whom he so earnestly desires to emulate. Getting up to mischief with women, gambling his money away or stealing what he can lay his hands on. The petty cash, no doubt, from Mr Harrop's desk drawer."

"Katherine." Her father stood up abruptly, pushing his chair away and striding to the window, his feet heavy on the carpet in his anger. He glared out of the window and the young gardening boy who was about to plant some bulbs in the wide bed picked up his tray and scuttled off, thinking it best to leave this part of the garden until later.

, Jack Andrews gripped the windowsill until his knuckles

showed white, fighting his inclination to strike out at this recalcitrant daughter of his, wondering why, since she spoke only the truth.

"It's true, Father. He stole that money. It did not belong to him and at the rate he was going, and who is to say it would ever slow down, he would bankrupt Waterway by the end of the year. With no one to care about it the mill will close down since you will be travelling with Mother and have no concern for it. Now I realise that it is only a fraction of the income you receive from the fortune you have invested and that you will still live in luxury, you and Mother."

"And you, Katy Andrews."

"Yes, and me, but what of the hundred or so men and women the mill employs? When Chris has beggared it, or Mr Harrop finds he no longer cares to accept the responsibility you have forced on him, with none of the benefits an owner might expect, what then, Father? What is to happen to them all then, Father?"

"Katy, you cannot do it, lass." Her father turned from the window, his face still flushed with his anger. His voice was pleading but already in its tone was a note of uncertainty, for he could suddenly see in her what had been in him at her age. A raw youth working on the railways; a rough navvie but with already in him the ambitious, aye, ruthless businessman he had become. He had met and loved Sara and she had become his star, leading him on to want more and more, and now his grandson, his daughter's child, was her star, her guiding light. She wanted something for him and perhaps with that inspiration to draw her on, to keep her steady, to keep her level and strong and bold, she might just achieve it.

What had he to lose? he asked himself, for he knew in his heart that his son would let it all slip through his fingers. He watched the expressions play across the lovely face of his daughter. Hope, eager hope, need, a hungry need to have some worthwhile goal in her life, excitement, anticipation in her glowing eyes, her cheeks flushed, her bright lips parted in a determined smile to let him know she would not accept defeat easily. So much in her. Such goodness and sweetness, such wild rebellion and defiance, such honesty and strength and yet a vulnerability which would make her prey to every predatory man who did business with her.

And yet ... Dear God, dear sweet Jesus, what was he

doing to her? What was he thinking of even to consider it for one moment? How would she and Chris exist together on the battleground which the mill would become? What profits would there be? And was Katy not already a pariah in her home town and would not this madness only make things worse for her?

"Father, please," she whispered, seeing the indecision in his face. "I have nothing to lose . . . please."

The men in the yard had grown accustomed in the last few weeks to seeing her canter through the open gateway and swing down from her mare. She would turn and beckon to one of the watchful small boys who hung about and who should have been at school. It was seven years since the Education Act had ordained that a school should be placed within the reach of every child in England, but until such schools were built the Act could not be made compulsory and it would be several more years before this was accomplished. Consequently, children from a young age still did work which was within their strength and one such work was running errands for the "maister" at Waterway Paper Mill. They would race one another, barefoot, cheerful ragamuffins, to hold a visitor's horse, or, in the case of the pretty young miss who had come to sit mysteriously in the maister's office, to lead her mare away to the stable at the back of the rectangular mill building. There was a man there whose job it was to look after the giant work horses which pulled the waggons carrying rolls of finished paper to customers, or brought the cotton waste, sent from the mills of Lancashire by train, from the railway station. The man would unsaddle the little mare, rub her down, give her tit-bits, petting her until her mistress called for her again.

Today Miss Andrews was dressed in an outfit of a beautiful rich shade of russet red. The material was barathea, a mixture of twilled hopsack, silk and worsted, consisting of a wide divided skirt over tight trousers and high boots and a neat little jacket which nipped her waist and clung smoothly to her high young breasts. She wore a cream stock tied about her neck, like a man's, and a wicked little cap with a peak, like a jockey's, in a velvet which exactly matched the colour of her outfit. She looked neat, businesslike, modest and yet there was something about her and her outfit that was certainly not the latter. Perhaps it was the way she walked, or held her head and her graceful back, the thrust of her full breasts or her brilliant smile as she thanked the boy who took her mare.

But whatever it was it brought the whole yard to a complete standstill until she vanished from their sight up a flight of steps which led to Mr Harrop's office. The men would sigh, not knowing they did so, some winking, or nudging one another in the way men did, as though to suggest how much better she might be employed if they had the keeping of her; then they would get on with their work, for what the maister's daughter did was nowt to do with them. It'd not last long, they told one another, just like the young master had not lasted long. Give her a week or two breathing in the reek of rotted rags, of chloride of lime; the stink of the boiling, pasting and mingling houses and all the other throat-catching aromas which hung about inside the mill like some almost visible miasma. She would soon be offended by the fine, cloying dust of the china clay, the sulphate of lime which coated her fine gown and choked her breath in her lungs and throat so that she could barely speak, gritting behind her eyelids until they were red raw. Let her get her splendid boots ruined at the "wet end" of the machine where the operatives worked barefoot and she'd soon run back to her baby and her sewing and whatever else fine ladies like her did all day long.

"Good morning, Mr Hardacre," she called out to the clerk who sat at his desk by the window of the outer office. "A fine morning, is it not? The sort of morning when one should be galloping up Spond Moor and not crouched over a desk in a stuffy office, don't you agree?"

Mr Hardacre, who had never been on a horse in his life and could think of nothing he would like less than dashing about the dangerous moorland on one, bobbed his head and thinned his already thin and disapproving lips. If that was what she would rather be doing, then why didn't she, his grim expression said, for he, at least, had no time to pander to the whims and fancies of Mr Andrews's spoiled – in more ways than one – daughter.

With another backward smile at the clerk, she knocked on Mr Harrop's door and without waiting for an answer, opened it and went inside. Mr Harrop, who had just lifted his coat tails to warm his buttocks at the glowing fire in the grate, let them drop hastily, moving to his desk, so flustered by her appearance, since he had been convinced her father would put a stop to this nonsense once and for all, he almost sat down behind it while she was still on her feet.

"Mr Harrop, good morning. No, please, do sit down. I just thought I would let you know I was here. I'm sorry I'm somewhat late but my son held me back. You know how it is." She smiled engagingly.

No, Mr Harrop didn't know how it was, for though he had three sons and four daughters of his own not one of them, at any stage of their growth, had ever held him up from his true purpose in life. His work.

He had been patient with her, prepared to put up with her for an hour or two, since she had got him out of a hole over the men's wages. He had been quite amazed at the strength of her perception, her sharp grasp, and at once, of everything he had explained to her but it would not do, not at all and surely with this visit to her father in Scarborough she would have been made to see it.

"Good morning, Miss Andrews," he answered as patiently as he could, "how pleasant to see you," treating her as though she were a casual visitor who had ridden over for the exercise. "But really, there is no need for you to abandon your son, you know. I'm sure he— "

"Oh, I have not abandoned him, Mr Harrop. I have left him in the charge of his new nursemaid. A fine young woman who is the niece of my cook and absolutely to be trusted. They are devoted to one another already which is just as well."

"Oh, and why is that, Miss Andrews?" Beginning already to feel the first trickle of dread ice through his veins. If this young woman thought . . .

"If I am to spend part of my day here, Mr Harrop, I must have a woman I can trust implicitly to look after my child, would you not agree?"

"Miss Andrews . . ." Mr Harrop stood up as though to display his male authority, his face becoming as red as a brick, but even standing he was still shorter than she was. "Miss Andrews, I really think you should be aware that I cannot approve of your apparent determination to work in my office and I'm sure your father must agree. You have shown an aptitude, I admit, for figures and— "

"As it happens my father does not agree, Mr Harrop," she interrupted him smilingly. "I intend to do more than just work here; much, much more, with your help, of course," she added hastily. "I could not do it without you, Mr Harrop, I am well aware of that, but all mill owners have to start somewhere, don't they?"

"Mill owners?" he said faintly.

"Yes, I have the documents here, Mr Harrop. My father has made me a gift of Waterway Paper Mill, you see. I am the millmaster. In fact, the new owner. 'Sink or swim,' he said, and I have no intention of sinking."

26

Jamie Hutchinson laid a gentle hand on his wife's naked breast, cupping it, rubbing his hard palm across the almond nub of her nipple, before bending his head to take it delicately between his lips. His tongue teased it, circling the little pink bud while his hand moved to stroke her neck and shoulder, the tips of his fingers tracing her fragile collarbone. His mouth moved from one breast to the other, slowly, lingeringly, tasting, making no rough or violent gestures, his hands exploring the surface of her skin with a touch which was almost featherlike, fingers trailing from her throat between her breasts, across her concave belly to the copper fluff of curls which flowered between her legs. Inquiringly they stroked and parted the soft lips they veiled and obediently her legs opened to allow a tender finger to enter her. Jamie sighed, for instead of the moist welcome he had hoped for she was painfully dry.

Removing his hand he brought it up to cup her face and with infinite patience began again, kissing her closed eyes, the high bone of her cheek, smoothing his warm, moist lips along her hairline and down to the small shells of her ears. His tongue probed delicately and his teeth nibbled her earlobe then his mouth moved to follow the line of her jaw. He was careful to touch no part of her body which could be considered erotic or sensual, sliding his mouth and his fingers along the inside of her slender arms, the backs of her tapering legs, the arch and instep of her foot, then up her body to the nape of her neck. He loved her body with all the sweet tenderness he had in him which was endless, beginning to caress her breasts again, biting them a little, moving down from them to her belly and finally between her thighs.

"Please, oh please, go on, Jamie," she whispered. "I don't

mind, really . . . please . . ." just as though she could take no more of his patient attempt to kindle her body to the flame which was consuming his. His penis was a hard rod against her thigh, painful with need and with a muttered oath he plunged it into her, his body welding itself shudderingly to hers, his head thrown back, his voice erupting into a groan which seemed to speak of deep pain.

When it was over he turned abruptly and lay with his back to her, tense and dissatisfied, she was well aware, then slowly, with a deep sigh which could have been compassion, turned back to her. He put his arms about her and she tucked her head in the hollow of his shoulder, her body curving, fitting itself against his, sighing too, for she knew she had not pleased him.

"I love you so much, Jamie," she ventured hesitantly. "You know that, don't you?"

"Yes, my little dove, I know that." His voice was infinitely tender. He pulled her closer, beginning to stroke the tangled mass of her curls which were spread across her pillow, cupping her cheek, lifting her chin so that he could kiss her but at once he sensed her withdrawal. Not distaste, never that, for she willingly nestled against him, in their bed at night, on his lap in the big rocker before the kitchen fire. There were times when he unbuttoned her bodice and fondled her naked breasts, even undressing her completely to lay her across his knee in the firelight and she made no objection, but somehow those exciting, sensual days before the loss of their child could not be recaptured. She allowed him to make love to her. She did her best to respond, he knew that, sometimes dragging her nails across the skin of his back until he flinched, in her determination to be as once she had been to him but somehow she was no longer with him, part of him, riding him to glory as he did his best to ride her.

"I'm sorry, Jamie."

"It doesn't matter, my dove. It will come back."

"You are so patient with me and yet I fail you . . ."

"No, no. Chloe, you don't fail me, never. You are my life, my heart. I live for you, you must know that." His voice was hoarse with urgency and he lifted himself on to his elbow to look down into her face. "I have loved you from that first moment on the train, remember? Your face so pale and anxious. Your eyes quite haunted with something."

"I was afraid."

"I know and I wanted to protect you from it whatever it was. I felt a great desire to make you smile, to see you free of what troubled you. To lift you up in my arms and carry you away to some safe place where I would pamper and pet you."

"Jamie, you didn't." She began to laugh, reaching with her hand to smooth back the rough shock of dark hair which fell across his forehead. Her hand lingered at his fiercely dipping eyebrows then moved down to touch a finger to his mouth. He took it between his lips, biting it gently, then bent to kiss her. Her mouth was warm, moist, parted, but she closed her eyes so that he would not see the shadow which came to muddy the clear, blue-green depths of them. She longed to be able to cling to him, her legs wrapped about his body as he plunged into her, her voice crying out in joy as once it had, but inside her that small, secret place where her baby had been shrivelled and shrank and withdrew from his male penetration, not wanting to suffer again the loss she had known.

He, who loved her, sensed it, lying back and drawing her against him, soothing her to sleep with gentle hands. For a long time after her quiet breathing told him she was deep in dreams he lay, one hand behind his head, staring at the pattern of light and dark on the ceiling, listening to the patter of the leaves of the hawthorn tree against the window and the sighing murmur of the moorland wind in the grasses. Downstairs Captain moved restlessly, padding across the flags to sniff at the bottom of the kitchen door, growling a little in his throat as a dog fox barked somewhere over the brow of the hill. There was a moon, full and white-faced, slipping in and out of cloud so thin it was like gauze, lighting the bedroom at intervals, since the curtains were undrawn and the familiar, well-polished shapes of the wardrobe and chest of drawers made shadows against the whitewashed wall. There was a pleasing scent of wild flowers, poppies, speedwell and white bryony, arranged in a plain glass jug by Chloe and placed in the low, wide, window bottom, and from downstairs the aroma of woodsmoke from the damped-down fire.

It was eight months since Chloe had lost their daughter and he wondered despairingly when she was going to recover from it. She was well, and seemed happy, singing about the place, laughing with Adah-May whom she was teaching to read, going about her household and farm work with every sign of strength and enjoyment. The same, but not the same and he could not put his finger on what it was that was wrong. She spent a couple of afternoons a week over at Cloudberry End, with Katy's approval, driving herself in the gig which Thomas had taught her to use, then walking with Jack in his fine new perambulator in the grounds of the house, taking him up into the woodland and playing with him on the mossy floor beneath the wide canopy of summer trees. The nursemaid, Biddy, was none too pleased about it, Matty had told her son, since Jack was her charge and she resented what she saw as Mrs Hutchinson's interference, and though Matty dearly loved the sweet-faced woman who was her daughter-in-law, she really did agree with Biddy, she said. Oh no, Katy didn't mind, she knew that, hoping, as they all did, that perhaps the companionship of Jack would help to assuage the pain of her loss. And, of course, wasn't Katy consumed with her new passion to become a businessman, for God's sake, and as long as Jack was happy she didn't mind who had him. Down at the mill with her brother Chris – who put in an appearance now and then in order to give credence to his claim to be working – the pair of them locked in deadly combat, it was said, and providing her son was at the door to greet her when she came home what did it matter whose arms he was in.

Jamie shifted slightly in the bed, easing Chloe from his chest, then, when he was satisfied she was still asleep, slipping from the bed. He moved towards the window, stepping lightly, his tall, lean, naked body quite beautiful in the luminous wash of the moonlight. The fine covering of hair on his chest and belly was dark against the strange pallor of his skin, thickening into a springing bush between his thighs. His penis was not completely flaccid, indicating his lack of complete sexual fulfilment and he felt an irritated need to attend to himself as men were forced to do during long weeks at sea. Irritated and shamed, for what he had just done with Chloe was the act of a man who gratifies himself with little thought for his partner's needs. That was not true, of course, he told himself, for he had done his best to awaken desire in her but was that not because her desire pleased him?

Seating himself on the sill, his back against the frame, his knees drawn up to his chin, his arms loosely clasped about them, he stared out blindly over the deserted farmyard to the slope of the hill beyond the gate. He should be asleep. He was a farmer who must be up and about with the dawn, which came early at this time of the year, and yet he was restless and edgy, tired and yet not ready to sleep. He had made love to his wife, his beautiful, loving wife who meant all the world to him, who was his world and yet he could not quiet the turmoil which still churned at the pit of his belly. What was the matter with him? Most men would consider themselves lucky beyond words to have a lovely, compliant wife in their bed, a wife who gave herself gladly whenever she was asked, so what the bloody hell was the matter with him? What was it he sought? What was it he missed in Chloe? She was as loving, as welcoming, as affectionate, as agreeable in all matters as she had ever been but there was some unique thing lacking which he knew had been there before the child's death.

He sat for perhaps ten minutes, breathing in the scent of summer bracken and fern, of the heather and gorse which climbed the hill, the distant spice of bilberry and cloudberry which grew in the rich peat moorland. He thought he could detect the scent of his early potato crop and the ripening acres of corn he had planted in the spring. Up on the rough grazing of the moor his sheep were fattening and his first two years as a small, mixed farmer had proved successful beyond even his own hopeful dreams. He had a tiny herd of cows, Fresians, bought with the proceeds of his first year's profit which Chloe and Adah-May milked with Tommy's help, and if he sat down and compared his good fortune with a hundred other men in the valley he could only give thanks for what he had. He had been the luckiest man in the world, he told himself, on that day he had stepped down from the train at Crossclough, with Chloe beside him, his future, though he had not known it then, stretching out like a scented carpet for him to walk on, so why was he so . . . so restless, so unquiet, so jumpy about nothing? Of course the loss of their child had been a sorrow, a blow to his heart as well as Chloe's but they would survive it. They had survived it. There would be other children. It did not need passion to make a child.

Now why had he said that? he asked himself painfully, glancing across at the bed where his wife slept. She had pushed back the bedclothes and her white body gleamed like pearl against the sheet, the darkness between her parted legs a deeper shadow and he found himself drawn towards her, yearning to put his hand on her, on the secret, hidden part of her woman's body and find it wet and waiting.

With a half-strangled cry he reached for his breeches and without waiting to put on his boots ran noiselessly down the stairs and out of the cottage.

"No, not you," he snarled at the surprised dog, shutting him in the kitchen, then, pulling on his breeches, he began to run. Across the yard he went, vaulting the gate and then the wall on the other side of the track, running on his bare, calloused feet, the result of his years of going barefoot on the deck of a ship, across the rough-textured grass of the field where his herd rested. They lumbered to their feet, stumbling away from him in panic into the moon-streaked darkness. Another wall and then he was out on the open moorland, going higher and higher until his heart thundered in his chest, threatening to burst out of its cavity. Up and up, leaping small cloughs down which the everlasting water ran until he reached the top of Round Hill.

He stopped, leaning forward, his hands on his knees, his head hanging down and when she spoke his name he was not surprised, for it seemed quite natural that she should be there. As his breath quietened he could hear the quiet chomp of the mare's teeth as she tore the grass from the ground, and the chink of her bridle.

"Dear God in heaven . . . oh, dear sweet Jesus," he groaned as he tore his breeches down across his lean buttocks, delivering himself into Katy Andrews's hands with a great moan of relief.

Her body was a rich, creamy white in the strange moonshine as she divested herself of her own breeches and shirt and boots, all she had on and when he knelt over her, breathing in the warm, flowery scent of her, lost in the exciting beauty of her turbulent body, he wondered who it was who was groaning in what seemed to be agony. Her lips opened like a thirsty flower to his, her warm tongue greeting his and from both of them escaped a long, shuddering sigh as their bodies fused together, breast to breast, belly to belly, thigh to thigh. His body pierced hers at once with no attempt to woo or prepare the way, both of them mad for it, tearing and biting and scratching at one another as he sank himself so deep inside her she moaned with the pain of it. Deeper and deeper her body swallowed his, taking away his desperation, his restless and wild longings, serving him, holding, drawing him in until he thought he would die of it. It was like being flung on a wave, one of those which thundered, a wild and vivid turquoise, on to the golden beaches of the Indies where he had once sailed. He felt he was standing on the edge of a dangerous precipice, or carried away on an uncontrollable runaway horse, going faster and faster until his body was pounded beneath the wave, dived like a bird over the precipice, galloped to the edge of no world he had ever known on the horse's back. Until he had emptied into her all that seethed in him. Passion and grief and love, yes, love for this woman, he admitted it now, and guilt for his wife who lay sleeping innocently in his bed at Valley Bottom Farm.

Afterwards he held her in his arms smoothing her trembling body, for it seemed she could not control the storm of her weeping. He kissed her forehead and eyebrows and, helpless again to withstand the supple, willing loveliness of her body, cupped her breasts, his breath quickening again, feeling the rock hardness of her nipples between his fingers as she came up against him, slipping his hands to span her neat waist, the full curve of her hips, holding her buttocks, straining her to him. Her arms were tight about his neck, her mouth as hot as flame upon his and though deep somewhere in his swirling, colour-filled mind he thought he heard a soft, familiar voice cry out to him, when her hand found his penis, hard and jutting in masculine arrogance, he was lost, without sight, or hearing, or thought. She moved over every curve and crease of him, exploring his groaning flesh, tasting it, every one of her senses satisfied, every one of his answering her need, calling out his name again and again. She lay under him and upon him, rolling with him in her arms, limpet-like, across the dark, upland, tufted grass, carrying him on and on until his body was nothing but an exploding jangle of feeling, every inch of him a sensation, a tingling, a joy.

"I love you, Jamie," she breathed into his open mouth, "I love you, I love you," echoing the words his wife had said to him no more than an hour ago.

"Katy . . ."

"Please, Jamie, you cannot, must not ask me to stop. I must say it. I have loved you, wanted you, waited for you for years and this is mine. This and this," her hand smoothing his muscled shoulders, his long hard back, his chest and his flat belly, moving to the crisp hair in which his maleness grew, feeling him tremble as she took it in her hand. "Now, here, it is mine. I know you love Chloe."

"Yes."

"And so do I."

"Katy . . ."

"No, my darling, allow me to speak. I ask nothing of you. I will take nothing of Chloe's, but please, if you care for me, about me, tell me . . . tell me so that I can treasure it. Stay with me a while, please."

"Katy . . ."

It seemed he could say nothing more, could say nothing of how he felt, about her, about this, about the singing joy which surged through him, a joy he had never before known, indeed had been unaware existed, and yet a languorous melting of his bones beckoned him to sleep, to sleep with his head on her full, ripe breast.

"What in hell's name were you doing up here?" he managed at last, feeling her beginning to shiver in his arms now that the fire of their lovemaking was burning low. He drew her close, wrapping them both in her warm cloak which was slung across the rock at their back. He knew he should leave, walk away from the temptation of her long, lithe body which was clasped tight against his, but she was glorious, her breasts big and full and tipped with rose, pressed against his chest, one long leg wrapped across his body, her hair drifting in scented disarray about his throat and mouth. He did not want to lose the feel of her, the warmth of her, the passion of her, not yet, not yet. Just another moment was all he asked for.

"I might ask you the same," she answered, her breath warm on his chest, hardening his nipples and causing his own breath to flutter in his throat. God, he was ready for her again, this wonderful, sensuous woman who had been, not very long ago, the wilful young girl whom he had thought of as nothing but a bloody nuisance.

"I couldn't sleep. I thought a run, but you haven't answered my question." His hand took her breast and he heard the indrawn gasp of her breath.

"Which was?" she managed to say.

"What are you doing up here at this time of night?"

"I often come up here."

"Well, you shouldn't. You don't know who you might come across."

"That's true." He felt her smile against his chest and his arms tightened about her. She was brave and bold was Katy Andrews, funny and bright and she caused a pain in him he found hard to describe.

"I'll take you home," he said gruffly.

"Oh, don't be so bloody silly, Jamie. I ride these moors day and night on my own and will come to no harm. This is my favourite place. It's sheltered from the wind and on a summer's day, or evening, is as warm and secluded as one's own bedroom. I ride up almost every night when Jack's in bed."

She was telling him that this, if he wanted it, would always be here for him. There was no need for words now. He knew her, knew of her love for him, her passion which would never end and which, always, before and after this, belonged to no other man but him. She was his, if he wanted her. She belonged to Jamie Hutchinson. She was his woman.

She sat up and the cloak slipped away from her. His eyes dropped to the soft weight of her breasts as they fell forward. The clouds raced across the blue-black night, leaving the moon unclothed, like the woman, filling the hollow in which they lay with a milky white radiance, coating her body in a silvery pearl which was quite breathtaking. He reached out, mesmerised, laying his hands on her throat, sliding them down to cup her breasts, leaning to take first one into his mouth and then the other until she purred like a cat. Her back arched, her legs fell open and he took her again, covering her mouth with his, gagging her cries as she called out his name to the lustrous moon.

The dawn was breaking, a sliver of apricot showing above the line of Bleaklow Hill when he slipped, shivering a little, into the warm space beside his wife. She murmured in her sleep, uttering what seemed to be a gurgling laugh, then turned to him, throwing an arm across his familiar chest. Her breath was sweet and soft and so was her cheek as she pressed it against his shoulder and his heart was filled to bursting point with his love for her. He lifted his arm, drawing her gently against him and with a little sigh she settled. He held her, this precious woman, this vulnerable precious woman and he felt the pain tear at him, split him, rip him apart, for could a man love two women at once? He had not meant to make love to Katy, nor to dishonour her, if that was the word, for she was a woman worthy of any man's love. A woman not to be taken lightly to satisfy a man's appetite and it was not like that. They had come together like two stars on a converging course, bound to collide, not planning what they had done but bewitched by it just the same. For that, he supposed, they could be forgiven since they had not intentionally set out to hurt Chloe.

But if he went again! If he slipped from his bed on another night when his restless, dissatisfied body took him from his wife's side. If, knowing she was up there waiting for him, he sought out Katy Andrews, then he, and Katy, would do his wife a wrong which could never be pardoned. By Chloe, or by himself.

For three weeks he made love to his wife with an urgency, a frequency which alarmed her. She did not question it, or his almost feverish need to have her constantly near him, coming down the hill to the farmhouse at any time of the day on any pretext, putting his arms about her, clinging to her, kissing her even in front of Adah-May who was horribly embarrassed by it all. Chloe did not know what it was that troubled him unless it was a desperate need to get her pregnant again and though she herself shrank from it since she did not think she could bear the pain of loss again, should it happen, she submitted to it as lovingly and as willingly as she could.

"Is our Jamie all right?" his mother asked diffidently on the day she came over to Valley Bottom Farm to help Chloe preserve the plums which had multipled on the tree growing on the sunny side of the farmhouse. Its branches hung low with rich, ripe fruit which Adah-May had picked and washed and in the dairy the clean stone jars stood waiting. Water was boiling in the kitchen range and rounds of paper over which they would pour melted mutton suet were cut in readiness for sealing the jars. The plums would make a welcome change throughout the winter when fresh fruit was impossible to come by. They had already preserved pears and apricots, bought cheaply in the market at Crossclough and Chloe's preserve cupboard stood neat and almost full, waiting for this last batch.

"Yes, why do you ask?" Chloe blushed deeply, her breath catching in her throat, for how could she reveal to her husband's mother Jamie's passionate need of her these last few weeks? How could any woman say to another that her husband's attentions, dearly as she loved him, were . . . well, not becoming tiresome, for that smacked of some rift in their marriage, but were performed in the manner of an automaton. It was as though he were using his skills as a lover to coax her to act in a certain way which apparently was lacking. There was an almost desperate appeal in him which demanded something of her she could not, as yet, give him. She needed time. How much? a voice inside her asked, for it was August now and her miscarriage had taken place last October.

Only think, that voice which whispered in her head, whispered now. If she had lived, that sweet, small girl, she would have been ten months . . . No, no, *no*, she would not let it in, that thought. She would welcome Jamie's body into hers and soon she would have another child, a little girl like the tightly furled bud who had not been allowed to flower, who had never breathed, or smiled, or clasped her hand as young Jack Andrews did.

He loved her that night and she took him into her with love, closing her eyes as his body pounded out some message hers could not understand.

She woke in the night and he was not there, probably gone to the privy at the far end of the yard. She sighed a little as she turned her face to the open window. He would return soon, she told herself and she would make love to him as once she had done, but when he came she had fallen asleep again.

27

Even above the din of the beating room you could hear them arguing. The huge, oval tubs in which all the ingredients for the making of paper were mixed, the revolving horizontal roll set with knives so that it resembled a paddle wheel; the constant clack of wheels and pulleys, straps and wires, all made a stridency which assaulted the brain and deafened the ears, but the men were used to it, cheerfully shouting to one another above the tumult, and they had also become used to the constant bickering which went on between the new maister and her brother.

They were standing face to face, almost nose to nose beside the pile of bulging sacks containing china clay, two of which were open, spilling their pure white contents on to the stone-flagged floor. It was as though a light flurry of fine snow had fallen, powdering the area about the sacks, clinging to Chris Andrews's highly polished black boots and to the expensive, well-fitting, dark grey trousers he wore. It drifted as some vagrant draught caught it, floating to settle on the fine cut of his matching grey frock-coat and pale lemon waistcoat and the men about the vats nudged one another, grinning as the young dandy fastidiously brushed the china clay from his sleeve.

The men could not hear the actual words of the exchange above the clatter of the machines but at one point they were convinced that young Master Andrews was about to strike his sister and they all held their breath in delighted fascination. They looked very much alike in their fury, the red-hot flush of temper beneath their fine, creamy, pale skins, their eyes, though of a different colour, narrowed and dangerous, like two cats who have met in an alley. They almost appeared to be arching their backs and spitting, as alley cats do, their hands turned into claws, ready to do one another a mischief and, as Ned Coleman said to Bert Garvey, he almost fell into his bloody vat he was so intent on watching the pair of them squaring up to one another. The new owner stamped her foot and a little puff of china clay rose to eddy about the already liberally coated hem of her plain, coffee-coloured skirt.

Lately, as though to parallel her new position as mill owner, Miss Andrews had taken to driving to the mill in her father's carriage. She often took papers, files, ledgers home with her to study in the evening and it was awkward carrying them on her mare. Consequently she was dressed in the fashion of a young lady of position, smart and up to the minute in her sheath-like skirt, discarding the small train which would have made it unsuitable for the exigencies of her working day. The skirt was short by the standards of the day, the hem two inches from the ground, revealing the fine bones of her slim ankle and her shoes, coloured to match her skirt, worn with matching stockings and laced over with a tongue. She wore a jacket bodice and under that a tight, buttoned waistcoat of a shade several shades deeper than her skirt and top. At her neck was a creamy stock, tied like a man's. She looked businesslike but still decidedly female, for the outfit clung to her full breasts, her neat waist and curving hips, and everywhere she went heads turned to look at her.

And she went everywhere. It was five months since the explosion of incredulous outrage that had rocked the community of Crossclough, rippling out from her father's paper mill, sweeping the length of the Longdendale Valley, up to the small town then on west into Lancashire and east into Yorkshire. Men who bought her father's fine writing paper and bond paper, wrapping paper and the paper on which newspapers were printed were aghast, for how were they to deal with a woman, a young and beautiful woman, they had heard, with a reputation which did not bear thinking about? Perhaps, they asked one another, it would be possible to ignore her, despite her ownership of the mill, for Mr Harrop was still manager, they had been told, and all they had to do was to state that they would much prefer to conduct their business with him.

But it was the actual inhabitants of the town itself and its outlying districts who were turned on their collective ears when the news reached them that the Waterway Paper Mill was now in the hands of the disgraced "scarlet woman" of Crossclough, a gift from her poor father who must surely be off his head. The whisper that his son had run off with the firm's funds had gone from house to house, farm to farm and cottage to cottage and they were not unduly surprised, since the lad had owed money to every wine merchant and tailor and bootmaker in Crossclough and was it not just like him to take to his heels across the Channel when they began to press him?

But still, a son was a son and though he would rather be a young squireen, riding to hounds and shooting grouse and pheasant at the right season, his father, as manufacturing fathers did with their sons, would have soon licked him into shape, surely?

The tales about Katy Andrews and her absolute determination to run the paper mill exactly to her own requirements, which were many and varied, it seemed, flowed into Crossclough like the myriad, fast-moving streams which sparkled down the cloughs to the reservoir. She had taken over her father's old office which he had furnished in the style of his study at home. It had gas lights on the wall, since the windows were small but there was an oil lamp with an independent cylindrical reservoir feeding the wick on the big, leather-topped desk, providing a good light for studying the numerous accounts, ledgers and invoices which Mr Harrop reluctantly thumped in front of her.

The walls of the office were lined with softly glowing wood. There were several pictures of stern, bewhiskered gentlemen hung on them, presumably of the previous owners, a deep and comfortable leather chair in which Mr Harrop often found her with her feet curled up beneath her, and a good fire burning in the black-leaded grate. Her father, having a fancy for the small luxuries to which he was accustomed in his own home, had arranged a glass domed clock on the mantelshelf, a couple of Dresden vases and a globe set in brass on a table beneath the window. There was a decent carpet patterned in rich shades of red and green and, on the desk, a matching pair of silver and brass cheroot and match holders with distinctive eagle claw feet. A handsome military chest, the drawers of which were stuffed with papers relating to his business, stood against the wall.

She loved it. She would enter her office at just after nine in the morning, later than Mr Harrop since she liked to organise her son's day before she left. She would smile and incline her head towards the grim-faced Mr Hardacre, telling him what a lovely day it was, what a wet day it was, what a cold day it was, though he could see it for himself, he brooded sourly, cursing the day Mr Andrews had put his good, sound business into the hands of this silly female.

She would take off her hat then move slowly round her desk, savouring it, letting her senses enjoy the anticipation of sitting down behind it, of placing her hands on the soft, dark green leather of its top, before ringing the bell to summon Mr Harrop and all the papers necessary for the day's business. He would sit opposite her, his face surly, doing his best to be polite since she was the owner. He was inclined to be patronising as he opened the company's books, or handed her the weekly reports, the audits compiled by Mr Hardacre, who knew a great deal more about paper-making than she did, the accounts and wages books.

"This letter came from Birkenshaws," he would say, letting her make of it what she would, no longer the tolerant, grateful gentleman who had been willing to indulge her whim in the weeks following Chris's disappearance with the firm's cash. He knew the letter would make no sense to her, for how was she to differentiate between "long elephants", "small hands" and "grocery papers"? But Katy was not too proud or foolish to ask, and once he had explained what their size and purpose was, she did not need telling again, he'd give her that. Her mind clung like a terrier's to the facts and figures he poured into it, a sponge which would never be saturated, a jug which would never be full, but when she made it clear she meant to speak to every man and woman in her employ since she paid their wages; that she intended scrutinising every job, every small cog that made up the machine which was the manufacture of paper; that she wanted to see it, hear it and understand it, he was mortified, insulted as her father had told her he would be. It was bad enough having her poking her nose into every damned drawer and every paper that drawer contained in the office, where at least she was out of sight, but to contemplate striding about the bleaching room, the beating room and along the path of the great white ribbon on the paper-making machine, the drying room and on to the cutting room was quite out of the question, he told her bluntly.

She took no notice, of course, since Katy Andrews meant to burrow into the mind of every man and woman who worked at the Waterway Paper Mill, including Mr Hardacre's for it was only in this way, since Mr Harrop was so reluctant to part with information, that she would learn the running of the business. And, she told herself bravely, if he refused to fit in with her, and not the other way around, then she would fire him and employ another manager.

The thought of the power she had took her breath away in much the same fashion it had done when she had her first sight of the magnificent Fourdrinier paper-making machine, various modifications of which produced different papers. It was a miracle of man's inventive mind, her father had told her and now that she had seen it she knew the reason why.

Her only problem, she told herself, since she was confident that she would soon become an accepted and familiar figure in the mill, was her brother Chris. He had swaggered home a week or two after her father had paid his debts, leaving him only the necessary cash for his journey, yelling at the front door of Cloudberry End to Janet to get someone to carry his bags in and fetch him some hot water, since he was to change and be off out within the hour.

Katy, since it was a Sunday, had been in the nursery with Jack and at the impatient sound of her brother's voice she moved along the upstairs hallway to his room.

"Aah, so Father persuaded you home then?" she enquired casually, leaning on the door frame, her arms crossed over her breasts.

"Oh, you're still in residence, are you?" he answered shortly. "And yes, it seems he did for I am here," not looking at her as he threw open his portmanteau and shook out a jacket. "Where's that bloody girl?" he went on, more to himself than her. "This jacket needs pressing before I can wear it."

"You're off again, I take it? May one ask where?"

"No, one bloody well may not, since what I do is none of your concern."

"Is that so?" the anger snapping through her. "Well, perhaps when you come home drunk at three o'clock in the morning and cannot get out of your bed the next day I shall make it my concern since I employ you."

He turned then and began to laugh. "Dear God, girl, do you honestly believe I intend to work for you in that God-forsaken place of Father's?"

"Mine, brother, and you have no say in the matter. It is my mill and I am the master there, a fact you had best get used to. You had your chance and you threw it away and so you are answerable to me."

"Oh please, let us keep this within the realms of sanity. If Father wishes to play his little games then that is up to him but as I couldn't work there, or chose not to work there when I had nobody but old Harrop to nag at me, are you such a fool as to imagine I would do it for you? Sweet Jesus, even I know more than you do about making paper and that's not saying much. Oh, I'll show my face often enough to placate Father and make sure of my allowance but as for working there, forget it. Now, if you don't mind, I've things to do before I go and meet my friends."

"Would those be the friends who helped you beat Paddy Andrews to a bloody pulp?"

He hesitated then, his face set, turning a little paler, she thought.

"What if they are?"

"And are you to make further plans to deal with him as you did before, now that he's up on his feet again and you can no longer run away with the firm's money?"

"Really, Katy, you talk a load of drivel."

"Is it? Is it drivel, or has Paddy made threats against you?"

"What could that cripple do to me, for God's sake?" His voice was contemptuous but he appeared uneasy.

"Nothing, if you keep out of his way but he's a devil when he's crossed, Chris."

"Well, you should know, my pet, since there's no one more intimate with him than you."

"You're a bastard, Chris Andrews," she said, smiling pleasantly, "but you are a bastard who is now working for me and unless I get my money's worth I shall fire you and we'll see if Father feels like paying you your allowance then."

He turned up on most days and on others simply vanished, slipping off, she supposed, with his friends on a bit of shooting, and once, when the hunting season began, vanishing for a whole week. He was often pale and tense and she knew he was suffering from the effects of a night's drinking but she turned a blind eye, unconcerned with his absences since it meant an avoidance of the inevitable arguments and she had enough of those with Mr Harrop.

The business flourished, still run by Mr Harrop while Katy moved quietly about, picking every man's brains who would speak to her, which was most of them for they could hardly turn their back on the one who paid their wages. They let her see, many of them, that they thought she should be at home with her child and her sewing. They had no need of her, for it had all gone smoothly under Mr Harrop's guidance.

They were not to know that though the mill did not need her, she needed the mill.

Mr Harrop blocked her way at every turn. There was this foolish idea of hers that they should begin to import timber and adapt their machines to the making of wood pulp, and he was against it, for what was wrong with esparto grass, or even rags and cotton waste for that matter?

"It's out of date or will be soon, that's why, and it is costly to process, owing to the large quantities of chemicals that are needed for treatment purposes," she answered tartly.

If he was surprised at the amount of knowledge she had stored in her brain in five short months he did not show it.

"And the grass has to be brought all the way from Tunisia so why not fetch timber instead?" she continued. "Now I want you to go to Liverpool and find out what is being brought in."

"Liverpool! You mean I am to stroll about the docks and buttonhole every docker I meet as to the where-abouts of— "

"Of course not. There will be timber merchants, importers, and you have only to find out who they are. Believe me, if I could go myself, I would."

"Aah, so you admit it is no place for a woman?"

"I admit to nothing, Mr Harrop and I will do it if I have to. It seems to me that if we can find out who is importing timber, or more importantly turning it into wood pulp, or even if the wood pulp is being introduced directly into the country, then we should be halfway towards our goal."

"It is too soon," Mr Harrop said stubbornly.

"It is over thirty years since that chap in Germany, I forget his name, patented a method of preparing pulp from wood, Mr Harrop. He ground it by mechanical means, I believe, and six years later paper was made from ground wood on a commercial scale. Thirty years, Mr Harrop, and you are telling me it is too soon."

Again, if he was surprised by her grasp of the paper-making industry, he did not let her see it, his irritation at being told his business by this damned headstrong girl almost too much for him.

"Miss Andrews, I cannot— "

But her enthusiasm for this new method of manufacturing paper, which as yet was in its infancy, fired her on and she would not let him continue.

"And what about those two fellows in America? In 1854 they patented a method of making pulp from wood by treatment with caustic soda and there are other treatments."

"I have heard of them, Miss Andrews, but— "

"Chemical treatments in use right now for producing good-quality cellulose from wood. The sulphite process, it is called. Oh yes, I have read about it quite extensively. My father was interested, you see, being a forward-looking man," implying that Mr Harrop was not, "and his papers on the subject are in those drawers. We cannot be left behind, Mr Harrop. Think of the vast resources of timber in the world."

"Aye, and the difficulties which still exist in turning it into pulp."

"Oh please, Mr Harrop, don't be such a fuddy-duddy. We must keep up with the times."

She did not mean to be rude but Mr Harrop took instant offence. A slip of a girl in the business no more than five minutes telling him, who had worked in it all his life, what he should be doing! It was intolerable.

His head snapped sharply and his face became a bright, beetroot red, his expression one which his wife and children would have recognised at once. His hand went to his collar as though it were choking him and he stood up with a movement which would have had his family cowering in their chairs.

It did not frighten Katy Andrews who in the past months had begun to grow in confidence, in her control of herself, in her knowledge of her own clever mind, which was as sharp, as quick, quicker, than this man's and many of the men with whom they did business. All she required was experience. She had the rest.

She needed him though. She needed him until those very men had become accustomed to the brutal fact that she was the master here, the decision-maker and that business was to be done with her.

"I'm sorry, Mr Harrop," she told him gently. "That was unpardonably rude of me."

Mr Harrop sat down abruptly since this was his office they were in and slowly his dangerous colour died away. He was not at all sure what to make of this lovely, self-possessed young woman who had risen, phoenix-like, from the ashes of the wild hoyden who had once been Jack Andrews's daughter. Still was, of course, but something, presumably her fascination with her father's mill, *her* mill, damn it, had altered her, but surely it could not only be that?

She rose to her feet and smiled, murmuring that she would speak to him later. He watched her swaying back as she moved towards his office door then let out his breath on an explosive sigh which he was not sure was relief, anger, or a male's admiration for a beautiful woman.

The men in the beating room watched her come from Mr Harrop's office, eyeing her splendid figure as she strode between the enormous vats, wondering, like the man whose office she had just left, what it was that was different about her lately. It couldn't be all down to the satisfaction she seemed to find in her new career as millmaster, surely, for what was there about it to put that sheen of glowing burned honey and polished amber in her skin, of rosy, bursting vitality in her long-striding, straight-backed figure? Her hips and buttocks in her tight, sheath-like skirt rolled boisterously and her breasts moved enticingly as though they were unfettered beneath her jacket. Her hair seemed to be lit with fire and her eyes, narrowed and slumbrous, were deep with some apparently golden secret she was keeping to herself.

She smiled a lot and was often heard to laugh outright, usually when she was in the room where the women sorted the rags and flax and hemp, the linen and cotton waste which Mr Harrop was determined to continue using and which came every day in great waggon-loads from the cotton towns of Lancashire. She seemed to find some affinity with the women and, against Mr Harrop's wishes, since it could only cut their profit, he snapped at her, had devised ways to make their days easier. She employed one of them, an older "sorter" who was "none too clever on her pins" though the woman would have admitted it to no one, for jobs were hard to come by, particularly at her age. A small room was furnished where the women, on a rota basis, might stop work for ten minutes morning and afternoon and drink a cup of the decent tea the woman provided.

The men had been astounded, and affronted, but when she had offered them the same service they had refused her as she had known they would. What did they want with a bloody cup of tea and a gossip, they muttered, but at least it had been offered. Her wages were good, that's all that mattered and, as many of the women in the rag sorting room were their own wives, they were mollified.

Aye, the talk of the valley was Katy Andrews with her new ideas, which soon got round as these things do, and her liberal fancies for the comfort of her female workers, who were mothers, many of them, but, unlike her who had servants to wait on her hand and foot at the end of the day, went home to scrubbing and washing and ironing and the care of perhaps half a dozen young children.

She was happy. She had never been so happy, so gloriously alive and glowing with an inner fulfilment which had begun two months ago on Round Hill when Jamie had come to her one silvered moonlit night. She had ridden up there each night after that, leaning her patient back against one of the outcropping rocks which grew out of the rough turf and which had sheltered them on that first night, waiting, her face quite expressionless, her eyes unblinking as they tried to part the veil of darkness which hid him, the darkness which would, she knew without doubt, bring him back to her. There had been something more between them than mere physical need, her body knew that at once. It was wrong, completely wrong, with no good in it for anyone, no justification for what they had done. She was aware that no matter how much she loved him he could, in the end, only do her harm. And Chloe. She should not be here, waiting in the secret hollow on the top of the hill. It was madness but she was possessed by her own need and capacity to love only this one man and she would wait here until he came.

It was three weeks before he did, tearing at her clothing with no tender gestures, no gentleness and she did not require it. There was an urgency in them that nailed their naked bodies together, an urgent need to possess and be possessed, her body wanting his, wanting to be crushed and hurt as he claimed her. Gasping and clutching and biting and then a fierce penetration that split her asunder, invaded her, enraptured her, terrified and thrilled her at the same time, leaving her docile and bemused. His!

Two months, and in that time he had come to her four times and on the fourth time his voice had called out her name as he came shudderingly to the climax of his endeavour.

"Katy . . . aah, Katy, I love you, girl."

It was enough. It was everything, and only on the days when she came face to face with her cousin Chloe, which was several times a week, did her heart die a little. This was adultery, which seemed a silly word, for what she was doing to Chloe was nothing short of murder but how could she stop? Only the night before she had cradled Jamie's dark head against her breast, holding it there with strong, possessive arms, kissing his tumbled hair with a fierceness which was ready to fight and kick and scream to protect what was hers, which was little enough. And when she smiled at Chloe who had come to ask if she might take Katy's son down to the station to see the trains, with Thomas driving the gig, naturally, since Chloe would have her hands full with the active little boy, how could she refuse? Jack was fifteen months old now, a tumble-legged, darting, inquisitive handful who must be watched over every minute of the day, for his fertile mind encouraged him to investigate everything in this fascinating world, from the taste of soil to the lethal clippers Angus used on the hedges. Chloe adored him and though sometimes Katy felt a small, guilty dart of jealousy when she saw the way her son ran into Chloe's arms she put it from her in the knowledge that what Chloe took from her, she took a hundredfold from Chloe.

"Of course you may," she had answered, turning a false smile into a genuine one, since she felt a great deal of affection for her cousin. "It will give me a chance for a good gallop up on Spond Moor."

She sighed, then shook her head as Chloe looked at her questioningly. She had been wondering what she and Jamie would do when the dark cold of winter came to the peaks, which would not be long now but she could not allow her thoughts to be voiced to Jamie's wife. Already it was bitter when they lay naked together under the warm lined cloaks they took up with them and soon their meetings would be impossible. She had not spoken to Jamie about it for it was too new, too fragile, too precious, this loveliness between them and she hardly dared to press him on how it was to continue during the winter months.

"Oh, it's the approach of winter that makes me despondent, cousin, nothing more. At this time of year, for an hour, I can ride out when Jack is in bed but it will soon be possible on Sunday only and I'm keen to get Jack started on his first pony."

"Oh, darling, not yet. He is so small."

"I began at eighteen months or so, cousin," doing her best not to be irritated by Chloe's protective attitude towards the boy who was Katy's son after all.

It was a glorious autumn day when Storm picked her way delicately up the rocky track leading towards Luds Leap and the great sweep of wildly rolling moorland beyond. There was a wind blowing, beginning to have an edge to it and the leaves beneath the trees she had passed through were thick and crisp, richly golden and tawny on the ground. There were fir cones and pine cones and windblown branches to be jumped, but when she reached the top of the track Katy reined in the mare to look down to the neat pattern of green and brown fields in the valley. She could see men, tiny and slow-moving, working on the harvested corn and one of them, she knew, was Jamie.

She sat for a long moment, her leg in its tight breeches bent across the pommel, her elbow on her knee, then with a click of her tongue and a nudge with her heels she moved Storm on, into a trot, a canter, a gallop, on and on into the teeth of the wind across the tufted upland grass of Spond Moor.

There was a clump of gorse, waist high and thick, ahead of her. She slowed down, to a canter, a trot, then a walk and when Paddy Andrews rose up from behind it, grinning broadly, she allowed him to catch the mare's bridle in her heart-stopping terror.

28

Storm reared and bucked, rolling her eyes and flaring her nostrils. Her ears flattened in terror and she whickered shrilly in the back of her throat. Katy did her best to control her, to drag her out of Paddy's strong hands, to hang on herself but Paddy kept on laughing and hauling on the reins and, as the mare's fear grew and she plunged more and more frantically Katy felt the strength go from her hands, and from her thighs which did their best to grip the mare and with a despairing cry she fell from Storm's back.

At once Paddy let the animal go, laughing exultantly with no need of the shooing gestures he aimed at her with his hands as she raced off in the direction of Rakes Moss.

Katy had landed on her back, sprawling awkwardly with her legs flung apart, completely winded, white-faced and blinded by her hair which had torn loose. She was dazed. The sky at the back of Paddy's head was whirling round and round and she thought she might be sick, but Paddy's mocking face and air of triumph, which seemed to be telling her that he had always known he would win, stiffened her spine and brought her to a sitting position where she remained for a moment. She thought it might be a good idea not to be too eager to get to her feet just yet, since there was every possibility she might fall down, or be knocked down again by the man who grinned at her derisively, so she sat quite still, her arms round her bent knees, doing, she realised, what an animal which is cornered will do, which was to remain as quiet as possible.

"Well, well, well, will yer look what's fallen inter Paddy's little trap?" he said softly. "I bin watchin' thi' fer weeks now, girl, just waiting fer thi' ter ride my way. They do say as 'ow if tha're patient enough tha'll get what tha' wants in't th'end, an' by God, it's true. I've thought o' nowt else ever since last January when I medd up me mind ter walk again, did tha' know that, lass? I've dreamed o' this moment, times, an' now it's 'ere an' I mean ter enjoy every bloody minute. I don't rightly know what I mean ter do wi' thi', after I've 'ad me cock in thee, that is. I'll 'ave ter decide then, won't I, but in't meanwhile we'll 'ave them britches off thi' sharpish. Let's see if thee an' me're as good as we were together afore our Jack were born, shall we?"

She felt able to get to her feet now. She was in terrible danger here, certainly of rape, possibly of murder, for Paddy would never forgive her for her desertion of him and her abduction of his son. He was strong again, and mobile, it seemed, for it was miles from Woodhead and he could only have walked up here. All she had was her cunning mind, her wit which was sharper, clearer than his, and her two good legs. Storm had vanished, not, she prayed, into Rakes Moss, please God, which was nothing but a quaking, spongy bog which would swallow her in a moment, but gone just the same and it was up to Katy Andrews to get herself out of this perilous situation.

With one part of her mind she could hear the calling of sheep from higher up the moor and across the sky at Paddy's back lapwings floated like large snowflakes and peewits wheeled and tumbled. Why, she wondered, again with that layer of her brain which seemed another part of her, is our attention captured by small, inconsequential things when all we should be considering is the danger in which we are trapped? The spicy aroma of the dying gorse bushes in which Paddy had hidden was sharp and pleasant in her nostrils and yet she was convinced she could smell her own desperate fear. She was not going to let Paddy Andrews see it though. She dusted her hands on the seat of her breeches and attempted a careless smile. Paddy was no more than three feet away from her, his eyes narrowed and gleaming, alert, balanced as he used to be balanced when he fought in the ring, ready to dart in any direction which was to his advantage, his hands formed into loose fists.

"You look well, Paddy," she told him, her tone conversational as though they were two acquaintances who had bumped into one another on the pavement in Crossclough. But for the short peg of wood which emerged from the bottom of his left trouser leg he was exactly as she remembered him two years ago. It was quite incredible that this lithe and handsome man had been hidden for so long in the bloated tub of lard which had sprawled in a wheelchair drinking himself to death in the cottage at Woodhead. He was bronzed, his skin firm and freshly shaved. His hair was a tumble of dark, glossy curls over his eyebrows and his eyes were a deep, untroubled copper brown, the whites clear and healthy.

He grinned amiably, pleased with what he thought was her admiration, his teeth which had started to rot the only part of him he had been unable to restore, those and his leg, of course. She marvelled as her eyes ran over him how he had managed to bring himself back to this.

As though he read her thoughts he squared his shoulders and arrogantly threw out his chest. He preened, almost like a girl in her first ballgown, prepared to let her get a good look at him before he threw her down and did what he had come to do. He'll flex his muscles next, she thought, ready to be hysterical, fighting her need to laugh in his face, longing to make a dash for it but knowing his reflexes were – had been – like lightning. His hand would shoot out, grasping her wrist before she had barely moved and she must keep these three feet between them for as long as she could.

She was helped by his own need to play cat and mouse with her and that was all to the good for she wanted to lull his senses, keep him talking, playing for time until the right moment came.

"I know 'ow ter train fer a fight, Coppertop," he said, "an' though it were bloody 'ard, once I medd me mind up to it I wouldn't be beaten. Just like I wouldn't be beaten in't ring. I cut out the drink an' set messen on a diet what an old trainer once told me about. Them fancy pugilists up in London an' such don't keep fit on batter puddin's an' suet dumplin's. Meat an' veg, and stuff what don't fill thi' but don't put no weight on neither. An' I exercised. Jesus, it were 'ard at first."

A thoughtful look of remembered pain crossed his face and had it not been for the purpose of his endeavours she had it in her to admire him. A strong will and a strong constitution Paddy Andrews had which, in nine months, had changed him from a grossly overweight cripple in a wheelchair into this well-muscled, well-proportioned and handsome man who looked like a gypsy with his brown skin and eyes, his dark hair and audacious grin.

"Oh aye, I got messen back ter condition, Coppertop. Me an' me alone, fer them cousins o' mine don't like movin' their fat arses unless it's ter't Queen's Head in Crossclough. I walk fer miles an' I swim in't reservoir an' it were all fer one thing an' I reckon tha' knows what that is. I medd a mistake wi' that soft prick of a brother o' thine. I left it ter Josh an' Jake the first time. Chuck 'im in Deep End Clough, I ses, but they'd no stomach fer it, them two, so what they do?" He went on contemptuously, "They only bloody leave 'im at bottom, thinkin' he'd turn up 'is toes quite nicely wi' no blood on their 'ands. Second time it were my fault an' I should've known better. Me what's trapped rabbits ever since I were a nipper. I were on't track up by Saltersbrook when he come ridin' by on that there grey of 'is an' instead o' lyin' low I tried ter catch 'im. Course, I couldn't . . ." His face twisted at the bitter memory. "An' he were warned then, weren't he? Took off like some frightened lass ter France or somewhere, they said, but he's back now an' I'll 'ave 'im one day, tell 'im. He'll turn 'is back fer a minute when he's on't road ter them grand friends of 'is, an' I'll 'ave 'im."

"Paddy, surely now that you are yourself again, could you not leave it all behind?" She was talking nonsense, she knew it. Talking for talking's sake and she was not surprised when he began to laugh.

"Yer what? Leave it all be'ind? Like I left me bloody leg, yer mean? Coppertop, I might look all right ter thee, aye, an' to other women an' all, 'cause I can tekk me pick again now, but I'm not. Not in 'ere."

He thumped his teeth with what seemed like despair and his teeth bared in a snarl.

"I can't fight no more, tha' see. I'm twenty-two years old an' I can do nowt what I used ter. Oh, I can tekk a woman an' I'll show thi' 'ow in a minnit, an' father another brat but I can't do what were in me blood. I were good, a bloody good fighter an' I'd 'ave gone far. 'Ad a go at championship, but that's all finished. So, I've ter find summat else ter fill me days an' I've a fancy to 'ave thi' an't lad wi' me again, Coppertop. Thee an' me were good together so 'ow about it?"

She did her best not to let her revulsion show, arranging her face into what she hoped was a pleasant smile.

"Look, Paddy, if I were to give you some money, enough to set you up in a business, perhaps in America where your brothers are, would you not consider it? You could make a decent life, marry, have children."

It was a mistake to mention children. His face darkened and became suffused with red rage.

"That's another bloody thing, an' all. I seen that woman, that cousin o' thine an' if tha' want ter work at that bloody mill, well, suit thissen, but I mean to 'ave my lad wi' me."

"Over my dead body," she hissed. She lifted her lips in a snarl of pure female rage, the rage of a mother in defence of her young, ready to leap for him, for his eyes, for any part of him which might hurt, preferably in his trousers, for any part of him which might disarm him for a minute, but some instinct, some primeval instinct inherited from the women who had gone before, surfaced to her inflamed mind, calming it, telling her to keep away from him for it was only thus could she escape him.

"That could be arranged, Coppertop," he said softly, dropping into the stance she had seen him take up in the prize fighting ring. It was the moment. He had had enough of talking, of boasting, of showing off to her the marvel of his recovery and was ready for action.

Katy glared at him, but he began to grin even more broadly as anticipation flooded his body and swelled the crotch of his trousers into a bulge of enormous proportions.

She tried not to let him see which way she was going to move, feinting a little, first one way then the other but he was too quick for her, too experienced. His hard, calloused hand shot out and gripped her wrist, a vice-like grip which no power on earth could loosen. He dragged her to him, his other arm going about her waist and his mouth fastened on hers before she had time to turn her head away. His teeth sank into her bottom lip and she tasted blood, then, letting her mouth go for a second, he slapped her hard across the face, ordering her in an icy voice to be still. Her cheek burned and her eyes watered. She could feel the blood trickle down her chin and terror trickle through her veins. He would not just rape her, she knew that. She had scorned him, hurt him in a way a man such as he could not cope with and it would be so easy to throw her body, when he had finished with it, naturally, into some quaking morass where it would vanish for ever. Storm might get home. They would search for her but would not be surprised when they could not find her, for more than one careless wayfarer had vanished in these bog-ridden uplands.

His free hand fastened in the front of her shirt and with a grunt of pleasure he tore it open, freeing her breasts which swelled into his cruel hand.

"By Christ, tha're better than ever, Coppertop," he muttered hoarsely. "That's right, lass, struggle. I like it when tha' struggle, and now them britches."

His hand left her breasts and he hooked his thumb in the waistband of her tight breeches, forcing them down over her hips and buttocks. His fingers dug into her thighs, doing his best to wrench them apart, then fumbled between her bared legs.

"That's it . . . that's it," he kept saying as they swayed together in a ridiculous dance of lust, but he had made the mistake of not laying her down before removing her breeches, of being too sure of himself on his wooden leg, and before he could steady himself again she forced her own strong leg between his, twisting it out and round his peg, wrenching it from under him and pushing him violently at the same time.

Caught off balance he did what she had prayed he would do. It is instinct to put out a hand when you overbalance and are about to fall and Paddy did just that. He put out both hands, for a man with one leg does not have the same automatic manoeuvrability as a man with two. He crashed on to his back and in a second Katy had lurched away from him, her breeches still about her knees, four, six, ten feet away from him until there was enough of a gap to prevent him reaching her, pulling at her breeches, struggling to get them up again, using both hands now, for what did it matter that her breasts were still exposed.

"You bitch," he screamed, lifting every bird for miles around. "I'll kill you for this, I'll kill you."

"You'll have to catch me first, Paddy Andrews," she taunted him, her fear gone, hopping about from foot to foot, widening the distance between them until her breeches were up round her waist.

"And don't think I won't. Tha'll not be shut o' me, my girl, never. Wherever tha' go . . . up 'ere . . . I'll find thi' an' when I do I'll 'urt thi' in a way tha've not dreamed of."

He was on his feet now, staggering towards her, surprisingly nimble but she danced further away, light as a feather, free and exhilarated with it, for she knew he could never hope to reach her now. He was shaking with rage and frustration as she moved backwards, her hair a living flame about her face, her eyes glaring from beneath it.

"No, I don't think so, Paddy, for I'll have every man in the valley looking for you before nightfall when I tell them what you tried to do to me."

"Give over! Who the 'ell cares what 'appens to a piece like thee, Katy Andrews. Tha' were my woman once an tha've a bairn ter prove it."

"The police will be called."

"Oh aye, an' 'ow are they ter search the whole of the bloody moor, tell me that."

"Don't go back to the cottage, Paddy, I'm warning you. I'll have it boarded up and though, as you point out, I may be nothing in this community, my father is a respected man and has influence. You've threatened my son, his grandson and you'll not be safe in this valley if you show your face again. I'll have you hounded."

She was beginning to shake now, for though she had managed to outwit him she had been badly frightened. He had stopped moving towards her, standing quietly with a menace which was even more terrifying than his livid fury. He made no attempt to follow her as she turned in the direction of her home, watching her go. She could feel his eyes in the middle of her back, like a knife, and she wanted to keep turning round all the way down the track just to convince herself that he wasn't there, behind her, but she resisted it, holding her head high, holding her torn shirt across her breasts, though there was no one to see her except some sad-faced sheep.

She began to cry when she reached Luds Leap, the tears blinding her so that she could barely see the shifting stones of the clough which led down from it. She floundered through the tumbling water, careless of her boots, ricking her ankle, hardly noticing the pain but by the time she had reached the stable yard at Cloudberry End she was in control of herself.

"Miss Katy . . . Dear Lord, what's 'appened to yer?" Dicken was aghast, dropping the tangle of harness in his hands and running across the yard towards her. Jimmy appeared from the tack room, his pipe drooping from his slack lips and old Noah heaved himself to his feet from where he had been enjoying the last bit of warm sunshine trapped against the stable block wall.

They all three eyed the tattered remains of her shirt which was gaping immodestly despite her attempts to hold it together, then hastily averted their eyes from the inordinate amount of naked flesh that was revealed. What in the name of God had she been up to now? their combined expressions asked, for no matter how she seemed to have settled down to motherhood, to the running of the mill, which she was making a decent fist of, they'd heard, and her determined effort to be a worthwhile mistress of Cloudberry End, they could never quite believe she would not suddenly revert to the wild, uncontrollable girl they remembered only too well.

"I'm all right, really I am, Dicken, so don't fuss." She pushed her way through them, for they were inclined to crowd about her, continuing to stride towards the gate which led to the kitchen yard and the back door. Her breeches were stained. Her hair was flung about like that of a mad woman and she had what Dicken was convinced was the beginning of a corker of a black eye but she managed a smile somehow.

"Wheer's Storm, Miss Katy?" hardly liking to bother her, the state she was in but his concern, not only for her but for her handsome little mare, could not be suppressed.

"I don't know, Dicken. I . . . I came off her on Spond Moor and she . . . galloped off."

"Galloped off!" Dicken was clearly astonished for if there was one thing Storm could be relied on not to do that was to bolt like some wild, untried animal. Highly strung she might be, expensively bred but he had taught her himself to be as obedient as a well-brought-up child, to stand like a rock, and he had often said, fondly, that you could lead her on a bit of thread she was so sweet-natured. Unless she was frightened!

"What 'appened, Miss Katy?" he asked, almost accusingly. "Did she tekk fright or summat?"

"Yes, yes that was it. She took fright, threw me and raced off towards . . ."

"Aye?"

"Towards Rakes Moss."

"Jesus." The three men exchanged horrified glances, for everyone who lived in these parts knew the menace of Rakes Moss.

"She'll come home, Dicken. She won't get into the bog. She knows the moors as well as I do and she'll find her way home."

"Aye." The men sighed, relieved, for what Miss Katy said was true. Dicken had taught Miss Katy, and the mare, the ways of the bleak, inhospitable uplands and Storm would find her way home.

"I must go and tidy myself," their young mistress said vaguely, moving, now she was home and safe, in a somewhat erratic fashion towards the kitchen door. The men watched her go, then, without a word, wandered across to the gate, leaning on it side by side, shading their eyes to gaze up at the peaks where one of their "flock", one of their own, was lost.

"Shall us go an' look fer 'er?" Jimmy ventured anxiously.

"Give 'er 'alf an 'our, lad, then if she's not back thee an' me'll tekk Hal an' Jenny an' go an' fetch 'er 'ome."

The servants in the kitchen, as women do, were more inclined to shriek and drop things when their young mistress walked in on them in her wild and dishevelled state, but Mrs Kelsall, who had controlled three times as many as this lot in her day with no more than the raising of her hand, soon restored order. Like the grooms she knew something . . . well, unusual had happened to Miss Katy but the girl was in a shocked state and did not need histrionics.

"I came off my mare, Mrs Kelsall," she said, her eyes wavering in the most odd way, "but I'm not hurt at all. Now I'd be obliged if one of you," turning appealingly to the circle of sympathetic faces, "would run up to the nursery and check on my son. At once please."

"Master Jack?" Mrs Kelsall was perplexed.

"Yes, who else, and at once." Her voice rose to a pitch Mrs Kelsall thought might be hysteria but she did her best to get her young mistress to sit down and drink the nice cup of tea Lottie was fetching her. Master Jack was out in the garden with Mrs Hutchinson, she said and—

"Oh, Jesus . . . Jesus . . ." They cowered back, Lottie dropping the nice cup of tea with a crash which made Dilly squeal like a stuck pig. Even Mrs Kelsall recoiled from the shrieking, shaking, leaping dervish their mistress had turned into, their hands to their mouths in horror, their kind faces appalled and bewildered, for what could be wrong? Mrs Hutchinson regularly took young Master Jack for a walk in the grounds and on up into the woods which surrounded the house. Biddy had just gone back up to the nursery, grumbling that she had nothing to do half the time with the little lad off somewhere with Mrs Hutchinson, but expecting him back any minute for his midday meal and afternoon nap, she said.

"Miss Katy, dear God in heaven, what?"

"Run, Lottie, Janet, and you, Mabel." They were trained to obey an order instantly and they began to mill about, making little runs here and there but not knowing where they were suppose to run to, or what they were to do when they got there. "Quick, tell Mrs Hutchinson to bring him back."

"Back, Miss Katy?"

"Find him, for Christ's sake, find him. I'll go up to the wood while you look in the . . . in the garden and shrubbery. Oh, for God's sake, split up, don't all go together and look everywhere."

"Oh, my Lord, Miss Katy, lass, don't get upset. Mrs Hutchinson will be back soon. There's no need to . . ." Mrs Kelsall nearly said "go off at half cock" but it was not the kind of remark one made to one's employer, was it? Really, what was up with the lass? How had she got herself into this deranged state? Her bosom was practically on view for anyone to look at and young Chuckie's eyes were out on stalks. The sooner they got her out of the kitchen and in her own room the better. Lottie and Janet would see to her. Get her undressed and into a hot bath, perhaps even a little sip of brandy to calm her, though Jess Kelsall was aware that ladies did not normally drink spirits. Just this once wouldn't harm her, would it? she asked herself as she tried to catch the whirlwind which was her young mistress. Tearing across the kitchen she was, dragging the bewildered Janet with her, screaming at the open-mouthed Chuckie to run to the stables and get the grooms and what the hell did Mabel, who had come to a full stop in her confusion, think she was doing standing there like a bloody brick wall when she had been specifically told to run out and look for Jack.

"Katy. Katy, darling, what is it? What's the matter? Oh, dear Lord, what has happened to you? Here, Janet, hold Jack, will you? Oh, Katy, what has been done to you?"

Chloe was there in the doorway which led into the hall, advancing towards her, her face creased with concern, her arms, now that she had safely deposited a wide-eyed Jack into Janet's care, outstretched to Katy, but Katy ignored her. Her face broke up and tears seemed to come from every pore and crease of her flesh, simply flooding it as her distraught arms reached out for her son, seizing him from Janet with a force which nearly knocked the girl to the floor. The child began to wail, for this demented woman who crushed him to her, though she looked like his mama, did not seem like his mama. He struggled and all the women about the room longed to snatch him away, soothe him, pet him, tell him his mama was not well, but she held him to her, her arms wrapped tight about him, her face buried in his neck as he strained away from her.

"Katy, don't . . . he's frightened."

"Don't touch him, he's mine, all I care about."

"I know, darling, but you must not alarm him so. Give him to Janet who will take him to the nursery and you and I will go to your room and you shall tell me what happened."

"Nothing . . . nothing happened. I fell off my mare . . ." for somehow, she didn't know why, she could not bring herself to mention Paddy Andrews's name in front of all these gawping maidservants. She felt dirty . . . perhaps when she had had a bath . . .

As though she had caught her thoughts Chloe said, "Then you need a bath, a change of clothing."

"Oh, Chloe . . . Chloe."

"I know, sweetheart, I know." Chloe sensed the utter terror in her cousin and though she had no idea what had caused it she was prepared to let Katy tell her when she was ready. "You are tired and hurt but you are safe now and so is Jack."

Safe from what? the expressions on the faces of the astonished servants had time to register as their mistress became calmer.

"I'm sorry . . . oh, I'm sorry, baby." She let the fear, the pain, the rigid tension slip completely away from her, turning the child in her arms, kissing him gently, smiling, smoothing his hair from his face, kissing him again until he recognised his real mama. "There, that's better. Silly Mama, getting so upset. I must have bumped my head when I fell from my horse. Silly Mama fell from Storm's back, darling . . . silly Mama."

They all began to smile and sag with relief, still not knowing what the fuss had all been about, but recognising that there had been some dreadful demon inside their young mistress. A demon which had terrified her, and them and her son but it was gone now, whatever it was. Mrs Hutchinson would see to her in that tranquil way she had. Biddy would tend to the boy and Mrs Hutchinson, who was the sweetest, most tender-hearted woman any of them had ever known, bless her, would see to Miss Katy. She would bring peace and serenity to this house which was often so sadly short of it.

29

It was one of the hardest winters anyone could remember in the Longdendale Valley. Snow began to fall just after Christmas, a violent maelstrom of air sweeping across the dark uplands and peaks, throwing up great drifts of banked snow against walls and gates and the sides of unprotected cottages and farmhouses, gathering and growing until it reached the eaves of some roofs and at its lowest was no less than four feet.

"It'll not be the last," Mabel, who had been born in a cottage up Barmings way, retorted darkly. "It'll get worse afore it gets better."

"Don't talk daft, girl," Mrs Kelsall said firmly. Mrs Kelsall had lived on the Lancashire side of the Pennines most of her life, the west Lancashire side where the air was somewhat gentler and had not yet been privy to a blizzard such as the one which blew vigorously down the backbone of England, from the Lake District to the Derbyshire Peaks. She had seen snow, naturally, but nothing like the stuff which, overnight, isolated not only Cloudberry End from Crossclough where Mrs Kelsall ordered all her provisions, but her kitchen from the stable block which was no more than a hundred yards away. When she opened her kitchen door she was vastly put out to find a wall, waist high, barring her progress, stretching in a featureless white expanse as far as her eye could see, which was to the gate which led into the stable yard. Young Chuckie, though, had thought it was marvellous, offering to make her a path through the yard to the stables.

"Lad, what do I want to get to the stables for, tell me that, and if they want to get here," which of course they did since her kitchen was where the food was, "they must dig their own path. Now, get on with them potatoes, if you please, for the mistress'll want dinner on the table just the same, snow or no snow."

Of course Miss Katy, like them all, was snowbound for several days, unable to get down the driveway, let alone struggle along the bottom road to the mill. It snowed again, and then again, blinding snow which obliterated the peaks in a white, ferociously moving curtain and everyone who was forced to go out in it came back with the stuff frozen on to their clothes and eyelashes, floundering about like blank-faced snowmen at the kitchen door, needing the giggling help of the maidservants and the implements with which they beat the carpets to remove it.

Katy fretted about the house, wondering out loud how she was to get that order to Birkenshaws by the weekend as she had promised and what shape her waggon horses were in, for if she could not get down to the mill, could Harry Ellison whose job it was to stable and feed them?

And where in hell's name had her brother got to since before Christmas? Not a word, not a message, but then had she expected anything else? she asked herself. As he had said he would, he showed his face at the mill enough times to support his claim that he worked there and for the rest she supposed he went about with Johnny Ashwell and Tim Warren, doing with them what young gentlemen of their class did. Presumably he had spent Christmas at Ashwell Hall, riding to hounds on Boxing Day, shooting and gambling and raising hell and would drift back when the snow had melted.

Nothing had been seen or heard of Paddy Andrews since the day he had caught her up on Spond Moor last October. He had simply vanished, taking his dog with him, and though the constable in Crossclough had assured Miss Andrews and her cousin Mrs Hutchinson when they made the complaint, respectfully, of course, since they were related to one of the most powerful men in the community, that he would certainly keep a look out for him, would even pass it on to other divisions of the police force since a man with one leg would not be hard to spot, there was not a lot more he could do. The man had not hurt her, had he? the constable had asked delicately, believing in his own private thoughts that a woman such as this one could not be hurt. Yes, a threat was a serious thing and if she had a witness . . . yes, he knew it had happened up on the moor but . . . well. Of course, he agreed it would be a good idea to board up her grandmother's cottage in Woodhead and he'd certainly keep an eye on it and she must be sure to let him know at once if her cousin, Paddy Andrews, her attacker, was sighted anywhere near her home.

Storm had returned later that day, whinnying her delight to be safe home, petted and cossetted and treated like a lost child who has returned by the three grooms and by Katy herself, who by then was calm, bathed, brushed and had been cossetted herself.

She had not seen Jamie alone for weeks. Once they had managed an hour in a crumbling sheepfold up through Pasture Wood by Rollick Stones but it had not been satisfactory since the cold had penetrated the very bones of them and all they could do was huddle together and try to keep warm. Without the feverish passion of their lovemaking to take away their senses, they had both been aware that their guilt at what they did to Chloe was ready to overwhelm them and it would not take much to persuade Jamie that the enormity of the crime they committed against her cousin, his wife, could not be continued.

"I love her, you know," he told Katy abruptly, not wanting to hurt her in any way but compelled to ensure that she knew the truth.

"Yes, I know, my love, I know," her own voice heavy with sadness, for he was telling her that there would never be anything but this for them. That Chloe was his wife, the woman he had chosen and that he would never abandon her. Katy knew it but it made no difference to her need for him. She was famished, thirsty, in pain without him, her heart beating, or so it seemed, more sluggishly in the hours which did not contain him. His image was the first one she saw each morning and her last thought was of him at night before she slept. To get through the winter was all she could think about and then, with the long days, the mellow nights ahead of them when spring came, they would recapture the enchantment of those first weeks on Round Hill. Perhaps, in the meanwhile, they could find somewhere. If she could manage it, holding the thought of it tenderly like some precious child, they might use some sheltered, private corner of the mill in which to have an hour or two alone. It would at least be out of the bitter winter weather and, after all, she had the keys.

Not yet, though, since she was not certain Jamie would agree to it. He was still in the first, guilt-ridden torment of longing for her, bewitched by her body and what it did to his but was not yet ready to speak of the future, of future meetings and where they might be and she was afraid to seem too eager for fear he would recoil from it. The meeting on the moor had been spontaneous, unplanned, but to slip down to the mill, unlock doors furtively, smacked somehow of deceit, intrigue, degrading, and though she was prepared to do anything to keep him, did he feel the same way? She was not sure she wanted to put it to the test.

The snow lasted for a week and in the first few days of January began to melt in the sudden milder weather. Clouds were thin, streaking the pale blue sky and the hurrying tumble of water could be heard once more. The sun shone and the far carrying, musical whistle of the teal fluted across the valley. It would come again, the snow. Again and probably again before spring arrived but it was grand to be able to step outside your own kitchen door again, Mrs Kelsall told Chuckie as she set him to sweeping the yard and the last remnants of the slush which hung about at the base of the walls.

"That there Biddy's got an awful cold, Mrs Kelsall," Janet was heard to say, indiscreetly Mrs Kelsall was inclined to think, for Miss Katy and Mrs Hutchinson were in the hall and heard the housemaid say it as she closed the green baize door which seperated it from the kitchen.

"That's got nothing to do with you, Janet," Mrs Kelsall said sharply, but of course the pair of them were up the stairs like two birds in flight but with only one nestling between them. Mrs Kelsall often wondered which of them loved that little chap the most and was often surprised at the way Miss Katy let Mrs Hutchinson remove the boy, whisking him away to play in the garden as though he were her own. You'd think Mrs Hutchinson, who was, after all, a farmer's wife, would have enough to do about her own kitchen and dairy, wouldn't you? She had that girl to help her but even so all the farmers' wives Mrs Kelsall had known had been at it from cockcrow to sunset. Her husband spoiled her, and so did that mother-in-law of hers, but as she'd said before and would say again, it was nobody's business but theirs. Still the little mite should be with his nursemaid, or his mama, in her opinion, though you couldn't fault Mrs Hutchinson in the way she cared for him, but a child needed stability, a bit of discipline which he didn't get in this household of women. Miss Katy kept saying she was going to put Master Jack up on his first pony since he was eighteen months old now but she'd not done so yet.

Biddy sniffled and snuffled her way up to her room on the top floor, protesting volubly since it was only a head cold and Master Jack was a strong, healthy little chap who never ailed a day. Nevertheless she promised to stay in bed if Mrs Hutchinson insisted, wondering, like Mrs Kelsall, why Miss Katy allowed her cousin such free rein in what was, after all, Miss Katy's house and with Miss Katy's son. Still, they were cousins, so perhaps that was why, watching from her dormer window as her mistress and her mistress's cousin, with Master Jack on her lap, set off down the drive in the little gig with Miss Katy at the reins.

The man watched as the two women drove up the track, keeping in the shadows, his hand on the dog's head to ensure he would not make a noise. He had seen the brothers set off an hour ago, their own young dog at their heels, both of them carrying a shepherd's crook, both of them warmly wrapped up as though they meant to go above the snow line which still lay at a thousand feet, about halfway up the Black Hill. They would be searching for sheep that might have wandered off the safer pastures and would not be back for hours.

The girl, big lump of a thing an' all, was tied up securely in the dairy with one of her own dishclouts stuffed in her mouth and would cause no trouble for a while. He'd be away in half an hour, anyroad.

"I'll be back before dark, Chloe," he heard Katy say. "Thomas will fetch me in the carriage. Now are you absolutely sure you can manage? You won't be able to get far without his perambulator and you know how active he is."

"Oh, go on, Katy. You know we'll be fine. I'll take him for a walk round the farm and he can come to no harm."

"I know. I've put his boots in his bag."

"Good, and then he can have his lunch and a nap, can't you, sweetheart? Now give Mama a kiss and then you and I will go and see the chickens. Oh, Lord, he's off already and he hasn't got his boots on."

There was the sound of laughter and the high, delighted

squeal of the child and the dog pricked his ears and snuffled a bit, wanting to growl a warning, but his master kept a hand across his broad muzzle, muffling the sound.

"Where's Adah-May, Chloe?" Katy called as she carefully manoeuvred the horse and gig to face in the other direction, a difficult task on the narrow track.

"She'll be in the dairy. No, darling, don't stamp in that puddle until Aunty Chloe has put your boots on. Now wave to Mama."

The child did so, then turned obediently towards the farmhouse, holding Chloe's hand with perfect trust.

"We'll have a warm drink first, I think, darling, and you shall have one of Aunty Chloe's gingerbread men. I made them especially for you, did you know that?" she was saying as she opened the door, guiding the child's feet across the threshold, smiling down at him as she closed the door behind them.

The boy saw the man first, his eyes round and dark in his rosy face and he pointed his plump finger as though to draw her attention to the visitor.

"What . . .?" That was the only word she got out, then he was upon her, shoving her fiercely to one side so that she fell heavily between the chair and the table. He was snarling a little in his haste as he picked up the startled child.

"I'll 'ave that an' all," he said, grabbing at the bag in her hand, since the conversation he had overheard in the gig had led him to believe that there were spare duds for the boy in it and he'd be needing them where he was going. He'd have to be quick, for the boat left Liverpool tomorrow.

"Right," he went on, "I'll be off wi' me son, then. Tell that bitch I've gorrim, will tha', an' that 'e'll 'ave a good 'ome wi' me."

She was stunned. Her head had hit the table as she went down. It had all happened so quickly she couldn't seem to get her bearings or drag her dazed wits about her, but the last words brought her round as though a bucket of ice-cold water had been dashed over her.

She leaped to her feet with the speed and grace of a cat, a she-cat defending her young, for mixed inextricably in Chloe Hutchinson's mind was the confusing belief that Jack was *her* child and not Katy's. Not all the time, of course, but when he was with her, when she had him all to herself she had begun to pretend that he was hers.

She began to scream and in the dairy Adah-May's eyes bulged and her face sweated a beetroot red as she strained against the washing line with which the man had tied her up.

"No . . . no . . . put him down," Chloe shrieked, leaping at Paddy Andrews's back and fastening her slender arms about his throat like the paralysing tendrils of ivy which grew up the wall outside. Enraged by the attack on his master the dog sank his teeth into her ankle, drawing blood, but she merely shook him off and the dog, old now and past such things and having done his duty, slunk to Paddy's side.

The boy began to wail, struggling in the strong grip of his father, his face crimson, his mouth opened wide to reveal his little baby teeth, his eyes spurting tears of terror.

Paddy quivered, amazed that this fragile-looking woman could be so strong, but of course she was no match for him, nobody was. The dog had given her a fair nip an' all but it didn't seem as though it was going to stop her, the silly cow. He didn't want to hurt her. She was nothing to him. She'd done him no harm, though he remembered she'd given him a bit of lip on that day she'd come down to Woodhead. Spirited little thing she was, and Paddy admired spirit.

He reached up and prised her arms loose, shaking her off much as she had done with his dog, flinging her back towards the rocking chair where she sat down heavily, but like a rubber ball she bounced out of it, hurling towards him at the speed and with the same ferocity as one of them bloody trains which roared through Crossclough Station.

"Give . . . him . . . to . . . me . . ." she panted, doing her best to snatch the screaming, terrified boy from his arms, kicking and biting and scratching and all the while his bloody dog would keep barking and it was all beginning to get on Paddy's overstretched nerves. He'd have to shut her up, get her off him or he'd never get away before her husband got back. He was sorry, really he was, because he didn't want to hurt anyone, only Katy. That was where his bitter rancour was directed. Not even at Chris Andrews who had crippled him, but at her who had humiliated him. It was she he was punishing by taking the boy. Besides, he was his son and he'd a right to him, hadn't he? As much right as her. A handsome lad, he'd thought proudly as he'd watched him toddle across the yard, a proper lad an' all, stamping in them puddles, and he'd fetch him up right in America.

First the woman though.

"Look," he said, his voice reasonable. "I don't want to 'ave ter tie thi' up but I will. I'm tekkin 'im . . ."

"No . . . oh, no . . . no, I won't let you. Please give him to me."

"Yer can't stop me, lass. He's mine."

"No, no, he's not. He's mine."

"Yourn?" Paddy looked puzzled for a moment but he had no time to be arguing.

"Yes. Oh please, don't hurt him."

"Nay, I don't mean to 'urt 'im, lass. Not me own son, but tha've got ter stop interferin' wi' me or I'll 'urt thi'."

"No, give him to me," and she launched herself against him with such force he almost fell over.

"Oh, fer Christ's sake, woman." He'd tried to be patient, to explain to her what he was doing and why he was doing it, but she'd not heed him and so he did the only thing left to him. Lifting his hand, he hit her with the back of it, snapping her head on her neck with such force her hair fell in a wildly flying swirl about her face. The blow split her cheek to the bone, knocking her across the room and she lay where she had fallen.

He waited a moment to see if she would get up again then, when she remained where his hard fist had flung her, he called to his frantically barking dog and, shouldering the bag, he hitched the crying child closer to his chest, opened the door and set off towards the small stand of trees which bordered the bottom road by the reservoir.

He avoided the track, keeping out of sight of the road until he reached a point where it zigzagged between Torside and Rhodeswood reservoirs. He crossed it hurriedly, intending to make his way across Peak Naze Moor to Hadfield where he would catch the train to Manchester, changing there for Liverpool. He'd get lost there in those crowds, as he had done for the past three months. He'd have to dirty the boy up a bit, for he'd stand out like a sore thumb in his fancy outfit but that was no problem.

There was a small sound behind him. A chink of stone on stone and when he turned round she was there. There was blood pouring down her face on to her cloak which was still tied about her shoulders. Her hair was drifting in a great coppery cloud about her head and down her back. The ground was heavy with the thawed snow and her little feet, clad only in thin kid shoes since she had travelled in the gig, sank into it, already as wet as though she had waded through a stream. Her ankle, where the dog had mauled her, was torn and bloody.

She stopped when he did, making no attempt to go for him as she had done before, merely standing, like a pale wounded animal, her eyes unblinking and fastened on the child who was hiccupping in deep distress on Paddy's shoulder. He had gone past the stage of frightened weeping, retreating, as children do, into the quiet, shocked state that is nature's protection.

"Give him to me, please," she said softly, holding out her arms. The boy saw her and raised his in a gesture which was heart-rending.

Paddy felt his temper flare and race through him like a flame through dry wood.

"Now look 'ere, tha' daft cow, if yer don't leave me alone I'll 'ave ter give thi' a clout that'll knock thi' out, see. I can do it, believe me."

"If you can reach me," she answered, in much the same tone Katy Andrews had used to him three months ago. Her eyes dropped to his wooden peg and Paddy was incensed, since he knew what she said was true. He could manage well enough on the often steep and craggy tracks he walked and clambered over, providing he could go at his own speed, pick the spot where he placed his right foot and, more carefully, his wooden peg. His left leg had been removed above the knee and the well-crafted but unjointed piece of wood on which he balanced so adroitly was stiff and awkward. There was no possible way he could reach anyone who was determined to keep out of his way and this lass knew it.

He'd not be bested though!

"Why, yer bloody fool, d'yer think I'd let this stop me?" he roared, hitting his left leg. "If I catch 'old o' thi' I'll kill thi', I'm warnin' thi'."

"I know that, Mr Andrews. That's why I'm keeping away from you but I mean to follow wherever you go and you can't stop me, so won't you put Jack down and just go? I won't tell anyone about this, I promise you, but please, give me my boy."

"My boy, yer daft sow, an' yer can go ter buggery. I'm off, an' if yer keep after me I'll set me dog on yer again."

"I'll take that chance, Mr Andrews, for I'll not leave that baby in your care. Wherever you go so shall I."

"Damn thi' ter hell, woman." His voice was hoarse with his frustrated fury, for how the devil was he to get across the moor with her on his heels and, more to the point, when he reached Hadfield how was he to get himself and the lad on to a train to Manchester? Once they had reached a town, anywhere where there were people, she'd only to scream out that he was pinching her bairn, not even that, for with a face on her like she had every able-bodied man in sight would rush to help her.

Well, he'd just have to lose her, that's all. His threat to set his dog on her was no more than that really for the poor old bugger could hardly walk, let alone charge at anyone with a pair of nimble legs on them and had only got her last time because she was hanging on to himself. There was something wrong with his rear end which manifested itself in a most disgusting way and Paddy was doubtful he would get him across Pike Naze Moor, never mind the train to Liverpool and the boat to America. He'd have left him with Josh and Jake but they'd only neglect the poor old sod and he'd been a loyal and trusted . . . well, friend to Paddy, the only one he'd ever had really.

"Suit thissen," he said curtly, calling up his dog and turning in the direction of the moor. It was just two thirty but the midwinter darkness was already beginning to fall.

"Take me up to the farm, Thomas, will you? Chloe has Jack and I promised I'd pick him up before dark."

"We'd best look sharp then, lass. I doubt I'll get carriage up that track, an' if I'm not mistaken theer's goner be a heavy frost ternight. It'll already be slippy up theer."

"Yes, then let's get on, shall we? You can wait for me on the road at the bottom of the track. It won't take me long to walk up there and get Jack."

The journey to Valley Bottom Farm did not take long. It was half past four but already the clear, frosted night was upon them and the winter stars were rising. They were bright for they had not yet reached their aloof suspension in mid-heaven, resembling a scattering of pin-heads on the purple-blue velvet of a pincushion. Though Katy was wrapped about with warm rugs and even a hot brick at her feet provided by the grateful little woman in the "tea room", as the equally grateful women rag sorters called it, she could feel the cold penetrate her bones and catch her lungs and her breath was a thick vapour about her head. The ground was iron hard, the horses straining up the hill, the panting of their chests and the creaking of their harness the only sound in the icy air.

As she struggled up the frozen track, slipping a time or two, refusing Thomas's offer to go for her, since Jamie might be there and just a glimpse, a word, a smile would be a crumb to feed the hunger of her longing, she was surprised to see the windows of the farmhouse were not lit. What was Chloe up to? Had she fallen asleep by her own hearth, Katy's child in her arms, the pair of them warm and dreaming in the peace of her kitchen? If that was so it meant Jamie was not yet home from wherever he had spent his day, probably up in the pasture checking on his small flock, or searching for a lost ewe which had not the sense to stay where it was safe.

Realising sadly that she was not to see Jamie, Katy felt a heavy pang of disappointment as she struggled with the gate to the yard which had become frozen to its hinges. She cursed fluently, ready to swear at whoever had left it closed, but as she turned from it she was brought to a paralysed halt and her heart was squeezed by a grip so strong she thought she might fall over.

The farmhouse door stood wide open, just as though someone had gone through it at great speed with no thought of closing it behind them to contain its warmth. The icy hand gripped her even more agonisingly and she wanted to scream out to Chloe but she could force no sound to her frozen throat.

But even though her heart already knew what had happened her mind refused to function and she stood for ten long seconds staring stupidly at the open door. What? . . . what? . . . what? her brain kept repeating, though of course her mother's heart knew.

"Chloe . . . Chloe . . . Jack?" she began to babble, tripping over the hem of her gown, despite its shortness, as she flung herself towards the open doorway.

"Chloe . . . Chloe, for God's sake, cousin, don't tease me, don't do this to me . . . please, oh please." She knew she was gibbering like one of those monkeys she had seen in the zoo as a child, for one part of her brain which still operated coolly at some basic level knew quite well that Chloe was incapable of playing such a cruel trick. The kitchen fire was still in, though it was obvious no one had replenished it for many hours and its sluggish light revealed no unusual disturbance, nothing out of place but . . . oh Jesus . . . oh sweet Jesus . . . where?

She began to scream then, knowing . . . knowing!

"Chloe . . . Jack . . . oh, please, where are you . . . where?" She pounded upstairs, swirling wildly round Chloe's neat bedroom, then down again, falling heavily at the bottom, catching the small of her back on the last tread, springing up again much as her cousin had done when Paddy Andrews had knocked her into the chair, and again, as it had done up on the moor with Paddy, a small part of her brain told her she would have a nice bruise there tomorrow and all the time her screams echoed about the kitchen and up to the very rafters of the farm roof then out in the yard where she blundered in her blind terror. They carried shrilly to the man waiting by the carriage, to the half-frozen girl in the dairy and to the brothers who were striding down the dark field at the back of the farm towards warmth and food and shelter on this bitter, bitter night.

When they reached her she was about to clamber over the drystone wall and stumble off into the dark peril of the moor in search of her son. She had found Adah-May gobbling senselessly in the dairy but Katy was out of her mind by now and since Jack was not there she whirled out again and on to the barn, the henhouse, the stable where the little horse which pulled the gig snorted in fright.

"Chloe . . . Chloe . . . Chloe . . ." she was screaming, "where's Jack? Where's my baby? What have you done with my baby?" beating her fists on Jamie's broad chest while Thomas and Tommy, white-faced and trembling, stared in growing horror at the half-demented maid, trussed up like one of Chloe's own chickens bound for market and at Katy Andrews who seemed ready to kill anyone who stood in her way, and at Jamie, whose own face had crumpled to the texture and colour of suet.

"Where is she, Jamie? Where's my boy? Oh please . . . please . . ."

"Katy, Katy, calm down, darling. Tell me . . ."

"He's got her . . . and Jack, Jamie. No, I haven't time to

be sitting about the kitchen, dammit, let me go ... let me go ..."

They lit lamps and stoked up the fire and all the while Katy Andrews screamed and fought like some mad woman escaped from bedlam and Adah-May huddled in a chair by the fire, repeating time and time again, "'E tied me up ... 'e tied me up," which, since they already knew that was no help to them at all.

They found the blood, a small pool of it on the far side of the fireplace, a scattering of it across the kitchen floor and out into the dark yard and for five minutes, all of them in such a state of shock and disbelief, they milled about, calling her name, calling Jack's name as though the pair of them were hiding in some childish game beyond the wall.

It was Thomas who was the first to collect himself. His stepson was having a hard time, not only with Katy but with his own mortal terror and Tommy, who was only a lad, was waiting for someone to tell him what to do.

"Can thi' drive carriage, lad?" his father asked him.

"Aye, I reckon so, Pa." Tommy could not help but feel a thrill of excitement.

"Then go hell for leather fer tha' ma, an' fetch Dicken an' Jimmy. Quick, lad, but mind them 'orse's legs on the ice."

30

They had climbed up the steep slope to Bramah Edge then dropped down again on to Peak Naze Moor itself, slipping and slithering on the black reefs of gritstone. Its frozen waves were perilous, for a fall could scrape the flesh from your bones, or shatter a limb and Chloe's feet were already bleeding inside her shoes. She marvelled at the agility of the man ahead of her who somehow, despite his wooden leg and the child in his arms, managed to keep his balance. Her heart was in her mouth, for if he should drop Jack the boy would be seriously injured.

From a distance they might have been taken for man and wife, the man carrying the burden of their child while the woman struggled wearily at his back some way behind, but they met no one in this vast wilderness of moorland and gritstone and wet, boggy peatland. This was murderous country, the gritstone hacked through by ice when glaciers made the deep valleys, and the summit of the Dark Peak was a peat-mantled tableland where it could snow for almost a quarter of the year. When it did so, or when it rained, the bogs became quaking pools and the becks were treacherous with flash floods scouring the cloughs, tearing everything down as they went.

The recent snow, thawed only a day or two ago, had caused such a saturation and every step they took their feet sank almost ankle deep into the sodden ground.

He turned on her again and again, his face a distorted mask of red fury, threatening her that if she did not bugger off and leave him alone he would do for her, but even in his rage knowing he must reach her first which made his fury greater. When he did she merely stopped, patient as a dove, saying nothing, her eyes on the boy in his arms. She was exhausted, for every step in the boggy ground required an enormous effort. Her ankle was on fire where the dog had sunk his teeth and her cheek still bled. She had no idea where they were, only that she must keep up and she believed the pain she was in helped in some strange way. She must not let Jack out of her sight. She didn't know what was to happen, what she was to do at some point in this nightmare, she only knew she must keep up, keep steady, keep her wits about her, for this man was not only powerful but he was deadly. He had had his chance in the kitchen and rejected it, thinking she was no threat to him but if he could reach her now he would kill her, she knew that. He dare not put the boy down to try, since he knew she would evade him, dart forward and scoop Jack up and run like the wind to where Paddy Andrews could not go.

They had lost the dog on the far side of Bramah Edge. He had done his best to scramble up the steep, slippery tumble of moving stones, heaving and panting, encouraged by the man but always falling back and for a while she had thought Paddy meant to pick the thing up and carry him along with the boy, wondering at the depth of his feeling for the ugly animal.

He had cursed, obscenities Chloe had never heard before, torn between his child and his dog and the child had won, not, she was aware, because of any fondness he might have for his son but because Jack was the only weapon he had to use against Katy.

"Let me have him, Mr Andrews," she pleaded, as Paddy knelt by the dog, his hand tender on his broad head.

"Sod off," was all he said, his mind not on her but the animal, then rising to his feet he turned, stumbling away, moving his head this way and that as though in an effort to shut out the piteous cries of the abandoned creature.

"Where are you going, Mr Andrews?" she called out to him as he lumbered up the steep, stony track used by sheep to reach the sweeter grass towards the summit of Peak Naze Moor. A thousand feet up it was and the snow fringed it, but Paddy Andrew had trained himself for this, planned every step of the way and it did not seem to concern him unduly. He was making for the rutted track which lay on the far side of the stretch of moorland and which, earlier in the century, had served a quarry. From there it was down to the main road which would be deserted as night fell and which would take him to Hadfield and the railway station there.

"Mind yer own bloody business," he snarled, twitching the child, who had fallen into a deep, death-like sleep, from one shoulder to the other. Blasted kid was heavy and Paddy was feeling bad, still inclined to grieve over his poor old dog left to perish on the moor all alone and he didn't deserve it, poor old sod. He was in no mood to chat to this persistent bitch who, before long, must be got rid of. They would reach the track in an hour and by then it would be completely dark and safe to venture on to it but not with this bloody woman at his back. Christ, he hadn't bargained for this but it made no difference, he'd still get his revenge on the bitch who had brought him to such a bitter end.

His peg sank suddenly into a dark patch of oozing, quaking ground which sucked at it greedily and he had a moment as he frantically pressed down on the firm ground with his good foot to thank God it was his peg which had gone in. Using his own foot he was quite easily able to apply the pressure needed to free himself, sweating a little at the closeness of his escape. Get stuck in there and you'd be a goner! A mate of their Walter's had lost a whole bloody horse and cart in a bog up Featherbed Moss way when he blundered off the path and any man who was careless, as Walter's mate had been, did not live long to regret it.

He stood for a minute or two, getting his breath back, for the long walk on his wooden leg, a walk he would have eaten up in the old days, was taking it out of him and he realised it was because he was hurrying, hurrying to get away from the woman at his back.

But there, out of the blue, was his answer. There was always a solid path across these patches of deadly bogs, or so his pa had told him and Paddy Andrews, born and bred in these parts as his pa had been, knew how to find them. If he could lure her after him – and what need did he have to lure her since she followed him like a bloody shadow – he had only to get her into the middle of the bloody thing, perhaps no more than a step or two for that would be enough, then, leaving her helpless, sinking, for she'd not know how to tread, the silly cow, he could make his way down to Hadfield in nice time for the train.

He was smiling as he turned, smiling as he had never done before, a wide grin of evil intent which warned Chloe at once that he was up to something. He was not cunning enough to hide it and her heart began to thud and she felt a great desire to turn and run. But he couldn't get her, could he? All these miles they had walked, she following him at a safe distance and he had not been able to get to her, had he, so what devilment was in his mind now? There was something. His eyes had narrowed speculatively as though he was weighing something up and despite herself she took a step backwards.

There was barely enough daylight left to see the misted outlines of the peaks which rose up about them. The coarse, tufted green of the grass and the rusty brown of the short winter bracken were becoming indistinct, blurred into an indistinguishable contour of dips and hollows, cut here and there by narrow tumbling water. It was intensely cold and the water which lay inches deep about her feet had a thin crackle of ice on it. She shivered, dragging her cloak about her, and waited.

"Well, I'm goin' across 'ere, seein' as 'ow it's a short cut," he told her, taking a cautious step forward on to a patch of ground which had a slightly different colour to it than the rest, but it was his voice, his words, for why should he tell her where he was going, that warned her more than the curious colour and texture of the ground he was stepping carefully across. He seemed to put his foot, his good foot forward first, gently, tentatively, as though he was testing the ground before bringing up his peg leg to join it.

He stopped for a moment. "'Ave thi' 'ad enough, then?" he threw over his shoulder, not turning. "Are thi' ter give up or ..." and as he spoke, his voice mocking, he seemed to lose his balance. He threw out his wooden leg to steady himself and immediately it sank twelve inches into the ground and in an effort to draw it out his good foot went in too and in thirty seconds Paddy Andrews was up to his knees in the clutching, sucking, clawing embrace of the morass. A morass just as lethal as the one which had taken the horse and cart of his brother Walter's mate.

He began to scream in panic, for a man with one leg has not the strength or dexterity of a man with two who might have struggled out, threshing about like some earth monster which has been caught in the primeval swamp from which it crawled. He let go of the bag containing Jack's duds and it disappeared with a nasty squelch, gone in a moment and Paddy's efforts to free himself became more frantic.

For ten seconds Chloe stood there, her eyes wide with shock, convinced that in a minute Paddy would claw his way to the safer ground, for he was caught only to the knees, then Jack began to whimper, his own mind catching the despairing fear of the man who held him, the man who knew better than Chloe Hutchinson what desperate peril he was in and at once life and movement and thought returned to the woman who watched.

"Jack!" she screamed as she sprang forward, racing across the last bit of firm ground towards the bog, but even as her icy feet reached it and prepared themselves to run lightly across it to get Jack, some instinct made her hesitate. Paddy was going down, faster and faster as his struggles became more frenzied, and if she didn't do something quickly he would be gone, taking the child with him. She was here, on firm ground, no more than six feet from him and surely it would serve no purpose to fling herself into the same brown slime which had Paddy in its deathly grip. She needed something, something to throw across the quaking mass for Paddy to grab hold of. But what? She looked about her desperately for a piece of wood, something, anything, but there were no trees up here, no handy branches to lay across the morass which was taking Paddy, and Jack into its stinking embrace.

Someone was moaning, crying piteously, calling out for help, a voice rising to a piercing shriek of despair and she knew it was herself. Herself, for there was no one else here. Chloe Hutchinson was the only one standing between death and the child she loved.

She steadied and so did her voice.

"Paddy, listen to me . . ."

"Oh Jesus, Jesus save me."

"No, there's only me, Paddy, only me. I can take off my cloak and throw it to you. You can crawl across it. I'll help you, pull you out."

"Do it, fer Christ's sake, do it, yer bitch. I'm goin' . . ." and it was true for already the ooze had reached his chest and Jack's little feet were beneath its viciously clutching surface.

"I will, but first you must throw me the baby."

"Fer pity's sake . . . oh lass, fer pity's sake . . ."

"Throw me the baby, Paddy and I swear I'll throw you my cloak. A fair exchange, I think, don't you, but be quick about it before it's too late."

How can you be so calm? a voice was shrieking inside her head, a voice which was telling her to forget caution and fling herself across the bog, to grab at Jack and pull him from Paddy Andrews's arms and if she couldn't, then she'd go down with him for how was she to live if Jack died?

"Paddy?" He could barely hear her over his own demented screams. The ooze had reached his shoulders but incredibly, perhaps an instinct which is inherent in a father, even the worst, to protect his own, he was holding Jack above it, both hands about his waist, the child slack with shock, almost unconscious.

"Here," Paddy roared and with one tremendous effort he threw the boy, like a man chucking a ball into a football match, a perfect arc which took Jack across the stretch of bog and into Chloe's frantic arms.

But that last movement was his undoing and without another sound, his eyes still open, his gaze on his son's face for the last time, Paddy Andrews slipped beneath the oozing slime of the bog.

They almost had to tie Katy Andrews to her cousin's rocking chair to keep her in the kitchen and only Jamie Hutchinson's arms about her, which seemed a bit queer to those Cloudberry End servants gathered there, appeared to keep her steady as she fought to be allowed to go and search for her boy. Deep liver-coloured hollows in which her haunted eyes were sunk, her cheekbones standing out where the flesh of her face appeared to have been burned away, and him no better, really, the pair of them clinging together like each was a life raft to the other.

It did no good, said Saul Gibbon, who knew the area as no other man did and who had been called on to help them in the search, blundering about in the dark, even if it was a clear night. Starlight, like moonlight, was queer, casting shadows that looked solid enough to walk on and giving the illusion there was firm ground where none existed and a man could smash his ankle on a rock, or blunder into one of the stretches of bog which waited up there to trap the unwary. He was sorry to have to say it, as Katy Andrews moaned and Jamie Hutchinson bowed his head, but they had to be warned.

And they didn't know which way they'd gone, did they? Aye, tomorrow morning at first light there'd be a score, fifty men up here to set off in search of the little lad and Mrs Hutchinson but no good would come of rushing about like headless chickens in the dark. That blood which led out from the kitchen, bobbing his head apologetically in the direction of the distraught mother of the missing child and the equally distraught husband of the missing woman, might give them a clue as to the direction to take and in the meanwhile Miss Andrews'd be better served by getting a good night's sleep.

It was just like that time Miss Katy herself went missing, did they remember it, they asked one another as they gathered at dawn in the farmyard where chickens squawked their displeasure. She was a right beggar for causing trouble, that one, they murmured, as they watched her mount her little mare, her cloak flung about her shameful breeches and a warm jacket one of the women from Cloudberry End had been instructed to bring over. She and the grooms from her stable were to ride up towards Spond Moor, fanning out, going north and west, while Ned Garvey and Harry Ellison, both decent riders and provided with a mount by Katy Andrews, were to go east. The rest of them were on foot, moving off from the farm in an ever-widening circle, calling and beating the bushes which, after the night's heavy hoar frost were white and frozen, ready to snap off if treated roughly. There was a bit of a mist which could hamper them to start with but Saul was of the opinion that it would soon clear and a cold, bright day would follow.

Matty and Adah-May were to remain in the farmhouse in case Chloe returned, Matty said, though her expression revealed she did not really expect it to happen. She would be here to make hot drinks and good nourishing soups in case of need, she added brightly, though her eyes said she was dying inside.

They covered every square inch of the moorland within a ten-mile radius of Valley Bottom Farm, looking behind and under each shrub and gorse bush, every rock, every stretch of frozen bracken and heather, every hole and gully and clough, even bloody rabbit holes, Arnie Bagshaw reported, close to tears as anyone could see, when the men came in exhausted, blank-eyed and almost furtive, for they found it difficult to meet the despairing gaze of Katy Andrews and Jamie Hutchinson. Saul Gibbon had not come in yet, having gone off towards Pike Naze Moor for some reason of his own, taking Barty Pickles and Barty's brother, Joseph, who were shepherds like him and good trackers.

It was just as dusk fell that they found them, Saul and Barty and Joseph. They had been no more than half a mile from the road which led from the moor down to Hadfield, the bairn and the woman, and had Mrs Hutchinson known of it she could have walked it in ten minutes.

But the poor lass was in a bad way, anyone could see that, with blood frozen solid to her face and tears frozen solid to the end of her long silken eyelashes. She'd taken off her good, warm cloak and wrapped the little lad in it, then lain down against the base of a rock, afraid to move, she had managed to whisper, in case she fell into the bog. She'd curled her body about the boy, her back to the vicious cold, the bairn tucked snug between her and the rock. All night and the best part of the next day she had been there when they found her, babbling through the alarming crackle in her chest which heralds pneumonia, of dark slime, of Paddy Andrews and cloaks and such and they knew her to be delirious.

They wrapped her up and brought her home to her husband, the little lad crying for his mam, who snatched him out of Barty's arms and held him to her with a great deal of crying of her own.

They put Mrs Hutchinson in her warm bed, her weeping mother-in-law and her frantic husband, but for some reason the men, even though it had all ended happily, could not quite bring themselves to leave, hanging about the farmyard, smoking their pipes and talking quietly. They glanced up at the lighted window where the lass was, they all knew it, fighting for her life. Brave lass, sweet-natured and kind, many of them and their wives knew it first hand. She'd saved that little lad's life and if there was anything they could do for her they'd do it, so if no one minded, bobbing their heads at Katy Andrews who came to the door to hand out cups of steaming tea, they'd just hang about a bit.

They were still there a week later, not all of them and not all at once but there was always someone there, a working man, or perhaps his wife, keeping a vigil for the lass who, they knew now, was not to recover.

Her face on the pillow was little more than a pale smooth oval, fragile as a snowflake, or the snowdrops which push through the greening land Chloe Hutchinson would never see again. Gone was the pink of rose in her cheeks, that sheen of good health which had lain about her since her marriage to Jamie Hutchinson. The scar on her cheek was a livid reminder of what had been done to her, of what had killed her. Only her hair was alive, rich and coppery, a smoothly brushed halo of curls which glowed in the candlelight, or in a stray beam of sunlight which came to lie across her pillow. Her breast rose and fell on her light, painful breathing, the drugs the doctor had given her making her drowsy though she did not sleep much. The harsh crepitation of the pneumonia seemed to fill the room and Matty, who had barely left the chair by the fireside, wept silently.

Just before dawn on the seventh day she awoke and spoke quite clearly.

"He saved . . . his life . . . in the end."

It was no more than a whisper, a sigh, a breath of softness in the warm room and at once Jamie bent over her, smoothing back her hair in an agony of love.

"Don't talk, little dove . . . save your strength."

"Katy?"

"Is downstairs."

"Must see her."

"Rest, darling, rest."

Chloe opened her eyes. They were a clouded blue-green, glowing with her love for him but already beginning to haze a little as death touched her and his tears dripped on to her hands which were as light and frail as a bit of swansdown.

"No, Jamie . . . you must . . . not weep . . . I love Jack. I could not have . . . borne it . . . if he . . . had died."

"I know, my lovely girl."

"Tell Katy . . . to come."

They brought her up, though she knew quite simply she could not bear it, for how was she to manage without the serenity and sweetness of Chloe whom she had known for less than three short years in her life? But she must not cry. She must not add to the burden of Chloe's going, as Jamie was, with tears.

"Katy . . ." It was the merest whisper.

"Yes, darling, I'm here. What is it?" She took one of Chloe's hands and held it to her cheek, smiling a little. "Tell me."

"Paddy . . ."

"I know about him, darling."

"He died in the . . . bog."

"Yes, they told me."

"But you must . . . he . . . redeemed himself, Katy. He threw . . . Jack to me . . . saved him."

She closed her eyes and for a long aching time was quiet. Katy watched her, scarcely aware of what Chloe had told her in her own painful grief. She thought she would not wake again and what did the revelation about Paddy Andrews, who had caused all this, matter to her now?

Chloe's breathing became sharp and shallow as the night wore on and the doctor shook his head. Katy rested her head beside Chloe's, sleeping a little but a light touch on her hair roused her and she lifted her head and looked into Chloe's eyes.

"Yes, darling, I'm here." Sliding her own strong arm about her cousin's shoulders she drew her gently into her arms. Chloe was no more than a bit of thistledown but she seemed to gain a little strength from the force of Katy's love.

They clung together, watched by the man who loved them both, the wild, forceful vigour of Katy Andrews holding back the dying spirit of Chloe Hutchinson for a brief moment. It was too late now to tell Chloe how she felt, how she loved her, for already the white, waxy face cradled against her shoulder had taken on the sunken look of death, but Chloe saw it in her eyes and a small tender smile tugged at her mouth.

Kissing her brow, smiling into her cousin's fading eyes Katy passed her into the arms of her husband and went downstairs.

Those gathered in the yard saw the curtains being drawn across her window. They bowed their heads, standing for a long moment in respectful silence and a woman, Archie Bagshaw's wife, threw her pinny over her head and wept, then, without speaking, they quietly left for their homes.

It was the same in the churchyard on the day of her funeral. The little chapel at Woodhead was like a ship floating in a sea, a great sea of silent people, all of them mourning the woman who had gone. Katy was astonished, filled with a wondering sorrow that she had not known of the esteem in which her cousin had been held. Archie Bagshaw, who had delivered her letters, held a handkerchief to his eyes and sobbed visibly, to his wife's distress, and Fred Beardsall, who collected the tickets at the station and who, it appeared, had a sickly wife whom Chloe had regularly visited, was quite shattered, leaning against the stone wall as the coffin was lowered into the ground.

Katy had brooded on whether she should write to Chloe's father to let him know she was dead, for after all she was his daughter and he had a right to know. But did he? To the best of her knowledge he had not written one line to Chloe in the years she had lived here so it had seemed inappropriate, not something Chloe herself would have wanted. All the people who loved her, and whom she had loved were here at her graveside, every one of them, and surely that was all that mattered?

"Crossclough must be empty," Tommy was heard to remark brokenly to his father, the pair of them clinging to Matty. Mrs Kelsall and her "girls" were there, all of them silently weeping, for a loud outburst, which was what they felt like showing, would not have been seemly. Not for Miss Chloe. She had been so ladylike, so gracious and serene in all she did, surely at her funeral they must behave in the same tranquil, respectful manner in which she herself would have acted.

Only Adah-May made a show of herself and she was no more than a child in a woman's body, poor soul. She was led away by her mother to weep inconsolably at the back of the chapel among the first snowdrops. She'd picked some, it was said, when the grave had been filled in and put them with the wreaths and dozens of simple bunches of flowers which covered it.

The biggest surprise was the appearance of Jack and Sara Andrews who had been known to hold their niece in some disfavour, something to do with Mrs Andrews's past relationship with her own sister who had been Mrs Hutchinson's mother. They had come to support their daughter and to check up on that grandson of theirs, no doubt, for the bairn had had a nasty experience and clung to his mother more than he once had.

They had all gone at last, drifting sadly away along the bottom road, most walking, for they were ordinary folk, towards their homes in Crossclough or Saltersbrook or

Woodhead, some to climb into their carriages and make their way to Valley Bottom Farm where Mrs Jenkins had provided refreshments.

"Will you come with us in the carriage, darling?" Sara asked her daughter, touching her hand gently, only realising now how much her cousin had meant to Katy, bewildered by it in a way, for the enmity between them had once been ferocious.

"No, Mother, I'll be up directly."

"Very well, darling." Her mother followed Katy's gaze up the gently sloping ground of the churchyard to where the bowed and lonely figure of Jamie Hutchinson stood by his wife's grave. "But don't . . ."

"I won't, Mother. I do have some sensitivity."

"Of course," though once Katy Andrews had not been known for it.

She made no move to join him. She remained out of sight at the gate, watching over him to see he did not falter, in much the same way she watched over her son. The day was grey, sharp with a hint of the snow to come and she saw him shiver but he did not move and neither did she. She would leave him soon when she was convinced he was steady. She would let him grieve as a man should for the woman he had loved, but not for long. Soon she would go to him and they would speak of farms and paper mills and his child which grew inside her and soon, before too long, she would ask him to marry her.

There would be talk, of course, but when hadn't there been talk in the valley about Katy Andrews?